The
MX Book
of
New
Sherlock
Holmes
Stories

Part XXVIII
More Christmas Adventures
(1869-1888)

First edition published in 2021
© Copyright 2021

The right of the individuals listed on the Copyright Information page to be identified as the authors of this work has been asserted by them in accordance with the Copyright, Designs, and Patents Act 1998.

All rights reserved. No reproduction, copy, or transmission of this publication may be made without express prior written permission. No paragraph of this publication may be reproduced, copied, or transmitted except with express prior written permission or in accordance with the provisions of the Copyright Act 1956 (as amended). Any person who commits any unauthorised act in relation to this publication may be liable to criminal prosecution and civil claims for damage.

All characters appearing in this work are fictitious or used fictitiously. Except for certain historical personages, any resemblance to real persons, living or dead, is purely coincidental. The opinions expressed herein are those of the authors and not of MX Publishing.

ISBN Hardback 978-1-78705-926-9
ISBN Paperback 978-1-78705-927-6
AUK ePub ISBN 978-1-78705-928-3
AUK PDF ISBN 978-1-78705-929-0

Published in the UK by
MX Publishing
335 Princess Park Manor, Royal Drive,
London, N11 3GX
www.mxpublishing.co.uk

David Marcum can be reached at:
thepapersofsherlockholmes@gmail.com

Cover design by Brian Belanger
www.belangerbooks.com and *www.redbubble.com/people/zhahadun*

Internal Illustrations by Sidney Paget

CONTENTS

Forewords

Editor's Foreword: Never Enough Holmes Adventures – Even at Christmas! by David Marcum	1
Foreword by Nancy Holder	16
"It is the Season of Forgiveness" by Roger Johnson	18
An Ongoing Legacy for Sherlock Holmes by Steve Emecz	20
Undershaw: Eliminating the Impossible by Emma West	23
A Sherlockian Christmas (*A Poem*) by Joseph W. Svec III	33

Adventures

No Malice Intended by Deanna Baran	35
The Yuletide Heist by Mark Mower	45
A Yuletide Tragedy by Thomas A. Turley	69

(Continued on the next page . . . .)

The Adventure of the Christmas Lesson 86
    by Will Murray

The Christmas Card Case 105
    by Brenda Seabrooke

The Chatterton-Smythe Affair 126
    by Tim Gambrell

Christmas at the Red Lion 137
    by Thomas A. Burns, Jr.

A Study in Murder 156
    by Amy Thomas

The Christmas Ghost of Crailloch Taigh 173
    by David Marcum

The Six-Fingered Scoundrel 201
    by Jeffrey A. Lockwood

The Case of the Duplicitous Suitor 218
    by John Lawrence

The Sebastopol Clasp 237
    by Martin Daley

The Silent Brotherhood
    by Dick Gillman 261

The Case of the Christmas Pudding 277
    by Liz Hedgecock

(Continued on the next page . . . .)

The St. Stephen's Day Mystery	297
by Paul Hiscock	
A Fine Kettle of Fish	311
by Mike Hogan	
The Case of the Left Foot	332
by Stephen Herczeg	
The Case of the Golden Grail	360
by Roger Riccard	
About the Contributors	401

These additional adventures are contained in
Part XXIX: More Christmas Adventures
(1889-1896)

Baskerville Hall in Winter (A Poem) – Christopher James
The Sword in the Spruce – Ian Ableson
The Adventure of the Serpentine Body – Wayne Anderson
The Adventure of the Fugitive Irregular – Gordon Linzner
The Father Christmas Brigade – David Marcum
The Incident of the Stolen Christmas Present – Barry Clay
The Man of Miracles – Derrick Belanger
Absent Friends – Wayne Anderson
The Incident in Regent Street – Harry DeMaio
The Baffling Adventure of the Baby Jesus – Craig Stephen Copland
The Adventure of the Second Sister – Matthew White
The Twelve Days – I.A. Watson
The Dilemma of Mr. Henry Baker – Paul D. Gilbert
The Adventure of the Injured Man – Arthur Hall
The Krampus Who Came to Call – Marcia Wilson
The Adventure of the Christmas Wish – Margaret Walsh
The Adventure of the Viking Ghost – Frank Schildiner
The Adventure of the Secret Manuscript – Dan Rowley
The Adventure of the Christmas Suitors – Tracy J. Revels

Part XXX: More Christmas Adventures
(1897-1928)

Baker Street in Snow (1890) (A Poem) – Christopher James
The Purloined Present – DJ Tyrer
The Case of the Cursory Curse – Andrew Bryant
The St. Giles Child Murders – Tim Gambrell
A Featureless Crime – Geri Schear
The Case of the Earnest Young Man – Paula Hammond

(Continued on the next page . . . .)

The Adventure of the Dextrous Doctor – Jayantika Ganguly
The Mystery of Maple Tree Lodge – Susan Knight
The Adventure of the Maligned Mineralogist – Arthur Hall
Christmas Magic – Kevin Thornton
The Adventure of the Christmas Threat – Arthur Hall
The Adventure of the Stolen Christmas Gift – Michael Mallory
The Colourful Skein of Life – Julie McKuras
The Adventure of the Chained Phantom – J.S. Rowlinson
Santa's Little Elves – Kevin Thornton
The Case of the Holly-Sprig Pudding – Naching T. Kassa
The Canterbury Manifesto – David Marcum
The Case of the Disappearing Beaune – J. Lawrence Matthews
A Price Above Rubies – Jane Rubino
The Intrigue of the Red Christmas – Shane Simmons
The Bitter Gravestones – Chris Chan
The Midnight Mass Murder – Paul Hiscock

**These additional Sherlock Holmes adventures
can be found in the previous volumes of**
The MX Book of New Sherlock Holmes Stories

PART I: 1881-1889
Foreword – Leslie S. Klinger
Foreword – Roger Johnson
Foreword – David Marcum
Sherlock Holmes of London (A Verse in Four Fits) – Michael Kurland
The Adventure of the Slipshod Charlady – John Hall
The Case of the Lichfield Murder – Hugh Ashton
The Kingdom of the Blind – Adrian Middleton
The Adventure of the Pawnbroker's Daughter – David Marcum
The Adventure of the Defenestrated Princess – Jayantika Ganguly
The Adventure of the Inn on the Marsh – Denis O. Smith
The Adventure of the Traveling Orchestra – Amy Thomas
The Haunting of Sherlock Holmes – Kevin David Barratt
Sherlock Holmes and the Allegro Mystery – Luke Benjamen Kuhns
The Deadly Soldier – Summer Perkins
The Case of the Vanishing Stars – Deanna Baran
The Song of the Mudlark – Shane Simmons
The Tale of the Forty Thieves – C.H. Dye
The Strange Missive of Germaine Wilkes – Mark Mower
The Case of the Vanished Killer – Derrick Belanger
The Adventure of the Aspen Papers – Daniel D. Victor
The Ululation of Wolves – Steve Mountain
The Case of the Vanishing Inn – Stephen Wade
The King of Diamonds – John Heywood
The Adventure of Urquhart Manse – Will Thomas
The Adventure of the Seventh Stain – Daniel McGachey
The Two Umbrellas – Martin Rosenstock
The Adventure of the Fateful Malady – Craig Janacek

PART II: 1890-1895
Foreword – Catherine Cooke
Foreword – Roger Johnson
Foreword – David Marcum
The Bachelor of Baker Street Muses on Irene Adler (A Poem) – Carole Nelson Douglas
The Affair of Miss Finney – Ann Margaret Lewis
The Adventure of the Bookshop Owner – Vincent W. Wright
The Case of the Unrepentant Husband – William Patrick Maynard
The Verse of Death – Matthew Booth
Lord Garnett's Skulls – J.R. Campbell
Larceny in the Sky with Diamonds – Robert V. Stapleton
The Glennon Falls – Sam Wiebe
The Adventure of *The Sleeping Cardinal* – Jeremy Branton Holstein

(Continued on the next page . . . .)

The Case of the Anarchist's Bomb – Bill Crider
The Riddle of the Rideau Rifles – Peter Calamai
The Adventure of the Willow Basket – Lyndsay Faye
The Onion Vendor's Secret – Marcia Wilson
The Adventure of the Murderous Numismatist – Jack Grochot
The Saviour of Cripplegate Square – Bert Coules
A Study in Abstruse Detail – Wendy C. Fries
The Adventure of the St. Nicholas the Elephant – Christopher Redmond
The Lady on the Bridge – Mike Hogan
The Adventure of the Poison Tea Epidemic – Carl L. Heifetz
The Man on Westminster Bridge – Dick Gillman

PART III: 1896-1929
Foreword – David Stuart Davies
Foreword – Roger Johnson
Foreword – David Marcum
Two Sonnets (Poems) – Bonnie MacBird
Harbinger of Death – Geri Schear
The Adventure of the Regular Passenger – Paul D. Gilbert
The Perfect Spy – Stuart Douglas
A Mistress – Missing – Lyn McConchie
Two Plus Two – Phil Growick
The Adventure of the Coptic Patriarch – Séamus Duffy
The Royal Arsenal Affair – Leslie F.E. Coombs
The Adventure of the Sunken Parsley – Mark Alberstat
The Strange Case of the Violin Savant – GC Rosenquist
The Hopkins Brothers Affair – Iain McLaughlin and Claire Bartlett
The Disembodied Assassin – Andrew Lane
The Adventure of the Dark Tower – Peter K. Andersson
The Adventure of the Reluctant Corpse – Matthew J. Elliott
The Inspector of Graves – Jim French
The Adventure of the Parson's Son – Bob Byrne
The Adventure of the Botanist's Glove – James Lovegrove
A Most Diabolical Plot – Tim Symonds
The Opera Thief – Larry Millett
Blood Brothers – Kim Krisco
The Adventure of *The White Bird* – C. Edward Davis
The Adventure of the Avaricious Bookkeeper – Joel and Carolyn Senter

PART IV – 2016 Annual
Foreword – Steven Rothman
Foreword – Richard Doyle
Foreword – Roger Johnson
Foreword – Melissa Farnham
Foreword – Steve Emecz
Foreword – David Marcum
Toast to Mrs. Hudson (A Poem) – Arlene Mantin Levy
The Tale of the First Adventure – Derrick Belanger

(Continued on the next page . . . .)

The Adventure of the Turkish Cipher – Deanna Baran
The Adventure of the Missing Necklace – Daniel D. Victor
The Case of the Rondel Dagger – Mark Mower
The Adventure of the Double-Edged Hoard – Craig Janacek
The Adventure of the Impossible Murders – Jayantika Ganguly
The Watcher in the Woods – Denis O. Smith
The Wargrave Resurrection – Matthew Booth
Relating To One of My Old Cases – J.R. Campbell
The Adventure at the Beau Soleil – Bonnie MacBird
The Adventure of the Phantom Coachman – Arthur Hall
The Adventure of the Arsenic Dumplings – Bob Byrne
The Disappearing Anarchist Trick – Andrew Lane
The Adventure of the Grace Chalice – Roger Johnson
The Adventure of John Vincent Harden – Hugh Ashton
Murder at Tragere House – David Stuart Davies
The Adventure of *The Green Lady* – Vincent W. Wright
The Adventure of the Fellow Traveller – Daniel McGachey
The Adventure of the Highgate Financier – Nicholas Utechin
A Game of Illusion – Jeremy Holstein
The London Wheel – David Marcum
The Adventure of the Half-Melted Wolf – Marcia Wilson

PART V – Christmas Adventures

Foreword – Jonathan Kellerman
Foreword – Roger Johnson
Foreword – David Marcum
The Ballad of the Carbuncle (A Poem) – Ashley D. Polasek
The Case of the Ruby Necklace – Bob Byrne
The Jet Brooch – Denis O. Smith
The Adventure of the Missing Irregular – Amy Thomas
The Adventure of the Knighted Watchmaker – Derrick Belanger
The Stolen Relic – David Marcum
A Christmas Goose – C.H. Dye
The Adventure of the Long-Lost Enemy – Marcia Wilson
The Queen's Writing Table – Julie McKuras
The Blue Carbuncle – Sir Arthur Conan Doyle (Dramatised by Bert Coules)
The Case of the Christmas Cracker – John Hall
The Man Who Believed in Nothing – Jim French
The Case of the Christmas Star – S.F. Bennett
The Christmas Card Mystery – Narrelle M. Harris
The Question of the Death Bed Conversion – William Patrick Maynard
The Adventure of the Christmas Surprise – Vincent W. Wright
A Bauble in Scandinavia – James Lovegrove
The Adventure of Marcus Davery – Arthur Hall
The Adventure of the Purple Poet – Nicholas Utechin

(Continued on the next page . . . .)

The Adventure of the Vanishing Man – Mike Chinn
The Adventure of the Empty Manger – Tracy J. Revels
A Perpetrator in a Pear Tree – Roger Riccard
The Case of the Christmas Trifle – Wendy C. Fries
The Adventure of the Christmas Stocking – Paul D. Gilbert
The Adventure of the Golden Hunter – Jan Edwards
The Curious Case of the Well-Connected Criminal – Molly Carr
The Case of the Reformed Sinner – S. Subramanian
The Adventure of the Improbable Intruder – Peter K. Andersson
The Adventure of the Handsome Ogre – Matthew J. Elliott
The Adventure of the Deceased Doctor – Hugh Ashton
The Mile End Mynah Bird – Mark Mower

PART VI – 2017 Annual
Foreword – Colin Jeavons
Foreword – Nicholas Utechin
Foreword – Roger Johnson
Foreword – David Marcum
Sweet Violin (A Poem) – Bonnie MacBird
The Adventure of the Murdered Spinster – Bob Byrne
The Irregular – Julie McKuras
The Coffee Trader's Dilemma – Derrick Belanger
The Two Patricks – Robert Perret
The Adventure at St. Catherine's – Deanna Baran
The Adventure of a Thousand Stings – GC Rosenquist
The Adventure of the Returned Captain – Hugh Ashton
The Adventure of the Wonderful Toy – David Timson
The Adventure of the Cat's Claws – Shane Simmons
The Grave Message – Stephen Wade
The Radicant Munificent Society – Mark Mower
The Adventure of the Apologetic Assassin – David Friend
The Adventure of the Traveling Corpse – Nick Cardillo
The Adventure of the Apothecary's Prescription – Roger Riccard
The Case of the Bereaved Author – S. Subramanian
The Tetanus Epidemic – Carl L. Heifetz
The Bubble Reputation – Geri Schear
The Case of the Vanishing Venus – S.F. Bennett
The Adventure of the Vanishing Apprentice – Jennifer Copping
The Adventure of the Apothecary Shop – Jim French
The Case of the Plummeting Painter – Carla Coupe
The Case of the Temperamental Terrier – Narrelle M. Harris
The Adventure of the Frightened Architect – Arthur Hall
The Adventure of the Sunken Indiaman – Craig Janacek
The Exorcism of the Haunted Stick – Marcia Wilson
The Adventure of the Queen's Teardrop – Tracy Revels
The Curious Case of the Charwoman's Brooch – Molly Carr

(Continued on the next page . . . .)

The Unwelcome Client – Keith Hann
The Tempest of Lyme – David Ruffle
The Problem of the Holy Oil – David Marcum
A Scandal in Serbia – Thomas A. Turley
The Curious Case of Mr. Marconi – Jan Edwards
Mr. Holmes and Dr. Watson Learn to Fly – C. Edward Davis
Die Weisse Frau – Tim Symonds
A Case of Mistaken Identity – Daniel D. Victor

PART VII – Eliminate the Impossible: 1880-1891

Foreword – Lee Child
Foreword – Rand B. Lee
Foreword – Michael Cox
Foreword – Roger Johnson
Foreword – Melissa Farnham
Foreword – David Marcum
No Ghosts Need Apply (A Poem) – Jacquelynn Morris
The Melancholy Methodist – Mark Mower
The Curious Case of the Sweated Horse – Jan Edwards
The Adventure of the Second William Wilson – Daniel D. Victor
The Adventure of the Marchindale Stiletto – James Lovegrove
The Case of the Cursed Clock – Gayle Lange Puhl
The Tranquility of the Morning – Mike Hogan
A Ghost from Christmas Past – Thomas A. Turley
The Blank Photograph – James Moffett
The Adventure of A Rat. – Adrian Middleton
The Adventure of Vanaprastha – Hugh Ashton
The Ghost of Lincoln – Geri Schear
The Manor House Ghost – S. Subramanian
The Case of the Unquiet Grave – John Hall
The Adventure of the Mortal Combat – Jayantika Ganguly
The Last Encore of Quentin Carol – S.F. Bennett
The Case of the Petty Curses – Steven Philip Jones
The Tuttman Gallery – Jim French
The Second Life of Jabez Salt – John Linwood Grant
The Mystery of the Scarab Earrings – Thomas Fortenberry
The Adventure of the Haunted Room – Mike Chinn
The Pharaoh's Curse – Robert V. Stapleton
The Vampire of the Lyceum – Charles Veley and Anna Elliott
The Adventure of the Mind's Eye – Shane Simmons

PART VIII – Eliminate the Impossible: 1892-1905

Foreword – Lee Child
Foreword – Rand B. Lee
Foreword – Michael Cox
Foreword – Roger Johnson
Foreword – Melissa Farnham

(Continued on the next page . . . .)

Foreword – David Marcum
Sherlock Holmes in the Lavender field (A Poem) – Christopher James
The Adventure of the Lama's Dream – Deanna Baran
The Ghost of Dorset House – Tim Symonds
The Peculiar Persecution of John Vincent Harden – Sandor Jay Sonnen
The Case of the Biblical Colours – Ben Cardall
The Inexplicable Death of Matthew Arnatt – Andrew Lane
The Adventure of the Highgate Spectre – Michael Mallory
The Case of the Corpse Flower – Wendy C. Fries
The Problem of the Five Razors – Aaron Smith
The Adventure of the Moonlit Shadow – Arthur Hall
The Ghost of Otis Maunder – David Friend
The Adventure of the Pharaoh's Tablet – Robert Perret
The Haunting of Hamilton Gardens – Nick Cardillo
The Adventure of the Risen Corpse – Paul D. Gilbert
The Mysterious Mourner – Cindy Dye
The Adventure of the Hungry Ghost – Tracy Revels
In the Realm of the Wretched King – Derrick Belanger
The Case of the Little Washerwoman – William Meikle
The Catacomb Saint Affair – Marcia Wilson
The Curious Case of Charlotte Musgrave – Roger Riccard
The Adventure of the Awakened Spirit – Craig Janacek
The Adventure of the Theatre Ghost – Jeremy Branton Holstein
The Adventure of the Glassy Ghost – Will Murray
The Affair of the Grange Haunting – David Ruffle
The Adventure of the Pallid Mask – Daniel McGachey
The Two Different Women – David Marcum

Part IX – 2018 Annual (1879-1895)

Foreword – Nicholas Meyer
Foreword – Roger Johnson
Foreword – Melissa Farnham
Foreword – Steve Emecz
Foreword – David Marcum
Violet Smith (A Poem) – Amy Thomas
The Adventure of the Temperance Society – Deanna Baran
The Adventure of the Fool and His Money – Roger Riccard
The Helverton Inheritance – David Marcum
The Adventure of the Faithful Servant – Tracy Revels
The Adventure of the Parisian Butcher – Nick Cardillo
The Missing Empress – Robert Stapleton
The Resplendent Plane Tree – Kevin P. Thornton
The Strange Adventure of the Doomed Sextette – Leslie Charteris and Denis Green
The Adventure of the Old Boys' Club – Shane Simmons
The Case of the Golden Trail – James Moffett
The Detective Who Cried Wolf – C.H. Dye

(Continued on the next page . . . .)

The Lambeth Poisoner Case – Stephen Gaspar
The Confession of Anna Jarrow – S. F. Bennett
The Adventure of the Disappearing Dictionary – Sonia Fetherston
The Fairy Hills Horror – Geri Schear
A Loathsome and Remarkable Adventure – Marcia Wilson
The Adventure of the Multiple Moriartys – David Friend
The Influence Machine – Mark Mower

Part X – 2018 Annual (1896-1916)
Foreword – Nicholas Meyer
Foreword – Roger Johnson
Foreword – Melissa Farnham
Foreword – Steve Emecz
Foreword – David Marcum
A Man of Twice Exceptions (A Poem) – Derrick Belanger
The Horned God – Kelvin Jones
The Coughing Man – Jim French
The Adventure of Canal Reach – Arthur Hall
A Simple Case of Abduction – Mike Hogan
A Case of Embezzlement – Steven Ehrman
The Adventure of the Vanishing Diplomat – Greg Hatcher
The Adventure of the Perfidious Partner – Jayantika Ganguly
A Brush With Death – Dick Gillman
A Revenge Served Cold – Maurice Barkley
The Case of the Anonymous Client – Paul A. Freeman
Capitol Murder – Daniel D. Victor
The Case of the Dead Detective – Martin Rosenstock
The Musician Who Spoke From the Grave – Peter Coe Verbica
The Adventure of the Future Funeral – Hugh Ashton
The Problem of the Bruised Tongues – Will Murray
The Mystery of the Change of Art – Robert Perret
The Parsimonious Peacekeeper – Thaddeus Tuffentsamer
The Case of the Dirty Hand – G.L. Schulze
The Mystery of the Missing Artefacts – Tim Symonds

Part XI: Some Untold Cases (1880-1891)
Foreword – Lyndsay Faye
Foreword – Roger Johnson
Foreword – Melissa Grigsby
Foreword – Steve Emecz
Foreword – David Marcum
Unrecorded Holmes Cases (*A Sonnet*) – Arlene Mantin Levy and Mark Levy
The Most Repellant Man – Jayantika Ganguly
The Singular Adventure of the Extinguished Wicks – Will Murray
Mrs. Forrester's Complication – Roger Riccard
The Adventure of Vittoria, the Circus Belle – Tracy Revels

(Continued on the next page . . . .)

The Adventure of the Silver Skull – Hugh Ashton
The Pimlico Poisoner – Matthew Simmonds
The Grosvenor Square Furniture Van – David Ruffle
The Adventure of the Paradol Chamber – Paul W. Nash
The Bishopgate Jewel Case – Mike Hogan
The Singular Tragedy of the Atkinson Brothers of Trincomalee – Craig Stephen Copland
Colonel Warburton's Madness – Gayle Lange Puhl
The Adventure at Bellingbeck Park – Deanna Baran
The Giant Rat of Sumatra – Leslie Charteris and Denis Green
   Introduction by Ian Dickerson
The Vatican Cameos – Kevin P. Thornton
The Case of the Gila Monster – Stephen Herczeg
The Bogus Laundry Affair – Robert Perret
Inspector Lestrade and the Molesey Mystery – M.A. Wilson and Richard Dean Starr

Part XII: Some Untold Cases (1894-1902)

Foreword – Lyndsay Faye
Foreword – Roger Johnson
Foreword – Melissa Grigsby
Foreword – Steve Emecz
Foreword – David Marcum
It's Always Time (*A Poem*) – "Anon."
The Shanghaied Surgeon – C.H. Dye
The Trusted Advisor – David Marcum
A Shame Harder Than Death – Thomas Fortenberry
The Adventure of the Smith-Mortimer Succession – Daniel D. Victor
A Repulsive Story and a Terrible Death – Nik Morton
The Adventure of the Dishonourable Discharge – Craig Janacek
The Adventure of the Admirable Patriot – S. Subramanian
The Abernetty Transactions – Jim French
Dr. Agar and the Dinosaur – Robert Stapleton
The Giant Rat of Sumatra – Nick Cardillo
The Adventure of the Black Plague – Paul D. Gilbert
Vigor, the Hammersmith Wonder – Mike Hogan
A Correspondence Concerning Mr. James Phillimore – Derrick Belanger
The Curious Case of the Two Coptic Patriarchs – John Linwood Grant
The Conk-Singleton Forgery Case – Mark Mower
Another Case of Identity – Jane Rubino
The Adventure of the Exalted Victim – Arthur Hall

PART XIII: 2019 Annual (1881-1890)

Foreword – Will Thomas
Foreword – Roger Johnson
Foreword – Melissa Grigsby
Foreword – Steve Emecz
Foreword – David Marcum
Inscrutable (*A Poem*) – Jacquelynn Morris

(Continued on the next page . . . .)

The Folly of Age – Derrick Belanger
The Fashionably-Dressed Girl – Mark Mower
The Odour of Neroli – Brenda Seabrooke
The Coffee House Girl – David Marcum
The Mystery of the Green Room – Robert Stapleton
The Case of the Enthusiastic Amateur – S.F. Bennett
The Adventure of the Missing Cousin – Edwin A. Enstrom
The Roses of Highclough House – MJH Simmonds
The Shackled Man – Andrew Bryant
The Yellow Star of Cairo – Tim Gambrell
The Adventure of the Winterhall Monster – Tracy Revels
The Grosvenor Square Furniture Van – Hugh Ashton
The Voyage of *Albion's Thistle* – Sean M. Wright
Bootless in Chippenham – Marino C. Alvarez
The Clerkenwell Shadow – Paul Hiscock
The Adventure of the Worried Banker – Arthur Hall
The Recovery of the Ashes – Kevin P. Thornton
The Mystery of the Patient Fisherman – Jim French
Sherlock Holmes in Bedlam – David Friend
The Adventure of the Ambulatory Cadaver – Shane Simmons
The Dutch Impostors – Peter Coe Verbica
The Missing Adam Tiler – Mark Wardecker

PART XIV: 2019 Annual (1891 -1897)

Foreword – Will Thomas
Foreword – Roger Johnson
Foreword – Melissa Grigsby
Foreword – Steve Emecz
Foreword – David Marcum
Skein of Tales (*A Poem*) – Jacquelynn Morris
The Adventure of the Royal Albert Hall – Charles Veley and Anna Elliott
The Tower of Fear – Mark Sohn
The Carroun Document – David Marcum
The Threadneedle Street Murder – S. Subramanian
The Collegiate Leprechaun – Roger Riccard
A Malversation of Mummies – Marcia Wilson
The Adventure of the Silent Witness – Tracy J. Revels
The Second Whitechapel Murderer – Arthur Hall
The Adventure of the Jeweled Falcon – GC Rosenquist
The Adventure of the Crossbow – Edwin A. Enstrom
The Adventure of the Delusional Wife – Jayantika Ganguly
Child's Play – C.H. Dye
The Lancelot Connection – Matthew Booth
The Adventure of the Modern Guy Fawkes – Stephen Herczeg
Mr. Clever, Baker Street – Geri Schear
The Adventure of the Scarlet Rosebud – Liz Hedgecock

(Continued on the next page . . . .)

The Poisoned Regiment – Carl Heifetz
The Case of the Persecuted Poacher – Gayle Lange Puhl
It's Time – Harry DeMaio
The Case of the Fourpenny Coffin – I.A. Watson
The Horror in King Street – Thomas A. Burns, Jr.

PART XV: 2019 Annual (1898-1917)
Foreword – Will Thomas
Foreword – Roger Johnson
Foreword – Melissa Grigsby
Foreword – Steve Emecz
Foreword – David Marcum
Two Poems – Christopher James
The Whitechapel Butcher – Mark Mower
The Incomparable Miss Incognita – Thomas Fortenberry
The Adventure of the Twofold Purpose – Robert Perret
The Adventure of the Green Gifts – Tracy J. Revels
The Turk's Head – Robert Stapleton
A Ghost in the Mirror – Peter Coe Verbica
The Mysterious Mr. Rim – Maurice Barkley
The Adventure of the Fatal Jewel-Box – Edwin A. Enstrom
Mass Murder – William Todd
The Notable Musician – Roger Riccard
The Devil's Painting – Kelvin I. Jones
The Adventure of the Silent Sister – Arthur Hall
A Skeleton's Sorry Story – Jack Grochot
An Actor and a Rare One – David Marcum
The Silver Bullet – Dick Gillman
The Adventure at Throne of Gilt – Will Murray
"The Boy Who Would Be King – Dick Gillman
The Case of the Seventeenth Monk – Tim Symonds
Alas, Poor Will – Mike Hogan
The Case of the Haunted Chateau – Leslie Charteris and Denis Green
          Introduction by Ian Dickerson
The Adventure of the Weeping Stone – Nick Cardillo
The Adventure of the Three Telegrams – Darryl Webber

Part XVI – Whatever Remains . . . Must Be the Truth (1881-1890)
Foreword – Kareem Abdul-Jabbar
Foreword – Roger Johnson
Foreword – Steve Emecz
Foreword – David Marcum
The Hound of the Baskervilles (Retold) (*A Poem*) – Josh Pachter
The Wylington Lake Monster – Derrick Belanger
The *Juju* Men of Richmond – Mark Sohn

(Continued on the next page . . . .)

The Adventure of the Headless Lady – Tracy J. Revels
Angelus Domini Nuntiavit – Kevin P. Thornton
The Blue Lady of Dunraven – Andrew Bryant
The Adventure of the Ghoulish Grenadier – Josh Anderson and David Friend
The Curse of Barcombe Keep – Brenda Seabrooke
The Affair of the Regressive Man – David Marcum
The Adventure of the Giant's Wife – I.A. Watson
The Adventure of Miss Anna Truegrace – Arthur Hall
The Haunting of Bottomly's Grandmother – Tim Gambrell
The Adventure of the Intrusive Spirit – Shane Simmons
The Paddington Poltergeist – Bob Bishop
The Spectral Pterosaur – Mark Mower
The Weird of Caxton – Kelvin Jones
The Adventure of the Obsessive Ghost – Jayantika Ganguly

Part XVII – Whatever Remains . . . Must Be the Truth (1891-1898)
Foreword – Kareem Abdul-Jabbar
Foreword – Roger Johnson
Foreword – Steve Emecz
Foreword – David Marcum
The Violin Thief (*A Poem*) – Christopher James
The Spectre of Scarborough Castle – Charles Veley and Anna Elliott
The Case for Which the World is Not Yet Prepared – Steven Philip Jones
The Adventure of the Returning Spirit – Arthur Hall
The Adventure of the Bewitched Tenant – Michael Mallory
The Misadventures of the Bonnie Boy – Will Murray
The Adventure of the *Danse Macabre* – Paul D. Gilbert
The Strange Persecution of John Vincent Harden – S. Subramanian
The Dead Quiet Library – Roger Riccard
The Adventure of the Sugar Merchant – Stephen Herczeg
The Adventure of the Undertaker's Fetch – Tracy J. Revels
The Holloway Ghosts – Hugh Ashton
The Diogenes Club Poltergeist – Chris Chan
The Madness of Colonel Warburton – Bert Coules
The Return of the Noble Bachelor – Jane Rubino
The Reappearance of Mr. James Phillimore – David Marcum
The Miracle Worker – Geri Schear
The Hand of Mesmer – Dick Gillman

Part XVIII – Whatever Remains . . . Must Be the Truth (1899-1925)
Foreword – Kareem Abdul-Jabbar
Foreword – Roger Johnson
Foreword – Steve Emecz
Foreword – David Marcum
The Adventure of the Lighthouse on the Moor (*A Poem*) – Christopher James
The Witch of Ellenby – Thomas A. Burns, Jr.

(Continued on the next page . . . .)

The Tollington Ghost – Roger Silverwood
You Only Live Thrice – Robert Stapleton
The Adventure of the Fair Lad – Craig Janacek
The Adventure of the Voodoo Curse – Gareth Tilley
The Cassandra of Providence Place – Paul Hiscock
The Adventure of the House Abandoned – Arthur Hall
The Winterbourne Phantom – M.J. Elliott
The Murderous Mercedes – Harry DeMaio
The Solitary Violinist – Tom Turley
The Cunning Man – Kelvin I. Jones
The Adventure of Khamaat's Curse – Tracy J. Revels
The Adventure of the Weeping Mary – Matthew White
The Unnerved Estate Agent – David Marcum
Death in The House of the Black Madonna – Nick Cardillo
The Case of the Ivy-Covered Tomb – S.F. Bennett

Part XIX: 2020 Annual (1892-1890)

Foreword – John Lescroart
Foreword – Roger Johnson
Foreword – Lizzy Butler
Foreword – Steve Emecz
Foreword – David Marcum
Holmes's Prayer (*A Poem*) – Christopher James
A Case of Paternity – Matthew White
The Raspberry Tart – Roger Riccard
The Mystery of the Elusive Bard – Kevin P. Thornton
The Man in the Maroon Suit – Chris Chan
The Scholar of Silchester Court – Nick Cardillo
The Adventure of the Changed Man – MJH. Simmonds
The Adventure of the Tea-Stained Diamonds – Craig Stephen Copland
The Indigo Impossibility – Will Murray
The Case of the Emerald Knife-Throwers – Ian Ableson
A Game of Skittles – Thomas A. Turley
The Gordon Square Discovery – David Marcum
The Tattooed Rose – Dick Gillman
The Problem at Pentonville Prison – David Friend
The Nautch Night Case – Brenda Seabrooke
The Disappearing Prisoner – Arthur Hall
The Case of the Missing Pipe – James Moffett
The Whitehaven Ransom – Robert Stapleton
The Enlightenment of Newton – Dick Gillman
The Impaled Man – Andrew Bryant
The Mystery of the Elusive Li Shen – Will Murray
The Mahmudabad Result – Andrew Bryant

(Continued on the next page . . . .)

The Adventure of the Matched Set – Peter Coe Verbica
When the Prince First Dined at the Diogenes Club – Sean M. Wright
The Sweetenbury Safe Affair – Tim Gambrell

Part XX: 2020 Annual (1891-1897)
Foreword – John Lescroart
Foreword – Roger Johnson
Foreword – Lizzy Butler
Foreword – Steve Emecz
Foreword – David Marcum
The Sibling (*A Poem*) – Jacquelynn Morris
Blood and Gunpowder – Thomas A. Burns, Jr.
The Atelier of Death – Harry DeMaio
The Adventure of the Beauty Trap – Tracy Revels
A Case of Unfinished Business – Steven Philip Jones
The Case of the S.S. Bokhara – Mark Mower
The Adventure of the American Opera Singer – Deanna Baran
The Keadby Cross – David Marcum
The Adventure at Dead Man's Hole – Stephen Herczeg
The Elusive Mr. Chester – Arthur Hall
The Adventure of Old Black Duffel – Will Murray
The Blood-Spattered Bridge – Gayle Lange Puhl
The Tomorrow Man – S.F. Bennett
The Sweet Science of Bruising – Kevin P. Thornton
The Mystery of Sherlock Holmes – Christopher Todd
The Elusive Mr. Phillimore – Matthew J. Elliott
The Murders in the Maharajah's Railway Carriage – Charles Veley and Anna Elliott
The Ransomed Miracle – I.A. Watson
The Adventure of the Unkind Turn – Robert Perret
The Perplexing X'ing – Sonia Fetherston
The Case of the Short-Sighted Clown – Susan Knight

Part XXI: 2020 Annual (1898-1923)
Foreword – John Lescroart
Foreword – Roger Johnson
Foreword – Lizzy Butler
Foreword – Steve Emecz
Foreword – David Marcum
The Case of the Missing Rhyme (*A Poem*) – Joseph W. Svec III
The Problem of the St. Francis Parish Robbery – R.K. Radek
The Adventure of the Grand Vizier – Arthur Hall
The Mummy's Curse – DJ Tyrer
The Fractured Freemason of Fitzrovia – David L. Leal
The Bleeding Heart – Paula Hammond
The Secret Admirer – Jayantika Ganguly

(Continued on the next page . . . .)

The Deceased Priest – Peter Coe Verbica
The Case of the Rewrapped Presents – Bob Byrne
The Invisible Assassin – Geri Shear
The Adventure of the Chocolate Pot – Hugh Ashton
The Adventure of the Incessant Workers – Arthur Hall
When Best Served Cold – Stephen Mason
The Cat's Meat Lady of Cavendish Square – David Marcum
The Unveiled Lodger – Mark Mower
The League of Unhappy Orphans – Leslie Charteris and Denis Green
        Introduction by Ian Dickerson
The Adventure of the Three Fables – Jane Rubino
The Cobbler's Treasure – Dick Gillman
The Adventure of the Wells Beach Ruffians – Derrick Belanger
The Adventure of the Doctor's Hand – Michael Mallory
The Case of the Purloined Talisman – John Lawrence

Part XXII: Some More Untold Cases (1877-1887)

Foreword – Otto Penzler
Foreword – Roger Johnson
Foreword – Steve Emecz
Foreword – Jacqueline Silver
Foreword – David Marcum
The Philosophy of Holmes (*A Poem*) – Christopher James
The Terror of the Tankerville – S.F. Bennett
The Singular Affair of the Aluminium Crutch – William Todd
The Trifling Matter of Mortimer Maberley – Geri Schear
Abracadaver – Susan Knight
The Secret in Lowndes Court – David Marcum
Vittoria, the Circus Bell – Bob Bishop
The Adventure of the Vanished Husband – Tracy J. Revels
Merridew of Abominable Memory – Chris Chan
The Substitute Thief – Richard Paolinelli
The Whole Story Concerning the Politician, the Lighthouse, and the Trained Cormorant –
        Derrick Belanger
A Child's Reward – Stephen Mason
The Case of the Elusive Umbrella – Leslie Charteris and Denis Green
        Introduction by Ian Dickerson
The Strange Death of an Art Dealer – Tim Symonds
Watch Him Fall – Liese Sherwood-Fabre
The Adventure of the Transatlantic Gila – Ian Ableson
Intruders at Baker Street – Chris Chan
The Paradol Chamber – Mark Mower
Wolf Island – Robert Stapleton
The Etherage Escapade – Roger Riccard

(Continued on the next page . . . .)

The Dundas Separation Case – Kevin P. Thornton
The Broken Glass – Denis O. Smith

Part XXIII: Some More Untold Cases (1888-1894)
Foreword – Otto Penzler
Foreword – Roger Johnson
Foreword – Steve Emecz
Foreword – Jacqueline Silver
Foreword – David Marcum
The Housekeeper (*A Poem*) – John Linwood Grant
The Uncanny Adventure of the Hammersmith Wonder – Will Murray
Mrs. Forrester's Domestic Complication– Tim Gambrell
The Adventure of the Abducted Bard – I.A. Watson
The Adventure of the Loring Riddle – Craig Janacek
To the Manor Bound – Jane Rubino
The Crimes of John Clay – Paul Hiscock
The Adventure of the Nonpareil Club – Hugh Ashton
The Adventure of the Singular Worm – Mike Chinn
The Adventure of the Forgotten Brolly – Shane Simmons
The Adventure of the Tired Captain – Dacre Stoker and Leverett Butts
The Rhayader Legacy – David Marcum
The Adventure of the Tired Captain – Matthew J. Elliott
The Secret of Colonel Warburton's Insanity – Paul D. Gilbert
The Adventure of Merridew of Abominable Memory – Tracy J. Revels
The Affair of the Hellingstone Rubies – Margaret Walsh
The Adventure of the Drewhampton Poisoner – Arthur Hall
The Incident of the Dual Intrusions – Barry Clay
The Case of the Un-Paralleled Adventures – Steven Philip Jones
The Affair of the Friesland – Jan van Koningsveld
The Forgetful Detective – Marcia Wilson
The Smith-Mortimer Succession – Tim Gambrell
The Repulsive Matter of the Bloodless Banker – Will Murray

Part XXIV: Some More Untold Cases (1895-1903)
Foreword – Otto Penzler
Foreword – Roger Johnson
Foreword – Steve Emecz
Foreword – Jacqueline Silver
Foreword – David Marcum
Sherlock Holmes and the Return of the Missing Rhyme (*A Poem*) – Joseph W. Svec III
The Comet Wine's Funeral – Marcia Wilson
The Case of the Accused Cook – Brenda Seabrooke
The Case of Vanderbilt and the Yeggman – Stephen Herczeg

(Continued on the next page . . . .)

The Tragedy of Woodman's Lee – Tracy J. Revels
The Murdered Millionaire – Kevin P. Thornton
Another Case of Identity – Thomas A. Burns, Jr.
The Case of Indelible Evidence – Dick Gillman
The Adventure of Parsley and Butter – Jayantika Ganguly
The Adventure of the Nile Traveler – John Davis
The Curious Case of the Crusader's Cross – DJ Tyrer
An Act of Faith – Harry DeMaio
The Adventure of the Conk-Singleton Forgery – Arthur Hall
A Simple Matter – Susan Knight
The Hammerford Will Business – David Marcum
The Adventure of Mr. Fairdale Hobbs – Arthur Hall
The Adventure of the Abergavenny Murder – Craig Stephen Copland
The Chinese Puzzle Box – Gayle Lange Puhl
The Adventure of the Refused Knighthood – Craig Stephen Copland
The Case of the Consulting Physician – John Lawrence
The Man from Deptford – John Linwood Grant
The Case of the Impossible Assassin – Paula Hammond

Part XXV: 2021 Annual (1881-1888)

Foreword – Peter Lovesey
Foreword – Roger Johnson
Foreword – Steve Emecz
Foreword – Jacqueline Silver
Foreword – David Marcum
Baskerville Hall (*A Poem*) – Kelvin I. Jones
The Persian Slipper – Brenda Seabrooke
The Adventure of the Doll Maker's Daughter – Matthew White
The Flinders Case – Kevin McCann
The Sunderland Tragedies – David Marcum
The Tin Soldiers – Paul Hiscock
The Shattered Man – MJH Simmonds
The Hungarian Doctor – Denis O. Smith
The Black Hole of Berlin – Robert Stapleton
The Thirteenth Step – Keith Hann
The Missing Murderer – Marcia Wilson
Dial Square – Martin Daley
The Adventure of the Deadly Tradition – Matthew J. Elliott
The Adventure of the Fabricated Vision – Craig Janacek
The Adventure of the Murdered Maharajah – Hugh Ashton
The God of War – Hal Glatzer
The Atkinson Brothers of Trincomalee – Stephen Gaspar

(Continued on the next page . . . .)

The Switched String – Chris Chan
The Case of the Secret Samaritan – Jane Rubino
The Bishopsgate Jewel Case – Stephen Gaspar

Part XXVI: 2021 Annual (1889-1897)
Foreword – Peter Lovesey
Foreword – Roger Johnson
Foreword – Steve Emecz
Foreword – Jacqueline Silver
Foreword – David Marcum
221b Baker Street (*A Poem*) – Kevin Patrick McCann
The Burglary Season – Marcia Wilson
The Lamplighter at Rosebery Avenue – James Moffett
The Disfigured Hand – Peter Coe Verbica
The Adventure of the Bloody Duck – Margaret Walsh
The Tragedy at Longpool – James Gelter
The Case of the Viscount's Daughter – Naching T. Kassa
The Key in the Snuffbox – DJ Tyrer
The Race for the Gleghorn Estate – Ian Ableson
The Isa Bird Befuddlement – Kevin P. Thornton
The Cliddesden Questions – David Marcum
Death in Verbier – Adrian Middleton
The King's Cross Road Somnambulist – Dick Gillman
The Magic Bullet – Peter Coe Verbica
The Petulant Patient – Geri Schear
The Mystery of the Groaning Stone – Mark Mower
The Strange Case of the Pale Boy – Susan Knight
The Adventure of the Zande Dagger – Frank Schildiner
The Adventure of the Vengeful Daughter – Arthur Hall
Do the Needful – Harry DeMaio
The Count, the Banker, the Thief, and the Seven Half-sovereigns – Mike   Hogan
The Adventure of the Unsprung Mousetrap – Anthony Gurney
The Confectioner's Captives – I.A. Watson

Part XXVII: 2021 Annual (1898-1928)
Foreword – Peter Lovesey
Foreword – Roger Johnson
Foreword – Steve Emecz
Foreword – Jacqueline Silver
Foreword – David Marcum
Sherlock Holmes Returns: The Missing Rhyme (*A Poem*) – Joseph W. Svec, III
The Adventure of the Hero's Heir – Tracy J. Revels
The Curious Case of the Soldier's Letter – John Davis
The Case of the Norwegian Daredevil – John Lawrence
The Case of the Borneo Tribesman – Stephen Herczeg
The Adventure of the White Roses – Tracy J. Revels

(Continued on the next page . . . .)

Mrs. Crichton's Ledger – Tim Gambrell
The Adventure of the Not-Very-Merry Widows – Craig Stephen Copland
The Son of God – Jeremy Branton Holstein
The Adventure of the Disgraced Captain – Thomas A. Turley
The Woman Who Returned From the Dead – Arthur Hall
The Farraway Street Lodger – David Marcum
The Mystery of Foxglove Lodge – S.C. Toft
The Strange Adventure of Murder by Remote Control – Leslie Charteris and Denis Green
        Introduction by Ian Dickerson
The Case of The Blue Parrot – Roger Riccard
The Adventure of the Expelled Master – Will Murray
The Case of the Suicidal Suffragist – John Lawrence
The Welbeck Abbey Shooting Party – Thomas A. Turley
Case No. 358 – Marcia Wilson

The following contributions appear in this volume:
The MX Book of New Sherlock Holmes Stories
Part XXVIII – More Christmas Adventures (1869-1888)

"No Malice Intended" ©2021 by Deanna Baran. All Rights Reserved. First publication, original to this collection. Printed by permission of the author.

"Christmas at the Red Lion" ©2021 by Thomas A. Burns, Jr. All Rights Reserved. First publication, original to this collection. Printed by permission of the author.

"The Sebastopol Clasp" ©2021 by Martin Daley. All Rights Reserved. First publication, original to this collection. Printed by permission of the author.

"An Ongoing Legacy for Sherlock Holmes" ©2021 by Steve Emecz. All Rights Reserved. First publication, original to this collection. Printed by permission of the author.

"The Chatterton-Smythe Affair" ©2021 by Tim Gambrell. All Rights Reserved. First publication, original to this collection. Printed by permission of the author.

"The Silent Brotherhood" ©2021 by Dick Gillman. All Rights Reserved. First publication, original to this collection. Printed by permission of the author.

"The Case of the Christmas Pudding" ©2021 by Liz Hedgecock. All Rights Reserved. First publication, original to this collection. Printed by permission of the author.

"The Case of the Left Foot" ©2021 by Stephen Herczeg. All Rights Reserved. First publication, original to this collection. Printed by permission of the author.

"The St. Stephen's Day Mystery" ©2021 by Paul Hiscock. All Rights Reserved. First publication, original to this collection. Printed by permission of the author.

"A Fine Kettle of Fish" ©2021 by Mike Hogan. All Rights Reserved. First publication, original to this collection. Printed by permission of the author.

"Foreword" ©2021 by Nancy Holder. All Rights Reserved. First publication, original to this collection. Printed by permission of the author.

"It is the Season of Forgiveness" ©2021 by Roger Johnson. All Rights Reserved. First publication, original to this collection. Printed by permission of the author.

"The Case of the Duplicitous Suitor" ©2021 by John Lawrence. All Rights Reserved. First publication, original to this collection. Printed by permission of the author.

"The Six-Fingered Scoundrel" ©2021 by Jeffrey A. Lockwood. All Rights Reserved. First publication, original to this collection. Printed by permission of the author.

"Editor's Foreword: Never Enough Holmes Adventures – Even at Christmas!" *and* "The Christmas Ghost of Crailloch Taigh" ©2021 by David Marcum. All Rights Reserved. First publication, original to this collection. Printed by permission of the author.

"The Yuletide Heist" ©2021 by Mark Mower. All Rights Reserved. First publication, original to this collection. Printed by permission of the author.

"The Adventure of the Christmas Lesson" ©2021 by Will Murray. All Rights Reserved. First publication, original to this collection. Printed by permission of the author.

"The Case of the Golden Grail" ©2021 by Roger Riccard. All Rights Reserved. First publication, original to this collection. Printed by permission of the author.

"The Christmas Card Case" ©2021 by Brenda Seabrooke. All Rights Reserved. First publication, original to this collection. Printed by permission of the author.

"A Sherlockian Christmas" (A Poem) ©2021 by Joseph W. Svec, III. All Rights Reserved. First publication, original to this collection. Printed by permission of the author.

"A Study in Murder" ©2021 by Amy Thomas. All Rights Reserved. First publication, original to this collection. Printed by permission of the author.

"A Yuletide Tragedy" ©2021 by Thomas A. Turley. All Rights Reserved. First publication, original to this collection. Printed by permission of the author.

"Undershaw: Eliminating the Impossible" ©2021 by Emma West. All Rights Reserved. First publication, original to this collection. Printed by permission of the author.

The following contributions appear in the companion volumes:
Part XXIX – More Christmas Adventures (1889-1896)
Part XXX – More Christmas Adventures (1897-1928)

"The Sword in the Spruce" ©2021 by Ian Ableson. All Rights Reserved. First publication, original to this collection. Printed by permission of the author.

"The Adventure of the Serpentine Body" *and* "Absent Friends" ©2021 by Wayne Anderson. All Rights Reserved. First publication, original to this collection. Printed by permission of the author.

"The Man of Miracles" ©2021 by Derrick Belanger. All Rights Reserved. First publication, original to this collection. Printed by permission of the author.

"The Case of the Cursory Curse" ©2021 by Andrew Bryant. All Rights Reserved. First publication, original to this collection. Printed by permission of the author.

"The Bitter Gravestones" ©2021 by Chris Chan. All Rights Reserved. First publication, original to this collection. Printed by permission of the author.

"The Incident of the Stolen Christmas Present" ©2021 by Barry Clay. All Rights Reserved. First publication, original to this collection. Printed by permission of the author.

"The Baffling Adventure of the Baby Jesus" ©2021 by Craig Stephen Copland. All Rights Reserved. First publication, original to this collection. Printed by permission of the author.

"The Incident in Regent Street" ©2021 by Harry DeMaio. All Rights Reserved. First publication, original to this collection. Printed by permission of the author.

"The St. Giles Child Murders" ©2021 by Tim Gambrell. All Rights Reserved. First publication, original to this collection. Printed by permission of the author.

"The Adventure of the Dextrous Doctor" ©2021 by Jayantika Ganguly. All Rights Reserved. First publication, original to this collection. Printed by permission of the author.

"The Dilemma of Mr. Henry Baker" ©2021 by Paul D. Gilbert. All Rights Reserved. First publication, original to this collection. Printed by permission of the author.

"The Adventure of the Christmas Threat" *and* "The Adventure of the Injured Man" *and* "The Adventure of the Maligned Mineralogist" ©2021 by Arthur Hall. All Rights Reserved. First publication, original to this collection. Printed by permission of the author.

"The Case of the Earnest Young Man" ©2021 by Paula Hammond. All Rights Reserved. First publication, original to this collection. Printed by permission of the author.

"The Midnight Mass Murder" ©2021 by Paul Hiscock. All Rights Reserved. First publication, original to this collection. Printed by permission of the author.

"Baskerville Hall in Winter" (A Poem) *and* "Baker Street in Snow (1890)" (A Poem) ©2021 by Christopher James. All Rights Reserved. First publication, original to this collection. Printed by permission of the author.

"The Case of the Holly-Sprig Pudding" ©2021 by Naching T. Kassa. All Rights Reserved. First publication, original to this collection. Printed by permission of the author.

"The Mystery of Maple Tree Lodge" ©2021 by Susan Knight. All Rights Reserved. First publication, original to this collection. Printed by permission of the author.

"The Adventure of the Fugitive Irregular" ©2021 by Gordon Linzner. All Rights Reserved. First publication, original to this collection. Printed by permission of the author.

"The Adventure of the Stolen Christmas Gift" ©2021 by Michael Mallory. All Rights Reserved. First publication, original to this collection. Printed by permission of the author.

"The Father Christmas Brigade" *and* "The Canterbury Manifesto" ©2021 by David Marcum. All Rights Reserved. First publication, original to this collection. Printed by permission of the author.

"The Case of the Disappearing Beaune" ©2021 by J. Lawrence Matthews. All Rights Reserved. First publication, original to this collection. Printed by permission of the author.

"The Colourful Skein of Life" ©2021 by Julie McKuras. All Rights Reserved. First publication, original to this collection. Printed by permission of the author.

"The Adventure of the Christmas Suitors" ©2021 by Tracy Revels. All Rights Reserved. First publication, original to this collection. Printed by permission of the author.

"The Adventure of the Secret Manuscript" ©2021 by Dan Rowley. All Rights Reserved. First publication, original to this collection. Printed by permission of the author.

"The Adventure of the Chained Phantom" and accompanying illustrations ©2021 by J.S. Rowlinson. All Rights Reserved. First publication, original to this collection. Printed by permission of the author.

"A Price Above Rubies" ©2021 by Jane Rubino. All Rights Reserved. First publication, original to this collection. Printed by permission of the author.

"A Featureless Crime" ©2021 by Geri Schear. All Rights Reserved. First publication, original to this collection. Printed by permission of the author.

"The Adventure of the Viking Ghost" ©2021 by Frank Schildiner. All Rights Reserved. First publication, original to this collection. Printed by permission of the author.

"The Intrigue of the Red Christmas" ©2021 by Shane Simmons. All Rights Reserved. First publication, original to this collection. Printed by permission of the author.

"Christmas Magic" *and* "Santa's Little Elves" ©2021 by Kevin P. Thornton. All Rights Reserved. First publication, original to this collection. Printed by permission of the author.

"The Purloined Present" ©2021 by DJ Tyrer. All Rights Reserved. First publication, original to this collection. Printed by permission of the author.

"The Adventure of the Christmas Wish" ©2021 by Margaret Walsh. All Rights Reserved. First publication, original to this collection. Printed by permission of the author.

"The Twelve Days" ©2021 by I.A. Watson. All Rights Reserved. First publication, original to this collection. Printed by permission of the author.

"The Adventure of the Second Sister" ©2021 Matthew White. All Rights Reserved. First publication, original to this collection. Printed by permission of the author.

"The Krampus Who Came to Call" ©2021 Marcia Wilson. All Rights Reserved. First publication, original to this collection. Printed by permission of the author.

Editor's Foreword:
Never Enough Holmes Adventures –
Even at Christmas!
by David Marcum

"It arrived upon Christmas morning . . . ."
Sherlock Holmes – "The Blue Carbuncle"

Dr. John H. Watson met Sherlock Holmes on January 1st, 1881, in a laboratory at St. Bartholomew's Hospital, where Holmes, not-quite twenty-seven years old, was taking advantage of the empty facilities to conduct medico-legal experiments related to blood identification. Watson, himself only twenty-eight, had been grievously wounded at the Battle of Maiwand just a little over five months before, and during his subsequent recovery, he'd nearly died from enteric fever, also known as typhoid. By the time he made the month-long journey back to England on the troopship *Orontes*, he was still just barely recovered, and his mood was certainly grim as he faced an uncertain future.

Watson wrote that he had "*neither kith nor kin in England*", and though it isn't recorded, one can only imagine how bleak was the Christmas of 1880 for this poor veteran, living on his meagre wound pension, and getting through every long dull day in an unfriendly city while residing in a small unfriendly hotel off the Strand. Unexpectedly running into an old friend, Stamford, in the bar of the Criterion on New Year's Day, and then subsequently being swept along to a meeting at Barts with a potential future flatmate, must have been the most excitement that had intruded into Watson's life since his return.

Based on their initial discussion at Barts, Holmes and Watson met the next morning to look at rooms in Baker Street. Watson moved in later that day, and Holmes the day after. The argument could be made that this arrangement saved Watson's life. He went from the desolate daily existence he'd had for weeks, slowly living beyond his means and with no set promise for a better future, to good rooms, a motherly landlady who helped him regain his health, and the mental distraction of a most unusual new flatmate. Within just a few months, Watson would learn that Holmes was a *Consulting Detective* – the first – and Watson began participating in various investigations as his health allowed. This certainly contributed more to his recovery than simply sitting around a bleak hotel room would have ever done.

Holmes lived in Baker Street from 1881 until autumn 1903 – around nineteen years, not counting the three-year period from April 1891 to April 1894 when he was absent and presumed dead following his battle with Professor Moriarty atop the Reichenbach Falls. Watson knew him that entire time – again, with the exception of The Great Hiatus, and that period of time in the mid-1880's when Watson spent some time in the United States – though he actually shared the Baker Street rooms with Holmes for quite a bit less than that – cumulatively around fifteen. His time there was broken up by those occasions when he married and lived elsewhere, with residences and medical practices in Paddington, Kensington, and Queen Anne Street.

Throughout all of these years, both of Holmes and Watson were involved in a great many investigations of varying levels of importance. There are those who think that Holmes's entire career consisted only of those cases related in the pitifully few sixty stories of The Canon, along with the one-hundred-forty or so "Untold Cases" such as the Giant Rat or the Red Leech – and unbelievably some people don't even want to acknowledge the legitimacy of the entire Canonical Sixty. However, over the course of a career that lasted decades, Holmes certainly carried out many thousands of investigations. (In "The Final Problem", Holmes states that "*In over a thousand cases I am not aware that I have ever used my powers upon the wrong side*" – and that estimate from the spring of 1891 must have been drastically low. Those who want – who *need* – to picture Holmes sitting around in his dressing gown for day after day and week after week in the Baker Street sitting room doing nothing, filthy and depressed and drugged and broken, and only able to function through Watson's caretaking while waiting desperately for a rare client to engage him for just a sliver of his vastly empty time are mistaken. That is not The Great Detective.

In fact, Holmes and Watson's lives were crowded with adventures. These overlapped and twisted and twined through one another, and the excitement never let up. Could anyone like Sherlock Holmes have lived a life of any other sort? Certainly not. And Watson, the recovered soldier and man of action, needed such a life just as much. Their days and years were full – and this would have been true in late December during the Christmas season just as much as any other time of year.

1881, that first year the two shared rooms in Baker Street, was when they became friends, and as Watson's health returned and he joined Holmes's investigations more and more, his assistance would prove to be initially useful, and then indispensable. By Christmas of that year, Holmes's practice would have been well established in the Baker Street rooms (following his move a year earlier from Montague Street), and

Watson would have had a good understanding of both Holmes's methods and personality. When Christmas rolled around, they would have already been working well together as a team for a number of months, so Christmas-themed investigations would pose no more difficulties than what had already occurred through the previous year.

For those who simply wish to read Holmes's adventures as they find them, each of the stories in this collection will be very satisfying. But for those who delve a bit deeper, there will be some who notice that there is a bit of overlap. Several cases, for instance, occur around Christmases in the same year, and those paying closer attention might see that they even occur on the same day. Don't let that worry you – it can all be rationalized. This is not a contradiction or an error, meaning that one story has to be chosen as the other as the "legitimate" account of what really happened on that day, and the other is a mere fiction. As someone who has kept a massive and detailed Chronology of both Canon and traditional pastiche for decades, I can assure you that it all fits together quite neatly.

Holmes and Watson's adventures often overlapped, with a piece of one case possibly consisting of just a short conversation lasting a few minutes before the day's events shifted to a piece of another case, and then back again. When Watson wrote the stories, he carefully selected the relevant threads for each separate case from this tangled skein of many concurrent cases, *The Great Holmes Tapestry* as I call it, to construct a self-contained and straight-ahead narrative of just one adventure. He didn't necessarily include what else was happening at the same time in another cases to avoid confusion. Thus, when written from beginning to end, a story will tell just that single investigation without pulling in threads from some other side-by-side case which would spiral the story beyond its scope. Think how twisted and intertwined the events are in your normal everyday life. How much more convoluted, then, were the lives of Our Heroes? As a deep-dive Holmes Chronologicist for forty-five-plus years, I assure you that all of the pieces of the puzzle fit. I'm thankful that Watson has taken the time to separate these events into digestible and self-contained pieces.

That's how the fifty-seven Christmas stories in this new collection can fit within the more limited years of Holmes and Watson's experiences and fixed number of Christmases. Some of these cases occur in the days leading up to Christmas, some on the day, and some afterwards. Some of the stories are inextricably plotted with the trappings of Christmas. Others are set during late December, and even though they could have occurred at any time of the year, they are certainly influenced by the season that surrounds them. In some tales there is festivity, and in others tragedy.

Watson might be having a bad year in this one, and Holmes in that one – the same as each of us have both high and low Yuletide seasons.

Sometimes more than one case takes place on a certain Christmas day, but they are cleverly written so that when reading them, it seems as if they stand alone. "*It arrived upon Christmas morning . . .*" said Holmes to Watson in "The Blue Carbuncle". He was describing a goose – a most remarkable bird – that held a bonny and bright little blue jewel. But he might have been describing any of the many stories that came his and Watson's way on and around the various December Twenty-fifths . . . .

And it isn't just the brilliant fifty-seven Christmas adventures in these three volumes that have to be taken into account – for there are quite a few other narratives beyond the extent of this set of books that also tell what Holmes and Watson were also doing at Christmas. Below is a list of *still more* Holmes and Watson Christmas Adventures. I highly recommend that the true student of The Entire Lives of Our Heroes seek them out as well. Read them and enjoy them – and study them too. Make notes as you go, and you'll start to understand just how the entire *Great Holmes Tapestry* of both Canon and pastiche fits together so brilliantly . . . .

<u>Short Stories</u>

The MX Book of New Sherlock Holmes Stories – Part V: Christmas Adventures (2016 – 30 stories)
- "The Case of the Ruby Necklace" – Bob Byrne
- "The Jet Brooch" – Denis O. Smith
- "The Adventure of the Missing Irregular" – Amy Thomas
- "The Adventure of the Knighted Watchmaker" – Derrick Belanger
- "The Stolen Relic" – David Marcum
- "A Christmas Goose" – C. H. Dye
- "The Adventure of the Long-Lost Enemy" – Marcia Wilson
- "The Case of the Christmas Cracker" – John Hall
- "The Queen's Writing Table" – Julie McKuras
- "The Blue Carbuncle" – Sir Arthur Conan Doyle (*Dramatised for Radio by Bert Coules*)
- "The Man Who Believed in Nothing" – Jim French
- "The Case of the Christmas Star" – S.F. Bennett
- "The Christmas Card Mystery" – Narrelle M. Harris
- "The Question of the Death Bed Conversion" – William Patrick Maynard

- "The Adventure of the Christmas Surprise" – Vincent W. Wright
- "A Bauble in Scandinavia" – James Lovegrove
- "The Adventure of Marcus Davery" – Arthur Hall
- "The Adventure of the Purple Poet" – Nicholas Utechin
- "The Adventure of the Empty Manger" – Tracy J. Revels
- "The Adventure of the Vanishing Man" – Mike Chinn
- "A Perpetrator in a Pear Tree" – Roger Riccard
- "The Case of the Christmas Trifle" – Wendy C. Fries
- "The Adventure of the Christmas Stocking" – Paul D. Gilbert
- "The Case of the Reformed Sinner" – S. Subramanian
- "The Adventure of the Golden Hunter" – Jan Edwards
- "The Curious Case of the Well-Connected Criminal" – Molly Carr
- "The Adventure of the Handsome Ogre" – Matthew J. Elliott
- "The Adventure of the Improbable Intruder" – Peter K. Andersson
- "The Adventure of the Deceased Doctor" – Hugh Ashton
- "The Mile End Mynah Bird" – Mark Mower

Holmes for the Holidays (1996)
- The Watch Night Bell – Anne Perry
- The Sleuth of Christmas Past – Barbara Paul
- A Scandal In Winter – Gillian Linscott
- The Adventure in Border Country – Gwen Moffat
- The Three Ghosts – Loren D. Estleman
- The Canine Ventriloquist – Jon L. Breen
- The Man Who Never Laughed – J.N. Williamson
- The Yuletide Affair – John Stoessel
- The Christmas Tree – William L. DeAndrea

- The Christmas Ghosts – Bill Crider
- The Thief of Twelfth Night – Carole Nelson Douglas
- The Italian Sherlock Holmes – Reginald Hill
- The Christmas Client – Edward D. Hoch
- The Angel's Trumpet – Carol Wheat

More Holmes for the Holidays (1999)
- The Christmas Gift – Anne Perry
- The Four Wise Men – Peter Lovesey
- Eleemosynary, My Dear Watson – Barbara Paul
- The Greatest Gift – Loren D. Estleman

- The Rajah's Emerald – Carolyn Wheat
- The Christmas Conspiracy – Edward D. Hoch
- The Music of Christmas – L.B. Greenwood
- The Christmas Bear – Bill Crider
- The Naturalist's Stock Pin – Jon L. Breen
- The Second Violet – Daniel Stashower
- The Human Mystery – Tanith Lee

Sherlock Holmes: Adventures for the Twelve Days of Christmas – Roger Riccard (2015)
- The Seventh Swan
- The Eighth Milkmaid
- The Ninth Ladyship at the Dance
- The Tenth Lord Leaping
- The Eleven Pipe Problem
- The Twelfth Drumming

Sherlock Holmes: Further Adventures for the Twelve Days of Christmas – Roger Riccard (2016)
- The Partridge in a Pearl Tree
- The Two Turtledoves
- The Three French Henchmen
- The Four Calling Birds
- The Five Gold Rings
- Six Geese at a Gander

Sherlock Holmes: Adventures Beyond the Canon – Volume I (2018)
- "A Gentleman's Disagreement" – Narrelle Harris *(A sequel to "The Blue Carbuncle")*

The Confidential Casebook of Sherlock Holmes (1997)
- "A Ballad of the White Plague" – P.C. Hodgel

Curious Incidents 2 (2002)
- "Green and Red trappings" – Valerie J. Patterson

The Sherlock Holmes Stories of Edward D. Hoch (2008)
- "The Christmas Client"
- "The Christmas Conspiracy"

The Misadventures of Sherlock Holmes (1944)
- "Christmas Eve" – S.C. Roberts

The Chronicles of Sherlock Holmes – Volume Two – Denis O. Smith (1998)
- "The Christmas Visitor" (Originally published in 1985)

Sherlock Holmes and the Watson Pastiche – Karl Showler (2005)
- "Fulworth Christmas"

Sherlock Holmes: A Case at Christmas – N.M. Scott (2016)
- "A Case at Christmas"

Sherlock Holmes: To a Country House Darkly – N.M. Scott (2017)
- "Christmas on Dartmoor"

The Secret Files of Sherlock Holmes – Frank Thomas (2002)
- "Sherlock's Christmas Gift"

The Secret Adventures of Sherlock Holmes – Paul E. Heusinger (2006)
- "The Christmas Truce"

Watson's Sampler: The Lost Casebook of Sherlock Holmes – William F. Watson (2007)
- "The Matter of the Christmas Gift"

Tales from the Stranger's Room (2011)
- "The Adventure of the Christmas Smoke" – David Rowbotham

A Christmas Carol at 221b – Thomas Mann (2018 – Novella)

A Julian Symons Duet – Julian Symons (2000)
- "The Vanishing Diamonds"

The Chemical Adventures of Sherlock Holmes – Thomas G. Waddell and Thomas R. Rybolt (2009)
- "A Christmas Story"

The Singular Exploits of Sherlock Holmes – Alan Stockwell (2012)
- "A Christmas Interlude"

Magazine Adventures

- "The Christmas Poisonings" – Barrie Roberts, *The Strand Magazine* (Issue No. 7)
- "The Affair of the Christmas Jewel" – Barrie Roberts, *The Strand Magazine* (Issue No. 9)
- "The Ghost of Christmas Past" – David Stuart Davies, *The Strand Magazine* (Issue No. 23)
- "The Christmas Bauble" – John Hall, *Sherlock Holmes: The Detective Magazine* (Issue No. 28)
- "Watson's Christmas Trick" – Bob Byrne, *Sherlock Holmes: The Detective Magazine* (Issue No. 46)

Novels

- *Sherlock Holmes and the Yule-Tide Mystery* – Val Andrews (1996)
- *Justice Hall* – Laurie R. King (2002)
- *Sherlock Holmes's Christmas* – David Upton (2005)
- *A Christmas to Forget at 221b* – Hugh A. Mulligan (2002)
- *Sherlock Holmes: Have Yourself a Chaotic Little Christmas* – Gwendolyn Frame (2012)
- *Sherlock Holmes & The Christmas Demon* – James Lovegrove (2019)
- *Young Sherlock Holmes* – Film Novelization by Alan Arnold (1985)

Film, Television, and Radio Adventures

- *Young Sherlock Holmes* – Film screenplay by Chris Columbus (1985)
- "The Adventure of the Christmas Pudding" *Sherlock Holmes* – Screenplay by George Fass and Gertrude Fass (April 4th, 1955 – Television Series)
- "The Night Before Christmas" *The New Adventures of Sherlock Holmes* – Script by Denis Green and Anthony Boucher (December 24th, 1945 Radio Broadcast)
- "The Adventure of the Christmas Bride" – Script by Edith Meiser (December 21st, 1947 Radio Broadcast)

- "The Man Who Believed in Nothing" – Script by Jim French (December 23rd, 2001 Radio Broadcast – Also published in *The MX Book of New Sherlock Holmes Stories – Part V: Christmas Adventures*)
- "The Christmas Ogre" – Script by M.J. Elliott (December 20th, 2015 Radio Broadcast. Text version published as "The Handsome Ogre" in *The MX Book of New Sherlock Holmes Stories – Part V: Christmas Adventures*)

And what has appeared in print doesn't even begin to match the level of excellent writing about Holmes and Christmas that one can find at fan-fiction sites on the web. In fact, for the last several years there has been a writing activity at *fanfiction.net* in which a group of authors compose and post something for the entire month of December, either a complete story, ranging from very short to full-length, to something serialized across the whole month. I've archived them in multiple binders and chronologicized them too, and it's amazing how it all fits together.

For more about the various Sherlockian Christmas stories, please see my essay "Compliments of the Season", an entry from my irregular blog, *A Seventeen Step Program*, at:

https://17stepprogram.blogspot.com/2018/12/the-compliments-of-season-sherlock.html

In the 2015 Foreword to the MX anthology volume *Part V: Christmas Adventures*, I wrote, ". . . *if there are already so many of them out there, why another book of Holmes Christmas adventures?*" As I explained then, for someone like me – and hopefully you too! – there can *never* be enough traditional tales about Holmes and Watson, two of the best and wisest men whom I have ever known. (And after reading and collecting literally thousands of stories about them for over forty-six years, I do feel like I know them.)

The other reason relates to the ever-increasing popularity of these MX Anthologies, and how it was time for *More Christmas Adventures*.

When I first had the idea for a new Holmes anthology in early 2015, the plan was to communicate with possibly a dozen or so "editors" of Watson's notes and see if they were interested in contributing. I had modest hopes that there might be enough new stories – maybe a dozen? – that could justify a new anthology. But the idea grew and grew until the first collection was three massive volumes of over sixty new adventures – really one big book spread out under three covers – and containing more new Holmes tales than had ever been assembled before in one place – at one time. (We've since surpassed that.)

A big part of what made the project so special was that the authors donated their royalties to the Stepping Stones School for special needs students, which was planning at that time to move into one of Sir Arthur Conan Doyle's former homes, Undershaw. By the time the first three books were released in October 2015, renovations were well under way at the school's future home, and it also quickly became apparent that the need for future volumes of *The MX Book of New Sherlock Holmes Stories* was very strong – many contributors reached out to me, wanting to contribute again, as did authors new to the party. The process for producing more anthology volumes was in place, a desire for more traditional Holmes stories is always there, and the school can always use more funding as provided by the sale of the books, so it was decided that what had initially been a one-time three-volume set would become an ongoing series.

Therefore, it was announced that there would be another anthology – but there was so much interest that it was quickly determined that *two* sets per year would be necessary, a general *Annual* in the spring, and another with themed stories in the fall. It turned out that the contributions for these spring and fall editions were so numerous that multiple volumes were required for each set. (Fortunately MX Publishing recognizes the value of these large collections, and doesn't try to limit their size as would some publishers – thus depriving the world of more great Holmes adventures. Rather, we add more and bigger books.)

With this set, we're now at 30 volumes, with more in preparation for Spring 2022, and I'm thinking ahead to a theme for Fall 2022. Right now we're nearing 700 stories from 200 contributors from around the world. We've raised over $85,000 for the school, with the very real possibility that it will go over $100,000 in early 2022.

At the time of publication, and as you will see mentioned in Acting Headteacher Emma West's foreword, it's been announced that the Stepping Stones School *at Undershaw* is changing its name *to Undershaw*, with the motto "*Eliminating the Impossible*". With this action, the school further reaffirms its connection with the Sherlockian world, and I'm personally thrilled that these books can continue to assist in the great and important work that they do – while also bringing more and more traditional Canonical adventures about the True Mr. Sherlock Holmes to light, and into the hands of a world that is starving for them.

* * * * *

"Of course, I could only stammer out my thanks."
– *The unhappy John Hector McFarlane,* "The Norwood Builder"

As always when one of these sets is finished, I want to first thank with all my heart my incredible, patient, brilliant, kind, and beautiful wife of over thirty-three years, Rebecca, and our amazing, funny, brilliant, creative, and wonderful son, and my friend, Dan. I love you both, and you are everything to me!

During the editing of these particular volumes, I've been in the second half of my first year at my dream job – which has required a massive amount of figuring out new things in a hurry. (I've been dreaming about it every night, and – according to my wife – talking in my sleep for the first time in thirty-three years.) When the agency where I was a federal investigator closed in the 1990's, and I was figuring out what I wanted to do with my life, we lived near a beautiful park, and as I would walk there nearly every day with my son, seeing the trails and springs and streams and culverts big enough that kids were exploring them, and I realized that I was interested in infrastructure – and particularly working for that particular city. That led to my return to school to be a civil engineer. After a number of years working at various engineering companies, and getting my license along the way, and still wanting to work at the city, I was finally able to. Now I'm in an office just a few hundred feet from that same park. That has kept me extremely busy for the last few months, which kept me from replying to emails as fast as I would have wished, not to mention reading and editing stories as quickly as I did just a year ago, so I'm very grateful to everyone who patiently waited to hear back from me about their stories.

I can never express enough gratitude for all of the contributors who have donated their time and royalties to this ongoing project. I'm constantly amazed at the incredible stories that you send, and I'm so glad to have gotten to know so many of you through this process. It's an undeniable fact that Sherlock Holmes authors are the *best* people!

As mentioned, the contributors of these stories have donated their royalties for this project to support Undershaw, a school for special needs children located at one of Sir Arthur Conan Doyle's former homes. As of this writing, and as mentioned above, these MX anthologies have raised over $85,000 for the school, with no end in sight, and of even more importance, they have helped raise awareness about the school all over the world – which I'm told by the school is actually more important than the funds. These books are making a real difference to the school, and the participation of both contributors and purchasers is most appreciated.

Next is that group that exchanges emails with me when we have the time – and time is a valuable commodity for all of us these days! As mentioned, I don't get to write back and forth with these fine people as often as I'd like, but I really enjoy catching up when we do get the chance: Derrick Belanger, Brian Belanger, Mark Mower, Denis Smith, Tom Turley, Dan Victor, and Marcia Wilson.

There is a group of special people who have stepped up and supported this and a number of other projects over and over again with a lot of contributions. They are the best and I can't express how valued they are: Hugh Ashton, Derrick Belanger, Deanna Baran, Craig Stephen Copland, Matthew Elliott, Tim Gambrell, Jayantika Ganguly, Paul Gilbert, Dick Gillman, Arthur Hall, Steve Herczeg, Paul Hiscock, Craig Janacek, Mark Mower, Will Murray, Tracy Revels, Roger Riccard, Geri Schear, Brenda Seabrooke, Shane Simmons, Robert Stapleton, Kevin Thornton, I.A. Watson, and Marcy Wilson.

Next, I wish to send several huge *Thank You's* to the following:

- *Nancy Holder* – I first began corresponding with Nancy in 2019, and I've been pushing for her to write a pastiche for this collection ever since. (*Nancy: You're still invited!*) I was able to meet her in person at the Sherlock Holmes Birthday Celebration in New York City in January 2020, and found that she's just as nice as she'd been by way of email.

In mid-2021, as this book was being prepared, she stepped up and agreed to write a wonderful foreword rather late in the game, showing what a truly consummate professional she is. Even though I haven't convinced her to write a Holmes adventure yet, I'm thrilled that she's part of these books. Huge thanks!

- *Steve Emecz* – Some people have a picture in their minds of a publishing company with several floors on some skyscraper, hundreds of employees running around like ants, with vast departments devoted to management, marketing, editing, production, shipping, etc. That is not always the case. Those old giant dinosaur publishers are still around, and they might squeeze out a Sherlockian title or two every year, but they don't represent the modern way of doing things. MX has become the premiere Sherlockian publisher by following a new paradigm. And they manage to get all of this done with a truly skeleton staff.

Steve Emecz works a way-more-than-full-time job related to his career in e-finance. MX Publishing isn't his full-time job –

it's a labor of love. He, along with his wife Sharon Emecz and cousin, Timi Emecz, *are* MX Publishing. In addition to their very busy real every-day lives, these three sole employees take care of the management, marketing, editing, production, and shipping, and they absolutely cannot receive enough credit for what they accomplish.

From my first association with MX in 2013, I've seen that MX (under Steve's leadership) was *the* fast-rising superstar of the Sherlockian publishing world. Connecting with MX and Steve Emecz was personally an amazing life-changing event for me, as it has been for countless other Sherlockian authors. It has led me to write many more stories, and then to edit books, along with unexpected Holmes Pilgrimages to England – none of which might have happened otherwise. By way of my first email with Steve – *Only eight years ago!* – I've had the chance to make some incredible Sherlockian friends and play in the Holmesian Sandbox in ways that I would have never dreamed possible.

Through it all, Steve has been one of the most positive and supportive people that I've ever known.

Many who just buy books and have a vague idea of how the publishing industry works now might not realize that MX, a non-profit which supports several important charities, consists of simply these three people. Between them, they take care of running the entire business – all in their precious spare time, fitting it in and around their real lives.

With incredible hard work, they have made MX into a world-wide Sherlockian publishing phenomenon, providing opportunities for authors who would never have had them otherwise. There are some like me who return more than once to Watson's Tin Dispatch Box, and there are others who only find one or two stories there – but they also get the chance to publish their books, and then they can point with pride at this accomplishment, and how they too have added to The Great Holmes Tapestry.

From the beginning, Steve has let me explore various Sherlockian projects and open up my own personal possibilities in ways that otherwise would have never happened. Thank you, Steve, for every opportunity!

• *Brian Belanger* – Over the last few years, my amazement at Brian Belanger's ever-increasing talent has only grown. I initially became acquainted with him when he took over the duties of creating the covers for MX Books following the untimely death of their previous graphic artist. I found Brian to be a great collaborator, very easy-going and stress-free in his approach and willingness to work with authors, and wonderfully creative too.

Brian and his brother, Derrick Belanger, are two great friends, and five years ago they founded *Belanger Books*, which along with MX Publishing, has absolutely locked up the Sherlockian publishing field with a vast amount of amazing material. The dinosaurs must be trembling to see every new Sherlockian project, one after another after another. Luckily MX and Belanger Books work closely with one another, and I'm thrilled to be associated with both of them. Many thanks to Brian for all he does for both publishers, and for all he's done for me personally.

• *Roger Johnson* – I'm more grateful than I can say that I know Roger. I was aware of him for years before I timidly sent him a copy of my first book for review, and then on my first Holmes Pilgrimage to England and Scotland in 2013, I was able to meet both him and his wonderful wife, Jean Upton, in person. When I returned on Holmes Pilgrimage No. 2 in 2015, I was so fortunate that they graciously allowed me to stay with them for several days in their home, where we had many wonderful discussions, while occasionally venturing forth so that they could show me parts of England that I wouldn't have seen otherwise. It was an experience I wouldn't trade for anything.

Roger's Sherlockian knowledge is exceptional, as is the work that he does to further the cause of The Master. But even more than that, both Roger and his wonderful wife, Jean, are simply the finest and best of people, and I'm very lucky to know both of them – even though I don't get to see them nearly as often as I'd like, and especially in these crazy days! In so many ways, Roger, I can't thank you enough, and I can't imagine these books without you.

And finally, last but certainly *not* least, thanks to **Sir Arthur Conan Doyle**: Author, doctor, adventurer, and the Founder of the Sherlockian Feast. Honored, and present in spirit.

As I always note when putting together an anthology of Holmes stories, the effort has been a labor of love. These adventures are just more tiny threads woven into the ongoing Great Holmes Tapestry, continuing to grow and grow, for there can *never* be enough stories about the man whom Watson described as *"the best and wisest . . . whom I have ever known."*

David Marcum
September 8th, 2021
A most important day,
for all kinds of reasons

Questions, comments, or story submissions
may be addressed to David Marcum at

thepapersofsherlockholmes@gmail.com

Foreword
by Nancy Holder

Sherlock Holmes and Christmas: Two fixed points in a changing world. The Great Detective, cracking the case with a dramatic flourish (and, often, a somewhat lengthy explanation). His faithful Boswell, marveling at the genius of Our Mutual Friend. Roasting chestnuts, glittering Christmas trees, carolers in hoop skirts and bonnets. A Victorian Christmas in all its holly-and-ivy splendor.

We who know and love The Canon – the fifty-six original stories and four novels written by John H. Watson (with an assist from Sir Arthur Conan Doyle) – wax nostalgic for the traditions of a time and place we will never see. At least I do, and I have spent the majority of my Christmases in Southern California, where guys in flip-flops spray artificial snow onto the windows of taco shops and sushi restaurants, and we watch *A Christmas Carol* with the air conditioning on – as do, I assume, my many friends in Australia, Hawaii, Florida, and so many other pleasant climes. Simply going by the cards I receive in December, Christmas as celebrated in late nineteenth century Britain and Ireland is the Ur of winter celebrations, and we perpetuate its hold on us with wholehearted devotion.

As a dedicated Sherlockian, I usually crack open "The Adventure of the Blue Carbuncle" to usher in Holmes at Christmas. This is the only story in The Canon that takes place at (or very near) Christmas. A review of the beloved tale is pretty much *de rigueur* at any December Sherlock Holmes cookie swap and/or Christmas jollification. How many of us have debated the various fine points of the story – (Why leave John Horner in the clink overnight? Does Peterson reap the reward for the gem?) – while sipping tea, brandy, or mulled wine and munching gingerbread? Nearly all of us – no matter if we celebrate Hanukkah, Diwali, Kwanzaa, or as is the case at my house, more than one winter holiday. For the duration of this one story, we happily transport ourselves to a Victorian Christmas.

But while "Blue Carbuncle" may be the only Christmas story in the Canon, it is, of course, not the only Christmas story featuring Holmes and Watson. MX Publishing, who published a lovely, hefty Christmas assortment in 2016, have done it again – a Santa sack brimming with Yuletide pastiches sure to please the traditionalists among us. Hewing close to the Canon, with no supernatural or fantastical elements, these are the kinds of stories sure to warm the heart (even if it's 98-degrees

Fahrenheit outside) and take us back to where we want to be for our winter holidays – with Holmes and Watson, wrapped in gas lamp frost, where it's always (or close to) 1895. Dozens of talented, clever, careful authors have penned wonderful stories tailored to this season of joy, wonder . . . and Sherlock. Whether it's Christmas in July where you are, or snowy with a chance of sugarplums, I urge you to unwrap and savor. What lovely gifts await you.

Nancy Holder, BSI
Near Seattle
July, 2021

"It is the Season of Forgiveness"
by Roger Johnson

In our minds, what do we associate with the stories of Sherlock Holmes? Crime, naturally, and mystery. Observation and deduction, leading to solutions, certainly. Gaslight and fog, yes. The mighty metropolis of London too.

But Christmas? There is, as we all surely know, only one Canonical investigation that takes place at Christmas time – it's "The Adventure of the Blue Carbuncle", and Dr. Watson's narrative famously begins: "*I had called upon my friend Sherlock Holmes upon the second morning after Christmas, with the intention of wishing him the Compliments of the Season.*" Not Christmas Eve, then. Not Christmas Day itself, nor the one immediately following – Boxing Day – but *two days* after Christmas. One might be tempted the dismiss its credentials (I mean *two days*?) but of course the whole account is imbued with the spirit of the season, and that spirit casts its benign shadow over our mental image of the Detective and the Doctor.

Last year Belanger Books published an appealing little book called *Sherlock Holmes: A Three-Pipe Christmas*, edited by Dan Andriacco. At its heart are "The Adventure of the Blue Carbuncle" by Arthur Conan Doyle, "The Adventure of the Unique *Hamlet* " by Vincent Starrett, first published in 1920, and "The Adventure of the Unique Dickensians", an exploit of Holmes's disciple Solar Pons, written by August Derleth and first published in 1968. The stories are accompanied by essays, whose authors include the editor of this volume and the author of this foreword. How entertaining the essays are, you must judge for yourselves, but the stories are excellent and the book as a whole is delightful.

Starrett was one of the immortals of Holmesian scholarship. So was S.C. Roberts, whose charming one-act play "Christmas Eve" you'll find in his classic *Holmes and Watson: A Miscellany*, first published in 1953 and now available in a new edition from the British Library.

The combination of Christmas and Holmes continues to appeal, to authors and readers alike. A notable recent novel, for instance, is *Sherlock Holmes and the Christmas Demon* by James Lovegrove. And the association is strong on stage and screen as well. It's a rare Christmas in Britain when theatregoers don't have the choice of a new or old Holmesian comedy, or more rarely a drama, among the seasonal fare. In recent years we have enjoyed *Sherlock Holmes and the Warlock of Whitechapel*,

Tweedy and the Missing Company of Sherlock Holmes, Sherlock Holmes and the Hooded Lance, Potted Sherlock, Mrs. Hudson's Christmas Corker, Sherlock Holmes and the Case of the Christmas Carol, The Adventures of the Improvised Sherlock Holmes, and any number of riffs on *The Hound of the Baskervilles*.

Mention of that particular classic reminds me that one of the better aspects of the 2002 TV film *The Hound of the Baskervilles* was the decision to set the story around Christmas time, and make the legendary Hound a character in a seasonal Mummers' play. And the last of the classic Granada Television series with Jeremy Brett as Holmes, "The Cardboard Box" broadcast in 1994, also relocated its narrative to Christmas to good effect.

Young Sherlock Holmes and the Pyramid of Fear (1985) begins with a decidedly weird Christmas episode and ends with a sad but hopeful one. More than thirty years earlier, an entertaining episode of Sheldon Reynolds's television series *Sherlock Holmes* was "The Adventure of the Christmas Pudding". Like *Young Sherlock Holmes*, it can be enjoyed today. And we mustn't forget the outstanding TV dramatisations of "The Blue Carbuncle", in 1968 with Peter Cushing and Nigel Stock as Holmes and Watson, and in 1984 with Jeremy Brett and David Burke. Two different interpretations – compare Madge Ryan's performance as the Countess of Morcar with Rosalind Knight's, for instance – but both excellent.

Sherlock Holmes and Christmas – inseparable? The stories in this book suggest that they are. And, as always, editor and authors won't get a penny from it, because all proceeds will go towards the maintenance of Undershaw, Arthur Conan Doyle's former home in Surrey, which now houses the Stepping Stones School for youngsters with special educational needs.

Roger Johnson, BSI, ASH
Editor: *The Sherlock Holmes Journal*
August 2021

An Ongoing Legacy for Sherlock Holmes
by Steve Emecz

Undershaw
Circa 1900

The MX Book of New Sherlock Holmes Stories has now raised over $85,000 for Undershaw, a school for children with learning disabilities, and is by far the largest Sherlock Holmes collection in the world.

Undershaw is the former home of Sir Arthur Conan Doyle, where he wrote many of the Sherlock Holmes stories. The fundraising has supported many projects continuing the legacy of Conan Doyle and Sherlock Holmes in the amazing building, including The Doyle Room, the school's Zoom broadcasting capability (including Sherlock themed events), The Literacy Program, and more.

In addition to Undershaw, our main program that we support is the Happy Life Children's Home in Kenya. My wife Sharon and I have spent seven Christmas's with the children in Nairobi.

It's a wonderful project that has saved the lives of over 600 babies. You can read all about the project in the second edition of the book *The Happy Life Story*.

In 2021, we are working on *#bookstobooks* which sees us donating 10% of the revenues from *mxpublishing.com* to fund schoolbooks and library books at Happy Life.

Our support for our projects is possible through the publishing of Sherlock Holmes books, which we have now been doing for over a decade.

You can find out more information about the Undershaw at:

https://undershaw.education/

and Happy Life at:

www.happylifechildrenshomes.com

You can find out more about MX Publishing and reach out to us through our website at:

www.mxpublishing.com

Steve Emecz
September 2021
Twitter: *@mxpublishing*

The Doyle Room at Stepping Stones, Undershaw
*Partially funded through royalties from
The MX Book of New Sherlock Holmes Stories*

Undershaw:
Eliminating the Impossible
by Emma West

Undershaw
September 9, 2016
Grand Opening of the Stepping Stones School
(Photograph courtesy of Roger Johnson)

I am delighted to share the news that Stepping Stones School has a new name. From 1st September, 2021, we will bear the name *Undershaw*, inspired by the building that houses our school. Stepping Stones has such a strong legacy as a school full of life, dynamism, and hope for a more inclusive future for our children. Undershaw is that school. Our staff, students, and families are proud of our community and excited for what the next stage holds.

> We stand for aspirational education free of discrimination.
> We stand for specialists supporting each young person their way, at their pace.
> We stand for our students developing the life and work skills necessary to navigate their adulthood and secure fulfilling and lasting careers.

We stand for breaking down barriers and creating a cultural shift in how workplaces of the future view diversity and inclusion so that they recognise the true talents and abilities of our learners.

These attributes run at the heart of everything we do, and I am thrilled that we are about to embark upon a new chapter in our story.

Sir Arthur Conan Doyle built Undershaw as a place of convalescence for his wife. It had an honourable purpose then, just as it has now. Together we have reignited the passion of Undershaw, firstly in 2016 by renovating the building as a state-of-the-art specialist centre for our students, and lately as an inspirational name for our school, as we take our philosophy forward and find our place in a wider societal conversation. Undershaw encapsulates our essence as we take the very best from the past and use it as the landscape for framing our future.

You have partnered with us for many years. Thank you for sharing our passion and ethos. Thank you for your benevolence. Above all, thank you for your good company. We could not do it without you. We have loved having you with us on the journey and hope you are excited to join in on our next chapter as we take Undershaw into 2022 and long into the future.

Emma West
Acting Headteacher
September 2021

Sherlock Holmes (1854-1957) was born in Yorkshire, England, on 6 January, 1854. In the mid-1870's, he moved to 24 Montague Street, London, where he established himself as the world's first Consulting Detective. After meeting Dr. John H. Watson in early 1881, he and Watson moved to rooms at 221b Baker Street, where his reputation as the world's greatest detective grew for several decades. He was presumed to have died battling noted criminal Professor James Moriarty on 4 May, 1891, but he returned to London on 5 April, 1894, resuming his consulting practice in Baker Street. Retiring to the Sussex coast near Beachy Head in October 1903, he continued to be associated in various private and government investigations while giving the impression of being a reclusive apiarist. He was very involved in the events encompassing World War I, and to a lesser degree those of World War II. He passed away peacefully upon the cliffs above his Sussex home on his 103rd birthday, 6 January, 1957.

Dr. John Hamish Watson (1852-1929) was born in Stranraer, Scotland on 7 August, 1852. In 1878, he took his Doctor of Medicine Degree from the University of London, and later joined the army as a surgeon. Wounded at the Battle of Maiwand in Afghanistan (27 July, 1880), he returned to London late that same year. On New Year's Day, 1881, he was introduced to Sherlock Holmes in the chemical laboratory at Barts. Agreeing to share rooms with Holmes in Baker Street, Watson became invaluable to Holmes's consulting detective practice. Watson was married and widowed three times, and from the late 1880's onward, in addition to his participation in Holmes's investigations and his medical practice, he chronicled Holmes's adventures, with the assistance of his literary agent, Sir Arthur Conan Doyle, in a series of popular narratives, most of which were first published in *The Strand* magazine. Watson's later years were spent preparing a vast number of his notes of Holmes's cases for future publication. Following a final important investigation with Holmes, Watson contracted pneumonia and passed away on 24 July, 1929.

Photos of Sherlock Holmes and Dr. John H. Watson courtesy of Roger Johnson

28

30

The MX Book of New Sherlock Holmes Stories

Part XXVIII
More Christmas Adventures
(1869-1888)

32

A Sherlockian Christmas
by Joseph W. Svec III

I'm dreaming of a Sherlockian Christmas,
just like those of long ago,
when the clues do glisten,
and Holmes and Watson listen,
to hear footprints in the snow.

I'm wondering, of where could they lead to?
Perhaps a winter's, Wisteria lodge?
Or a Red Circle, bright,
shinning in the night,
when bullets, they will have to dodge.

I'm pondering on Bruce Partington's Plans,
You know it keeps my thoughts afloat,
more than a Dying Detective.
It is really quite effective.
Just like, a secret submarine boat.

I'm musing on Lady Frances Carfax,
and also of, The "You Know Who's" Foot.
And Sherlock's Last Bow
won't really be, we all know,
or Doyle would be quite hard put.

Yes, I'm dreaming of a Sherlockian Christmas
with every rhymed line I write.
May your clues be clear and so bright,
and may all your deductions be right.

34

No Malice Intended
by Deanna Baran

It was a gray December afternoon, and I had spent the greater part of the day attending the wife of a young administrative officer at their home in Dorset Square. He had formerly been stationed in the Madras, but due to injuries sustained during a bad day at pig-sticking, his tenure abroad had been abruptly cut short. He had removed his household from those humid, tropical beaches and returned to the cooler climes of our own island to heal, and perhaps pick up less dangerous hobbies. His wife celebrated the occasion by presenting him with a son, and it was for the purpose of escorting this young fellow into the world that I was drawn into their company that particular day. I was fond of the young officer, whose healing progress I had supervised for nearly a year. We enjoyed trading stories of India – mine from a military perspective, as things had been ten years ago and rather more easterly, and his more current and definitely in the western parts of the Subcontinent, with an emphasis on the whimsies of government administration in a foreign land.

Having left the young mother doing well, the young master in her affectionate embrace, and all supervised by the proud and doting father, I took my leave. The clouds of nostalgia did not dissipate as I took to the sidewalk, and in such a mood, I realized that Dorset Square was not too far distant from the dwelling of my friend Holmes. I judged sufficient time in my schedule to stop by and see if he was present in his chambers, and if so, say hello and hear a few words of his latest occupation.

Thus it was that I found him seated upon the floor, an open trunk at his side. Numerous books were spread in a rough semicircle about him, and he was in the midst of consulting a rather large text with densely printed pages. I called an amiable greeting as I approached.

"Hallo, Holmes. Some of those look rather like schoolbooks. Don't tell me you plan on returning to the lecture-halls at this stage of life – this time as the lecturer?" For it was foolish to imagine him sitting quietly and taking notes as anyone else in the world lectured to him, he who was master of so many diverse fields.

"Accurate as to the first, and certainly not as to the second," said Holmes, not lifting his eyes from the page. "As it is, most of these are old chemistry texts from days past, and I found myself wishing to consult them, as the information is pertinent to a certain problem facing me. I have memory of the book, and upon the part of the page upon which I might find that which I seek. All that remains is to find the actual page. It was a rather offhand comment upon an obscure point, but once I find it, it may hang a man."

I busied myself with reading the titles of the other books he had unpacked. Most were dry and academic, but there was a slim volume that looked interesting enough for the effort involved in bending over and retrieving it. "*The Art of Making Fireworks, Improved to the Modern Practice from the Minutest to the Highest Branches*'," I read aloud. I spent a few moments admiring the elaborate hand-colored frontispiece. "This book surely wasn't yours. Perhaps it was your grandfather's when he was a boy?"

"Used bookstalls have been the source of many treasures," said Holmes. "What boy doesn't have an amateur enthusiasm for explosives, a casual disregard for the safety of his own fingers, and an indulgent bachelor uncle to cultivate such interests?"

"I'm pleased you survived childhood with all your fingers, then, if these were the sorts of exploits you pursued in your youth."

"Even in the modern era, chemistry remains in its infancy, yet it is how we understand the realities of the cosmos," said Holmes placidly. "All the fairy tales in the world aren't a pin against the magic of chemistry. It pervades existence. What youth doesn't want to make sense of this great, messy, complicated universe around him? The world would be a better place if more people understood the chemistry that permeates and sustains our daily lives. The magnificent complexity of the natural world, and the invisible latent powers that control it, combined with the indifference of the universe – it keeps one humble. The oratory of Demosthenes, the charismatic leadership of Napoleon, the splendid power of Her Majesty upon whose dominions the sun never sets – all utterly powerless when confronted with a really superlative exothermic reaction."

Having little success in visualizing anything to keep Holmes humble, I allowed this odd discourse to go unanswered. Instead, I flipped through the little book, reading the subject headings as they caught my eye. "*Odiferous Nalloons. Fire Fountains.*' All good and well, presuming that one has access to three pounds of saltpetre, or actually knows what oil of spike and Assa odorata are."

"Chemistry is best reserved to the chemists. It protects those precious fingers when their owners are disinclined to preserve the value of a fully functioning hand," was all that Holmes responded, his attention having returned to his own volume. After a pause, he added, "Benzoin."

We proceeded in silence a little longer, before I noticed a slip of paper at the very end of the book. "You seem to have kept a little piece of doggerel for a book-mark," I observed.

No malice intended,
No malus in ten lived.
We are all of us pleased
We're neither investments nor trees
Else your children, nephew, and wife
Would have quite the short life!

A dry smile flitted across his lips. He rose, set his book upon the table, and arranged himself more comfortably in his armchair, inviting me to take my accustomed place across from him. "Shall I tell you the history of that book and that little rhyme?"

Recognizing the opportunity for a story, I readily accepted the invitation. Holmes rang for tea, which soon appeared, accompanied by a variety of savouries, and under these congenial circumstances, he began to relate his tale . . . .

Like most boys of his age and background, he had been sent away to school. Although it was usual to return home in between terms, that particular year, circumstances were such that Michaelmas ended and young Holmes faced the prospect of remaining alone amidst the depopulated corridors of school for Christmas and the New Year, stranded with the few other gloomy boys who were also unable to return home for one reason or another.

A casual schoolmate of his, with whom he was fond of fencing and performing minor feats of chemistry, was more sorry about this prospect than Holmes himself had been upon receipt of the news. Price was himself an orphan, having lost both mother and father in a boating accident, and felt loneliness very keenly, especially in the midst of the holiday season. It was thus that he imposed upon young Holmes to accompany him to spend Christmas with himself, his guardian uncle, aunt, and cousins, as they lived in a fine rambling home in Berkshire with plenty of room to accommodate unexpected guests. Not to mention, Price wanted to show him the amateur laboratory he'd set up for himself in the abandoned cowshed. They could perform much more daring experiments there than Holmes could possibly do on the school grounds.

Holmes didn't require much more persuasion after that. Leave to do so was requested and granted.

Uncle Henry and Aunt Elizabeth responded to the intrusion with courtesy and grace, and accepted Holmes's presence without a protest. The boys were allowed the freedom of roaming the grounds and pursuing their whims during the short winter day, climbing the dead branches of what was once an orchard, watching Aunt Elizabeth's first-class Arabians taking their exercise in the winter paddock, helping the hired man feed the pigs, marching over barren snowy fields, and observing the antics of a colony of rabbits dwelling in the abandoned cowshed. In the last of the day's sun, the entire family gathered to pass a congenial hour together in the parlor. Uncle Henry himself presided over a spirit lamp in the corner to prepare hot cocoa. All consumed books and chocolate in front of a warming, cheery fire, before partaking of supper and then turning in for the early onset of night.

The pair spent a few hours every morning entertaining the young cousins, much to the relief of the nurse and the governess. After the first few days of exploring, however, the two youths spent most of their daylight hours out in the abandoned cowshed, which was most fortunately kept heated against the winter weather by a small stove. It was as Price had advertised: A very respectably-equipped amateur laboratory, where the sights and odors of their experiments would not cause alarm in the housekeeper. Likewise, Price's extensive collection of ingredients, materials, and equipment were kept safe from causing danger to inquisitive cousins, the eldest of which was a good ten years younger than they themselves, and none of which were very good at following instructions against meddling. Holmes was in awe that such luxury was the possession of a mere boy – even though the premises were shared by the rabbit colony – and vowed to someday have something twice as good, once he could afford it.

It was during this period that Price suggested that they make presents for everyone in the form of Christmas crackers. In Holmes's book, the small volume destined to come to my attention over twenty years later, he had a recipe for making Waterloo crackers, which involved small pieces of cartridge-paper, a little powdered glass, and grains of silver. When the two ends were pulled, it would snap with a loud report. Once those had been manufactured, it was a simple matter to put together cardboard, decorative paper, and small little prizes customized to the recipients – a little slip of paper with a humorous rhyme on it, sugared almonds, a little trinket. With this goal in mind, the boys worked steadily upon their Christmas project, experimenting with the recipe to make bigger and better bangs.

It was not all play, however. Uncle Henry would occasionally take Price into the library for an hour or two to go over accounts with him. As the trustee of the estate until the young heir reached the age of his majority, it was Uncle Henry's job to manage the investments in the meantime, and he was scrupulous in keeping Price informed of the state of the finances, for the good and for the bad, but most often for the bad.

"Every time I come home," Price complained to Holmes after one particularly depressing session, "he always has bad news about this disaster or that disaster. I swear, my parents should have just buried their fortune in a hole in this cowshed floor and let the rabbits protect it, for all the luck he's had with it."

"Oh?" asked Holmes. "So these premises are your premises, and not your uncle's home?"

"When I am grown, I expect they will find residence elsewhere," agreed Price. "But yes – this house, this land, it is all mine. No good it does me, for all that, as Uncle Henry is always talking about the roofs needing mending and the drains having troubles or the fields not bearing. And if his investments keep going the way they have, there will be precious little left to pay for those roofs and drains and fields by the time they're my responsibility to maintain."

"Do you think he's failing on purpose?" asked Holmes.

"It's just the way he is," said Price carelessly. "My father was always the successful one. Uncle Henry was always in his shadow. He's always very humble about not being able to do anything right, but everything he sets his hand to, he seems to fail in. He tries to invest, and the ship founders, or the government collapses. He tries his hand at agriculture, and spends a hundred pounds cultivating the orchard, but a late frost wipes out any chance of apples, and a hard frost proceeds to damage the roots. He buys a share in an up-and-coming racehorse, and it sprains a ligament. Those sorts of things. He's always very apologetic about circumstances beyond his control. What can one do?"

"Request an audit and a more scrupulous trustee, perhaps?" asked Holmes. But as they were both young, Christmas was near, and as they weren't very familiar with the *minutiae* of economics and investments, they did not dwell too hard upon the poor performance of the trust's ventures.

Soon the time came to exchange gifts after dinner on Christmas Eve. Aunt Elizabeth was resplendent in a new sable mantle and supervised the distribution of nuts and sweets with much fondness and affection. There were many small glass curiosities she had brought back from their latest trip to Venice, which she distributed to her offspring, and then promptly had them borne away to prevent breaking. Uncle Henry gave his children each a small blank sketchbook upon which they were to practice drawing nature studies. For his beaming wife, however, he provided a seemingly endless supply of jewelry, which, Holmes observed, seemed to have been acquired in Florence and purchased under her supervision. Holmes and Price were each content with receipt of a small packet of peppermint humbugs, and expressed their gratitude.

The two boys then displayed the basket of their homemade crackers, of which they were enormously proud. They made a great deal of handing everyone their personal cracker. They took great pains to inform their audience that the crackers within were not mass-produced from the factory. Rather, each was personally crafted with the intended recipient in mind. There was a great fuss as each person pulled them open with a satisfying bang, and sifted through the treasures revealed. Mottoes were read aloud and laughed at. Trinkets were admired. Edibles were consumed at gratifying speed.

Only Uncle Henry's cracker seemed to fall flat. He began reading aloud: *"No malice intended, no malus in ten lived. We are all of us pleased we're neither investments nor trees . . . ."* But by the time he got to the end, his voice had faltered and he had an odd look on his face.

Price thought he had crossed a line and embarrassed his uncle in front of the guest, so he tried to cover the embarrassment by telling him cheekily, "It was a joke. About the apple orchard and everything else that seems to go wrong here. Malus, you know."

And Uncle Henry laughed politely, but the odd expression did not disappear from his face. He seemed to be thinking very hard all night long, and was visibly distracted all through the Vigil service that night.

"Something isn't right," Price confided to Holmes a few evenings later.

"What's wrong?" asked Holmes.

"I'm not feeling well," he admitted. "Or rather, I haven't been feeling well. Not since Christmas." He seemed to be gathering his courage, deciding whether or not to confide his darkest suspicions. "I think someone is contaminating my food."

"You mean, you think you're being poisoned," said Holmes, immediately perceiving his true meaning.

"Yes," said Price glumly. "It sounds ridiculous once one says it aloud, doesn't it? Everything I eat and drink, you drink and eat, the cousins eat and drink, and Uncle Henry and Aunt Elizabeth eat and drink. I've been paying attention to the menu. Everything is served from common dishes. There's no way for someone to target me. And who would want to? Maybe at school, there might be a few rotters who have it out for me. But at home? Hardly. Night after night . . . I don't think it's much, but all the same, that's what I think."

"Poison can be introduced in a variety of ways," said Holmes knowledgeably. "Some you ingest. Some is in the air. Some is by contact. Tell me your symptoms."

He pursed his lips. "Gastric distress," he finally said primly. "And . . . well, other things."

Holmes nodded his sympathy. "I haven't heard of anyone else in the house having, um, gastric distress. But, presuming that you haven't made enemies of gypsies or an ancient cult or Amazonians with access to unknown poisons, the ones you mostly read about in the papers are likely to be arsenic, cyanide, and strychnine. Arsenic is a metal and affects the digestion. Cyanide gets in the way of oxygen. And strychnine works on the nerves. There are others, like your vegetable poisons, and those are harder to detect. But of the three, the first I'd test for is the arsenic."

"But what would you test? And how would you test for it?" asked Price fretfully. "I certainly can't hide samples of everything I eat in my napkin and bring them out to the cowshed."

"You remember the Marsh Test and the Lafarge case," said Holmes with enthusiasm. "We can test food and drink. And, umm, biological samples. Like hair. Or fingernails. Or, umm . . . other things."

It didn't take long to acquire the preferred biological sample. Holmes placed it in a clean flask with a small lump of zinc and sulfuric acid. He plugged one end with a cork pierced by a tube. Under this tube, he held a steady flame, to allow any invisible gas to become heated. As he dragged the open end against the surface of a small, chilled dish, it left behind dark, spotty deposits.

The two youths peered at the results and exchanged a look. They both knew its ominous meaning.

"But it doesn't say how it got into your system – if it was deliberate, or if it was accidental," mused Holmes. "Still, I think this is evidence, and we ought to take good care of it in case something happens to you."

"Something is happening to me, and I don't like it," said Price unhappily. "It's all well and good to chase down my murderer, but I'd prefer not to be in a situation where I'm in need of avenging in the first place."

"It isn't difficult to know whom to suspect," said Holmes thoughtfully.

"What do you mean?"

"It's certainly not the young cousins. It's not the nurse, or the governess, or the cook, or the housekeeper, or the housemaid, or the hired man. Who's the one person who would profit by your death?"

"Uncle Henry, of course."

"It may be your aunt, but I primarily suspect your uncle. We shouldn't discount the possibility she may be his accomplice. I don't know if she's the sort of woman who would go along willingly with a scheme. How long have they been married?"

"Six years. She was a wealthy widow when they married, but had no offspring from her first husband."

"And how long has he been your guardian?"

"Four years. My parents had their accident when I was eleven."

"And how much is in your trust?"

"It used to be more, but at this point, I expect it to bring perhaps £450 per annum."

Holmes raised an eyebrow but refrained from commenting. One couldn't live like a duke upon it, but one could certainly be a gentleman of the leisured class with such a sum to rely upon.

"What would happen if it was discovered the trust was being mismanaged?"

"That's a bit strong," objected Price, momentarily forgetting that his fears had been validated just moments before. "He just has strong bad luck."

"But what if that's his story to cover for the mismanagement?" pressed Holmes. "Perhaps there were no collapsed governments, or no injured racehorses, or no shipwrecks. Perhaps he was merely helping himself to your money, knowing that you wouldn't notice, and it would be a long time before he would be held accountable? What if an accident befell you before you came of age? It would be a tragic pity, of course, but people do die young. And then he'd be able to enjoy your trust rather more openly, rather than merely maintaining your house and your land and your servants, and skimming a little here and there."

"That's a lot of assumptions," said Price glumly. "But there's no way to get him to tell the truth if we were to ask him."

"The way he reacted to the malus poem is confession enough for me," said Holmes stoutly. "He seems to have changed after that night. I think it struck a guilty chord in him. He might have thought you were indirectly accusing him. Malice aforethought. The intent to kill. It sped up his plans. What he might have brought about in the years ahead, he now needs to do before you go back to school and start spreading your suspicions."

"But I don't have any suspicions." Price's eyes were bright with tears by this point. "Or, at least, I didn't."

Holmes looked at him with concern. "You can't breathe a word of your thoughts," he warned, "or else he may panic and forget all about subtlety."

At this point, Holmes, sitting with me at the tea table many years later, suddenly broke off his narration.

"Pray don't pause there. What happened?" I pressed.

"Young Price was not brought up to subterfuge. His countenance was an open book. It was impossible for him to disguise his emotions with the knowledge that his guardian uncle fully intended to harm him. So, as I warned, he panicked and forgot all about subtlety."

"Were you able to protect him?"

Holmes gazed thoughtfully into his teacup. "I had, of course, deduced the source of the poison, even though I didn't confess to it at the time. Have you?"

"Holmes, you know I haven't the faintest idea."

"It hinged upon the cocoa ritual, where the entire family gathered to read in the parlour. The task of preparing the cocoa was not delegated to a housemaid, or to the children's staff, or to the cook in the kitchen. Instead, Uncle Henry prepared it with his own hands, in a corner, upon a spirit lamp. It was the simplest thing for him to adulterate his nephew's drink, yet allow everyone else's cocoa to remain wholesome."

"Was this your working hypothesis, or were you positive?"

Holmes gave me an indulgent look. "Knowing that Price had unwittingly given his uncle notice that all was known, I was a thousand times more concerned for his sake. Thus it was that, through some sleight of hand and misdirection, I was successful in switching his drink with his uncle's that afternoon. No one knew. Not even Price. I never told anyone, that day, or any other day. I struggled internally with that choice of action for many years afterwards, for, with the knowledge of his nephew's suspicion, the uncle seemed to have accelerated his plans and chose that evening to administer a lethal dose. Which, through my actions, he had the misadventure to consume himself. He was none the wiser until the poison began to perform its fateful work. Such was his enthusiasm with administering a fatal dosage that he passed swiftly, even before the servants, at a gallop upon an Arabian, had reached the doctor in town, let alone brought him back. I suspect that was deliberate . . . but he had no way of knowing that he would be the one in need of the doctor. For that matter, neither did I . . . ."

"That must have been a burden to bear," I sympathized. "To have that sort of responsibility on one's soul, at such an early age."

"When I chose to do it, I did not feel as though I had a surplus of options," admitted Holmes. "The estate was isolated from the town. Who would have lent me one of Aunt Elizabeth's handsome Arabians on the pretext of an errand? It would have been an hour's walk to summon a policeman, and another hour back. Once arrived, what was he to do? Wait patiently in the cupboard until the day he was needed? As a guest, and as a youth, I was powerless. I suppose Price could have written to his family's solicitors and requested assistance, or some other course of action. He could not have peremptorily turned his aunt and uncle from the house with their children, not without inviting certain scandal. The timeline of events was too accelerated for us. At the time, it was only my intention to give

Uncle Henry a dose of his own 'gastric distress'. I did not yet have the experience to recognize a cornered beast ready to fight for his own life."

"What happened afterwards?" I asked.

"Aunt Elizabeth hadn't been a party to any of it, yet she had been the reason for the whole thing," said Holmes. "She was an exigent woman. Uncle Henry had run through his own money trying to keep up with her demands for material luxuries. Only the best from the jeweler, furrier, and dressmaker. Superior equines. Lavish travel. Those sorts of things. After he came to the end of his own funds in his quest to satisfy his wife's insatiable appetite for the finer things in life, it was the most natural thing in the world to start squandering his nephew's fortune to maintain his wife at the level to which she was accustomed. Hence the almost comical string of pretended bad luck, as he tried to get his nephew accustomed to the idea that perhaps he would not be as wealthy as his solicitors had prepared him to be. She kept the gifts, of course, despite their having been acquired with embezzled funds. After all, what would young Price want with dresses and jewels? But she and her children left the country very swiftly after Uncle Henry's death, and last we heard, she had married a German aristocrat abroad, so perhaps it never occurred to her to return the ill-gotten valuables."

"Did his crime ever come out?"

"There were no deathbed confessions, if that's what you refer to. No apologies or expressions of sorrow. In fact, it was a rather grim passing, and not merely because of the arsenic. That might make part of a compelling little pamphlet in the future, by the by – *Glimpses Upon a Criminal's Deathbed, Whereupon the Last Moments of Nefarious Villains Are Described*. Sensational and dramatic, just as the reading public likes, and one-hundred-percent truthful, as all the best cautionary tales are.

"But back to Uncle Henry. It took a few years to piece things together to appreciate the scope of his misappropriation. It was ultimately kept very quiet to avoid needless embarrassment. According to what I heard, there was some strong suspicion that Uncle Henry had been a significant factor in the drowning deaths of my friend's parents, thus giving him control of the fortune in the first place. However, that line of investigation was never pursued, as far as I was made aware."

"How dreadful to think that such a thing could happen."

"If you cast your mind back, you'll recall I've relayed the sentiment to you on previous occasions that the vilest alleys of London are no match for the sins committed in our charming British countryside. If one runs afoul of hooligans near the gas-works, assistance is only a police-whistle away. But in the isolation of the country, there is much justice destined to be delayed until it may be heard by a higher court than any in this realm."

The Yuletide Heist
by Mark Mower

I have recounted more than once that, when the mood took him, my good friend Sherlock Holmes was something of a consummate storyteller. At such times, he would regale his listeners with narratives that were both gripping and puzzling. Most often, these were tales of adventure and intrigue in which he had played no small part. And it was in the December of 1896 that he chose to share with us one of his most absorbing stories – a mystery he referred to simply as "The Yuletide Heist".

On the Christmas Eve of that year, we had a full house at 221b. Assisted by Billy the Page, Mrs. Hudson had spent the better part of the day preparing a veritable feast for our consumption that evening. Holmes had insisted that the pair should join the festivities at the large refectory table which had been assembled in our upstairs apartment. Alongside the four of us, the other invited guests included Inspectors Lestrade and Eastland from Scotland Yard, Dr. Henry Tamworth, an academic from King's College, Cambridge, and Mrs. Celina Grimble, a long-standing member of the Wandsworth Ladies' Reading Circle with whom I had corresponded for some years. We were a disparate group to be sure, but the atmosphere and bonhomie that evening was both cheery and heart-warming.

Our meal had commenced with a piping hot dish of Palestine Soup, made with delicious Jerusalem artichokes and a variety of exotic spices. The main course was a further Mrs. Hudson speciality – a lavish and extravagant serving of roasted goose with sage-and-onion stuffing, ham, potatoes, oysters, peas, and cabbage. And during the consumption of this, Holmes began his unusual narrative.

"I have often reflected," said he, "on the extraordinary lengths that some criminals will go to in perpetrating their felonious deeds. A simple and uncomplicated plan of action will often be discarded in favour of a more elaborate scheme designed to misdirect and unseat the most dogged of investigators. And yet, it is sometimes this particular or peculiar *over-complication* which serves to expose the man or woman concerned."

"I'm not sure I follow," announced Inspector Giles Eastland, his round, chubby face flushed with a distinctly crimson hue which had no doubt been brought on by the three glasses of strong Madeira he had managed to consume since being seated at the table. "Are you saying that some criminals are too clever for their own good?"

Holmes eyed him keenly. "Yes, it is sometimes simply that. But there is more. It is often in the formulation of a most cunning plan that our offender leaves more tangible clues than he might otherwise. That was certainly true in the case of the Tichborne Claimant [1]. Arthur Orton's confession last year came as no surprise. Throughout his long and unsuccessful claim to be the missing heir to Sir Henry Tichborne's baronetcy, he devised a most fiendish and over-complicated background to support his assertion. In my view, it was this over-elaboration which ultimately enabled his scheme to be laid bare."

"I have to agree with you there," said Mrs. Grimble with some gusto. "Frightful man he was. And what a cock-and-bull story he told!"

There was some merriment at this, although Mrs. Hudson – who was sat beside her – seemed somewhat shocked by the remark and shot a glance at young Billy, who appeared to find the comment particularly humorous and had chortled loudly.

It was Inspector Lestrade who spoke next, raising his fork on which was still positioned a sizeable piece of goose meat. "I take the point, Mr. Holmes, but give me a straightforward case any day. A cleverly devised criminal enterprise may leave more by way of breadcrumbs, but always increases the amount of legwork that needs to be undertaken. Sometimes, we detectives have neither the time nor the energy to pursue such matters."

I believe I saw Holmes suppress a grin at this. "My dear Lestrade, it is in those more challenging and colourful cases that the greatest satisfaction is to be had. It is the very reason I set myself up as the world's first consulting detective!"

Mrs. Hudson beamed at Holmes as she passed a dish of roasted potatoes across to Dr. Tamworth. To this point, the aged and somewhat emaciated anatomist had said little, while eating a great deal, and now seemed intent on filling his plate for a second time. As a longstanding acquaintance of the detective, he had often been invited to dine with us at Baker Street, and with a sharp wit and inherent curiosity about all of life's mysteries, had regularly proved to be an affable dinner guest. It was he who then addressed my colleague.

"Then tell us, Mr. Holmes, of all the cases that you have investigated over the years, what is the one single affair which most aptly illustrates your point? I would be keen to hear about a convoluted crime which was, by its nature, over-planned, to the extent that it enabled you to solve it more easily than you might otherwise."

"Me too!" opined Mrs. Grimble.

The nodding heads confirmed that we were all in agreement. With a distinct twinkle in his eye, Holmes began. "Well then, it seems I have little choice but to lay before you one of the most fascinating cases of my early career, in the days before the good doctor became my most trusted associate."

Mrs. Hudson gave me an approving nod and, having taken a sip of her dry white sherry, settled back into the dining chair and fixed her gaze upon Holmes. Like the rest of us, she clearly relished the opportunity to hear the detective talk about a case in his own words. Beyond the flickering of the gas lamps and the gentle crackle of the coal burning merrily in the hearth, there was an expectant silence.

"I was still living in Montague Street in the December of 1878. The year had been a busy one, and as Christmas approached, I anticipated that my caseload might ease somewhat. Yet this was not to be. I became embroiled in two or three minor investigations in both the lead up to the 25th of December and the few days beyond that. But it was on Monday, the 6th of January of the following year, that I received an urgent telegram from a prestigious private bank on Victoria Street. For reasons of confidentiality, I will refrain from naming the institution concerned.

"In short, the bank wished me to investigate the circumstances surrounding a most audacious theft. A sizeable sum of cash had been stolen from an elaborately protected bank vault which sat one floor beneath the bank's three-storey building. The robbery had been planned to allow the thieves the maximum amount of time between taking the money, and the point at which the loss of the cash would be discovered. The bank had placed the last deposits in the vault on the 23rd of December and having closed for the Christmas and New Year period, it was only on the morning of Monday the sixth that the vault was reopened and the crime detected. The thieves had, therefore, a full two weeks to cover their tracks after pulling off the theft.

"In the scheme of things, the bank considered this to be a significant, yet surprisingly manageable, loss. While the vault had contained around five- to six-hundred locked safety deposit boxes – containing jewellery and other assets estimated to value more than £5 million – it was clear that none of these had been tampered with. The thieves had confined themselves to the carefully stacked bundles of banknotes which sat on a central plinth on the floor of the vault. And yet, even here, their ambitions had been conservative. While the vault held more than £1 million in cash deposits, of various currencies and denominations from around the world, the gang had taken only £100,000 in sterling banknotes. Given this situation, the bank was keen to avoid any sort of public scandal and desired only to prevent its depositors from withdrawing their cash and other assets, which would effectively plunge the business into liquidation. The directors believed that they could make some accounting adjustments to cover the loss and took the decision *not* to call the police. However, they could not risk the same thing happening again, so called me in to determine how the theft had been executed, so that steps could be taken to strengthen the bank's security arrangements and prevent any future robberies."

At this point, Holmes paused to raise a glass of cabernet sauvignon to his lips to refresh his palate. Inspector Lestrade took the opportunity to interject, his pinched and drawn features hiding none of his disdain for what he had just heard. "It is disappointing to learn that a prestigious financial institution would choose to conduct its affairs in such a way. I mean no slur on your abilities and credentials, Mr. Holmes, but a crime of this magnitude should surely have warranted the attentions of Scotland Yard's finest."

Inspector Eastland nodded in agreement, but Holmes refused to be drawn too far down that path. "I take your point, gentlemen, but I had little choice but to accede to my client's terms for carrying out the investigation. I must admit that I was a little surprised when I arrived at the bank around ten o'clock that morning to find no police presence. In fact, beyond the half-dozen bank staff and directors who knew of the robbery, there was only one other person present – an engineer from the firm which had installed the locking mechanism of the solidly constructed vault door. He had been called in at short notice to ascertain whether the lock had failed or had been tampered with in any way."

My own curiosity was piqued by this. "So had it? It seems clear to me that some simple form of lock-picking would be the most obvious way to steal from the vault, having gained access to the building."

Holmes smiled. "If only the solution had been that straightforward. But the engineer was completely baffled. He said that the mechanism appeared to have worked exactly as it should have done and could see no way in which the thieves could have entered the vault. To understand the significance of this, I will explain how the elaborate security system worked.

"Firstly, we start with the building itself. The ground floor foyer consisted of a large open area in which were situated the front desk and counters used by the bank staff and a few ancillary storage rooms. While there were large windows on both sides of this space, they were set high up in the room and could not be opened. All were intact and showed no signs of having been interfered with when examined that Monday morning. The entrance to the foyer was through two large front doors which faced onto Victoria Street. At night, and during the weekends, a uniformed concierge would sit at a desk to the side of these doors. Two men were employed for this task, sharing the different shifts between them. Stanley Bliss, the elder of the two, had been with the bank for over twenty years. His counterpart, Harley Coulter, had been employed for a little under ten months. Alongside the bank's manager and under-manager, they were the only staff that held keys to the front entrance door and other areas of the building. There were no other doors to the property, and my subsequent investigations showed that all of the locks to the doors and bolts to the windows of the building were intact and working as they should."

Inspector Eastland spluttered in response to this. "Now, there's a telling clue, right there! My intuition tells me that the newer man was at the centre of this. Without keys, there could be no theft. There would be no way of gaining access to the vault." He shifted heavily on his chair and took in a deep breath.

"I'm not sure I agree," said Mrs. Grimble somewhat brusquely. "I've been reading crime and mystery books for some years since I first discovered *The Moonstone* by Wilkie Collins, and I never missed one of Dr. Watson's publications. At this stage in the narrative, there could be other ways in which the robbers gained access to the locked vault – an underground tunnel, maybe, or the use of explosives, or perhaps by leaving someone on the inside who could then open the vault door and reset the locking mechanism after the cash was stolen."

Eastland seemed unable or unwilling to respond to this challenge and reached once more for his Madeira glass. Holmes sought to answer both sets of comments.

"These are exactly the sort of considerations that occurred to me that wintry morning. But let me tell you more about the security and the vault itself. It will help to address some of the splendid ideas suggested by Mrs. Grimble. A locked door at the back of the foyer provided access to all the other areas of the building – a staircase to the upper floors and a slope leading down to the vault room. Further locked doors provided access to all the corridors of the upper floors, and it was the bank's policy to ensure that every single room throughout the building had an individual lock and marked key and was always secured when the staff were not at work. This included a final locked door which stood at the entrance to the vault room."

It was the bright-eyed and fresh-faced Billy who then spoke. "Please excuse the interruption, sir, but I just wanted to be clear. If the thieves had wanted to get to and from the vault using the Victoria Street entrance, they would have required three different keys."

"That is a perfect summary, my young friend."

"And all of that before they could even attempt to open the vault."

"Indeed."

"Well, Mr. Holmes, that does suggest that one of the concierges had to be involved. Sat behind the doors to one side, he could not have failed to see the robbers enter."

"Billy, we will make a detective of you yet! I was about to tell you more about the vault, but your polite interruption is a timely one, for I should have said more about the responsibilities of the concierge. On any working day, the bank closed its doors to customers at three-thirty in the afternoon. Staff working at the bank would then spend time reconciling all the day's transactions, typically leaving for home at five o'clock. For a further hour, the building would be occupied by only the manager and under-manager. During that time, they would be responsible for locking the vault and securing the two doors back to the main foyer. At a few minutes before six o'clock, the concierge would arrive at work, using his own keys to enter the building. He would then wait for the manager and under-manager to appear in the foyer before commencing work. When the two managers had left for the evening, the concierge would be the only person left in the building."

"This is lending more weight to my colleague's assertion that one of the uniformed men must have been involved," said Inspector Lestrade, giving a sly wink to Eastland, who looked to perk up a little at the show of support.

"We will come to that," replied Holmes, with just the merest hint of agitation in his voice. "First, let me continue with the routine observed by the concierge. During the first hour, he would check all the doors on each floor, starting with the door to the vault. While he would never expect to find this unlocked, it was quite common for some of the doors on the upper floors to be left unlocked as staff departed for the evening. The bank was a stickler for routines and paperwork. Ticking off his progress using a printed checklist, the concierge was required to approach every door, and check that nothing was amiss in each room. This included checking that all the windows were firmly secured. Having to unlock and relock so many doors was time-consuming but necessary, as far as the bank was concerned. Until the theft, it had never experienced any form of break-in. This routine of checking would be repeated twice more during the night – once at ten o'clock, with a final tour of the building at four the following morning. Each tour would take a minimum of forty-five minutes. Stanley Bliss admitted that he and his colleague were never in a hurry to complete the task as it broke up the monotony of the ten-hour shift."

"During which time, the front entrance was left unattended and exposed," opined Mrs. Hudson, frowning with some disapproval.

Holmes nodded in agreement. "Yes, for all the bank's well-planned procedures, this was a clear area of weakness. Anyone with a knowledge of the routine would realise that they had three periods of at least forty-five minutes in which they could enter and leave the building with little risk of detection."

I could not help but interject. "And of those, the ten o'clock and four o'clock slots would be preferrable, given that the normally busy Victoria Street would be much quieter."

"That was my working assumption."

Dr. Tamworth, who had been listening most attentively, was clearly convinced by the emerging hypothesis, but appeared eager to get the heart of the matter. "That all sounds credible, but does not address the issue of the allegedly corrupt concierge. Someone on the inside must have been involved to allow the thieves to gain access to the three keys needed to get to the vault. If we are convinced that the bank managers were innocent, then it must have been one of the two uniformed men."

"Not necessarily," answered Mrs. Grimble, once again playing Devil's Advocate. "Any of the four sets of keys we have been told about could have been copied and placed in the hands of the criminals. Furthermore, this could have been done with or without the knowledge of the key holder. They may have been stolen for that purpose and replaced before the loss was realised."

Inspector Eastland was having none of it. "That's a lot of keys that would need to be cut."

Mrs. Grimble was quick to react. "No, just the three. As Billy observed so eloquently, only three keys were needed to get from the front entrance to the door of the vault."

Billy piped up in support of the bespectacled Mrs. Grimble. "Yes, and Mr. Holmes said that all of the keys were 'marked'. I took that to mean that they could be individually identified according to which lock they were supposed to fit." He looked across at Holmes who was pleased to nod in confirmation.

"The keys were indeed marked – etched with some numbers and letters according to the floor and room concerned. This made it easier for the three specific keys to be identified and copied away from the bank."

Inspector Lestrade seemed surprised at the revelation. "So it wasn't one of the concierges who let the thieves in on the night of the raid?"

"Not as such. It was later to become clear that the robbery had occurred on Christmas Eve. Stanley Bliss had been on duty on that night. As far as the bank was concerned, he was beyond suspicion given his dedicated years of service. My subsequent investigations cleared him of any involvement. And while it would have been tempting to believe that the more recently employed Harley Coulter had acted in concert with the felons, this also proved not to be the case. On the night in question, Coulter had a solid alibi. He had visited some relatives in Lincolnshire and had stopped overnight at an hotel in Scunthorpe. No, our inside man proved to be none other than Dominic Tuttle, the former concierge whom Harley

Coulter had replaced. Before leaving the job, he had three duplicate keys cut to enable the robbers to reach the vault. I will explain how we netted him a little later. For the moment, let us turn to the vault itself.

"In the room designated, the bank had installed the most sophisticated and expensive vault locking system on the market at that time, designed and built by a prestigious Swiss clock manufacturer. The door had no keys or combination locks. It was opened, instead, by a clockwork mechanism housed on the inside of the door. Once set, it could not be tampered with and had been built to withstand both heavy drilling and explosive charges.

Each evening, the manager and under-manager would set the timer on the inside of the door and, where required, ensure that the clockwork mechanism was wound to the correct point. The timer would be set for a period of up to twelve days and was fixed to open only at eight o'clock on the chosen morning. Once the door had been closed it could not be unlocked until that time. The lock was serviced once a year and the timing mechanism adjusted accordingly. In its ten years of service, it had never failed or lost more than a fraction of a second in time. It was a remarkable piece of engineering."

Mrs. Grimble looked a little crestfallen. "So my ideas about tunnels and people being left in the vault can be discounted then, Mr. Holmes?"

"Yes, on this occasion. The vault had remained intact, and there was nothing to suggest that anyone had been hidden in the space. However, it might interest you to learn that the door could be opened from the inside. It was a failsafe mechanism built in to prevent one of the bank staff inadvertently locking themselves in. However, given the responsibility placed on those setting and locking the door, this task was never left to anyone other than the manager and under-manager who would, in concert, double-check the settings. When I first arrived at the bank, they gave me every assurance that there had been no one inside the vault when the door was shut on the evening of the 23rd of December."

"Well, that's a pretty mystery then!" said a smiling Dr. Tamworth. "You said earlier that the engineer who was called in on the morning of the 6th of January could find nothing wrong. That being the case, I can see no logical way in which the safe could have been opened prior to that."

"Nor I," agreed Mrs. Hudson. "Now, I'm sure we are all eager to learn more, Mr. Holmes, but could Billy and I be allowed a short amount of time to clear the plates and serve afters? I have a steamed plum pudding with brandy for those that still have the space. And if your appetite is more limited, there are cranberry and mince pies."

There was an enthusiastic response to the housekeeper's announcement. My colleague agreed to a short interval, and while the plates were cleared and the desserts served, most of the menfolk took the opportunity to have a smoke in front of the fire. I spent the time talking to Mrs. Grimble about some of the cases in which we had been engaged earlier that year, including those that I later entitled "The Veiled Lodger", "The Sussex Vampire", and "The Missing Three-Quarter". She was also fascinated to learn that we had finally brought to justice a certain Edwin Halvergate, one of Professor Moriarty's long-standing foot soldiers, who had taken it upon himself to lead what remained of the academic's criminal fraternity in the wake of the events at the Reichenbach Falls.

It was approaching eight-thirty that evening when the dessert plates had finally been cleared and a few gifts that had been hanging on the Christmas tree were distributed to our guests. With everyone's glass replenished with their favourite seasonal tipple, Holmes resumed his narrative.

"As you might imagine, I used the first couple of hours at the bank to interview all the relevant staff and directors and to carry out a thorough inspection of the building, paying particular attention to the vault and all of the areas leading to it. Given that he had already completed his work in examining the locking mechanism, I also took the opportunity to quiz Alex Dunlop, the vault engineer, before he departed."

"A-ha!" said Inspector Lestrade, with a knowing look on his face. "Very wise, I'd say. In your position, I'd have done the same – to find out more about the annual service."

"Indeed. And a very fruitful line of enquiry it proved to be. For Dunlop had *not* been the engineer who had carried out the routine maintenance two days prior to the Christmas shutdown. In fact, he had never visited the bank before the 6th of January, and had only been called in to assist as the regular engineer, Frank Chilvers, had failed to show up for work that morning."

"Highly suspicious," agreed Inspector Eastland, now resembling the deep hue of the port he was imbibing at some pace.

"Yes, but that wasn't the only irregularity. Dunlop had checked the firm's maintenance records before setting off for the bank. Frank Chilvers had signed off on the completion of the annual service, but his maintenance log was inaccurate."

Mrs. Grimble was as fascinated as the rest of us. "In what sense?"

"As far as the records were concerned, the work required a single engineer, but when quizzed, the manager and under-manager confirmed that the annual service had been undertaken by *two* engineers. In fact, when I asked about this, the two men had to concede that it had been unusual. In ten years, they had never known the task to require more than one person. The under-manager then recalled that Chilvers had mentioned something about the second engineer being 'an apprentice' and recollected that the young man in question had looked extremely youthful, if not a little effeminate. He remembered seeing the lad struggling to wheel in the trolley which carried the large toolbox that the engineers brought with them for the service."

"That is extremely suggestive," replied the ardent crime reader, "but serves only to further complicate our attempt to unpick the *method* by which this crime was carried out. And how did you act on this additional information, Mr. Holmes?"

The detective gave Mrs. Grimble the broadest of smiles. "My investigations then required me to leave the bank and put in some good, old-fashioned legwork. I will be honest in saying that my inspection of the building yielded no further clues. The thieves appeared to have been extremely diligent in covering their tracks. Not so much as a hair, footprint, or finger-mark had been left in the vault."

"Finger-marks, Mr. Holmes?" said Billy, with a look of some confusion. "Why would you look for a finger-mark?"

Somewhat to the surprise of those around the table, it was Dr. Tamworth who answered. "I am sure that Mr. Holmes will forgive me, but this is an area of study in which I have long been interested. Marcello Malpighi, a professor of anatomy at the University of Bologna, was the first to identify the ridges, spirals, and loops that define the nature of finger-marks, as far back as 1686. In 1788, another anatomist, the German Johann Mayer, concluded that these marks are unique to each individual. More recently, academics and law enforcement agencies have sought to develop classification systems for identifying and recording them. When we have a workable system, it should be possible to match any marks taken from the scene of a crime to the recorded finger-marks of the criminal involved."

Inspector Eastland looked unconvinced and Lestrade merely rolled his eyes before commenting. "Yes, but he didn't find any finger-marks, so that wouldn't have been much use."

Mrs. Grimble seemed to find this exchange amusing, but pressed Holmes further. "Come now, Mr. Holmes, we want to know what happened next?"

"Well, my enquiries the next day were focused on locating the whereabouts of Frank Chilvers, the lock engineer, and Dominic Tuttle, the former concierge. The bank provided me with an address for the latter, which proved to be a shabby two-up, two-down house in Shoreditch. The landlady of the property informed me that Tuttle had lived there for about three years, but had announced before Christmas that he was moving out, and did so just two days later. She was not at all pleased, particularly as

Tuttle refused to say where he was moving when asked about a forwarding address for any post he might receive."

Mrs. Hudson smiled broadly. "I'm sure that the landlady *did* find out where he was heading. There isn't much that escapes the notice of a good housekeeper."

"How right you are, Mrs. Hudson! For the very meticulous landlady had occasion to observe some papers while dusting in her lodger's room on the day before he departed. It seems he had already purchased a ticket for the train ferry crossing from Dover to Calais, and had made arrangements for the onward rail journey to Paris where he was booked to stay at the Hôtel de Lalande."

"Very neat," observed Inspector Eastland, "and awfully expensive, no doubt. So I imagine you were thinking that Tuttle had to be one of the thieves who had arranged to escape to the Continent after the theft and before the robbery was discovered."

"That was one of my thoughts. The other was that Tuttle had been paid handsomely for supplying the duplicate keys and had made the arrangements knowing he was likely to be investigated as a former concierge. Either way, his actions served only to highlight his probable complicity. In my view, an unnecessary *over-complication*. Had he continued to reside in Shoreditch and had refuted any suggestion that he had supplied the keys, there would have been little that I could have done to bring him to justice. Try as I might, I could never prove where he had arranged for the keys to be cut.

"For the moment, we will leave our comfortably accommodated Mr. Tuttle in his Parisian hotel room and turn instead to Frank Chilvers. His firm had an office and workshop in Clerkenwell from which it carried out services and repairs to the wide variety of clockwork mechanisms that the Swiss-owned business had installed across the capital. Chilvers was in his mid-thirties and had worked there for over a decade. He was a trusted employee. I visited the office the day after the robbery had been discovered. The firm's fears that Chilvers may have had a hand in the robbery had grown when the man failed to appear at work for a second day. A work colleague had then been sent to Chilver's rented property in Farringdon but found it empty, and had no success in discovering the engineer's whereabouts. I was a little more fortunate.

"My enquiries at the office in Clerkenwell revealed two pieces of information which proved to be crucial. The first was that he had graduated from Cambridge with a first-class honours degree in engineering. As well as being a talented engineer, the man was highly literate and able to speak a variety of European languages – skills which his Swiss employer valued a great deal. The second was that he had romantic inclinations towards a young lady with whom he had been reacquainted eighteen months earlier. His work colleagues knew only that her name was 'Ellen Cox', for Chilvers had always been tight-lipped about revealing anything further of the woman."

"A-ha!" squealed Mrs. Grimble. "We have our romantic interest! Like any good mystery story, there has to be some amorous element."

Once again, Mrs. Hudson looked troubled by the lady's outburst and I saw her calmly, yet surreptitiously, move the carafe of Madeira away from Mrs. Grimble's immediate grasp as Holmes continued his narrative.

"Having returned briefly to my rooms in Montague Street, I then travelled up to Cambridge by rail that afternoon to visit this Ellen Cox."

"How did you know she lived in Cambridge?" I asked, incredulously. "You had but her name."

"I believed that if Chilvers had been *reacquainted* with the young lady, there was every likelihood that the pair met originally when Chilvers was a student. Working on the basis that the woman might still reside in Cambridge, I consulted my collection of street directories for the town and had a lucky break. There was an entry for a Miss Ellen Cox in one of the directories, which showed that she was the owner of a private residence close to Appleton Meadows on the outskirts of Cambridge."

"A very desirable area in which to live," announced Dr. Tamworth. "I wish my academic salary afforded me such a location."

"Yes," replied Holmes. "Appleton Meadows is an open space to the south of Cambridge, which sits alongside the River Cam. It is a popular destination for students, hikers, and naturalists – many of the latter being drawn to the marshy woodland areas which host species like the butterbur and musk beetle."

"Very picturesque, I'm sure," intoned Inspector Lestrade, "but let's hear more about your visit to the young lady and how this led you to Chilvers."

Holmes was not ruffled by the gruff remark. "Well, a fifteen-minute cart ride took me from the railway station to the pretty village of Appleton. And it didn't take me too long to locate the property, named – appropriately enough – *Appleton House*. It was a sizeable building, created in the early part of the century – square in shape, attractive in design, and covering a plot of maybe five acres, the highlight of which was a broad rectangle of land which stretched down to, and gave unparalleled views of, the meadows themselves.

"A young servant girl greeted me at the door and took my card when I announced that I wished to speak to Miss Cox. A few minutes later I was shown into the spacious parlour of the property where I was met by a smiling, albeit slightly bemused, woman in her early thirties. She was around five-feet-four-inches in height, with a delicate, pale complexion and bright blue eyes. The braided buns of her light blonde hair suggested that she might have been of Scandinavian descent, but the clear, clipped tones of her diction gave no hint of a foreign accent. She wore a simple powder-blue dress with a high neckline, over which she had fastened a thick tartan shawl with a brooch resembling a scarab beetle.

"The lady directed me towards a comfortable armchair close to the fire and instructed the maid to prepare a pot of tea for us, before taking a seat on a sofa opposite me. 'How may I help you, Mr. Holmes? Your card says you are a *Consulting Detective*. I don't think I have ever met one of those before.'

"I smiled. 'Indeed, Miss Cox. You will have to forgive my impromptu visit to your beautiful home, but this is a matter of some urgency. I am trying to locate the whereabouts of a man I believe you know – a Mr. Frank Chilvers.'

"The statement had an immediate and telling effect. Miss Cox shifted in her chair and brought her hands together tightly. She blinked three or four times and then sought to regain her composure. 'Frank Chilvers? Yes, I did know a man by that name some years ago. We met at the university. Frank was studying in the school of engineering, while I had been given permission to attend some mathematics lectures given by a friend of my father's, even though I wasn't formally recognised as an under-graduate. I will be candid, Mr. Holmes: We did walk out together for some months, but when my father found out, he forbade me from seeing or speaking to Frank, whom he considered to be an unsuitable match.'

"'And why was that, if you do not mind me asking?'

"She responded confidently. 'I was always due to inherit a small fortune. My great-great-grandfather was a successful jeweller, and both my father and grandfather carried on in the same vein, bringing further wealth to the family. However, as an only child, the line stopped with me. My father was overprotective and wanted to ensure that the man I married was my social equal. Frank was the son of a carpenter, and while he was a gifted engineer set for a good career, had still to make his way in the world. My father believed that if he married me, he would have no incentive to do so, and would shirk his responsibilities, relying on my inheritance – something he told Frank in no uncertain terms. After our graduation, we went our separate ways. I took a job at a private school for girls, while Frank moved to London to work for an engineering firm.'

"'And have you seen him since that time?' I then asked.

"This time her reply seemed a little less assured. 'No. I have lived here at Appleton House all of my life. My mother died when I was but six years of age. Father passed away four years ago, leaving me the house and the family inheritance. And I have been alone since that time. I have had no cause to reach out to Frank, and I imagine he would feel the same.'

"While we drank our tea, she asked why I was trying to reach Chilvers. I had no desire to reveal my hand, so made no mention of the bank theft, saying only that he had failed to turn up for work and his employer had been concerned as to his whereabouts. The explanation seemed to placate her, for she made no further mention of the man and the conversation drifted on to other topics. A short while later, I thanked her for her time and said that I would need to find a way of returning to the railway station. Her face took on a look of some concern, as she explained that I was unlikely to find any sort of cab, cart, or carriage in the vicinity. She then suggested I might like to walk through to the bottom of her garden, where I would find a footpath running through the meadows alongside the river which provided a direct and most charming route back to the town. I agreed to do so.

"We left the parlour and walked through the house towards the rear of the property. As we did so, we passed a large, brightly lit study to our right. Inside I could see tables, cabinets, shelves, and plinths displaying many clocks, automata, and other mechanical devices. I was at once intrigued and asked her about them. She explained that the collection had belonged to her great-great-grandfather, and she could not bear to part with them. I stared into the room for some time, deep in thought, before turning to see that Miss Cox was regarding me keenly.

"'A fascinating collection,'" said I, trying to play down my elation at seeing the devices.

"'Indeed,' she replied rather enigmatically. 'An inheritance like none other.'"

"At the rear of the house we passed into a large, glass-domed conservatory filled with exotic plants from across the globe. A small wood-burning stove had been placed to one side to keep the plants at an acceptable temperature, even in the depths of an English winter. Miss Cox unlocked some double doors at the far end of the conservatory, and we stepped into the garden.

"The view which greeted me was as perfect as it was engineered – an exquisitely ordered arrangement of borders, beds, and pergolas, down the centre of which ran a broad lawn with not so much as a hint of a weed. Beyond the vista of the garden was a panoramic view of Appleton Meadows in all their natural glory. The contrast between the two could not have been more distinct.

"In the very epicentre of the formal garden was a circular area of lawn, in the middle of which sat a large brass sundial. As we passed the timepiece, I saw Miss Cox extend her right hand to touch the dial, gently and fleetingly, with obvious affection – a gesture which I imagined she always made when passing by.

"At the very end of the garden was a small gate to the left, which placed me on a path leading down to the river's edge and the route back to Cambridge. I thanked Miss Cox for her time and set off at a pace, eager to make it to the railway station as quickly as I could for the journey back to London. With what I knew, I could afford to waste no further time."

There seemed to be some confusion in the room at this point, and it was young Billy who voiced the concern we all appeared to share. "I don't understand what you learnt from Miss Cox, sir. While she admitted to knowing Frank Chilvers, she said she had not seen him since his student days. Even if she had been lying, I cannot see how that would have helped you to find the engineer."

"You have a splendid enquiring mind, Billy," Holmes retorted. "But I think you have failed to realise why the encounter with Miss Cox was so revealing."

"He's not the only one," admitted Mrs. Grimble. "I think I must have missed something too!"

Inspector Lestrade smiled broadly and sought to explain. "I think what Mr. Holmes is trying to say is that Miss Cox's reaction to his appearance was odd and very telling. In fact, it wasn't a *reaction* at all. Not once did she ask Mr. Holmes *how* he came to know of her and her connection to Frank Chilvers. And if it had been true that she hadn't had any contact with the engineer for many years, she would surely have asked Mr. Holmes *why* he wished to know. I'm guessing that the moment she saw the card announcing that a *Consulting Detective* wished to speak to her, she knew someone was on to Frank Chilvers. By implication, this suggests that she already knew of the bank robbery."

Holmes agreed. "From my earlier enquiries, and what I had subsequently seen in the house, I knew that Miss Cox had to be involved. And I was already speculating that the bright young woman was likely to be the architect of the theft. I just had to find out why."

Inspector Eastland was clearly struggling to keep up. "How could you possibly believe that she was involved, given what you've told us?"

It was Mrs. Hudson who answered, with some satisfaction. "Inspector Eastland, remember the *apprentice* engineer who helped Frank Chilvers to service the locking mechanism? That wasn't an effeminate young man – it was Ellen Cox herself!"

"Indeed, Mrs. Hudson. Her role was pivotal, as I will explain shortly. But let me first explain what happened next. I returned to London in the early evening and made my way to the Diogenes Club, an establishment frequented by my older brother, Mycroft. As some of you in the room will know, my brother has a fair degree of influence within government and diplomatic circles. I told him about the robbery and explained the nature of my quest: Principally, that I needed the French authorities to arrest Frank Chilvers and Dominic Tuttle at the Hôtel de Lalande and have them returned to England. I couldn't risk letting Ellen Cox get a message to them saying that their robbery had been exposed."

"How did you know that Chilvers had joined Tuttle in fleeing to France?" asked Dr. Tamworth.

"I didn't know for certain, but believed that to be the most logical outcome. Like Tuttle, Chilvers had already cleared out of his rented property. It would make sense for the two to travel together on the pre-arranged journey and to hide out in France."

"I disagree," said Mrs. Grimble. "Surely they would have been taking a most extraordinary risk, having carried out the robbery, and being in possession of some or all of the stolen cash?"

"No," came the reply. "They would not have risked that. I conjectured that the proceeds of the robbery would be left in safe hands. Namely, those of Ellen Cox, who would no doubt return to Cambridgeshire to hide the loot. Having done so, it was then simply a matter of waiting until the coast was clear and getting word to her two accomplices that it was safe for them to return to England."

There was general hubbub in the room after this, with everyone voicing their thoughts and ideas. It took my colleague some moments to regain his ground and to carry on with the narrative. "My plans worked to perfection. Mycroft's rapid intervention and hastily arranged telegrams to his counterparts in France yielded the desired results. Early the next morning, both Chilvers and Tuttle were detained by officers from the Paris Police Prefecture. By the evening of the same day, they were on the train ferry back to England in the custody of two burly officials from the British Embassy. Having arrived back in London, they were placed under house arrest in the Farringdon property which Chilvers had vacated some days earlier."

"Did they admit to the crime?" asked Billy eagerly.

"No. I visited them the following day and explained that I was investigating the robbery on behalf of the bank. Both men refused to say anything. Chilvers even questioned the legality of the house arrest."

Inspector Eastland had an opinion on this. "I don't mean to sound churlish, Mr. Holmes, but he had a point. Under what powers were you acting? Did you involve Scotland Yard after all?"

Holmes brushed aside the concern. "The arrangements were made by the Home Office. As the men had refused to give a clear account of why they had travelled to France, they were being detained as suspected spies.

In fact, a mysterious note found in the possession of Frank Chilvers gave some credence to the notion that they were withholding information. Their detention was one of Mycroft's ruses, of course, but it gave me time to resolve all of the outstanding queries in the case."

"That's a little sneaky, Mr. Holmes!" said Dr. Tamworth, relishing the tale.

"True. But everything began to fall into place very quickly after that. My investigations into Ellen Cox's financial affairs revealed some startling information. After she had inherited the house and the financial legacy from her father, she had invested most of her wealth in some schemes suggested by her bank. Apparently knowing little of the nature of these investment schemes – which mainly involved risky overseas property ventures – she sustained substantial losses. The bank which advised her was none other than my client."

Mrs. Grimble clearly had a penchant for melodrama. "So the robbery was an act of revenge!"

"I'm not sure I would put it quite like that. But her losses stood at around £100,000 – the same amount stolen from the vault during the raid."

"How extraordinary!" said I, every bit as enthralled as the others. "But if that was the motivation, how the devil did they carry out the theft? I still don't see how they managed to open the vault door."

Holmes was relishing the denouement. "That, of course, was the really clever aspect of the case. To understand the method, we must first delve back into Ellen Cox's family history. The room full of clocks, automata, and other mechanical devices I had seen at Appleton House had indeed been owned by the young lady's great-great-grandfather. But these were no mere ornaments. They had been crafted and engineered by the man himself. When I first saw them, I knew that her relative had to be the famous *James Cox*. She was being evasive in describing him as a 'successful jeweller'. In fact, James Cox was a jeweller, goldsmith, inventor, and entrepreneur, famous for producing elaborate and expensive automata like the Peacock Clock, a large automaton showcasing three life-sized mechanical birds. The clock was eventually bought by Catherine the Great, the Empress of Russia, in 1781.

"More significant than any of these creations was his construction of a timepiece in the 1760's which he claimed to be a perpetual motion machine [2]. Working in collaboration with a man named John Merlin, Cox created a clock which needed no winding. The device was powered by changes in atmospheric pressure, which resulted in the movement of the clock's winding mechanism. It was sufficient to enable the timepiece to run indefinitely, and a clever safety mechanism prevented any overwinding of the machine. The source of the clock's energy was a large barometer containing one-hundred-fifty pounds of mercury."

Dr. Tamworth was quick to respond. "That's correct. I have read accounts of the timepiece, but while I'm no expert in this field, I believe I'm right in saying that the clock was not a true perpetual motion machine, for such an operation would have defied the laws of thermodynamics."

This was all too much for Inspector Eastland, who looked as if he were about to suffer a fatal seizure. "Thermo . . . *what?*" he spluttered. "Scientific mumbo-jumbo! What does this have to do with the bank robbery?"

There was general hilarity at the officer's outburst. Even Lestrade allowed himself a loud guffaw in response. As Mrs. Hudson filled my brandy glass for a second time, Holmes sought to clarify things.

"In the bank, on that first day of the investigation, I began to speculate on the nature of the vault's lock. And it occurred to me that if the existing clockwork mechanism had been overridden in some way, the door could then have been primed to open at a time different to that set by the bank's manager and under-manager. But my problem was one of power. Without the clockwork mechanism, or some form of alternative gas or electrical power, the timer would not have worked. But having seen Ellen Cox's display of timepieces, the solution presented itself. What if the clockwork mechanism had been overridden and replaced, instead, by something resembling *Cox's Timepiece?*"

As ever, Billy was quick to point out an obvious anomaly. "Yes, but when the vault engineer was called to the bank on the day the robbery was discovered, he said he could find nothing wrong with the lock. How could that be the case?"

Holmes's face lit up, as if he had been anticipating just such a challenge. "He found nothing wrong, because the clockwork mechanism had been restored to its original function."

Mrs. Grimble seemed unconvinced. "Then I'm as confused as ever. First you say the mechanism was tampered with, now you are saying it was fine. Which was it?"

"Actually both," admitted Holmes. "My theory was this: Two days before the bank's Christmas shutdown, Chilvers had arranged for the annual service. While presented to the bank as an *apprentice*, Chilvers's very capable assistant was Ellen Cox. Having grown up surrounded by her great-great-grandfather's mechanical contraptions, she knew as much as there was to know about the operation of his famous mercury-powered timepiece. I speculated that Ellen had become reacquainted with Chilvers following the death of her father, possibly after learning that her investments had gone sour. When Chilvers told her that he was responsible for servicing the bank's elaborate locking system, the two hatched a plan. Between them, they constructed a smaller and much lighter version of Cox's Timepiece, which could be housed temporarily within the space ordinarily occupied by the vault's clockwork mechanism. They had plenty of time to plan for this, and it was well within reason to imagine that Chilvers had copied all the required blueprints to engineer the replacement lock with complete precision.

"It was my belief that the heavy trolley which the 'apprentice' had been seen to be struggling with was carrying the newly-constructed timepiece hidden within what looked like a large toolbox. During the service itself, the couple removed all the superfluous clockwork components, hiding them in the toolbox. They then installed the new timepiece, powered by its mercury barometer. What was left of the original lock was set to deceive. It could still be wound up as before and the clock could still be set. But while the bank's managers believed they were setting the clock for the 6th of January, this had no effect. The mercury timepiece was now controlling the operation of the lock with its own timer. The would-be thieves had set the door to open for two days at eight o'clock in the morning, consistent with the normal routine at the bank. But the third, and final, unlocking was set to occur on Christmas Eve when the theft would take place.

"It was then a matter of carrying out a successful robbery. We already know how the thieves entered the building. Chilvers would have met Dominic Tuttle on the many occasions he had visited the bank to carry out the annual service. It was probably the simple inducement of money which persuaded Tuttle to go along with the plan.

"With the concierge elsewhere in the building, they would have gone straight to the vault with the trolley carrying their tools and the clockwork parts removed earlier. And with the door now open, the three would have stuck to their assigned tasks given the limited time available. As the non-technical member of the gang, I imagine Dominic Tuttle was responsible for bagging up the money. Ellen Cox most likely focused on removing the mercury timepiece and placing it on the trolley. Frank Chilvers would then have used his expertise to replace all the original clockwork components. With this being the lengthiest part of the operation, I envisaged that Cox and Tuttle would use the time to wheel the trolley back to the entrance door of the bank, carrying both the cash and the timepiece. And when Chilvers had completed his work, the lock could be reset to open on the 6th of January. Beyond that, they had but to lock the entrance door behind them and wheel their trolley to the cart or carriage in which they had arrived. In many respects, an almost perfect theft."

Inspector Lestrade had to concede. "Well, Mr. Holmes. I must agree with you. If your theory proved to be correct, this was indeed an unnecessarily *over-complicated* affair. But I'm fascinated to know how you *proved* any of it. With your detainees refusing to say anything and Ellen Cox still sitting on the stolen cash, what proof had you?"

"You're quite correct. That was my final challenge. Having crafted such an elaborate plan, I knew that Ellen Cox would have taken every precaution in hiding the cash until it was safe to retrieve it. And yet, once again, it was her over-thinking of the arrangements which proved to be her downfall. I mentioned earlier that when Frank Chilvers had been arrested in France, he was found to be in possession of a mysterious note. Mycroft had the document sent on to me, and it proved to be the one final piece of information I needed to crack the case. The typed note read as follows:

Whispering whirls of water flow, down winding willowed waterways,
as seasoned sun soothes shallow depths, of summer's silent stream

Mrs. Grimble could barely contain her delight. "Such beautiful alliteration, and so evocative. This has certainly proved to be a most entertaining mystery, Mr. Holmes, but what did it mean?"

"The note was still contained within its envelope – one that had been sent from England on the 27th of December 1878 and addressed to Chilvers at the Hôtel de Lalande. It was postmarked '*Appleton*'."

Billy was quick on the uptake. "Then it was a coded message from Ellen Cox!"

"Yes. I was later to find out from the lady herself that it was part of a love poem written for her by Chilvers after his first visit to Appleton House, way back in the summer of 1866 when the two had first met. It took me some time to work out the full significance of the extract, for it was a clever attempt at concealment – "

To my surprise, it was Mrs. Hudson who interposed. "Forgive me, sir, but I believe I know what the note was meant to convey. The extract was to remind Chilvers of their shared time together all those years ago, but more specifically, was telling him that the stolen cash had been successfully hidden – somewhere close to Appleton Meadows!"

There was a round of applause and much raising of glasses in salute to the housekeeper's proclamation. Holmes was ebullient in his reply. "Capital, Mrs. Hudson! But there was more. The note communicated the *precise* location of the plunder, for it contained directions to the hole in which both the cash and the mercury powered timepiece had been buried within a sealed metal strongbox. I realised that the alliteration of the poem had been used to great effect, given the predominance of W's and S's at the start of most of the words. In fact, there are six *W*'s and seven *S*'s. I concluded that these were compass directions from a given point: Six feet '*West*' and seven feet '*South*'. I had then to work out from where to start the search . . . ."

Dr. Tamworth was not to be outdone. His quick mind and strong analytical abilities had presented him with the solution before Holmes could elaborate further. "I have it, Holmes! You alluded to it earlier, when you described Ellen Cox's passage through the circular area of lawn in the epicentre of the garden. The source of her affection was the sundial. That was the starting point!"

Holmes acknowledged that he was correct. There was a further round of applause and a series of toasts to the ageing academic who seemed a little overwhelmed by the response. My colleague took the opportunity to retrieve his churchwarden from the mantelpiece and filled the bowl with some strong shag tobacco. When the pipe was lit, he sent a plume of thick grey smoke up into the air above the hearth.

"So with the retrieval of the cash and this timepiece, your theory proved to be correct," said Inspector Eastland, rallying for a further top up of his glass.

"Yes. The money was returned to the bank. Rather surprising, the directors refused to press charges against the three, being determined to keep the matter from the public gaze. In fact, they seemed content that the investigation had highlighted several security flaws which they could address in making the bank secure for the future. It was a decision which angered my brother, given the lengths he had gone to in securing the arrest of the two men and arranging for them to be transported back to London.

"Dominic Tuttle eventually returned to France, where he took up a position as a sign-writer for a Parisian carriage maker. Ellen Cox and Frank Chilvers went on to marry and still reside at Appleton House with their three young children. They have a thriving business creating bespoke timepieces for wealthy and discerning collectors."

Mrs. Grimble had been moved to tears. "Such a marvellous tale, Mr. Holmes. I would encourage Dr. Watson to set it down on paper one day. I'm sure it will delight the legions of readers across the world who now follow your exploits."

The evening was almost at a close, a clock on the shelf closest to Holmes's bureau announcing that it was ten o'clock, with just two hours until Christmas was once again upon us. While Billy and Mrs. Hudson began to clear the table of bottles, glasses, side plates, and napkins, we said our farewells, with each guest expressing their appreciation for the food and entertainment which had been provided. Inspector Lestrade was the last to leave, shaking our hands firmly before retrieving his cape and brown Derby from the coat-stand and heading off down the stairs. We heard the door bang behind him and sat down to enjoy a final smoke and to reflect on the evening.

"Exhausting," said Holmes.

"Exhilarating," I replied. "You really must let me record the case. I know it will be popular."

"If you must, but there is one final detail you may wish to add. I will, of course, leave that to your discretion as the chronicler of my adventures." He pointed towards the doors of the large oak cabinet which sat to one side of the sitting room. "If you care to look inside there, you'll find a Christmas present. But please, take care, it is exceptionally heavy, unbelievably rare, and needs to be handled with the utmost delicacy, for it must be kept upright."

I stepped over to the cabinet and opened both doors. Within the space was a parcel some two feet in height and a foot-and-a-half in width. I turned back to Holmes, who merely laughed at my hesitancy. "Go on, man – open it!"

I peeled back the layers of thick green wrapping paper, being careful not to disturb the item within, although I could already tell that it was resting firmly on the floor of the cabinet. The unwrapping revealed a most exquisite clock, set with the most beautiful gemstones I had ever seen, and framed within a case constructed of gold, silver, and platinum. The effect was stunning.

"It's a mercury powered timepiece," said Holmes by way of explanation. "The same internal mechanism which was used to open the locking mechanism of the vault. Some months after the conclusion of the case, I received a message from Ellen Cox, who had by then become Mrs. Ellen Chilvers. She invited me to revisit Appleton House, where I was greeted warmly by her and her new husband. They had asked me to their home to give me the clock as a gift. The original workings had been rehoused within the ornate case you now see. While extremely grateful to them, I have never really known what to do with it. In all my time here at Baker Street, the clock has been tucked away at the bottom of a wardrobe. But I will say this: When I retrieved it earlier this week, it had not lost so much as a second in time."

I was struggling to find the words to thank my dear friend, for it was, without doubt, the most lavish gift I had ever received in my life. "This must be worth a small fortune," I exclaimed. "I don't know what to say other than thank you. In the circumstances, I'm afraid you might be a little underwhelmed when you see what I have bought for you in return!"

We both laughed and I stubbed out what remained of my cigar. "Then you had planned to tell that story tonight well before being invited to by Dr. Tamworth?"

"Yes, it was a small deceit. Having rediscovered the clock, I knew it would be a tale sufficient to entertain our guests for what might otherwise have been a long and very dull evening!"

"Agreed. But there is one point on which I remain unclear."

"And that is – ?"

"Why did Mr. and Mrs. Chilvers feel the need to give you such an extraordinary gift? I'm surprised they even invited you to the house, given that it was you who scuppered their intricate plan."

"I must admit to being a little dishonest in my earlier retelling of the story. It wasn't at all surprising that the directors of the bank chose to bring no charges against the three, for that was what I recommended them to do to prevent a public scandal. And it was true that the episode enabled the bank to improve its security arrangements. My actions probably helped the gang to escape prison sentences of between ten and fifteen years. For Ellen and Frank, who had already endured many years of enforced separation, that would have been too much to bear. Her motivation in planning the crime was anger, not greed. Anger that a trusted institution could be so reckless with her family's legacy. The stolen money was returned to the bank. In my view, that was justice restored. To prosecute them beyond that would have been wholly unjust. Sadly, that was not the view shared by my brother. When the bank agreed to my recommendation, Mycroft was furious. It was many weeks before he would speak to me again."

It had been a memorable evening, and with the gift I had received it was one which I was never to forget. The clock was always given pride of place in all the properties in which I thereafter resided. I had only to glance at the delicately balanced hands of that perpetually driven timepiece to be reminded of that special Christmas and my absolute respect and devotion for the man who was Mr. Sherlock Holmes.

Notes

1. The Tichborne Case captivated the press and public in the 1860's and 1870's. Arthur Orton, a butcher's son from Wapping, claimed to be Roger Tichborne, who was believed to have been shipwrecked in 1854 on the passage to Australia. Responding to Lady Tichborne's advertisements in the Australian press, he came forward to claim the Tichborne inheritance in 1866, saying that he had been living under the name Thomas Castro and working as a butcher in the remote settlement of Wagga Wagga. While Lady Tichborne accepted him as her long lost son, his legal claim failed, and in 1874 he was convicted of perjury and sentenced to fourteen years in prison. In 1895, he confessed to being Arthur Orton, although he later retracted this.

2. *Cox's Timepiece* was an object of curiosity and wonder and had a long history of public display. From 1768 until 1774, it was exhibited in Cox's own museum in Charing Cross, London. By 1796, the clock was on display in Thomas Week's Royal Mechanical Museum in Titchbourne Street, where it remained until 1837. The astronomer James Ferguson once described the timepiece as *"the most ingenious piece of mechanism I ever saw in my life."*

A Yuletide Tragedy
by Thomas A. Turley
for Marcia Wilson

Each year, I am accustomed to fall into the doldrums around Christmas. We Scottish Protestants, of course, are historically indifferent to "Christ's Mass". My own ambiguity originated at the age of six, when my English mother perished in a carriage accident while returning from Christmas Eve festivities. Nonetheless, her firm insistence that we celebrate the Saviour's birth is an early memory I cherish. [1]

Now I have a fresher cause for sad Yuletide reflections. When I contrast my present life – secure in my profession, respected by my colleagues, blessed with the finest and most loving wife a man could have – to the time when I returned from India following the Afghan war, I realise again how much I owe to my late and much lamented friend. For it was on this day, ten years ago, that I found myself arrested for a murder, a charge quickly refuted by Mr. Sherlock Holmes. Needless to say, this is not a story that will ever see the pages of *The Strand,* that new journal which has published my accounts of several of our cases. This tale I record only for my recollection.

Thirteen months before, I had arrived in London hardly recovered from enteric fever and my wounds at Maiwand, having neither friends nor family to welcome me. My career as a soldier was likely at an end. Nor had I any source of income other than my meagre pension, for my brother Henry inherited the residue of our father's lost estate. When I last had heard from him, he was en route to America to squander it. [2]

I took up residence in a small private hotel off the Strand, a neighbourhood familiar from my student years. It had grown raffish in the interim, but my own abode remained respectable, albeit comfortless and drab. My early days were spent in aimless wandering about the city, attempting to recover my lost strength. Exhausted by these efforts, it was some time before I found the energy to venture forth at night. When I did, my destination was too often the Criterion or other public house, or a gambling den where I contrived to lose what little money I possessed. On occasion, I drifted into Whitechapel, near the old hospital, which offered other dubious allurements to a lonely man. These I managed to resist, thanks more to my injuries and lack of funds than moral fortitude.

Even so, I was not immune to feminine attractions. Among my fellow lodgers was a young lady named Abigail Jordan, who occupied the room above my own. The coughing fits I heard at night, and her wan demeanour when we passed upon the stairway, indicated that my neighbour was in far from perfect health. Pale, blonde, and willowy, Miss Jordan appeared to be about my own age, with a muted, fragile prettiness she made no effort to enhance. One evening in December, I was summoned to attend the lady by the manager, doubtless to avoid the cost of calling in a practicing physician. She had suffered a slight hemorrhage, confirming my surmise that she was in the early stages of consumption.

On that night, I found my patient feverish, restless, and at times delirious. I therefore learned more of her sad history than she would otherwise have wished to tell. A former governess, Miss Jordan had been ravished by her employer and discharged by his wife. Being alone and unknown in the district, she was too humiliated to report the crime. Her parents were deceased, and her only other relative, a clergyman, had declined to aid his niece when told of her "ruination". After moving to the city, Abby (as I came to call her) began by taking students as a private tutor. That option was no longer open once she became ill. As my neighbour jested when we shared a dinner after her recovery, her pallid looks and slender figure left her unlikely to obtain employment as an *ingénue* or artist's model. Moreover, Abigail was determined to fall no lower than she already had. At the time we met, she was trying to earn her living as a typist, (like old Frankland's daughter in the Dartmoor case).

Our disabilities engendered sympathy between us, and had life continued as it was, those feelings might one day have blossomed into love. Within a fortnight, however, I met Sherlock Holmes and moved to Baker Street. There I began rebuilding my own life, assisted by our kindly landlady and my strange new friend. Overcoming my memories of Maiwand and an initial reluctance to return to Barts [3], I began working as a *locum tenens* there and at other London hospitals. When Holmes and I came to know each other better, he revealed to me the unique vocation he had chosen. Soon I was assisting (to the best of my ability) the world's only "private consulting detective" in investigations, starting with the grisly affair I later recorded as *A Study in Scarlet*. Under a new regimen of nutritious meals, regular habits, professional relevance, and an intriguing fellow-lodger, I quickly recovered strength and confidence. The lost months of deprivation slipped into the past. Abby Jordan, to the extent I thought of her at all, was left behind without regret. She was not destined, however, to pass forever from my mind.

Late in the summer, having completed my nine-month recuperation, I presented myself to the army board at Netley. I was rejected – to my unconcealed dismay – on the grounds that my leg wound left me slightly but permanently lame. In the opinion of three retired surgeons, two of whom had never set foot on a battlefield, Surgeon-Major Watson was unfit for further service to the Queen. He was discharged with the Board's thanks and an extension of his pension.

When I arrived at Waterloo Station that evening (after bitter hours of reflection on my own "Waterloo"), I did not return at once to Baker Street. The idea of facing Holmes and Mrs. Hudson in a state of anger and dejection was too much to bear. Instead, I elected to "make a night of it", a thing I hadn't done since moving from the Strand. I regressed to the Criterion's Long Bar, where – dwarfed to insignificance by the splendour of that lofty, tiled, and gilded cavern – I drank to the old gentlemen who had so kindly scuppered my career. As round succeeded round, several of my former cronies joined me, but they eventually grew tired of my ill humour and left me to myself. The only companion who remained was whisky.

Sometime after ten o'clock, I was distracted from my misery by a familiar laugh. I turned to behold my former neighbour, Abby Jordan, dressed in a maroon evening gown. Above its low-cut bodice gleamed a ruby necklace that was far beyond her means. Rouge had given Abby's cheeks a hectic flush, which seemed to mimic fever. Indeed, she looked much sicker than when I had seen her last. Having attended the comedy playing in the theatre [4] below us, she and her escort had come into the barroom for a late-night drink.

"Why, *Johnny!*" Abigail cried nervously as I approached them through the crowd. "I haven't seen you for an *age!*"

"Hello, Abby," I replied, pleased to find a target for my fury. "You've come up in the world since last we met. Or would *down* be a more accurate direction?"

"Whatever can you mean?" she murmured in embarrassment, while her companion fixed me with an indignant glare. He was at least forty, pop-eyed and chinless beneath a curling moustache, but splendidly attired in evening dress. "Who *is* this person, Abigail?"

"Surgeon-Major John Watson," I informed him coolly before Abby could respond. "Late of the Berkshires, with whom I served at Maiwand."

"Oh, a *war hero*," sneered my interlocutor, "though Maiwand was hardly one of our successes, what? Well, I'm glad you told me, Surgeon-Major. Otherwise, I might have mistook you for a drunken vagabond."

Abigail gasped as I drew back to strike him, but before the blow could land my arms were pinioned from behind. Two of my fellow-drinkers kept me firmly, if not unkindly, in hand as we retreated to the Criterion's front entrance. In a moment, I found myself alone upon the street.

"What were you *thinkin'*, Johnny Watson?" one of my protectors thundered as they turned away. "That toff's a pal o' the Prince o' bloody Wales!"

It was with remorse, and an excruciating headache, that I awoke the next morning in my bed in Baker Street. On arriving downstairs, I found the sitting room deserted, but a pot of coffee stood steaming on the breakfast table, where a place was laid for me. Beside my plate, atop a box of fine Havanas, was a note from Sherlock Holmes:

> *My dear Watson,*
>
> *From your non-appearance until the wee hours of the night, Mrs. Hudson and I deduced that your interview at Netley yesterday did not go well. She asks you to ring the bell should you desire any breakfast. I trust that you will still accept the gift below, although its intended purpose is now altered. We are very glad, at least, that you will not be leaving us.*
>
> *Yours sincerely,*
> *Sherlock Holmes*

Owing no doubt to my jangled nerves, my friend's tact and understated sympathy came near to reducing me to tears. I didn't ring for breakfast, instead making my way to my old lodgings off the Strand. There, as I suspected, Miss Abigail Jordan still resided.

My one-time neighbour was reluctant to admit me, but after my abject apology she accompanied me to a nearby restaurant where we had dined before. While I picked half-heartedly at bread and cheese, Abby told me of her paramour, whom she refused to name save by the appellation "Monty". Originally, he had employed her to type the history of England he was writing. Their relationship progressed from there. Abigail insisted stoutly that she was *not* his mistress, although "Monty helps me sometimes with expenses." As for the ruby necklace, which I noticed on a dressing table while briefly in her room . . . .

"It isn't really mine, you know. Monty lets me wear it when we go someplace nice. To Simpson's, or the theatre, or . . . well, a *nicer* hotel."

"How generous! No doubt it's borrowed from his wife."

"Certainly *not!*" cried Abigail indignantly. "It belonged to his late mother. Monty isn't married, Johnny. That would be *immoral!*"

My incredulous laugh provoked a bout of coughing. Abby wouldn't allow me to examine the handkerchief she held against her mouth.

"What do *you* care, *Doctor* Watson?" she snapped breathlessly. "I haven't even *seen* you since you moved away."

The result of this rebuke was that Abigail and I resumed a professional relationship. After our initial consultation, she reluctantly agreed to visit the Brompton Hospital [5] clinic and undergo a thorough examination. It revealed (as I had feared) that over the past eight months her condition had deteriorated markedly. Both lungs were affected, and she was seriously ill. Unfortunately, I, as a mere *locum tenens*, lacked the authority to admit Abby as a full-time patient. I repeatedly urged her to inform her paramour, who – if he indeed had royal connexions – could make an appropriate subscription or solicit a recommendation from a governor. [6] Abigail refused either to make the overture herself or to allow me to do so. She likewise continued to withhold the man's identity. I might have discovered it by a return to the Criterion, but such a course seemed to violate my patient's trust. For the same reason, I hesitated to enlist the help of Sherlock Holmes, to whom I had never mentioned Abby Jordan. Our relations in those early days did not include confiding the details of our private lives.

By December, it was evident that Abigail's admission to hospital could no longer be delayed. After a short remission in the autumn, she was wracked by fever, chest pain, and an almost constant cough, which produced not only blood but decaying matter from her lungs. Rapid weight loss and an elevated pulse showed that without prompt intervention her life would soon pass to its end. In desperation, I approached Dr. Richard Powell [7], my old mentor at the University of London. He, as a member of the Brompton staff, had the power to admit out-patients from the clinic. When we reviewed Abby's case, I proposed trying artificial pneumothorax, injecting air into the pleural cavity, thereby collapsing the lung and permitting it to heal. The procedure was coming into vogue upon the Continent, but Powell discounted its utility in such a late-stage case. [8] Nevertheless, he readily agreed that Abigail should be admitted the next day. Although it was mid-evening by the time I left, I hastened to our old hotel to take her the good news.

I shall not forget the last time I saw Abby Jordan. My nascent romantic feelings had diminished long ago. The chief emotion I now felt for her was pity. Had my patient not overborne my wishes, I should have urged Powell to admit her months before. Instead, thanks to her stubbornness, it was likely that Abigail's decline had reached a point of no return. Even so, her bravery, and even cheerfulness in the face of death still touched me. On that final night, she held up several dresses for me to examine, coyly asking which one she should wear to Brompton. We arranged that I would call for her at eleven in the morning. When we said good-night, the lips that brushed my own in parting were as bloodless as her hollow cheeks.

"You had a very late night, Watson," remarked Sherlock Holmes. We had eaten a companionable breakfast, enlivened by my friend's enthusiasm over his latest chemical experiment. Now he was again ensconced amid the beakers and test tubes on his work-table, concocting a noxious variation on the theme. Even with the dismal task before me, I counted myself fortunate to have an excuse to spend the morning elsewhere.

"Yes," I acknowledged, in answer to his comment. "One of my long-time patients has taken a severe down-turn. I'm arranging to have her admitted to hospital today."

"To Brompton, I perceive?"

"Indeed." For once, I forbore to ask how the detective had arrived at this perception. He raised his eyebrows slightly but, with the reticence that still marked our early months together, didn't offer to explain. Instead, he walked to the bow window, for we could hear a loud commotion in the street.

"Gregson," Holmes noted, as the tall, flaxen-haired inspector alighted from a cab. The uproar came from a gang of urchins ("Not mine," smiled the Irregulars' employer.) who had been gruffly denied alms.

"*And* Lestrade!" I added in surprise, for a smaller but familiar figure had emerged to join his rival. It was rare sight to see Scotland Yard's two best, but most competitive, detectives co-operating on a case.

My friend, his experiment forgotten, began clearing the clutter of breakfast dishes that lay on the settee. Although fully dressed, he hadn't put on his coat and now dived into his bedroom to retrieve it. The bell downstairs had rung, and we could hear the ill-matched treads of the two policemen as they climbed the stairs, preceded by our landlady. She, having announced our guests, frowned resignedly at the chaos on the breakfast table. "More coffee, gentlemen?" she sniffed.

"Thank you, Mrs. Hudson," Holmes replied meekly, recognising that he had made a fortunate escape. He waved the inspectors to the now-pristine settee, while we settled into our usual chairs beside the hearth. I couldn't but notice that both Gregson and Lestrade seemed ill at ease.

"*Gentlemen,*" my friend welcomed them, with a touch of mockery. "How may we assist you in this season of good cheer?"

"This time, it's Lestrade and I who are assisting *you*," retorted Gregson, "or, rather, Dr. Watson. Not," he added, grimacing in my direction, "that we'll be bringing you much cheer." Shaking his head, he turned to his companion.

"Do you know a young lady, Doctor," Lestrade somberly enquired, "by the name of Abigail Jordan?"

My heart sank, as goes the *cliché*, for I knew at once that Abby was no more. "A patient of mine," I answered woodenly. "She has advanced consumption. I'll be taking her to Brompton Hospital later in the morning."

"I'm afraid not," said the detective. "Miss Jordan was found murdered in her room this morning. She was discovered by the hotel maid at half-past-seven, lying in a pool of her own blood."

"A bit more than a patient to you, Doctor, was she not?" insinuated Gregson. "So I've heard it, you both lived in her hotel before you moved to Baker Street. In fact, you were quite friendly for a time."

"See here, Gregson – !" began Sherlock Holmes, while Lestrade whispered urgently, *"Tobias!"* I gave the burly inspector a direct look as I replied.

"Miss Jordan and I were 'friendly' – in the sense you mean – for perhaps two weeks before I left the Strand. Prior to that time, and afterwards, our relationship was that of physician and patient. A patient, incidentally, who was quite seriously ill."

"When was the last time you saw her?" This came smoothly from Lestrade.

"Last night, as it happens. I stopped by to let her know that I had found a place for her at Brompton. When I left her, Miss Jordan was indisputably alive, if far from well."

"I suppose someone can corroborate the time you left?"

"Considering that I encountered no one else at the hotel, I presume that someone *did*. Otherwise, you and Gregson wouldn't be here. It was shortly after nine o'clock."

Both officers visibly relaxed. "Quite right, Dr. Watson," beamed Tobias Gregson. "An old fellow named Cumberbatch, who identified himself as the hotel's manager, told our man you departed at precisely nine-thirteen. I'm surprised you didn't see him."

"I'm not. He had probably scuttled round the corner. Cumberbatch was notorious for lurking outside the female lodgers' rooms."

"Well, Gregson," remarked Holmes with some asperity, "if you and Lestrade have finished badgering the innocent, perhaps we can now leave for Arundel Street and begin searching for the murderer." He rose decisively, but the policemen didn't follow him. Instead, they exchanged a wary glance.

"I'm sorry, Mr. Holmes," Lestrade replied, "but Gregson and I cannot permit that. You see, it's not our case."

"Whose, then?" my friend queried, relapsing in his chair.

"Athelney Jones is the inspector in charge. He's liable to appear at any time to arrest Dr. Watson."

Although I had by that time met several of the other Scotland Yarders, the name was new to me. "Who is Athelney Jones?" I wondered stupidly. Holmes's snarl of dismay did not bode well.

"By far the worst detective on the force!" my friend opined. "He has only his energy to recommend him. The man should never have been made a constable, much less put in charge of an investigation."

"You've said as much for most of us," snapped Gregson, "at one time or another. Lestrade and I recognise that Jones can be a little . . . *hasty* in jumping to conclusions. That's why we came here when we heard the Doctor's name was mentioned. We want to see fair play."

"It's very good of you," Holmes murmured in surprise. He seemed quite abashed.

"Indeed," I gratefully seconded. "But how did you find out so soon?"

The flaxen-haired inspector grinned. "Constable John Rance was the first man on the scene. You put quite a bug in his ear, Mr. Holmes, during the Lauriston Garden affair, and I'm bound to say his performance has improved since then. When Athelney latched onto Dr. Watson as a suspect, Rance managed to get word to us."

As though our talk had summoned Jones, we could hear a loud voice booming in the ground-floor hall. He climbed the stairs at a slower pace than his two colleagues and was wheezing by the time that he arrived. Mrs. Hudson briefly announced "Inspector Jones," but said no more of coffee as she turned away.

Athelney Jones, if nothing else, was physically imposing. Red-faced and corpulent, he stood perspiring heavily in a woollen muffler and overcoat, breathing so stertorously that I became concerned. Even so, the inspector's porcine eyes keenly marked me as his suspect. An incongruity belatedly occurred to him.

"What are you two doing here?" he demanded of his fellow Yarders.

"Just happened to be passing, Athelney," Lestrade assured him easily. "Don't let our presence distract you from your duty."

Thus encouraged, the inspector turned his stare back to me. "Dr. John H. Watson?" Without rising, I nodded from my chair.

"I arrest you – "

"Inspector *Jones!*" cried Sherlock Holmes, jumping to his feet as though startled from a nap. "Where are my manners? Let me take your hat and coat. Watson, pray turn my armchair around for the Inspector. I fear the basket chair may not support him. *Where* is Mrs. Hudson with that coffee?"

As if on cue, our landlady entered with the promised beverage. Crumpets, jam, and marmalade accompanied the coffee, and before he was aware of it, Inspector Jones was joining us in a second breakfast. He applied himself with gusto befitting a man of his vast girth, but Lestrade and Gregson also did the table justice. While we ate, Holmes repeated an abstruse recounting of his chemical researches. Only when the pot was emptied, the crumpets gone to crumbs, and the four of us reduced to stupor did my friend relent. Taking cigars from the coal scuttle, Holmes distributed them to the policemen. He then lit up his own briar pipe, while I took the last Havana remaining from his gift from my coat pocket. Soon all of us were smoking amiably.

"If you will forgive 'talking shop' in this congenial setting," he addressed Athelney Jones, "I understand that there has been a murder. Dr. Watson has explained to your two colleagues his role as the victim's long-time physician. His visit last night was to arrange her admission to hospital today. As I believe you are aware, the Doctor was seen leaving Miss Jordan's room shortly after nine o'clock. Did your examination of the body allow you to estimate her time of death?"

"No-o-o, that hasn't been established," admitted the inspector, "but she was dead enough by the hour she was found. Truth to tell, I didn't examine the body very closely. Terrible lot of blood there was. Best leave it to the medical examiner. Trouble is, he's out of hand. Won't be back until tomorrow. I sent the body to the morgue."

"So you don't know the time of death," reiterated Gregson. "What about the murder weapon? Was her throat cut? I take it your witness didn't hear a shot?"

"Difficult to say," mused Jones. "No weapon was found at the scene." He glanced about our sitting room suspiciously. *"Something* produced all that blood! Plenty of sharp instruments in a doctor's bag. Maybe we ought to take a look for it 'round here."

"I'll be happy to show you my medical instruments, Inspector," I offered instantly, having noticed the ill-concealed disgust of Gregson and Lestrade. The little Breton [9] had nearly bitten his cigar in two. Tobias Gregson merely looked contemptuous, but then he generally did.

"Ah, but what would that *prove?"* the fat policeman wondered. "Easy thing to wash a knife or scalpel. Why, you might have thrown the murder weapon in the Thames! A bagful of clean instruments proves very little, Dr. Watson."

"Then let me ask you this," I countered, for a theory of the crime had just occurred to me. "Was Miss Jordan's jewel box rifled? Did you find a ruby necklace in the room?"

Sherlock Holmes, who had been sitting with his face between his hands, showed a renewed glimmering of interest. Jones's colleagues likewise gave me their attention. The inspector himself remained unmoved.

"Oh, no, it was all cheap costume stuff. I am satisfied that robbery wasn't a motive. This was a crime of passion, gentlemen! No doubt committed by a jealous lover, past or present. Doctor, I hope you recognise yourself in that description?"

"By no means, Inspector. But I *am* aware that Abby Jordan had a lover, a gentleman who allowed her to wear a ruby necklace. The fact that it was missing from her jewel box, I submit, may suggest his presence at the scene."

"Well, now!" marvelled Athelney Jones. "I had thought it was Mr. Holmes who was the theorist, but I see that you are one as well. A mysterious lover with a ruby necklace! Can you tell me more about him, Dr. Watson?"

"Not a great deal," I admitted. "I met him once at the Criterion, but he didn't give his name. Abigail would only refer to him as 'Monty'. He was about forty, bug-eyed with a curling moustache, and obviously wealthy. Abby said he was unmarried. He was writing an historical work that she was typing for him. I heard from others that he was friendly with the Prince of Wales."

"Better and better! A gentleman known to royalty who takes his typist as a mistress. Gives her ruby necklaces, but keeps her in a cheap hotel. I really must congratulate you, Doctor. You have quite a future as a novelist!"

Only then did I realise how preposterous the story sounded. To my chagrin, Gregson and Lestrade were also looking doubtful. Holmes quickly intervened on my behalf.

"And *you*, Athelney Jones, missed your calling as a music-hall comedian! Happily for all of us, it should be a simple matter to confirm or refute Watson's theory. If you will allow me to assist in the investigation, I shall undertake to clear the case in time for you to eat an early dinner."

The inspector wagged an admonitory finger. "Ah, Mr. Holmes, that would not do. A friend of the chief suspect involved in the investigation? Why, I should be laughed out of Scotland Yard!"

"If it hasn't happened by now – " began Lestrade, but Inspector Jones had already risen in his place to charge me. "Dr. John H. Watson, I arrest you for the wilful murder of one Abigail Jordan." ("Only one?" scoffed Gregson.) Anything you say henceforth may be used in evidence against you."

"I'm aware of that," I answered, moving from the table to retrieve my hat. "Well, Holmes, it looks as if our plans for Christmas may have changed."

"I promise you, Doctor," said my friend, with more emotion than I had ever heard from him, "that you will return to your place at this table long before December twenty-fifth. Jones, this arrest is a disgraceful travesty!"

"Don't promise him too much, Mr. Theorist," sneered the Inspector, nodding in self-satisfied farewell as he guided me onto the landing.

Thus ended my part in the investigation of Abby Jordan's murder. What I learned of subsequent events came from Lestrade, who visited my cell the night of my incarceration, and from Sherlock Holmes after my release. With the two Yarders' help, their occasional nemesis resolved the case almost as quickly as he promised, if not quite in time for the arresting officer "to eat an early dinner".

The instant the door had shut behind us, Tobias Gregson began to expound a plan of action. When reminded of Jones's ban upon my friend's involvement, the flaxen-haired inspector growled, "The day I take orders from *that* tub of guts – "

"It's no violation of procedure, Mr. Holmes," agreed his rival. "So long as one of us is with you, you're merely 'assisting the police with their enquiries'. If he don't like it, Brother Athelney can howl at the moon."

It was decided that Holmes and Lestrade should visit the Criterion, while Gregson tracked down the medical examiner. In this attempt he failed (the doctor having left the city), ensuring that Abigail's autopsy would be delayed until the following day.

The other two detectives were more fortunate. Happily for the cause of justice, the mysterious "Monty" was well-known at the Criterion. Both the theatre manager and an off-duty bartender identified him readily. Abby's paramour was The Honourable Montgomery Gorst, second son of Viscount Landry and M.P. for an obscure borough in Cheshire. He was indeed unmarried, an amateur historian, and (for reasons I couldn't quite fathom) a minor member of the Marlborough House Set. [10]

Armed with this information, my friends made their way to my former residence. There they subjected Cumberbatch, the manager, to a more searching interrogation than had Athelney Jones. As Holmes described it to me later, "The key, Watson, was to flatter the old rogue's vanity. He was proud, you see, to have 'a viscount's son' about the premises. When I adopted a smirking, 'man-to-man' approach, Cumberbatch freely admitted that 'Monty' paid him liberally to permit access to Miss Jordan 'after hours' and to report other male visitors she might receive. You will be relieved to know that there were none, yourself aside.

"Gorst was aware of your visits by daylight in a medical capacity, but when his spy sent word to him on that last evening, he arrived at the hotel just after your departure. Old Cumberbatch trailed his benefactor to the hallway outside Miss Jordan's room. There he overheard the beginnings of a quarrel before prudently returning to his desk downstairs. When 'Monty' reappeared in the lobby fifteen minutes later, his face was ashen and he could barely speak. He threw Cumberbatch a ten-pound note and made him swear to tell no one of Gorst's presence there that night.

"Fortunately, like most men one can buy, the manager did not 'stay bought'. He had been willing enough to dupe Athelney Jones – no difficulty there, of course – but he didn't reckon on Inspector G. Lestrade. My esteemed colleague from the Yard had promised to keep silent, but I could hear him grind his teeth throughout the interview. When it became apparent that Cumberbatch had thrown you to the wolves, I thought Lestrade would strike the man. It was most fortunate for him that I was there."

Having already received a more colourful account from the Inspector, I was aware that Cumberbatch now occupied his own cell in Scotland Yard, charged with withholding information from a police officer. Lestrade had cooled sufficiently to acknowledge that the charge would probably be dropped, but I wasn't sorry to see the hotel manager given a good scare.

It only remained to apprehend the suspect. With evening fast approaching, Lestrade and Holmes took a cab to his Westminster rooms. They arrived as The Honourable Montgomery Gorst was sitting down to dinner, having booked a late-night train to his family's estate in Scotland. To give the elusive M.P. credit, he made a clean breast of the matter after one pitiful attempt at bluff. He admitted confronting Abby in her room, angrily querying the nature of my latest visit. As the argument grew heated, poor Abigail became extremely agitated. "Suddenly," recounted Gorst, "she began to cough up blood, and it poured from her mouth in a torrent. My God, Mr. Holmes, she was dead before she hit the floor." At that point, understandably, her lover panicked. Snatching up his mother's necklace, he promptly fled the scene, pausing just long enough to toss another bribe to Cumberbatch.

It was not a very creditable story, but to both detectives it had the ring of truth. The Scotland Yarder threatened "Monty" with arrest should he try to leave the city, posting a pair of stalwart constables outside his door. Inevitably, his version of events would be upheld or disproven by the autopsy. "If that slug Jones hadn't funked examining the body," Lestrade grumbled, "we could have had Gorst in a cell tonight."

In the end, Abby's paramour was vindicated. That afternoon, after failing to find the medical examiner, Tobias Gregson had gone to Brompton Hospital. There he practically ordered Dr. Richard Powell to assist in the *post mortem*, which finally took place early the next day. It confirmed "Monty's" innocence as well as mine. No injuries were found upon the body. Having suffered a sudden, catastrophic hemorrhage, Miss Abigail Jordan had died of shock and loss of blood. [11]

I was released before luncheon by the abject Athelney Jones, whose colleagues had made any recriminations on my part superfluous. Holmes had a few choice words for him as we departed Whitehall Place, and many months would pass before he agreed to work with Jones again. Eventually, the rotund detective played a role in what was definitely *my* most memorable case, *The Sign of the Four*, that brought me my dear Mary. Sad to say, his deductive skills had improved but slightly in the interim.

The outcome of the Jordan case was far less satisfactory. Lestrade and Gregson fully intended to arrest Montgomery Gorst for bribing old Cumberbatch and failing to report a death, thereby perverting the course of British justice. They were warned off by no less an authority than the Commissioner, who (as Holmes learned afterwards from his brother Mycroft) had been called into the presence of the Prince of Wales. This was the origin of my friend's contempt for that royal gentleman. Meanwhile, thanks to my deliverers, I appeared at Abby's inquest only as her doctor, while her paramour didn't appear at all. As expected, the coroner's verdict was that she died of natural causes. Only I knew that Abigail's life had been abbreviated by abusive or neglectful men. To my shame, I must count myself among them.

As Holmes had promised, I returned to Baker Street in time for a Christmas party. Scotland Yard's two rivals were persuaded to attend, and our landlady outdid herself for the occasion. Mrs. Hudson's graciousness, the gruff congratulations of Inspectors Gregson and Lestrade, and my friend's quiet amiability made this Yuletide celebration the most pleasant I had enjoyed in years. After our guests departed, I asked Holmes why he thought they had stood by me without question. He seemed surprised that I should ask.

"Well, I cannot speak for Scotland Yard. All men bear the mark of Cain, but you don't strike me as a likely murderer. I reasoned that had you planned to kill this unfortunate young woman, you would not first have troubled to secure her admission to Brompton Hospital. Jones's 'crime of passion' was ruled out by your demeanour the next morning. Unless, of course, you are a master of deceit! I must say, Watson," he added with a smile, "that thus far in our acquaintance you have shown no sign of it."

Ten years have passed, and another Christmas is upon us. As I conclude this tale, that happy night in 1881 seems long ago. Besides convincing me that I had found a home in Baker Street, it fully established a relationship of mutual respect and confidence between the best of the official force and Sherlock Holmes. Henceforth, although the ties between them might occasionally be strained, they were not broken. Lestrade, Gregson, and nearly all their colleagues now mourn Holmes as sincerely as I do. They recognise that Scotland Yard has suffered a great loss. Over the past decade, the amateur they once had scorned has made these Isles a better place. He sacrificed his life to end a scourge upon humanity. It is a legacy for which our friend was satisfied to die, and which those of us who worked with him shall always honour in his memory.

NOTES

1. The exact circumstances of Mrs. Watson's carriage accident remain obscure. Conflicting accounts of Dr. Watson's parentage may be found in W.S. Baring-Gould's *Sherlock Holmes of Baker Street* (Avenel, NJ: Wings Books, 1995 [1962]) and in a purported autobiography, *The Private Life of Dr. Watson: Being the Personal Reminiscences of John H. Watson. M.D.*, edited by Michael Hardwick (New York, E.P. Dutton, Inc., 1983). The account here seems to mix elements of both. In David Marcum's "The Stolen Relic", the Doctor recalled having *"traveled south to visit my mother's people during the Christmas season. It was only then that I was able to see a traditional English celebration . . . while being raised in Scotland, where Christmas is not celebrated as such."* See *The MX Book of New Sherlock Holmes Stories, Part V: Christmas Adventures*, edited by Marcum (London: MX Publishing, 2016), p. 93.
2. Three years later, Watson would follow his errant brother Henry to America, a tale he eventually told in "A Ghost from Christmas Past". The story also recounted another Yuletide tragedy: The loss of his wife Constance in 1887. See *The MX Book of New Sherlock Holmes Stories, Part VII: Eliminate the Impossible*, edited by David Marcum (London: MX Publishing, 2017), pp. 130-152.
3. Dr. Watson described his horrific experience at Maiwand, and the emotional residue it left behind, in a forthcoming story entitled "The Fashionably Dressed Girl", written by David Marcum.
4. Designed by Thomas Verity and completed in 1873, the Criterion's Byzantine splendor was a *"monument to Victorian exoticism . . . ."* The Long Bar was on ground level, with the restaurant, dining rooms, and ballroom on the floors above. Beginning in 1883, the Criterion's basement theatre was remodeled, for the original system for pumping air into the gas-lit auditorium proved less than adequate. Besides Watson and Stamford, the Criterion was patronized by such Victorian/Edwardian luminaries as Oscar Wilde, Christabel Pankhurst, H.G. Wells, Bertrand Russell, Lloyd George, and Winston Churchill. W.S. Gilbert produced several of his own plays at the theatre. See Wikipedia's separate articles on the theatre and restaurant, and the blogs Historic Dining in London:
   (http://historicdininglondon.blogspot.com/2010/08/criterion-piccadilly-circus.html)
   and Victorian Web:
   (https://victorianweb.org/ art/architecture/verity/1.html).
5. Because tuberculosis was incurable in the nineteenth century, consumptives were turned away from hospitals in early Victorian Britain. Brompton was founded, initially as an outpatient facility, in 1841 by Philip Rose, a young solicitor whose clerk had been refused admission elsewhere. Prince Albert laid the cornerstone of a new hospital in 1846. By 1879, it had expanded to *"368 beds and dealt with thousands of patients (in- and out-) each year."* In 1948, Brompton came under the National Health Service. It soon shifted to

"other areas of lung and heart medicine" as tuberculosis became less of a concern. Having later combined with other heart and chest hospitals, it *"is still the largest cardiothoracic centre in the UK."* See "The Hospital for Consumption and Diseases of the Chest, Brompton" (March 10, 2015) by Rebecca Nielsen
(https://thefightagainsttuberculosis.wordpress.com/2015/03/10/the-hospital-for-consumption-and-diseases-of-the-chest-brompton/).

6. Like others of its era, Victorian Brompton was a voluntary hospital, *"financed entirely from charitable donations, legacies, and fund raising"* so that most patients were not charged. However, in order to be admitted, *"patients needed a recommendation from a governor or a subscriber, although the medical staff could refer a small number of patients seen in the Out-Patients Department . . . ."* See the Wikipedia article "Royal Brompton Hospital":
    (https://en.wikipedia.org/wiki/Royal_Brompton_Hospital)
    and "Lost Hospitals of London: Royal Brompton Hospital"
    (https://ezitis.myzen.co.uk/royal brompton.html).

7. Like Watson, Richard Douglas Powell (1842-1925) studied medicine at University College, London. He served as house physician there, under Sir William Jenner, before his move to Brompton. In 1887, Powell received an appointment to the Palace as Physician-in-Ordinary to Queen Victoria and, later, to Edward VII and George V as well. He was created a baronet in 1897. See Powell's biography by the Royal College of Physicians
    (https://history.rcplondon.ac.uk/inspiring-physicians/sir-richard-douglas-powell).

8. The operation of artificial pneumothorax, or collapsing the lung, was conceived and first attempted by the Scottish physician James Carson in the 1820s. See the article "Two Forgotten Pioneers: James Carson and George Bodington," by R.Y. Keers. Thorax, vol. 35 [1980], 483-489.
    (https://thorax.bmj.com/content/ thoraxjnl/35/7/483.full.pdf).
    Although, as Watson notes, artificial pneumothorax was common in Europe by the 1880's, it was not performed at Brompton until 1911. Nor did Brompton open a successful European-style sanatorium (at Frimley, thirty miles southwest on London) until 1905. The combination of fresh air and good nutrition that sanatoria provided improved the health of many consumptives. The German microbiologist Robert Koch identified the bacillus that caused tuberculosis as early as 1882. However, it was only *"in 1946, that the development of the antibiotic streptomycin finally made the effective treatment and cure of TB a reality."* Besides sources previously cited, see the blog "Consumption: The Most Feared of Diseases" by V.L. McBeath, 2021:
    (https://valmcbeath.com/consumption-the-most-feared-of-diseases/#.YL_LWzZKhTZ)
    and "A Sanatorium in Focus: Brompton Hospital Sanatorium, Frimley" (March 17, 2015) by Rebecca Nielsen:

(https://thefightagainsttuberculosis.wordpress.com/2015/04/17/a-sanatorium-in-focus-brompton-hospital-sanatorium-frimley/).

9. The little detective's Breton heritage is revealed by Sherlockian pasticheur and illustrator Marcia Wilson, whose novels trace the family lives and backstories of Lestrade and other Scotland Yarders. Three books have appeared so far: *You Buy Bones* (which is roughly contemporary with this story) and two *Test of the Professionals* novels, *The Adventure of the Flying Blue Pidgeon* and *The Peaceful Night Poisonings*. All are available from MX Publishing, and more are sure to come. As David Marcum has remarked, "*Marcia Wilson has found Scotland Yard's tin dispatch box.*" Her wonderful novels have made real people of the characters Conan Doyle created as mere foils for Sherlock Holmes.

10. While it may seem pointless in a story avowedly written for himself, Watson appears to be disguising an historical figure with an alias, a practice he employed until very late in his career. "Montgomery Gorst" is conceivably a stand-in for Montague John Guest (1839-1909), who was also a scion of the aristocracy, a Liberal M.P., and the author of *Lectures on the History of England*. Guest's 1880 caricature in *Vanity Fair* (included with other portraits of the Marlborough House Set in the National Portrait Gallery's collection) bears a resemblance to the Doctor's description of Abby Jordan's paramour:

    (https://www.npg.org.uk/collections/search/portrait/mw257662/Montague-John-Guest-Statesmen-No334?LinkID=mp101525&role =sit&rNo=5).

    The Marlborough House Set, of course, was the slightly disreputable coterie around Albert Edward, Prince of Wales.

11. Although rare, sudden death from a massive pulmonary hemorrhage was not unknown among patients with tuberculosis. In 1900, an article from the *Journal of the American Medical Association* warned that those liable to hemorrhage should be kept "*unperturbed from anything: anger, fear, worry, and apprehension are equally dangerous . . . [that might] bring on a large bleeding . . . .*"

    (https://jamanetwork.com/ journals/jama/article-abstract/476748).

    A 2013 article from the *Journal of Forensic and Legal Medicine*, written by physicians from an area in which tuberculosis is still endemic, might provide some comfort to Athelney Jones. In this case: "*A 55-year-old male was found dead lying in his room in a pool of blood without any obvious injuries under suspicious circumstances. . . . The autopsy revealed the death was due to asphyxiation as a result of massive hemoptysis secondary to fibro-cavitatory tuberculosis.*"

    (https://www.sciencedirect.com/science/article/abs/pii/S1752928X13000863).

The Adventure of the
Christmas Lesson
by Will Murray

I had stepped out of Self's, the tobacconist shop on Oxford Street, my arms burdened with bundles, when who should I run into but no less than my flatmate, Mr. Sherlock Holmes, striding up the street, his mouth steaming in the frigid air like the chimney of a steam locomotive.

It was a week before Christmas, and London was enduring a bitter cold wave. This was in 1881. As the year drew to a close, Holmes and I had been dwelling at 221b Baker Street since very nearly the first of that memorable year.

"Upon my word!" I exclaimed. "Fancy running into you."

"How are you?" he asked distractedly. Without waiting for my response, he took note of my laden arms and remarked, "I perceive that you're Christmas shopping."

"I am, indeed. I presume that you're about the same brisk business?"

"In actual fact, I'm not. I'm presently struggling with a problem, and I'm bereft of a solution."

"A new case?"

"A murder. A man beaten to death with a blunt instrument. A crime with no suspects, no motive, no clues. There is only the corpse and the circumstances in which it was found, not steps from his very door. The widowed wife is beside herself."

"Tragic," I mused. "Have you nothing to go on?"

"Nothing. It's quite vexing, but by now you know me well enough to appreciate the more difficult the conundrum, the more deeply I sink my teeth into it."

I laughed. "You're like a dog with a bone, as always."

"I will not take your likening me to a canine personally. Although I'm sometimes called a 'sleuth hound', I take pride in that I walk upon two legs and that I carry my brain higher above the earth than most animals."

I could see that my friend was troubled by his lack of progress. Attempting to lighten his mood, I remarked, "As you might imagine, my dear Holmes, one of these packages is intended for you. Perhaps you would like to apply your deductive skills to divining what I've purchased on your behalf?"

"That's hardly a challenge, for I smell through the wrapping the familiar odor of Ship's black shag tobacco, which as you well know is my preferred brand. And you have just quitted the tobacconist."

"Ah," I returned. "But as you can plainly see, I'm carrying several packages. Are you jumping to a conclusion instead of reaching a sound deduction?"

Holmes hesitated. I could see that I had stung him. His high brow furrowed, whilst the entirety of his expression became firm. His eyes, which were the grey of storm clouds, took on a penetrating demeanor.

"You have me, Watson. While I won't surrender my initial supposition, I must admit that I leapt rather rashly when I should have stepped methodically. Examining the size of the packages you're carrying in your arms, I see now that there are many possibilities."

"You admit defeat, then?"

"Never! I will counter your challenge with this promise. By Christmas Day, I will have correctly deduced what you've purchased as a gift for me. In that sense, I don't withdraw my initial suggestion. I merely wish to hold it in abeyance until I've had time to apply my undistracted brain to the problem. Presently, I'm deeply preoccupied with the other, more serious question.

"I will hold you to that promise, friend Holmes, while releasing you from the former commitment."

Hearing that, he said, "You must excuse me now. I have undertaken this walk to loosen my mental machinery in the hopes of jarring from the meagre collection of data I've accumulated the first scent of a solution."

I laughed again. "Ever the sleuth hound. Very well, I'll let you go on your way. No doubt you'll have much to tell me over supper."

My shoulder was acting up in the cold, a consequence of a bullet wound I had suffered in the recent Afghan War. I decided that my parcels were too much for it to bear, so I found a hansom cab and hired it to take me back to Baker Street, where I set the various presents upon the windowsill overlooking the street below. My thoughts as to Holmes's hasty deduction I will not share, lest I spoil my story.

I'd only known Sherlock Holmes for just a year, but I knew him well enough to realize that when he saw me so burdened with packages, this reminded him that he hadn't yet commenced his own Christmas shopping. Perhaps he was waiting for me to go first, since our acquaintance was still rather thin.

I wasn't surprised when Holmes turned up hours later, and in his hand was a square box, professionally wrapped. This he placed without comment on the windowsill next to my array.

"This is quite a varied collection," he remarked. "I didn't know you knew so many people in London worthy of receiving gifts at Christmas time."

"Has it not crossed your mind that some of these gifts are intended for the same person?"

"It had not," said Holmes sharply. "I confess that I'm not in the habit of giving Christmas gifts to those outside of my immediate family, but now I see the error of my thinking."

Changing the subject, I inquired, "Have you made progress in your murder?"

"Very little. It is vexing in the extreme."

Holmes retreated to his preferred chair by the hearth, while I took my own favorite. And we two proceeded to smoke.

Holmes was preoccupied with his pipe and tobacco, whilst I made do with a cigar. Watching him charge the briar bowl, I noted that his expression remained tight and tense. By this point in our association, I knew him well enough to comprehend by this indication that he hadn't made appreciable progress in his latest investigative foray, for I had previously observed a tightening of his expression as he penetrated a matter – releasing facial tension only after he had made dramatic progress, or was winding up the affair.

Once the old pipe was lit, it was as if both the briar and the one who smoked it were giving off sparks. Although Holmes's sparks were entirely mental, I could nevertheless feel them leaping about his immobile person.

"Here is the problem, Watson: Mr. Nigel Addison left his home late one night for reasons that are obscure. Not two-dozen steps from his front step, an unknown blackguard approached him from behind and, using a cudgel, all but dashed his brains out over the cobbles. A constable making his rounds found him within the hour, shivering in a frozen welter of mixed fluids and gasping his last."

"Beastly business."

"Scotland Yard could make nothing of it. Inspector Gregson turned to me out of sheer desperation. I made a thorough examination of the surroundings. It was unfortunate that I wasn't called in on the night of the murder, but upon the following morning, for there may have been many clues that have been missed."

"Was that Thursday night last?"

"It was."

"Did it not rain overnight?"

"Lightly, but yes, it did."

"I should think that any clues lying about would have been ruined by the overnight precipitation."

"Possibly, possibly, but not definitely. By the time morning had come, however, there fell a cold spell, congealing a great deal of the residue of precipitation into ice."

"I see. The weather was against you, then?"

"There is no question about it. Perhaps one day Scotland Yard will learn to call me on the instant, and not in the barren aftermath."

"So nothing was found?"

"A splash of mud that had frozen in the cold. One could only imagine from which muddy patch it had been hurled, but it may or may not have had any bearing on the case. There is no way of telling. It might have been made by the victim in his last moments. I fear that this is one case in which no clues are to be discovered."

"I seem to recall you once saying words to the effect that there is *always* a way of telling. That even footprints stamped upon a pond's surface can be detected by a clever man."

"Yes, yes, I may have said something to that effect, but please don't hold me to that. I was theorizing. There, I was being a generalist. Presently, I'm a specialist. And I cannot crack this uncommonly confounding common case."

"Now how will you proceed?"

"Without data, I cannot proceed. I'm not a crystal gazer. I don't peer into blown glass seeking for the face of the guilty. I must have clues, something tangible to go on."

"A bone to chew, as it were."

"If you must put it in such an uncouth way, yes. If I only had a bone to masticate, I might crack it open and taste of the hidden marrow. That would surely get me going. But I've nothing. Nothing at all."

"Pity."

Holmes smoked in silence for a protracted period. I studied his expression, but it didn't alter one particle. It was impassive. For all the animation he displayed, he might have expired. Only his eyes showed human fire.

I was about to take up the evening newspaper when Holmes looked up abruptly. His sharp eyes sought my own, and locked with them. For an electric moment, I felt the force of his personality, the acuteness of his brain.

"Watson, why don't you accompany me to the location of the crime."

I recoiled at the thought. "It's too late and much too dark to go poking about, is it not?"

"No, no, I don't mean this instant. Tomorrow morning will do. I've gone over the scene thoroughly, but a fresh pair of eyes might be of use."

"I'm flattered that you imagine that I might be of help," I said frankly.

"In the past," Holmes reminded, "your presence has stirred my cerebral juices. I don't expect you to perceive what I cannot. My mental tools are much too sharp. But your comments and questions might push me towards a fresh perspective."

"Very well. I agree. Tell me more of the case."

"You may learn all you need to know by consulting the account in the newspaper at hand. Read it, but save your questions for the morning. I must think . . . ."

With that, Sherlock Holmes withdrew into a world of thought that I occasionally glimpsed, but could never fully fathom . . . .

The following morning, Holmes and I bundled up against the cold, he in a Burberry great coat and I wearing my Mackinaw. So attired, we stepped out onto Baker Street and hailed a passing cab.

It wasn't terribly long before the driver deposited us before a modest clapboard home in Hoxton. It was a homey little place, and suggested to me that the owner had been of middling means when he purchased it. I knew, of course, from the address that this was the former residence of the late Nigel Addison.

As the cab clattered off and away, Holmes and I walked around the cobbled thoroughfare. Ice was everywhere. Some of the nearby trees showed a gleaming rime of frost where the intense cold had congealed the moisture left by the prior rain.

Our breaths visible, Holmes lead me to a spot and stopped. It was a patch of garden, now slumbering beneath the winter hoarfrost. No trace of gore was now visible, the rains having carried it all off.

"Upon this exact spot," he said, "was discovered the bleeding body of Mr. Addison. The constable could get nothing out of him except that he called once for his wife, whose name is Alice. This meant nothing to the constable, who didn't recognize Addison as a man lying so close to his doorstep that he could have crawled to it, had he summoned the strength to do so."

"How dreadful!" I exclaimed.

"Quite. By the time the police had got it all sorted out, Inspector Gregson knocked on the proper door and broke the terrible news to Mrs. Addison. She all but fainted. Smelling salts soon brought her around, of course. I'm told that her wailing and carrying-on went on nearly the entirety of the night. She is still quite grieved."

"Had Addison any enemies?"

"None have come to light," said Holmes, staring down at the patch of earth where the poor man had been found. What had been a muddy section was coated with ice, but numerous small upheavals suggested booted feet had tramped the mud before it had frozen over. None of the marks, however, suggested discernible footprints.

I asked, "Is there any question that it was murder?"

"No murder weapon has been found, but the wounds on the man's skull showed plainly that he was struck from behind with a heavy instrument, conceivably a ballpeen hammer, for two wounds were found at the back of poor Addison's head, a small round concavity and a larger square penetrating wound. The first blow stunned the man no doubt, but the second was the death blow, although the poor fellow lingered for some time before succumbing."

"A robbery?"

"His wallet was found in his pocket," advised Holmes. "If robbery was the motive, the murderer panicked and fled before he could avail himself of his prize."

"The newspaper said there were no witnesses," I put forth.

"None have come to light," agreed Holmes.

"It is strange," I opined, "that something as simple as a murder should be so impenetrable to a brain worker such as yourself."

"To understand a crime such as this, one must seize upon a beginning of understanding – the first impulse, as it were. Motivation is key. However, absent motivation, one must have something of equal value. Had the murder weapon been dropped, it would be to my mind as if a lump of gold had fallen into my hands. I could do much with a murder weapon. Had this man fallen into dirt or mud, I would have something to go on. A footprint would be enough."

I looked around. The ground was exceedingly hard and icy. There were cobbles adjacent to the spot on which we stood. Cobblestones would scarcely give up any clues.

"You said something about a splash of mud," I reminded.

"A frozen and congealed splash of mud." Holmes indicated a spot with a finger. "There it is. I doubt that you could make anything of it, but you're welcome to try."

I went to the spot. It was perhaps two yards from where the body had been found and not half of that from a frozen patch of water in the equally frozen ground.

"A person stepping in mud before it froze would have created a similar splash, I would say."

"Yes, but which person? The murderer or the victim? The footprint of the murderer would tell us much, but the victim's would reveal little."

As we discussed the matter, the front door of the late Mr. Addison's home opened and a rather stout woman poked her head out and stared fixedly at us with squinting black eyes.

As we turned, she cried out to us, "What is it you want? Are you men from the police?"

"We are not," called back Holmes. "But we are here at their behest. May we speak to you?"

Holding onto the half-open door, the woman hesitated for some moments. Finally, she said, "I don't see how it could help. Nor can I imagine what harm could come of it. You may come in, but hurry, the cold is seeping into my house, which is drafty enough as it is."

We hurried to the door and the woman let us in before we doffed our hats and made our introductions.

"I'm Sherlock Holmes. Inspector Gregson passed on to you my request for an interview, which you were unable to entertain, owing to the suddenness of your bereavement."

"Yes, yes, he told me so. I couldn't speak with you. I couldn't speak with anyone. Oh sir, I am beside myself with grief. How could such a tragedy have befallen me?"

I endeavored to get a word in edgewise by saying, "I'm Dr. John Watson, accompanying Mr. Holmes in his investigation."

The woman barely acknowledged me. Her eyes, rimmed in red, were fixed upon Holmes's austere countenance.

"I'm not familiar with your name, Mr. Holmes," she averred, "but the men from Scotland Yard speak highly of you."

Holmes nodded politely. "I have been of some small assistance to them in the past. And as much as they were making little headway towards the resolution of the matter of your husband's murder, they invited me to have a look."

"What title do you hold, Mr. Holmes, that Scotland Yard should think so highly of you?"

"I'm a consulting detective. It's a fresh field, and I'm pleased to call myself a pioneer. I've made a study of many scientific disciplines. In that way, I bring knowledge and insight into the problems of crime solving which Scotland Yard has yet to acquire."

"I see. What questions do you have for me?"

"Your husband went out rather late. Why was that?"

"He was in the habit of taking an evening stroll. Sometimes he would be sitting and smoking and reading the newspaper, and he would be seized by the desire to go out of doors. It didn't matter the weather. Something would come over him and he would dash out, with hardly a word."

"Was this before the rain commenced?"

"About two hours after. I took to my bed when Nigel didn't return, for he sometimes walked until beyond the midnight hour, slipping back in so as not to wake me. I had no understanding of what had happened until the police were knocking on my door with the terrible news."

Up to this point, Mrs. Addison had been in charge of her composure, but when she spoke of the knock on the door that had altered the trajectory of her life, she dissolved into tears and then, unable to call them back, sobs wracked her thin frame.

I could see that she was on the verge of being unable to hold herself together, so I took her in hand and escorted the poor woman to the couch, and sat with her there.

Following behind us, Holmes towered over the woman, his features were not without sympathy, but yet stern withal. He gave the woman time to compose herself and then he resumed his questions as if she hadn't made any outburst. At the time, I thought he was rather insensitive to the woman's grief, but over the years I came to realize that when pursuing an objective, he was psychologically unable to waver.

"A man going out at such a late hour," he commented, "might go to a public house, a gambling establishment, or to visit a friend."

"My husband's friends were few. As for the other considerations, Nigel didn't partake of strong spirits and I have never known him to gamble."

"That leaves only one other possibility," suggested Holmes – rather indelicately, I thought.

Mrs. Addison's tone turned as crisp as the frost on her windows. "If you're implying an infatuation with another woman, I would discard that thought, sir. I've never known him to look at another. I don't think the thought ever crossed his mind. He was a man of business, and liked to sit by his hearth rather than visit others. His only quirk, if I may call it that, was his unaccountable desire to go off into the late evening and walk for all hours. I imagine he liked to be alone with his own thoughts. He had business concerns, and walking helped him to unravel them."

"I understand that his business was a simple one," said Holmes.

"It is simple, but it had its challenges. He was a cooper, you see. Barrel staves were his stock in trade."

"Did Mr. Addison show signs of being worried about anything?"

"None at all."

"Did you and your husband recently quarrel?"

"We rarely quarreled, Mr. Holmes. And when we did, they were rather common household disagreements. As an example, he didn't like me to serve mutton too often, but mutton is one of my favorite dishes, so we compromised by having it only twice a month. That seemed to satisfy him, even if it didn't completely satisfy me. I prefer a nice mutton stew once a week, but I'm a married woman – " Her voice caught. " – I *was* a married woman, and made do in order to please my husband."

Once more, the tears flowed. I saw that they were genuine. There was no mistaking her bereavement.

"I'm exceedingly sorry, Mrs. Addison," said Holmes in an uncommonly gentle voice.

We permitted the woman some moments to deal with her overflow, after which she resumed speaking.

"I would forebear from eating mutton for the rest of my life, if only my Nigel could be restored to me, for without him, I don't know what to do with myself!"

There was no doubting the genuine feeling in her words. She plucked the linen handkerchief in her hands, and her nervousness and her unrestrained woe were as if a rain cloud had enveloped her person.

I looked at Holmes. He met my gaze and nodded almost imperceptibly.

"We're sorry to have troubled you, Mrs. Addison. It was necessary to hear from your own lips every pertinent detail of your husband's last hours. He was in good spirits when he left?"

"I would say that he was rather distracted, as he sometimes was before he launched into his solitary walks."

"Did he have a good appetite before he left?"

"He seemed a bit peckish, and he ate what I set before him."

"And what was that?"

The woman looked slightly startled. "Why, it was mutton. Isn't that strange? The last meal poor Nigel ate was the one thing he least enjoyed – but still, he finished his meal. He didn't go out into the night hungry. I can assure you of that. I fed that man quite well for so long as we were married. And if he were seated at the dining room table once again, I would serve him again and again without complaint."

"I have no doubt that you would, **Madam**," said Holmes. "I think we are finished here. If anything comes to mind, please write it down and convey it to Scotland Yard at your earliest opportunity. We aren't progressing very rapidly in the investigation, and I fear that the more time that passes without result, the less likely it will be that we will uncover your husband's murderer."

"The man who killed my husband could go free if only my husband could be restored to me," the poor thing said plaintively.

"That is a very admirable and Christian sentiment," I said to the woman.

"Thank you. I appreciate your kind words, Dr. Watson."

With that, we took our leave.

Once out in the cold, Holmes returned to the frosty patch where Nigel Addison had been discovered and once again directed his attention at the immediate surroundings.

"I presume that you considered a lover's spat as a prelude to the murder?" I asked Holmes.

"Of course. Do you take me for a fool? A spouse always stands foremost in the glare of suspicion, but to my eyes, that woman's grief was genuine. Her emotions are strong, but they are also pathetic. Understandably so. A murderer wouldn't display such feelings."

"So we are left with an unknown murderer and an unknown motive?"

"Regrettably, yes."

"If that patch of ice hadn't frozen over, you might have a footprint to examine."

"Conceivably," said Holmes absently. "But not definitely. You were forgetting that it had rained that night. Any clear footprint might have been obliterated by the rain."

Holmes was staring at the patch of ice and suddenly his face lit up in a surprising way. His mouth fell open.

"You have succeeded in scouring the rust from my brain. Of course! It is obvious. Why didn't I think of it before?"

"If it is obvious," said I, "it isn't obvious to me."

"Fortunate that the cold has persisted," muttered Holmes, stepping up to the frozen patch. It was modest in size, probably not much more than the size of a window pane.

I had seen signs in the past that Holmes was an uncommonly strong individual, but now he surprised me greatly when he knelt down and began to dig his gloved fingers into the edges of the ice crust.

Using both hands, he pried the clump of ice from the frozen ground and turned it over.

"Behold!"

I looked at the dirty underbelly of the ice and saw a distinct protrusion.

"What is that?"

"Oh, Watson. Use your wits."

The impatient lash of his words made an impression on me. I peered down into the frozen hole, and saw a footprint fixed in the hardened mud. The ice had filled the impression and created a mold of it.

"I see now! Yes, it is clearly a footprint. But whose?"

"I judge this to be the boot print of a man whose foot is size eleven."

"What size was Nigel Anderson's feet?"

"I examined the body and I judged to be closer to ten."

"Could this be the footprint of the murderer?"

"It may very well be. This is the start I've been looking for, and I thank you for your prodding. Now I have something of substance to analyze. Let us find a cab. I must take this berm of ice back to Baker Street and study it ere it melts."

This is exactly what we did. Holmes set the ice in Mrs. Hudson's sink, where it would drain as it softened, for there was no preventing this melting. Holmes worked as rapidly as he could, making sketches and studying the details until he had recorded everything he needed.

I was in the sitting room when he came up with several sheets of paper on which he had inscribed drawings and measurements.

"This is the footprint of a man weighing, I imagine, nine stone. He is a fellow of middling means. The boot heel is barely scratched. Therefore it is a new boot, or one infrequently used."

"Well and good," said I, "but I don't see how far along the road to success this trifling information takes you."

"A murder investigation is often a piecemeal thing. Now I have pieces to ponder. From these, I hope to acquire a greater understanding of the person who perpetrated this cowardly act."

Settling into his comfortable chair, Holmes spread the papers on his lap and began charging his pipe. I knew this ritual well. He might smoke all through the night, studying and pondering, studying and pondering, until a full picture resolved itself in his mind and he could make sense of it all.

For my part, it seemed to me that he had barely scratched the surface of the matter. I couldn't see the road from here to its just conclusion. I only knew that Holmes would walk every step to its finish, if it were in his power to do so.

I left him to his mental toil whilst I resumed reading a book that I'd laid aside some days past.

The men of Scotland Yard are nothing if not thorough. One would think that finding a man wearing a certain pair of boots would be an impossible task, but when a London constable has turned his attention to the solving of a crime, he becomes attuned to the task the way a foxhound fixates upon the fox.

Not three days later, a constable in Houndsditch happened to notice a pair of boots sticking up from an alley trash heap. These boots were conspicuous in that they didn't look very much worn. Moreover, the left heel exactly matched Holmes's sketches, the descriptions of which Scotland Yard had made certain to share with the various constables.

The dutiful officer didn't immediately rejoice at his discovery. No, he was too practiced for any such display. Instead, he poked about the trash heap further and uncovered a burlap sack containing a ballpeen hammer that was old and work-worn.

Thinking that this might possibly be the instrument of Nigel Addison's destruction, he took these items back to Scotland Yard, where they were pored over most carefully by Inspector Gregson.

Of course, Sherlock Holmes was called in to examine them. As he later told me, he pronounced the boots definitely the discarded footwear of the murderer, for the fact that they had been tossed away after so little use was suggestive that the owner wished to be rid of them for reasons that could only be unsavory. Of the hammer, he was less certain.

"Proximity to the murderer's boots was suggestive," he said. "But not conclusive. But it may not matter, for the ballpeen hammer was rather a common thing, and quite worn with age. My hopes remain with these boots. We do now have a path forward to discover who the owner is – or was."

Alas, for Holmes's unbounded confidence, succeeding days opened up no further lines of inquiry. His investigation soon all but petered out.

Returning to Baker Street one afternoon after visiting Scotland Yard, Holmes confessed to me, "We are at another blind end. The way forward is blocked by the blankest of walls. The bootmaker was of no help. The boot style is a common one – manufactured in Manchester and distributed all throughout England. As for the hammer, its blunt faces proved to be too small to have inflicted the fatal wounds."

"Regrettable," said I. "All you have to show for several day's efforts is a discarded pair of boots. Although if you find your man, this will help make your case, would it not?"

"It is all but superfluous," lamented Holmes. "The boots are a common type. Its size is ordinary. Nothing about them points to an individual. And it is an individual that Scotland Yard wishes to apprehend."

"Have there been other instances where murders were committed in a similar fashion?"

Holmes shook his rather disheveled head. "Scotland Yard has been on the watch for such a recurrence. If there is a murderer intent on repeating his act, he has yet to strike. It is our one remaining hope that the bounder will strike again. But if he doesn't, we walk an investigative path that is utterly featureless."

With that, poor Holmes sunk into his armchair and into a tobacco-clouded funk. He remained there until Christmas.

When Christmas finally arrived, the cold spell had mercifully abated, and a rare snowfall dusted London's varied rooftops.

Mrs. Hudson served a wonderful Christmas goose, and I availed myself of two hearty portions, for I preferred my goose hot, as opposed to warmed over on a later occasion.

Holmes did his best to join in the festivities. He didn't evince any special appetite, I saw, but consumed his share, and he didn't spurn the mince pie, but I could tell by his constrained demeanor that his unresolved problem still weighed upon his mind.

"The goose was excellent, Mrs. Hudson," I complimented as the meal drew to a close.

"Thank you, Doctor. I alternate each Christmas between goose and mutton. Do you like mutton?"

"I do, indeed, but I find that like goose, my interest diminishes when it isn't hot out of the oven."

"But you will eat it hot or cold?"

"I never turn down a meal, especially one cooked by someone as expert as you're in preparing them."

At this remark, Mrs. Hudson turned. "And you, Mr. Holmes? What are your preferences for future Christmas dinners? I ask since it appears that you and Dr. Watson have become quite comfortable in your present lodgings, and I imagine that we shall all be sharing next year's celebration."

Rather absent-mindedly, Holmes admitted, "I invariably eat what is put before me. As for mutton, I find that it pleases me much the same, whether hot or cold."

"I'm glad to hear it. Some do not care for mutton at all."

This last comment plucked a chord in Holmes's ever-active brain. His dreamy expression altered significantly. And I could tell from the quick gleam in his eyes that his mind was going back to our conversation with Mrs. Addison.

I thought little of it for, once the meal was concluded, we commenced the distribution of gifts.

Holmes started. "For you, my good doctor. With my sincere compliments. I trust this will be only the first Christmas in which we exchange *cadeau*."

"And this," I returned, taking a green-paper enwrapped box from the windowsill, "now belongs to you."

Together we unwrapped our presents and I was both surprised and pleased to find a new pair of house slippers which Holmes had purchased for me. I immediately put them on.

"They fit me perfectly," I declared.

"Of course," said Holmes with a smile. "I would hardly buy my flatmate a pair of slippers without first measuring his old pair."

Holmes then unwrapped the present I had handed him. After disposing of the gay wrapping, he opened the box and extracted from it a ceramic shaving mug.

The expression on his face, I was disappointed to see, was crestfallen. He actually lost a hint of color.

"Are you not pleased, Holmes?"

From a pocket, Holmes withdrew a slip of paper and handed it to me. I unfolded it and read the lines.

My Dear Watson:

After considerable cogitation, I have arrived at an inescapable conclusion. It is that you have purchased a leather tobacco pouch, which you've filled with Ship's black shag. I thank you in advance. This note is to assure you that I've arrived at the decision on the date inscribed below.

Beneath the initials *S. H.* was the date: *December 20, 1881.*

I said, "Surely you cannot object to a fresh shaving mug, for I noticed that your old one is cracked."

"It isn't that, Watson. I'm most grateful for your thoughtfulness. It's just that I was certain that I'd arrived at the correct conclusion. I don't see how I could have failed. All the clues were present. My conjecture rested on a sound foundation, supported by the odor of tanned leather, mixed with the aroma of black shag. I would have bet my modest savings upon it."

"Well, you've never claimed to be perfect. This is merely a demonstration of an unassailable fact of life, is it not?"

"Quite so, quite so," murmured Holmes, but I could tell that he was shaken. This, on top of his failure to solve the murder of Nigel Addison, seemed to undermine his confidence.

We spent the remainder of the afternoon drinking port and attempting to make merry, but Holmes didn't seem to be fully present. His mind was clearly elsewhere.

That night, he walked out into the night and I knew that this was no evening constitutional, but rather an effort to clear his head and rearrange his thoughts.

I confess that I felt terrible. And deeply wished to speak with him, but he didn't return until after I had gone to bed.

The next morning over breakfast, I announced, "I have a confession to make, Holmes."

He barely looked up from his smoked herring. "What is that?"

"That you were correct in your initial deduction. I did, in fact, purchase for you a leather pouch which I charged with black shag tobacco. However, since you had already anticipated this, I switched presents and gave you the one you now have."

"What is this?"

"I said that I exchanged presents. I did in truth intend to give you strong shag tobacco for Christmas. I make no bones about it. Since you had already jumped to that conclusion by whatever intellectual reasoning you applied, the element of surprise was lost. I thought that I should restore it."

Holmes's expression turned peculiar. "You changed your mind?"

"I believe that is self-evident. I meant you no harm, but I saw last night that you were troubled by your failure to reach a correct conclusion. Let me assure you that your conclusion was correct. I simply altered the game, as it were."

"That was a factor I hadn't anticipated," mused Holmes. "The processes of my formulating a conjecture didn't include the unexpected element of human contrariness."

"One can never set aside the human element," I pointed out.

"No," he mused, "one must not. It is a fatal error not to take in all possibilities, including the contingency that one might change one's mind, or regret the rashness of one's actions."

"I hope you don't think I was rash in my actions. I only wished to preserve the spirit of the occasion, which is traditionally one of surprise and delight."

Holmes smiled in his reserved way and a sincere light leapt into his eyes. "Watson, you have delighted me more than you can imagine, for I suddenly see a possibility I had previously discarded."

"What possibility is that?"

"I beg you to excuse me," he said, finishing his coffee with alacrity. "I must fly to Scotland Yard and see Gregson. Let me thank you for opening up a fresh line of inquiry. I fear that I've foreclosed on a distant possibility that now seems quite likely."

At that, he left me with an open mouth and utterly uncomprehending wits. It wasn't the first time. Nor would it be the last.

I didn't see him for the remainder of the day.

Night was falling, and with it a gentle snow, when I heard Holmes's familiar footsteps tramping up to the sitting room.

He went straight away to his comfortable velvet-lined chair and fell heavily into it. I saw him glance to the mantelpiece and for a moment I feared that he might take some solace in his morocco case containing a solution of cocaine. Instead, he reached for the Persian slipper where he kept his store of tobacco. From this, he extracted the new leather pouch I had secreted there in a gesture of reconciliation and, using his pipe bowl, dug out the appropriate amount of fresh black shag, for I had deliberately neglected to inform my good friend that I had merely withheld his original Christmas gift, intending to present it to him upon his next birthday.

Methodically, he lit his pipe and inhaled slowly. I could tell from his expression that he was appreciative of the tobacco.

"I daresay from your demeanor that progress today has been scant," I prodded.

"The contrary. The murderer is now firmly behind bars. I might add, it is largely thanks to your perspicuity."

"Me? Why, my good fellow, I had little enough to do with your investigation."

"But you had everything to do with providing me with insights that I might not otherwise have formulated. For that, my dear Watson, I'm eternally grateful."

Holmes began puffing on his pipe. He seemed indisposed to continue speech. I gave him the benefit of the doubt and waited patiently. He seemed to become lost in his thoughts.

Finally, when I could stand it no more, I simply asked, "Well, out with it. Name the culprit."

"Indulge me, while I give you a tour of the method by which I arrived at the correct conclusion."

"Very well. Proceed in your own way."

"Thank you. Now, you will recall the footprint in the frozen mud. I had determined that the boot had seen little use, for the left heel wasn't appreciably worn. This was especially evident in the ice mold. This suggested a new boot, but in speaking with the manufacturer I learned the boot had gone out of style five years previously. Therefore, this was a pair of boots which the owner seldom wore. Yet he wore them on this occasion. This fact led me to believe that the murderer chose to wear boots to which he wasn't normally prone to wearing. Therefore, this murder was premeditated. The boots prove it."

"Very good."

"There was also the fact that I had noted that the boot wearer had stepped into the mud with his heel pressed down more firmly then his toe. This isn't normal. One steps with one's forefoot. Not one's heel. Was the wearer of the boot attempting to disguise his footprint? Not if he rarely wore the pair. Therefore, there could be only one other possibility. They weren't his boots in the first place, but ones that he had borrowed or acquired or conceivably stolen. He walked in an unfamiliar pair of boots and didn't step normally."

"I follow your reasoning thus far," I offered.

"Scotland Yard had previously spoken to Mr. Addison's few friends, his neighbors, and other acquaintances. All spoke well of him. In fact, most claimed not to have known him intimately. He was something in the manner of a homebody. No enemies could be found, and therefore no motive for murder. The circle, thus, at last shrank to a mere handful of possibilities, none of which stood out."

"The fewer suspects, the better, I suppose."

"Only if one was applying the proper logic to the few," declared Holmes. "There is always the possibility that a stranger murdered Addison. Or, in the alternative, someone who hadn't yet risen to the level of a suspect."

"As I considered all these features, my thoughts kept returning to the one person I had excluded almost from the start. I don't consider myself an especially intuitive person, but as soon as I heard these words, my heart all but stopped."

"Are you referring to Mrs. Addison herself?"

"I am. The selfsame Mrs. Addison who is now languishing behind bars at Scotland Yard, and who weighs nine stone, which I judged to be the weight of the murderer. I must confess that her continual weeping has rather unsettled me. The woman seems genuinely remorseful. And there lies the crux of the matter."

"I cannot believe that poor bereaved woman murdered her husband – and you didn't believe it at first either. Whatever compelled her to do so?

"Murderers sometimes confess from the outset, but not all of those confessions are advertent. Many aren't obvious to the ear. You will recall that Mrs. Addison spoke of her husband's distaste for mutton, the very last meal he consumed. But I get ahead of myself.

"When I laid before Inspector Gregson my theory, we went directly to the Addison residence and confronted her. Instantly, she confessed all. The murder weapon, a ballpeen hammer, was found in a tool box. It had been washed of blood and brain matter, but when Alice Addison disposed of the telltale boots, she inadvertently ridded her household of the wrong hammer, disposing of it in the same trash heap into which she consigned the murder boots. An understandable mistake for a wife unfamiliar with her husband's tools. You see, when Mrs. Addison contrived to strike her husband down with one of his own hammers, she, for whatever reasons, put on a pair of boots that she revealed had been given her late husband as a Christmas gift five years back. Unfortunately, the boots were a half-size too small, and he wore them but once before giving up on them. Nor did he bother himself with getting them exchanged for the proper size, considering this to be his wife's duty and responsibility. For her part, Mrs. Addison insisted that the boots were a proper fit and only needed to be broken in. A resentment smoldered over the unresolved issue. Evidently, affairs between Mr. and Mrs. Addison had been deteriorating for some time.

"At the heart of their unhappiness was a simple matter: Mutton. Mrs. Hudson called it back to mind there over Christmas dinner. I had dismissed it as a trifle, not having ever been married myself, but I thought it odd that she had brought it up in reference to her late husband, only to reveal in almost the next breath that his last meal had been the detested mutton. You see, muttering of mutton was in the nature of an indirect confession."

"She killed him because he was offended by the meal?"

"It was a culminating factor. There were many others, equally banal. The marriage was in disrepair, but no one outside of the two of them knew it because no one was acquainted with the couple on close terms. As Mrs. Addison explained it, her husband wanted Christmas goose for dinner, whilst she desired mutton chops. She reluctantly agreed, but, wishing not to surrender her favorite meal, she served him mutton stew that night without giving him proper warning – for Mr. Addison sometimes excused himself from a supper of mutton to eat at a local pub, simply to avoid it. When Mrs. Addison explained that they had compromised, she was speaking in the past tense, the compromise of mutton had been falling apart to the point where he adamantly refused to eat it. And she had been forced to remove it from the family menu, as it were.

"In as much as it was her favorite dish, certain emotional pressures built up, until she finally, stubbornly, served the hated meal. Mr. Addison wasn't pleased. There was no row as such. As was his habit, he ended the disagreement by silently storming out into the night. The mutton no doubt had cooled by this point, and Mrs. Addison, seeing her favorite dish congealing in a manner reflective of her marriage, drew on her husband's neglected boots, took up one of his hammers and followed him out of the night.

"There, she did the terrible deed. Despite calling out his wife's name with his last breath, I doubt Addison ever knew what struck him down— or whom. It was all over in two blows – the first robbing him of his senses and the next, of his life. Retreating to her own home, Alice Addison hurried off to bed in the pretense that nothing had happened.

"I don't know if she slept or not, but when the official knock came upon the door, the total enormity of her actions struck her with full force.

She understood that she had made a terrible mistake. Almost immediately, she regretted it. As she explained to us, she would have turned back the clock and undone the bloody deed, if only she could. She hadn't been thinking. She had been seized by her emotions much the way a tree is seized by fire that is out of control."

"I see," said I. "Poor woman. She killed her husband and then changed her mind, but she couldn't change the outcome of her passions."

"No, she could not. I had obviously considered Mrs. Addison to be a suspect when I first met her, if for no other reason than to discard the possibility. I noted that her feet were too small to have fit into the boots, and that since they were men's boots, and her grief was so genuine, there seemed to be no reason to be suspicious of her. And yet, not until the coincidence of our Christmas dinner conversation, and your clandestine exchanging of intended gifts, did the possibility that I was wrong occur to me. Simply put, I had discarded a suspect prematurely. It is a valuable lesson. Equally valuable for future calculations is the fact that one may perpetrate a dastardly deed and come to regret it most sincerely."

"A tragic story," said I.

"Most tragic," agreed Holmes, puffing on his pipe thoughtfully. "And once again you have my gratitude, Watson. I don't think I would have penetrated the fog of my own prejudices had it not been for your perceptive insights."

"And I, too, am grateful to you, friend Holmes."

"How so?"

Lifting my feet to the hearth fire, I said, "These house slippers are infinitely more comfortable than my old pair."

Holmes smiled, and drew a long pull upon his pipe. Then we fell to reading. The sordid story of Mr. and Mrs. Addison is something we didn't wish to further discuss, so we laid the matter aside until I decided to recount it for the edification of the general public.

The Christmas Card Case
by Brenda Seabrooke

Several days before Christmas, the grey sky spat gritty snow over London. I saw the last of my patients for the day before noon. I hadn't established a practice yet, but when my monthly pension ran out from my battlefield wounds at Maiwand, I filled in for doctors who needed to be away from London for a time. In the days leading up to Christmas, I was working for a Dr. Daniels in a poor but respectable area of London. I dressed burns, sewed up cuts, splinted limbs when needed, or placed them in plaster casts. I listened to hearts hardly able to continue and prescribed what I could to help the patients get on with their lives. One such hadn't appeared for her appointment. I was concerned for Miss Lucy Meers and resolved to look in on her during the holidays. I found her address in Dr. Daniels's files and copied it into the little book I carried with me always.

On my way back to Baker street, I mailed the last of my Christmas cards to colleagues, patients, and friends, and also a package to Millicent Watson, my late father's second cousin twice removed, in Scotland. I assumed she was still living since I hadn't heard otherwise. This year's gift was a selection of teas from Fortnum and Mason. It wasn't exactly a case of *in loco parentis*, but I sent something every Christmas since my parents were gone. Cousin Millicent was my one last connection to family. She must have been close to ninety by then and lived with her late husband's great-niece.

Wind blew a flurry of flakes into my face as I turned the corner into Baker Street and hurried to 221 where, since the previous January, I had shared rooms with a singular fellow who styled himself the world's first consulting detective. I was still discovering bits of information about him, and I wondered if I should purchase a token gift for him. I had the feeling he didn't celebrate Christmas, just as he'd ignored Easter. He cared nothing for the acquisition of the material objects that most people pursued beyond the practical. Case in point: He kept his pipe tobacco in a Persian slipper nailed to his side of the mantelshelf after he'd acquired it in a case last summer *. He had an affinity for smoking and drinking, and a gift of either tobacco or brandy wouldn't be amiss. I stopped in the tobacco shop and bought a box of Habaneros. For Mrs. Hudson, I already owned a small blue vase given to me by a patient, and with my limited resources, that was the extent of my Christmas gift-giving in 1881.

Holmes was in and Mrs. Hudson had prepared an excellent mid-day meal for us, eaten in silence after my one or two attempts at conversation were answered with a single syllable. I gave up and repaired to what had become my chair on the left side of the hearth, with Holmes taking the right.

The fire in the grate snapped and hummed, lulling both of us into a postprandial torpor following the excellent lunch. The mantel clock ticked agreeably. Holmes lit a cigarette and rose to stand by the window, watching the weather. I didn't have the energy to light one and join him.

"I'm glad I don't have to be out in this any longer," I remarked. I'd seen patients all morning and felt a comfortable slide into sleep that awaited me.

Holmes laughed and tossed his cigarette into the fire. "Don't get too comfortable, Watson. I suspect that our situation may change in one or two minutes, if not sooner."

I'd not long to wait to see if his prognostication would become actual. I'd found this often to be the case with the world's first consulting detective. His powers of observation were acute. He noticed minute clues that enabled him to construct scenarios of occurrences, and sometimes he even seemed to see them in the air that were no more substantial than a winter snowflake.

Today seemed one of those times when a knock at the street door brought our landlady to our sitting room.

"A lady to see you, Mr. Holmes."

"Show her in, please, Mrs. Hudson."

At that moment she ushered in a young woman in her late twenties, about our age. She was dressed for the weather in a dark blue walking suit with snowy lace at the throat, and a hooded cloak of the same hue which removed the necessity of a hat or bonnet. Her hair was a rich shade of chestnut, styled in the French way.

"This is Mrs. Ingoldsby."

"Please sit by the fire and let it take the chill away," Holmes said, indicating the basket chair. As she perched on the edge of the seat, he drew up his own seat.

"You are Sherlock Holmes?" She had a pleasant voice, but seemed perturbed by something.

"I am. This is my colleague, Dr. Watson. How can we help you?"

I nodded at her.

She produced a velvet bag and rummaged in it as she told us. "I really don't know if it's anything. My husband says it's just one of those things that happens – people come and they go. That's just the way of things."

"And your husband is?"

"Jarred Ingoldsby. At the Foreign Office."

"Indeed. May we offer you a brandy on this braw cold day?"

"No, thank you. The fire is sufficiently warm."

"Does this concern your husband?"

"Oh no. Well, I don't think it does. No, I'm sure it doesn't."

"Is it perhaps blackmail?"

"No, nothing sinister. In fact it may be nothing."

"It must be something to have brought you here."

"Tell us about it," I said in my best doctor-to-patient tone.

Holmes looked amused as if he recognized what I was doing – as I'm sure he did. He often seemed to know what people were thinking and doing before they were aware of it themselves.

"Every year on the sixth of December, my husband and I receive a Christmas card. There's never any name on them. The handwriting is unfamiliar to either of us. But this year, no card has appeared. I'm concerned that something has happened to the sender. I wouldn't like to think this person has fallen into something dangerous, or died without us ever being able to reply because we don't know who it is. I realize it's late, but I've been busy with our daughter and twin sons, and also my husband's obligations." She finished looking in her dark blue bag and drew out a thick bundle of postcards tied with a green ribbon, which she handed to Holmes.

He took the cards but didn't look at them. "The sixth of December – it may have significance. That's the day celebrated in Holland as St. Nicholas' Day – the night before Sinterklaas and his helper would have brought toys and sweets to good children who left their shoes outside the door awaiting his gifts. Does your family have a Dutch connection?"

"No, not that we know about, on mine or my husband's side. We're completely mystified every year as to who sends them, and why that date, and we've racked our brains to try to find the answer. It's become our Christmas mystery."

Holmes took the bundle and removed the ribbon. The fire settled into a warm purr as he studied each card. Mrs. Ingoldsby watched him anxiously. By then, I was becoming familiar with his methods. He examined the front of each card, and then the back. When he'd looked through all of them, he glanced up.

"Can you tell anything?" asked our visitor.

"Oh yes, several things. They were all sent by the same person – either a woman, or possibly a man imitating a woman's handwriting. I would venture that it was mostly likely a woman The writing itself is excellent rounded copperplate. The writer learned his or her lessons well, and most likely early in the Queen's reign. The author used proper black ink and a quill pen. So we know she is most likely an older woman, perhaps of limited means. What does this suggest to you?"

"Why . . . I don't know. She could have been a neighbor, I suppose."

"Indeed. Someone you or your husband knew in the past. But who would be intimate enough to send you unsigned cards?"

Holmes then perused the scenes printed on the cards. "I'll consult a stationer, but I believe these cards were printed quite some time ago. If you look at the women's clothing in the illustrations, a frothy polonaise bustle style is shown. By last year, this bustle had subsided into the princess line named for Alexandra the Princess of Wales who popularized it. The horizontal waistline has disappeared into a smooth long-line look involving tucks and darts, with volume appearing lower."

"Why Mr. Holmes, you amaze me!" Mrs. Ingoldsby cried. "You know more about the style of women's dresses than I do."

He amazed me, too, but I dared not say it. I hadn't even noticed that bustles had completely disappeared from the world in 1880 – though I was busy in a war during much of that time. Good riddance in my opinion.

Holmes smiled briefly. "It is an important part of what I do to know styles. No doubt many bustled dresses were remade to fit the new style. The point of this discussion is that these cards depict women in out-of-date clothing. Sometimes depictions do this on purpose, but Christmas cards tend to represent the immediate present, or go much farther back – the days of Jane Austen, or even classical times. In those cases, the depictions wouldn't show a decorated tree, since those were first introduced by Queen Charlotte at Windsor Castle in 1800 and didn't become popular until Prince Albert surprised Queen Victoria with one in 1840. Only then did the custom spread."

The clock on the mantel chimed four times. Mrs. Ingoldsby abruptly sat forward and gathered her cape. "Oh, I must go. You've provided me with a great deal of information already, Mr. Holmes. Will you look into this matter for me, as small as it is?"

"Certainly. I don't believe I've ever had a case involving Christmas cards."

Mrs. Ingoldsby gave him her visiting card. He glanced at it and slid it into a pocket. "I'll be in touch."

We both stood and I escorted her downstairs to the front door where a cab awaited. I helped her into it. "I do hope my problem isn't too trivial for Mrs. Holmes's time and attention."

"It isn't," I said, as if I knew. Even after a year of knowing him, and occasionally assisting in his investigations, I wasn't entirely sure yet what intrigued Holmes and what he considered trivial. Clearly kingdoms wouldn't topple over these Christmas postal cards, but the affair might lead to something bigger than it seemed.

When I returned to the sitting room, Holmes had found his magnifying glass and was studying the cards inch by inch. "What do you think?"

"I think from the little we have gleaned that some soul wished to keep up a connection with her betters – perhaps she was a former servant – but was too timid to put her name or address on the cards. It was enough for her to send one every year."

"Astute of you. You'll be a detective yet."

Was there a touch of jest in his tone? "It isn't so different from diagnosing a patient's illness and finding either a cure or relief from pain."

"That simple, is it?"

"Yes. It is that simple."

"You're right. You are already a detective of sorts, though not as versed in ordinary clues as you're in observing medical clues. If someone comes in with a hollow cough, your first thought might be tuberculosis. A closer look, however, plus some palliative medicine to enable the patient to sleep without coughing, might reveal a case of grippe."

"You are correct. You might make a doctor yourself."

A smile flashed over his mouth and then was gone. Was he making sport of me? If so, I think that I gave as good as I got.

"You did, Watson. You did."

I didn't quite know how to take this – or how he knew what I'd been thinking. "Brandy?" I asked to change the subject.

"I hear Mrs. Hudson with our tea. Perhaps later."

Later that evening, after a joint of sirloin accompanied by tender peas, carrots, and potatoes in beef gravy, we finally had our splash of brandy and Holmes returned to the stack of cards. "The first Christmas card was printed by John Callcott Horsley the artist for his friend Sir Henry Cole in 1843. It merely said '*Merry Christmas*'. The custom caught on when illustrations were added and postage was dropped to a penny, and then to a half-penny, along with the cost of the cards as well. I suspect the sender thriftily bought up a packet of ten several years ago, after the holiday had passed, and when they subsequently cost even less – perhaps three pence instead of five. It was then that the idea was born to send them to someone from the author's past and better days."

"You can tell all of that from simply looking at the cards?"

"Certainly not. Some of that I remember from when it occurred. And at one time I needed knowledge about Sir Henry Cole for an investigation – that fact was still in my little brain attic."

"Indeed."

"Look at the pictures and tell me what you see. Describe the cards to me."

He handed over the stack. I looked through them one by one, spreading them out on the recently cleared table. First I sorted them according to pictures. "These are mostly scenes of Christmas morning, it seems. The first one is a pair of robins perched on a berried holly branch with snow on the ground. The rest have scenes of Christmas trees, most with children in them. This one has an older woman with the children, and two have a fireplace behind them. The fireplaces differ, and the trees slightly as well. This one has cats and rabbits around a decorated tree. This one is the same, but instead with cats and mice."

"Small differences. The cats and rabbits aren't wearing clothing, while the mice are."

"True. The final card shows Father Christmas watching children dancing around a decorated tree."

"Excellent. You've categorized them. What differences and similarities do you see?"

"The card with robins depicts no children or decorated trees or Father Christmas. All of the other cards depict a decorated tree. Nine have human figures in them. All ten have some seasonal greenery, either a tree or holly."

"Again, excellent. Is there anything else that they all have in common?"

I looked at each card carefully – too carefully.

"Come, come, Watson. How can you not see it? Why isn't it jumping out at you? Or flying in circles around you?"

I gave him a blank look. "They all depict Christmas . . . ."

I looked again at each card. Holmes became impatient.

"The birds, man. The little red birds."

"Oh that. They're so small I can hardly see them."

"In your defense, I did use the glass to spot them, but they can be seen by the eye. Each card has a tiny red bird tucked away somewhere. On the Christmas trees in different places, or almost hidden in the holly on the robin card."

He handed me the magnifying glass and instantly the tiny birds jumped into view. "Yes, I see them now."

"Observe, they were all hand-drawn and colored with some sort of dye instead of ink – possibly beet juice. If you hold the cards a certain way in the light, you can see the slight indentation made by the quill."

"Someone was sending a message."

"Possibly. If so, we must find out what the message is."

"However will we do that?"

"We'll start with the postmark. These cards were all mailed at the Houndsditch Post Office. Our sender must live near there – at least up until last year when the last card was sent – as these have been consistently sent from that post office for years. Tomorrow I'll pay that office a visit."

In the morning, I had no patients to see. Dr. Daniels had returned from his journey and, as I had no new assignment, I accompanied Holmes to the post office. "If anyone remembers the cards, it's most likely to be the postmaster," he said.

No patrons waited in line and we had the building to ourselves. The man behind the counter, who confirmed he was the postmaster, looked old enough to have been there for some time.

Holmes took the bundle of cards out of his inside pocket. "I hope you'll be able to help us. I'm Sherlock Holmes, and this is my associate, Dr. Watson."

The rather stooped man with gray hair brightened. "Dr. Watson? It's you then, is it? I'm Jonas Case. I came to you when you was *loco*-ing for Dr. Samson."

Indeed, I couldn't recall every patient that I'd seen while serving as a *locum* in various practices all over the city, but I did remember this one. "Mr. Case – of course! You had a bad case of grippe."

"I did. That medicine you give me fixed it right up. What can I do for you gentlemen, ah Mr. – "

"Holmes," I said quickly. "Sherlock Holmes. He is a consulting detective, and I'm assisting him in an investigation."

"How do, Mr. Holmes."

"Fine, thank you, Mr. Case." He lifted the cards. "We're trying to locate the sender of these. They were sent from this postal station on the fifth of December every year for the last few years – until this year. Do you recognize them, or remember who might have sent them?"

The old man took the cards. "Not many as sends Christmas cards in these parts." He flipped through them, looking on the side with the address. "Don't have writing on the greetings part." He then turned them over and recognition brightened his pale face. "But I do indeed know the sender. It's Mrs. Ava Beale. Lives nearby."

"Would you happen to have her address?" I asked. "She may be ill since she missed sending a card this year."

"I do. She lives over on Wirthy Lane. Round the corner, not far. I'd show you myself, but I can't leave."

"Thank you, Mr. Case," I replied. "I'm sure we'll find it. Take care of those lungs now. Get out and breathe fresh air when you can." I tipped

111

my hat, as did Holmes, and as we left, new customers came in to buy stamps.

"Around the corner, he said." Holmes headed around toward the nearest turn. After some searching, we found it. Wirthy Lane was a mean little street. Some of the houses had small upstairs balconies that jutted overhead above the street, blocking any sunlight that might be trying to reach the place. After several enquiries we found the house in question, a rickety shamble of a building whose origins lay several centuries in the past. We were told that Mrs. Beale lived upstairs in half of a balcony that someone had enclosed a century or more ago. We climbed the inner stairs carefully. They shook with every step.

When we arrived at the street side of the first floor, Holmes knocked on the door opening onto the landing. "Mrs. Beale? Mrs. Ava Beale?"

No reply.

"Mrs. Beale, my name is Sherlock Holmes, and with me is Dr. Watson. We're here about the Christmas greeting that you failed to send this year."

"How do you know that?" came a weak voice.

"On each card for ten years you drew a red bird – possibly this was meant to represent yourself, as your name '*Ava*' means '*bird*'. Mrs. Ingoldsby, of the family that received the cards, has engaged us to find you and see if you're all right. She's worried because no card arrived this year on St. Nicholas' Day."

"Oh!" The low cry could have been a sob of happiness, or despair or relief. The door finally opened and a tiny frail bird of a woman stood there, clutching a frayed shawl.

"Please come in," she almost whispered, "though this is no place you would like to be."

The sliver of a room was icy, and would have been impossible to heat, despite the fact that someone had papered over the many cracks in the walls. Mrs. Beale hadn't done much to keep it warm, besides setting a charcoal pot on a square of bricks. A north-facing window let in pallid light, and I suspected before our arrival that the poor woman had been wrapped tightly in the neatly folded blanket lying upon the corner pallet bed.

Mrs. Beale may have been pretty in her youth, but the difficulties of her life had aged her. With only one chair in the room, we stood to talk. I was worried that she might keel over simply from the exertion of speaking with us. "As a doctor, Mrs. Beale, I must insist that you sit while we speak."

I took her arm and settled her on the plain wooden chair, and then busied myself looking for tea things. I found a cup and a battered kettle, but no tea – or any other foodstuff for that matter. I shook my head at Holmes and opened my empty hands to show there was nothing to eat or drink in this room. Clearly this was unacceptable for human habitation.

"We shall consult Mrs. Hudson. Come, Watson, not a moment to lose."

"Is there anything you want to take with you?" I asked her.

The woman was shocked that, within seconds of our arrival, we were preparing to leave and take her with us. "Just a chest," she replied. "There. It serves as a table."

Holmes lifted and half-carried her out the door and down the stairs, leaving me to struggle with the small trunk, which proved far heavier than I had expected.

"I don't think I can walk far," Mrs. Beale said when we reached the pavement.

"We'll get a cab," Holmes replied.

"Not likely in this neighborhood," I muttered.

"You there, lad," countered Holmes, gesturing to a small ill-dressed boy watching from across the street. "Find us a cab and there's a coin in it for you." He held up a sixpence with one hand while the other supported Mrs. Beale.

I set the trunk close to my feet, just touching my leg. In this neighborhood, an inch farther away and it would be whisked away before I missed it. I took off my overcoat and slid it around Mrs. Beale just as a strong gust of wind armed with snow grit nearly blew us away.

The boy returned within minutes. "Ee's comin!"

Holmes gave him the sixpence and, noting his raggedness, something extra. I heard the coins clink.

Almost immediately, a hansom turned into the street. Normally hansoms carry two passengers, but Mrs. Beale hardly made a third person. Even so, we fit snugly inside which wasn't bad considering the coldness of the day.

Once inside the hansom with the trunk at my feet, Holmes unwound his muffler and tossed it to the boy. "Take care now," he said as the cab drove us away.

Presently Mrs. Beale spoke. "This is the warmest I've been since my husband died."

Holmes looked at me over her head. "We'll see that you will be warm from now on."

I nodded. Somewhere in London, we ought to be able to find a place for her. Mrs. Hudson would have some suggestions. If not, then perhaps I could ask some of the patients that I'd seen and come to know. The lady was not going back to that terrible room.

"Agreed," Holmes said, nodding my way.

This time I wasn't surprised he'd discerned my thoughts. How could I have been considering anything else? We couldn't help everyone in need in London, but we could help Mrs. Beale.

"Upon my soul!" Mrs. Hudson said when she saw our visitor. We explained the details of the investigation, how we'd located the poor woman and the conditions in which we'd found her. Our capable landlady took over and soon Mrs. Beale was filled with hot soup and crisp scones dripping with butter. She'd had a bath and now wore some of Mrs. Hudson's things until hers dried from the quick washing that the maid gave them.

Mrs. Hudson tucked the little old lady under a shawl in front of the fire in her own sitting room and then climbed the stairs to report to us. "She's had a dreadful time of it, poor thing. Her husband was a clerk for a company cataloging libraries. The last place he worked, over fifteen years ago, was at the home of Lord Belding, in the library at Sheldon House. It was extensive and required a number of years to sort out. During that time, Mr. Beale was given the use of a cottage and he brought his wife with him, letting their own cottage out for rent for the time. Mr. Beale was a deal older than his wife, and they never had children of their own, and neither possessed any other family. While they lived in the cottage, Mrs. Beale became fond of the Belding children, taking them on picnics and what-not.

"That's when she met Mr. Ingoldsby. He was a ward of the Belding family after his parents were killed in India. She was especially close to him during the time she spent at Sheldon House. Years later, she saw his name in the newspaper and started sending the Christmas cards, although anonymously. They were a connection to her past, and it made her happy to do so."

"Thank you, Mrs. Hudson," said Holmes. "I believe you've discovered the remaining questions related to the matter, and you've been most kind as well."

"I couldn't have done otherwise, poor soul. She isn't to go back to that room. She can stay here until we find a place for her."

Holmes didn't look surprised. Nor did I.

I took my bag downstairs to Mrs. Hudson's sitting room to make sure that Mrs. Beale was well and to determine if she needed any additional medical attention. Her pulse and heart rate were a trifle weak, but that was to be expected. She had a normal temperature reading. Holmes came down as I was finishing my examination and waited impatiently until I was done.

"Now Mrs. Beale, please tell us the rest of your story – after you and your husband left Sheldon House."

"We went on as before. With the extra money from the long let of our little house, my husband was able to purchase a small annuity for our old age only he died not long after and I was left. I stayed in the cottage for another year or so, taking little jobs of sewing or caring for others as I could, but as costs rose, I was forced to sell my home and seek out rooms, nice at first, but then meaner and meaner, until I fetched up in Wirthy Lane." She heaved a great sigh, as if letting out the very misama of that dreadful place.

"And then what happened?" Holmes asked.

"At the end of every month, I always go to the bank to receive my annuity check and cash it. Two months ago, a pair of ruffians lay in wait for me. They were rough and took all of my money. Last month, the same thing happened again. I managed to buy enough food to last me with the little I'd saved back from previous months, but my rent is due on the last day of every month, and after paying at the end of November, a few weeks ago, I had nothing left for food or rent."

"And that is why the cards stopped," I said. "You couldn't afford even the price of postage on December 5th."

"Yes." Tears collected on her lashes. "They were the most important part of my year. I had such pleasure remembering those happy times, drawing the little bird somewhere on the pictured side. I thought of what a sweet little boy Mr. Ingoldsby had been, and how well he'd grown up. I thought of him as if he were my own, and now he has little ones of his own. And this year I couldn't even do that – couldn't even send him a card." A tear slid out of her left eye and glistened like a jewel on her cheek before disappearing into the shawl wrapping her to her chin.

"This year you will do even better than that," Holmes said. "This year you can draw little birds in person, for we shall take you to see the Ingoldsbys. I've telegraphed them, and they invited you to tea tomorrow. They suggested today, but I thought you needed to rest for awhile."

Mrs. Hudson agreed, as did I. In her frail condition, Mrs. Beale might be overcome at seeing the little boy she obviously still loved so much. "Her memories of Mr. Ingoldsby were what sustained her through her penury, her hunger and cold," I said when we went back upstairs. "Would that everyone had food and warmth and happy memories. The world would be a different place if that were true. You might be out of a job, and mine might be much easier if people grew up eating well and living in warm dry housing."

"Indeed, yours would be easier. Certainly rickets and other results of malnutrition would abate. Tuberculosis might even disappear. But you can rest assured that greed, malfeasance, and hate would still be with us, driving humans to crime."

"A bit cynical for the Christmas season," I countered.

"For any season, but the heart of man doesn't improve much with the comforts of a fire and nourishing food. Think of the rich amongst us who have everything and continue to commit crimes."

Alas, I had to concede he was correct in his thinking, but I still clung to the belief that many crimes would cease with comfort, and the release of fear of starvation and freezing to death.

Mrs. Beale wore her best dress for tea at the Ingoldsby's, pulled from her trunk and ironed by the maid. It was a soft rose color with a bit of lace here and there. Her hair was carefully pulled up and arranged. Mrs. Hudson lent her a cape with a hood.

"We want to look our best," she said as she tweaked the lace and bustled around us as we were leaving. Finally Holmes said, "Would you like to accompany us? I'm sure the Ingoldsbys won't mind an additional guest for tea."

Mrs. Hudson drew back, aghast. "Certainly not! This is a family affair. With the addition," she amended, "of the both of you who made it happen." Turning to Mrs. Beale, she said, "Enjoy yourself, my dear. And don't worry about a thing. We will make something happen for you."

"Thank you."

Holmes had a growler waiting at the kerb. We settled ourselves in and the cab moved into traffic.

"Such a pleasure to be riding in a cab again," Mrs. Beale remarked. "I was too cold to enjoy it yesterday. Indeed, I believe I must have been half-asleep for much of the journey."

She had actually slept for the entire trip, but I didn't remind her of it, for then she might recall why, and those days were over now. No need to dwell upon them. Mrs. Hudson would find a place for her.

The cab stopped before a handsome Georgian brick house with a black front door under an elegant fanlight, the brass polished to bright shine even on so late of an overcast afternoon. A spray of holly branches held by a red velvet ribbon echoed the design of the fanlight.

"Festive," Holmes murmured as he helped Mrs. Beale out while I paid the cabby with a generous tip for the holiday.

Holmes tapped the door-knocker and it was instantly thrown open by Mrs. Ingoldsby herself, while a butler stood slightly to her left – No doubt in case we proved to be ruffians! – with a disapproving expression on his face.

"Come in, come in! Welcome to our home! We are so excited to meet the sender of those lovely cards. I'm Caroline Ingoldsby. George isn't home yet – he was delayed – but will be here as soon as he can."

Behind her a pair of boys of the same height came into view. Apparently they were the twins although they didn't look alike. With them was their younger sister wearing green velvet, and they all danced with excitement. "Mama let me wear my new dress," confided the little girl, Melinda, when her mother had introduced them. The two boys were William and Phillip.

I thought then that Mrs. Beale would be overcome, but she took to the children immediately as we moved to a large sitting room, cozy with a fire, comfortable furniture, and wallpaper striped in shades of blue. A large brown dog on the hearth and a grey cat slept in a basket.

"What a lovely room," remarked Mrs. Beale as we were seated. A Christmas tree stood in a place of honor, decorated with paper ornaments probably made by the children: Chains, cornucopias of sweets, and a paper nativity scene tucked into a gap in the branches.

Holmes pulled the packet of cards from his coat and handed them to Mrs. Ingoldsby. She crossed the room and placed them on the mantelshelf, along with a number of others already tucked into the greenery. We were immediately served a sumptuous tea fit for a king before Mrs. Beale was drawn into helping the children in making paper birds with horizontal wings for the tree.

"They look like they can fly!" Melinda said.

Meanwhile, Holmes softly explained to Mrs. Ingoldsby what had transpired. "Mrs. Hudson is looking for a place for her – "

"Certainly not!" the lady of the house interrupted. "She must stay here. We shall sort this all out. She shouldn't be working at her age and frailty."

Just then, I became aware of someone standing quietly nearby. Mr. Ingoldsby had arrived so silently that the children and Mrs. Beale hadn't noticed. He watched the scene for a minute. We stepped toward him, and his wife softly introduced us as he continued to observe the lady with his children, engrossed in their task. "We'll put a birdie on every branch," Phillip said.

A change came over Mr. Ingoldsby's demeanor. He stepped further into the room. "Birdie," he called softly.

Mrs. Beale turned her head and saw him there, this tall, handsome man. "George!" she exclaimed, rising and then apologizing. "I mean, Mr. Ingoldsby. You are so grown up."

"If you're still Birdie, then I'm still George," he said. "You made a lonely orphaned boy feel loved. I cried when I came back from an outing and found that you had gone. No one would ever told me where you went or how to find you. I didn't even know your name beyond 'Birdie'." He looked toward his children and said, "She taught me to make those same birds,"

"Is that why you called her Birdie?" Mrs. Ingoldsby asked.

"I think so."

"My husband called me that," Mrs. Beale explained. "My given name is Ava, a form of *Avis*, which means '*bird*' in Latin. You spent time at our cottage at the estate, George, helping me peel apples and putting cores out in the trees for the birds."

"How ever did you find her?" Mr. Ingoldsby asked, looking toward Holmes.

Holmes repeated some of what we'd just related to Mrs. Ingoldsby, omitting the sadder parts of the story, and instead concentrating on how we'd located her. "And now our work is done. We must take our leave."

"Please – let me know your fee," Ingoldsby said.

"Certainly not. This is my gift to you for Christmas."

"It's so generous of you!" Mrs. Ingoldsby said. "I can't thank you enough."

"Nor I," Ingoldsby said. "I suspect this story will become an oft-told tale at bedtime."

"One with a happy ending," I added.

"But we haven't reached the ending," Holmes informed me a few minutes later, after we had taken our leave.

I nodded. There was the matter of the toughs who'd robbed Mrs. Beale . . . but that could wait until after the holiday.

Mrs. Hudson had been busy in our rooms. Holly, mistletoe, and pine greenery sprigged every picture frame and the mantelshelf. She was waiting in her traveling clothes to hear how our meeting went. We told her as briefly as possible.

"I'm so happy for her. I wish more stories could end this way. And I wish you both had somewhere to go for Christmas. I've left you a joint and trimmings. I trust you can take care of yourselves, but if you change your mind, my sister will welcome you at her house tomorrow."

"That's kind of you, Mrs. Hudson."

"Wait – I have a gift for you." I rushed upstairs to my room and brought down the blue vase clumsily wrapped in brown paper. Holmes gave her a small package from his room as well.

"I believe I'll open them here." She removed the brown paper and exclaimed over the blue glass vase.

"It matches your eyes," I said. I noticed that it looked small. "Sorry it isn't larger."

"Why, thank you, Dr. Watson. It will look lovely in my sitting room and will be perfect for small bouquets which are my preference when my other vases are either too small or too large. It's perfect. Thank you."

Holmes gave her a crystal candy dish already filled with boiled sweets.

After our perfect dinner we relaxed by the fire, but I was called out on a case. Mrs. Cummings' baby decided to be a Christmas present. After I delivered her baby, Mr. Cummings thanked me for coming out on Christmas Eve.

"It's no bother. You saved me from a boring evening by the fire, and now you have a little one to celebrate with."

"My wife wants to name him Noel, so we've decided to name him after you. John Noel, it is."

Childbirth is a miracle whenever it happens, but on Christmas Eve it's a special miracle. When the family wasn't looking, I slipped a sixpence and an orange from my bag into the stocking that Mr. Cummings had hurriedly hung by the chimney for John Noel.

Snow passed us by that Christmas, despite earlier flutterings. Snow is beautiful, but I don't care for the mess that we humans have to deal with. We should retire to a snug cave somewhere in snowy climes and sleep off winter.

The streets that were busy with carol singers and last-minute shoppers earlier were silent now. Since the weather was cold but not vicious and I was in the area, I decided to stop and see Lucy Meers. I found her address in my pocket and decided to walk, as it was only one street over and a little way down.

The Meers family was surprised to see me. Their daughter Lucy had been too feverish to come to her appointment. I listened to her chest. The rales had subsided and her fever was almost normal. "Whatever you are doing works. Continue doing it," I instructed her parents. "Give her plenty of liquid and whatever food she can keep down. Let me know if she worsens."

As I repacked my black bag on the table in a dark corner of the room, I surreptitiously slipped fruit into an empty bowl, apples and oranges. Perhaps they would think Father Christmas paid them a visit in the night when it came to light in the morning.

No cabs were about in that neighborhood so late, so I walked in the clear night back to Baker Street, overlooked by stars of a particular brightness.

I slept late the next morning. Christmas Day was quiet. With Mrs. Hudson away, Holmes and I did for ourselves from the ample dishes that she'd left for us. Around eleven o'clock, a private messenger brought two parcels to the door, one for each of us. The contents were identical, very old fine French brandy.

"Calvados," Holmes said unwrapping his first. "From Normandy. Cider brandy distilled by Gilles de Gouberville in 1553. How fortunate it was called after the region and not Gouberville. I don't fancy sipping e*au de Gouberville*."

I laughed. "I suspect people would sip this under any name."

"Your romantic streak holds sway, Watson. Or is it because of Christmas? '*A rose by any other name would smell as sweet.*' Let's hope this doesn't have the same result as what occurred in *Romeo and Juliet*."

He brought out a package wrapped in brown paper and handed it to me. I removed my identically wrapped gift from my black bag and gave it to him. "Hmm," he murmured. "Can it be?"

Yes it could. We had each given the other the identically-wrapped same box of Habaneros from the nearby tobacconist shop.

We lounged by the fire. The day was snowless, but still very cold. I was content to listen to the sounds of the fire and hoped that no more babies decided to arrive on this day.

Holmes left around two to pay some calls, but he didn't specify as to whom. I suspected he would drop by Scotland Yard to see Gregson and Lestrade, if not others who might be on duty this day.

I caught up on professional reading and one or two yellow-book stories of derring-do, and dozed periodically after my long night out, and was much the better for it. Holmes returned around nightfall. We decided to save our gift bottles for the end of the year.

"I'm glad Mrs. Beale's case ended well," I remarked over ordinary brandy.

"Oh, it isn't ended. Indeed not. Mrs. Beale's part was merely small beer, albeit devastating to her. No, much more is to come."

He drifted off in a smoky reverie and would say no more. I decided to turn in.

Mrs. Hudson returned late on Boxing Day and insisted on cooking. "I brought back a fine gammon, fresh from the country."

The next three days saw me busy with diseases of winter and broken bones at Barts, several trying cases in which overeating had been a factor, a matter of poisoning from a green dress, and other of the sundry disasters that man is heir to.

I received a note from my relative Millicent Watson, who was still alive and well. She was quite appreciative of the exotic – to her – assortment of teas, and also to be remembered by her great-great nephew. I saw little of Holmes during those days except in passing, and once or twice breakfast or dinner. I wasn't in the habit of asking him about his plans, but took his activity to mean preparations for the next-to-last day of the year were going forth.

As we sat down to dinner on Thursday, Holmes said, "The thirtieth is upon us on tomorrow. I hope you'll be available from nine in the morning to accompany us to the bank."

"Is that the time Mrs. Beale usually goes to pick up her annuity?"

"It is."

"Will we be her only protection?" I wasn't sure that I was up to taking on toughs yet after my battle injuries and long fever bout.

"No. She wrote down all details of her walk to the bank and back, and where she was accosted both times. We'll have men in those areas, and also stationed along the route to the bank. Lestrade and his men will be out in force, albeit discreetly placed."

I was comforted by that, but the next morning after a quick breakfast, I slipped my Bull Dog into my pocket and hoped I wouldn't have to use it.

I busied myself with some of my patients' notes for an hour or two. Mrs. Hudson provided a light lunch which Holmes declined to partake. I'd noticed this was often the case with him when something was about to happen.

"Holmes, you do know that food provides energy and keeps us going."

"I can't spare the energy to digest it and wait for the transformation to that energy. I already have sufficient for the task at hand."

At half-twelve, Holmes picked up a satchel and hurried me down to the street where a hackney awaited us. "I ordered it earlier," he explained.

"Surely a hansom would be sufficient."

"We're stopping for Mrs. Beale. I wanted her to ride in comfort."

I refrained from saying that anything on wheels would be a comfort to one who had walked for the last ten years. Mrs. Beale deserved her comforts.

George Ingoldsby escorted her to the cab and to my surprise, though possibly not to Holmes's, he insisted on accompanying us. Mrs. Beale wore her old cloak, and under it her best old clothes that she saved for bank days. Holmes insisted that nothing must be different today from her previous trips to the bank.

As we drove through the crowded streets toward Mrs. Beale's old neighborhood, Holmes went over the plan with her again. "You must not be emboldened and try to resist them. We want them to take possession of your property."

"We'll have them in the act," Ingoldsby added.

Holmes stifled a laugh and I looked away. The man seemed to be living an escapade from *Boys' Own Paper*. Perhaps he read stories of that sort to his own sons.

Holmes stopped the cab out of sight of Mrs. Beale's former abode. He opened his bag pulling out a different coat, which he put on. Then he did a few things to his face and hair before clapping a battered hat onto his head.

Ingoldsby and Mrs. Beale stared at the transformation. "Whatever are you doing?" Ingoldsby asked.

"I can't follow Mrs. Beale dressed as a toff without being taken for one, can I?" He spoke in a rough accent.

Ingoldsby could scarcely understand him. Then he laughed. "I say, Holmes, you're a corker!"

Holmes smiled faintly and replied in his own tones. "I leave no stone unturned, nor anything to chance."

I saved that away for future remembrance. It fit with my observations, but I hadn't yet framed it in that way.

He gave us our final instructions. He helped Mrs. Beale from the cab and loitered around the corner while she entered her former lodgings, only to immediately exit and begin her walk to the Shadwell Bank. The cab carried Ingoldsby and me to the bank by another route, and we were inside the sturdy red brick building when she arrived. She went about her business as usual, while we looked over a sheet containing printed figures at one of the tables close to the entrance. When she left, we concluded our imaginary business with one another and, with a handshake, we followed her – first me and then Ingoldsby.

Outside, we pretended to bump into each other and, with animated gestures, conversed as we followed the route back to Mrs. Beale's former lodgings. I didn't see Holmes or the Scotland Yard detectives, or even the duty constables. I assumed that they'd been sent to the farthest reaches of their beat in order to give the thieves a false sense of security. As we neared the meaner streets, the crowds roughened, and I suspected Holmes must be in the middle of them, but invisible as he blended in. He'd even rubbed dust and dirt on his clean shoes and trousers before we separated, lest they give him away. As he said, he left nothing to chance.

From a distance we followed the brave little bluebell that stood upright on Mrs. Beale's straw hat. As she passed a dark, dirty alley, even worse than Wirthy Lane, three toughs suddenly burst from it, dragging Mrs. Beale out of our sight. We weren't close enough to hear what they said, but could imagine them saying something along the lines of, "Your money or your life!"

We sped to the corner where we heard her reply querulously, "Please – this is all I have! I'll starve!"

One of the men laughed, but the other didn't because his laugh was suddenly choked out of him when he was grabbed from behind by a rough fellow with dust on his shoes. He could only made slight gagging sounds, as a baton of some sort was now tight across his throat. At that moment, two other rough fellows came down the alley toward us. They were disguised constables, but they stopped short, for Mrs. Beale had a knife at her throat.

"Back up!" the tough who had seized her ordered. "This is *my* pigeon!"

"Not much meat on them bones," one of the constables said.

"Naw," added the other. "We don't 'tend to share. Give over."

"I said get back!" the knife-wielder snarled. "Covy Joe won't take kindly to you muscling in."

"That's who you work for?" the first disguised constables asked with scorn.

"Yeah," came the reply as the knife was brandished. "He's smarter'n whoever you dungs are workin' for!"

Mrs. Beale gasped, but stayed on her feet.

"I doubt that," one of the constables said, but they started to back away slowly.

Meanwhile, Holmes had allowed the unconscious partner to collapse in a quiet heap, and then he slid without sound along the alley wall and closer behind the attacker. No one else moved. Something had to be done, or the attacker would soon become aware of Holmes.

"I say there," I interrupted in my plummiest English accent, with apologies to my Scottish forebears. "I believe that I'm lost. You fellows wouldn't happen to know where the Shadwell Bank is located?"

The tough's attention was drawn my way for a moment as he weighed the seriousness of my presence. At the same time, Ingoldsby shrank back as if he wanted no part of this scene, a typical response of the upper class, and perfect for this occasion.

Holmes took advantage of the situation and struck the criminal a hard blow to the head with his baton. The constables were quick. One snatched Mrs. Beale out of harm's way while the other cracked the attacker's knife arm with another baton that appeared in his hand. Holmes took care of the third one. "You're under arrest," he said, turning him over to a constable.

Ingoldsby came closer, and Inspector Lestrade joined us. Mr. Ingoldsby reached Mrs. Beale first and took her arm. "Are you all right, my dear Birdie? That ruffian didn't hurt you?"'

"No, I'm quite well, thanks to all of you." She righted her brave little straw hat, with the upright bluebell quivering somewhat.

Lestrade ordered the police wagons brought up. I gave each of the criminals a glance. The one that Holmes choked was waking up, while the second had a nasty bump on the back of his head, and the third's right arm below the elbow might very well be broken. I informed Lestrade that they would need medical attention, but I wasn't prepared to provide any without my medical bag.

At the inspector's nod, the constables loaded the three thieves into separate wagons and gave instructions to have a doctor at attention when they arrived. Ingoldsby then invited the constables and Lestrade over to his house for a libation, but unfortunately they had to decline, as they were all on duty and had the business at hand to complete. "Come tomorrow, then," Ingoldsby offered. "At anytime. We want to think you for taking three more criminals off the street."

Holmes and I had nothing there to further occupy us. With Ingoldsby and Mrs. Beale, we adjourned to the waiting cab where Holmes pulled off the old coat and cleaned his face, using a rag from his satchel. He wiped his shoes as well. Then he drew out a small clothing brush and returned his trousers to their former state. The old hat and coat went back into the bag.

The three of us watched him with fascination. This was the first time that I'd seen him make such a transformation in front of me.

"You are presentable again," I remarked when he donned his own coat, Inverness, and fore-and-aft cap.

"He is always presentable," Mrs. Beale said, "as whatever the occasion calls for."

"Well said." Holmes favored her with a smile.

The entire story was told again for the benefit of Mrs. Ingoldsby over a celebratory tea and libations. When Holmes seemed to reach a saturation point in conviviality, we made our farewells. Before we left, the children presented us with a stack of paper birds. "For your tree," Melinda said.

I hadn't the heart to tell her we had no tree.

"I can't thank you enough," Mrs. Ingoldsby said.

"Nor I," Mrs. Beale echoed.

Back in the flat, I placed the paper birds in the mantel greenery where they perched festively, and then I sank down in front of the fire while Holmes dumped more coal on the embers and worked the bellows.

"That went well," I said.

"Indeed. But I wonder: Will we hear more from this Covy Joe? And how many toughs does he have on his string?"

124

"Let's not borrow trouble for the future," I said. "Let the old year end on a high note."

"It has, but we must keep in mind that those three toughs are mere sardines in the swill of the River Styx."

"How poetic of you. And literary."

Holmes snorted. "Facts, my dear Watson. I deal in facts only."

NOTE

* See "The Persian Slipper" *The MX Book of New Sherlock Holmes Stories Part XXV – 2021 Annual (1881-1888)*

The Chatterton-Smythe Affair
by Tim Gambrell

Some cases investigated by my good friend Sherlock Holmes were so brief as to appear almost inconsequential, warranting little more than a footnote or an aside within our grander narratives. One such occurred the very first Christmas after Holmes and I had taken rooms at 221b Baker Street. However, I feel this case is worthy of coverage in more detail.

It was on or around December 23rd. We were just settling in for the evening when we found ourselves interrupted by Inspector Athelney Jones. The poor man was clearly flustered, and we provided him with a seat by the fire and a large constitutional brandy. As he composed himself, I looked to my companion. Holmes's expression gave nothing away. It was well known by me, even at this early stage, what little regard Holmes held for our visiting police inspector.

After the second brandy and a few pleasantries regarding the season, the inspector tried to come to the point. Or, rather, he embarked upon the journey to inform us of the point of his visit. I could tell he was anxious. Jones's Welsh accent always broadened with nerves. Holmes, meanwhile, busied himself about his pipe.

The inspector told us that the previous day, he had been called to Lord Chatterton-Smythe's residence in Mayfair. The young Miss Chatterton-Smythe, only introduced into society the previous season, was missing a very valuable signet ring – a family heirloom. It was part of the inheritance from her late maternal grandmother, Lady Trevithick. It was incredibly valuable and had been insured for a large sum of money, but to the young miss and her mother it held far greater sentimental value.

The Chatterton-Smythes kept a quiet household, with only a small number of servants, according to the inspector. The staff had searched the whole house, to no avail. When the ring had not reappeared, Lord Chatterton-Smythe suspected foul play and raised the alarm. That was the situation as Inspector Jones and his constables found it upon their arrival.

The family wanted the ring recovered with all haste and minimal fuss. Lord Chatterton-Smythe challenged the police to search the house thoroughly from top to bottom, including all the servants' persons and their effects. The staff had been consigned to their quarters and told not to leave on pain of dismissal – unless summoned, of course. His Lordship offered to be searched by Jones himself. Lady and Miss Chatterton-

Smythe were searched by Her Ladyship's maid (once she herself had been searched), supervised by the inspector.

"I take it you have found no trace of the ring?" Holmes snapped, clearly tiring of the inspector's lengthy and detailed account.

"Indeed, Mr. Holmes, that is the case," Jones replied. "We even took all the decorations off the Christmas tree, in case it had somehow been caught on there, or placed there as a practical joke."

I interceded at this point. "And the family are convinced the ring hasn't left the house?"

"As they live and breathe, Doctor Watson. The young miss had worn it to a society ball a few days prior, but it was seen by all on her finger at the house afterwards. She herself recalls placing it back inside her jewellery box on the dressing table when she retired."

"You looked for secret compartments and so forth within the jewellery box?" asked Holmes.

Jones nodded. "It's one of those wind-up boxes that plays a tune and has a ballerina dancing inside. At least, it *did* play a tune until we took it apart to look for the ring."

Holmes gave a drawn-out sigh. "Are you here to ask for my help, Inspector?"

The inspector cleared his throat in an affected manner. "Having completed the search and drawn a blank . . . you see, Lady Chatterton-Smythe stepped in. She's quite a formidable woman."

This I had heard.

Holmes glared. "Get to the point, Inspector."

"Well, she, as it were, demanded that I bring in someone more . . . ." His words faded.

"Competent?" my companion suggested.

Jones glared at him, his face like thunder. But he offered no contradiction. "That was the general gist of what she said, yes."

Holmes tutted. "And your superiors at Whitehall Place suggested you call on me?"

Jones tugged at his collar. "Actually, Mr. Holmes, I haven't spoken to my superiors. I don't believe they would honour Her Ladyship's request without considering that I had failed in my job. I've seen how colleagues are treated when they've been demoted."

At this, Holmes barked a laugh. "So rather than lose face, you've come to me."

"In a nutshell, Mr. Holmes, yes. Call it a Christmas favour. Season of Goodwill and all that."

Holmes looked across the room at me. I wasn't certain if he was seeking my opinion or not. The embers of the fireplace reflected in his eyes. I nodded to him, regardless, and he nodded back his affirmation. He wouldn't pass up the challenge.

Meanwhile, Athelney Jones continued. "In all honesty, I don't think even you can solve this one. I swear that ring isn't within the property. My men have stripped and searched every inch of it. And every person too. If it has actually been stolen, then without considerable good fortune, I fear it's a lost cause."

"What time in the morning are they expecting us?" I asked.

Jones rubbed a hand across his mouth. "That's another thing, gentlemen," he said. "We have to go there immediately. Tonight."

"By Jove!" I cursed. "Really?"

"Of course," said Holmes. "The inspector was almost certainly released from the house purely to recruit someone more senior or competent, on the proviso that he returned immediately thereafter with said person, and that the investigation recommence with all haste."

Jones nodded. "That is, to all intents and purposes, precisely what happened."

"You have a cab outside?" Holmes asked.

Jones nodded again and attempted in vain to draw another drop of brandy from his glass.

"Excellent! I've no doubt we'll have this sorted and be back home before midnight. Come along, Watson," And he strode purposefully from the room.

The Chatterton-Smythe's London residence in Mayfair was large and grand as one would expect. Even the foggy wash from a nearby streetlamp couldn't hide the fact. As we pulled up outside, I really hoped we wouldn't have to search the place from top to bottom. It had already been undertaken twice, as we knew. I noticed a few curtains twitch and move in nearby windows. Some houses had a tree, specially decorated for Christmas, in their front windows. This leant a spark of seasonal joy to an otherwise cold and overbearing evening.

One of the inspector's constables was on guard outside. He looked beleaguered and spoke in hushed tones with Jones. The inspector nodded and motioned for the constable to allow us entry, before turning to address Holmes and me.

"It would appear Her Ladyship remains in ill-humour. I was expected to return with more haste than I have. We should brace ourselves."

And with that, we climbed the steps and entered.

I'm certain that I can dispense with a detailed description of the luxuriousness we found within. I would never suggest that the houses of titled persons are all alike, but wealth and status affords a commonality, at least, that spares the writer from describing the various comforts and treasures in minutiae – unless, of course, they impact upon the story. These did not, other than being somewhat in disarray, since the house had been searched twice of late.

What I can detail, however – as it is a vision that will remain with me forever – was the thunderous expression on the face of Lady Chatterton-Smythe. She was waiting for us just inside the door. A vision in deep blue crushed velvet, her chestnut brown hair tied up in an intricate bun. Immediately she assaulted poor Inspector Jones for being a useless fool and a blackguard, and not treating the family with due urgency and respect. I will freely admit to feeling very sorry for the inspector, being dressed down publicly like that.

What I will also never forget is the miraculous change that came over Her Ladyship when Sherlock Holmes stepped forward and removed his hat. All at once her face brightened and her manner softened.

"Can it be the young Mr. Sherlock Holmes?"

Holmes inclined his head politely. "Indeed, your Ladyship. It is an honour to serve you. Doubly an honour since you appear to know me."

"My dear young man," she replied, "in my circle we still discuss, with great fondness, the service you did for Lady Carmichael back in seventy-seven. I'm delighted that the inspector's superiors have seen fit to call upon your services for our little problem."

Holmes smiled and inclined his head again. Jones smiled, also, no doubt relieved that he had serendipitously improved matters for himself no end.

Lady Chatterton-Smythe looked at me. "I see you have a valet in your service now, Mr. Holmes."

I tried hard not to express any shock or surprise. Holmes immediately jumped on the confusion and explained who I was and why I was there.

To give Her Ladyship her due, she was as profuse in her apologies as she was thunderous in her criticism. I felt thoroughly welcomed and no more was said on the matter.

We were led through into the sitting room, where Lord Chatterton-Smythe was enjoying a cigar and a brandy in what was clearly his favourite chair, near the grand fireplace. His Lordship was a man of late middle age. His thinning steel grey hair was more than made up for by his prodigious whiskers. I noticed a scar across the back on his right hand as he clasped his glass. He glanced at us from above a pair of half-moon glasses.

Young Miss Chatterton-Smythe – Lavinia – was there also. She was dressed similarly to her mother, but her hair was left loose. Although very much the image of her mother, she'd had the misfortune to inherit her father's prominent front teeth. She could be heard sniffling away into a handkerchief in the far corner, near a splendidly large and grandly decorated Christmas tree.

Her Ladyship instructed the inspector to announce Holmes and me. We bowed civilly to his Lordship.

"Would you care to take a seat, Doctor Watson?" Her Ladyship said, gesturing to my stick.

I thanked her for her kindness and told her I preferred to stand for now.

"You may go," she told Jones, immediately after.

"Go, your Ladyship?" he queried, nervously.

"Yes," she said, gesturing him away with a flapping hand. "Go and interrogate the staff again – find out which one of them has stolen the ring."

"Are we certain that is what has happened?" asked Holmes. "I need the inspector here with me, for now."

Jones's face was a mess of simultaneous relief and nerves.

"It's obvious, Mr. Holmes," Her Ladyship replied. "The house has been thoroughly searched. Twice. It isn't here. One of the staff must have removed it. They might all be in on it, even."

His Lordship spoke up for the first time, interrupting his wife. "I know that's what we thought before, but frankly I don't see how it can have happened. You and Lavinia were there the whole time."

Her Ladyship ignored her husband. "They'll have left it somewhere secret, of course, while they wait for everything to calm down. But you mark my words, Mr. Holmes. We'll have half of London looking out for it. They won't get even a thousandth of what it's worth."

Holmes looked at the inspector, who merely shrugged at him. Then he stepped forward and addressed the room.

"My Lord, your Ladyship, Miss Chatterton-Smythe. I apologise in advance for potentially asking you to repeat information you have already given to the inspector here, but I must beg your indulgence."

His Lordship exhaled a mouthful of cigar smoke and inclined his head, signifying that Holmes should proceed.

"The signet ring is very valuable, I am told."

"Diamond-studded gold," His Lordship stated.

Holmes nodded. "What is its worth, precisely?"

"It was last valued at fifty-thousand pounds – "

My sudden, forced breath drew some looks.

" – and insured accordingly," His Lordship concluded.

"And you are absolutely certain that the ring returned to the house?"

"Yes," muttered Miss Chatterton-Smythe, through her handkerchief. "It seems impossible that anyone could have removed it from my jewellery box. Yet, as Mama says, someone must have."

"My daughter has been unwell since our last society ball, Mr. Holmes," Her Ladyship advised, placing a motherly hand on her daughter's head. "Until yesterday morning, when the ring was found to have disappeared, she had taken to her bed. The jewellery box resides in her chamber."

"I see. And her nurse?"

"I tended to her myself, Mr. Holmes," Her Ladyship replied. "A mother's prerogative."

"Indeed. No argument from me. So, can I assume that there would have been few, if any, opportunities for anyone to have removed the ring unobserved?"

"None," she confirmed.

"And therein lies the mystery," sobbed poor Miss Chatterton-Smythe.

Holmes slowly turned to Athelney Jones, sweeping his eyes around the room as he did so. "The ring remains somewhere within this house, Inspector."

Jones held out his hands, in a helpless gesture. "But we've taken the house apart. There's nowhere it can be."

"Have you checked the drains?"

"Yes," the inspector coloured somewhat at being openly interrogated by Holmes. "As far as we can, at least."

"I'm sure you've done your best," Holmes agreed. He then turned to me. "Doctor Watson, a medical view, if I may. Could someone, perhaps, have swallowed the ring?"

"Hoping to regurgitate it later, you mean?"

"That is a possibility, I think you'll agree."

Agree I did, although I stated that I thought it a very dangerous endeavour. "It has the potential to cause severe discomfort to an individual and isn't guaranteed of success. Further, an item of that size could get lodged anywhere within the oesophagus or digestive tract. The diamonds would most likely cause internal lesions and bleeding, which would – "

Holmes held up his hand. "Thank you, Watson," he said. "I'm sure such an act would smack of desperation. I'm not convinced this is the work of an opportunist thief. I just wanted to make sure we had considered all possible angles."

Holmes then wandered over to study the decorated Christmas tree.

"This is quite splendid, I must say."

I saw Mrs. and Miss Chatterton-Smythe glance at each other, no doubt wondering what Holmes was up to.

131

"It isn't at its best," grumbled His Lordship. "Taffy's clodhoppers snuffed out the candles and ripped all the decorations off it this morning. Took half the pine needles with them, too. I had them replace as much as they could while he was off enlisting your help, but they've made rather a hash of it. And I dare not get the candles re-lit until I know the blessed thing isn't likely to go up in flames."

"I'm sure it still looks truly splendid from the street." Holmes checked his eye line. The tree was directly opposite the large front bay window, no doubt framed by it from the outside. The candle-lit decorations would have easily been seen to glitter and sparkle magically from the street. I thought briefly of the others I had seen nearby when we arrived. Holmes indicated some of the hanging charms and sweetmeats. "May I handle them?"

"Feel free," His Lordship agreed.

"Careful, Mr. Holmes," said Her Ladyship. "Some of them are very fragile. And valuable."

He glanced at Lady Chatterton-Smythe. "I'll be gentle – although I suspect if they've survived the fingers of the Metropolitan Police, they are probably hardier than you make out."

I joined Holmes to better see what he was up to. He was gently cupping some of the glass baubles and silver bells in his hand. They clearly were very delicate creations and intricately decorated. They were individually tied to the branches of the tree with small red ribbons.

"What do you make of these, Watson?" he asked.

I told him I thought they were delightful. Decorating a tree for Christmas was not a tradition I had ever entered into. It was mainly the proviso of the wealthy and some charitable organisations.

"And you see how they have been spread out, one to each branch?"

"Presumably so as not to overload the tree in any particular spot," I replied.

Lady Chatterton-Smythe spoke up again. "Could we return to searching for the ring, Mr. Holmes?"

He glanced at Her Ladyship. "Oh, but I am, your Ladyship." Then he turned to Lord Chatterton-Smythe. "And I believe I have found it."

His Lordship was immediately on his feet. "What the blazes – ?"

Inspector Jones was similarly at our side in an instant.

Holmes stepped back a pace from the tree. "Look at these small branches. The baubles and bells are all very light and delicate, so they hang without causing the branches to strain or bend significantly. The gingerbreads and sweetmeats, however, are slightly heavier and cause some of the branches to flex." He pointed to one branch in particular. "But if we look here, we have a branch that is flexing considerably, but with only a bauble hanging from it. So, either the branch is weak or broken, or the bauble is heavier than the others."

Lord Chatterton-Smythe uttered a curse. The ladies held a hand to their mouths in surprise.

Holmes very gently lifted the ribbon from the branch, which sprang back, shedding some of its pine needles in the process. He placed the object in my hand. It was clearly considerably heavier than the others. Taking it back, he examined the top of it. There was a metal clasp with a loop, from which to tie the ribbon. With some slight encouragement, this clasp popped off, revealing an opening into the hollow ball. And within, along with plenty of cotton wool to prevent it from rattling, was the missing signet ring.

"Amazing!" announced His Lordship.

"I noticed it almost as soon as I entered the room," Holmes said. He walked over to Miss Chatterton-Smythe and handed her the ring, Then, he turned to Athelney Jones. "You can release the staff, now, Inspector, and send your men back to the Yard."

"In fairness, I think they'll be going home, Mr. Holmes," Jones replied. "It's been a long day." Relief was evident in his face.

Lord Chatterton-Smythe held up a hand. "Hang on, though. There's still the mystery of how the ring got there bauble in the first place."

Holmes let out a long, low breath. "Are you going to tell him . . . Lady Chatterton-Smythe?" He turned to look her squarely in the eye. "Or shall I?"

Miss Chatterton-Smythe burst into tears and immediately fled from the room. Her Ladyship remained seated but seemed to sink further into her chair, raising a hand to support her brow.

"Go, please, all of you," she said, her usually firm voice breaking at the edges. "This is now a private matter that must remain within these four walls. I thank you, Mr. Holmes, for your perspicacity. Inspector Jones, I feel I should apologise for some of the treatment I have given you and your men."

I glanced at Athelney Jones in time to catch his reaction. The fact that it was only *some* of the treatment for which Her Ladyship was apologising clearly did not sit well with him. I took him by the shoulder and guided him swiftly from the room. Holmes followed close behind.

"We will see ourselves out," I called back, "and you may rely on our confidentiality."

"Speak for yourself, Doctor Watson," grumbled the inspector as Holmes closed the sitting room door behind us.

"Never mind that now," I said. "Let's just do as we need. Release the staff from their rooms, get them back to their daily tasks, and then the rest of us can go home." I checked my pocket watch. "To bed," I added.

Holmes looked at me and smiled. "I told you we'd be done with this and home by midnight, Watson, didn't I?"

It was some days into the New Year before we saw Inspector Athelney Jones again. He called on us to say that he had received a commendation, following a letter sent to his superiors at Scotland Yard. The correspondence was regarding his diligent and efficient handling of the recent case. It was on paper crested with the family coat-of-arms and signed by both Lord and Lady Chatterton-Smythe. There was a post-script, stating that following the distress of the incident, the family would be retiring to their country seat in Buckinghamshire.

"Well done, Inspector," said Holmes.

I congratulated him also and handed him a celebratory drink.

"Thank you both," he replied, "although I'd be lying if I said I wasn't still put out about the treatment I received at the time."

Holmes finished his own drink and wandered over to his desk. "Think of it as a test of character."

I could see that Jones wasn't convinced.

Holmes removed an envelope letter and held it up. "I should, perhaps, mention that I, too, received a letter."

This was news to me. He opened it and scanned his eyes down the page.

"Her Ladyship thanks me for my attendance at such an awkward hour, *etcetera*, *etcetera*. Further, she advises that should I ever need a letter of recommendation upon any endeavours, she would be more than willing to provide one."

Jones nodded. "Very generous, I'd say."

Personally, I felt it was the least she could do, since she had deliberately wasted all our time. We hadn't offered Jones a seat, but he took one anyway, indicating he felt there was more to be said on matters.

"What else can we do for you, then, Inspector?" I enquired.

He waggled a finger at me. "I still want to know what was going on in Mayfair. With the hidden ring. Was it a family game gone awry?"

I looked at Holmes. In all honesty we had barely spoken about the affair ourselves since.

"Are you aware what Lord Chatterton-Smythe is worth, Inspector?" Holmes asked.

Athelney Jones shook his head. "More than me, I know that much."

Holmes stepped to the window as he continued to speak. "I know that the family's fortunes have reportedly been on the wane for some time now. You yourself commented to us that the family retained very few serving staff. I suspect His Lordship was hoping for a favourable match for his daughter to assist matters with creditors."

"I see," said the inspector, nodding sagely. "Shame about the teeth. No reason to play daft pranks with family heirlooms, though."

Holmes raised a pointed digit. "And there, my dear Inspector, you are completely wrong. Consider, perhaps, that financial matters were quickly coming to a head. Also, that it was clear that the young miss, and her prominent teeth, weren't yet going to obtain a favourable match. Now, should the signet ring be confirmed by the police as lost or stolen without trace, the family could have claimed the value on insurance. Fifty-thousand pounds, remember? I have no doubt that would have resolved any immediate issues for the family and allowed them to keep up a pretence in society."

"Insurance fraud?" Jones was appalled. "By the titled high and mighty?"

I admitted to being rather unimpressed, myself. "But the ring would have to remain hidden ever after – or at least for a very long time," I pointed out.

"I agree," said Holmes, "but no doubt it was considered a justifiable sacrifice for long-term relief."

"I can't comprehend wearing a piece of jewellery of such value anyway," I said. "I'd be forever on my guard. I'd never relax."

Jones frowned. "So the family were all in on it, but not the staff?"

"Oh no, Inspector. I wish you would use your eyes, man." Holmes was easily annoyed where Athelney Jones was concerned.

Jones's face creased with frustration, but before he could vent forth, Holmes continued.

"You must have seen the way Her Ladyship and young Lavinia behaved. His Lordship, however, was completely in the dark, and would no doubt have remained so until after he had claimed the insurance money. No. Miss Chatterton-Smythe was ill, as stated, and Her Ladyship nursed her back to health. While they were in the room together, I imagine they talked over the financial situation and came up with the scheme between them. It was hardly the ingenious work of a criminal mastermind, after all. But if successful, they'd improve the family finances. And without direct knowledge by, or involvement from, his Lordship."

Holmes paused to light his pipe before continuing.

"So, Her Ladyship removed the ring from the jewellery box and concealed it within the decoration. Doubtless the family had owned it for several years, and one on which they knew the ribbon cap could be easily loosened. My discovery of the ring meant that Lady Chatterton-Smythe had to come clean about the whole affair with His Lordship. Hence young Lavinia running from the room and us being asked to leave immediately. Hence, also, the letters we received. And hence, further, the family leaving London. It would not surprise me to find that in the next few weeks, the house in Mayfair is put up for sale."

"I see," said Athelney Jones, when it was clear that Holmes had finished his summing-up. He sniffed and rose from his seat. "Well, thank you for that, Mr. Holmes. I think I'd better leave you to your day."

"Indeed you had, Inspector," I said, ushering him to the door. "Thank you for dropping by, and well done again on the commendation."

"A happy New Year to you both," he said as I left him in the capable hands of Mrs. Hudson.

I closed the door and turned back to Holmes.

"I can't help thinking we have done Inspector Athelney Jones a greater service than perhaps he deserves," I said – aware that I was being rather uncharitable.

"The man's an imbecile," spat Holmes. "A commendation, indeed. We should have left him to be demoted. And the next time we see him he'll be back to telling us yet again that he knows best."

"Very likely," I replied. "A leopard never changes his spots. And neither, I suspect, does a Welshman!"

Christmas at the Red Lion
by Thomas A. Burns Jr.

The year of 1881 was singular for many reasons. First and foremost, it was the year that I first met the man who was to become my best and most trusted friend, Mr. Sherlock Holmes. After agreeing to share lodgings with him in Baker Street, I learned that he was a consulting detective – a profession unique in the world of crime. He graciously allowed me to participate in one of his investigations – the murders of Enoch Drebber and Joseph Stangerson, which occurred that spring. As my physical condition precluded working more than half-time as a physician, Holmes began to call on me for assistance more and more, until, "Watson, get your hat and stick – the game is afoot!" became a familiar refrain.

Now, as Christmas rapidly approached, we had settled into a comfortable relationship, although I sensed that it had become a bit strained of late. Holmes had been injured in a recent case, which limited his mobility. We had originally agreed to share lodgings because neither of us had kith nor kin in England, but while Holmes was largely content to burrow in and hibernate during the Yuletide, I found myself growing melancholy and restless as the holiday neared. Even in Afghanistan, I had my comrades-in-arms with whom I could celebrate the season. Our landlady, Mrs. Hudson, had informed us that she would leave us a cold supper for Christmas Day whilst she was off with relatives, which I counted as a poor substitute for Christmas feasts I'd experienced in past days. When I suggested to Holmes that some modest decoration of our sitting room would not be amiss, he pooh-poohed the idea saying, "The twenty-fifth of December is just another day." He thereupon went back to the study of one of those abstruse subjects of which he was so fond, lounging on the sofa amidst a pile of books and papers, which I was sure he was going to set ablaze with his constantly smouldering pipe.

Sitting in my chair, vainly trying to become interested in the morning paper, my heart leapt as I heard our landlady's tread on the stairs, followed by a knock at the door. "Come in, Mrs. Hudson!" I cried. Seeing that she bore a silver tray with a business card, a frisson of joy coursed through me. A client! Surely this would exorcise the demons from my soul. She moved to the sofa and offered the card to Holmes.

Holmes plucked the card from the tray and examined it half-heartedly. After a moment, he said, "Tell them I'm otherwise engaged, Mrs. Hudson."

No! "Surely these people must be in some imminent distress if they wish to consult you this close to Christmas," I said.

He regarded me with a half-smile, which suggested that I had confirmed a deduction of his. He said to the landlady, "Oh very well, we'll give Dr. Watson an early Christmas gift. Let's have them." Mrs. Hudson nodded in acquiescence and went downstairs. Holmes rolled into a sitting position, shuffling his papers off the couch onto the low table in front of it, giving me an accusatory look that spoke volumes: *I'm doing this for you*, it said. "Bring two chairs near the fire for our guests," he ordered, and I hastened to do his bidding.

In a minute's time the door opened again and the landlady showed a couple into our sitting room. I rose from my chair, but Holmes remained seated. Our gentleman caller was tall and stocky, about thirty years old, wearing a black, double-breasted greatcoat and a fedora against the cold. He had dark hair and a handlebar moustache. The lady was attractive and somewhat younger, with brown hair peeping beneath a wool hat, a pert nose, and red-rimmed eyes. She was clad in a cloth overcoat with fur on the lapels and 'round the collar.

Mrs. Hudson took their coats and hats. The gentleman offered his hand to me.

"Hugh Jasper," he said, "and this is my wife, Trinity." I took his hand and nodded to his wife. With the overcoat gone, it was quite obvious that she was with child.

"I'm Dr. Watson, and this is Mr. Sherlock Holmes." Holmes nodded laconically, still not rising to greet his guests. "Would you care for coffee, chocolate, or tea to remedy the morning chill?"

"Anything hot will be welcome," answered Jasper. I nodded to Mrs. Hudson, and she left the room.

"You'll pardon me for observing that you have an unusual given name, Madam." I said.

"My father was a churchman, Doctor. All of us children were christened with such names."

Jasper appeared to be somewhat put out as he addressed the detective. I hoped it wasn't because of my remark. "You were recommended to me by Arthur Bathgate, Mr. Holmes."

"Yes," said Holmes. "I handled a trivial matter for him, regarding a less-than-honest servant. But what has happened to mar the joy of the season for a watchmaker and his wife?"

As many do when surprised by one of Holmes's deductions, Jasper started. "However did you know how I make my living, Mr. Holmes?" he asked. "Did Arthur inform you I was coming to consult you?"

"No, Mr. Jasper. Your squint, your monocle, and your long, thin fingers provide ample evidence of your profession. But please be seated and tell me what brings you here on a cold Monday morning?"

Before sitting, Jasper withdrew an envelope from an inside pocket and handed it to me. "This arrived in the morning post along with our Christmas cards."

It was addressed to *Mr. Hugh Jasper, 41 Great Windmill St., SW1*. I handed it over to Holmes, who extracted a folded paper from inside. He sniffed it, made a face, then unfolded it and held it up to the light streaming in the window. Handing the contents to me, he said, "A typewriter can be as distinctive as handwriting, but that is of help only if one can find the individual machine."

The note was indeed typewritten. I read:

The child that Trinity Jasper carries is a bastard.

I offered the letter back to Jasper, but he turned his face away as if I held a foul thing. "It shouldn't be necessary to say that that accusation is a vile canard," Hugh Jasper averred. "However, I was prepared to let it go uncontested until I arrived at work this morning."

"What happened to change your mind?" asked Holmes.

"My employer, Mr. Peter Burkmeier, has a shop in the Strand. He approached me with a note similar to this one, which he said he received in this morning's post. It alleged that I was unhappy with my position in his shop because he paid me insufficiently."

"Is that true?" Holmes asked. "What was Mr. Burkmeier's reaction?"

Jasper's eyes dropped to the floor. "I suppose few workmen feel that they are receiving proper compensation for their efforts. As to his reaction – of course I told Mr. Burkmeier that I was perfectly happy with my situation with him. He seemed to believe me."

"And to whom, besides your wife of course, have you expressed such displeasure?" Holmes asked. "Any co-workers?"

"Oh, I don't know!" replied Jasper in an exasperated tone. "It isn't like I go round telling my troubles to every Tom, Dick, and Harry I meet in the street. And I do know better than to air my grievances at work."

A knock came at the door and I rose to admit Mrs. Hudson, who was bearing a tray containing a silver tea service. She placed it on our dining table and served everyone.

After she had departed, Holmes said, "I'm at a loss, Mr. Jasper. What exactly is it that you would have me do for you? Identify who sent these missives? Typically, poison pen writers are erstwhile friends or acquaintances, usually women, who take umbrage with the subject of their persecution, which they assuage by sending their hateful letters. Fortunately, their bile is quickly spent in most cases, and the vitriolic messages cease. In this case, I fail to see much benefit to you from identifying the writer. You couldn't even sue for libel, because one of the allegations is true and the other false one wasn't publicly communicated. I suggest we wait and see if the campaign is continued."

Trinity Jasper spoke up for the first time. "Perhaps Mr. Holmes is right, Hugh. No real damage has occurred."

"I simply cannot have someone going about saying such awful things about you and our child," Jasper said.

"But the deed is done." Holmes said. "The most that could be gained is informing the writer we are on to her, but even that wouldn't prevent her from making future allegations – especially truthful ones." Jasper's expression made it evident that he didn't like what he was hearing. Holmes continued. "Mr. Jasper, have one of these excellent biscuits and finish your tea. Then go home, and you and your wife make a list of all the people you know, thinking about what, no matter how seemingly inconsequential, you may have done so one of them might choose to respond in this way. However, I'll wager that by the time you have finished, the letters will have stopped and you can enjoy a happy Christmas."

Hugh Jasper wasn't the only dissatisfied individual that morning. Holmes placed Jasper's letter on the mantelpiece with his unanswered correspondence, then went back to his pipe and his papers after the Jaspers had departed. I was thus left to wallow in my holiday funk once again. I briefly considered a stroll in Regent's Park, but it was much too cold to subject my war wounds to such conditions. I dallied away the rest of the day reading a newly published novel by Wilkie Collins, *The Black Robe*, which I found exceedingly long-winded. It had a rambling plot about a scheming Jesuit seeking to deprive a man of his ancestral home by converting him to Catholicism. I was glad to put it down and retreat to my upstairs bedroom as darkness finally fell.

When I awoke, my fire consisted of only a few dark coals. My bedchamber was damp and chilly, which doubtless accounted for the pain in my wounds and joints. Arising, I lighted a candle and looked out my window. The back yard was shrouded in darkness, but the glass was coated with tiny droplets that swelled and ran into each other as I watched. Knowing there would be no more sleep for me, I donned my dressing gown over my pyjamas and made my way downstairs. As expected, Holmes hadn't arisen. I put a couple shovels full of coal on the fire and rang for Mrs. Hudson to bring coffee. God bless the good woman – she promised me an early breakfast within half-an-hour.

The church bells were ringing half-eight when Holmes arose. He went immediately to the sofa and his papers, and I rolled my eyes to the ceiling as I contemplated another day like yesterday. Then the downstairs bell sounded, momentarily followed by Mrs. Hudson's rap upon our door. "Come in!" I cried, and she did, bearing a folded paper on a silver tray, which she immediately offered to Holmes.

"Ha!" he ejaculated. "The plot thickens!" He flipped the paper to me as he rose and made for his room. "If your constitution will allow, I would appreciate your assistance this morning."

It was a wire posted from Soho. it ran:

Scotland Yard here. For God's sake come at once.

H. Jasper

"Obviously dashed off in a great hurry, since he neglects to inform us where "here" is. I think we can safely assume he's at home in Great Windmill Street. Get dressed, Watson! Our client awaits!"

We threw on our clothes, greatcoats, and hats, and Holmes took up his cane on the way out the door. I felt distinctly better as our hansom rattled through the streets, even though the cold drizzle hadn't abated. Number 41 Great Windmill Street was easily identified, as a constable was posted outside. The Jaspers' rooms were in a four-storey red brick edifice that looked as if it had been built sometime during the previous century. As the officer moved to deny us entry, Holmes mentioned Lestrade's name, and the policeman quickly stepped aside.

Trinity Jasper responded to Holmes's rap upon the door with his cane. "Mr. Holmes, thank God for you!" she cried. "That horrible little man wants to take Hugh away!" She led us to the sitting room in which two great windows overlooked the street. Hugh Jasper sat on the sofa while Lestrade loomed over him like an owl over a mouse. Trinity ran to her husband's side, taking his hand as she sat next to him.

"What has Mr. Jasper purportedly done to deserve your undivided attention, Lestrade?" Holmes asked.

Jasper spoke first. "The inspector thinks that I burned my employer's place of business. But I assure you Mr. Holmes, I did not!"

Lestrade took up the tale. "Somebody threw a paraffin bomb through the window of Mr. Burkmeier's shop in the Strand during the wee hours this morning, Mr. Holmes. This gent here claims he was in bed with his missus at the time, which we both know isn't an alibi at all. And he tells me he can't think of anyone else with a grudge against his boss who would do such a thing."

"But that's where I was!" cried Jasper, his wife nodding vigorously. "I was at Red Lion until closing last night, then I came home to Trinee and we went right to bed."

"And why, pray tell, are you so sure Mr. Jasper did the deed, Inspector?" Holmes asked. "Surely anyone can throw a bottle of paraffin through a window. Is there something else that makes you suspect that my client is to blame?"

"If he's innocent, why did he engage you, Mr. Holmes?" Lestrade answered pointedly.

"Mr. Jasper, may I reveal the details of our engagement to the inspector?" Holmes asked. Jasper nodded, and Holmes told him about the letter that Jasper had received. "I suspect you may have gotten a similar communication, Lestrade?"

Lestrade looked at the floor as he said, "We did receive a letter at Scotland Yard in the first post, which accused Mr. Jasper because he thought Mr. Burkmeier was treating him unfairly."

"Typewritten and unsigned, I'll wager." Lestrade nodded. "I don't suppose you have it with you?" The inspector produced the missive from his coat pocket. Holmes retrieved from his pocket the letter that Jasper had brought to Baker Street yesterday and compared the two. "Look here, Lestrade. See the notch on the top of the lowercase *e*, and how the bow of the capital *J* is flattened on the bottom? It's very likely these two letters were produced by the same machine. Don't you agree this suggests someone else attacked Mr. Burkmeier's establishment and is trying to put the blame on Mr. Jasper?"

"That's a possibility, Mr. Holmes. It's no good saying it isn't. But it's also possible Mr. Jasper engineered this whole scheme to deflect suspicion from himself."

Holmes's face indicated what he thought of Lestrade's suggestion, but he wisely didn't say so. Instead he said, "I'll take the responsibility that Mr. Jasper keeps himself available to you if you have further questions for him. Surely you don't have to separate him from Mrs. Jasper at Christmastime, especially given her delicate condition?"

"Well, if you'll be responsible for him . . . ." Lestrade said.

"Very well, then," replied Holmes. Mrs. Jasper sprang up and raised her arms to embrace Holmes, but he caught her wrists and lowered them to her sides, shaking his head. Lestrade departed after warning our client to remain in the city until further notice.

After the inspector had gone, Holmes addressed Jasper. "Tell me, sir, do you spend considerable time at the Red Lion?"

The client looked at Holmes with indignation. "I do fancy a gill or two after a long day at work, Mr. Holmes, if it's any of your business."

"Oh, I assure you it most definitely is my business, sir. You wouldn't have told any of your fellow drinkers there that you were dissatisfied with your remuneration from Mr. Burkmeier, would you?" Jasper didn't answer, but he didn't have to. His face told the tale. "If you don't mind," Holmes continued, "I would ask you to avoid the Red Lion this evening."

"And why should I do that?"

"Because I would like to visit the establishment myself, and I don't want you to interfere with what I'm trying to do."

Again, Jasper's face revealed that he didn't like it, but Trinity spoke up. "Please Hugh, it's just for one night. I can even go up early and bring you some beer to have here." Jasper nodded his assent.

Back on the street, we found that our cab was gone since we hadn't asked the driver to remain, and a light rain was still soaking the cobblestones. Looking north, I spotted the Red Lion on the corner of Archer Street, dark and empty at this hour of the morning. We walked toward Shaftsbury Street and Piccadilly Circus to find another hansom. My leg began to throb almost immediately, and Holmes seemed to fare little better. Abruptly he stopped and poked at something with his stick. I looked down and saw that it was just a dead pigeon, its feathers darkened from the dirty water flowing in the gutter. The detective raised his head and looked about, then extended his cane to point to another bird lying against the side of a building. "Curious," he said. He stooped and picked up something from the pavement which he placed in a piece of paper that he folded and put in his pocket.

I was rapidly becoming cold, damp, and ill-tempered, and had no interest whatever in the local fauna. "Let us be off to Baker Street, where we can have a late breakfast and some of Mrs. Hudson's excellent coffee."

"Be off, then," he said, and we went on our way.

Several cabs were immediately available when we arrived in Piccadilly Circus. By this time, my leg was throbbing, so I boarded one, but Holmes directed the cabbie to wait. "Indulge me for a moment Watson, if you will." He moved off to the west along Piccadilly. When he returned in a couple of minutes, he gave the cabbie an address in the Strand instead of Baker Street.

"Mr. Burkmeier's watch shop," Holmes replied, no doubt seeing my sour expression. "I don't expect to learn much there, but it's best to leave no stone unturned."

Sadly, Holmes's prediction proved correct. Onlookers crowded the area in front of the establishment even in the rain, drawn to the tragedy as flies to a corpse, which made the shop easy to locate. The storefront was nothing but a burnt-out shell, with ugly black streaks running up the outside of the stone building that housed it. It was a mercy that the entire neighbourhood didn't go up. Holmes shook his head and didn't even bother to get out of the cab. Then, to my surprise, instead of directing the cabbie homeward, Holmes gave him an address in Rathbone Place. When I inquired as to why, his cryptic response was, "You'll see."

Rathbone Place proved to be a seedy area filled with dilapidated tenements built in the previous century. After directing me to wait in the cab, Holmes hopped out and disappeared inside one of them. In a few minutes, he returned with a bulky parcel wrapped in brown paper.

In response to my inquiry, Holmes said, "I have found it useful to maintain several boltholes around the city where I can go during an investigation if I wish to remain inconspicuous. In addition to some non-perishable foodstuffs and a place to sleep, I maintain some useful accoutrements for various disguises there. It would hardly do to turn up at the Red Lion this evening in gentleman's garb if we want to gain the confidence of working-class drinkers, so I have secured us more appropriate clothing."

We waited a couple of hours after the sun went down to strike out for the Red Lion. Holmes had provided a pair of wool trousers, a collarless, long-sleeved white shirt, a wool scarf, and a driver's coat for me, while he dressed in a pullover atop a pair of plaid trousers and two sack coats against the cold. We scuffed up our own shoes, and two flat caps completed our outfits. All of our garments were ill-fitting and none too clean, ensuring that we'd fit in well with the working-class crowd at the Red Lion.

When I asked him what he hoped to accomplish on our foray this evening, he said, "I'm nearly certain that the writer of these hateful missives is well-acquainted with our client, and what better place to become so than the local pub. Our purpose is to meet the Jasper's neighbours and find out what's been transpiring in the area of late. Has anyone else been receiving poison pen letters? But we must be circumspect. If we give the locals the impression that we're spying, they'll shut up like clams on the beach."

We walked to Marylebone Road for a hansom to Piccadilly Circus. "I'd prefer to have the driver drop us further from the Red Lion than that," said Holmes, "but I fear that neither of us is up to a longer walk on such a cold evening." Indeed, the temperature hung just above freezing and snow flurries were starting to swirl around us as we embarked on our night's adventure. By the time we alighted, the snow was beginning to adhere to the cobblestones, and I wished I had brought a stick as Holmes had done, but mine were much too fine and would clash with my workingman's outfit.

As we turned the corner from Shaftsbury Road, the Red Lion, which occupied the corner of Great Windmill Street and Archer Street across from Ham Yard, was a glowing blue-and-gold beacon of comfort amidst the whirling snowflakes. Indeed, there is nothing that bespeaks *home* to an Englishman more than a good old pub. I know it was what I missed most whilst in Afghanistan. The public house is as much of a symbol of England as St. George's cross, rare roast beef with Yorkshire pudding, and the White Cliffs of Dover. It is a place where class distinctions fade and camaraderie reigns, where a cabman and a gentleman may converse on equal terms – a place where a man's thoughts and actions are determined solely by himself. Not by his wife, his employer, his minister, or some government functionary. As Holmes pressed the brass latch on the heavy oak door and pushed it open, the warm beery effluvium that inundated us actually brought tears to my eyes. I now knew what the prodigal son felt upon returning to the bosom of his loving family.

Two huge gas chandeliers provided ample light. We passed a parlour on the right as we entered, furnished with stools and small round tables that could hold pints of beer and plates of bread, cheese, and onions. Beyond it, an *L*-shaped oaken bar ran the length of the room with the bottom of the *L* extending into the parlour. A mound of sawdust lay beneath the brass rail at its base, where a drinker could conveniently rest his foot.

There was a row of candles in front of the mirror behind the bar, whose top was festooned with garlands of crimson-berried holly in honour of the season, and a sprig of mistletoe dangled from an overhead beam near the centre of the great room. On the left, a brown-painted wooden bench sat next to the windows looking out on Great Windmill Street, providing ample seating for drinkers weary of standing. The custom was mostly male, though there was one woman acting as barmaid whom I thought to be the landlord's wife, as well as three other ladies whose profession was much older, I fancied. Even though the pub had opened only a quarter-of-an-hour before, nearly two-dozen people now occupied it.

We shouldered our way through the throng and elbowed up to the bar ("Watcher self, matey!"), where Holmes ordered two pints of the best. The landlord plied the large white china handle of the beer engine, filling two mugs held in one ham-sized hand before plopping them down in front of us. "That'll be a tanner gents," he said, and Holmes laboriously counted out three pence in payment for his. The landlord looked to me for the remainder, and I scowled at Holmes as I paid.

Because both of us had game legs, we moved to the side parlour to see if we could find a table. We were in luck. Two chairs were open. As

145

we settled in, a nearby man handed Holmes a hat saying, "The refuge over at Ham Yard is collectin' fer the holiday banquet at the Leicester Soup Kitchen." Both of us tossed in a penny each and passed the hat along. Everyone dug into their pockets to give what they could in the spirit of Christmas until the hat came to a chap in the corner, who held up both hands as if he were warding off evil when it was offered to him. He was a singular-looking fellow, a giant of nearly twenty stone from the look of him. A top hat hovered over his long, fat face, which resembled nothing but a swollen old boot. He was dressed rather better than the rest of the customers, in a maroon frock coat and shiny black trousers.

"C'mon, Horseface, you've got more brass than any of us!" a drinker jibed, only he didn't refer to the gentleman as *Horseface*, but rather something more profane that rhymed with it. "If youse don't pony up," said another, "we won't let youse play Father Christmas on Saturday night." That comment evoked a round of derisive laughter, which caused the redoubtable Horseface to spring up suddenly, tipping his drink over as well as a couple of the others.

"Oi mate, yer payin' fer that!" shouted an outraged lush, but the big man ignored him as he parted the crowd like the Red Sea on his way out the door, muttering curse as he went.

"A cheerful fellow," said Holmes to no one in particular.

"Aye, 'e's a rum 'un, Mr. Throckburton is," agreed a patron. "Thinks 'e's a toff, 'e does. Don't know why 'e 'angs around wit' our lot."

Holmes crooked a finger, and I leaned in close. "Let's split up, old man, cover more ground. Remember, be circumspect." Holmes arose and moved toward the great room, leaving the table to me. Another chap slid into the vacant chair, saying, "'Aven't seen you 'ere before, matey. Now, d'ye follow football?" I said that I did, and we were soon embroiled in a spirited discussion about the recent defeat of Kensington by St. Patrick's Rovers at Turnham Green. Later, the talk turned to the railway tragedy in the Finsbury Park tunnel in North London the previous Saturday.

"If it was me was in charge," averred one worthy, "I'd 'ang that signalman up in Piccadilly Circus!"

"Gan wit' yer!" said another. "Don't blame the poor hunks of a signalman. 'E's just a workin' stiff like us. Them tracks ain't enough fer all them trains that runs on 'em, and the bluidy gov'ment won't come up wit' the brass to build more."

Oftentimes it seemed as if things would come to blows, but somehow, magically, that never transpired. Before I knew it, time was called and I was shaking hands with all of my new friends prior to meeting Holmes out on the street.

146

"Well, what have you discovered?" asked Holmes as we hustled off in search of a cab.

"Other than that Kensington is poorly coached and the budget for the Underground is in sore need of an increase, not much," I told him.

"Perhaps you should be a bit less circumspect next time." Holmes said, not unkindly.

"And what have you learned?" I asked him.

"That the Jaspers weren't the first people in the neighbourhood to receive poison pen letters. Last spring, a family moved out of the area after a man was accused of a questionable relationship with his stepdaughter. That's further evidence that our miscreant is a local."

By the time we arrived back at Baker Street, three pints of beer and two treks through the snow had me totally fagged.

"I shall do some more investigating on my own tomorrow," said Holmes. "Given your delicate condition, you had best take the day to recover."

I must confess that I felt somewhat annoyed by Holmes's solicitude, but I realized that he was correct. Overall, I was much stronger than I had been earlier that year. However, the effects of my trials in Afghanistan still weighed upon me. I slept in until ten the following morning, waking to find blue skies outside my window and the previous night's snow but a frosty memory. Mrs. Hudson informed me that Holmes had departed before the sun rose, again clad in workingman's clothes. I lingered over breakfast, reading *The Morning Post* and Mr. Dickens's *Daily News* cover-to-cover before falling asleep again in my chair over Verne's *Giant Raft*. I hadn't been awake but fifteen minutes when Holmes returned, just as the sun was going down.

"Well, how did it go?" I asked him.

"I've been shadowing our client's wife, Trinity Jasper, as she went about her daily chores. It appears that someone else is also interested in her peregrinations."

"Who, pray tell?"

"That is unclear, although I have my suspicions. I noticed a four-wheeler, its windows heavily curtained, ambling along in her tracks. When I approached it closely enough to see the number plate, I found it didn't have one. However, either the driver or the passenger must have noticed my interest, because it suddenly sped away." Holmes continued, "I also heard a rumour on the street that the fire-bombing in the Strand was contracted, but no one seems to know by whom. Tomorrow, I shall cast my net wider."

I rang the landlady for supper whilst Homes repaired to his room to eradicate all vestiges of the labourer from his person. We were just lighting post-prandial pipes after a leisurely meal when we heard the front bell, followed by rapid footsteps on the stairs. Our door burst open without even a knock and Inspector Lestrade stood on the threshold.

"I thought you'd want to know," he said. "Your client Hugh Jasper was waylaid by a gang of toughs on his way home from the Red Lion. He's been rushed to Barts."

Holmes's expression was incredulous. "What? Of course! The pigeons!" He looked to me. "Get your hat and coat. We're off to Barts."

Lestrade had a four-wheeler waiting downstairs, anticipating that Holmes would want to be away as soon as he heard the news. We clattered off for a quick trip because the streets were largely empty due to the cold. On our arrival, we found our client in a ward, unconscious. Mrs. Jasper was there, her face a portrait of anguish as she sat by his bedside, holding his hand.

Holmes approached her. "Madam, I am so sorry," he said. "I should have foreseen this."

How could you have? I thought.

"It wasn't your fault, Mr. Holmes," she said.

"Would you mind terribly moving aside, so Dr. Watson can examine your husband?"

She complied. A bandage on Jasper's forehead concealed a nasty gash which was doubtless responsible for his present state. He had other bruises and abrasions on his face, arms, and legs, but these looked to be mostly superficial and would cause nothing more than some aches and pains for a day or two. I said as much.

"How serious is the head wound?" Holmes asked.

I piloted him away from his wife, who had returned to her husband's side, before answering. "It's hard to say. It's likely he hit a kerbstone when he fell. It could be life-threatening if the skull is fractured, or he could awaken in the morning with nothing more than a headache. The next twenty-four hours should tell the tale."

Holmes entreated Mrs. Jasper to go home, but she refused. "I don't want him awakening all alone in a strange place," she said. I told her that it was likely he wouldn't awaken for several hours, but she was adamant.

"Very well," said Holmes. "But if you decide to leave, I want you to send for me so that I may accompany you. Your tormentor seems to have dangerously escalated his campaign. I don't want you injured as well."

"I will, Mr. Holmes", she promised.

On the morning of December 22nd, I rose at dawn to find an icy fog hanging over the city. As she said she would, Mrs. Jasper had sent Holmes a message the previous night when she was ready to return home, and he had escorted her without incident. We had just settled down to breakfast when Mrs. Hudson admitted a lad of twelve or thirteen, clad in layers of ill-fitting garments to protect him against the cold.

"Ah, Wiggins!" Holmes greeted him. "You have my thanks and Mrs. Hudson's for obeying my wishes that you leave your comrades behind on these visits." Wiggins was the leader of a gang of street Arabs dubbed by Holmes as *"the Baker Street division of the detective police force"* who often assisted him when information had to be gleaned from the streets. "You will have heard of the arson attack in the Strand?"

Wiggins nodded. "Yes, Mr. 'Olmes."

"Rumour has it that it was bought and paid for. And there was a second attack on a gentleman in Great Windmill Street last evening, which also may have been contractual. I want you and your minions to see if you can discover who the perpetrators were." Holmes removed a bag of coins from his pockets. "The pay scale is as usual: A shilling a day, with a crown for the individual who discovers what I want to know. If you can discover who hired this business done as well, there's a sovereign in it for you." The boy's eyes widened at that – a sovereign was more money than he saw in months.

"Time is of the essence," Holmes continued. "Report to me every morning whether you have results or not."

He handed the money to Wiggins, who said, "Aye-aye, sir," then turned on his heel and dashed out of the room.

"If he brings such energy to his future endeavours, that boy cannot help but rise above his station," said Holmes. "Now there is nothing to do but wait. Fortunately, I have a little monograph in preparation that requires my attention."

A couple of hours later we received another visit from Mrs. Jasper. "I'm on my way to hospital to sit with my husband," she said. "I received this in the first post today and thought you should see it right away." She held out an envelope to Holmes, who took it and removed a sheet of paper.

Opening it, he said, "Hmm. Same typewriter." He read aloud:

You are free now. Your lying husband got what he deserved. I will come to you soon.

"What does that mean – '*I will come to you soon*'?" asked the lady, her voice trembling.

"It means that I will dismiss your bodyguard that I'd arranged and be traveling to Barts with you myself, and that I will see you safely home when you are ready," Holmes said. "Watson, please remain here and take the report from Wiggins should he return."

149

After Holmes and Mrs. Jasper had departed, I tried in vain to interest myself in my newspapers and books, to no avail. The poison pen writer's last message indicated that the case had taken an ominous turn, and I feared for my friend's safety, as well as the lady's.

It was sunset before Holmes returned. I inquired of our client's health.

"Much the same," said Holmes. "The doctors don't know *when*, or even *if*, he will awaken."

"If a good and a poor outcome are equally probable, we must maintain a positive outlook," I said.

"Good old Watson!" said Holmes. "If optimism was a remedy, you could work miracles."

"Sometimes it is, old man, sometimes it is."

It was Friday morning, the twenty third of December, before Wiggins graced us with his presence again. He stood before Holmes with his hat in his hands, a dejected expression, looking at the floor – a clear indication that he and his mates had been unsuccessful.

"I don't expect miracles, Master Wiggins. Perhaps you should just tell the lads to give it another day," Holmes said.

The boy continued to study the carpet. "I don't think that will do much good, Mr. 'Olmes. They already done their best."

Holmes looked at Wiggins with an odd expression. "I'm sure they have," he said. He hesitated, then continued, "Come, Wiggins. What's really the matter?"

"Ain't nuthin' the matter, sir. We just failed youse, that's all."

Holmes was silent for a moment more, then, "I don't believe that you did fail me. I think that you succeeded. It was some of your mates that attacked Mr. Jasper, wasn't it, Wiggins? And who threw the paraffin bomb?"

Now Wiggins gazed straight at Holmes, fear shining in his eyes. "How do you know that?" His voice shook.

"Aside from his head wound, which he likely received when he fell, the rest of Mr. Jaspers's injuries are superficial, consistent with the theory that he was waylaid by a group of young boys. Who were they Wiggins? Anyone in my employ?"

"I ain't no snitch," Wiggins said.

Holmes seemed to consider carefully before speaking. "All right then. If you won't reveal who the perpetrators were, how about the person who hired them? He isn't one of your mates too, is he?"

"Naw, he ain't." said Wiggins. "But I don't know 'is name. All I knows is that 'e lives at the Albany."

150

The Albany was an exclusive set of bachelor apartments not far from Piccadilly Circus.

"Can you describe him?"

"I ain't never seed 'im. I just know that he pays some of the lads to do little jobs fer 'im, like you do."

"But I don't pay you to break the law, do I, Wiggins?"

"Nossir."

"Very well. You tell your mates that if Scotland Yard and I have to come looking for them, we will find them, you know. We can't have them burning down buildings and attacking people in the streets. When we do find them, they will suffer the full penalties prescribed by the law. Of course, if they were to turn themselves into me, perhaps some arrangement could be made . . . ."

"I'll tell 'em, Mr. 'Olmes." Holmes held out a coin. "And youse don't need to pay me. I didn't do nuthin' fer youse. "

After Wiggins departed, I asked Holmes, "So now what will you do?"

"Go to the Albany, of course," he said. "And I have a pretty good idea who I'm going to find there."

It was Christmas Eve, and snow was falling in earnest as I walked up Great Windmill Street towards the Red Lion. After returning from his sojourn to the Albany the day before, Holmes had spent the balance of the afternoon playing with his chemicals or scraping on his fiddle. When I remonstrated that he was no longer working on the case, he told me he had done all that was necessary. He directed me to travel to the Red Lion by myself that night, saying he would join me later in the evening.

The drinkers in front of the place milled about as they waited for admittance. Just as I walked up, the landlord threw the door wide and the crowd surged inside. Chaos ensued for a while as everyone converged on the bar, simultaneously shouting orders, and the landlord plied the handles of the beer engine as fast as he could, sometimes holding as many as four mugs in one hand, until all had been served. An alcoholic yeasty fragrance soon filled the air. Out of the corner of my eye, I caught a glimpse of Lestrade in the crowd, a gill in hand, showing no indication of his profession.

Because I had my back to the door as I endeavoured to garner my pint, I hadn't seen Throckburton enter. However, when I went to the front parlour he was in his usual place, taking service of his libation from the barmaid. I took a seat nearby and waited for the night's performance to begin.

It wasn't long before the front door opened and Holmes entered, clad in the foppish finery of a workingman masquerading as a toff, with Trinity

151

Jasper on one arm and his cane hanging from the other. Her hair was done up high with jewels twinkling between the strands and a green garland around her brow, and she was resplendent in Christmas attire: A floor length crushed velvet skirt in emerald green with a matching hooded top, worn over a white blouse with a ruffled front under a red tartan vest. She resembled anything but a wife disconsolate over her husband in hospital. The festive couple approached a table and Holmes glared at the occupants, who immediately rose to offer the fine lady and her escort a seat. The barmaid came and took their order, returning quickly with a pint for Holmes and a bottle of stout for the lady.

I took an opportunity to glance at Throckburton – that worthy sat like a statue, glaring at the pair with obvious venom.

Holmes drained a quarter of his glass with a generous swig and banged it down on the table.

"Cor!" he hollered. "Wot sort o' a pub is this? Ain't ye got no music on Christmas Eve?"

In short order one man brought out a squeezebox and another a fiddle, and they struck up "God Rest Ye Merry Gentlemen". The crowd eagerly joined in singing, with Holmes's vibrant baritone soaring above all. "Hark the Herald Angels Sing" and "Good King Wenceslas" quickly followed. When the musicians segued into a lusty rendition of "Landlord Fill the Flowing Bowl", Holmes stood and took Mrs. Jasper by the hand, pulling her into a gay dance. Several other enterprising wights snatched up the ladies of the evening and joined the fun, while the barmaid retreated to safety next to her husband behind the bar. Holmes still had his cane hanging from an arm, but as he danced, his leg showed little sign of infirmity. When the song was done, Holmes steered Mrs. Jasper under the mistletoe, puckered his lips and leaned forward to perform the traditional Christmas ritual.

"Fer the love of God, no!" bellowed Throckburton, springing up and overturning another table full of drinks. Enraged, he charged Holmes, who spun Mrs. Jasper behind him and stabbed at the big man's diaphragm with his cane. Throckburton grabbed the stick with both hands, intending to pull it out of Holmes's grasp, but Holmes slapped his hand down on Throckburton's, locking his thumb to the stick, and rotated it up and around, carrying his attacker's arm with it and spilling him onto the floor.

"Not so easy when you're not hiding behind a poison pen, is it now?" Holmes taunted.

"Ye should of listened!" Throckburton yelled at Mrs. Jasper as he struggled to his feet. "I would have taken you away from that lout. 'E isn't worthy of ye!"

Wary now, the giant threw a right at Holmes, his left ready to block the cane if Holmes swung it at his head, but the detective slapped the punch away with his arm and brought the stick up between Throckburton's legs instead, simultaneously stomping down on his foot, pinning it to the floor. Holmes then twisted the cane against the immobilized leg, buckling both of his adversary's knees. There was an audible snap as Throckburton tumbled to the floor once again. This time he didn't rise – rather he sat there bawling like a baby, both hands clasped around his ruined knee. He gave Lestrade no trouble as the inspector clapped the darbies on, but a couple of constables had to be summoned to carry the big man from the premises.

I sat back in my chair, removed my napkin from around my neck, and sighed. Holmes and I had just finished Mrs. Hudson's cold Christmas supper, and what a fine feast it was! She had provided us with oysters, a cold salad of potatoes, beets, celery, and eggs, and a whole turkey with cranberries. We couldn't even touch the plum pudding with whisky sauce.

Holmes had a wire from Lestrade earlier that evening. After using Throckburton's statements during the fight at the Red Lion to secure a warrant, a search of his rooms at the Albany had turned up a typewriter that proved to be a perfect match to the one that produced the poison pen letters. Additionally, by touting Holmes's unparalleled abilities as a detective, Wiggins had convinced the boys who had fallen under Throckburton's spell to come forward and identify him as the man who hired them to bomb Mr. Burkmeier's shop, and to waylay Hugh Jasper.

"I have a friend in a high position in the government who can doubtless convince the Crown Prosecutor to accept a punishment other than prison for the lads," Holmes said. "A year or two at sea should serve nicely. On the other hand, Mr. Harrison Throckburton has many years of walking the wheel to look forward to."

"When did you know it was Throckburton who sent the poison pen letters?"

"I suspected that the writer was from the Jaspers' neighbourhood from the beginning. I had an inkling that he or she might be dangerous when I saw the dead pigeons in Great Windmill Street on leaving our clients' flat that first day. One dead pigeon is happenstance, two coincidence, but I saw no less than sixteen on our walk from the Jasper residence to Piccadilly Circus. When I left you there to go a little further west, I found more. A wire to Dr. Swithers at the British Museum confirmed that no avian pestilence was currently rampaging throughout London, so why so many dead birds? The answer was obvious – someone was poisoning them. A test of some corn I picked from the pavement

153

confirmed that hypothesis. It contained a fair amount of arsenic. Cruelty to animals has been linked to all sorts of criminal behaviour, so I stored the hypothesis in my brain-attic that those birds just might be victims of our writer.

"It was Throckburton's outburst at the Red Lion Wednesday night that caused me to suspect him. He had all the characteristics of a poison pen: Unattractive, petty, and egotistical. The only contraindication was his sex. Women comprise the majority of poison pen writers. However, the attack on the watchmaker's shop strongly suggested a man might be implicated.

"After Wiggins told me about the involvement of his mates and that the man who hired them lived at the Albany, all it took was a look at the post boxes in the lobby to confirm that one 'H. Throckburton' was a resident there. I could see him in my mind's eye, strolling from the Albany to the Red Lion, a pocket-full of poisoned corn, scattering death in his wake."

I interrupted. "Why would he choose the Red Lion as a place to imbibe if he thought everyone there was beneath him?"

"He was slumming, Watson. His sort craves an atmosphere in which he can consider himself superior to everyone around him. I was certain that the boys would identify him as their employer. Less so that their accusation would carry enough weight to convince the Crown Prosecutor because of the social distance between them and Throckburton. I needed more – I needed that typewriter, which I was sure I would find in his flat."

"So you convinced Trinity Jasper to aid you with that charade at the Red Lion," I finished for him.

"Once I explained the situation to her, she was only too happy to do so. I felt sure that the vile letters were motivated by unrequited lust, and that Throckburton now harboured the insane notion that she might be attainable to him with her husband out of the picture. Incidentally, I had a wire from Mrs. Jasper a while ago that her husband had awakened for a few moments earlier today, which his doctors consider a very encouraging sign. Anyway, I was sure that seeing her with another man who wasn't himself would provoke a strong reaction from Throckburton. You saw that I wasn't mistaken."

"Indeed I did." Knowing Holmes's views about women in general, and seeing his behaviour with Trinity Jasper at the pub, I couldn't resist adding, "It's a shame that she is taken. You two certainly made an attractive couple."

Holmes cocked an eyebrow at me. "I have noted that you evidence a definite strain of pawky humour, Watson. I expect that someday, I will lose you to a wife. Your expression upon seeing the solicitude that Mrs.

Jasper showed to her husband in hospital left no doubt in that regard. Now, it is a peculiarity of many who covet the married state that they expect that everyone else would also be better off married, but I can assure you there are no nuptials in my future. For every happy marriage that you can show me, I can show you one plagued by infidelity, thievery – or murder."

"But don't you think that the joy of the season would be enhanced by the presence of family?"

"For some yes, and for you, certainly, but not me. My work is all I need."

I looked at the small fir tree on the sideboard, hung with gaily coloured bits of paper and cotton wool, which Holmes had finally allowed me to bring into our rooms in honour of Christmas. Even with my good friend beside me, the lack of a family wore heavily on my heart. I only hoped that, for his sake, Holmes was speaking truly.

A Study in Murder
by Amy Thomas

The Christmas holiday of the first year of my acquaintance with Sherlock Holmes was supposed to be an understated affair. Mrs. Hudson had promised us a moderate feast, and Holmes had said he might favor the house with a few holiday airs on his violin. I had notes on a few of my patients I wished to finish and, on the whole, I expected it to be an uneventful, if pleasant, interlude.

That intention was shattered by a loud rapping at the door on Christmas Eve, just as dawn was breaking. I heard Mrs. Hudson stirring, and then her shrill voice, "Mr. Holmes! Dr. Watson! Come at once!"

I threw my clothes across me, too sleep-addled to even imagine what sort of sight might greet me or what reason there might be for such a commotion. Holmes joined me, looking fresh and alert, as we made our way outside the house, to where Mrs. Hudson was on the front stoop.

I rubbed my hand across my face, trying to fully awaken, and noticed a crowd gathering down the street. "Over here, Doctor!" I heard a shout and saw a man beckon.

"He won't need no doctor now," another observed as I made my way over.

As a doctor, I have seen many corpses. As a soldier, even more. I can't claim that the sight shocks me as it might someone of a different profession, but still I didn't expect to see one in the middle of a London street on the morning before Christmas.

"Get the children away from here!" I barked, seeing a few peering at the edges of the group gathered around the body.

To my surprise, Holmes was the one who answered my order. I was dimly aware, as I started my examination, that he was herding the children with surprising gentleness and making sure they returned to their nearby homes.

The corpse looked like a common laborer, in the middle-thirties to middle-forties, not rich but not destitute, judging by his healthy frame and well-kept but unremarkable clothing. His cause of death was imminently obvious from the knife wound that went through his back into the vicinity of his heart and the blood pooling around it. An altogether nasty business, and one, it seemed, that hadn't happened long ago.

"No signs of life," Holmes said quietly, materializing behind me.

"None," I said. "It's your domain now."

He knelt down next to me, oblivious to the crowd gathered around. Fortunately, their horror of the dead kept the direct interference to a minimum, though the crowd continued to look on in amazement and, perhaps, fascination. "The police will be here at any moment to clumsily destroy the evidence," Holmes said. "I have to work quickly."

I hadn't seen many such examinations at that point in time, but I watched Holmes methodically survey the body, then the clothing. He took a few things into a small bag that he had on his person, fabric remnants and a bit of blank paper he'd found in a coat pocket.

Soon the police arrived, led by Inspector Lestrade, whom I hadn't seen in some days. I supposed he'd been called out since the obvious implication was murder.

"Mr. Holmes," he said. "Doctor. Lucky I was close."

"Very," said Holmes, looking up. "Almost lucky enough to indicate you as a suspect." At the best of times, Holmes couldn't resist baiting the man, and this was far from the best of times.

Lestrade didn't seem to see anything amiss in this after all. "So I would be, except that I was having a Christmas pint with my sister, whose house is just two streets over."

"This man has been stabbed," said Holmes, "obviously."

"Yes," said Lestrade, turning to one of his junior officers. "Digsby, make an examination." The younger man nodded in silence and knelt down beside Holmes to make his own findings.

"Digsby is a scientist turned detective," Lestrade said proudly, much as if he were showing a prize hog at a county fair.

"I wonder if he's good at either," Holmes said drily, leading Digsby, who was well within earshot, to look toward him with a grin.

"I haven't your flair for the dramatic, Mr. Holmes," he said, "but I'm methodical."

"If true," Holmes answered, "that would make you valuable beyond the majority of your peers."

"I'll share my findings," Digsby rejoined, "and you can judge for yourself."

Lestrade quickly turned to the crowd, and I heard him take the man's name from a bystander who apparently knew the fellow – Charles Witten. A distant address was then provided, as well as the fact that the man had been married.

"Chartwell," Lestrade instructed another of his young officers, a tall and observant-looking fellow, "go to the man's home and speak to the widow." Chartwell turned and left with a woman onlooker who offered to show him the way. "We've no information yet, but she ought to be told."

A third officer, Williamson, hung about and watched Holmes's investigation before asking the crowd around if anyone had seen anything. Predictably, many thought they had seen something suspicious, but nothing they said led to anything concrete.

Holmes was quick with his work, and without a word, he rose, leaving Digsby still beside the body. "Come, Watson," he said, and Lestrade was left calling after us. My companion paid him no mind. The crowd was fascinated by the corpse, so once we were out of its direct purview, we were no longer a notable attraction.

"What are you about?" I asked.

Holmes didn't answer for a moment. "A fool's errand," he said. "Someone had to have put the man there so close to our door and, judging by the corpse, not long ago. Perhaps there might have been tracks, except that the murderer picked an open street – risky, but with the probable likelihood of drawing a crowd to obliterate evidence more quickly than Scotland Yard." He was frustrated as his steps turned back toward 221, and as soon as we arrived, he seated himself at his chemical table with the evidence he'd collected.

"Harrowing morning," I commented, when Holmes finally looked up that evening.

"Murder always is," he replied, "though I grant you that when bereft children are involved, the thing somehow always seems worse."

I studied the man opposite me. I hadn't known Holmes long before I had detected the peculiar dichotomy of his work and his humanity. He had a remarkable ability to detach himself from human sensibilities at will, then re-engage them when the situation demanded it. I wondered if, should I accompany him on enough of his cases, I, too, would develop this ability, but I strongly doubted it. It appeared to be a peculiar feature of his particular character.

"What are you thinking of?" he asked. "Have you a theory?"

"According to what I heard," I observed, "the man didn't live nearby."

"No," Holmes agreed. "I'm inclined to think he was left near this address on purpose."

I stared at him for a moment. "You think the murderer was trying to signal to you, personally?"

"Perhaps," he answered. I thought this ridiculous, but the longer I thought about it, the less ridiculous it seemed.

Just before ten o'clock, Lestrade sent a summary of Digsby's findings around to Baker Street, and Holmes read through them with interest while he smoked an evening pipe.

I could hear our landlady muttering about Christmas decency as she climbed the stairs, preparing for the morrow and passing the closed sitting room door, while Holmes read off the inventory of Digsby's analysis. "He's forgotten to list the man's missing watch," Holmes said. "He had a chain on him, but the watch itself was missing. Otherwise, however, he's done a surprisingly decent job."

"Killed for his watch?" I asked.

"Doubtful," said Holmes, "though perhaps the murderer would like us to think so. People have been killed for less, but rarely when it would have been so easy to secure the thing another way.

"Who is he?" he finally asked himself. "Who is this man who summarily stuck an unnecessarily large knife in a man's back on Christmas Eve morning."

"Or she?" I asked. I had recently read of the vicious murder of seven members of a household by their affronted maid, and the idea was heavy on me.

"Unlikely," Holmes said. "Women's methods are generally more clever and less direct. Ten female poisoners for everyone who stabs or shoots. Furthermore, it would have taken a strong form indeed to have managed to drive the knife so far into the man's back. We would be looking for a woman of abnormal strength and character. I would rather run down the more obvious leads first. It isn't impossible, but let us call it highly unlikely, at least until other possibilities are eliminated."

I could not deny it – the story I had read was of poisoning. Holmes was in no way reluctant to declare women suspects of any crime he investigated, but I had quickly learned that when he made a quick judgment that ruled out a category of people, he had his reasons.

"I do hope the bereaved family has something for Christmas dinner," I mused as I passed Mrs. Hudson the following morning, suddenly regretting that I hadn't thought of it before.

The lady gave me a strange look. "I forget sometimes how short your acquaintance has been with Mr. Holmes," she said, "and how little you know him." She walked away, leaving me to wonder what she'd meant.

I did some deducing of my own. Holmes had gone out very early and had a cheerful air when he'd returned, empty-handed but exceedingly lively. Was it possible, I wondered, that he had made such a human gesture that hadn't even occurred to me?

"I gather you've made Christmas brighter for the Witten family," I said. After all, I was a doctor, not a detective. I had to ask what I couldn't deduce.

159

"I supplied turkey and side dishes aplenty," he answered readily. "It's hardly reparations, but at least it preserves something for the children."

I was touched by his thoughtfulness. "You're an enigma of a man," I said.

"What you mean," he replied, still in unusual good humor, "is that you didn't expect such a thing of such a calculation machine as I am."

This was closer to reality than I liked to admit. "Something like," I said.

"Even the coldest warm at Christmas, Watson," he said. "And I was once a child who eagerly awaited the day."

I tried to imagine that and found it difficult. In some people, the child is forever evident. Others seem to have been grown up forever, and Holmes, I suspected, had been one of these. A rather silly train of thought, so I consciously abandoned it.

The second of the murders took place on Boxing Day, when Holmes was still in the midst of making enquiries about the first, though he had confided to me his frustration at his lack of progress. The widow of the first had claimed her husband had no enemies, the ephemera Holmes had taken from the body shed no light beyond general observation of habits and character, and Lestrade was, unsurprisingly, of no help.

I wasn't even out of bed before, once again, excessively loud rapping at the door and Mrs. Hudson's shrilly startled voice once again dragged me out of my precious sleep. Again, I met Holmes in the hallway. He was rarely a deep sleeper at the calmest of times, and he looked exactly as I had left him the night before contemplating the first of the atrocities. The only difference was he had changed into his dressing gown, and his hair was unusually mussed.

"I trust you slept well," he said, "for it certainly seems despicable creatures are determined to make sure no one in London has a peaceful holiday." Soon, the idea of creatures would be reduced to one, singular object.

I had rarely seen Holmes so annoyed during our relatively short acquaintance. He didn't normally seem to take cases as personally as he had obviously started to take this one. I hadn't thought he was a particular traditionalist where holidays were concerned, but I saw that he could enjoy a fine feast and good wine as much as any man when he wasn't preoccupied with other matters, and he possessed the ability to be irritated when the privilege to do so was denied him by the perpetrator of a crime.

This time, we were led far away from Baker Street and through some of the most fashionable parts of the city, certainly a stark contrast to the previous incident. I wasn't alone in my apprehension of the strangeness of this, for after a ride of ten minutes, Holmes muttered, "Lestrade had better have a good reason for connecting this murder to the other one and insisting on calling me out."

It turned out, he had. As soon as our conveyance turned into a street filled with imposing houses that seemed to glare down in disapproval, we saw the unfortunate Mr. Ralph Evans lying dead in front of his home in the exact same manner as the previous victim.

It was so obvious as to be unmistakable: The murderer didn't wish to hide his connection to the other case. The man's wound was an identical knife through the back, though his manner of living and social standing couldn't have been more different from his simple predecessor's.

It occurred to me in a mad, inappropriate way that the murderer might be some kind of social equalizer, out to show that poor and rich alike could die by a sharpened knife point. I could tell that my mind was running away with me at the gruesome sight, and I took a deep breath and went over to where Holmes was surveying the corpse, determining to force myself to be professional. Unlike the previous instance, there were few onlookers, save some concerned faces peeking out of windows in the houses around, servants who seemed to be checking the situation to report back to masters and mistresses within.

Holmes looked as intently at the corpse as he had the other one, but he soon stood back up from his perusal. "Exactly the same," he said. "The murderer is insulting the police – and me. He wants everyone to know he's the same man and that he's operating freely under our noses."

"Why here?" I asked.

"To show that no one is safe," he said shortly.

Lestrade had Digsby and Chartwell with him once again, but they were joined by a man called Redding this time, an extremely young policeman who turned white as a sheet when he approached the corpse with his colleagues.

"All right, Redding?" I asked very softly, seeing a need I might fulfill.

"I've – never seen a murdered body up close, Doctor," he said, turning blue eyes on me. "I don't mean to be soft."

"The first time is always difficult," I said, thinking of the first battlefield corpse I had encountered during my service, a very far remove from the cadavers I had examined in medical school or the placid morgue residents I had met as a young physician. There was always something different about corpses created by violent death. I placed a hand on his shoulder, feeling that I couldn't do more without attracting unwanted attention to him. I let go and walked toward Holmes, who was a way off, watching wordlessly.

"I despise self-aggrandizing murderers," he said darkly. "They're often the hardest to catch because they love the sport of it, so there's no grand, unifying motive other than general enjoyment of the thing."

"You think there's no connection between the two dead men, then?" I asked.

"I will be duly diligent to prove the absence of such a connection," Holmes said, "but this doesn't appear like a murder committed for anything other than the pride, and perhaps the enjoyment of the murderer. I've encountered few of this sort, but they're particularly pernicious. The killer might have a type he prefers to kill – I would call that more likely than a meaningful connection between the two men."

"How despicable," I said.

Lestrade had, by this time, begun knocking on doors to find out what anyone from the big, quiet houses on the street might have seen or heard. He tolerated Holmes going along with him, but at his request I stayed behind with the officers and the corpse. He didn't want the affluent people of the neighborhood to be troubled by any more representatives of the law than necessary.

Finally, after an hour, the corpse was taken away, and Holmes accompanied me home, with his notebook full of notes and his head full of ideas and information that he pondered all the way home without speaking.

"It nearly a new year," said Holmes when we finally reached Baker Street. "A year ago, I hadn't expected to find someone to share my rooms who would so perfectly tolerate my conflagrations and complement my work."

"Are you complimenting me?" I asked, both in wonder and amusement.

"That is for you to decide, I suppose," he answered. "Does it take goodness or madness to put up with the likes of Sherlock Holmes?"

I didn't answer his question, and he was immediately back to his notebook, in which he circled some things and crossed out others, seemingly to create a workable timeline of what had happened. I had a medical text in hand, and I read it while I waited for Holmes to speak or not speak, as he would.

"A murderer is a slippery class of being," Holmes mused. "On the one hand, nearly any man or woman is capable, if pushed to an extreme, but only a very few have the capacity – or appetite – to continue doing it more and more, unlikely to stop unless killed themselves or incarcerated."

"Are such people really human?" I asked, more of a rhetorical question than anything, though Holmes answered it.

"Of course they are," he said. "If we call everything we don't understand 'inhuman', we are in danger of coming out with a definition of humanity that is very narrow indeed." I hadn't thought of it like this.

"You, yourself, were a soldier," Holmes said. "The pacifist would see your cause as no different from that of our killer, albeit more officially sanctioned."

I didn't like this train of thought. "Surely there is a difference."

"So there is," Holmes agreed, "though its definition lies in the crossroads of objective truth and subjective experience. It is a thing most people feel, but would be extraordinarily hard-pressed to explain."

"It does feel different on a battlefield when the other man is holding a gun," I commented.

"I have no doubt," Holmes agreed, "though I have no personal experience to support the assertion. You serve as my experiential proxy."

"Going at each other with guns and knives is hardly civilized in its moment," I said, trying not to let overwhelming images barrage my mind, "but it's significantly more so than one man going at another who's unarmed."

"Power," said Holmes. "The killer likes the feeling of power. When you were in Maiwand, you did your duty. It wasn't a pleasure. For this man, it must be, whereas many would be horrified at subjugating another."

He went quiet for a moment before continuing. "I have little doubt we're being taunted, from the difference in the victims' circumstances to the fact that the body found near here was transported after death, while our unfortunate Mr. Evans perished in front of his own house. A repeat murderer might be expected to have a routine – at least, the majority of them do. This is a routine of *not* having a routine. Unpredictable." He said the last word like it was a pejorative of the deepest dye.

"But how did no one see anything?" I asked.

"The killing happened before daylight, supposedly," said Holmes. "No screams or sounds of struggle were heard, likely because the man was stabbed so quickly and with such force. I don't take it as a matter of course that everyone is telling the truth, but such a street isn't one where neighbors pay obvious attention to one another's business."

I hadn't thought until then of how difficult it must be for Holmes to solve puzzles centered around the wealthy and how they lived, locked into their ivory towers. The poor, by necessity, had little such privacy, and might inadvertently produce a myriad of false trails and clues, but this was surely preferable, I thought, to having nothing to go on in the starkly cold halls of the wealthy.

That the third corpse was presented practically on our doorstep was perhaps to be expected, though it irked me that it gave credence to Holmes's surprisingly frivolous suggestion that the murderer was leaving him the puzzles as a holiday gift. Mrs. Hudson, to her credit, didn't faint or flee when she came across the unfortunate gentleman on New Year's Day. She simply stepped back inside and called for Holmes and me.

"Again," said Holmes, once outside and looking down at the young man. Once more, it was cold, and there were signs that death had been at least a few hours earlier. As with the other victims, the wounds appeared to be knife-inflicted, with the primary one in the chest and two more superficial cuts on the arms.

"He fought," I said. "Those extra scratches are from an altercation."

"Just so," Holmes answered, "and unlike our other two. Why, I wonder, did our murderous friend decide to change his method this time?"

"If your theory is right," I replied, "he did it simply to throw you off."

"We're being taunted, Watson," he said. "The killer wants it to be obvious that he's the same man who dispatched the others. He's laughing at me and at the police, from what he believes to be his exalted vantage point." I didn't disagree, but I also didn't voice my impression that the man had reason to feel confidence, for, from what I could see, we were no closer to catching him than we had been on the occasion of the first corpse's discovery.

Lestrade, who took a half-hour to arrive and was his usual blustering self, but I could see real concern on his face. He was envisioning public outrage if a multiple murderer remained uncaught, and he'd begun to think it might really be a possibility. I have read speculation that the police are excited by the attention that comes from major crimes being committed in their jurisdictions. In reality, little is further from the truth, at least as far as Lestrade and his officers were concerned. No self-respecting police office wanted to be saddled with the next unsolved murder that might inflame the city with panic and lurid interest.

"What do you see?" he asked Holmes, with considerably more humility than he had shown previously.

"Much the same as the others, on first glance," said Holmes. "That in itself is a clue."

"Any chance of someone copying the murderer of the others?" asked Lestrade.

Holmes looked up from his perusal of the remains, identified as Michael Evans from documents in his pocket. "That's a surprisingly decent question, and I will pursue the possibility, but the detail is indicative of the same man. An imitator could inflict the same wounds, but would be unlikely to do so with precisely the force or angle needed. Not if he read about it in the papers." Digsby soon materialized, and Lestrade visibly relaxed with his rising star right-hand man by his side.

I was suddenly glad to be unmarried, though I had lamented my singular condition many times. I could not, at the present moment, imagine being responsible for lives other than my own, at a time when it seemed a murderer might strike anywhere in London at any time. All corpses are equal, suddenly, when everything else is stripped away.

"Is there a relationship between the three men?" Holmes asked, once we had returned to our lodgings and he'd had a chance to review all that we'd learned about the victims, including the most recent. "All three were native Londoners, and all three were married. Beyond that, I can find little to connect them. Witten was fifty-eight, Clarke was barely nineteen, and Evans was thirty-one. One was well-to-do, one was a laborer, and the youngest spent his days at public houses and opium dens.

"Perhaps that's the point?" I said. "Might the murderer have particularly looked for victims with no connection to one another?"

"If my theory is correct," said Holmes, "but I'm trying to find deeper connections that may be less apparent than the surface ones before I settle upon it."

"Have you encountered many murderers who murder for the sport of it?" I asked, genuinely curious about how often he had seen such a thing, as we were young men. I had little indication of his former life, and I considered any potential glimpse a gift.

"I have seen it, but rarely," he said shortly. "It's a chilling thing, Watson, to look into the eyes of a man whose only motive is the love of bloodshed. Such killers are extraordinarily difficult to apprehend, as they don't have the traceable motivations of their murderous peers. They exist, however. I have often wondered how many of them are sent off to some far-flung locale to fight for Queen and Country, when otherwise they would be honing their skills on the London streets."

This thought was unpleasant in the extreme, but I considered it. "I suppose men seek out employment that suits their particular interests, even these."

"You dislike the idea," Holmes replied. "I don't blame you. It must be repugnant to one of your sensibilities."

"Not to you?" I asked.

Holmes shook his head. "Not to the same degree. Little of human behavior still holds the power to surprise me, and I expect it will even less as I continue in my present career."

"Do you not wish to understand it?" I asked, wanting to know him better.

"Only as far as understanding the thoughts of the criminal aids in apprehending him or her," Holmes replied. "For purely academic purposes, I have no interest whatsoever. My concern is whether someone is guilty and, beyond that, if they are likely to continue to prove dangerous to those around them."

I couldn't argue with the rationality of this, though it differed sharply with my own need to categorize and analyze things I couldn't comprehend. For Holmes, it was enough that a human being had done a thing. I felt compelled to think over what combination of circumstances both inward and outward might produce such abhorrent behavior. I believe Holmes thought this sort of pursuit a waste of time unless it directly impacted his pursuit, and, for him, it would have been. I, however, couldn't help it. I couldn't let go of searching for reason where none was obvious and explanation in the midst of chaos.

After a while, Holmes seemed pensive, for which I didn't blame him. "A worthy opponent, Watson," he said. "I'd have no qualms at all if he'd chosen to steal money or pilfer jewels. I would gladly enter into a friendly competition. That isn't, however, possible when confronted with three brutally-murdered corpses, complete with grieving wives and bereaved children. I cannot afford to take any longer to find him, lest he continue to strike, particularly since his crimes provide few clues in themselves. They speak more by what they don't show. The killer's lack of mistakes shows an extensive knowledge of the Yard's investigative practices.

"Do you mean to suggest a policeman?" I asked, astonished.

"Not necessarily," he replied, "but someone with access to the knowledge of their methods. Every type of information that I'm normally able to discover in a situation like this seems to be missing – possibly intentionally. Only those who have heard me stress the importance of such evidence, such as policemen, would know where I'd be looking. I suppose that coroners and some in the legal profession might fit the bill as well. It's also possible, though unlikely, that an ordinary man could have sought and found such information – perhaps a relative or friend of a policeman. I will have to create a precise list of likely possibilities. It doesn't narrow the field completely, but it does suggest where we might concentrate our efforts."

"I don't suppose you're suggesting that Lestrade is genuinely a suspect?" I ventured, thinking through the past few days. "He has, after all, attended each case and is heavily involved in the investigations."

Holmes threw back his head and laughed. "Thank you, Watson," he said after a few moments. "I haven't had as good a laugh as that for some time. Lestrade may be many things, but a murderer isn't among them, nor does he possess the capability to carry one out with such cunning as these."

"Very well," I said, slightly annoyed. "I don't know him as well as you do."

Holmes smiled, still mirthful. "You mustn't take your missteps so hard. Given the limited scope of your knowledge of Lestrade, it isn't as catastrophic a failure as it might have been. In fact, if he were his own subordinate, I've no doubt he would suspect himself." I didn't find this to be complimentary in the slightest, but I held my peace.

"I will need an exhaustive list of any official persons who responded to any of these incidents. I have observed in cases like these, where the murderer appears to find joy in the act itself, it isn't enough to merely kill. A proximity to the body and observance of its discovery is also often sought. I'd not be surprised to find that the murderer lurked around the discoveries."

For the first time, it truly occurred to me that I might have stood near or even next to a prolific murderer within the past few days. The thought was both concerning and exciting. I started to consider the faces of everyone I could remember seeing, and suddenly each and every one seemed to take on a sinister character.

"How do you go through life without suspecting everyone of a crime?" I asked Holmes after a while.

"Why do you I assume I do not?" he asked. "Everyone is capable of crime in the right – or I suppose *wrong* – circumstances."

"Dismal view of human nature," I answered.

"You were a soldier," he retorted. "I cannot believe you think so differently."

"No, you're right," I said. The difference was, until that moment, I hadn't allowed myself to think of these things much at all since my return to England.

"Digsby is a useful man," Holmes commented after a while.

"You sound less flattering than your words would indicate."

"Too useful," he continued. "Almost as if he knows what he'll find before he gets to the bodies."

"Oh, Holmes," I remonstrated, "you can't seriously think that because the man is a reasonably competent officer among inferiors that he must be a murderer."

"No," said Holmes, "but I intend to lay a trap for him. If he is our man, he has an extraordinary amount of hubris. It will prove to be his downfall, as it has many others."

I shook my head. "I cannot believe it."

"Your similarity to the doubtful apostle does you credit, Watson. You have no cause to believe it yet. If I am correct, we will soon know."

167

I forced myself to entertain the possibility. Holmes was too likely to be correct, which I already knew. But he didn't offer me one of his chains of deduction, which he was almost always willing to do. That, I surmised, meant he was not sure, at least not yet.

The following day, Digsby came to Baker Street in response to a note requesting his findings on the third corpse, which he hadn't yet sent around for Holmes's perusal. He was a pleasant-seeming, serious sort of young man, and Mrs. Hudson seemed charmed by him as she led him up to our sitting room.

"Good afternoon," he greeted Holmes and me. "It's a great pleasure to visit the lodgings of someone of your reputation." This was addressed to Holmes, who was visibly unimpressed but maintained civility.

"Please make yourself comfortable, and Mrs. Hudson will bring around tea, for I take it you don't imbibe stronger substances during your hours of duty," said Holmes.

"Quite so," said Digsby. "Inspector Lestrade sets his men a strong example." I supposed there were worse things. Lestrade might be as unimaginative as a piece of gravel, but no one could doubt his moral certitude.

Holmes took out a small notebook. "I should like to compare findings of the unfortunate Evans, if you please."

Digsby nodded. "I doubt I have anything to add that you haven't already documented."

For a few moments, they spoke about the man's wounds and the manner in which he'd been found. I was nearly drowsy with the repetition of what I had myself seen, when Holmes casually began to shift the conversation.

"It is clear," he said, "that much about these three crimes is similar, so let us consider the differences, which may be more helpful."

"Station in life," Digsby supplied. "Age of each victim. Marital status."

"What about the findings on the corpses?" Holmes asked. "There was a paper with his name on it found in the pocket of the third man. What about the first? Did the police find any paper?"

"Yes," Digsby answered readily, "but it had nothing written on it."

Holmes maintained his breathing, but I thought I detected almost-imperceptible excitement, and I understood it. Holmes himself had found and pocketed a piece of paper in the first man's pocket before Lestrade and his officers had even arrived. He had never mentioned it or given it to them.

"I think," said Holmes, "we had better call Inspector Lestrade."

Lestrade came at once. Upon his arrival, he was shown into the sitting room. "What is the meaning of this?"

"Merely that I suspect one of your men of triple murder, and I fancied it would be less welcome to make such an accusation in the middle of your office." He turned to Digsby. "Tell us more of the paper found with the first body."

"Paper?" growled Lestrade. "What paper?"

Holmes explained how he had retained it after initially searching the first body, and how it was a bit of knowledge that only he and I had known about – and possibly the killer as well. "But Mr. Digsby knew about it."

"I – never saw it!" Digsby replied unprompted. "Chartwell told me of its existence, but when I asked Inspector Lestrade about it, he said he didn't have such a thing. I didn't wish to question a superior officer, so I dropped the subject. Isn't that right, Inspector?"

Chartwell, I recalled clearly, hadn't reached the scene of the murder any sooner than Digsby, a fact that was obviously forefront in Holmes's mind. And yet he'd mentioned the paper as if he knew of it – were Digsby to be believed.

Lestrade, meanwhile, confirmed the young man's statement. "Digsby did ask about a piece of paper, but it seemed irrelevant."

"That serves as something of a confirmation to your story, Digsby," said Holmes. Then he simply looked at Digsby for a long moment. I didn't know his thoughts, but I supposed he might be, as I was, judging the man's veracity.

"What else did Chartwell say about it?" he asked after a moment.

"He said it was a piece of paper, perhaps the sort that might be used to pack sweets – that it had little yield in terms of clues and nothing written on it."

Lestrade was clearly appalled. I had seen the man in several emotional states, but this one was new. "One of my officers?" he asked, his desire to disbelieve Holmes obviously trumped by his conviction otherwise. "Do you mean – ?"

"Betrayal," Holmes replied, "and of the vilest sort. I should have seen this. My obliviousness is inexcusable. If this is true, Chartwell took every possible advantage of his position. I've known officers to commit crimes, of course. There are depraved men everywhere, but not necessarily of this disgusting, remorseless sort. I'm thoroughly disappointed in myself for allowing such a thing to go on unchecked, when, at any moment, I might have stopped the man with a word."

"How could I – " expressed the policeman in shock.

In that moment, I came to understand more of the relationship between Lestrade and Holmes, for I expected my friend to make a sharp retort, but instead he answered simply, "We are all blind when it comes to our closest allies." It was the nearest to making an allowance for human frailty that I had yet heard Holmes come.

The next step of the business was to confront Chartwell, and Lestrade realized immediately that time was of the essence, for if he wasn't apprehended and was responsible, he might at any point sense trouble and flee. The four of us went immediately to Scotland Yard and Lestrade's office, where he had the presence of mind to calmly order Chartwell to be sent to him. This would have been a more difficult business, but the man was at that moment calmly engaged in correlating the statements of those who had been interviewed around each of the three murders.

Digsby was sent out, but under discreet guard, for it was still possible that he had fabricated his story to implicate Chartwell when he realized that Holmes was getting close. And if Chartwell were guilty, Digsby's presence in the office have made the examination impossible.

As soon as Chartwell was brought in, Lestrade asked, "Chartwell, do you know what happened to the bit of paper discovered on our unfortunate first victim? It seems to have been misplaced."

"I gave it to Digsby as soon as I found it," Chartwell said defensively. "He'd missed it – he knew nothing about it, and I thought it should have been in his possession, given that he usually works with the evidence and I with the people."

"And yet," Lestrade mused aloud, "that paper wasn't found by any of us. It was pocketed by Mr. Holmes here, before you or Digsby or I even arrived. Very irregular procedure, but quite useful now, it turns out, for you could have only known of its existence if you'd had contact with the corpse some time before its discovery."

Chartwell, who until that point had impressed me as a remarkably bland sort of man, turned white, then red, his awareness of his own mistake immediate. Then he attempted to flee. Thankfully, both Holmes and I had anticipated this, and we both lunged for him and caught him between us.

"Really," said Holmes, "a man of your singular intellect resorting to such feral behavior." Chartwell gave him a look of pure malevolence but stopped struggling.

"The problem with this sort, Watson," Holmes continued, exactly as if we were having a friendly conversation over tea, "is that they always think themselves the cleverest. They never consider the likelihood that anyone else might come along and spoil their game. Pride is the downfall of this kind of killer." I refrained from commenting that it might, perhaps, take a similar sort to recognize the signs.

Chartwell tried then to sputter that it was Digsby who had told him about the existence of the elusive but useless paper. However, everyone in the room knew that the game was up, including Digsby, who had quietly entered to watch the arrest.

That evening in our rooms, in front of a cozy fire that made murder seem far more remote than it really was, Holmes and I spoke of the case. "Lestrade was quick to agree to suspect one of his own officers," I observed.

"He is many things," Holmes said, "but he isn't corrupt. He has a dogged willingness to see justice done that is almost admirable, except for its inflexible lack of creativity."

"Surely the papers would like to know the story of one of the police being the culprit," I said.

"It won't be published now," said Holmes. "Undoubtedly, Scotland Yard has already determined to suppress it for the sake of the public peace."

"Just as well," I answered. "The public shouldn't spend the whole winter recalling gruesome murders. Perhaps this reprieve is a merciful one. For now, I'm happy to get back to petty thievery and deception."

Just then, Mrs. Hudson came in with a celebratory repast. Though I had told myself I wouldn't partake too heavily, I couldn't resist the sumptuous offerings. Even Holmes, who didn't like to overindulge while working and sometimes even came dangerously close to starving himself, partook freely. He was, I saw, able to celebrate his successes just as he lamented his failures.

"There's a peculiar satisfaction in the solution," I observed to Holmes that night, over the fire and my final evening drink. "I have little sympathy for Chartwell. He'll get what's coming to him, and he leaves no one to mourn him."

"Yes," Holmes agreed, filling his pipe with his usual precision. "My only regret is that it took me three times to stop him."

"Left to Inspector Lestrade, he'd have managed to murder half of London," I snorted.

"Perhaps," Holmes replied, "but Lestrade is hardly the standard."

"What is, then?" I asked, genuinely curious.

"Perfection," he replied simply, and I didn't doubt he was telling the truth. Perhaps it wasn't a happy way of being, but he certainly knew himself.

"I hardly think anyone could have done it more quickly," I said. "The killings were unmotivated, other than by his sheer joy in perpetrating them.

His victims were unrelated, and he didn't behave like the usual jilted lover or enraged inferior. He knew how to erase evidence of himself."

"Yes," said Holmes. "He behaved like the sort he is, and it is a sort for whom we must be prepared. We are inclined to look for motives that make sense according to the normal human mind, and to look for connections where there are none. In cases like this one, the absence of some things is more important than the presence of others."

"Why mention the paper to Digsby at all?" I wondered. "That is his action that baffles me."

"Pure vanity," Holmes said. "Like leaving the third corpse at our address – another way of taunting Lestrade and taunting me, but he met his match." Holmes sat back in his chair with an air of immense satisfaction.

"I suppose we don't like to think of killers with no motive beyond killing itself, since anyone might be their next target. It suggests an existential dread and puts a face upon it."

"An immensely poetic turn of phrase," said Holmes.

My first Christmas spent with Sherlock Holmes was, I would later realize, a reliable indicator of what was to come in our association. Three murders, Lestrade failing to solve anything, and my friend as alive and excited as I had yet seen him, punctuated by Mrs. Hudson trying to feed us holiday delicacies at every possible opportunity. It would have been grotesque, that combination of the macabre and the festive, except that the two united in Holmes, somehow. He was the center of the madcap pageant that led us from one corner of London to the other and finally sent a policeman to the scaffold.

"Perhaps when we're old men, the tale may be told," Holmes said with a smile, and I tried to imagine it, though at that moment, I could not. Of course, as I complete this account, that time has come. I shall finish this day just as Holmes and I finished that one, with an excellent dinner, a pint of something good, and one another's company.

Mrs. Hudson's granddaughter is calling, so I finish my musings here and only say that those early days, as strange as they were, are to me priceless. I will toast their memory tonight with Sherlock Holmes by my side.

Just as Holmes observed during that first Christmas, I, too, hadn't expected to find myself in such a situation. It wasn't the rooms, nor the cases, nor even Holmes that surprised me the most. No, what gave me the most surprise when I considered my situation that Christmas was its happiness.

The Christmas Ghost
of Crailloch Taigh
by David Marcum

Although I would have wagered that being alone was the best medicine after the day I'd just experienced, Holmes knew better, and insisted that I join him downstairs in the inn's small bar.

We had journeyed to Stranraer the day before, traveling north across a cold and bleak landscape that looked blasted in the weak December light. I knew that come spring, the land would awaken as it always did, and these blue-gray empty fields, dotted with barren leafless trees and scattered black buildings under a low metallic sky, would again be filled with color and life and ever-renewing vitality. But for now, this emptied and grim terrain matched the mood of the task which called me back to the town of my birth.

Just days before Christmas, I'd been summoned there to take care a bit of long-delayed business that had suddenly become urgent and then final. I don't propose to recount it here – it's not my story to tell. I simply reference its unpleasant nature so that one might understand how Holmes and I came to be there, and my perspective as we tarried overnight before returning to London on the following morning's train.

A couple of hours before, our business finished, we had entered the inn, located on the southern outskirts of town. It was far too late to start the journey home, though I didn't fancy staying any longer that I had too. In the closed carriage on the way to our temporary lodgings, I tried to both thank Holmes, who had offered to accompany me on my unpleasant journey, and to apologize for him being there, so far from Baker Street just before the holidays. He would have none of it, attempting to distract me with an amusing anecdote concerning one of the old ladies he'd encountered earlier in the day while I was otherwise occupied. I appreciated the effort, but I simply didn't want to hear it, and he soon fell silent.

I would have been content to sit upstairs, brooding in my room, but after I'd retreated there for a few minutes, Holmes knocked and reminded me that I hadn't eaten at all that day, and the whisky I'd carried upstairs would sit better on a full stomach. So we went down and found a table at the back of the low-ceilinged room. The young missus whose husband owned the inn approached our table and heard our choices from the night's menu. I found that I had an appetite after all and favored the roast pork, crisped along the fatty side, while Holmes ordered some of the local seafood – caught fresh by fisherman who didn't rest simply because of inclement seasonal weather.

The mood in the bar was subdued but not unpleasant, and I found myself beginning to thaw. After all, this Stranraer business wasn't unexpected, and finally I could draw a line under it, for good or ill. Holmes perceived that my attitude had shifted, and when he tentatively asked a few questions about how things had been resolved, I was able to answer with objectivity.

The food was excellent and the local whisky tolerable. The fire was warm, and the modest but sincere Christmas decorations scattered around the room helped to further ease my tension. During a lull in our conversation, I looked more closely at our surroundings. There were half-a-dozen or so locals, sitting in small groups, talking softly and comfortably, and not put out at all by the presence of a pair of London strangers. These men themselves showed no indication that this night, with Christmas just days away, was any different from any other that they might spend here, but there was still something festive about the place. The owner's wife, a beautiful lass in her twenties with thick dark hair and the glow of a woman who was obviously expecting her first in just a couple of months, still moved with a dancer's grace, and hummed various Christmas carols in soft tones as she went about her tasks.

Her husband held station behind the bar. Introduced to us as William Fraser, he was a tall fellow with black hair and broad shoulders, and his outlook matched that of his wife. He clearly had pride in his establishment, and a joyful satisfied expression as he watched his wife and child-to-be moving about the room, or carrying meals from the kitchen.

I had settled lower in my seat, feeling the unpleasantness of the day finally sloughing away, when the front door opened abruptly, flying back and lowering the room's temperature by twenty or more degrees almost immediately. Most of the men sitting around had the same reaction as the womb-like warmth of the room was stripped away in an instant, causing them to jerk upright in their chairs as one while making raucous complaints and grumbles toward the figure who stood in the doorway.

Realizing what he'd done, the new visitor bent to push the door shut, but too late – the damage was already done.

The grumping men settled back, attempting to regain their warmth and comfortable leisure. I glanced at our hosts. Fraser was looking at the newcomer with sudden ill-concealed distaste – unexpected, as he'd been quite genial to this point – while in turn his wife watched her husband, a troubled expression upon her face.

"Mr. Holmes?" said the man in a strident voice with an unmistakable Dartmoor accent. He looked around for half-a-second after speaking before seeing us at the back of the room. As we apparently looked different enough to stand out as strangers, he moved with decision in our direction. He stopped on Holmes's side of the table, clearly having been told the appearance of the man he sought. "I bring a note from Mr. Bloom."

The name meant nothing to me, and I could see that Holmes was in the dark as well. Instead of taking the envelope thrust in his direction, Holmes asked, "And who might that be?"

The room had grown silent as all those present made no secret about listening to this conversation. Behind the bar, Fraser gave a small but dark chuckle when Bloom's messenger seemed taken aback at Holmes's ignorance of his master. "Lucius Bloom," he answered, his voice a bit less confident now. "He's one of the men associated with the waterfront properties – a most important man, you know. He helped to form the harbor syndicate." He shook the envelope again, as if it were a lure on a line. "He heard that you were here, in Stranraer, and needs to engage your services."

Holmes nodded in my direction. "Dr. Watson and I plan on returning to London in the morning. Christmas will be here soon, you know."

I nearly laughed aloud, in spite of my day. The idea that Holmes might turn down a case because of a holiday was unthinkable. But I didn't openly express this thought. Clearly Holmes was fishing his own line here, nudging further information from the messenger with his apparent indifference. And he still did not take the note. "Tell us more of Mr. Bloom. I'm afraid that his reputation hasn't made it to London quite yet – and in fact, he hasn't been mentioned to us since our arrival in Stranraer either, Mr. . . . ?"

This seemed incomprehensible to the man standing before us. While I'm not Sherlock Holmes, I have managed to successfully learn some of his methods during the time that I've known him. I could see that the man holding the note was in his early thirties, and was likely unmarried. He was well-dressed and looked as if kept himself in good physical condition. He was thin, but not in an unhealthy way, and there were no blemishes on his skin that might indicate unhealthy habits. His nails were quite short, and in places appeared to have been bitten to the quick. He appeared to have a certain amount of nervous energy as he shifted from one foot to the other. The creases in his well-polished shoes indicated that he moved about quite a bit, and that his duties didn't keep him behind a desk too often. What wasn't obvious from his appearance, but was already quite clear otherwise, was his unappealing awe for Lucius Bloom.

"My name is Grayson," was the reply to Holmes's question, "but that isn't important. As you will read if you'll accept this note, Mr. Bloom requests your presence at the manor immediately. Tonight! He won't tolerate another day of this . . . this abuse!" His voice had risen, and he took another step closer to Holmes. If my friend hadn't taken the envelope at that moment, I expect that Grayson would have thrown it at him.

I looked past him. The other occupants of the room seemed to have returned to their own business, as our conversation was too low for them to hear. Still, glances were often turned our way.

With a neutral smile, Holmes accepted the note, looked at the front and back of the envelope, and then pulled out a folded sheet. The paper of both was cream-colored, appearing thick and expensive – facts that I verified just a moment later when Holmes handed both to me.

Mr. Sherlock Holmes, [it read]

I've learned that you're in the area and am writing to avail myself of your services. I'm disappointed in myself that doing so hadn't occurred to me earlier. I would have hesitated to request that you be inconvenienced to travel all this way from London, but things have reached the point that I might have considered it, in spite of the distance.

I apologize for writing so late in the evening, and requesting that you leave the comfort of your temporary lodgings, but as the events seem to occur only at night, and only at this time of year, possibly you can conduct a quick investigation now before the next manifestation occurs.

I've asked my man, Grayson, to deliver this note discreetly, [I raised an eyebrow at how that had turned out.] *for what is happening is no one's business beyond these walls. If you'll agree to accompany him back to the manor, he can explain what's been taking place as you travel, so you'll be ready to begin upon your arrival.*

Again, I apologize for the abrupt and inconvenient invitation, but I'd be a fool not to seek your help while it's available.

Very Best,
Lucius Bloom

I looked up and met Holmes's gaze. Clearly the tone meant to be conveyed in Bloom's note had been missed by his rather enthusiastic and demanding employee.

"Have you read this?" asked Holmes, his voice even lower than before.

"I have not!" replied Grayson, missing the cue to speak more softly, and outraged that such might be suspected of him. "I have no need. I'm fully aware of everything that has taken place, from – "

"If you have not read it," Holmes interrupted, frowning and lowering a hand, advising Grayson to be quiet, "then apparently you do not know that your employer hoped for your discretion in the matter. Now is not the time to explain." He looked my way and I nodded. "We will accompany you. Give us five minutes to ready ourselves and get our coats. We'll join you outside."

"Very good," said Grayson with a sharp nod. The matter was done, the mission accomplished, and without further interaction, he spun, walked to the door, opened it with much less force than before, and then departed.

As Holmes and I stood, our landlord spoke, his voice cutting through the low murmur of conversation. "Once again, the high and mighty Mr. Lucius Bloom – " There was a definite contemptuous sneer that slid into his voice. " – thinks that he can just send his toady into the night and order people to do his bidding." His tone was surprising – bitter and scathing, and nothing like what I'd heard from the man in the short time I'd known him. Looking quickly around the room, I could see that the other patrons were also rather surprised at this was unexpected behavior.

"William – " began his wife, but he raised a hand.

"I'll be silent, Em. But you and I both know what I think of that man. He'll get what he deserves someday. Mark my words."

I could tell that Holmes would have liked to question William Fraser a bit before we left the inn, but it was impossible with so many strangers sitting about and our transportation awaiting us outside. We both went upstairs to make ready for the journey, and soon I was stepping into the narrow dark hallway and pulling my bedroom door shut behind me. I'd already heard Holmes move along the passage and go downstairs, so I was surprised to find the landlord's wife standing silently in the corridor when I turned.

"Don't mind William," she whispered glancing toward the back stairs as if fearing she would soon be caught. "He . . . he's a good man. But he has some ideas – about rich folk – that he'd be better off forgetting. And certainly never mentioning aloud."

"Do you know anything about Bloom's household that might be of use to us?" I whispered. "I've never heard of the man before now, and I'm sure that the same is true for Mr. Holmes. Anything at all might be useful."

She shook her head. "He's an Englishman who moved here and bought the old manor many years ago. I've heard that he's hard but fair. But – " Then she looked again toward the stairs. "You must go! Your friend is waiting. And William thinks that I'm in the kitchen." With that, she turned toward the back of the building, and within seconds she'd started carefully down the steep rear stairs.

I wanted to share this small exchange with Holmes, but it would have to wait. Insignificant as it was, it was no business of Grayson's.

Downstairs, I crossed the room toward the door even as I saw Mrs. Fraser entering by way of the kitchen, conspicuously wiping her hands with a towel. Her husband watched me with a scowl on his face as I joined Holmes at the front door and he didn't glance toward his wife, apparently having no idea that she had slipped upstairs to speak with me.

The sudden shock from the warm room to the dark night made me instantly pull my heavy coat tighter. The temperature had dropped quite a bit from just a few hours earlier, and there was a fresh breeze coming from the direction of Loch Ryan that carried a dampness that made my eyes sting and my throat ache with each freezing inhalation. The particular sensation made me recall very faint memories of my youngest years.

There was a hint of snow, and the sky had that peculiar pinkish look which indicated that more was on the way. As little protection as it was, I was glad to be in the closed carriage with the door shut and the shades tied down over the windows. I knew that Holmes would have wished to see what we passed on our way to Bloom's manor house, but that would have been nearly impossible on that dark night. At best, we might have observed a few lit windows in distant houses. Nothing else would have been visible.

"Now," said Holmes as we settled ourselves and the carriage rolled forward, "Mr. Bloom's note said that you would discreetly explain what has been occurring." His voice was low, as if he didn't want the driver to hear what was being discussed.

"I'm aware that Mr. Bloom wants me to brief you," was Grayson's rather haughty reply, "but I only know so much myself. His daughter is being terrorized by a Christmas ghost."

That statement hung unanswered between us for a long moment. I was curious by what it implied, but also wondering what Holmes's reaction might be. He had often said that a foundational tenet of his practice was that "No ghosts need apply." I half-wondered if he would bang on the carriage roof with his stick before ordering the driver to turn us around. And yet he surprised me. "How?" he asked simply.

"Mr. Bloom's daughter is now eight years old," Grayson replied. "For the last five years, at Christmas-time, she has received mysterious gifts – treats, or small toys. Sometimes picture books. They are wrapped in bright festive paper and ribbons, and usually left in her bedroom – on the bedside table, or on the mantel, or on a chair. On occasion they are found in other parts of the house."

"And they are discovered on Christmas morning, when she awakens?"

"Oh, not just then. There are a dozen of them each year, as if counting down the Twelve Days of Christmas, leading up to the twenty-fifth. They start appearing in mid-December, culminating with the nicest gift on Christmas Day."

"Do they have a theme?" I asked, thinking of the unique and increasing series of gifts described in that old carol – and how tedious it would be to receive flocks of birds and maids and lords and drummers, especially for a small girl, year after year.

"Not at all – except they are something that a child would appreciate. They have remained appropriate to her age. When she was quite young, the books were those that are read to small children. The same for the toys. As she has aged, they have become more elaborate."

"The girl's name?" asked Holmes.

"Elsbeth."

"And her parents are naturally concerned."

"Just Mr. Bloom," was the reply. "His wife died a year or so after Elsbeth was born. I'm told that she had a weak heart."

"Today is the twenty-third," I said. "The gifts have been appearing this year as usual? Then tonight should be the tenth of this series."

"That's correct. No matter what precautions are taken, the gifts are delivered, one way or another, to some part of the house."

"And I'm sure that efforts have been made to stop this from occurring," said Holmes. "Or to discover and catch whomever is responsible."

"Of course," replied Grayson with a bit of disdain, as if even asking the question was foolish. "This has been occurring for five years now – with a total of nearly sixty gifts. Often Mr. Bloom has stayed in the bedroom himself to see who is coming in and leaving gifts. He's had staff do the same – I've spent my share of sleepless nights there without any success. On the nights that one of us stays in Elsbeth's room, a gift is left there if we fall asleep while on watch, and elsewhere in the house if we remain alert. He's had Elsbeth sleep in other rooms, but she protests this, and so he always lets her return. If she were my child, I'd have no hesitation about moving her to another room entirely – or at least for the

179

month of December! I might even leave Stranraer for the entire time – "
Then he shut his mouth abruptly, as if voicing aloud any implied criticism
of his liege, particularly before strangers who were an unknown factor and
might betray him, was a very foolish thing indeed.

At that point, the carriage took a decided lurch to the right, and I could
feel that the nature of the roadway had changed beneath us. Soon we were
slowing. "Where are we?" asked Holmes.

"Crailloch Taigh," was the reply. "Mr. Bloom's manor house Just a
few miles west of the inn, not far from where Crailloch Burn joins
Pilanton. It's a fine old house, neatly restored. It's a pity you can't see the
approach in daylight."

"Perhaps we will," said Holmes.

The carriage pulled to a stop and we climbed down underneath a large
porte cochere, extending from what seemed to be a very large house. It
was too dark to get a full sense of the place, being so close as we were to
the front door, but the walls on either side extended for quite a ways before
vanishing into the night. Looking beyond the carriage, I could see that the
curved drive behind us similarly stretched beyond vision toward the road
and the distant lights of Stranraer. I turned back toward the house in time
to see the door open. I joined Holmes and Grayson as we stepped inside.

We were met by a tall cadaverous fellow, apparently the butler, in
formal clothing who offered to take our hats and coats. As he did so, I
examined our surroundings. The entry hall was a wide room with a high
ceiling, running back nearly forty feet toward a substantial staircase,
ascending into darkness. Although the room was dimly lit, I could see that
the walls were covered with a number of striking paintings. One seemed
to be in the style of Whistler, and I wondered if it was an original.
However, before I could step over and examine it further, we heard the
sound of rapidly approaching footsteps, and in a moment, a big heavy-set
man with thick iron-gray hair and a wide moustache joined us.

"Gentlemen," he said, thrusting out a hand, "I'm Lucius Bloom."

I was surprised to hear his American accent. "This way," he said,
holding out an arm toward a nearby doorway. "Would you care for
something to drink? Whisky? Port? Something hot?"

"A cup of coffee," said Holmes. "If it isn't too much trouble. It has
been a long day, and your note was unexpected."

I nodded in agreement. "Something hot would be welcome."

"Of course." Bloom turned to the cadaverous man. "Blair, if you
please?"

The butler nodded and departed. As we entered a tasteful sitting
room, with Bloom behind us, our host turned. "That will be all Grayson,"
he said, moving to shut the door in the face of the man who had brought

us there before he could cross the threshold. The last I saw of our summoner was a stoic expression, punctuated by disappointed eyes.

"So," said Bloom, rubbing his hands and indicating seats before a blazing fire, "how much did Grayson tell you?"

As we settled, I had a chance to further study the American. He was older than I had initially believed – at least sixty – and seemed to exude a great vitality and strength. I suppose that I had been expecting someone much more unpleasant, based on both the initial attitude evinced by Grayson, and also by our landlord's comments, indicating that he didn't have much respect for Bloom at best. But his note had been humble enough – a request rather than an arrogant demand as we saw so often from the wealthy – and I found the man to pleasant and seemingly forthright. However, he was clearly rather worried as his eyes cut back and forth between Holmes and me.

"The gist of his statement was that for the past five years, Christmas gifts have been left for your daughter, usually in her bedroom, whether or not she is there, and even if someone has remained in the room to guard it."

"That's right – somehow the next morning, the gifts are there. If it's only Elsbeth sleeping there, then they're placed in obvious locations. On the table beside her bed, for instance. The thought that someone approaches her so closely in her sleep . . . ."

He closed his eyes, overcome at the thought. Then he swallowed. "But if someone is on guard, and unfortunately falls asleep, then the gift will be discovered later: Behind a chair, perhaps, or underneath a tossed-aside piece of clothing. If the watcher remains awake – and I can assure you that I have remained awake many times – then the gifts are found elsewhere in the house, even if there are other guards on duty in the other rooms as well."

"It sounds as if you have made quite the effort to catch this ghost," I said. "Knowing that the visits will occur must surely oppress any holiday cheer."

Holmes then glanced pointedly around the room. "Our sample is very small in terms of what we've so far seen of your home, but I haven't observed any Christmas decorations."

For the first time since meeting him shortly before, Bloom's countenance hardened, and I saw the man who was responsible for his success in life. His eyes narrowed, and his mouth tightened. "That's right. I'll have none of it. I find the whole season to be most unpleasant."

"Indeed," Holmes replied. "I understand that your wife died five years ago. Might I venture a shot to state that her passing occurred at Christmastime?"

Bloom's mouth twitched as his lips tightened, and then he took a sharp breath, as if to make a quick retort. But then he stopped and swallowed. "That is correct. Thus, I have no use for such frippery."

"And your daughter?" I asked. "She has never had a Christmas celebration then?"

"She has not," Bloom replied shortly. I could see that he was becoming more defensive, but I raised a placating hand.

"Not everyone does," I said. "I was born here in Stranraer, and spent my early years not far from here. We didn't observe Christmas. My father was strict Church of Scotland, which has no use for Christ's Mass – 'Too Popish!' he would always say. I only learned of the traditional British Christmas on those few occasions when we traveled south to visit my Grandfather on my mother's side."

I didn't mention that there were many others who didn't celebrate because they were unable – living in terribly deprived conditions where simply finding their daily bread was the most blessing that could be hoped for. I knew that there was far too much of that all around us, often within mere blocks of great wealth. In fact, I had no doubt that, not far in any direction from Bloom's fine home, I could locate any number of individuals and families to whom the idea of a Christmas celebration was somewhere between altogether unknown and tragically laughable.

"May we examine your daughter's room?" asked Holmes.

"Of course. This way."

Bloom stood and led us into the hallway, where we met Blair returning with a tray containing a pot of coffee and three cups. He was expressionless as we passed him, but I thought I could see sympathy in his eyes nonetheless as we walked past him toward the wide stairway and he saw how my gaze lingered on the pot. "I'll keep it hot for you, sir," he said softly.

We went up one floor and wound along the back of the building to the east wing. "The manor is quite old," Bloom explained, "with records about the original foundations dating back over four-hundred years. It was in ruins when I bought it, nearly thirty years ago when I came here from Philadelphia to expand my business. I found that I loved Scotland, and stayed. I hope that you can see it in daylight – I'm quite proud of how it's turned out. I brought in the finest architects and builders."

He paused before a wide door made of dark oak – possibly in place since the building was first constructed. He knocked, and a girl's voice answered. Bloom opened the door, well-maintained and silent, to reveal a most cozy room, well-lit, and tastefully decorated to suit a young girl.

Seated near the fireplace was Bloom's daughter, a girl of about eight, alongside a matronly lady who was holding a book. They had apparently been reading before putting the girl to bed, as she was attired in a nightgown and slippers. With a look toward Holmes and me, the girl slid forward on the settee to place her feet upon the floor and then ran to her father, who bent to receive her enthusiastic hug.

"Oh, Papa," the girl cried, releasing him and glancing again our way, "please don't let them stop the Ghost from visiting! It's so much fun!"

The hint of a frown appeared between Bloom's eyebrows, but it vanished in an instant. "You know that I'm concerned that someone can get in here so easily," he said. "If someone wants to send you gifts, why can't they have them delivered by post?"

A good question, I thought, and indicative that there was more to this than simply getting a gift into the girl's hands.

Meanwhile, the elderly woman stood. "This," explained Bloom, "is Mrs. Treathaway. She's been Elsbeth's nurse since the passing of her mother six years ago."

The woman nodded. "Nice to meet you both."

"Mr. Holmes and Dr. Watson are going to see what they can determine about our ghost," added Bloom. He turned toward my friend. "How would you like to begin?"

"I understand," Holmes answered, "that on occasion Elsbeth sleeps elsewhere during this season. Perhaps this would be possible tonight as well?"

"Certainly." Bloom turned to Mrs. Treathaway. "Can you gather her things?"

The woman nodded. "After Elsbeth is settled," added Holmes to the nurse, "may we speak?" He received an acknowledgement, and then Mrs. Treathaway began assembling a few items to carry away, including the book she had just been holding.

Holmes knelt down and faced Elsbeth. "So you aren't afraid of the ghost?" he asked.

She shook her head. "He always brings me gifts, for as long as I can remember."

"'He'? Are you sure that the ghost is a 'he'?"

She nodded, and glanced toward her father. "I've seen him."

At this, her father sputtered in surprise. "What? You've never mentioned *that*!"

The girl nodded and took her father's hand – seeming to instinctively know that doing so would calm him a bit. "Just this year. I've pretended to be asleep. I didn't know he was here until he was setting one of the presents beside my bed. I tried to breathe normally and kept my eyes almost closed, but I could see him. He isn't a ghost at all – he's *Father Christmas*!"

183

"And how do you know what Father Christmas looks like?" asked her father. The question surprised me for an instant before I remembered that Bloom hadn't allowed Christmas into his house since his wife died.

The little girl gave a wise smile, older than her years. "I know you don't like Christmas because of Mama, Papa, but I still know about it. I see the decorations when I'm in town, and I know about it from the other girls. I know Mama died then, and that's why you don't want to be reminded of it, but it doesn't bother me that way. That's why I'm so happy that Father Christmas has found a way to help me celebrate . . . ."

Bloom swallowed, as if rocked by unexpected emotions. After a moment, he dropped to one knee and pulled her closer, even as Holmes rose to both feet. "You are getting older, my girl. Perhaps we should talk more often about . . . about these things." Then he released her and stood. "But still, I can't have anyone – even Father Christmas – entering and leaving the house uninvited." He looked toward us. "Gentlemen – if you can help us learn the truth . . . ?"

I nodded, and Holmes answered. "I will examine the room, and then one of us will stay in here tonight, with a suitable false Elsbeth constructed in the bed. Hopefully the fact that strangers to the household are here won't disrupt the good Father's generous inclinations. I suspect that someone who has been so consistent for five years won't be dissuaded by a couple of visitors from London."

With that we said goodnight to Elsbeth, who was led away by Mrs. Treathaway. Then, Holmes requested that Bloom and I wait in the hallway while he made his investigation alone.

Outside, I could see that Bloom was becoming rather nervous. I mentioned it to him, and he laughed. "It's the same every night leading up to Christmas – wondering how he'll get in, despite our precautions, and if this is the night we'll catch him."

"What precautions have you taken?"

"Anything from elaborate to nearly giving up in defeat. When this started, I initially accused the staff – of one or all of them of being responsible. At the time, Mrs. Treathaway was quite critical of my . . . my avoidance of anything to do with Christmas. I thought that she was the one providing the gifts to get around my wishes. But I could tell that her concern regarding an intruder in the house was sincere, and was stronger than any desire to expose Elsbeth to aspects of the holiday.

"During the first year, and the first twelve gifts, each night became increasingly worrisome. No matter where we watched or waited, somehow the gifts appeared. The next year, I didn't believe that it would continue, but it did, and I arranged for a number of local men to supplement the staff, watching much of the inside, and outside as well. It did no good. The same for the third year. By last Christmas, I was ready to give up and just get through the days as best we could."

"It sounds as if you allow Elsbeth to spend some nights in the room alone – even knowing that a stranger is entering."

"She has never been alone. On those nights when no one is in the room, I stand guard in the hall with the door cracked. But even then, there are times when I have turned away for a short period, or my spirit momentarily weakens, and I assume that's when this 'Father Christmas' finds his way inside. I would move her out of the room entirely, as we've done tonight, but she does love it there so, and whether she's in there or elsewhere, the intruder gets inside."

At that moment, Holmes opened the door and joined us. "I've made my examination and found a few points of interest." He held up a hand. "Watson will tell you, Mr. Bloom, that I like to hold my cards close at this stage of an investigation. I propose that, after we speak with Mrs. Treathaway, we prepare for the rest of the night." He looked toward me. "Watson, would you mind taking the shift in the rather comfortable looking chair in Elsbeth's room, somewhat disguised as Mr. Bloom here, while I take up a post in the hallway? Feel free to sleep – you will be safe enough – and if you do wake up, make no effort to disturb Father Christmas's work. I propose to let him come and go unopposed tonight, in order to learn more about him so that we can bring this to a conclusion tomorrow night. Agreed?"

It was, and we then went in search of the nurse.

She had little to tell us. A very quiet woman, she answered mostly in one-word responses, but one had the sense that she had secrets to keep. Perhaps, however, it was simply the cast of her face, with a small upturn at one side of her mouth that seemed to imply hidden knowledge that amused her. She confirmed Bloom's introduction that she'd been the girl's nurse for six years, and that she had been a part of the household staff before then – quite a few years back in fact. "Since the time of the master's first wife," she explained. We glanced toward Bloom.

"Elsbeth's mother was my second wife," he explained shortly. "My first wife came with me from America. She died a quarter-century ago. A year or so after that, I met my second wife. On a trip to the Continent. She was . . . she was quite a bit younger than me. We'd been married for quite a while before Elsbeth came along. She was . . . something of a surprise, and by then my wife had . . . weakened. She never quite recovered from giving birth. Since her passing, it's just been the two of us – Elsbeth and me. I don't plan to remarry a third time."

"And did you have any children from our first marriage."

185

Bloom shook his head. "Sadly, no. My first wife was unable to bear children. My second wife and I believed that to be true in her case as well. That's why my girl was such a blessing."

Mrs. Treathaway had nothing further of importance to add, stating only that she had no idea who the ghost – or Father Christmas – might be, and while she disagreed with the ghost's methods – and here she looked pointedly at her employer – she admired his motivations.

"Motivations?" asked Holmes. "You understand them, then?"

"Certainly," she said with her secret and possibly unintended smile. "He wants that girl to have her Christmases."

We left her where we'd spoken, in the hallway outside Elsbeth's temporary bedroom. Bloom went in to say good night one more time, and Holmes and returned to the girl's regular room.

Inside, Holmes set about constructing a false Elsbeth in the girl's bed, made from pillows artfully bunched under her sheets and blankets. Meanwhile, I related my short conversation with Mrs. Fraser while I arranged the chair where I would sleep, setting it according to Holmes's instructions at a certain location facing the bed. I asked if this placement was in relation to something he'd seen during his examination while Bloom and I waited in the hallway, and he grunted in agreement without elaboration.

"What Mrs. Fraser told me . . . ." I said. "Is it important?"

"Initially, everything is important," was his cryptic reply.

When all was arranged in the room, Holmes wished me a good night and stepped into the hallway, pulling the door closed behind him. I settled into the chair, turned down the table lamp, and settled in the darkness, only dimly lit by the dying embers in the tidy little fireplace. After the day I'd had, it wasn't long before I was fast asleep. My last thought was that I'd forgotten to tell Blair that I no longer needed the coffee.

The chair was comfortable, and when I awoke to morning light, I had no particular aches to complain of. I was surprised to have slept the whole night through, and had no difficulties in remembering where I was. I thought that nothing must have happened, because I'd been aware of no visitors in the night. Throwing aside the heavy quilt in which I'd wrapped myself, I stood, noticing the shape in the bed remained as Holmes had arranged it. There was nothing different about the bedside table.

Then I turned and saw, on the small settee behind my chair where Mrs. Treathaway had been reading to Elsbeth, a large box wrapped in red paper and a green ribbon.

Father Christmas had been here, just feet away from me, while I slept in ignorance. I felt a chill run up my back.

186

The fire was out, and after being wrapped in the quilt all night, I was suddenly cold. I checked watch and saw that it was early, not long after six a.m. I left the bedroom, looking for Holmes. Unsurprisingly, he wasn't still on duty in the hallway. I found him downstairs, in the room where we'd first spoken with Bloom, sitting quietly with his pipe and a cup of coffee. He stood and nodded my way, passing without speaking toward the hallway and then the rear of the house. Soon he returned with a second cup. As he handed it to me, I said, "Did you see him?"

"I did."

"Who is it?"

He shook his head. "I'm not ready to reveal that quite yet. I need to understand a few more things first – motivations and history."

I took a sip. "I expect that it's Grayson, although I don't know what would motivate him so."

"You simply don't like him."

"That's true. I wonder if he's been here long enough to have started this five years ago."

"He has. I found the cook, Mrs. Ames, to be most gregarious when I spoke with her earlier this morning."

"Well, let's wake Bloom and haul Grayson in front of him and be done with it then."

Holmes shook his head and smiled. "Ever the man of action. No, as I said, I'm not ready yet for the dramatic *denouement* that you so crave. In truth, the only reason to awaken Bloom is to have him arrange for our transportation back to the inn.

But our host was already awake. He wasn't surprised at all to learn that there had been another visitation and another gift, and while he also wanted to know what – and whom – Holmes had seen, he was satisfied that the matter would be wrapped up within another day. He left to arrange for the carriage, and within a short while we were headed back toward Stranraer.

It had snowed some more during the night – not an excessive amount, but enough to re-whiten the landscape and cover the trees in a sugary dusting of white. As we drove away, I looked back at the manor, as did Holmes, and saw that it was quite large indeed. Although there were a number of more modern features tacked onto it here and there, the overall ancientness of the structure was unmistakable.

The roads were safe enough, and we were conveyed without incident to the inn door. By daylight, I could see that it was only a few miles' journey, and would be quite beautiful during the warmer months. Thanking our driver, we turned to go inside. However, Holmes stopped me for a moment, seeming to be in thought as he pinched his ear while staring at the ground outside the main door. Finally, he nodded to himself and we continued inside. As it was still quite early, the main room was empty, although I could hear sounds of activity in the kitchen beyond the bar.

We went upstairs to freshen up for the day, and when I was finished, I walked down the hall to knock on Holmes's door. He was ready to go downstairs as well, but beforehand he gave me instructions.

"I intend to throw a small party," he said. "A little Christmas celebration for the locals we met last night, and the Frasers. If you could let them know that I'll be buying drinks and refreshments for whomever wants to attend this afternoon, it would be much appreciated. Around three o'clock, I think – the more, the merrier."

I smiled and accepted that I would understand the reason for this at some point. "Anything else?"

"Yes," Holmes said. "There's no need for you to venture forth today. Spend time downstairs, talking and listening and asking questions. See if you can get Mrs. Fraser to tell you about the locals. Start by asking about her and her husband – people always like to talk about themselves, and it will be a good point from which to pivot to the wider community."

"And you?" I asked. "While I stay in, I expect that you'll go out."

"An accurate assumption. After breakfast, I want to visit and ask some questions of my own. Perhaps I'll spend time with the local vicar at the nearby church. What better way to acknowledge the approach of Christmas than in the presence of a holy man?"

I laughed and Holmes smiled, and we ventured downstairs to request some breakfast.

Much of that day passed in a rather dreamlike haze. We arranged to stay for another night beyond what we'd originally requested – not a difficulty, as we were the inn's only guests – and then Holmes departed while I settled myself into a cozy corner of the bar. I began with coffee in the morning, resisting the temptation to begin too early with beverages that would have the opposite effect. I had a book to read, and made great progress through it, but I also engaged in conversations and became acclimated to the flow of the place as various patrons arrived and departed, all on their own schedules.

Toward midday I ordered a meal, and when Mrs. Fraser placed it before me, I took the opportunity to start a conversation. As there were no other visitors needing her just then, she accepted my offer to join me. Easing into her chair across the table, she explained that as her delivery date approached, she found it harder to get through the days, and she indicated that soon she would desist and they would hire a replacement. They would have done so sooner, she said, as her husband was most

188

insistent that she not exert herself, but she hated to concede that she needed to go easier.

The pub, she explained, was a family affair which her husband had inherited from his widowed mother. She had opened it with some inherited money when he was a very small boy, and he'd grown up here. He had gone away for a while to serve in the military, but there was never any intention that he make a career of it, and after receiving a slight wound, he'd returned home. Soon after that they had married, and not much later after that his mother had passed. Now, after several years of patient waiting, they were to have a child of their own. I congratulated her again on their good fortune.

Our talk turned to the local area, and she commented on how this location south of the town and the loch had changed during her lifetime. I heard the stories and gossip about several of the more colorful locals, but she conspicuously deflected my attempts to steer the conversation toward the Bloom household. When I did so, she glanced nervously toward the bar, where her husband sat on a stool, reading a newspaper. Soon after, seeing that I had finished eating, she stood and took my plate. I wasn't able to question her again as more people drifted in through the passing afternoon.

Mrs. Fraser had been pleased but frankly puzzled about Holmes's idea of throwing a small Christmas party, but she allowed that it would be a welcome event. Holmes himself returned a little before three o'clock, a Pied Piper leading a number of locals inside to mingle with those who had already heard about it. Within a short time, the room, which I'd already grown accustomed to being a quiet and peaceful sort of place, was full of a loud and raucous but good-natured celebration.

I spent time moving from group to group, and I heard a number of interesting tales, along with unexpectedly meeting several old-timers who had known my father. In spite of whatever they remembered about him in truth – for he had been a difficult man at times, with a grim outlook – they were quite willing to only refer to him in the best possible terms.

I lost track of Holmes rather quickly, in spite of my attempts to see what he was up to – for he would have never suggested such a gathering without having another purpose in mind. I only noticed him again when the party started to thin and die an hour or so later. Three or four men seemed inclined to stay and try and keep it going, but when Holmes signaled to Fraser that he was done buying drinks, their interest quickly flagged. In another hour, the scene was very similar to how we'd found it the night before when returning from my very difficult day – the same regulars in their typical places, and Holmes and me at our table in the back, having chosen to repeat our previous menu choices. Why seek after something new when satisfaction is already established?

As we ate, Holmes explained that we would go upstairs after a suitable time and then wait until a man that he'd met the previous day when involved in my business, a local who now owed him a favor, would enter by way of the front door. He would ask to speak to the Frasers, delivering a meaningless message, while Holmes and I surreptitiously departed by way of the back stairs and out through the kitchen. Then we would return to the manor, where with any luck, the matter of the false Father Christmas would be explained.

I still had no idea what to expect, but that wasn't unusual. Holmes had the twin aspects of preferring a dramatic revelation, for which I always made a perfect audience, and also that he preferred to keep as much information to himself as he could, in case his interpretation of the facts somehow went awry. I had once been frustrated by it, but no longer. Additionally, I was a doctor and a former soldier, and in each capacity, I was trained to accept and carry out orders when needed – the former during surgeries when one rarely second-guessed a senior surgeon during a procedure, and the latter when following instructions might mean the difference between life and death.

All went according to plan. We rose and wished everyone good night. Then we went upstairs. I sat smoking in my room, reading further in my book, while Holmes waited in his down the hall, watching out the window toward the front of the inn. In about an hour, he softly knocked on my door, indicating that the distraction had arrived. I pulled on my coat and hat, and we slipped along the hall and down the back steps, which Holmes had already ascertained could be descended quietly. The cook having long since departed, we were able to exit while both Frasers were out front. A walk of five minutes brought us to an alley where a hansom cab stood waiting. Holmes spoke softly to the driver, and then we were in transit to the manor house.

Bloom met us outside the front door, where he'd apparently been waiting impatiently for some time, if the amount of cigar ash at his feet was any indication. Of Grayson or the staff there was no sign. "I've sent them away, as instructed," Bloom explained. "Do you really know who it is?"

"I do," said Holmes. "All will be revealed – later tonight."

"Good, good. Where do you want me to hide?"

"In your own bedroom," announced Holmes, raising his hand as Bloom started to protest. "I assure you that we'll call as soon as we have him – but nothing must occur beforehand to spook him." He indicated that we should go inside. "Shall we get into place?"

Bloom accompanied us upstairs toward his daughter's room. "I did as you asked," he said. "I had everyone loaded up and sent north, to a smaller house that I keep near Ballantrae. No one had time or opportunity to send word that they would be away – I made sure of that. I . . . I told them that we would have a Christmas celebration there." He swallowed. "I . . . I didn't want to, but you should have seen . . . seen how pleased Elsbeth was. Perhaps . . . perhaps I've made a mistake. Keeping Christmas from her. If nothing else, perhaps . . . this whole business has softened my heart, just a bit."

"You won't regret it," I said as we reached his daughter's doorway. "I grew up without Christmas. I'm glad now that I celebrate it. I can't imagine not doing so."

He nodded, and then asked if we needed anything. Hearing that we didn't, he said good night and retreated down the hall. When he'd vanished around the corner, I asked softly, "Will he stay away?"

"I expect so. In any case, I'll be here in the hallway to wave him away should he come creeping back."

"And I'll be back in my chair?" I asked, wondering if I'd sleep as well tonight as before, especially after spending such a tranquil, warm, and untaxing afternoon.

"No, not at all. I have a different spot picked out for you."

Inside, the room was as we'd left it that morning, although there were some small signs that Elsbeth had retrieved a few items since then for her journey. The bed still contained its false figure curled in supposed sleep. Holmes stepped that way, rearranged the pose somewhat, and then nodded in satisfaction. "And now for your station."

I looked around. There was no obvious place in here to hide – no bureaus or cabinets to step behind. I wondered if I'd be standing behind the drapes all night when Holmes inexplicably moved to the wall beside the fireplace. With a bend and flick of his fingers, he stepped back to allow a segment of the wall room to swing silently open, revealing a black passage behind.

"Behold: One of the remnants of the original manor – with the works oiled, guaranteeing unhindered and undetected passage by Father Christmas."

I moved forward with a wondrous look. This wasn't the first such passage that I'd seen, but I always reacted the same way – as if I were a boy reading of such things in adventure books about knights and pirates, castles and treasures, and exciting deeds both noble and otherwise.

"I spoke at length today with the vicar. When I'd gained his trust and explained what was occurring, he told me some of the house's history – how such passages were necessary for the original owner of this building

– a merchant who often ran afoul of enemies or thieves, and also those of opposing religions who used their beliefs to justify their attempts at his murder."

"And did he tell you where to find this doorway, and how to open it as well?"

"No, I learned that for myself last night when I initially examined the room while you and Bloom waited in the hallway."

"So you already knew how Father Christmas would enter."

"I did. And I saw him do so from my place at the cracked doorway while you slept. He was dressed as Elsbeth said – in the traditional costume. He never approached the bed, or even stepped near your chair. I suppose on those nights that he finds a guard, he waits for his chance and then enters no further than necessary. He simply left the gift on the settee and returned to the passage, closing the door behind him without a single sound."

"And you know who he is. You saw his face."

"As clearly as I see you – and yes, in spite of his false beard, he was unmistakable."

"Then why wait another day? Why didn't you confront him this morning?"

"Because the vicar told me other stories besides the history of the house. I think that by waiting, and catching him tonight when he least suspects it, we can help mend something that has been broken for too long."

Holmes lit his dark lantern and then led me into the passage. Immediately after entering, he paused to point out a boot mark in the dust. "This passage was swept clean when I first examined it last night – obviously kept that way to avoid any indications being tracked into the bedroom. I scattered just a bit of ash here during my inspection to show footprints, if possible, and I was successful. You didn't observe, but there were some new prints in the bedroom – although they weren't easily noticed on the wooden floor."

He walked on, and we had to keep our heads ducked and our shoulders tucked to avoid the low ceiling and narrow stone walls. I wondered just how far the passage went, and if there were others. Seemingly reading my thoughts, Holmes replied, "There are openings to other rooms – which is how, I expect, Father Christmas has been able to leave gifts elsewhere when Elsbeth's bedroom was too well guarded. I was also able to backtrack through this passage to find the exit – several hundred yards behind the house, well-hidden behind a thick and ancient growth of yew trees lying next to a rocky embankment."

He stopped before a small turning to our left, about fifty feet from where we'd entered the manor's walls. I could see that it went about ten feet or so before turning out of sight to the right.

"This leads down to a wall behind the kitchen. You'll hide here until our visitor passes. By the time he reaches the bedroom, you will have come along behind, bottling him up while I enter from the hallway. Tonight, with no guard in the room, he will fully enter to leave a gift beside the bed. It's nearly eleven now. If he keeps the same schedule as last night, we shouldn't have to wait very long – even Father Christmas wants to finish up and get home earlier rather than later."

I wanted to ask who to expect, and whether there would be any danger. It has been my experience that even the most tame creature can turn and fight when surprised or threatened. But Holmes seemed to expect no danger – he hadn't warned me or asked if I had my service revolver, although of course he knew that I did, as I'd learned long ago to never, ever travel without it.

With a nod, as he considered that all that I needed to know was explained, he handed me the dark lantern and retreated down the black passageway.

I looked around, made sure that there was a comfortable place to stand without any nails or other intrusions that might snag my coat, and settled to pass the time. With a sigh, as this wasn't my first occasion in this type of situation, I lowered the flame and closed the lantern's doors. Except for the comforting smell of hot metal, ready to illuminate the passage when needed, there was no indication that I was here.

I was always curious to see how much time passed during those periods on Holmes's investigations when I waited in darkness before something happened. Generally my internal clock wasn't too disappointing. It was never as long as I thought, but then again it wasn't as if I were off by hours. I had time to recall a great many things, including past Christmases, and times before that as a boy in Stranraer. This latter was no doubt related to the sad business that had called me back to the town of my birth just a few days before. My mind wandered eventually to those more tedious things – the lists of things to do and accomplish that eat up one's day-to-day life and cannot be avoided by those making an effort to function as successful adults – when I heard the faintest shuffle in the passageway beyond where I hid.

I began to perceive a small glow as Father Christmas approached – for who else could it be? Apparently he brought his own dark lantern, not caring to cross the untold distances within the walls without some sort of assistance. I couldn't blame him. If the spaces were as Holmes described, with branches going here and there to multiple rooms, there was lot of

193

opportunity to become lost. And who could say that the other routes were as well-kept as the small segment that I had I witnessed?

It occurred to me to wonder just how Father Christmas knew about these lost passages. I supposed that the answer would be forthcoming.

When the light had reached its peak at the junction of the narrow corridor where I hid and then started to dim, I knew that he had passed, and I slowly allowed the smallest amount of light to escape my own lantern. Unlike Holmes, I didn't trust my own ability to navigate my way back to the main house in the dark. After standing in the blackness for nearly two hours, even the small amount of light from the lantern seemed extraordinarily bright, and was more than sufficient. I silently stepped out of my spot and moved back toward Elsbeth's bedroom.

Turning into the main passageway, I could see the crack ahead where the bedroom entrance was already opened. I quickly covered the remaining distance, pausing just inside the doorway, and holding my breath, while hoping that the intruder couldn't hear the pounding of my heart which seemed deafening in my own years. Then, I had to wait no longer. The light in the room grew much brighter, causing me to suddenly squint, and I heard Holmes stating that the game was up. I surged forward.

Father Christmas had his back to me, facing Holmes, who stood in the bedroom doorway. He was a tall fellow with broad shoulders, and underneath his white wig, I could see that he had black hair. I glanced down at his boots, which had tracked ash from the passageway across the floor, much as he would have done the previous night.

He wasn't aware of me yet and, ignoring Holmes's command, he quickly pivoted back toward my direction and his escape. He was carrying a package – this one much smaller than that of the night before – and when he saw me, it slipped from his fingers. There was a small tinkling of broken glass, and he lurched to a stop, looking down at the gift. He gave a small groan, looked back in my direction, and then knelt almost without thought to pick it up.

"You can get her another one, Mr. Fraser," said Holmes softly, stepping in and pushing the bedroom door shut behind him. "Although perhaps meeting you – properly, if you haven't already met her otherwise – would be a greater gift."

Holmes took another step forward, and just after he did so, the door behind him reopened to reveal Bloom, still in the clothes in which we'd last seen him – and carrying an ugly revolver.

"So you have him, then," he said, his eyes cold. "Didn't take long. Thank you, Mr. Holmes. I can take it from here."

"I think not, Mr. Bloom," said Holmes, turning and stepping between the two men. I shifted as I withdrew my own service revolver, revealing it to our client and covering him so that there was no doubt that Fraser was – at least for now – under my protection. Fraser might have bolted for the passage at that point, as I was no longer in his way, but he simply turned and faced Bloom as well, a frown on his face as he reached up to pull off the white beard and attached wig.

"Don't worry, Mr. Holmes," said Bloom. "You misunderstand. I won't shoot him – unless he tries to flee. But I will see him arrested and put away. Five years of intrusions! Five years of ruining my peace of mind, invading my home, and destroying any sense of security. And the threat to my daughter – "

"There is no threat to Elsbeth," said Fraser, his voice low.

"What?" asked Bloom. "You know her name?"

"He does," said Holmes. "She is his half-sister. Mr. Fraser is your son."

My surprise was only equaled by that of Bloom himself. He took a step back as if pushed, the gun lowering in his hand toward the floor. He stumbled against a chair and dropped into it. I saw him uncurl his finger from the trigger.

Looking at them both, I could now see a resemblance, and was angry with myself for not noticing it before. I had known Holmes long enough by then that I should have done as he always advised and looked beyond surface appearances. I had been lulled when looking at Bloom's features by his heftiness and aged features, as well as his grey hair. Now that I'd been told, I could see that their relationship was undoubtedly true.

"His son?" I asked. "Did you learn this from the vicar?"

"I did," replied Holmes. "He's been remarkably discreet, considering what he has known all of these years. I verified it from the baptism records – where it has rested unnoticed for all of these years simply because no one here has ever cared enough to examine them. Mr. Fraser's mother felt the need to have the child's father recorded accurately and honestly, in spite of the fact that she could have shown her late husband, Mr. Fraser, as the father."

"But – " I gestured to Bloom. "He obviously didn't know. How did that happen?"

Fraser took a step forward, looking rather disconcerting with his big frame garbed in the Father Christmas attire, which I could see now had the aspect of a cheap seasonal costume. "He didn't know. My mother never told him, and after he sent her away, he never bothered to check on her."

"I didn't know," breathed Bloom in agreement, his eyes on his son. "She led me to understand that our . . . relationship, such as it had been, would best be kept secret. For her own reputation, more than my own."

Fraser looked back at Bloom, and one could almost see him rethinking whatever beliefs had sustained him for so long. I recalled his comments the night before, when Grayson had arrived at the inn to request our presence – how he seemed to have no use for Bloom, and no respect either. And then, a few moments later, Mrs. Fraser had tried to make excuses for him when she'd spoken to me in confidence.

"My mother and father worked here, at the manor," explained Fraser. "My father – Silas Fraser – was apparently a bad man, but what could a woman do? From what she told me, Mrs. Bloom – the first Mrs. Bloom – was something of a cold harridan. She made his life – " He jerked a thumb at the seated man. " – a living hell. They . . . they . . . It's difficult to speak of one's mother this way. But she and . . . this man . . . found one another. Comforted one another, here in this house. Even after his first wife died – especially then. But after several years more of that, he sent her away. She and my father both. Turned them out."

"I didn't know," muttered Bloom. "I had met my wife – my second wife – and I knew that having your mother remain here . . . so close . . . would never work out. I . . . I cared for her. Seeing her every day, and given how we'd felt about each other, while my first wife . . . I didn't just turn them out. I gave them money. That's what they – she and Fraser – used to buy the inn. And I didn't communicate with her afterwards. I thought that's what she – your mother – wanted. And I was newly married. I loved my wife, you see. I couldn't hurt her that way, or be dishonest to our vows. I made a clean break of it."

"Which is why," countered Fraser, rather coldly, "you never knew that she was with child – with *me* – by the time you sent her and my father away. He died soon after, and people believed that I was his son."

Bloom looked up at him then. "But how do you know that I am your father, and not him?" Then he blinked and shook his head, a sad smile upon his face. "But no, I can see the resemblance between us. There is no doubt." He raised a hand to his eyes. "So close. So close, and I never knew. I remember when she . . . when your mother died, and I knew of you, of course, but I always thought that you were Fraser's son." He looked up again. "But there is no doubt."

"None," agreed Fraser. "And in any case, my mother was certain that it was you – and she would certainly know, wouldn't she? Not long after they bought the inn, my father died – a drunken accident, from what I was told – and several months after that, I was born. No one questioned who my father was – but she told me the truth when I was old enough. My mother had good help, and ran the place well until she died. She brought me up right, and it's mine now, and I run it right too."

196

"I'm sure you do," said Bloom softly. Only then did he notice that he still held the gun in his hand. He placed it quickly on a nearby table, as if he were hot and burning his hand.

"But why this business with Father Christmas?" I asked. "What has that accomplished?"

"I knew that I had a sister. From all I've heard, she's happy and well cared for. But for some reason, this man – my . . . father – refused to let her celebrate the holiday. A girl should be able to celebrate Christmas! How dare he keep that from her? Maybe what I'd heard wasn't true – maybe she wasn't as happy as everyone believed. I decided that I would celebrate for her – and in doing so be the brother she didn't know she had."

"And you knew of the passageways into the manor that allowed your access?" Holmes asked.

Fraser nodded. "Some of us who have grown up here know them. It's a secret that gets passed along. Not everyone who knew ever used them, obviously, but we would sometimes sneak inside when I was younger, my friends and I. But during the occasions when I've entered over the last five years, I haven't seen any signs that anyone else has been in or out in a long time. Maybe they're forgotten now – possibly all of the others who knew of them kept it to themselves, rather than tell their own children. Some of them aren't safe. The passageways are old – far older than the building that stands here now."

"As the vicar confirmed for me earlier today," confirmed Holmes.

"I suppose that you visited last night and again tonight," I said to Fraser, "because you refused to be stopped this close to Christmas, even knowing that a trap might be set."

"I wasn't sure," replied the innkeeper. "I knew that Grayson had summoned you here last night, but I didn't know why. I thought that it might simply be related to business."

"Then you don't know that Holmes is a detective?" I asked, glancing at my friend. "You haven't heard of him?"

Fraser shook his head. "No. Should I have?"

I smiled. This would be a point of discussion on the train back to London. It was always good to have a few examples such as these for those occasions when Sherlock Holmes needed to be humbled a bit.

"The affair at the inn this afternoon," I asked Holmes. "What did that accomplish?"

"I knew from watching last night who Father Christmas was." He pointed toward the doorway into the walls. "As you can see, Mr. Fraser, I had left some ash on the passage floor to record your footprints. Although I knew who you were when we returned to the inn early this morning, I saw those same footprints in the inn doorway, left in the newly fallen snow. I spent the day asking questions, confirming that Mr. Bloom is well thought-of in the community, by both current and former employees from the house, as well as those at his various businesses, and local merchants, and even his business competitors. Only your negative comments last night seemed out of place. It was the vicar who confirmed why."

"But the Christmas party – " I prompted.

"Ah, yes. That little distraction kept Mr. and Mrs. Fraser busy long enough for me to search their quarters and find the Father Christmas costume. You can see my mark that I placed there on the right knee – something that looks rather like an *H*."

"And of course Mrs. Fraser knows," I added.

"She does – and how could she not? For twelve nights at Christmas, for the last five years, her husband has stepped out not long after midnight." He looked at Fraser. "Has she tried to discourage you?"

Fraser nodded. "She has. But I'd already been doing it for two years when we married, and I didn't want to stop."

"She has been very supportive, I'm sure, but I believe that she'll be pleased that this matter will now be resolved."

Fraser looked surprised – we all did – as Holmes spoke louder. "You may come in now, Mrs. Fraser."

The door to the hall opened and the innkeeper's wife stepped through. Walking beside her and holding her hand was young Elsbeth Bloom, her eyes wide as they fixed on the tall dark-haired man wearing the Father Christmas costume.

"It's you," she breathed. "It's really you."

"Not Father Christmas," said Bloom, finally pulling himself to his feet. "This is . . . this is your brother, William Fraser." He looked from his daughter to the tall young man standing beside him. Then, tentatively, he took a step toward his son, and then another. He put out his hand as if to shake, but then with a choked sob, he lurched forward and pulled Fraser into an embrace.

The younger man seemed surprised, and his chest inflated for a second as he inhaled deeply, as if in preparation to pulling loose and stepping back. Then – and one could see him meet his wife's steady smiling gaze as the conscious decision to relent washed across his features – he relaxed and raised his arms, returning his father's hug.

Mrs. Fraser nodded to Elsbeth, who released her hand and ran forward, throwing her arms around both men – each of whom freed an arm in turn to pull her closer. Mrs. Fraser looked toward Holmes, her eyes rimmed with tears, and silently whispered, "Thank you."

As other members of the household slipped into the now-crowded bedroom – Grayson, Mrs. Treathaway, Blair, and others that I hadn't met

– Holmes tapped my arm and nodded toward the hallway. We slipped past the last of the staff entering the room, went downstairs, and retrieved our hats and coats.

Outside, Holmes tugged his wool fore-and-aft cap tighter on his head, pulled his coat close, and asked, "Are you up for a night walk?"

It was cold but clear, and I found it – at least for the moment – quite bracing. I had mixed emotions about departing from the house at such a moving moment, but it belonged to the Blooms and the Frasers, and not us. I might regret it before we had walked the few miles back to the inn through the cold darkness, but for then I agreed.

"You've had a busy day," I said as we set out, moving slowly but steadily to avoid any unseen patches of ice on the otherwise cleared road.

"It was simply dotting I's and crossing T's," he replied. Once I saw who the visitor was, the rest was just frosting."

"And you made the assumption that there would be a happy ending. You summoned back Elsbeth and the staff from Ballantrae, knowing what time to have them arrive, based on last night's Father Christmas visit."

"It seemed logical. And Bloom really does have an excellent reputation as a good man. Additionally, the vicar confirmed that he had strong feelings for Fraser's mother. It was only circumstances and societal expectations that kept them apart. I knew that when Bloom understood the truth, he would be pleased. And likewise, a good man like William Fraser – and he must be good to have won such a fine lady as his wife – would not hold onto his bitterness."

"And you took Mrs. Fraser into your confidence. Nothing that I heard from her and related to you gave any indication that she wouldn't simply tell her husband of the trap, causing him to stay home tonight."

"Ah, that was a bit more of a gamble, but from what you told me, she didn't seem comfortable with what was going on, and a person of her character, based on the small bit that we witnessed, would certainly wish to see things open and aboveboard, and a family mended, rather than let it continue along the same course."

We walked on in silence for a while, and I found myself scanning the skies for a large star. It was something that I did every year – never with any success, but still I did it – looking for some signs of a Biblical miracle in these less-than-miraculous modern times.

Once again, as if reading my mind, but probably just noticing where my gaze remained directed, Holmes said, "There are many theories as to the true nature of the Bethlehem star. A comet, perhaps? The nova of some distant star? Possibly two or more planets that came into alignment at just the right time to glow particularly bright."

He began to explain the thinking about the latter, raising both hands to illustrate the motions of the planets. He was still doing so when we reached the inn, and he continued as we entered and I stepped behind the bar to retrieve a bottle of the local whisky. We built up the fire and settled at our usual table, neither of a mind to go to sleep.

From that topic we progressed to a number of others, including me finally discussing my true thoughts as to our visit to Stranraer. We were still talking in the early morning when the Frasers returned, their faces glowing. We stood as Fraser silently crossed the room to shake our hands, while Mrs. Fraser waited her turn to hug us both on that bright Christmas morning.

The Six-Fingered Scoundrel
by Jeffrey A. Lockwood

NOTE: Certain aspects of this narrative clearly indicate that it was one that ended up in Dr. Watson's Tin Dispatch Box, with little hope of publication in The Strand. *Editor George Newnes would have red-lined this mercilessly and without hesitation, possibly rejecting it entirely for its stepping beyond the public sensitivities of the time. However, today's modern audiences can be trusted to have a more enlightened viewpoint, and we can be grateful that Watson preserved a record of the affair. – J.L.*

We had not glimpsed the houses across the way from our sitting room on Baker Street for the past week, so thick was the December fog. During these dreary days before a holiday that Holmes found of little interest, he scraped at his fiddle in a desultory manner, although I occasionally requested a carol to lighten the mood. He chuckled derisively about there being a season of goodwill amidst the crime and misery of London.

Mostly unopened Christmas cards from various clients were piled by Mrs. Hudson on the sideboard, although Holmes had found one to his liking. Throughout the days, he smoked more Alexandrian cigarettes than I could count. At least the tobacco was keeping him from seeking out the cursed hypodermic to alleviate his tedium. To quicken Holmes's prodigious mind, he was currently working on what he called an "historical mystery of the highest order".

"Watson," said he, shuffling through some papers and closing a leather-bound tome, "I am near to solving the case of who wrote '*Sumer is Icumen in*' – the oldest known six-part polyphonic composition."

"Indeed," I replied, being absorbed by a report in *The Lancet* regarding how medical degrees could be simply purchased from some colleges in the United States. One can but marvel at the Americans' ingenuity for moneymaking, although the holiday season certainly revealed a British fondness for spending money.

"I think," he continued, taking my noncommittal response as encouragement, "the composer must have been Willemo de Winchecumbe, the precentor of the priory of Leominster in Herford, who signed his name '*W de Wyc*'."

I was mercifully spared a further disquisition on medieval musicology by a tentative knock at our door and the entry of a strapping lad with sparkling eyes, flaxen hair, and glowing cheeks that conveyed a sense of health despite the baneful weather.

"Do come in," said Holmes. "You must be chilled to the bone on a day such as this." He took the fellow's threadbare overcoat and led him to a place by the blazing fire. I suspected that my companion's hospitality was motivated by a hunger for something to assuage his growing *ennui*.

"I'm so sorry to disturb your evening," said the fellow. "But I have heard such inspiring things about your abilities, Mr. Holmes, and I find myself in desperate need of assistance. You see, there's been a suspicious death at the manor where I'm employed."

"Foul play?" asked Holmes with barely concealed delight. "Pray, continue, but please begin at the beginning. And it would be useful were I to know who you are."

"I am Andrew Bates, the footman at Carlisle Hall. My master is Leander Carlisle, owner of the Northampton Ironworks, along with the largest quarry in Northamptonshire."

"And your employer has met an untimely end?" asked Holmes.

"Not at all. Indeed, I think he may be somehow involved in the death of my fiancé, Sarah Dawson. You see, she is, or was – " His voice cracked. " – Lady Carlisle's maid. And my treasured love died terribly two days ago."

"Terribly?" said I, feeling deep sympathy for such a loss at this time of year. "Say more, if you can," Andrew gathered himself and looked disconcertingly at me.

"This is Dr. Watson, my trusted companion. As a first-rate physician, he often proves to be invaluable, and he invariably proves to be discrete."

Giving a slight and almost apologetic nod, Andrew continued. "Sarah began having horrible stomach pains and convulsions. She was confused and frightened, so Lady Carlisle sent for Dr. Clarkson, the family's long-time physician. He came within the hour and bled her to relieve the sickness, but she began trembling violently, slipped into a deep sleep, and soon died with her dear friend Elise at her side."

"Did this Dr. Clarkson offer an explanation for Sarah's affliction?" I asked, dubious that any competent physician would still use bleeding as a treatment.

"I overheard him telling Lady Carlisle that Sarah had suffered a nervous collapse. He used words that meant nothing to me, saying she had suffered a 'pair of oxen' and 'cattle empties'. Do you know what these mean?"

"My good fellow," said I, "they are big words to cover-up small knowledge. A 'paroxysm' is simply a convulsion, and 'catalepsy' refers to an unconscious trancelike state. Was she of a weak constitution?"

"Not at all. She'd been healthy, if a bit preoccupied, on the day she collapsed."

"And she wasn't normally distracted, I gather," said Holmes, sensing there was something more to the young man's story.

"Sarah had to be highly attentive to anticipate the needs of Lady Carlisle. But I must say that my beloved had been acting strangely for a fortnight. She'd been secretive and anxious. I wonder if that disposition might have foretold her affliction, or – "

"Or perhaps something involving Leander Carlisle?" inquired Holmes.

"I have only my suspicions. Master Carlisle had been unusually lenient to Sarah of recent, although typically harsh and demanding toward the rest of the staff. He spoke with her in his study on several occasions, but she wouldn't tell me the nature of their conversations. Perhaps they involved a matter concerning Lady Carlisle – a gentle and generous woman, far better than he deserves."

"Indeed?" said Holmes encouraging our visitor to say more.

"I shouldn't speak ill of my master, as he hasn't had an easy time of it. He bought the largest estate in the county for his first wife in expectation of having a large family. But a decade passed without children before she died of consumption, probably induced by the foul air blanketing Northampton from the smelter. And now Lady Carlisle hasn't provided him with a child in the five years of their marriage."

"How is it that you have been given leave to come to London?" asked Holmes.

"I haven't, exactly. You see, the Master and Lady are visiting her parents in Leeds for the weekend to decorate the family Christmas tree. The butler allowed me a day for myself to mourn Sarah's passing, so I must return tonight. I am desperately hoping that you might pay a visit to the manor and conduct a discrete investigation during the Carlisles' absence." Andrew hesitated and dropped his gaze to the hearthrug. "I should say that I have saved only a week's pay that I can offer you, and I'm afraid such a sum is insufficient."

"Do not concern yourself with that, as fair compensation will be a chance to engage my mind in a challenging venture, to provide justice for your betrothed if needed, and to work closely with my dear friend whose medical knowledge may be of consequence in this case. Indeed, consider it my Christmas present, as unusual as that might be – a gift like all others, fulfilling the interests of both giver and recipient."

After making arrangements for our journey, Andrew took his leave. Holmes went to the sideboard, poured two glasses of port, and rearranged his favored Christmas card against the bottle to display the image of a dead robin. "'*May Yours be a Joyful Christmas*'. A rather equivocal message for the season, don't you think?" said, I accepting the glass from my companion. He set his on the table beside his chair and retrieved the Persian slipper where he kept his tobacco, loaded his briar pipe, and methodically lit the bowl.

"The holidays are filled with ambiguity," said Holmes, settling into his chair, pulling meditatively on the curved stem and staring vacantly into the fire. "Children are torn between the fear of Krampus and the hope of Santa. I believe that Andrew would appreciate the image and wording of the card."

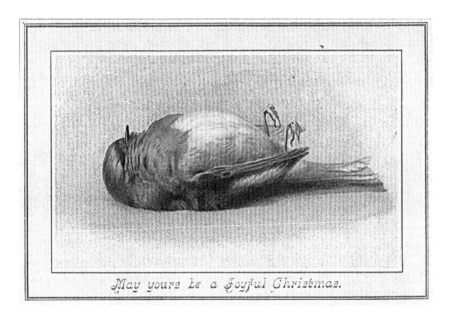
May yours be a Joyful Christmas.

The next morning, after a hasty breakfast that Mrs. Hudson firmly declared was insufficient to ward off the chill of our upcoming journey, we donned our overcoats and scarves, hailed a cab to the Euston Station, and secured a first-class carriage to Northampton. The hour's journey took us to a small, wayside station where we descended. The air in the small industrial city wasn't as foul as I've experienced in Sheffield further north, but it had a miasmic quality – even more dreary than London. Andrew had sent a wagonette pulled by a pair of cobs, driven by a taciturn fellow with a ready whip to deliver us to Carlisle Hall. The slushy road took us past fields blanketed in crusty, gray snow and shrouded with a sulphurous fog from the town's ironworks. Being a believer in the *genius loci*, Holmes murmured, "A wretched melancholy pervades this land."

We soon crested a hill and turned into an avenue lined by the somber skeletons of leafless trees that would surely provide a more verdant aura come springtime. In their branches were clumps of mistletoe, a harbinger of the season. The fog thinned and before us lay a forbidding building draped in ivy, except where openings had been trimmed for the heavy mullioned windows. Between its twin crenelated towers rose a chimney languidly issuing a sinuous column of black smoke.

Andrew greeted us solicitously at the porch, asking after our condition – the first sign of warmth in the world since our arrival. The house was decorated for the season with holly and ivy, as if to defy the grim event that had transpired. Holmes immediately requested an interview with Elise, the housemaid who had tended to Sarah Dawson during her final hours. The dainty lass was almost mute with shyness upon meeting Holmes, whose grey eyes, keen as rapiers, could intimidate the most stalwart of men. But he quickly shifted to the peculiarly ingratiating countenance that readily established the confidence of women, and she began to speak with quiet assurance about her dear, departed friend. After she explained that Sarah had been with the Carlisle family for many years, Holmes began his questioning.

"Tell me what you can about Sarah's condition," said Holmes. "My friend is a doctor of the highest competence, and perhaps he can shed some light on the dreadful event."

"It is my understanding that Sarah was felled by a nervous collapse," said Elise. "At least, that's what the house staff has been whispering, from what was overhead of the doctor's explanation to Lady Carlisle."

"Indeed," said I. "But tell us what you yourself witnessed."

"Well," she began haltingly, "Sarah began stumbling when she walked. Then a weakness and confusion came over her, so I put her to bed. She was sick in the stomach, and I did what I could to make her comfortable. She mumbled that her limbs had become senseless and her fingers were tingling. Her head pained her terribly, and next came spasms that gripped her whole body. When the doctor arrived, he bled her well, but the poor dear fell into a shuddering sleep from which she never awoke." Elise put her face in her hands and sobbed quietly.

I looked at Holmes, who nodded for me to continue. I patted her shoulder and, to affirm my medical suspicion, asked whether the household had been having any difficulties with rats.

"I'm afraid so, although I don't understand why that matters," she said moistly. "In recent days, they have moved from the stables into the kitchen seeking warmth. Or that's what Andrew says."

"Oh, has Andrew been dealing with the rats? Perhaps using arsenic bait?"

"You will need to inquire of him," she sniffled.

"Now then," said Holmes, "I must ask a difficult question of you: Was there gossip in the household regarding Sarah?"

Elise fell silent for some moments. "Master Carlisle told the staff that he wouldn't tolerate illicit relations in his household, and that any maid who was knapped would be summarily dismissed, whatever Lady Carlisle might wish." She paused before continuing, "His mention of m'Lady made clear that Sarah was the target of his disapproval."

"And was she having relations with Andrew?" asked Holmes with his usual directness. This might be the season to celebrate a virgin birth, but my companion countenanced no such medical impossibilities.

"I cannot say," said she, a blush rising to her cheeks.

"Cannot – or will not?" replied Holmes, to which she dropped her eyes without answering. "Well then," said he, "could you direct us to Sarah's room, as I should like to see what might be discovered regarding her personal effects."

"We shared a chamber," said Elise and pointed us toward a set of dimly lit stairs which led to a hallway above the kitchens.

"What have you gleaned thus far?" Holmes asked as we made our way down a gloomy passageway to the servants' quarters. There were no sprigs of mistletoe here to tempt the servants.

"I suspect poisoning," I replied, "and I would have diagnosed arsenic, but the symptoms aren't quite typical."

"Pray, continue," said Holmes, "for this is precisely why I brought you along."

"Arsenic can induce abdominal pain, tingling in the extremities, vomiting, and intestinal distress – all of which Sarah experienced. However, muscle cramps are more characteristic than weakness, and death generally takes a day or more from the onset of symptoms, which usually begin with a sharp burning pain in the esophagus, along with reddening of the skin."

"I judge by your tone that you nevertheless favor arsenic poisoning," said Holmes.

"The conditions of patients can vary, based on my knowledge of case studies. And the house staff evidently had access to rat bait."

"Indeed," said Holmes, "but arsenic is also a byproduct of the smelting process, so it would be widely available in this district. Beware Watson – the formation of premature theories upon insufficient data is as deadly for an investigation as arsenic bait is to a rodent."

"I wouldn't presume to name a suspect, although several of the servants might have something to gain from Sarah's death. Being the lady's maid is surely a coveted position."

"We are well-advised to consider everyone in the household at this point of the investigation – and also if it was actually a murder! Now, let us see what we might learn in Sarah's room," said he, opening the door into the tiny, windowless chamber. In his usual fashion, Holmes systematically and minutely inspected the floor, walls, and furniture. "Halloa! What is this?" he exclaimed, having searched through the drawers of Sarah's battered bureau and lifted out a package of yellowish, waxy powder from beneath her clothing.

"That is nothing remarkable," said I reading the label on the medicament. "Diachylon is used to treat the skin, and housemaids have ample opportunities to develop sores. Indeed, I saw that Elise's knuckles were raw, undoubtedly from scrubbing."

"However, this belonged to Sarah, not Elise," said Holmes, "and a lady's maid would hardly engage in excoriating labor. Nor would she have cause to hide the ingredients for a common poultice in the bottom of a drawer. Surely it isn't some holiday gift to be hidden. What, pray tell, does this substance comprise?" he asked poking inquiringly at the pasty mass and touching a finger to his tongue. "From the sweetness, I would deduce a lead compound," he said in answer to his own question.

"Lead Oleate is blended with a small amount of glycerin. This substance is applied to sheets of linen to serve as an adhesive plaster. I see nothing of importance to our investigation."

"My dear Watson," chided Holmes, "as so often is the case, you see but do not observe."

We made our way to Leander Carlisle's study with the guidance of his octogenarian butler, who introduced himself as Edmund Baxter. Andrew had explained the nature of our visit to the stooped servant. With a mischievous glint in his clear blue eyes as he led us to the study, Baxter explained that he looked forward to soon leaving both the manor – and his master. Holmes latched onto this remark like an east London cur clenching a discarded beef knuckle.

"I gather you are displeased with your employer," prompted Holmes.

"I plan to take my leave upon the New Year," Baxter said, "and at my age I shall not be seeking further employment, so I can be honest after years of discretion. I am quite aware that Master Carlisle has forced himself on several young maids in his employ which would be despicable enough, but he has done so even while Lady Carlisle, a truly sweet and decent woman, has been in the house and occupied with one or another

207

social obligation. She makes her husband appear respectable to those families in the county who regularly convene for hunts, dinners, and to cheat at cards."

"Returning to your Master's improprieties, might these have involved Lady Carlisle's maid?"

"Sarah Dawson was a buxom lass," he said wistfully, and then with a tone of condemnation. "I can have little doubt she caught the master's eye."

"We were informed that he reproached the staff for illicit relations," Holmes continued. "Do you think it possible he was covering his own indecencies?"

Having reached our destination, Baxter led us into an oak paneled room and closed the door as if what he had to say was somehow more sensitive than what he had already shared. "Indeed, Shakespeare might have written, '*The gentleman doth protest too much, methinks.*' But in this case, the protestor need not have worried about leaving evidence of his transgression, as he has been unable to sire a child."

"Perhaps he was laying a blind, just in case," said I. "In my medical experience, infertility is a fickle affliction."

"I hadn't considered that he might have planned so fiendishly to implicate Andrew should a child have resulted. But in any case, there would be no way other than the lady's testimony to trace parentage back to my master."

At this point, Holmes had begun his examination of the room. He took a magnifying glass from his coat pocket and peered intently at a photographic portrait of Leander Carlisle. "I discern that your Master has a long and severe scar on the lateral portion of his left hand, Baxter. Might you know its origin?"

"I am told that the wound below his little finger is the result of an accident as a young man. A similar scar is on his right hand as well."

"It would be remarkable that a mishap damaged both hands in the same manner," said Holmes, moving to a large photograph showing three generations of the Carlisle family.

"I cannot speak beyond what I've been told," said Baxter, as Holmes studied the photograph, "although Dr. Clarkson has attended to the family for many years and might know more."

"Were you given an explanation for why your master's father – at least I am deducing the relationship from facial similarities – wore gloves for an indoor portrait? Moreover, can you offer a reason why the littlest finger of the glove is so enlarged?" he asked, nearly pressing his nose to the photograph.

"You are remarkably observant. He always wore gloves, but nobody ever spoke of either the reason or their unusual form."

"I would imagine, however, that you can identify the sword-wielding woman portrayed in stained glass window on the far wall," Holmes said, shifting gaze from the photograph, past the fireplace to the opposite side of the room.

"That is Saint Barbara. Her feast day was just two weeks previous, I believe. She is the patron saint of miners. She represents the longing of miners for light."

"Quite," murmured Holmes, as he next began to study the items on the desk, before directing his attention to a credenza on which was mounted a stuffed rooster with a russet body and a shimmering green-black tail.

"That is a Red Dorking, who sired three champion cocks," said Baxter. "This breed is Master Carlisle's passion, although all but the magnificent specimen you see here were fated for the kitchen."

"A remarkable specimen in more ways than one," said Holmes.

"Meaning what?" I asked, not expecting an answer when Holmes had his nose scenting the trail.

"In due time, Watson. There is still a vital interview to be conducted," said Holmes, his brows knitting and eyes sparkling in a manner that bespoke a deep immersion into a chain of reasoning that I couldn't fathom. "Our next step should be a visit to Dr. Clarkson, who examined Sarah in her final hour. Baxter, could you arrange our transportation into town?" The old butler bowed and shuffled down the hall as Holmes paced in front of the stone-cold fireplace.

Within the hour we'd returned to Northampton as wet snowflakes began to fall. In the heavy air, the pungent odors of leatherworks mingled with the brimstone vapors of the ironworks as we arrived at the residence and consulting room of Dr. James Clarkson. He was a tall septuagenarian with a vulpine face, shrewd eyes behind gold-rimmed spectacles, and a haughty bearing. While Holmes tried his best to elicit from the fellow details about the death of Sarah Dawson, I took the opportunity to conduct a Holmesian inspection of the man's surgery. The doctor was evasive and pompous and my companion was getting nowhere – a rare situation, indeed.

"Well then, Watson, I think our task here is complete," said Holmes.

"Perhaps so, but might I ask a question of my colleague?" Holmes cocked an eyebrow and nodded his assent. "Tell me, Doctor, where did you earn you medical degree?" I asked, knowing the answer from having perused the certificates mounted on the wall to impress naïve patients.

"The American University of Philadelphia," he pronounced, "one of the finest institutions in America."

"Really now? I read in *The Lancet* just yesterday that one can simply purchase a medical degree for about eight guineas from your alma mater. And speaking of lancets, blood-letting such as you performed on Sarah Dawson has been rejected by the medical community for many years – except perhaps in Sleepy Hollows where patients and practitioners are uninformed."

"By Heaven, I won't be insulted by the likes of you! There's a prejudice just now against the use of the lancet, but – "

"But nothing. I must wonder whether the nature of your credentials, such as they are, would be of interest to the Carlisle family and the good people of Northampton – not to mention the General Council of Medical Education and Registration."

With this, Clarkson's indignation collapsed and he stammered, "What is it that you want of me?"

"Answer me honestly, and we shall leave you to your practice, as even inept treatments may be preferable to none at all, although this is woefully uncertain in your case." I said this in an uncharacteristically belligerent manner, but little angers me more than fraud perpetrated on people who are in ill-health. I had adopted the investigatory intensity of my now-silent companion who watched the proceedings with evident pleasure. "First, what do you know of the scars on the hands of Leander Carlisle?"

Clarkson cleared his throat and lowered his voice, as if to ensure that nobody could eavesdrop. "He bears the marks of surgery that I performed when he was a child. I removed an extra finger from the outside of each hand, a condition that he shared with his father, who hid the extra digits by wearing a pair of custom-made gloves at all times. They were embarrassed by this grotesque flaw in the family line. I believe the only member of the staff aware of the condition was Sarah, who tended the elder Carlisle in his last days. And now, if there's nothing more, I must ask you to leave."

"We shall, if you will now also answer my question," said Holmes. "What use might a young woman have for diachylon, other than as a plaster to treat skin afflictions?"

Clarkson sighed deeply in evident discomfort. "Of late, these substances are being widely used in this region as abortifacients." Holmes scowled at the evasive, technical term, so I whispered to him that this referred to preparations meant to induce the abortion of a fetus. "I blame the women of Sheffield," Clarkson continued, "who observed that many pregnancies were lost following the use of lead pipes in the city's water supply. From there, they began to experiment with diachylon. Among those who cannot support another child in an already hungry household, the practice of taking diachylon to bring on a woman's flow is far more prevalent than anyone would readily admit."

"Such as perhaps in the case of Sarah Dawson?" I asked.

"I should not wish to say, as my patients expect discretion rather than rumor-mongering," replied Clarkson directing us toward the doorway as he had clearly reached the limits of his patience.

On our journey back to the Carlisle Hall, so that Holmes could secure, in his words, "Two final pieces of the puzzle that might allow us to solve this case beyond any doubt." He put his hand on my shoulder in a manner that I'd rarely experienced in our years together. "My dear Watson," said he, "I don't believe that I have ever been more pleased – nay proud – to have you as a partner in an investigation."

Andrew met us upon our arrival and we were given the run of the manor so that Holmes could conduct his business expeditiously, since we hoped to catch the last train back to London before nightfall. My friend strode to Sarah's room, where he took a large sample of the diachylon secreted in her bureau drawer. Thence we dashed up to Leander's study, where Holmes adopted a frustratingly deliberate pace in his minute investigation of the stained-glass window. Finally, we rejoined Andrew on the balustraded gallery garlanded with greens and bedecked with stags' heads.

"Do you know what happened to Sarah?" asked Andrew nearly trembling in anticipation.

"I believe that I do," replied Holmes, "but knowing and proving are different matters. Moreover, determining the cause of her death may prove easier than establishing the perpetrator. Rest assured that I shall return within days, having acquired evidence needed for both. Until then, however, there is one last, difficult matter."

"Of course, anything," said Andrew.

"Where are your fiancé's remains?"

"Dr. Clarkson declared there was no basis for an inquest as her death resulted from natural causes. And, of course, he is very influential in this county regarding such matters. She was buried the next day in the Carlisle's graveyard, a furlong east of the house."

"Is it not unusual for a servant to be interred in the family cemetery?" asked Holmes.

"Sarah had been with the family since she was but fourteen, having been at the side of Master Carlisle's father in his final days. The old fellow was terribly senile and had come to mistake her for his own daughter who

211

had died tragically in her youth. And Sarah was much loved by Lady Carlisle, so I was not very surprised at her receiving a place in the back corner."

During our return to London, dusk cloaked the cold body of the rolling hills like a death shroud belying the holidays. Descending into my own darkness, I said to Holmes that to be certain of Sarah's fate would mean examining her body. Even so, there would be no way to differentiate a tragic accident from a desperate suicide, or a heinous murder. This was just as well, since the local magistrate would almost certainly refuse to issue a Writ of Exhumation given the standing of the Carlisle family. Holmes cocked his head and lifted an eyebrow, suggesting that he was conjuring a plan into which I would surely be drawn. And just as surely, I would be provided with only those details that my companion deemed necessary.

"Tell me," said he growing comfortable with the ungentlemanly terms used by physicians, "what do you know of pregnancies outside of wedlock from your years of medical practice?"

"The condition is rare among the upper classes because the girls are closely chaperoned. And in the middle class, the girls are either swiftly married or sent away to give birth and the babe adopted."

"And the working class?"

"Abortion is common, although not admitted by the authorities."

"What of a domestic servant, such as Sarah?"

"You know as well as I that the reputation of one's servants is taken to be a reflection on the house as a whole. Thus, a maid would likely be dismissed without a character reference, and hence without any prospect of further employment. This portends a desperate future, one that often leads to the vile houses along the Strand, Haymarket, and the Vauxhall Pleasure Gardens if they are pretty and young. Otherwise, they ply their trade on street corners and dark alleys."

Holmes nodded slowly, closed his eyes, and pressed together his finger-tips. For the remainder of our journey, the set of his jaw suggested a deep vexation boding ill for the object of his hardening conviction. I was reminded of the grim fate of King Herod, whose last days were so agonizing as to elicit a desperate attempt at suicide.

Back in Baker Street, Holmes sent me to pursue whatever knowledge was available regarding the unusual condition of the Carlisle men's hands. I divided my time between the reading room at the British Museum and the library at the British Medical Association on Tavistock Square, while Holmes pursued his chemical investigations on the acid-charred bench in our sitting room. All the while, poor Mrs. Hudson tried to guess when we would dine and never chose the correct hour, as I adopted Holmes's monomaniacal focus and often didn't return until well after any civilized dinner hour to find a joint of beef, a loaf of bread, and slab of butter arranged on the sideboard.

Upon returning on the fourth evening of our separate pursuits with an overflowing satchel of notes that I'd taken from my research, I encountered Archie Stamford leaving our apartment. Before I could inquire as to the reason for the presence of this disreputable pickpocket and forger whose iniquitous skills my companion sometimes enlisted, Holmes greeted me with an exuberant cry. "At last, Watson, it's as clear as crystal, and I couldn't have received a better gift if Father Christmas had come early to our rooms."

"And I, too, have achieved my ends," said I, quickly forgetting about Stamford. "But first tell me of your discovery."

"I adapted the Marsh Test, which as you know is a highly sensitive means of extracting arsenic. My modified methods revealed that Sarah's diachylon contained only lead."

"But isn't that what you expected?"

"Expected, yes, but the world is not required to meet our expectations – a fact that every child learns at this time of year. Now then, allow me to finish without interruption, my good man. I used sodium hydroxide to precipitate the lead from a carefully measured aliquot of her salve. And from this, I was able to ascertain that the diachylon contained nearly ten times the amount of lead that a competent apothecary would use in a formulation."

"So had Sarah ingested the material in an amount typically suited to induce an abortion, she would have taken a lethal dose."

"Precisely. And now what have you learned from the dusty tomes of medicine?"

"A great deal. The extra finger that appears in the Carlisle family line arises from a rare, inherited condition called *polydactyly*. The extra digit typically forms on the ulnar side of the hand, meaning the development of a second little-finger. This defect is more common in males, and is also frequently seen in some breeds of fowl – "

"Such as Dorking chickens," Holmes interjected.

"But how?"

"While you were enchanted by the plumage of Leander Carlisle's mounted cock, my eye was not so distracted. Birds typically possess four toes, but the one in his study had five on each foot. I would deduce that his predilection for this breed lies in the abnormality that it shares with his family."

"So how shall we proceed with the chemical and genetic knowledge we have obtained?"

"A return to Carlisle Hall is in order. This time we will bring along Inspector Lestrade, as I don't trust the local constabulary, given the sway held by Leander Carlisle in the county."

"And your plan?"

"In due course, Watson. Trust that Three Wise Men will be sufficient to the task. But before we leave tomorrow afternoon, acquire a shovel from Mrs. Hudson's garden shed and bring along the materials for making a flaming torch."

Upon our return to Northampton with Lestrade, Holmes promised a Christmas gift to the inspector in the form of a solution to a murder for which he could take credit back in London. While the two of them went to find us accommodations for the coming night, I was sent to the grounds of Carlisle Hall with a rather peculiar task. As dusk arrived along with a swirling mist, I made my way to the family cemetery, where I used Mrs. Hudson's garden spade to turn over a foot of soil above the grave of Sarah Dawson. Thence, my instructions were to put the lighted torch alongside the gravesite and draw the attention of the staff without being seen myself. A few pebbles cast against the back windows of house were sufficient to induce the groundskeeper to investigate the queer happenings in the graveyard. I had learned well to trust my companion and avoid inquiries as to the purpose of such strange undertakings.

By the time I managed my return to town, Holmes and Lestrade had settled themselves into the local tavern and were enjoying a heaping platter of boiled beef, potatoes, and cabbage. The meal was uninspired but it warmed me from the inside out. After the two detectives were done exchanging tales of recent exploits, we made our way to our rooms. The next morning, we arose to a driving sleet and arranged for a carriage to take us to Carlisle Hall. Baxter greeted us and Andrew took our coats, whispering that there was great consternation in the household caused by a mysterious happening involving Sarah's grave.

Baxter led us past a Christmas tree festooned with candles, ribbons, and sparkling ornaments to an agitated Leander Carlisle, a portly, large-featured man with the arrogant bearing of an industrialist who is used to giving orders and having them followed. We were soon joined by Lady Carlisle, a statuesque woman of striking beauty with confident, kind eyes.

"What is it you want?" he commanded, perhaps set aback by our arrival upon the heels of my nocturnal shenanigans. Holmes introduced us and suggested that our business might be best conducted in his study. Carlisle grumbled, but the presence of a scrawny, rat-faced Scotland Yard

214

detective was persuasive. Once inside the wood-paneled room, Carlisle attempted to gain the upper hand.

"Perhaps, Inspector Lestrade, you might investigate the criminal disturbance of a grave on my property."

"There's no need for that, as the perpetrator is in this room," Lestrade answered. Apparently Holmes had filled in his counterpart regarding my perfunctory grave digging while they were enjoying a beer at the tavern. For my part, I was still at a loss as to the Holmes's endgame. Lady Carlisle looked unsteady and gracefully took a seat in one of the leather chairs beside the crackling fireplace.

"Indeed, Dr. Watson and I exhumed the body under the supervision of detective Lestrade," said Holmes with bold deception. With that declaration, he withdrew a document from his coat pocket and placed it on the desk for Carlisle to examine. The official looking paper was titled, *"Writ of Exhumation"* and was issued by the High Court of Justice in London, complete with the Royal Coat-of-Arms and signed by the Honorable Justice Lord Alverstone. This explained the presence of the forger in our apartment the day before. Lady Carlisle squeezed shut her eyes, trying to maintain composure.

"What is the meaning of this?" Carlisle boomed.

"I would ask the meaning of the gloves your father wore," Holmes replied peering intently at the family photograph. "Or the meaning of the scars on the outside of your hands. Or perhaps your peculiar affection for Dorking chickens."

"I suppose that you are proud of yourself for having invaded my privacy to discover an inherited physical irregularity."

"Not only a physical defect," Holmes continued, "but a moral one as well. What I'm about to share will be terribly disturbing, so perhaps it would be best for you to take your leave."

"I am fully capable of dealing with whatever your investigation has revealed," she replied, now sitting straight-backed in the chair and lifting her chin defiantly.

"Very well, then. In Dr. Clarkson's surgery, an autopsy was performed by Dr. Watson with all of the respect and dignity possible, given the disturbing nature of the procedure. Do you wish to reveal your findings?" he asked, turning to me.

"I think it best if you do so as the private investigator of this unsettling case," I replied, since I had no inkling what fictional findings my companion sought for the purposes of his unfolding plan.

"He found, and has entered into the official record, the presence of a fetus judged to be ten weeks of age." Lady Carlisle gasped, and her husband braced himself against the desk. "And Dr. Watson further documented that the babe has six fingers on each hand." With this, Lady Carlisle stood and glared at her spouse. Her abhorrence shifted from the image of a beloved maid on the surgeon's table to the real presence of an adulterous husband.

"I demand an explanation, Leander. What have you done?"

"She seduced me in a moment of weakness!" he pleaded – no Angel Gabriel this time to explain away the pregnancy in this holiday-shattering revelation.

"I'm sure you felt safe that your tryst wouldn't yield a child," Lady Carlisle said in an increasingly unladylike manner.

"I offered her a generous payment if she would bring on her flow," he said, as if this would mitigate his infidelity and his wife's ire. I could also sense in his words the wound to his manhood that Lady Carlisle had inflicted by referring to his failure at fatherhood.

"I'm sure you did," said Holmes. "And you certainly approved of her plan to use diachylon. But a man of means, such as yourself, wouldn't want to lower himself to paying for a servant's silence. Or perhaps Sarah raised the stakes. In any case, you realized that you could save your reputation and your money by increasing the lead in Sarah's medicament to a deadly level, which would create the impression that she had accidently poisoned herself in attempting to abort Andrew's child, should the cause of her demise ever be determined. A near perfect plan, I should say."

"You should say nothing of the sort," Carlisle said in a last vain effort to escape justice. "If she took too much of the substance, that is not my fault."

"For a man of industry, you seem quite unaware of the capacity for a competent chemist to determine that the lead in her medicament was present at ten times the standard concentration. Nor did you anticipate that an observant investigator could detect that lead had been scraped from the joints between the panes of your stained-glass window. Under magnification, it was evident that these scrapings were finely minced and added to Sarah's diachylon."

"You damnable blackguard!" Lady Carlisle said to her husband, having abandoned all affectations of civility.

Carlisle turned to his wife and said pretentiously, "Given your maid's capacities, my lack of an heir evidently resulted from *your* feminine inadequacies. I suppose I went too far in trying to undo *with* Sarah what you were unable to do *for* me."

With that, Lady Carlisle stepped forward and delivered a slap that – had it been a man's cross-hit – would've dropped her husband on the spot. Uncomfortable with such domestic disharmony during what was rightfully

216

a time for family celebration, I let my eyes drift to the interlaced holly and ivy that the servants had used to adorn the study. According to tradition, the firm holly represents the man and the soft ivy the woman.

As Lestrade took an enervated Carlisle into custody and his wife looked on with prickly betrayal, Holmes began to softly whistle the tune of the "Boar's Head Carol", an ancient melody recounting the sacrifice of a beast for the Yuletide dinner. Was my calloused companion expressing a moment's empathy with the despondent and emasculated killer, or was Holmes enjoying a satirical twist on the centuries-old song? It was impossible to say, although even Ebenezer Scrooge had a change of heart.

The Case of the
Duplicitous Suitor
by John Lawrence

It was just a week before Christmas, 1885, and London was resplendent with the lights and decorations of the holiday season that always brought a degree of gaiety to that bone-chilling time of the year. I had been preoccupied late by a patient: A congested child with a hacking cough and a desperate young mother fearful the lad was taking his last painful breaths. A small amount of brandy dissolved in weak tea had helped relieve the youngster's distress, and a larger amount calmed the mother. It was shortly before dawn when I climbed into my bed, still shivering from the cold, weary and longing for a few hours' rest, only to be wakened in what seemed mere moments by a loud knocking on my bedroom door.

"Awaken, Watson!" the familiar voice of Sherlock Holmes cried from the landing. "The day is fast disappearing, and a case awaits!"

A quick examination of the clock on my bedside table indicated it was just after seven, but the damage to my slumber was done. Once awakened, an old army surgeon can never return to sleep, regardless how dark it is, so I quickly conducted my ablutions, dressed, and met Holmes downstairs in the our sitting room. I noted that Mrs. Hudson had thoughtfully arranged some evergreens on the mantel above the glowing fireplace to give a touch of the season to our rooms.

Holmes acknowledged my arrival with a nod of his head and a slight smile of greeting. Despite the early hour on a Sunday morning, he was already dressed and, from the stuffy atmosphere of the room, I guessed onto his second pipe of the day. Several newspapers had already evidently been read and their contents digested, along with a breakfast on the table consisting of sausages, scones, and grilled tomatoes. I poured myself a cup of Mrs. Hudson's thankfully hot and strong coffee and eased myself into a chair by the table.

"What is so urgent as to disturb my very unsatisfactory but essential rest?" I inquired.

"Yes, I heard you go out last night," Holmes explained. "Not too challenging a case, I hope?"

"I'm surprised you don't know the precise details of it," I replied somewhat tersely, waiting for the caffeine stimulant to ratchet me more awake.

"No, I don't, and for once, I will not engage in that parlour game."

"The one in which you guess what I have been doing, or with whom, or where I have been?"

"Quite so," he replied, "but not today. I awakened you because we are due to have a distinguished visitor this morning, and I didn't think you would want to miss his arrival."

"I certainly hope he and the case he brings to your attention are worthy of my having sacrificed a decent night's sleep," I replied. "Or whatever was left of it."

Holmes looked at me understandingly and walked over to where I sat, hungrily examining the pile of bangers and tomatoes. "Perhaps this will spark some interest," he said, dropping a folded piece of paper in front of me. "What do you make of this note?"

The letter was written on heavy, high-quality cream-coloured paper. The handwriting was scrawled, barely even legible to my eyes. The engraved name atop the stationery removed all doubt as to its provenance: Collins Bookseller at 255 Piccadilly Street, in St. James.

"A most reputable book-seller," I noted.

"If you wouldn't mind, Watson, might you read the message aloud?" he requested. "It will help me to digest the contents without taxing my eyes again on that dreadful handwriting."

He threw himself into one of the other chairs by the table and speared a plump sausage with a pen knife, likely one used recently to open the envelope containing the letter now nestled in my hand.

Dear Mr. Holmes, [it began]

I do not make it a practice to seek the advice and counsel of men in your line of work, but an inexplicable series of events has come to my attention that I am unable to comprehend. The circumstances are quite delicate, I think, and therefore I would favour describing them to you in person at your residence later this morning, rather than include them in this letter or delay relating them to you. With your permission, then, I will arrive at your door by eight a.m. and would appreciate the benefit of your consideration of this peculiar and disturbing matter.

The missive was signed *"Garthwaite Collins, Esq."* in the same scrawl as the text of the message itself.

"I think that's about it," I said, squinting slightly to be sure I had faithfully deciphered the perplexing penmanship of Mr. Gaithwaite Collins, Esq.

"Can you form any ideas from so curious a note?" he asked.

"Nothing beyond what he states quite clearly in the letter," I responded. "I suppose you are able to construct a grand story from it."

"Well, there is a bit that can be discerned, I think," Holmes said in response to his own question. "It seems clear the events of which the honourable Mr. Collins seeks my assistance pertain to someone other than himself, since the account has quite a secondary or detached description of the matter. Mr. Collins is a well-known merchant whose shop has provided me with some of the rare city directories I find so useful in my work. I know him to be an unmarried man, like myself, but of some advanced years, so it seems likely the matter has been brought to his attention by an acquaintance or colleagues, rather than a family member."

"That seems reasonable enough."

"Since he refers to the situation as 'delicate', I would think it most likely the person involved is a woman, probably a young woman, without parents – possibly only recently arrived in London, and perhaps a junior employee."

"How do you deduce that set of facts?"

"If the woman were young, she would surely seek the advice of her parents. If older, her husband, or more likely her lady friends, if the matter were truly 'delicate'. Since she has come to Collins, a man of sixty or more, I must assume she either has no parents or is estranged from them. Otherwise, even if the matter were urgent, she surely would reach out to them rather than turn to someone like Collins. So, she likely is young, without husband or close women friends nearby with whom to consult, and so she turns to a thoughtful and intelligent man she knows. How would she come to know him? Likely because she works at the bookstore or is a frequent client who has come to rely on him for advice about becoming acquainted with her new residence, I suspect that is the portrait of the person in need: A young woman, fairly new to London, without parents of friends and facing a disturbing situation involving a suitor that she can entrust only to someone older and yet compassionate."

"All that from this vague letter?" I pressed.

"And more, in all likelihood, but why prolong the mystery? I believe I heard footsteps on the stairs, and expect that Mrs. Hudson will imminently announce the arrival of Mr. Garthwaite Collins."

Holmes has no sooner finished speaking than Mrs. Hudson's familiar knock signaled her presence outside our rooms. "Mr. Garthwaite Collins," she announced as I opened the door and a tall, distinguished, white-haired gentleman strode through, glancing neither at our housekeeper nor me, but walking straight across the room to where Holmes stood puffing on a churchwarden.

"We have met before, Mr. Holmes," he began, offering no greeting. "At the Diogenes Club. You were visiting your brother."

Holmes nodded his head in recognition. "I recall, Mr. Collins. I believe we had a brief conversation in the Stranger's Room about the excellence of the hiking trails in the Grampian Mountains of Scotland."

"Astonishing!" cried Collins. "Believe me, I wouldn't have said the conversation was so memorable."

"Nor would I," Holmes replied coolly. "Now, I'm sure you didn't come here to discuss hiking in Scotland. Your note mentioned an urgent and 'delicate' matter. Pray, how may we be of service to you or – if I may presuppose – to the young lady who has confided the reason for her unhappiness to you?"

Collins stood with his mouth slightly open for a moment before shifting on his feet slightly. "Why, how did you know that?"

"It is, as I'm wont to say, my business to know things that others believe hidden. I merely read the inflections and suggestions in your letter to reach my conclusion."

Collins considered Holmes's explanation and then walked with a slight limp to one of the comfortable chairs near the fire and sat down. Holmes and I followed, and we all lit cigarettes as we prepared to hear the book merchant's account.

"You are quite right, Mr. Holmes," he began. "The young lady's name is Penelope Barrington, and she has been most terribly misused, I fear. Her father and I served together under General Outram during the Battle of Khushab. That was during the war with Persia."

"I am aware," Holmes murmured.

"Well, it was a nasty business, and we were in the thick of it for sure at Khushab. Many of our mates didn't make it out of there, but I did – with a bullet through my thigh. My friend, Philip Barrington, was even less lucky. He caught two rounds, one in the chest and one in his abdomen. Tore him up something terrible, but the doctors were on him in minutes and saved us both."

"I was an army physician myself," I said. "Took a Jezail bullet in my shoulder at Maiwand."

Collins glanced briefly at my shoulder and a momentary fellowship was struck between us before he continued his story. "We returned home considerably worse for wear. I became a book merchant, as you know, and have been fortunate to run a very successful establishment. Philip was less lucky. He did straightaway marry his sweetheart, Mary, and they lived happily enough for some years though without any children. Then Mary fell ill and died, leaving Philip a shattered man. A few years later, however, he was fortunate to meet a young woman – Dora – whom he wed, and within a year or two, little Penelope arrived. She was the apple of his eye for sure, and they would bring her round to the shop for me to admire from time to time.

"Ah, but time wasn't good for Philip. His injuries kept him in and out of doctors' consultancies for years, and he was fortunate that his father's good fortune in the spice trade in Indo-China kept him and his family secure and comfortable.

"Philip's luck went from bad to worse starting a year or so ago. His wife developed influenza and died suddenly last June. As if that wasn't disconcerting enough, he began complaining of all sorts of troubles and that his pain, which seemed perpetual, was steadily worsening.

"One day, he came to see me to ask that should something happen to him, would I be good enough to keep an eye on Penelope, perhaps provide her a job at my shop. Well, she was an attractive, literate, and pleasant enough young lady and I assured Philip she would be welcome if something befell him.

"Not six weeks later, he was a dead man. The old repairs in his gut had come undone, or some such thing, and he was full of infection. It was fortunate he didn't have to live long in that pain. Soon after, I received the note from Penelope, asking if I would honor her father's request. Well, 'a friend's last need' and all that, so naturally, I urged her to come down to London at her earliest convenience and I would get her settled into the book business."

"And was she an attentive employee?" asked Holmes.

"I hadn't a care or worry about her, not for a moment," Collins continued. "Oh, she was still quite sad about her father, you can understand, what with him dying so fast and in such discomfort. She had lost a bit of her bounce. But then Mr. Josephus Rexford came along, and things certainly seemed to be changing for the better."

"Josephus Rexford?" Holmes inquired. "Pray, who is he?"

"Well, I admit that is a bit of a mystery, that question," Collins said. "He came into the shop one day about six months ago looking for some books on European history, and Penelope was happy to show him our selection. He must have liked the books because he returned the next day and then the next, and each time, he would ask Penelope to join him back at the history section where they would peruse books and discuss their contents."

"And did Mr. Rexford actually purchase any books?" Holmes asked.

"Oh, yes, quite a few," Collins responded. "All sorts of books about the history and politics of Italy, Switzerland, Germany, and the like. Seemed quite knowledgeable about the subject, I might add, for we engaged in several conversations of our own whenever he visited the store."

"Can you describe him?" asked Holmes.

"Oh, quite a young gentleman," responded Collins, "or I should have never allowed him so much unescorted time with Penelope! Tall, well-dressed, perhaps in his early twenties, almost dashing. He often carries a cane with a large silver knob on the top – an affectation for someone his age, I believe. It seems to have a crest of some type, but it has always been too far away to discern any details."

"And how came he to the shop?"

"By foot, but there always seemed to be a carriage waiting for him upon his departure – a private carriage, not a cab for hire."

"And how does he speak?"

"Oh, he is very articulate – very precise in his diction, I should say."

"Any accent? Inflection? Any hint from where he might be?"

Collins paused thoughtfully, rubbing his lips with his index finger. "Now that you mention it, perhaps the slightest of accents, very faint and certainly nothing I could trace. I took him to be a well-educated young man and gave little thought to such matters. We have so many from overseas in England now."

"Did he mention his line of business?"

"Not to me, but as Penelope began spending some time with him, including in afternoon walks away from the shop, I assumed she learned more about him. I did ask. I considered my responsibility to Philip to include ensuring his daughter wasn't being taken advantage of, even by such a seemingly upstanding gentleman. But she didn't share much information with me, except to assure me that Mr. Rexford had attended Sandhurst, was quite wealthy, and engaged in private affairs of which he chose not to speak. I found the secrecy somewhat disconcerting, I must admit. One afternoon when Penelope was preoccupied with another customer, and as I found myself alone with him, I decided to do a little sleuthing of my own."

"Oh, excellent," Holmes murmured. "And what information did you uncover?"

"Well, not a great deal, to be truthful. He deflected questions about his source of income, but he assured me it was considerable and quite secure, although he declined to be more specific. As to his intentions with Penelope, he told me he intended to ask her to marry him. Well, you can imagine I was quite astonished since I knew so little about the gentleman's background, but what was there for me to do? I was neither her father nor legal guardian.

"Sure enough, several days later she fairly floated into the shop one morning, beaming with happiness and bubbling with laughter. Her glow far outshone the holiday lights that I had arranged to give the store the look of the Season.

"'Oh, Mr. Collins, I'm so fortunate!' she exclaimed. 'I'm to be married to Mr. Rexford!' She showed me a beautiful ring he had given her to commemorate the betrothal, one of several pieces of family jewelry he had apparently conferred on her, although he asked that she not wear them outside her flat until he had alerted his family of these gifts.

"I was, of course, delighted to see her so overjoyed, but I remained wary, not knowing nearly enough, in my estimation, about the man to whom she was now engaged to be married."

"Have you been introduced to his family?" Holmes asked.

"Certainly not."

"Has Penelope?"

"Not to my knowledge. I'm not even sure where his family lives, or what business they might be in. She said that many of them don't live in England. She and her betrothed intend to embark upon a trip to meet them all after their marriage."

"Well, Mr. Collins, this seems somewhat irregular, I admit, and you are certainly in an unenviable position, having some of the responsibilities of a guardian but none of the authority of a parent. You can continue to press Miss Barrington for more information. You may even insist upon a fuller explanation from Rexford himself. But I doubt you have much legal authority to demand information or act if it isn't proffered."

"Yes, I'm quite aware of the precariousness of my situation, Mr. Holmes, which is why I haven't sought legal recourse. But I have not yet told you the most singular part of this situation."

Holmes smiled gratefully, lighting another cigarette and taking a deep pull on it. The fire at the end glowed brilliantly orange as he settled back in the chair and blew out a cloud of gray smoke. "Then pray, Mr. Collins, do not keep me in anticipation," Holmes said.

"Four days ago, Penelope appeared my home after dinner. She was quite upset – even distraught, I might say."

"'Oh, Mr. Collins, he is *gone*!' she exclaimed, falling into my arms. 'Gone!'"

"Who is gone, Penelope?" I asked, anticipating the response.

"'Josephus!' she cried. 'He has left me, and intends to leave England altogether. Alone!'"

She reached into her handbag and presented me with a note.

My dear Penelope,

I despair that I should have to write these words, but I must rescind my offer of marriage to you, although it is against my wishes and my heart to do so.

Circumstances quite beyond my control have intervened and compel me to leave England and render this saddest of decisions, which will haunt me for the rest of my life. Yet duty and loyalty must rise above all else.

The reasons for my departure from this, my adopted home, will soon become clear, even as my separation from you remains painfully inevitable. I wish you to keep the gifts as evidence of my abiding deep love in hope they will allow you, in time, to remember me with affection.

Goodbye, my dearest! And I hope you will forgive this hasty and, for the moment inexplicable, departure.

J. Rexford

"The scoundrel!" I involuntarily exclaimed. "Toying with a young woman's affections!"

Holmes held up his hand and waved it from side to side.

"Let us be careful, Watson, not to jump to conclusions," he said. "There are many aspects of this matter that warrant deeper consideration." He turned to Collins. "Is there more?" he asked.

"Yes, there is," Collins replied. "A burglary!"

"No doubt at the home of Miss Barrington."

"Precisely," he confirmed. "Two days later, an intruder entered her rooms in broad daylight whilst she was at work."

"And, if I'm not presuming too much, the jewelry given her by her former suitor was stolen."

"Precisely, Mr. Holmes, as well as several other items of inconsequential value," answered Collins, "except for the engagement ring she had taken to wearing, which she now treasures as her only tangible memory of that rascal Rexford."

"I presume the burglar was nearly apprehended by the manager of the property?"

"Yes. How on earth would you know that?" Collins inquired. "He made a very hurried escape as the landlady entered the room for weekly cleaning."

"Oh, that is excellent!" Holmes replied, rubbing his hands together in what resembled glee.

"Well, I assure you that Penelope views the matter with a good deal less merriment than you," Collins said with some displeasure.

"I do not make light of these circumstances," Holmes assured him, "only that so clear a map has thoughtfully been left to lead us to an explanation for the facts as you have presented them."

"A map?" the book merchant repeated. "I must say I'm left only with questions. Who is Rexford? Was his courting of Penelope genuine or a ruse? Why has he suddenly disappeared, to the despair of the young woman he purports to love? What is this 'duty' that displaces his affection for his fiancé? And was this burglary a coincidence or related to Rexford's absconding? I must say, Mr. Holmes, I fail to see how the pieces fall together."

"Then how fortunate in that case that you have come to me," Holmes replied. "I should like to meet Miss Barrington at the earliest time. Would that be possible, say, tomorrow at your book store?"

"I am sure it would be," Collins replied. "She is as perplexed as I about the entire situation, and a good deal more distraught!"

The following morning, Holmes and I arrived at Collins' at ten o'clock, as we had arranged. As he had described, the entry-way was decorated Christmastime decorations creating a bright welcome to customers. We were escorted by the owner to a room in the rear where Miss Barrington awaited us. Collins hadn't exaggerated her radiant beauty that inevitably had been dimmed by recent concern. She was dabbing at her eyes with her handkerchief when we entered the room.

Introductions were made all around as we seated ourselves at a small table, and Miss Barrington turned her distraught face toward Holmes with a silent plea for assistance.

"Miss Barrington," he began, "through Mr. Collins I have learned the basic facts of your situation, but I would like to hear additional details from you directly "Can you explain to me the circumstances of how you met Mr. Rexford, the nature of your conversations, and the specific details of your engagement plans?"

"I am so grateful to you, Mr. Holmes," she began. "I know of your reputation and can appreciate that my situation must seem quite petty and unimportant compared to the types of cases that typically command your attention." She paused for a moment and turned to me. "And my gratitude goes out to you as well, Dr. Watson." I admit my heart fairly softened at such words from so charming a young woman.

"Josephus – Mr. Rexford, that is – is a good man, an honourable gentleman, of that I have no doubt."

"And yet," I interjected, "by all appearances, he has treated you most discourteously!"

"It is true, I suppose, but there must be an explanation, something that he is unable to share with me. Perhaps some terrible things he has done early in his life, or has been accused of, with which he wishes to spare me any association. Perhaps that explains his sudden departure."

"Would an honourable man have encouraged you to marry him, knowing such a black cloud hung over him?" Holmes asked. "Surely he must have realised that ignominious behavior – a criminal record, a military disgrace – "

"A past wife," I interjected.

Holmes threw a disapproving glance in my direction as shock registered on the young lady's face.

"Is there anything he shared about his life before he knew you that might have suddenly interposed itself and caused him to reconsider his promises to you?"

"Nothing!" she insisted. "I admit that, in some respects, I knew quite little about him. I don't know the precise nature of his work, only that it provided him with a generous remuneration that allowed him to live comfortably in London."

"And to proffer gifts of jewelry, I understand?" Holmes queried.

"Yes, beautiful jewelry," she confirmed. "Here is the one piece I was able to save from the intruder who pilfered my home the other day." She held out her left hand on which there was a gold ring with sparkling green emerald in a filigreed setting. "It is my only connection to him now," she said, her voice choking as the handkerchief rose again to her eyes.

Holmes's eyes stayed focused on the ring for several moments. "Do you mind?" he said, holding out his hand. She reluctantly removed the ring from her finger and handed it to the detective who examined it carefully with his hand glass. He uttered a short snort and handed the ring back to her. "And is there nothing else that he left behind? No personal items that might have indicated an intention to return to visit you?"

"He gave these cigars to me – as an 'early Christmas gift', he said." Collins brought the box to Holmes. "But they have no label indicating the manufacturer."

Holmes took the box and set it on his lap. He opened the top, which was hinged in the back, revealing a dozen cigars. Holmes pick one up and held it next to his ear, rolling it between his fingers and then sniffing it thoughtfully. He examined a small paper ring around the cigar, which appeared to be a colourful crest of some sort. Producing a small penknife from his waistcoat pocket, he cut it open with as much precision as a surgeon making his incision and separated the leaves, examining the mess of dried tobacco with his glass.

"Very good!" he declared. "I have, as you may know, made a study of tobacco ash, as Watson has recorded."

"But this tobacco hasn't been burned," Collins correctly noted.

"I usually analyze the ash because the unburned tobacco isn't available," Holmes explained. "However, when it is, as in this case, so much the better. Yes, these cigars are most instructive." He turned to Miss Barrington. "I will endeavor to determine what has occurred in hopes that knowing will give you peace of mind," he said. "But I think I can safely say you aren't responsible for any of the events that have transpired. Hopefully, in short order, I shall be able to lay all the facts before you."

Holmes and I departed the book store and hailed a carriage to return to Baker Street. As I was stepping into the cab, Holmes put his hand on the door. "Watson, I have several inquiries to make," he said. "I hope to return to Baker Street by five o'clock with the information I require to satisfactorily resolve this case."

I knew better than to query him about his plans, and instead nodded in agreement and departed in the cab. I watched him dash off and then gave the driver the address and settled in for the brief drive across central London. Later, I had lunch at a restaurant two blocks from our rooms and then, somewhat fatigued from the morning's activities and the heavy meal, resolved to spend a few hours catching up on some medical journals. I settled into a comfortable chair near the fire and began perusing an article on surgical treatments of club foot.

When I awoke, it was late-afternoon, the sitting room was dark, and Holmes was standing over me.

"Where have you been?" I asked.

"To the telegraph office, to begin with," he responded. "I sent a few telegrams that I thought might produce some useful answers."

"And did you receive the information you were seeking?"

"Very enlightening," he replied. He sat in his favorite chair, lit his pipe, and withdrew several telegrams which he began reviewing, scribbling some brief notes in the margins. Knowing he was connecting the pieces of the puzzle, I took my own chair and pipe and waited for him to finish his preparations.

After a half-an-hour, Holmes announced there was little else to be done until the next morning, when he expected we would be welcoming several visitors to our rooms.

"What visitors?" I inquired.

"Miss Barrington, for one," he responded. "And I expect we shall have additional guests."

"Mr. Rexford?" I inquired.

Holmes smiled thinly. "I should be very surprised if he doesn't make an appearance. But let us take ourselves to Wimpoles. I understand they have an excellent holiday pheasant there and, I would wager, a fine wine to accompany the bird."

We passed an enjoyable hour-and-a-half at the renowned Marylebone restaurant and then a stroll back to Baker Street to walk off the rich dinner. Carolers were strolling the streets and festive residents opened their doors to offer hot cider and sweets to the singers. Back before the fire, we smoked a pipe and discussed news from the Continent before the meal and stroll began to work their effect on me and I begged off to bed.

"Our first guest arrives at ten in the morning," Holmes cheerfully called as I closed the door to the sitting room.

The next morning, we had finished our breakfast and Mrs. Hudson had cleared the dishes and set a fresh pot of tea and some lemon cakes on the table when we heard a knock on the door precisely at ten o'clock. I opened it to find our landlady, accompanied by a tall young man, fashionably dressed, carrying a silver-topped cane.

"It's Mr. Rexford come to see you, Mr. Holmes," she announced.

Holmes quickly bounded up from his chair and strode to the door. "Thank you, Mrs. Hudson." He regarded the young man standing by her side and bade him enter the room. Our visitor entered and Mrs. Hudson closed the door behind him. He quickly surveyed the room, then turned his gaze to me for a moment before focusing his attention on my friend.

"You are Sherlock Holmes, I presume?" he said, his voice clear and, as Collins had noted, with a faint hint of an accent.

"Always an error to make presumptions," the detective responded, "but in this case, yes, I am Holmes."

"Josephus Rexford," the visitor replied, removing a pair of gray calfskin gloves and extending a soft hand that looked very much like one that had successfully avoided manual labor.

Holmes regarded the extended hand for a moment, then grasped it for a brief handshake and bade Rexford to take a chair.

Our guest sat as we settled into our own chairs, then took a deep breath.

"Of course, I am aware of your reputation, Mr. Holmes," he said. "I am, however, uncertain why I should be summoned to your consulting room by the advertisement in this morning's paper." He threw down a copy of *The Londoner-Journal,* a German language newspaper published in London. I could see that he had circled an advertisement with a red pencil. The English translation ran:

Mr. Sherlock Holmes would be delighted to meet Mr. Josephus Rexford at 10 a.m. at 221b Baker Street this morning. It is worth attending the meeting before your departure.

"I am not used to being summoned to conferences like a school boy," Rexford said in a somewhat irritated fashion.

"And yet, here you are!" Holmes replied flippantly.

Rexford studied my friend's face carefully. "To be frank, I could hardly pass up the opportunity to meet the famous Sherlock Holmes, even if the reason for the invitation remains vague to me, even now."

"I didn't imagine you could, Mr. Rexford," Holmes replied. "Or should I say, 'Your Highness'?"

Rexford's reaction could barely have been more startled than my own.

"I beg your pardon, sir?" he responded archly.

"Come now, do you underestimate my skills so profoundly that you did not imagine, even before you crossed my threshold, that I knew I was in the presence of Crown Prince Albert of Thurn and Taxis."

I sat upright in my chair, looking intently at Holmes and then at Rexford. Our guest betrayed no surprise. "I'm not sure I understand your implication, Mr. Holmes," he responded.

Holmes stood and walked to mantel. "Let us not be coy with each other about something so painfully evident. Discerning your identity required a minimum of effort, I assure you, and the reasons behind your duplicitous behavior regarding Miss Barrington is no less obvious to me. Would you like to make a clean breast of it, first to me and then to the young woman you have so distressed, or will you compel me to recite the facts of the case for you?"

Rexford rose halfway from his chair before settling back, his shoulders sagging slightly as he realized the pointlessness of continuing his charade.

"All right, Mr. Holmes, I shall not deny my identity any longer to you, although I'm torn about discussing the matter with Penelope. I admit my actions have been unconventional and she may well feel I have wronged her, but only because I wish to mitigate the sadness I presume the disclosure will bring her."

"With respect, sir," declared Holmes, "it is unfailingly preferable to acknowledge the truth, however unpleasant it may be, than to perpetuate a deceit, especially in matters of the heart."

Rexford, or Prince Albert, remained silent for a moment before beginning to speak. "How did you come by this knowledge, Mr. Holmes?"

he asked. "I believed I had concealed my path well enough to ensure my anonymity from the most diligent of pursuers."

"And so you have, Prince Albert," replied Holmes. "All but one. You had the extreme misfortune that Mr. Collins was concerned enough about Miss Barrington that he came to see me.

"As to how I came to possess the information revealing your true identify, I assure you it was a simple matter. Mr. Collins mentioned that you had studied at Sandhurst. Together with the disclosure that you spoke with a faint accent, I inferred that you, like many at the academy, might well be in England training to assume a high-ranking position in one of the states of Europe.

"I have some very trustworthy contacts associated with Sandhurst, as you might imagine, and I was able to procure your admissions material. Rexford was a name assigned for use at the academy, but wasn't your true name." Our visitor sat silently during Holmes's remarks. "But I was unable to learn your actual identify from the directors at Sandhurst. You may applaud their honoring a pledge of confidentiality. They did tell me that you failed to complete the training program and left after just a year-and-a-half of study."

"That is true, Mr. Holmes. I was uninterested in the study of military strategy from the outset and attended only under duress. All that marching and cavalry horses and weapons – well, I had no desire to continue those studies. I withdrew and came to London where I escaped the clutches of those who had pressured me to study military affairs.

"My true interest lay in books, in literature, in the study of art and music. Not exactly what my family had in mind for me. But in London, I could live almost anonymously, visiting museums, archives and – yes – bookshops, which is where I encountered Miss Barrington. You must believe me that I had no intention whatsoever to deceive her, and certainly no intention to become involved romantically. But as you know, Mr. Holmes, the brain cannot always dictate the sentiments of the heart."

"I have been fortunate in that regard," Holmes responded, "to have maintained the superior influence of the brain. But pray, carry on."

"Over the past few weeks, I found myself falling hopelessly in love with Miss Barrington. We shared so many interests and perspectives! But I also felt terribly guilty. Whenever she asked about my background, from where I came, or what I had done prior to our meeting, I had no choice, Mr. Holmes and Dr. Watson, but to prevaricate." He looked to me for understanding and I couldn't help giving a supportive nod.

"I couldn't reveal my true identity even to her without jeopardizing my anonymity. Oh, I know Penelope – Miss Barrington – would never voluntarily let slip she had befriended a prince, but I couldn't take that risk. At least, not until I had planned how to proceed. But I deeply care for her, and I gave her several pieces of family jewelry to demonstrate my deep affection."

"It was through the ring Miss Barrington still wore that I discerned your connection to the House of Thurn and Taxis," said Holmes. "That, and the particular cut of the tobacco in the cigars you gave to Mr. Collins – quite distinct as the style favoured by the princes of Germany.

"As to the ring, I have made quite a study of the crests of all the royal families of Europe. I quickly recognized the distinct dual lions and crosses of your family insignia stamped onto the back of the setting – the same crest, I note, on the handle of your very fine walking stick. Given the other mysteries surrounding your courtship, I decided to place the announcement that brought you to this meeting.

"And why did you place it in *The Londoner-Journal*," I inquired.

"I presumed that a German-speaking gentleman about to depart England, undoubtedly for Germany, was likely to be reading a newspaper that would include news about developments in his home country. Fortunately, my command of German remains passable. A quick perusal of recent editions at the newspaper office yesterday afternoon revealed the brief story about the unexpected death of Prince Maximilian of Thurn and Taxis. I had no doubt I had chanced on the precipitating event."

The prince stared at Holmes in astonishment, but then collected himself and continued his account.

"By then I had resolved to ask her hand in marriage," he said, returning to his narrative, "having determined there would be little conflict with any royal duties that might arise. My role, you see, was quite incidental since my older brother, Maximilian, had succeeded our grandfather in 1871 when he was but a child."

"He succeeded your grandfather?" I asked.

"Yes. Our father had died at a young age, just thirty-five. His life had been somewhat in turmoil, in part because of the great controversy surrounding his marriage to my mother, Helene, niece of the King of Bavaria. The king objected because my grandfather, despite his title, wasn't of a royal house. So, you can understand my hesitancy in entering into a marriage that might precipitate yet another family crisis – particularly if, as I intended, we remained residents of London rather than return to Germany as I had promised. Nevertheless, my love for Penelope took precedence over such concerns, even though I was uncertain how I might marry an English commoner, live in anonymity abroad, and still honor my family responsibilities, however minor, as a prince."

"And then, you learned that those responsibilities had changed," Holmes interjected. "But wait, I hear footsteps. Unless I'm mistaken, you

232

will have an opportunity to complete your explanation in the presence of the person who deserves to hear it most."

Holmes opened the door before Mrs. Hudson had even had the opportunity to knock and drew Miss Penelope Barrington into the room. She gasped slightly at seeing the man she knew as "Rexford", but then ran to his side.

"Josephus!" she cried. "Is it you?" She flew into his arms and buried her face in his shoulder, sobbing heavily as the prince looked awkwardly towards us. Turning to my friend, she implored, "Mr. Holmes, however did you find him?" Turning to "Rexford" she asked, "Where have you been? Why have you not communicated with me?"

Holmes drew up another chair for the distraught young woman and bade us all sit. Mrs. Hudson thoughtfully had brought fresh tea and we poured cups as we settled into our chairs.

"Miss Barrington, I'm afraid you have been ill-treated by this gentleman, although he doesn't believe he ever intended to deceive you for malicious reasons."

The young woman looked confused. "What is he saying, Josephus?" she asked.

Holmes looked sharply at the young man. "Shall I explain, or will you?" he demanded. The prince stared at his feet in embarrassment and nodded towards Holmes.

"Very well. Miss Barrington. You believe yourself to be engaged to, and in love with, Josephus Rexford. I have the unhappy duty to tell you there is no 'Josephus Rexford'. This young man, in actuality, is Crown Prince Albert I of Thurn and Taxis."

Miss Barrington looked incredulously at the man she had presumed to be her fiancé. "Is this true, Josephus?" she gasped.

The prince unhappily nodded his head without looking at her. "Yes, Penelope, what Mr. Holmes says is accurate." He looked up, his face was filled with remorse. "But I implore you to believe that I never had any intention of misleading you. I fully intended to remain in London after we married. I had no responsibilities as the head of my family and, with my brother already established as Prince, no prospects those conditions would change."

"But they did change, did they not?" Holmes insisted.

Again, the young prince nodded his head and looked at the floor.

"Yes, two weeks ago," he began. "I received a wire from Regensburg, our family seat at St. Emmeram Castle. It contained the dreadful news that my brother Maximilian had suffered heart failure and died suddenly, just as our father had at a young age. Maximilian was just twenty-three years old!" He buried his face in his hands and his shoulders heaved. In a few

233

moments, he was able to collect himself and after wiping his eyes with his handkerchief, he continued his recitation. "The wire informed me that I was now the head of the royal family: *The Prince!* It was a designation I have never coveted, not for a moment. You must understand! But fate had intervened, to my despair. Ignoring the request to return would destroy our family's history and disgrace our position!"

"Having learned of the death of the Prince," Holmes interjected, "it hardly required much conjecture to understand that you must be next in line and had been called home, however reluctantly, to assume your familial duties."

"Why could you not tell me this?" implored the young woman. "Did you think I would love you less if I knew you were a prince? Or more?"

Prince Albert looked distraught. "My life had changed," he explained. "My responsibilities had been altered in a manner I could never have imagined when I met you. My brother should have held this position for many decades, long enough to produce sufficient heirs to ensure the role of Prince would never descend upon my shoulders. I was, you must believe me, content to live in obscurity, here, in London, with you as my wife, Penelope.

"But that possibility was irrevocably changed by Maximilian's death. I find myself the Prince, against all my wishes, with duties and family obligations I cannot abandon, even for you."

"Then take me with you!" she implored.

The Prince's face grew dark, his brow knotted as he struggled to give voice to his emotions.

"I'm obliged to marry royalty," he finally said. "It is the custom, the expectation. As Josephus Rexford, I could marry you and spend my life without anyone caring or noticing. As Prince Albert the first, it is impossible to marry a British commoner, a clerk in a bookstore – even one as worthy as you."

"You realized the jewels you had conferred on the woman you intended to be your fiancé must remain within your family and therefore had to be returned," Holmes added. "But you didn't have the courage to explain the situation to Miss Barrington."

Again, the young man hung his head.

"You are correct, Mr. Holmes. I couldn't bring myself to recount this dreadful turn of events to you," he said, turning to the young woman. The tears that had been flowing down her cheeks had stopped now, and a more determined look was on her face.

"I would have returned them, of course," she said.

"I have no doubt," Albert answered. "But I couldn't bring myself to request that you do so, particularly at this time of the year!. I'm ashamed to say that I hired a man to enter you rooms whilst you were at the book shop to recover the jewelry. He was surprised during his pilfering of your rooms and in making his escape, swept up some pieces of jewelry that weren't among the heirlooms I gave you. I will certainly return them."

"But he failed to secure the ring Miss Barrington was wearing," I added, "contrary to your instructions never to wear the jewelry in public."

"Yes. I worried someone would find it strange that so valuable piece was worn by a clerk. So, I had asked Penelope to wear them only inside, at least until we were married."

The young woman reached to her left hand with her right and gave a gentle tug on the ring still on her finger. "Here is your ring, Josephus – or Albert, or whatever it is you wish to be called," she said, a measure of annoyance clearly in her voice. She reached out to hand the ring to the prince, who regarded it like an infernal device.

"No," he cried, waving it away, "I wish you to keep it. To remember me and our dreams of a life together."

Miss Barrington stood and stepped over to the Prince. She grabbed his hand and turn it palm upward, and then placed the ring in his hand.

"I have no need to be reminded of 'our dreams together'," she said curtly. "If I'm unfit to stand by your side as your wife, I'm uninterested in retaining the ring or in remembering you as many more Christmases – hopefully much happier ones – pass us by. I wish you a Happy Christmas in your palace, Your Majesty, and I bid you *adieu*." Miss Barrington turned abruptly and walked across the room, opening the door and disappearing onto the landing. We listened in silence as her footsteps marked the stairs down to the street.

The Prince looked about awkwardly, then placed the ring in his pocket.

"I – ah – I – " he began hesitatingly but Holmes waved his hand dismissively.

"I don't think there is much more to say," he declared, "except to bid you a safe journey back to Thurn and Taxis." He strode to the door and opened it, gesturing to the young Prince. Albert looked about awkwardly before curtly nodding and departing. Outside, in Baker Street, we saw a carriage and fine horse waiting for him.

"A sad story, wouldn't you say?" I asked that evening as we dined at Wilton's in St. James, the restaurant decorated with candles, holly, and ribbons for the approaching holiday. "Star-crossed lovers and all that, denied a chance at happiness by a quirk death and succession to royal duties. Pity. Such a nice couple."

"Nonsense!" Holmes rejoined. "I can think of no other case in my experience that demonstrated more acutely the absurdity a system of royalty without responsibility! It is one thing to make such marriage decisions when one has a nation or an Empire to run. After all, one cannot imagine the Prince of Wales marrying a school teacher, it goes without saying. But Thurn and Taxis? Pray show me on the map of Europe the location of that nation! Surely the princehood associated with such a fantastical place is but sheer fantasy, the perpetuation of centuries of the drawing and redrawing of national boundaries that resulted in the swallowing up of innumerable inconsequential principalities. Albert will have a title, but little else. He rules no territory. He has no subjects. And yet in order to possess so meaningless a title, he is willing to abandon the woman he had come to truly love and who loved him – not for his title or nobility, but as a man."

Holmes popped an oyster in his mouth and followed it with a long drink of chilled sauvignon blanc.

"No, Watson, we have witnessed an example of the outdated micro-nationalism that I fear will someday produce a far greater number of victims than has the duplicitous suitor, Prince Albert of Thurn and Taxis. And, I might add, a man of so little character does not, in my view, deserve the affection and trust of a woman as loyal and honourable as Miss Barrington."

We finished our dinner with a delectable brandy aperitif to brace us against the December chill. Walking back to Baker Street amid the jingling of sleigh bells on the carriages bustling about, a swirl of snow had begun falling and had begun to cover the grime of London's streets by the time we arrived at our rooms.

I gave little thought to this case until I read several years later that Albert I, the 8th Prince of Thurn and Taxis, had been wed to the Archduchess Margarethe Klementine, the third daughter of the Archduke Joseph Karl of Austria, a descendent of the Holy Roman Emperor. Eventually this royal pair would have eight children – all the men, save one who joined the Benedictine monks, who married princesses of similarly non-existent states.

As to Penelope Barrington, she happily recovered from the distress caused her by her brief engagement to the non-existent Josephus Rexford. Within the year, she was engaged and married to a young barrister who soon stood successfully for Parliament. Together they raised six children of their own and, as those who follow literature are aware, she became quite a noted poet in her own right.

The Sebastopol Clasp
by Martin Daley

Chapter I

It was a Tuesday in late December 1885 when Sherlock Holmes and I were enjoying a pipe while relaxing upon our two favourite couches in the drying room of the Turkish Bath on Northumberland Avenue. As Holmes had just completed a recent investigation and neither of us had any pressing engagements – not to mention that fact that my shoulder had been troubling me lately – I suggested we indulge in one of our guilty pleasures.

The heat and oils from the exotic establishment were acting as the perfect antidote to our lassitude, and our relaxing morning was approaching its conclusion when I heard a familiar voice ask through the heavy atmosphere, "Is that you, Watson?"

I opened my eyes to see an older man with a discernible limp padding across the tiled floor. "My goodness," I cried. "Woodward! What a wonderful surprise!"

"I *thought* it was my old companion," he said offering a hand.

"Holmes," I said by way of introduction, "this is Simon Woodward from Afghanistan. We were on the *Orontes* that bought us back to England." Holmes barely creased a forehead in acknowledgement. "Woodward, this is my friend, Mr. Sherlock Holmes."

"Yes, I've heard of you," said my old colleague enthusiastically.

"What are you up to these days?" I asked, a little embarrassed having lost touch with him after leaving Netley.

"Well, like you, my soldiering days are over," he replied with some melancholy. "Being a career soldier with a debilitated hip, regular work is difficult to come by. I tend to get by on the meagre pension they gave us and the odd temporary job as a clerk or a courier. When I can afford it, I come here, as I find it a good alternative medicine for this wretched thing." He patted his hip.

"Yes, I can understand," I agreed, rubbing my shoulder with a sympathetic smile.

We chatted for a few minutes as old soldiers do, balancing the strange paradox of being pleased to see one another, but sharing a reluctance to recall in any great details the dreadful experiences of the battlefield. As Woodward turned to take his leave, we agreed to meet again.

"In fact," he said, "it occurs to me that I'm getting together with a few old comrades from the Crimea on Christmas Eve. Why don't you come along?"

"I didn't realise you were in the Crimea?" With my question, I realised that – as well as we became acquainted on the long sea journey back home – we must have spoken little of our military experiences. Clearly, we were thankful to be alive and concentrated instead on what the future held for us both.

"Only briefly," said Woodward in answer to my question. "I arrived with the last deployment troops – just in time to see the fall of Sebastopol. I was a young Subaltern with the Lancashires. We were only there less than twelve months before returning home. When we left, a few of us vowed to get together for a reunion every ten years to commemorate our first campaign together. This year will be thirty years." Woodward's head dropped as he adopted another melancholic smile. "There are only half-a-dozen of us left. And on top of all that, I had my campaign medal stolen last year."

"I'm sorry to hear that."

"Never mind," said my old comrade. "What do you say about the invitation – a little celebratory dinner and a chinwag with a few old duffers?"

"I shall be delighted," I said.

"Excellent!" cried Woodward with genuine enthusiasm. "I shall send over the details to your lodgings." I gave him the address.

"What a pleasant surprise," I said, half to myself as I watched him leave.

"Do you believe in Fate or Providence?" asked Holmes, who had been lounging with his eyes closed throughout the whole exchange.

I looked across at my friend, surprised by his enigmatic question.

"I can't say I've particularly thought deeply about it. I suppose things always happen for a reason, whatever that reason might be – our own meeting for example, when I returned from Afghanistan. Why do you ask?"

"Your simplistic explanation is as good as any, I suppose," replied Holmes languidly. "Chance meetings often act as a portent for what lies ahead."

That night, we welcomed Inspector Lestrade to our rooms. He often called during the winter evenings to enjoy a whisky-and-soda and a cigar. I had come to appreciate that his visits were mutually beneficial to both the official policeman and the private consulting detective: Lestrade could pick Holmes's brains about the thorny issues with which he and his colleagues were wrestling, while Holmes enjoyed keeping abreast of the latest cases that had landed at the doors of Scotland Yard.

"Anything of interest lately?" asked Holmes as we stared into the blazing hearth.

"Not particularly," replied the policeman. "It's always the quietest time of year. I think the London criminal seems to take a break in preparation for the holidays."

"Typical!" sneered Holmes, failing to see any humour in Lestrade's comment.

"Come to think of it, it has been a strange year all round. We've been troubled by the rise of anarchism more than anything else. It appears as though the troublemakers of Europe are finding London their preferred destination these days – rioting, fire-bombing of businesses, looting of shops. Anything to disturb and disrupt."

"Can you not identify the culprits?" I asked.

"It's exceedingly difficult, Doctor. Their usual tactic is to throw a bottle full of kerosene through an office window in the middle of the night without any warning. By the time we move into the East End to investigate the next morning, it seems no one speaks English."

"How many deaths have these attacks caused?" asked Holmes, who had been listening attentively.

"Thankfully not that many," replied Lestrade, "because they are aimed mainly at businesses at night, when the buildings are mostly uninhabited."

"Mostly?"

"Well, there have been a few tragic losses – the most heart-breaking were the elderly couple who were lodging in a room above their shop in Bethnal Green while their house was being redecorated further down the street."

"Only their business was targeted then?"

"It would appear so. The only incident that has raised my suspicions was the killing of a retired army man in July. His home was attacked one night, but fortunately he managed to escape, only to be shot and killed a few days later. He was sitting in a coffee shop in the Tottenham Court Road when a gunman burst in. He seemed to have known who his victim was, as he didn't disturb any of the other customers who were beside themselves with fear at what they witnessed."

"Yes, I remember reading about that," I said. "Terrible business. From memory, the poor chap had enjoyed a distinguished career: Mentioned in dispatches in Balaclava, decorated for bravery in Lucknow, and distinguished service on the Northwest Frontier. How ironic that such a decorated, much-travelled veteran would meet such a sad end on a London street."

"We handed the matter over to Special Branch, who are looking into the Fenian outrages – probably one of them."

At the end of the evening, Lestrade invited Holmes and me to a small gathering at the station.

"We regularly get together at Christmas," he said. "We would be delighted if you would both join us."

Knowing my friend's strong aversion to society and ceremonial gatherings, I knew he wouldn't welcome such an invitation – however well intended – and made some non-committal gesture in response. It was therefore left to me to show our guest out. Before going up to my room, I looked in on my friend, who was still in his chair with his chin sunk upon his breast, gazing intently at the smouldering fire.

"Good night, old fellow."

The following day I spent the morning Christmas shopping. I think the whole of London – undeterred by the bitter temperature and the whisps of snow in the air – had the same idea. The Strand and Oxford Street were packed with every form of humanity: Pedestrians and street vendors jostled for room on the pavements, while carriages and omnibuses moved from side to side in order to avoid collisions on the roads. Notwithstanding such activity and the noise and confusion it generated, it proved to be a productive morning. I chose a new billiard cue for my friend Thurston, a nice set of cufflinks for Holmes, and a fragrant basket of pampering products from Gamages People's Emporium for our selfless landlady, Mrs. Hudson. The one thing I had underestimated was the journey back to Baker Street unscathed, whilst wrestling with the awkwardly shaped fruits of my morning's work. At one point I came close to being run over by an omnibus as I scurried awkwardly across Charing Cross Road whilst hailing a cab. Moments later, I was relieved to be in the sanctuary of the hansom, trotting towards our lodgings.

Managing to ascend the stairs without being seen by either Mrs. Hudson or my fellow lodger, I deposited my treasures in my room before going back down to our sitting room, where I found Holmes in his grey dressing gown, chuckling to himself at the Agony Column of the previous evening's *Pall Mall Gazette*.

"A successful morning's work, I take it, judging by your step on the stair," he said as I entered.

"Yes, it was, thank you. You seem in a very jolly mood."

"There is nothing more amusing and informative than the Agony Columns of the popular press."

Before he could elaborate on his statement, Mrs. Hudson knocked and entered.

"Mr. Holmes, there is a Mr. Bateman downstairs who wishes to see you. He says he's come directly from the Paddington Express and needs help with an urgent matter before he returns home."

Holmes interrupted his own amusement and acquiesced. "Very well Mrs. Hudson, show him up."

Moments later, a ruddy faced man of around sixty entered our room, apparently quite agitated, judging by his manner. He snatched his cap from his head.

"Mr. Holmes?" he asked, his eyes darting from one of us to the other.

"I am Holmes, this is my friend and colleague, Dr. Watson."

"I hope you can help me, I don't know what else to do."

"Pray calm yourself, Mr. Bateman," my friend said, soothingly. "Please sit down and tell us what brings a left-handed, widowed lamplighter from Reading to our tranquil abode."

Our visitor slowly lowered himself into a chair with such a look of incredulity it was almost comical.

"How do you know me, sir?" he asked.

"Our good landlady told me your name and informed me that you had just arrived at Paddington on the morning express. If I know my *Bradshaw*, the only non-stop train to arrive there near this time during the week is from Reading. As for your profession and personal circumstances, I note by your complexion that you clearly work outdoors. Beneath your sleeve, I can see that the wrist and hand on your left side is bigger than those on the right, indicating that you are clearly left-handed. When I see no fewer than seven droplets of oil spattered on your sleeve, I deduce that you are either an oilman or a lamplighter – probably the latter, seeing that you have to return immediately, presumably before it gets dark."

"Both, as a matter of fact," confirmed our visitor, inspecting his workman's coat.

"And as your jackets are open," added Holmes. "I see a wedding ring hanging from your watch-chain. Such a small item could never fit on those fingers, Mr. Bateman. I can only conclude that your dear wife is no longer with us."

"That is true, Mr. Holmes. Just around this time last year."

"We are sorry for your loss," I said.

"Now," asked my friend, "how can we help?"

"It's my son, Mr. Holmes. He was always a good lad. His best pal growing up was young Percy Armitage from Crane Water, near Reading. You helped young Percy's fiancée with that trouble with her father. When

I asked Percy if he had any idea where Edward was, he suggested I come and see you."

"So your son has disappeared?"

"Yes, he's been gone for weeks without a word or a by-your-leave. After his mother died, he's gradually become more irrational. First, he started drinking heavily. Mind you, he wasn't the only one . . . ." Bateman lowered his head in his own embarrassment. "Then he gradually got in with the wrong crowd. It ended up where he came here to London where he got a job at Pritchard's Brickworks in Stepney. I hoped he was making an effort to improve his life before coming home, but when I didn't hear from him for a while, I asked at Pritchard's, who told me that he had left. They didn't know where he's gone, and they haven't seen him since. I don't have much money, Mr. Holmes, but I was hoping you could help in the circumstances."

"Don't worry about my fee, Mr. Bateman," said my friend with a smile. "After all, we're approaching the season of good will. Now, give me Edward's last known address and we'll see what we can do."

"Thank you, sir," said Bateman, as he wrote down whatever details he could think of.

"As I have nothing else to do at this time," said Holmes after our visitor left. "I may as well start my enquiries into this disappearance. Are you game?"

"Of course I am," I replied, reaching for my hat and coat once more.

Chapter II

The natural place to begin our investigation was the large brickworks where the young man had been employed. Holmes sought out Bateman's foreman, who informed him that the young man from Reading had only been with them for a couple of months.

"He just disappeared," he said. "Didn't show up one day – haven't seen him since. Not a bad worker, but he seemed a troubled young lad, if you ask me."

"Do you know where he was staying?" asked my friend.

"I think he was at old Annie Carver's place on the Old Kent Road."

We followed the workman's directions, traversing the blackened streets of London's East End – two incongruous figures, drawing suspicious glances from those we passed – until we came upon a shabby-looking establishment not far from the junction with Albany Road. A faded sign reading *"Carver's Hostel"* hung above old weather-beaten double doors whose timbers had once been coloured green, but now, with most of the paint flaked away, were now a drab silver grey. Holmes

242

entered without a moment's hesitation and I followed, wondering how many waifs and strays had crossed this threshold over the years. The entrance hall was as modest as the building's exterior.

"Mrs. Carver, I presume?" asked my friend upon seeing an elderly lady through the open door of a room on the right.

The lady looked up from her knitting, apparently surprised to see such well-dressed gentlemen in her home.

"Yes," she said, with a combined air of suspicion and concern.

"Please don't be alarmed, Madam. My name is Sherlock Holmes, and this is my colleague, Dr. Watson. We're here because we believe an acquaintance of ours may be staying here: An Edward Bateman."

In the years in which I had been with Holmes, I'd often observed him obtaining information in the most subtle and discreet manner. This was usually done without revealing his own identity and by convincing the source that the information he was seeking was of little or no interest to the detective. On this occasion, he obviously felt there was no need for such subterfuge.

"Oh, yes, he was here a while ago," said the old lady, standing up and unnecessarily wiping her hands on her apron. "Had to ask him to leave."

"Really? Why was that may I ask?"

"I run a respectable house, Mr. Holmes. If anyone causes any trouble, they're out."

"What sort of trouble was he causing?"

"Coming in late, not following the house rules. But it was mainly the company he was keeping – one fellow in particular. Funny sort he was."

"In what way?"

"Foreign!"

Holmes and I exchanged an amused glance.

"Madam, there must have been something more than the man's nationality that you found unpleasant?"

"Had no respect," recalled Mrs. Carver pensively. "Used to come in here as if he owned the place. He always seemed to have a hold on the younger man. It got to a point I could hear them in Mr. Bateman's room, shouting and scuffling. I had enough and told him to leave."

"When was this?"

"About a fortnight ago."

"Do you know where Bateman went?"

"He said he was going to stay with Mr. Gregory."

"Mr. Gregory?"

"Yes, this Gregory bloke I've been telling you about."

"I don't suppose you have an address for this Mr. Gregory?"

"No," said Mrs. Carver with contempt, "and I wouldn't want to know either!"

"Thank you for help," said Holmes courteously. "What do you make of that?" he asked as we stepped back out onto the street.

"Well, he is clearly our man, and Mrs. Carver's experience appears to support his father's suspicions that he's fallen in with the wrong crowd."

"Indeed."

"We aren't exactly dressed appropriately to make enquiries at the local hostelries without raising further suspicion. I suggest we return to Baker Street and ponder our next course of action."

It was now well after three o'clock and the skies were darkening on the December afternoon.

We returned to our rooms where I found a note sent by my old friend Woodward, confirming his invitation to join him and his friends for dinner on Christmas Eve.

"The Café Royal!" I said. "Very nice."

Holmes showed little interest and shrugged at my enthusiasm. He retook his seat at his table amid the test-tubes and vials in which he'd been distilling various chemicals over the previous few days and resumed with one of his malodorous experiments. Anticipating some of the toxic odours that were bound to shortly fill our sitting room, I left him to it and retired up to my own room.

I wrote a brief response to Woodward, thanking him for the invitation and telling him how much I was looking forward to meeting up with him and his old comrades. Checking my watch, I decided I could just about make it to the post office in Marylebone Road. On my way out, Mrs. Hudson met me in the hallway and asked if I would do her a favour the following morning.

"Doctor? I've ordered a Christmas tree from Carswell's in the Edgware Market. I wonder if you would mind picking it up for me?"

"Of course. I'd be delighted. There's nothing that gets us in the mood for Christmas more than decorating the tree."

"Hmm," she murmured, indicating upstairs with her eyes. "Well, most of us anyway!"

I ran my errand and, on the way back, happened to pass by a small corner pawnbroker's. This gave me an idea for a gift for my friend, Woodward. Although the shop itself didn't have what I was seeking, Mr. Wiseman, the owner, told me that a larger pawnbroker, Etherington's, was likely to carry such an item. Knowing I was going to Edgware Market the following morning anyway, I decided I could make a detour that way at the same time.

244

Over dinner that night, I informed Holmes about Mrs. Hudson's request. I smiled as his sigh of derision reminded me of her anticipation of his response.

"I shall leave you both to it then," he said, without elaborating on what he had planned.

By the time I came down for breakfast the following morning, Holmes had gone. I myself left an hour or so later and found that the same throng of humanity jostling for space of the streets of the capital I'd experienced the previous day had barely dissipated. I made my way first to Etherington's.

I explained to the proprietor what I was looking for and was delighted when he reached into a drawer below his counter and produced the very article. It was a Crimean campaign medal that even had the distinctive curled clasp with the word *"Sebastopol"* pinned to its ribbon.

"That's perfect!" I exclaimed. The man was taken aback by my enthusiasm and I felt obliged to explain. "I have a friend who recently had his campaign medal stolen. He was in Sebastopol with his regiment towards the end of the war, and I thought it would make the perfect Christmas gift."

"Very good, sir," said the pawnbroker wrapping it in some brown paper.

I then walked to the market off Edgware Road where the shoppers inadvertently bumped and barged into each other as they searched for produce beneath the patchwork of awnings. I found Carswell's stall and informed the large, ruddy-faced man that I was here to pick up the tree ordered by Mrs. Hudson of Baker Street. He had two- or three-dozen trees tied up, and he began to sift through the labels. As he was doing so, I looked over to the next stall where a woman was inadequately dressed in a woollen shawl, fingerless gloves and a straw boater. Beside her was a steaming urn.

"Nice bowl of soup, sir?" she shouted above the din of the crowd when she observed me looking over.

As appetising as the invitation sounded on such a morning, I politely declined, knowing that in a few moments I would be wrestling with a Christmas tree that would be as tall as I was.

"'*Mrs. Hudson of Baker Street*'," announced the stall holder at last as he found the right label. "Here we go, sir."

As with the previous morning, I underestimated the task involved in picking my way through crowds with awkwardly shaped festive items. My mission on this particular morning was made all the more difficult with the narrowness of the walkways between the stalls and the varying heights of the different awnings. Following several "Excuse me's" and having to suffer many an affronted stare, I managed to extricate myself from the canvassed labyrinth and hail a hansom. Upon our arrival at Baker Street, I felt obliged to add a generous tip to my fare, as I was aware the driver would find his cab littered with pine needles. I gave an embarrassed smile as he was fulsome with his gratitude and wished me Compliments of the Season.

"Mrs. Hudson!" I called as I struggled through the front door.

"Oh, Doctor, that's wonderful!" she said, appearing from the kitchen.

"Where are you going to put it this year?" I asked.

"I thought this year I'd put it on the halfway landing where we could all enjoy it," she replied. I'm sure I detected more than a mischievous glint in her eye as she said it.

"Very well," I agreed making to heave it up the first flight of stairs. "The halfway landing it is!"

I reached the landing and saw that our resourceful landlady had already positioned a large bucket in which the tree would stand. I stood the tree in the large bucket and removed my hat and coat. Remembering I had Woodward's medal in my inside pocket, I removed it and placed it on the table before taking off my coat and re-joining Mrs. Hudson, who had followed me up to the landing with a large box of Christmas decorations.

No sooner had the two of us started to dress the tree when we heard the key turn in the front door downstairs – something that prompted us both to look at one another in a mixture of amusement and trepidation. As Holmes ascended up to the stairway landing, he stopped as he saw what we were doing.

"Good morning," I said casually.

My friend gave a sigh of resignation. "Good morning," he said at last as he squeezed passed us and on up to our sitting room.

Mrs. Hudson and I continued our task and after a few seconds I saw, out of the corner of my eye, that Holmes was standing in the sitting room and looking at the table.

"Everything all right, old fellow?" I asked, going up and crossing the threshold.

"What is this?" he asked.

I followed his gaze which was fixed on the medal I'd bought earlier that morning for my army friend. The brown paper that the pawnbroker had loosely wrapped the medal in had naturally unfolded as I lay it on the desk.

"It's gift for Woodward. You may recall that he told us his own medal had been lost when we spoke to him in the drying room the other day."

"*Fool!*" cried Holmes

The outburst caused Mrs. Hudson – who was obviously party to the exchange – to drop a red bauble that she was about to position, and it rolled a short distance away, fortunately not breaking.

"That is unworthy of you, Holmes!" I protested. "I'm making what I believe is a kind gesture to a former colleague who has had the misfortune of losing something that was extremely precious to him."

"Watson," replied Holmes kindly, finally tearing his gaze from the medal, "pray accept my apologies. I don't mean you, my dear fellow – I am scolding myself. If short-sightedness were a crime, our friend Lestrade would have every right to clap me in irons!"

"I don't understand."

"I have to leave once more," Holmes was passing Mrs. Hudson as he made this latest announcement.

The two of us were left staring at one another, bemused, as we heard the front door slam shut.

Chapter III

Mrs. Hudson did a wonderful job of decorating the whole house. Coloured ribbon and foliage adorned everywhere, from the entrance hallway to the staircase leading up to my bedroom. The centre-piece was the tree that I had helped decorate. She'd even cleaned up by late afternoon and when I went to close the curtains in our sitting room, snow had started to fall in Baker Street, as if to acknowledge our efforts in preparing for the festivities ahead.

It would be another hour before Holmes returned.

"Where have you been?" I asked as he brushed the snow from his hat and coat.

"I went to see Lestrade," he said, without elaborating.

"Was it to give yourself up?" I ventured, referring to the comment he made as he left.

"It may well be the case in time," said he with a smile, "but I hope to have an opportunity to redeem myself."

It would be twenty-four hours before Holmes said anything further on the matter. He was prompted by Billy, the page, who knocked and entered at his usual pace.

"Got a letter for you, Mr. Holmes!" he announced with great enthusiasm.

Holmes took the missive and ripped it open. He glanced the clock, which showed that it was almost five o'clock.

"Too late to reply," he mumbled to himself, and then to the page. "That will be all, Billy. Thank you. Come back first thing tomorrow when I'll ask you to post my reply."

"Very good, sir," said the boy before scampering off.

The detective tapped the note absentmindedly with the stem of his pipe and looked into the middle distance.

"Holmes?"

Breaking from his reverie, he retook his seat by the fire. "I fear that these may be much deeper waters than we first thought."

"Was the note to do with young Bateman?" I asked.

"Yes," replied my friend while staring at the flames.

"I don't understand your reaction when you saw the Crimean medal earlier," I said, unsure whether *that* was linked to Bateman or not.

"It wasn't the medal itself that caught my attention. It was the clasp attached to it. When I saw the word '*Sebastopol*', the casual conversations we've had over the past few days, first with your friend Woodward, then with Lestrade, and then finally with Mrs. Carver, were suddenly linked by a thread. If my suspicions are proved accurate, that delicate thread will develop into a substantial chain, the events of which may culminate in an eventuality that I dare not contemplate."

He raised his eyes from the fire and looked across towards me, but I was at a loss to understand what he was driving at. Before I could question him further, he asked, "Tell me do you know who is attending this dinner your friend has invited you to on Christmas Eve?"

"Not exactly," I answered, a little taken aback. "I know there are a few of his old army colleagues, but beyond that, I'm not entirely sure who they are. Surely you don't suspect some malevolent intention from them?"

"Not *from* them, Watson, but potentially *towards* them – and by association, towards my dearest friend."

I had seldom heard my friend speak with such intensity of feeling and I found myself touched by his words.

"I would like you to reach out to Woodward and find out exactly who his friends are," he resumed. "I have been carrying out my own enquiries today and together, I hope we can prevent any further tragedies."

"Tragedies? With regards to whom? Are we still talking about Bateman?"

"I made some discreet enquiries about Bateman this morning, based on what Mrs. Carver told us. I have an agent working on the matter as we speak."

"No doubt one of the children from what you've described as your '*Baker Street division of the detective police force*'," I announced with some humour.

248

"No," replied Holmes gravely, "this isn't a task for children. I'm hoping Bateman will provide the final piece in the puzzle that will send a dangerous man to the gallows and disrupt the activities of a much wider criminal enterprise."

"But listening to Bateman's father, the young man sounded like someone who had just come off the rails following the passing of his mother. Surely he can't have turned into a hardened criminal in such a short period of time?"

"I'm not talking about Bateman. I'm referring to the company that I believe he's keeping. Does the name Grigory Yubkin mean anything to you?"

I cudgelled my brain. "It does sound vaguely familiar."

"You may remember I brought his name up at the end of the Dial Square case." *

"Of course!" I cried, snapping my fingers in recognition. "He was the man you suspected of receiving the stolen ammunition from the factory."

"That is just one of his many misdemeanours." Holmes re-lit his pipe and sat back in his chair before resuming his narrative.

"Yubkin was from Crimea, where his father was a serving officer in the Russian army. He was killed during the siege of Sebastopol and young Grigory fled with his mother. She died a few years later while he was in his teens. He started a nomadic existence, gradually travelling west through Europe, invariably seeking out fellow dissidents. As you know, radical political activity has grown into anarchism across the Continent, and if there were any bombings or assassinations to be organised, our friend Yubkin is never too far away."

"As shocking as this is," I said, "what has this Yubkin got to do with this case?"

"Everything to do with it. Far from this being a relatively minor enquiry involving a missing person, I believe we have the opportunity of apprehending one of the most dangerous men in London.

"You will recall Lestrade telling us the other night about the Crimean veteran who was shot and killed in the coffee shop. I went to see our erstwhile colleague today and together we visited his colleagues in the Special Branch section who are investigating the murder – lamentably I might add! I discovered that the soft-nosed bullet used in the killing was one of the many consignments stolen from Dial Square over the past twelve months."

"They are a horrible thing!" I said, with some disgust.

"Indeed, designed to mushroom upon entry, causing instantaneous death. The assassin's ammunition of choice, I would suggest. What the police haven't linked – until I pointed it out to them of course – is that particular killing with two others in Paris and Lyon earlier this year."

"France?" I exclaimed. "Forgive me, Holmes, but your narrative is getting cloudier by the minute!"

"At the turn of the year, Yubkin was in France. His visit there coincided with two high-profile assassinations: Both senior army officials, and both veterans of the Crimean campaign – particularly the taking of Sebastopol."

"I now suddenly see what you are driving at."

My friend nodded slowly. "Yes. As well as fuelling the anarchy in others, I believe Yubkin is carrying out his own personal vendetta against those whom he feels are responsible for his father's death."

"That is why you want me to find out who is attending Woodward's dinner on Christmas Eve."

"It is. Your friend has already mentioned that he and his colleagues are veterans of Crimea. If my theory is correct, this puts them in danger of Yubkin, who is now back in London."

I sat trying to digest my friend's staggering deduction and the dangers that potentially lay ahead. Before I could articulate the feelings and thoughts that were wrestling for attention inside my head, Holmes spoke again.

"When we visited Mrs. Carver, she spoke of a 'Mr. Gregory', with whom young Bateman had become involved. If my suspicions are correct, she had misunderstood Bateman when he was talking about this friend. I think the young man has become embroiled not with 'Mr. Gregory', but with Grigory Yubkin."

"Yes, it's certainly plausible. I remember she commented that he was a foreigner. But where can they be?"

"I think I already know," revealed Holmes, much to my further amazement.

"You know?"

"Well, at least my agent does. I went to see him yesterday and put him on the trail. The note he sent me earlier told me that he had found our man Bateman."

"Who is this man of yours?" I asked,

"Shinwell Johnson," my friend announced, and then, in response to my puzzled expression. "He is a fellow who has enjoyed a checkered career himself, even enjoying more than one period at Her Majesty's pleasure."

Although this was the first time I'd heard Holmes speak of Johnson, I wasn't surprised that he had allied himself to the character he described, such was his determination to explore every avenue of enquiry when engrossed in a case.

"And this Johnson chap has found Bateman?" I asked.

"He has," said Holmes with a chuckle. "If anything is going on in the criminal underworld of this great city, Johnson invariably knows about it."

"So what do you propose to do now?"

"I will reply to Johnson and see if he can lure him to Baker Street."

"And then what?"

"Find out whether he knows about Yubkin's intentions or not." If it were possible, Holmes adopted a graver tone. "If Yubkin doesn't know about the dinner, we may have an opportunity to set a trap that will snare this dangerous character."

I sat for a few minutes coming to terms with what my friend was suggesting. "When you first told us about Yubkin at the conclusion of the Dial Square robberies, I remember you said that he was a small part of a much larger criminal enterprise. If you do succeed in apprehending him, would that not allow the friends he has in higher places to evade capture?"

"That's a risk we will have to take. If Yubkin is intent on carry on with his murderous rampage, as I suspect, we are duty-bound to stop him. If that means delaying the apprehending of bigger criminal fish, then so be it." Holmes looked directly at me. "You realise what I'm suggesting? I'm risking the lives of innocent men and my friend in order to snare this villain."

"I do," I replied meeting Holmes's stare, "and if it is in a good cause, which this clearly is, then I'm your man!"

Holmes smiled and returned his gaze to the fire.

Chapter IV

As Holmes had suspected, as well as my old friend Woodward, my dining companions were to include three senior officers, all of whom were decorated for services in the Crimea. It seemed too fanciful that this Russian chap would attempt to assassinate such a group of retired old soldiers, but knowing and trusting Holmes's instincts as I did, I wasn't prepared to ignore his concerns.

It was four days before Christmas Eve when we heard that my friend's contact in the East End had been successful in locating young Bateman. He intended to bring him to Baker Street that night after convincing him that he was also an ally of Yubkin and there was a task the Russian wanted the two to perform. At the appointed hour, we heard feet on the stairs and the two men entered our sitting room. One was a thick-set man with a ruddy complexion and various marks on his hard face that indicated a tough life. The other was a much younger man, thin with wispy fair hair and a saturnine expression.

"Gentlemen! Come in!" announced Holmes with a flourish. "Thank you for joining us."

"Mr. Holmes, sir," said the rough looking character who took up his station with his back to the door, blocking any exit.

The younger man looked confused and darted a glance between Holmes and the man who had brought him here.

"Do not be alarmed, Mr. Bateman," said my friend. "My name is Sherlock Holmes, and this is my friend and colleague, Dr. Watson. I must confess, Johnson here has brought you to Baker Street under slightly false pretences. But don't worry. It was done in order to help you."

"I don't understand," said Bateman, first to Holmes and then turning to Johnson. "You said it was something to do with Grigory."

"And so it is," said Holmes before Shinwell Johnson could say anything. "I'm aware that you have allied yourself to Grigory Yubkin. Whether you know it or not, Yubkin is an extremely dangerous man, guilty of, amongst other things, theft, anarchy, and murder."

The fact the Bateman didn't protest suggested he was at least aware of some of Yubkin's activities. "He is only fighting for what he believes in," he said at last, rather pathetically.

Holmes didn't hold back. "Murder and destruction aren't worthy causes." He composed himself before continuing. "Your father visited us a few days ago and asked me to locate you. He is concerned about you, Bateman. He has already lost his wife, and you have lost your mother. You must return home to Reading to be with him. I suspect you haven't been associated with Yubkin long enough to perpetrate any serious crimes yourself, but you could certainly be viewed as an accessory, even by association."

Bateman lowered his head as Holmes raised the subject of his mother's passing.

"It isn't too late," resumed my friend. "If you work with me I can help you, and you'll be back at your father's table enjoying a goose on Christmas Day. If you work against me, I'm afraid your own goose will be cooked, and you'll find yourself eating whatever is being served in the cells."

"What do you want me to do?" asked Bateman while looking into his lap.

"Has Yubkin said anything to you about an event on Christmas Eve?"

252

Bateman looked up. "Yes, he did mention something. He asked if I could help him. He mentioned something about 'having his revenge', but didn't really go into any details. I'm due to meet him tomorrow to get the details."

"Did he say anything about the Café Royal?"

"No, not that I can remember. Why?"

"There is a dinner taking place there on Christmas Eve involving old soldiers who served in the Crimean War. It's my suspicion that Yubkin wants to murder them to avenge the death of his father at Sebastopol."

"What do you propose that I do?" asked the young man.

"I would like you to go ahead with your meeting and confirm if my suspicions are correct. If they are, I'll make arrangements to have your friend arrested in the act of attempting his crime."

"And if it isn't what he is planning?"

"Then my friend here can enjoy his dinner with his friends in peace and we'll keep an eye on what else Yubkin is up to. Either way, I would like you to return to your father and give up on this life you seem so intent on."

Bateman knew he had no choice and finally nodded slowly. "Very well, I'll do it."

"Do you think he can be trusted?" I asked as I watched Bateman and Johnson make their way along Baker Street, now thick with snow.

"I believe so," replied Holmes, lighting his pipe. "Bateman was clearly emotionally vulnerable following the loss of his mother. He is only guilty of making some poor decisions during this period. I don't see him as a hardened villain – unlike some of the company he's now keeping. If all goes to plan, we shall be removing one dangerous man from the streets of London, while saving the soul of another."

On the night of the 23rd, two days following his first visit, Bateman returned to Baker Street with news of his meeting with Yubkin. It was as though the events of the previous forty-eight hours had brought the young man to his senses and he now realised the perils of the path he had chosen by leaving his father. He was also clearly extremely nervous about betraying his friend.

"You are correct, Mr. Holmes," he said after retaking his seat from earlier in the week. "Grigory is planning to be at the Café Royal tomorrow night. And I'm afraid that I may have made matters worse."

"How so?" asked Holmes.

"He told me that he had been monitoring the movements of a Colonel Richards for some months and it is him whom he intends to kill. But then I told him that other veterans would be there and this prompted him to change his plans."

253

"What was his reaction when you knew about the other veterans?"

"I simply said that Colonel Richards had been a friend of my father. He seemed to accept that. But Mr. Holmes," he added, "instead of taking a handgun to shoot Richards, he plans to take a handmade bomb and throw it into the dining room."

My blood ran cold at the thought, and it was my turn to fully comprehend the dangers that lay ahead.

"That is useful to know, Bateman," said Holmes. "At least we can now prepare properly."

"What do you intend?" asked the young man.

"I'll inform Inspector Lestrade and have him position his men at key locations in and around the foyer of the restaurant. When Yubkin enters – before he can ignite the fuse of his bomb – we will have him arrested."

"I have a request of my own," said Bateman, and then responding to Holmes's questioning expression. "I would like the police to arrest me as well, so that it doesn't look as though I've betrayed him. For the first time last night, I saw what a dangerous man he is, Mr. Holmes. I would hate to think there would be any retribution against myself – or more importantly, my dear father."

"I'm sure we can stage something that will protect your secret. As for any reprisals concerning your actions, I think you can rest easy on that score. I've never known anyone succeed in any retribution as they hang from the end of a rope."

After Bateman had left, Holmes sensed my nervousness.

"I wouldn't ask you to do this, if I didn't believe you were the man for the job."

"It isn't my own safety I'm concerned about. At least I know the dangers I'm facing. The others don't, and this is what is making me nervous."

"I believe it is the best way, my friend. The less people know about this, the better. We want everyone to be completely natural on the night so that Yubkin doesn't suspect anything is amiss. Any nerves he senses from young Bateman will be just that – first night nerves, as it were."

I nodded silently, still feeling uneasy about my dining companions' ignorance of the matter.

I slept fitfully, my mind constantly going back to the horrors of my experiences in Afghanistan. The following day wasn't much better. Christmas Eve has always been of my favourite days, with a sense of anticipation that was unrivalled throughout the year. But Christmas Eve that year was different: I was quiet throughout the day and had to be reminded at one point by Mrs. Hudson that I'd promised to collect our

Christmas goose from the poultry seller who set up during that time of year in Covent Garden.

Holmes had been away for most of the morning, briefing Lestrade on what was about to take place that evening. It was his usual habit to keep me in the dark about his periods of absence, but on this occasion – understanding my apprehension – he informed me that the Scotland Yard man was to have plain-clothed officers outside the restaurant, as well as other men in the foyer posing at staff. Holmes himself would be there to assist if necessary.

"Our night's work will be a serious one," he concluded as he reached into the drawer of his desk, "and I'm afraid that your army revolver will ruin the cut of your tails. You must therefore rely on me."

He checked the chamber of his pistol and then snapped it shut. It was five o'clock when Holmes buttoned up his pea-jacket and slipped the revolver in his pocket. Reaching for his heavy hunting crop from the rack, he left once again to meet Lestrade and prepare for the evening's events. I remained in Baker Street for a further hour-and-a-half. Such was my state of anxiety, I had three attempts before successfully knotting my white tie. There was part of me that felt ashamed about withholding the information about Yubkin from Woodward and his friends, but I knew that to betray Holmes's instructions wouldn't only be a treacherous act in itself – it would jeopardise the whole mission and put us all in further danger. I hardened my heart and put on my hat and coat.

As my hansom travelled towards Regents Street, I sensed the excitement amongst the people of London. From my cab I saw boisterous passers-by moving to-and-fro in the gas-lit streets, muffled in their coats and cravats. There were fathers who had finished work for the holiday, giddily playing with their children in the snow. A group of carol singers made their way along Wigmore Street, while a waft of roasting chestnuts permeated my nostrils as we passed a street vendor selling his produce by an open brazier. We arrived shortly before seven and as I climbed down from the cab and paid my fare, there was a quintet of Salvation Army bandsmen along the street softly playing "Silent Night", their faces lighted by the rays of a horn lantern carried by another uniformed member of the group.

The street was already busy as diners were arriving in their dozens. I thought how catastrophic it would be if Holmes were unsuccessful in his plan to stop Yubkin. I quickly dispelled the thought from my mind and made my way inside, trying to pick out the police officers that Holmes and Lestrade had positioned.

There were two uniformed doormen to meet and greet guests as they arrived. One seemed quite natural, continually touching the brim of his top hat and wishing everyone a good evening, the other stood stock still, looking straight ahead. Inside there were staff taking diners' coats and hats. One of the staff was the picture of awkwardness as he wrestled with an armful of coats, much to the concerned expressions of their owners. My attention was then drawn to a clatter of cutlery, dropped from a tray by someone coming out of the kitchen.

"Probably temporary staff employed for the holidays," I heard one woman say to her husband as I followed them into the vast dining room.

It was decorated with four large Christmas trees in each corner, while ribbons and bunting had been strung across the room from the ceiling. I saw my old friend Woodward waving at me through the crowd of people who were starting to take their seats.

"Watson!" he called. "How lovely to see you! Thank you so much for coming."

"My pleasure," I said, rather unconvincingly.

Woodward turned his attention to his seated companions. "These are my colleagues from the Crimea." Except for Colonel Richards, Yubkin's original target, their names barely registered – such was my distracted state of mind. "Gentlemen, this is Doctor John Watson, a dear companion of mine from Afghanistan."

After pleasantries were exchanged, I took my seat. As the old soldiers launched into their various reminisces and waiters appeared from the kitchen with the soup course, my mind was filled with what was happening elsewhere. It would be a further hour before I relaxed into the evening and it would be still later that night, over a cigar and brandy, before Sherlock Holmes properly enlightened me as to the sequence of events that I was unable to witness first-hand.

As he related later, Holmes had left me in Baker Street and met Lestrade and his men. The uniformed officers were kept out of sight while three were placed in positions of a fake concierge, a cloakroom attendant, and a member of the waiting staff. (I must confess to being delighted at this information and inwardly congratulated myself or my own observations).

"We waited in position for Bateman and Yubkin. All of the guests were inside and seated when the two arrived, just as the nearby church bells sounded eight o'clock. I must compliment Yubkin on his sense of propriety – he was dressed immaculately and would certainly pass for restaurant patron himself who had simply arrived late. Bateman was driving a small landau and waited discreetly along the street for his would-be confederate to exit the building before making a hasty escape. When Lestrade and I saw Yubkin get down from the landau, we quickly made our way into the foyer where we took up positions out of sight, alongside four other uniformed officers. Moments later, Yubkin appeared and, calm as you like, handed his coat to one of the cloakroom attendants. From our hiding place, I could see he was holding something in the back of his hand, concealed from the member of staff, who directed him towards the dining room.

"I must say Lestrade's men played their parts well, for as Yubkin made his way through the foyer, one of Lestrade's constables appeared from the dining room dressed as one of the waiting staff, carrying a tray of plates. He knocked into Yubkin as they passed, just as the Russian was reaching into his pocket, I suspected in order to light the fuse of the device he was carrying. It was just enough to distract him momentarily from his task.

"'*Now!*' I signaled, and the rest of Lestrade's men appeared from their hiding place and overpowered the man with a minimal of struggle. As they wrestled him to the floor, he dropped an object he was carrying, along with a box of matches. The unlit device started to roll away before I trapped it under my foot. A pretty little thing, I must say. It was a variation on the Orsini Bomb but with its own fuse – designed to cause the maximum of damage. None of the patrons heard a thing.

"When he was searched, Yubkin even had a seating plan in his pocket with your friend Woodward's table indicated, so he knew exactly what he was doing.

"The final act was to march him out of the restaurant and ensure that he saw Bateman being arrested also, so as to protect the young man's reputation in the eyes of his former friend. He will be back on his way to Reading as we speak, whereas our Russian friend is now in the Old Bailey."

"Good heavens!" I replied after hearing my friend's narrative. "You were just in time to prevent the most horrible of crimes."

Of course, I never knew any of this as I was inside the dining room at the time of the action. Whatever noise came from the scuffling in the foyer was drowned out by the clanking of cutlery and crockery, and the general hubbub of the diners. The first I'd known of my friend's successful operation was when I was tapped on the shoulder by the *maître d*, who held a silver tray on which sat a bottle of champagne.

"Sir," he said, "the gentleman in the foyer sent this over with his compliments."

I looked over the crowd to the door leading to the foyer to see the figure of Sherlock Holmes standing with just the hint of a smile on his lips. He touched the brim of his hat with his crop and was gone. I knew then that his mission had been successful. I thanked the *maître d'* and took the bottle.

Turning back to my dining companions who had been engrossed in their own conversation all night, and therefore completely oblivious to any potential dangers, I filled their glasses.

"Gentlemen, I would like to wish you all the complements of the season!" And then, raising my own glass: "Merry Christmas, everyone!"

NOTE

*   See "Dial Square" by Martin Daley, *The MX Book of New Sherlock Holmes Stories: Part XXV – 2021 Annual (1881-1888)*

POSTSCRIPT

The inspiration for "The Sebastopol Clasp" comes from my great-great-grandfather, Isaac Scott. It is no exaggeration to say that this old boy changed my life, almost a hundred years after his death. He was a soldier in the nineteenth century and served in the Crimean and Indian Mutiny campaigns. Sadly, his medals had been lost from the family some time ago. That notwithstanding, during my research into his life, I found out so much information about him that I decided to write a little book. With that, I was well and truly bitten by the writing bug and over thirty years on, I'm still loving it.

As far as fiction was concerned, my favourite literary characters had always been Holmes and Watson – still are of course – so I decided to set an adventure involving our two heroes in my home city of Carlisle. I even gave Isaac a walk-on part in the book, and to commemorate its publication, my wife – unbeknownst to me – commissioned an artist friend of ours to produce a Paget-esque drawing of the scene where Isaac meets Dr. Watson in a local park.

Imagine my delight when a medal collector in America tracked me down a few months ago and informed me he had recently bought Isaac's medals at auction. He offered to return them to me and we came to an agreement. I had the medals cleaned, mounted, and framed alongside the wonderful photograph I have of the great man. If you look closely at the medal on the left, this is his Crimean campaign medal, attached to which is a curly bar. That bar curly is . . . (Yes, you've guessed it) the *Sebastopol Clasp*.

Martin Daley
Carlisle
2021

WE CONTINUED TO CHAT DESULTORILY FOR SOME TIME, AS OLD SOLDIERS ARE BOUND TO DO...

ISAAC SCOTT (1834-1908)
PRIVATE 1622 17TH LANCERS

The Silent Brotherhood
by Dick Gillman

It was, as I recall, a rather changeable afternoon in late December 1886 when I first met Mr. Charles Melville Williams, a person whose absolute trust in Sherlock Holmes was to decide a matter of life and death.

Given the time of year, our rooms in Baker Street had little in the way of Christmas cheer. However, as I rose from the dining table, I passed the fragrant, pine Christmas tree whose presence was something upon which I had insisted. Pausing briefly to straighten a wayward angel, I found that my ministrations only brought a snort of derision from my friend, even though I fancy that he secretly welcomed the festoons of gummed paper chains and the colourful glass baubles that I had lavishly purchased from Harrods, no less.

Ignoring Holmes's retort, I looked out from the window of our sitting room. It seemed as if the December weather couldn't determine if it were to provide a glimmer of sunshine or to punish the scurrying figures of shoppers on the pavement beneath with a sharp flurry of snow.

We had taken something of a light luncheon consisting of wedges of delicious pork pie together with slices of ham-and-tongue and a little of Mrs. Hudson's chutney. I was delighted to find that this was followed by a splendid home-made treacle tart which, I must say, played to my sweet tooth.

Replete, we returned to our respective armchairs and enjoyed our first pipe of the afternoon. For my part, I had taken up my mid-December copy of *The Lancet*, and was now intrigued by an article therein.

Hardly had we settled when the ringing of our bell in the hallway below announced that we had a visitor. I looked up briefly towards my friend and noticed that he appeared to be so engrossed in his morning edition of *The Times* that he didn't stir.

Some moments passed and, as there was heard no sound of conversation between our landlady and our guest, Holmes raised his head and then slowly folded his paper. Leaning forward in his chair, he seemed now to be somewhat unsettled by this most curious occurrence.

Holmes inclined his head slightly and frowned as he listened intently to the footfalls upon our stairs before a gentle knock at our sitting room door announced Mrs. Hudson's arrival. As the door opened, I could see that she was accompanied by a well-presented, slim, and rather diminutive male figure. The gentleman before us was of some fifty years with swept back, iron-grey hair which topped an oval face with a neatly trimmed moustache.

Mrs. Hudson looked a little bemused as she announced, "Excuse me, Mr. Holmes. This gentleman appears to be needing your services. He has said not a word, simply passing me a note bearing his request."

Mrs. Hudson now held out a small piece of paper towards Holmes which, I noticed, he studiously ignored. Rising from his chair and extending his hand towards our visitor, he greeted him. "My dear Mr. Williams, how pleased I am to see you again."

I looked from Holmes to our guest, expecting some kind of response from our visitor to Holmes's welcome . . . but there was none, other than a warm smile and nod of the head.

Turning to our landlady, Holmes smiled before saying, "Thank you, Mrs. Hudson, Mr. Williams is known to me." Mrs. Hudson nodded and, with a slight frown and a questioning glance towards our guest, she made her way back down the stairs.

I rose from my chair and ushered Mr. Williams towards our chaise longue and, as I did so, Williams plucked from his inside jacket pocket an envelope which he passed to Holmes before settling so that he sat directly facing him.

Holmes pursed his lips slightly as he opened the envelope and then rapidly devoured the contents of the single sheet of paper within. As he read, the mere twitch of an eyebrow was sufficient for me to realise that its content was of some import.

Holmes remained silent for perhaps some thirty seconds, as did our guest, who still had uttered not a single word since his arrival.

Passing the envelope to me, Holmes then frowned before declaring, "Watson, I would like to introduce Mr. Charles Melville Williams, a gentleman who was a client of mine a little before your time." I smiled and nodded towards our guest who, in return, nodded politely – but I was still puzzled by his silence. Seeing my questioning expression, Holmes then turned once more to our guest and continued, "Mr. Williams, this is my friend and colleague, Dr. John Watson. He is my confidant in all matters."

Once Holmes had said this, Williams raised his hands from his lap and then began to make a series of intricate hand movements towards Holmes.

It was as if at that moment someone had struck a Vesta within my head. I suddenly realised that Williams was a mute, unable to speak, and was now communicating with Holmes by way of sign language. I had some rudimentary knowledge of signing, but I was unable to keep pace with what was now occurring.

Eager to be part of this affair, I opened the envelope Holmes had passed to me. Upon the single sheet of paper within, and in fine copperplate, a few paragraphs had been written which were, indeed, greatly concerning. The two men were signing rapidly, one to the other, and I reluctantly decided not to interrupt and to wait, somewhat testy, until their "conversation" was complete.

Watching Holmes intently, I was indeed impressed by this hither-before unknown talent. Although conducted in complete silence, the changing expression on Holmes's face was of grave concern to me. Of course, I knew that he would recount to me all that had transpired once Williams had left, but that didn't relieve my impatience.

After perhaps some five minutes of this silent exchange, Williams took from his waistcoat pocket a business card. Taking out a silver pencil, he carefully wrote upon the reverse a single word before passing the card to Holmes. As he studied the card, his face clouded. Looking up at Williams, he then slowly nodded.

Abruptly, Holmes rose. He shook Williams's hand and was about to guide him towards our sitting room door when I stepped forward. Using my most rudimentary knowledge, I signed, "Goodbye, Mr. Williams. I'm pleased to have met you." At this, Williams's face lit up and, on turning his back to me, signed something to Holmes who, in return, nodded gravely.

As Holmes closed our sitting room door, I was now desperate to learn all that had occurred. I was barely able to wait until Holmes was once more seated before blurting out, "For heaven's sake! Don't keep me in suspense!"

Holmes frowned slightly as he turned to me and deigned to raise a single eyebrow before sighing. "Pray don't tell me that you are an oralist, for I side with Socrates in this matter. His view that the deaf and dumb are those who have words without sound and that language is dependent on a sensory input but not on any particular sensory output is one with which I whole-heartedly agree."

My brows furrowed as I answered, angrily, "Indeed I am not! I believe there is a place for both the reading of the lips and the use of sign language in communicating with the deaf. I'm of the opinion that the 1880 International Congress in Milan on the teaching of the deaf was dominated by oralists. Their decision to move away from signing was deeply regrettable!" I took a moment to calm myself before asking, "I take it that Mr. Williams is a deaf-mute?"

Holmes nodded his head slowly. "Indeed, he has been both deaf and unable to speak from birth." Holmes paused to draw upon his briar before asking, "What do you make of the contents of his note? Would you be so

263

kind as to read it aloud?" Holmes then sat back, puffing contemplatively upon his pipe with his eyes half closed and knees drawn up close unto his chest.

Taking up the envelope, I pulled the sheet of paper from within and read aloud: "Mr. Holmes, I come to you as I fear that my life may well be in danger. It has been some years since we last met and, during that time, I have become the senior partner in an accountancy firm in the City."

I paused for a moment before continuing, "My affliction has had little effect upon my success in business and, indeed, I have embraced it. In doing so, I have become an active member in a reclusive, yet protective, society of similar souls. "The Silent Brotherhood" has members from every profession and the identity of its members is closely guarded."

I looked towards Holmes for further clarification, but he simply waved his hand as a signal for me to continue. "I am privileged to be the society's treasurer, a position that I gladly undertook, but it now appears that it carries with it some great personal risk."

Putting down the sheet of paper and looking towards my friend, I was keen to hear what this great risk might be, enquiring, "I trust that Williams expanded upon this in your conversation?"

Holmes took the pipe from his lips, saying, "Indeed, and it disturbs me more than a little. Williams explained that he is the custodian of both the private papers that detail the membership of the society and also a large fortune that has been accrued over many years. This has been by way of shrewd investment, gift, and bequest." Holmes paused, adding, "However, by some means, knowledge of the society's fortune and the potential for blackmail of its esteemed members has become known to criminal elements and, in the last few days, he is being followed."

I frowned, asking, "Does he not keep this treasure secure in the strongroom of his business?"

Holmes blew out a small cloud of smoke towards our already ochre-coloured ceiling and then slowly shook his head. "I fear not. Such is the secrecy of this society that its business must be kept far from the public gaze and, therefore, he has installed a substantial safe in his own home."

I considered all that Holmes had said for a few moments before asking, "I saw that he gave you his business card, and I'm intrigued as to what he wrote upon it."

Holmes reached into his waistcoat pocket. Passing the card over to me, I read Williams's name and address. Turning it over, I observed the single word that had been written thereon.

I frowned, asking, "What is the significance of this word – '*Heimdall*'?"

Holmes looked troubled as he explained, "You will agree that it is an uncommon word, and that is as it should be, given its purpose. It would appear that each member of this mysterious brotherhood of silence has chosen a word, a most secret, single word, which is of immeasurable value within the society." Holmes became even more serious as he continued. "It is an unbreakable token of trust. A member can only make it known to a person outside the brotherhood who is completely trusted, and that trust is absolute."

I sat back and considered this. "So Williams has given you this word as a token of his complete trust in you." I thought for a moment before saying, "It is a strange word, '*Heimdall*'. I have a notion that this is the name of a figure from Norse mythology."

Holmes nodded. "Quite so. Williams has placed upon me a great responsibility. However, only on finding you to be a kindred spirit, by way of your signing, has he allowed me to share the word with you." I sat back, wide-eyed, as this was something I hadn't even considered!

He continued as he wagged the stem of his pipe in my direction, saying, "The word itself is a conundrum. Heimdall was a guardian of secrets, just like Williams, but in contrast, Heimdall's hearing was such that he could hear a single leaf fall." Holmes paused. "I think, perhaps, Williams's choice of word is one which reveals some dark humour on his part."

I pursed my lips, asking, "How do you intend to proceed?"

"I think it is necessary for me to discover who might be following Williams, and to do so somewhat discreetly."

I looked towards my friend and observed that there was now a twinkle in his eye. On saying this, he rose from his chair and moved towards his bedroom.

The following morning I took breakfast alone. Holmes wasn't to be seen, but the carelessly tossed-aside remnants of his own breakfast and the scattered array of cutlery that littered Mrs. Hudson's fine damask tablecloth bore witness to his having been present sometime earlier.

It was as I took my final sip of coffee that our sitting room door burst open and in swept a ragged figure which I knew could only be Holmes in one of his many disguises. Bemused, I commented, "Ah, I see that you have once again embraced the role of an invisible man!"

Holmes threw off the tattered outer garments of his disguise before making his way towards his bedroom, crying, "Indeed! I'm the man whom nobody sees and yet, he sees all!"

Moments later, he returned as his true self. Allowing him time to light his pipe, I then asked, "And what intelligence did you gather?"

Holmes drew strongly upon his pipe before replying, "It is as Williams suspected. I took it upon myself to discreetly follow him and, as I did so, so did another." I sat forward in my chair, eager to hear more. "The fellow whom I spied was unfamiliar, but once at Williams's place of work, he broke off, and I then set out to trace this shadow back to his lair.

"The trail led to an alleyway near Charing Cross," he added, "which, as I settled within the shadow of a corner, was visited by a very unsavoury fellow with a pronounced limp." He now pointed the stem of his pipe towards me, saying, "You may recall a certain Henry Callow."

I frowned and pursed my lips as I searched my memory for the name. "Yes, yes! Was he not accused of grievously wounding some poor fellow in a wretched attempt at blackmail?"

Holmes nodded. "Indeed, and only the unproven intimidation of witnesses ensured his continued freedom." He remained silent for a few moments before adding ominously, "If Callow intends to rob Williams, it will not be some casual street theft, for the man is a brute."

Rising from his chair, Holmes hurriedly took up a telegram pad and dashed off a few lines before ringing rather furiously for Billy, our page. "Williams must be warned to be most cautious, given the nature of this man." His face darkened as he added, "I am indeed concerned, and intend to call upon him this evening to impress upon him my fears." Holmes then paused before asking, "Would it greatly inconvenience you if – "

Before he could finish his sentence I interrupted. "Not at all. Perhaps it might be best if we were to take an early dinner?"

His face brightened and, with a grateful nod, he sank back into his chair. Little further was said throughout the day, although Holmes busied himself for some hours poring through our ever growing collection of newspaper clippings.

By seven o'clock, we were dressed in overcoats, hats, and mufflers, and making our way down the stairs and out onto Baker Street. Waving his cane somewhat enthusiastically, Holmes quickly attracted the attention of a passing cabbie and then, on calling out, "Spanish Place, off Manchester Gardens," we quickly installed ourselves before setting off at a good pace for the short journey.

Manchester Gardens was unknown to me, an attractive lawned square having a side of some hundred yards and planted with mature trees. It seemed to be a small, hidden oasis in the centre of the city. The houses that surrounded it were Georgian in design and, as we drew to the kerb in Spanish Place, the dwelling before us was indeed impressive.

Stepping down, Holmes tossed the cabbie a sixpence and then stood before the elegant, columned porchway with its half-moon, wrought-iron traced window above the front door. He was about to reach for the door knocker when he suddenly stopped and then transferred his cane to his right hand, grasping it half-way down the shaft.

Leaning forwards, he reached out his gloved hand and gently pushed against the door which, surprisingly, opened at his touch. Seeing Holmes's posture, I followed suit, holding my own heavy, silver-topped cane in a similar fashion.

The oak-panelled hallway was in semi-darkness, but the prostrate figure of a liveried footman was visible in the gloom. Holmes stepped over the man and then nodded towards me. I nodded silently in return and knelt beside the fellow. Peering closely, it was clear that he had suffered a cruel blow to the head which had felled him and the absence of a pulse confirmed my fears.

Rising, I saw that Holmes had progressed down the hallway towards the flickering glow of light emanating from a partially open door at its end. Raising his cane, he silently advanced. Flinging open the door, he then sprang into the room with his cane at the ready.

As I approached, the waft of disturbed air from Holmes's sudden entry reached me. It carried with it the stench of stale sweat, vomit, and more. Reaching the doorway, the scene that greeted me appeared to be one taken from the very bowels of hell itself. Furniture within this large reception room had been tossed aside except for a single chair at its centre. Upon this, a bloodied, bare-chested figure hung limply.

Fearfully, I approached this scarecrow of a man and, in truth, it took me a moment to recognise the badly beaten features of Williams. He was, I observed, bound to the chair at both the wrists and ankles. Holmes was already moving around the room, taking in every detail. Occasionally he would pause and then drop to his knees as something drew his attention whilst gathering samples of detritus, which he placed carefully in small, gummed envelopes.

My examination of Williams was something of a gruesome formality, for he was clearly dead. His body and soiled clothes bore witness to his having been tortured to extinction. Lit only by the flickering flames from the grand fireplace and the two candlesticks upon the mantel, the scene was indeed macabre.

Having searched the room thoroughly and examined the still-securely locked safe, revealed from behind its concealing curtain, Holmes now turned his attention to Williams. Painstakingly, he examined the corpse and, without turning towards me, he asked, "Bring me a candle from the mantel – the left one, if you please."

I frowned as, to me, the two candles appeared to be identical in all respects. However, I complied with his request and watched as he used the light and his glass to provide further detail. Other than this brief request, Holmes said nothing throughout his examination.

Replacing his glass in his coat pocket, he then strode to the mantel and replaced the left-hand candle. Leaning close, he blew out the right-hand candle and, once it had cooled, he then pocketed it.

Seeming to be finished with his examination, he turned on his heel and then marched purposefully from the house. At the front door he paused, and then gave three sharp blasts upon his police whistle before walking briskly away. I hurried after him, surprised that he hadn't waited for a response to his whistled request for assistance.

On reaching the corner of Manchester Gardens, Holmes was fortunate to be able to hail a cab almost immediately. As I climbed aboard, I could see by the cab's lamps that his expression was that of riven granite. Wisely, I determined to hold my tongue. What I had seen in Spanish Place had sickened me. Even the joyous Christmas decorations in the windows of the houses we passed couldn't raise my spirits as we rode back in silence to Baker Street.

It was, perhaps ten o'clock that evening before Holmes spoke. By then, our rooms had developed that familiar, blue, ethereal fog as we smoked our second pipe of the evening together. Finally he broke the silence. "There is an abundance of wickedness here. Consider the unimaginable horror of being seized, bound to a chair, and then tortured to give up secrets – secrets that your body will not allow you to reveal, even if you were willing."

"It is unthinkable," I replied.

Holmes's eyes burned as he continued. "And yet it has happened. This must not go unpunished. The evidence is questionable, but it may be sufficient to satisfy a jury of Callow's guilt, and we must be sure." He rose and walked to the coat stand. Delving into his overcoat pocket, he removed the candle that he had taken.

Returning to his chair, he declared, "Wax is an excellent material for holding the form of something pressed into it while it is still warm. For example, a finger-mark."

I sat upright on hearing this, asking, "I observed that Williams had been subjected to hot wax being dripped upon his body. Do you believe that the candle bears the finger-mark of his torturer?"

Holmes pursed his lips, replying, "It is but a partial mark, but I gleaned something more from the area around where Williams was seated." Reaching into his jacket, he removed a small gummed envelope and tossed it towards me. "Tell me what you see."

Carefully, I broke the seal and peered at the contents. "There seem to be some fibres and small brown crystals."

Holmes nodded. "The fibres are from the carpet and are of no particular value, but the crystals are, I believe, brown sugar. They were discovered at the edge of an unevenly weighted footprint."

I frowned as the importance of this discovery eluded me. "And this is your evidence?"

Holmes again nodded, saying, "Perhaps. My research this afternoon into Mr. Henry Callow noted that his place of work was recorded as Blood Alley, West India Docks – a place where raw sugar is off loaded."

I rubbed my chin before asking, "Surely a competent defence barrister would argue that the presence of the sugar on the floor of Williams's sitting room could just as likely to have been the result of a clumsy maid as it having its origins from Callow's boot."

"Quite so, but the inference of his presence in Spanish Place and the opportunity to intimidate me into remaining silent might just be sufficient to tempt Callow to a meeting."

On hearing this, I countered, "A meeting? You cannot. The man is a monster! I must protest!"

Holmes turned towards me, took the pipe from his mouth, insisting, "It is essential that I do so, for this fellow is indeed a rarity. Consider this: Here is a man who will torture another unto death even though, after only a few minutes of his work, it would have been crystal clear, from the absence of any cries from Williams that his captive was a mute. And yet he continued."

Holmes paused and I considered what he had said, no matter how distasteful. "You examined Williams's body. There was no sign of any mercy by way of *coup de grace*." He fell silent for several moments before continuing, "I firmly believe Callow to be a criminal maniac and worthy of my observation. I fear that even if sufficient evidence was gathered to convict him, he might escape the gallows by way of insanity."

I sat back, eyes wide open, as my mind reeled from his suggestion. "I cannot condone your need to study this fellow for your own purposes." I paused to settle my thoughts before asking, "Given your 'diagnosis' of this fellow's condition, wouldn't such a meeting be dangerous in the extreme?"

Holmes smiled, "Fear not, for any such meeting would be on my terms, and I would have ample protection." He raised an eyebrow and held my gaze for rather longer than I expected. Indeed, he did so until I finally sighed and slowly nodded my acceptance.

On seeing this, he cried, "Capital! I shall pen him an invitation to take refreshments tomorrow afternoon. But where? I cannot meet him for luncheon at Simpson's!"

I thought for a moment of the locations where I had visited during my travels in the metropolis before suggesting, "Perhaps The Coal Hole, also in the Strand. That might have an ambiance more suited to the man. Afterwards, we might then progress from there to Piccadilly and choose a suitable Christmas gift for Mrs. Hudson?"

Holmes smiled and nodded in agreement. "Ah, Watson, ever the practical man. I trust you will be taking your service revolver to such a venue?" I didn't reply but simply inclined my head and smiled.

The next day, Holmes was true to his word and, by breakfast time, had already dispatched a telegram to Callow at the address he'd discovered in Charing Cross. I wasn't sure whether it would elicit a response but, by lunchtime, Mrs. Hudson was handing him a reply.

Tearing open the envelope, his face bore a grim smile as he read aloud, "'*Agreed. Callow.*'"

I frowned, saying, "A man of few words. I look forward to observing this wretch. At what time have you arranged to meet him?"

He appeared serious as he replied, "I've set the meeting for two o'clock when, I believe, the pub should be almost empty after the departure of its lunchtime trade. Might I suggest that we travel independently and for you to arrive some ten minutes before that time? I would like you to use your military skills and position yourself so that you're close at hand, should the need arise." I nodded, mindful of the responsibility I now had.

Little was said as we ate luncheon and with a single nod from Holmes, I rose from the table, donned my coat, hat, and muffler, and made my way downstairs.

The journey through the holiday-decorated streets to the Strand was uneventful and I arrived at The Coal Hole well before Holmes. I had purchased of a copy of *The London Daily News* so as to be in keeping with the character of the venue. I seated myself in the corner of the bar which provided me with a clear view of the other tables. Sipping at my half-pint of ale, my only comfort came from the reassuring weight of my service revolver in my overcoat pocket.

I had removed my hat and muffler and was now idly thumbing my way through the pages of newsprint when a shadow passed before me. Casually looking up, I noticed that a fellow of large frame and having an uneven gait was now seating himself a little to one side and not six feet from me. Given his stature, I assumed that this was Callow. Lifting my paper once more, I continued to pretend to read.

Perhaps a further five minutes passed before I heard a distinctive, familiar tread upon the wooden floorboards of the pub which announced Holmes's arrival. As casually as I could, I dipped my hand into my overcoat pocket and removed from it my service revolver. I had already

270

placed my folded muffler upon the table and concealing my revolver beneath it was done with ease.

Holmes sat half-facing me while Callow sat across from him. Still seeming to be intent on reading my newspaper, I leant forward slightly so that I might catch every single word that was spoken.

"Good afternoon, Mr. Callow, I am Sherlock Holmes." He took a card from his case and passed it to him. Callow, I saw, read it before tossing it back to him. Holmes retrieved it and placed the card carefully in his waistcoat pocket. "I see from the abrasions on your hands that you're still engaged in the business of transporting sugar."

Callow looked at his hands and then at Holmes, asking, "What else might you think you know about me?"

Holmes paused for a moment before replying, "Well, let us see. You are originally from Devon and didn't travel directly here this afternoon from your rooms in Charing Cross. You broke your journey, which required you to travel on two different omnibuses. Previously, before the accident in the Blood Alley Sugar Warehouse that broke your leg, you served in Her Majesty's Navy and spent some time in Ceylon – specifically, around the city of Jaffna." He paused, asking, "Does your leg allow you to do much in the way of badger hunting with your terrier?"

Callow now sat open-mouthed while Holmes continued, "The two different coloured bus tickets in your waistcoat pocket told me of your travels today. The opportunities to travel to Ceylon, other than in the service of Her Majesty, are indeed limited. The tattoo that peeks out from beneath your shirt cuff on your right wrist depicts a karava lion – a creature that is indelibly linked to Jaffna.

Holmes again paused, adding, "The short white hairs that reach to mid-calf on your trousers are those from a short-legged terrier. This suggests to me that it is descended from one of Reverend John Russell's Fox Terriers. They can be found amongst the badger diggers of Devon and Somerset, as can your accent, which you have retained."

Holmes gave a thin smile and then sat back, asking, "I believe I was enquiring about the abrasions on your hands being caused by your employment at Sugar Wharf?"

Callow looked down at his reddened and cracked knuckles and sneered. "Oh no, Mr. Holmes, that was from something quite different, as I think you well know. You said in your telegram that you had proof of me visiting a certain address near Manchester Gardens."

Holmes nodded slowly. "It must have come as something of a surprise when you discovered that Charles Williams was a deaf mute, and yet you continued with your evil work." He paused. "I could understand you killing the man if it were to simply conceal your identity."

I heard a muffled snort before Callow replied, "Yes, there wasn't a peep out of him, no matter what I did, and it is that what drove me on." I saw Holmes stiffen, his hands now drawn into fists of white marble as Callow paused and then seemed to look around him. "So what is this proof, and where are the police? Are you going to take me in yourself, Mr. Holmes?"

He slowly shook his head. "No, Mr. Callow. I visited Spanish Place and found traces of brown sugar in a boot print on the carpet next to Williams. This undoubtedly came from your boot."

I jumped in my seat as Callow slapped the table with his palm and laughed. "Ha! I'll wager half of London has sugar on their carpet! What else?"

Holmes smiled grimly before saying, "Wax is such a strange substance, is it not? From what I have seen, you appear to be familiar with its properties, Mr. Callow." He paused before adding, "The candle you used and left behind bears, what I believe to be, an impression of *your* finger-marks, and as you kindly returned my card, it now also bears *your* finger-marks." There was a moment of silence before he continued, "I believe that it will be indeed interesting to make a comparison of the two."

A deep, animal growl emanated from Callow and his voice now took on a harsh tone. "What then, Mr. Holmes, if I were to cut out that card from your waistcoat, and your heart at the same time?"

I had heard enough and my hand crept beneath my muffler as I saw Callow's hand move slowly into his opposite sleeve where there was a glint of steel.

Holmes eyes burned as he stared directly at Callow while saying, without emotion, "I fear that might be quite difficult for a dead man to achieve, Mr. Callow."

On Holmes saying this, I raised and cocked my revolver. The unmistakable sound of the cylinder of my Webley rotating and the hammer locking into position caused Callow to visibly stiffen. Slowly, he withdrew his empty hand from his sleeve and then rose, half-turning towards me.

His face was a mask of hatred as he bared his teeth. For a dreadful moment, I thought he might leap at me, but instead he rushed past and was away.

With more than a modicum of relief, I made my revolver safe and returned it to my overcoat pocket. On the surface, Holmes seemed unmoved by what had occurred, saying simply, "Come along. We have a Christmas gift to buy." I nodded in agreement, but I could see that anger now raged uncontrollably inside my friend.

Hailing a cab, I directed the driver to take us to the Burlington Arcade. This marvellous shopping gallery of almost two-hundred yards in length, with its glazed roof and many fine emporia, provided a sanctuary for those wishing to buy items in a safe and secure manner. Indeed, uniformed Beadles patrolled the arcade to prevent any boisterous behaviour that might annoy its patrons.

Here, Holmes and I perused perhaps a dozen different shop windows before finding a purveyor of fine China where we purchased a pair of exquisite Worcester egg coddlers. These were something that I'd determined we would both enjoy the contents thereof, almost as much as Mrs. Hudson would enjoy their use in her kitchen.

With our purchases neatly boxed and wrapped with brown paper and twine, we strolled along the arcade towards Burlington Gardens, stopping occasionally to admire the variety of festive displays in the shop windows. It was as we did this, that Holmes briefly tugged at my sleeve and appeared to point and gaze more closely at a display but saying softly, "We are being followed. Be a good fellow and let us make our way onwards at a little more sprightly pace." On him saying this, I suddenly had a vision of being restrained and at Callow's mercy. This, undoubtedly, had the desired effect on my tardiness.

As we entered Burlington Gardens, there appeared to be little in the way of cabs and when a four-wheeler approached, Holmes waved enthusiastically towards the driver and it drew to a halt beside us. Swiftly opening the door, we climbed hurriedly inside.

It was only then that we realised our error, for within the carriage were two armed and masked men who, without a word and at gunpoint, bound our wrists and placed black hoods over our heads. My gun was taken from me.

Thankfully, our journey only seemed to last for some ten minutes or so. As we dismounted rather clumsily, bound as we were at the wrist, I could hear the lapping of water some distance away. This I took to be the Thames, but I hadn't a single idea as to where we had been taken.

I must confess that fear now gnawed at my stomach. Knowing Callow's predilection for torture, I feared for my life and, increasingly, the journey to its end. Strong hands grasped my upper arms and after a minute or so I was made to sit. Lacking vision, I was acutely aware of the sounds of movement around me. I was curious as to the sound which, even though muffled by the hood, appeared to echo strongly.

With no warning, the hood was swiftly removed and I blinked at the sudden brightness. It took me a moment to take in my surroundings and it seemed as though I had travelled back in time. The room I found myself in had stone walls and an arched and vaulted ceiling, and was lit by burning torches held against the wall by curving, wrought-iron brackets.

Standing with their backs to the wall and facing me were ten hooded and masked figures dressed in long black robes which were girded at the waist with a silken cord. A little way before them stood a single tall figure, hooded and masked, and dressed in a silken bright-purple robe.

Glancing to my left, I discovered Holmes, seated and bound like myself. I then looked to my right and, to my utter astonishment, sat a similarly bound but seething Callow. I had no time to dwell upon this as my attention was drawn to the figure in purple who now addressed us.

Without preamble, the male voice announced, "You are here to answer for the life of our brother, Charles Williams." Pointing towards each of us in turn, he said, "A watch had been kept on his house, and you are the only persons seen to have visited him on his final day on Earth. One of you, or perhaps more than one, is responsible for taking his life." The man then paused before adding, ominously, "This we will now determine and the guilty will be punished."

My befuddled brain now realised that we were being held and were to be judged by "The Silent Brotherhood". The name in itself now appeared to be a paradox, but it was abundantly clear that it was this secret society who sought retribution. In some confusion, I looked towards Holmes who, from his expression, appeared to be calm and accepting of the situation.

The purple clad figure now spoke again. "I am the Grand Master, and the only member of this society who both hears and speaks. Brother Williams let it be known to me that he willingly revealed a secret to another. Your knowledge of this will prove your innocence."

I sensed movement behind me and I struggled briefly as I was firmly gagged. Looking left and right to Holmes and Callow, I saw that they too had suffered a similar fate. "Now you are like brother Williams, bound and mute. I will ask each of you, in turn, to reveal the secret."

My brain raced as I struggled to comprehend how this was to be achieved. "Mr. Holmes?" Holmes seemed to sit immobile but, after a few seconds, the Grand Master nodded and then spoke again, "Dr. Watson?" I panicked and then, suddenly, my mind flashed back to our meeting with Williams in Baker Street, and I knew how I might proceed. When I had finished, the Grand Master nodded and then asked, "Mr. Callow?"

For what seemed like an eternity, there was silence and then a torrent of muffled profanity was heard from the gagged Callow. The Grandmaster raised his arm and pointed towards Callow before signing a single word, one which I repeated in my head: *"Oubliette!"*

At this, a struggling Callow was seized by several of the brotherhood and bundled through a concealed doorway. At the same moment, our gags were removed and we were freed from our bonds.

The Grand Master now stepped forward and bowed slightly, saying, "I apologise for the discomfort, gentlemen. Trust isn't a gift that is given lightly and, to those who have received it, it is absolute." He paused before continuing, "We will delay you no further." At this he raised a hand and one of the brothers returned to Holmes the parcel that was taken from us in the carriage, and to me my service revolver.

Holmes nodded in thanks before asking, sombrely, "I take it that Mr. Callow will not have his day in court?"

The Grand Master was hesitant in his reply. "No. It wasn't simply my decision. All the brothers were in agreement. Given that the tidal range here is in the order of some twenty feet, he will not have that day, or any other." He then paused for a moment before continuing, "To preserve our anonymity, we must insist that you be hooded for your journey to – ?"

Holmes pursed his lips before saying, "221b Baker Street, if you please."

The Grand Master nodded, signed the address to one of the brothers, and then the black hoods were once more placed over our heads. I was grateful when the touch of a hand upon my shoulder was simply to guide me to the waiting carriage. Only on arrival at Baker Street were the hoods removed and, in silence, Holmes and I exited the unmarked carriage and climbed the stairs to our sitting room.

Reflecting on the afternoon's events with a pipe, it was perhaps some five minutes before I found I was able to state, "*Oubliette* is a strange word. I believe it has its roots in French and is related to '*forget*'."

"Indeed. In this case, I believe that it refers to those strange, bottle-shaped, and quite tall rooms built along the river with but a single trap-door entrance in the ceiling that were used as prison cells. Prisoners who were dropped or lowered into them were, indeed, 'forgotten' and simply left to die."

I considered this for a moment and then remembered the Grand Master's reference to the Thames. "And what is the importance of the height of the tide?"

Holmes was silent for a moment. "Some of these oubliettes were also used as latrines. I suspect that, in this case, the floor has an orifice that is open to the Thames and, as the tide rises, it is cleansed as it fills. Completely."

My eyes opened wide as I stammered and looked at my friend, "Then . . . ."

He simply nodded and would say no more.

The following day was Christmas Eve and I noticed that despite Holmes's feigned dislike for the trappings of Christmas, there were gifts for both Mrs. Hudson and me beneath the Christmas tree. To this I added my own, and I saw that Mrs. Hudson had also added two small parcels.

That evening as Holmes and I sat and smoked, my thoughts returned to the "Inquisition" by the Silent Brotherhood. "I've been wondering who might be the Grand Master of the Silent Brotherhood? Some important person in the City, perhaps?"

Holmes looked towards me, saying without emotion, "As soon as the man spoke, his identity was abundantly clear."

My pipe almost fell from my mouth as I sought to respond, gasping, "You – you know?"

Holmes nodded. "It would surprise you if I were to tell you his name, for he is a man who upholds the law most vigorously and has been known to regularly don the black cap." Holmes paused before continuing, "I must confess that I was greatly relieved when you were able to sign Williams's word of trust for, had you not, you may well have shared Callow's fate."

Hearing Holmes confirm my worst fear suddenly made me shudder, for this was something that I had pushed to the very far reaches of my mind. So terrifying was the thought, it was to become the source of many troubled nights for years to come.

After banishing my night-time demons as best as I could, Christmas Day finally arrived. Holmes had invited Mrs. Hudson to our sitting room and, with a glass of sherry to hand, we gathered around the tree and opened our presents together. Each one of us was, I believe, truly grateful for our gifts and, at breakfast on Boxing Day morning, both Holmes and I found the contents of a fine Worcester egg coddler quite delicious.

The Case of the
Christmas Pudding
by Liz Hedgecock

Chapter I

"To a medical man, the conclusion should be obvious."

I jumped, then stared at Holmes, who was regarding me with amusement. "Whatever do you mean?"

"Why, that a walk will do you much more good than a second mince pie."

"But I never said a word!"

"My dear Watson, gestures and glances may communicate as strongly as words, especially in the case of a man with your speaking countenance."

I glared at him, discomfited. "Since we are both meant to be at leisure, I did not expect to be observed quite so closely."

"The period between Christmas and the New Year is always slack, but that doesn't stop my eyes from seeing or my brain from thinking." Holmes's eyes took on a faraway look. "I wonder if the criminal fraternity make a point of ceasing their activity for the festive season, and whether that is through choice or necessity. Perhaps there is a monograph in it." He laughed. "Oh Watson, do stop fidgeting. This is why you would benefit from a walk."

"You must admit that it is rather uncomfortable to feel one is being observed like a specimen under a microscope."

"It was hardly difficult. During the last five minutes you have eyed the crumbs on your plate, gazed out at the sky, checked your cup to see how much tea remains in it, then looked back at the plate. I shall not mention the thoughtful hand on the stomach, nor the second glance out of the window. I daresay even Lestrade would come to the same conclusion."

I couldn't help laughing. "In that case, perhaps you should accompany me on this walk. You clearly require stimulation. In fact – "

I was interrupted by a short peal of the doorbell. Holmes raised an eyebrow. "Perhaps I am wrong about the criminal fraternity."

Billy's footsteps came upstairs, and the page himself appeared. "There is a visitor for you, Mr. Holmes. A lady."

Holmes frowned. "Rather odd that she hasn't written first."

"Perhaps she hasn't had time," I suggested.

"Perhaps. Does our visitor have a name, Billy? How would you describe her?"

"Her name is Mrs. North. She is well-dressed, pretty, and no older than twenty-five. Oh, and she says she has come from Hertfordshire."

"Mmm."

"Holmes, you have to see her," I protested. "It may be really important, especially as she has come into town."

Holmes sighed. "My holiday is over. Very well. Since you are so keen on the idea, we shall see your damsel in distress." Yet from the manner in which his grey eyes gleamed, I knew he had never intended to turn our visitor away.

Chapter II

She arrived in a flurry of apologies and confusion, and it was all Holmes and I could do to get her to sit. "Would you like tea, Mrs. North?" asked Holmes. "We have mince pies, too." This was said with a sly glance at me.

"Tea would be nice," she replied, "for it was a trying journey. London is very big, isn't it?"

"Mrs. North, please can you tell us why you have come to see me today. This gentleman is my friend Dr. Watson, and you may speak before him as confidently as if we were alone."

Mrs. North regarded me with wide china-blue eyes, and I silently agreed with Billy's assessment of her prettiness. "A doctor? A medical doctor?"

"I am indeed," I said, with a smile.

"Then perhaps you can help too. I was in two minds whether to come today, as this is such an odd matter. It seems silly, but I cannot make it out." She looked perturbed for a moment, and then began her story.

"My name is Dora North, and I live with my husband in Pasden, a village in Hertfordshire. We have been married for six months, and such a thing as this has never happened before. At first I thought nothing of it, but in the days since I have grown more and more worried about him. He has become withdrawn and cold towards me, and I have done nothing to deserve it." She bit her lip.

"Perhaps if you start from the beginning, Mrs. North, that will help us to puzzle this out," remarked Holmes. To a casual observer he would have appeared calm, but I noted the continual jiggle of his left foot.

"It began on Christmas Day," said Mrs. North. "We had arranged that my parents, who live nearby, would come to us on Christmas morning. We opened our presents together then, instead of on Christmas Eve, and ate

278

our Christmas dinner. Everything was wonderful, and my husband John was in unusually good spirits. He can be rather quiet sometimes." She paused, and gazed at Holmes with those wide blue eyes. "And then Cook brought in the pudding."

Holmes leaned forward. "Go on."

"Once the flames were extinguished, John undertook to serve the pudding. We each had a large helping, as Cook's puddings are uncommonly good. Mamma got the silver wishbone, Papa a silver sixpence, and John got the anchor, but when I cut my piece I found a charm in the shape of a D." She reached into her bag, brought out a folded handkerchief, and unwrapped it to show a letter D, quite plain and made of silver, with a little loop at the top for a link. Holmes took it, produced a pocket magnifying glass, peered at it for a few seconds, then handed it back.

"I exclaimed in delight and turned to thank John, for I assumed it was a surprise for me. But his face was as white as a sheet, and he stared at my little charm as if it were a poisonous snake."

"'Is this not from you, dear?' I asked, and with that same strange look he said that it was not."

"My parents both examined the charm, as surprised as any of us, and said they knew nothing of it. Mamma tried to make the best of it by laughing and saying that it was a little mystery, but John threw down his napkin and got up. When I asked where he was going, he said, 'To the kitchen. This must have come from somewhere.'"

"'But what about your pudding?' I asked.

"He looked at me with a mixture of anger and despair such as I have never seen on his face. 'I have lost my appetite,' he said and left the room. He did not return, and later a maid brought a message to say that he had gone to bed with a headache. Ever since then he has been very quiet, and I am at a loss to fathom why."

"I see," said Holmes.

"That is not the end of it," she replied, with an expression of mild reproach. "Yesterday evening, when we were alone, I asked him what he was thinking, as he had not spoken for a whole hour. 'I am planning to start a business on the Continent," he said. "You may accompany me or not, as you wish.'" Her face twisted in anguish. "I cannot live abroad. How could I be apart from my parents? And what else can I do? Perhaps he thinks I have done something – something improper, and a man has put the charm in the pudding to woo me, and I don't know what to do!" She burst into noisy tears and buried her face in her hands.

"Please don't worry, Mrs. North," said Holmes, when she had calmed herself a little. "We shall come back with you on the next train, and see if we can get to the bottom of this matter."

"That – would be – wonderful," she choked out. "I am so terribly afraid. It took all my courage to come here, knowing John might think I had sneaked off to go and meet – someone!" This brought on a fresh attack of weeping.

Holmes turned to me. "Watson, find your *Bradshaw*. There is no time to lose."

Chapter III

On the train journey to Pasden, Mrs. North told us a little more of her history. She was her parents' only child, and had lived in the same small village her whole life.

"We were all excited when we heard that the manor house was to let. People speculated on what the new owner would be like, since he was a stranger and quite young, and some said it was a shame that an outsider – one who had been abroad, no less – should take over the manor house. But they soon came round when he made repairs to the roof of the village hall, gave money for a May Day celebration, and organised food parcels for those in need."

She smiled in reminiscence. "I was astonished when John spoke to me at a village dance. I never thought anything like that would happen. Not to me, who had lived in the same sleepy village my whole life. How could I be of interest to a man who had seen America and amassed a fortune? But we became acquainted, and by degrees, acquaintance became friendship, then love. How could I not admire such a man?" Her expression changed from awe to distress. "Now everything is ruined, and I don't know why!"

Holmes put a hand on her arm. "We shall be at Pasden soon, and then we can begin our investigation. I promise I shall do my best to solve your case."

"Thank you," she murmured with tears in her eyes, and I felt a burst of anger against the man who could treat her so cruelly.

The village of Pasden was little more than a picturesque row of shops, a church, and a public house, so small that I wondered at it having its own railway station, but the manor house was a Georgian building of mellow stone with large windows and an imposing pillared entrance. Holmes inspected the building. "Several of the curtains are closed," he remarked. "Is part of the house not used?"

"Oh no, all the rooms are in use," Mrs. North replied. "John sustained an injury to his eyes when he was abroad, and as a consequence he finds bright light difficult to bear." She touched her right cheek for a moment. "On a sunny day like today, the servants ensure that any room he may use is shielded from direct light."

"Oh, I see," said Holmes.

He walked towards the front door, but Mrs. North hurried after him. "Perhaps it would be better if we began at the back of the house."

Holmes gave her a quizzical look. "I can certainly talk to the cook, as she is the expert on the pudding. You are right, Mrs. North. Let us start there." The relief on her face was unmistakable.

Mrs. Latham, the cook, was very willing to talk to us, although it took us some time to get her off the subject of the special recipe for the Christmas pudding which had been handed down from her great-great-grandmother and never failed, not once.

"So when do you make the Christmas pudding?" asked Holmes. "I assume it is prepared in advance."

She gave him a pitying glance. "Only a man would ask that. Why, on Stir-Up Sunday, of course. When else would I do it?" She sighed at my blank expression. "The last Sunday before Advent, like in the collect: "*Stir up, we beseech thee.*""

"I see," said Holmes. "So on a Sunday a few weeks before Christmas, who helps you?"

"Nobody helps me," Mrs. Latham replied indignantly. "The pudding practically makes itself. The only help I have is when everyone comes into the kitchen to stir the pudding and make a wish."

"Ah!" cried Holmes. "Is that when people put the charms in?"

"*I* put the charms in," said Mrs. Latham firmly. "I'm not having people putting dirty sixpences in my pudding. I keep the pudding silver packed away specially and I watch everyone while they stir." She folded her arms.

"So no one could drop an extra charm in the pudding without you noticing?" asked Holmes.

She shook her head. "Absolutely not." Her eyes narrowed. "Why are you so curious about my Christmas pudding, may I ask?"

"I work for a newspaper in London," said Holmes, "and our female readers are always interested in recipes and articles on cookery. Word of your pudding came to me, and I wanted to ask for your recipe."

I doubted Mrs. Latham would swallow that, but she preened like a peacock. "Oh, people often ask me for my recipes." Then she frowned. "But it was Christmas three days ago. Why would your readers want a pudding recipe now?"

"We work far in advance," said Holmes. "If you let me have a copy of your recipe, and a list of the charms that you put in it, I'll make sure your name is mentioned."

While the cook, all smiles, did Holmes's bidding and wrote down the recipe, he glanced at the doors and windows, which were stout and well maintained. "No signs of a break-in there," he murmured. "Mrs. North, might I have a word with your husband about the, er, article, if he is at home?"

"He will be at home," she murmured. "At this hour he is always in his study."

She took us to the study door, and Holmes knocked. "Come!" said a deep voice.

We entered to find the master of the house sitting in an armchair and reading the newspaper. John North was powerfully built, and wore a long bushy beard which would have been more appropriate for an elderly patriarch than a man in his mid-thirties, as I took him to be. As soon as he saw us he rose, and he easily matched Holmes in height. "Who are you?" he demanded. Even those few words carried a slight but distinguishable American accent.

"My name is Sherlock Holmes, and I am a consulting detective. Your wife visited me earlier today, and I have come to ask you some questions about . . . about one of the charms in your Christmas pudding."

"I see," said Mr. North. "Well, I'm afraid that I am busy, and I don't have time to help you. If you wish to know about the pudding, I suggest you speak to the cook." He sat down and picked up his paper. "Good day to you."

We left the room to find Mrs. North wringing her hands in the corridor, watched nervously by a young footman. "You see how he is?" she whispered. "Normally he is the gentlest, most obliging man." She gazed at Holmes. "I am so sorry. You have come all this way, and for nothing – "

He put his finger to his lips, then beckoned her further along the hall. "Please do not be distressed, Mrs. North. There are people we can speak to besides your husband, and that is what we shall do." He looked at the closed study door, and his eyes gleamed. "This case is far from over."

Chapter IV

"What else can we do?" asked Dora North, fretfully.

"You mentioned earlier that your parents live nearby," said Holmes. "Are they within walking distance, or do we need a carriage?" He eyed the footman, who immediately pretended not to be listening.

282

"They are but fifteen minutes' walk away. I visit them most days, sometimes twice, and only take the carriage in bad weather." Her eyes lit up as she spoke, and I saw how she would look when not burdened with fear and worry.

"Then let us set off. I take it they will not mind if you call unannounced?"

"Mind?" She laughed. "They will be delighted."

"There," Holmes observed, once we had left the manor house and were proceeding towards the village. "At last you have your walk."

"Indeed I do," I replied, slightly out of breath. We had moderated our pace out of consideration for our companion, but if anything she was in danger of outstripping us.

A few minutes later she gestured at a smallish villa on the outskirts of the village. "Here we are." She led the way down the path.

The door was opened by an elderly maid who beamed when she saw Mrs. North. "Miss Dora!" Then her smile vanished. "Who are these gentlemen?"

"Don't worry, Mary, they are just visitors. Are Mamma and Papa at home?"

"They are. I'll go and tell them you're here."

Mrs. North stepped into the hallway and beckoned us forward. "Come in. They won't mind."

Holmes and I stepped over the threshold as Mary returned. "They're taking tea in the – the parlour." She opened a door on the right and showed us into a room which would have been cramped with half the amount of furniture. Among it all sat a stocky man, perhaps in his fifties, with red cheeks and a bald head, and a slender, pale woman of around the same age who seemed to be composed mostly of frills. Both rose hastily as we came in. On the little table between them was a cake stand half-filled with sandwiches. "You'll have to introduce the gentlemen, Miss Dora," the maid said, out of the side of her mouth, "for I don't know who they are."

"Mamma, Papa, these gentlemen are Mr. Holmes and Dr. Watson, and they have come to help me with a puzzle. Gentlemen, these are my parents, Mr. and Mrs. Sugden."

"A puzzle, eh?" said Mr. Sugden. "What sort of puzzle would that be?" His expression was neutral, but his tone not particularly welcoming. He glared at his silent wife. "Invite the gentlemen to a chair, Letitia."

"Oh – oh yes. Please do sit, gentlemen."

I looked about me. Every chair in the room was covered with antimacassars, fancy work, or little cushions, and none appeared comfortable. I lowered myself into the nearest, which was as hard as I had expected, and focused on the couple.

283

"I had better ask for more cups, hadn't I?" murmured Mrs. Sugden.

"Yes, Letitia, you had," replied her husband, as she rose to pull the bell. "Not to mention plates."

"We shall not require plates," said Holmes, and I must admit to feeling annoyed, since we had missed lunch. "We only wish to ask you a few questions, and then we shall be on our way."

Mr. Sugden frowned. "What sort of questions? Where are you from? I haven't seen you in the village before."

"We have come from London," said Holmes.

"Oh!" breathed Mrs. Sugden, gazing at us.

Mr. Sugden raised his eyebrows. "I dare say you have, but why?"

Holmes glanced at Mrs. North, who gave him a tiny nod. "Your daughter is concerned about one of the charms that found its way into the pudding on Christmas Day."

"Ha!" barked Mr. Sugden, and his wife jumped. "All the way from London, for that?"

"Yes," said Holmes. "So it would be very helpful if you could tell me whether you saw or heard anything unusual at your daughter's house on Christmas Day." He regarded Mr. Sugden with a speculative eye.

"Not a thing," replied Mr. Sugden. "Well, not until young John took ill and went to bed. Most unlike him. He's as strong as an ox." He laughed. "Perhaps it was too much drink taken." Both his daughter and his wife gave him a pained look.

"Mrs. Sugden, did you notice anything unusual on Christmas Day?" Holmes asked.

She gave a nervous giggle. "Oh no, not at all. I mean, the charm with the letter was a present, wasn't it?"

"Don't be silly, Letitia. John said he had nothing to do with it, and we know we didn't." Mr. Sugden turned to Holmes. "Any more questions?"

"I'm afraid so. Were you at your daughter's house on the Sunday when the pudding was made? I understand everyone stirs it."

"Yes, we were, and yes, we did," replied Mr. Sugden. "We almost always visit Dora for Sunday lunch, and as Cook was making the pudding, naturally we took a turn at stirring."

"Mrs. Latham is an excellent cook," put in Mrs. Sugden.

"That she is," said Mr. Sugden. "Our Jessie could learn a thing or two from her."

"I do try," murmured his wife.

"If it weren't for Sunday lunch at Dora's, I'd have to go to London to get a decent meal," remarked Mr. Sugden, stretching out his legs. "I go once or twice a month now, to maintain a small interest in my business, and I miss the food most of all." He glared at his wife. "Anything else?"

284

"No, that is all." Holmes stood up and extended a hand to Mr. Sugden. "Thank you for your time, sir."

"You can hardly thank us for our hospitality, can you, seeing as Mary never brought those cups. The servants will run wild if you don't keep them in line, Letitia." Mrs. Sugden quailed under his gaze.

The walk back to the manor house was rather less pleasurable than the outward trip. "Is that your father's usual manner, Mrs. North?" asked Holmes.

Dora North considered. "He's not usually so peppery. I think he was cross that I brought guests without warning." She paused. "He is conscious that John is a wealthy man. As a family we were always comfortable, but it isn't the same."

"Yes, he did seem rather short with your mother," Holmes observed.

A little furrow creased her forehead. "Papa isn't the most patient of men, but he has always been gentle with me." She met our eyes. "I don't think my parents' marriage has a bearing on this case," she murmured. I felt ashamed of myself, though I hadn't spoken of it.

"My dear Mrs. North," said Holmes, "at present we don't know what has a bearing on the case."

She sighed. "You have spoken to Cook and my parents, and John will not help, so I suppose your investigation is at an end." She looked so utterly helpless that I longed to comfort her.

"Our investigation isn't at an end until we have exhausted every avenue," said Holmes. "Watson and I shall walk you home, and then decide our next move."

She gazed at him. "I cannot help feeling that it is hopeless."

We saw Mrs. North to the manor house, and with a heavy heart I took the *Bradshaw* from my pocket.

"Not so fast, Watson."

I glanced at him. "What do you mean?"

Holmes didn't speak again until we were in the lane. "Assuming you have no objections, I would like you to book us accommodation at the local inn for tonight." He took the *Bradshaw* from me. "I shall return to London to pick up a few things, and meet you for dinner."

"Really? Can you solve the mystery of the Christmas charm?"

"The charm isn't the mystery," he said as he strode along. "Dora North's husband is the mystery."

Chapter V

As promised, Holmes returned by dinner time carrying a large Gladstone bag. "I have brought your pyjamas and sponge bag," he said, extracting the items and laying them on the bed.

285

I eyed the bulging bag. "And – ?"

"Wait and see. Now, I propose we have dinner in our room, for reasons which will become apparent." I raised my eyebrows, but he merely smiled.

Half-an-hour later, we were both sated. "Would you like a pint of beer?" Holmes asked.

"I would," I replied. "There are few things more restful than a quiet pint of ale in a country inn, listening to the locals."

"I agree. Why don't you go down? I shall join you shortly. I have a small matter to attend to first."

I was sitting in a quiet corner, nursing the last third of my pint and wondering if Holmes would ever appear, when an elderly, bewhiskered workman shambled in and leaned on the bar. "Pint of bitter, please, landlord." When it arrived, he took a large gulp and sighed with satisfaction. "That hit the spot." If it hadn't been for his prominent nose and his height, which he had adopted a stoop to disguise, I would never have recognised in that workman my old friend Sherlock Holmes.

He turned to his neighbour, a dejected-looking young man who seemed somehow familiar. "Good day, young 'un?"

The young man shrugged. "I've had better. Came here to take my mind off it."

Holmes wore a look of concern. "Why, what's happened?"

"Master gave me a dressing-down," the man replied. "Not for doing anything wrong, just for being there."

"Oh," said Holmes.

"It ain't like him, that's the funny thing. He's normally easy-going, him and the mistress both. But she brought in a man from London asking questions, and the master wasn't happy."

"Bit rum," remarked Holmes. "Whereabouts do you work? I hope you don't mind me asking, but I'm looking to pick up a bit of trade. I'd rather not go barging in where I'm not wanted, like."

"Up at the manor house, as a footman. Been there two years, and this is the first time he's raised his voice to me. I didn't answer back – I wouldn't dare – so I went and sat in the kitchen. Cook said my face was turning the cream and if I had nothing better to do I could take an hour off." A smile flickered over his lips. "She'd tell you she rules the place with a rod of iron, but she's soft as butter really."

"Would that be a woman called Mrs. Latham?" asked Holmes. "I've heard of her. Very good cook."

"She is, and she knows it. Although she's a bit partial to – " The footman tapped his pint glass, which was almost empty.

"Let me get you another of those." Holmes held up a finger to the barman. "Partial to what?"

"A little drop now and then." The footman grinned. "One of the maids told me she sampled so much of the brandy for the Christmas pudding that she had a little nap at the kitchen table. Someone called for a recipe and had to leave without it because there was no waking her." He chuckled. "Good thing it's always high tea on a Sunday evening."

"Nobody's perfect," said Holmes. "If she's a kind soul, I might call in and see if she needs any knives sharpening." He winked at the footman, who smirked and took a long pull at his fresh pint. Presently Holmes finished his own drink, slid the glass across the bar, wished the footman well, and ambled out.

It was all I could do not to down my own drink and follow, but I made it last another five minutes before going up to our room. There I found Holmes in his normal clothes and, minus whiskers and wig, drying his face. "Fancy a stroll?" he asked when he emerged from the towel.

"Where to?" I enquired.

"To the manor house, and you know it. I have a fancy to enquire about a certain visitor on Stir-Up Sunday."

Ten minutes later we were in the grounds of the manor house and making for the servants' entrance. Dinner was clearly in progress. Cook was taking a joint of meat from the oven and a maid was draining potatoes. She saw us, banged the colander down, and came to the door. "What is it?" she snapped.

"We are writing a newspaper article on Mrs. Latham's pudding, and we wish to ask a question about the recipe."

The maid huffed and opened the door wider. "Recipe, recipe, always a recipe." She turned. "Mrs. Latham!" she shouted. "Man here for a recipe!"

Mrs. Latham looked over her shoulder. "Oh, it's you." She advanced, wiping her hands on her apron. "Sorry about the noise. It gets busy at dinner time." She jerked her head towards the scullery, where a skivvy was washing the plates and cutlery from the previous course.

"That's quite all right. May I?" Holmes nodded at the table.

"Of course," said Mrs. Latham, and took a seat herself.

"This is rather an odd question," said Holmes, "but I heard at the inn that someone had asked you for one of your recipes on Stir-Up Sunday: A Christmas recipe, I assume. Might we include it in the article as well?"

Mrs. Latham appeared puzzled. "A recipe? On Stir-Up Sunday?"

The maid who had answered the door to us rolled her eyes. "They'll be waiting in the dining room, Mrs. Latham. We're already late."

287

Holmes turned to the maid. "I don't suppose you remember? The person I spoke to was quite sure."

Her eyebrows drew together and she opened her mouth to reply, but at that moment the inner door banged open. John North stood in the doorway, the embodiment of rage. "What is going on?" He looked at Holmes, seething. "What are you doing here?"

For once, Holmes had no answer.

"I don't know what you're up to, but if I see you in my house or grounds again, I shall not be answerable for the consequences." Mr. North eyed the servants, who were practically standing to attention. "Your job is to get dinner on the table at a reasonable time," he said, in a milder tone, "not sit chatting with strangers. Do you understand?"

"Yes, sir," they muttered.

"Good. Now, please get on." He glared at Holmes and me. "And you: Get out."

"Well, that's that," I remarked, as we slunk down the lane with our tails between our legs.

"Perhaps," said Holmes, "and perhaps not." He strode forward, eyes gleaming, like a hound on the scent. "I suggest we catch an early train to London in the morning, but we are not beaten yet."

Chapter VI

When we arrived back in Baker Street, I found myself at a loose end. "What will you do this morning?"

"I have a couple of errands to run," Holmes replied. "Dull, but necessary. What about you? Will you frowst in a chair again?"

"I shall go for a walk." The truth was that I couldn't bear being cooped up in a room. I had spent the train journey fidgeting and worrying about poor Dora – I mean Mrs. North – trapped at the manor house with that bear of a man. I glanced at Holmes, hoping he hadn't somehow read my thoughts, but he merely remarked that the country air seemed to have had a good effect on me, and took his leave.

I spent the walk puzzling over the problem of the pudding, to no avail, and returned two hours later to find Holmes fizzing with nervous energy and holding a telegram. "This was waiting when I returned a few minutes ago. Look!"

I took the telegram, and read.

Please help STOP John has gone STOP Left goodbye note STOP North.

288

I gave the telegram back to Holmes. "Perhaps it is for the best. They are not well suited at all. She is so delicate, and he is so – "

"Physical appearance is not everything," Holmes chided. "Handsome is as handsome does."

I snorted. "It isn't like you to quote old saws."

"Never mind that." Holmes dashed to the desk and picked up a scrawled note. "I shall take this down for Billy to wire, and then we must be off."

I stared at him. "What, to the manor house?"

"Watson, there is no time for that!" Holmes ran downstairs as if John North himself were chasing him, and I had no choice but to follow.

Two minutes later we were in a cab. "This is our best chance," said Holmes. "When a man like John North says he is leaving, he goes far. I just hope we arrive in time."

"Are we going to the docks?" I asked.

"What? No, to Euston station. John North has the advantage of us, but we can still catch him if we get through this traffic." He glared at the busy street.

"What did you put in the wire?" I asked.

"I asked Mrs. North to come to London directly and wait at Baker Street until we return." Holmes looked out of the window and fidgeted. "Come on, come on!" he muttered.

At last we arrived at the station. Holmes flung half-a-sovereign to the cabbie, then dashed towards a porter leaning against a pillar. "Has the Liverpool Express gone yet?" he demanded.

The porter, completely unruffled, pointed at a distant, crowded platform where a train squatted. "You'll be wanting that one. It goes in a quarter-of-an-hour."

"Thank you," said Holmes, and we ran along, dodging porters and passengers and suitcases, until we arrived at the correct platform.

A station official stood facing the train, hands clasped behind his back. "Is this the Liverpool Express?" Holmes asked.

He inspected us from under his cap. "It is, gentlemen, but you may not board. The train isn't yet ready." He eyed the gathered passengers, who sagged at his pronouncement.

"Can you check the platform for Mr. North?" Holmes turned to the official. "We don't wish to board. I merely have a message for a former colleague of mine. I believe he intends to travel on this train."

The official raised his eyebrows. "He had better hurry, for we depart at noon."

289

I dashed up and down the long platform, but in vain. John North wasn't there. Then the official shouted, "Passengers, you may board." A frantic scramble ensued, and I was almost propelled onto the train by the rush of passengers.

Eventually I arrived at Holmes's side. "Any luck?" I panted.

He shook his head, and we both glanced at the station clock, which showed six minutes to twelve. We watched the approach to the platform for the tall, broad form of John North, but there was no sign of him.

"If you would move back, please, gentlemen," said the official.

Holmes looked crestfallen, and my heart went out to him. He had been so confident, and it had come to nothing. "Perhaps he is planning to take a later train," I said.

"I was so sure," he murmured.

The official stepped forward and raised his whistle.

Holmes eyed him. "Perhaps we could send a wire to the station in Liverpool – "

He stiffened as a tall figure ran towards us, and a loud voice shouted "Wait!"

As the figure came closer I recognised John North. He was sprinting for the train, somewhat hampered by a large new carpet bag and a voluminous ulster. His deerstalker, with the ear flaps tied, was under his chin.

Holmes moved forward to bar his way. "No, Mr. North – *you* wait."

John North glared at him. "Stand aside, sir."

Holmes stood firm. "No, I shall not. I know your secret – I know the truth – and I urge you to stay for your wife's sake."

Mr. North stood, breathing heavily, and suddenly he seemed smaller than before. "You know?"

"I do," said Holmes. "There is no need for you to run away, Mr. North. Please return with me, and we shall resolve this once and for all."

The official eyed us, his whistle at his lips. "Are you boarding this train, sir, or not?"

Still looking at Holmes, John North shook his head, and the whistle shrilled. The train huffed in response, and as it began to glide out of the station, Mr. North followed us from the platform like a sleepwalker. Holmes hailed a cab, and seconds later we were bound for Baker Street once more.

Chapter VII

"Is this really necessary?" I asked, as we waited in the manor house kitchen, doing our best to keep out of the way of the bustling servants.

"I have my methods, Watson."

"I don't mind," said John North. "Now that Dora knows, I don't mind anything." His smile erased the severity from his face and made him look years younger.

A maid came into the kitchen. "They're ready for the starter, Mrs. Latham."

"In that case," said Holmes, "our time has come." He led the way to the dining room then stood aside for John North, who took a deep breath, drew himself up, and entered. Mrs. North beamed at him, but her parents, sitting on either side of her, gaped as if he had risen from the dead.

Dora North rose from her seat at the head of the table and gestured to her husband to take it, but he waved Holmes forward. "I fancy this gentleman will be doing most of the talking. I shall go to the kitchen and ask for three more places to be laid."

A few minutes later, everyone was settled at table. "I shall begin, as I don't wish to delay your meal for longer than necessary," said Holmes. "This has been a most curious case. What seemed a Christmas novelty became perhaps one of the strangest matters I have ever dealt with."

"Mrs. North called me in to investigate the mysterious appearance of a silver charm in her Christmas pudding. The charm was in the shape of a letter *D*, and understandably she assumed it was meant for her. When her husband reacted angrily, her only explanation was that since no one at the table had put the charm in the pudding, he might suspect her of dalliance with another. I dismissed this idea at once – what suitor would reveal his hand so publicly? Moreover, Mr. North's instantaneous reaction to the *D* made it clear that the charm was intended for *him*. What could be so frightening about the letter *D*?"

Holmes poured himself a glass of water from the carafe on the table, took a sip, then continued. "My first line of enquiry was to investigate how the charm had got into the pudding. To that end I spoke to Mrs. Latham and found that the pudding was made on Stir-Up Sunday, a few weeks before Christmas. Everyone in the house had stirred the pudding, but she had watched throughout. This seemed watertight – unless someone was in league with the cook and had slipped the charm in with her knowledge. However, given Mrs. Latham's obvious pride in her work, this was unlikely. Mr. North declined to speak to me on that occasion – "

"Sorry," murmured John North.

Holmes smiled at him, then addressed the table in general. "My next move was to speak to Mrs. North's parents, Mr. and Mrs. Sugden, who were in the manor house both at Christmas dinner and during the making of the pudding, and see whether they had any information for me. They provided no fresh insights on the pudding or the charm, and therefore I decided to exploit local knowledge and repair to the village inn. There I learnt that an individual had called at the manor house on Stir-Up Sunday, found the cook taking a well-deserved nap, and, after waiting for some time, left again. I could hardly ask my interlocutor who that person was, so I determined to enquire at the manor-house kitchen, whereupon Mr. North threw me out."

"I am truly sorry," muttered John North, now distinctly pink beneath his beard.

"Oh no, it was extremely helpful. It gave me the opportunity to note that, though you were in a brightly lit kitchen and you allegedly had weak eyes, you didn't shield them from the light."

Mr. and Mrs. Sugden gave him a surprised look, but said nothing.

"Dr. Watson and I returned to London the next morning. I told Watson I was running errands, but in reality I was continuing with the case. When I examined the charm, I saw a maker's mark: The letters *IG* beneath a crown. That denoted a famous jeweller's: Garrard in Regent Street. After making enquiries there, I discovered a special order had been placed several weeks earlier for a bespoke silver charm in the shape of a *D*. The order was paid for that day and eventually posted to an address in Hertfordshire."

Holmes gazed around the table. "Why would the person who ordered the charm choose such a way to deliver their message? Why wouldn't this person speak to Mr. North? My conclusion was that this person wasn't confident in his or her knowledge, or too intimidated to challenge him. Far easier to put the charm in the pudding and await a result. If he or she was wrong, Mr. North wouldn't react, his wife would assume the charm was for her, and no harm would be done. If he did react – and he did – there must be a foundation for our mystery person's suspicions."

"This is ridiculous!" Mr. Sugden huffed with disdain. "Who would do things in such a roundabout, underhanded way?"

Slowly, Mrs. Sugden stood up. "I did it," she said, and her voice was steady, though she shook like a leaf.

Chapter VIII

"What?" Mr. Sugden shouted. "What do you mean, Letitia?"

"I saw it, and I had to do something."

"You saw what?" demanded her husband angrily. "Of all the stupid things – "

"She was trying to protect her daughter," said Holmes.

"I couldn't tell what it meant," said Mrs. Sugden, her voice a little stronger, "but I knew it was bad. I formed a plan, and went to London to do some early Christmas shopping. I had hoped to put the charm in the pudding when I stirred it, but Cook was watching, so I returned later that afternoon when I thought she might be asleep or, um, distracted. The pudding bowl was on the table with a cloth over it, so I slipped the charm in." She covered her mouth with her hands and gazed at her daughter with wide eyes that, though faded by time, would once have been the same shade of blue as Mrs. North's. "You don't know how worried I was – "

"What did you see, Letitia?" bellowed her husband.

John North rose from his seat and turned the lights up. "She saw this." He presented his right cheek to us, moving the hair of his beard this way and that, and bit by bit revealed a pale, raised scar which formed a large D. "The beard hides it well, but the hair has never grown where I was branded."

"What!" shouted Mr. Sugden, his eyes almost popping out of his head. "What are you, a common felon?"

"When I was a boy, I lived in a Whitechapel slum with my mother. As often happens, I fell in with the local gang: The Dorset Street Lads. I was big for my age, and they said I would be useful. At first I was just a lookout, but after a year the older lads judged it was time I earned my keep. They wanted me to turn pickpocket, but I refused, and I could defend myself. I had to get out, but I didn't know how."

He paused, and swallowed. "One day I was keeping watch as usual and along came a policeman. I whistled, and the lad I was looking out for came pelting round the corner, gave me a bundle of handkerchiefs, and fled. I was so surprised that I was caught red-handed. It was my first offence, but because of my size they thought I must be older than I was and made an example of me. I was whipped and sent to the reformatory school for two months." He winced. "I shall not say what happened there, but I knew I would never go back."

Mrs. North gave him her hand, and he enclosed it in his own large one. "As soon as I got out I went to the gang leaders and told them I was leaving, but they said no one ever left the gang. When I tried to run they caught me, tied me up, then heated an iron and branded me on the cheek. D for '*Dorset Street*' and D for '*Deserter*'." He touched his face self-consciously.

A tear ran down Dora North's cheek in sympathy. "I thought your scar was from the injury that hurt your eyes, dearest."

John North hung his head and resumed his narrative with difficulty.

"I had to leave, both for my safety and my peace of mind, so I slipped onto a train bound for Liverpool. I had seen the White Star Line posters on my occasional trips outside the slum – I could read well enough to pick out the word '*America*' – and the gang would never follow me there."

"I managed to stow away for half the voyage, and luckily when the crew found me they were lenient. They put me to work in the kitchen and gave me a straw mattress to sleep on, and at the end of the voyage they even gave me a few dollars to get started. I began as a boot boy in a New York hotel, and as soon as I could hide my disfigurement with a beard I sought new opportunities. To summarise, fifteen years later I had several people working for me in a thriving business, and I had made more money through investments."

He sighed. "But I missed home. So when I was fairly sure that I could live independently if I never did another day's work in my life, I sold up and came back to England. It had been twenty years since I left and I was confident no one would recognise me, having discovered on my return that my mother had died. To make sure, I took up residence in a quiet village."

Holmes nodded. "Having noticed your curious scar in the kitchen, I recognised it as a gang mark, which suggested you had had dealings with the Dorset Street Lads. After visiting the jeweller this morning, I proceeded to the newspaper archives and spent a fruitful hour searching for news of gang members sentenced to imprisonment between fifteen and twenty-five years ago." He smiled. "I looked for young lads, since I thought it unlikely anyone would have been able to brand you once you reached your full size." Holmes reached into the inner pocket of his jacket and passed Mr. North a scrap of paper. "I believe this refers to you."

John North read the paper. "Yes, that was me. *'Jack South, twelve, convicted of petty larceny and sentenced to a whipping and two months' imprisonment.'*" He grimaced. "It was a terrible experience, but it probably saved me from the gallows."

"You turned your whole life upside down," said Holmes. "You changed your name from Jack South to John North and arrived in America a different man."

"I am so sorry." Mrs. Sugden's voice trembled. "If I had known . . . I do hope that one day you can forgive me."

"Forgive him?" shouted Mr. Sugden. "He is a common criminal, and married to our daughter! His name isn't even his own – you heard him!" He stood up. "Dora, you had better come with us. Who knows what this man might do."

"No!" cried Mrs. North, moving to her husband's side. "John is no criminal. He is my husband, and I love him."

Mr. Sudgen glared at her. "If you are determined to throw your lot in with this man . . . ." He transferred the glare to his wife. "Letitia, we are leaving. When that man began his story I assumed this was another of your idiotic fancies, but it appears that for once you are right."

"I was wrong," said Mrs. Sugden, "and my son-in-law's story has made me realise my mistake. When I saw the mark on Mr. North's cheek, I thought he was a murderer – or worse. I was terrified Dora might be in danger, but I also feared she had married a man whom she would grow to hate."

She gave her husband a look that spoke volumes. "You have always been forthright, but you never used to bully and shout at me – not until Dora left our home. It is time for you to mend your ways, Ernest, and treat me as your wife, and not an object of ridicule and a scapegoat." She turned to John North. "Once again, I am truly sorry, and I hope you can forgive me."

Mr. North came round the table and took her hand. "I wish you had come to me first. Then I would have told you the story. Apart from that, there is nothing to forgive."

Mrs. Sugden began to weep, and John North put a large, hesitant arm around her shaking shoulders. Dora North rushed to her mother, while Mr. Sugden put his hands in his pockets, walked to the window, and stared into the night.

Holmes caught my eye, and we slipped away. "Our part in this affair is concluded," he murmured. "If we hurry, we can catch the last train to London. But first I shall tell the kitchen to send the starter in. Perhaps food will smooth things over."

I gazed out of the window as the train rattled along.

"A penny for your thoughts, Watson. We are ten minutes from Euston Station, and you have barely said a word the whole way home."

"It was so very unexpected," I replied. "I honestly thought Mr. North would be the villain."

"Under that beard and that imposing stature, he is a good and soft-hearted man. You saw how he was with the servants."

"Yes." I sighed. "But it seems unfair that you have given the Norths such a generous Christmas present while we leave empty-handed."

"Quite the contrary. Do you remember when John North came into the kitchen and returned the slip of paper I had given him? Folded inside was a cheque which more than repays the time and trouble we have spent on this case."

"Oh." I returned my gaze to the window.

The snap of Holmes's watch case made me turn round. "Five more minutes," he said. "Since we have barely eaten with all the excitement, I propose we repair to the Strand on arrival and treat ourselves to a slap-up dinner at Simpson's, on the promise of Mr. North's handsome cheque."

I managed a smile, though I didn't much feel like it. Perhaps hunger was making me low-spirited. "What a good idea." Then I paused, remembering a pair of imploring china-blue eyes. "I shall forego dessert, though. I shall not be able to look a pudding in the face for a very long time."

The St. Stephen's Day Mystery
by Paul Hiscock

"Come and sit by the fire."

Holmes ignored me and continued to look out of the window onto the street below.

"Nobody will be out there today," I said. "The snow is deep and crisp and even, just as it should be on the Feast of Stephen. Join me for a pipe, or avail yourself of the fine selection of cold cuts Mrs. Hudson has left for us."

Holmes let the curtain drop and turned to me.

"On the contrary, Watson. The snow outside now lies dinted, and there is a trail leading to our door. I believe we can expect a visitor."

Sure enough, as he spoke, I heard footsteps on the stairs, and a moment later Mrs. Hudson showed a gentleman into our rooms. She took his overcoat and hat, tutting slightly as the snow from them fell onto the rug, before leaving us to our business.

Holmes gestured towards the visitor's chair.

"Please sit down, Mr. . . . ?"

"Gooding, James Gooding. Thank you."

He sat, and placed his briefcase next to the chair.

"Very well then, Mr. Gooding. What compelled you to leave your festive celebrations and seek us out on such a wintry day? It must be a matter of some urgency to tear you away from your wife and children – especially your youngest who is enjoying Christmas for the first time."

"Are you already acquainted with my family, Mr. Holmes? Perhaps you knew my father-in-law, Mr. Overy? He was a figure of some note before he passed."

"No, I was not aware of you or your family's existence before your arrival here today. However, there is plentiful evidence of them upon your person. Firstly, there is your necktie. You have touched it repeatedly since you arrived, and it is rather garish compared to the rest of your attire. It was a present from your wife, and you are wearing it to make her happy, even though it makes you feel self-conscious. Then there is the ribbon hanging from your jacket pocket. I imagine you didn't notice when your daughter placed it there for safekeeping. Then there are the marks on your trousers. Judging from the width and spacing, the lines on your lap were made by the wheels of a well-oiled toy train, while the sticky handprints on your lower legs are a tell-tale sign of a young child just learning to stand."

"You are quite right in every respect, Mr. Holmes. I played with my three youngest children this morning, just as you describe, before circumstances forced me to come here."

"They are lucky to have a father who enjoys spending time with them," I said. "Not every child is so fortunate."

"I would do anything for my family. Indeed, it is for the sake of them, or more specifically my nephew, that I have come to ask for your help."

"Tell us what happened," said Holmes.

"My brother and his wife died a few years ago, and their son, Peter, came to live with us. We did our best to make him feel welcome, but it has been difficult. He was angry about his parents' death when he first moved in, and over time has become increasingly rebellious. I had hoped to settle him in a good career, maybe even at the bank where I work, but he has fallen in with an unsavoury crowd and spends all his time drinking and getting into trouble with them. There have even been a few incidents involving the police. So far it hasn't been anything too serious – public drunkenness and a couple of fights – but we have been worried that he would get into more serious trouble if he carried on along his present path."

"I am sorry to hear that," I said. "It sounds like he is still struggling with grief at the loss of his parents, but I don't understand how you think we can help him."

"We persuaded him to join us for Christmas dinner yesterday, but as soon as we'd finished eating, he left to join his friends. I wasn't surprised, and honestly I was grateful that he spent that much time with us. However, now I wish I had insisted that he stayed, as those so-called friends persuaded him to become their accomplice in an act of burglary."

"Where did the burglary take place?"

"I don't know, Mr. Holmes, and that is why I need your help. All I have is this."

Mr. Gooding picked up his briefcase and took out a flat square box. He opened it, revealing a silver necklace.

"May I see?" asked Holmes, and Mr. Gooding passed the box to him.

"My mother-in-law has trouble with her memory, and this morning, my wife walked into the drawing room to find her wearing this necklace, which neither of us recognised. At first she insisted it was her Christmas present, but eventually we established the truth. She had found the box hidden behind the Christmas tree this morning, and assumed that it was a gift that had been overlooked. She kept asking when my late father-in-law was going to come down so that she could thank him for it."

298

Holmes passed the box to me and I studied the necklace. At first, I must admit I was disappointed. During his investigations, Holmes has recovered an array of priceless jewels, and I have been fortunate enough to hold such exquisite items as the Denham Emerald and the Blue Carbuncle. This necklace wasn't in that league. It was a pretty piece, set with small blue sapphires, and something one might find in any quality jewellery store in London. However, it was still valuable, and its theft was no small matter.

"You believe your nephew stole it," I asked, "and hid it there?"

"It is the only explanation that makes sense. He certainly couldn't have afforded to buy it. Furthermore, the drawing room is below my bedroom, and I heard him crashing about in there when he came home late last night."

"Did you confront him about it?" I asked.

"Of course, but he denied everything, and stormed out of the house."

"Since you have chosen to bring the necklace to us, rather than the police," said Holmes, "I assume that you hope to resolve this matter quietly."

"I thought that, if you could find the owner, I might be able to make restitution to him or her without involving the law. I know I cannot protect Peter forever, but I want to give him one last chance to turn his life around, if I possibly can."

Holmes closed his eyes and sat in silence for a minute. Then, like a jack-in-a-box, he sprang out of his chair.

"Very well, Mr. Gooding. In the spirit of the season, we will help you and your nephew. If you will please leave the necklace with us, we will endeavour to reunite it with its rightful owner. Where should we reach you when we have news?"

He handed Holmes his card, which Holmes in turn passed to me. The address was in Ealing.

"Very well," said Holmes. "You should expect to hear from us soon."

Once Mr. Gooding had left, I opened up the jewellery box again and examined the necklace.

"I am not sure how we are going to find its rightful owner," I said. "There weren't any robberies mentioned in this morning's paper. Should we go to the police? It ought to have been reported to them."

"No. You and I are far too well known by the detectives of London. As soon as they hear we are taking an interest in a case, they will charge in, and we will lose any chance of resolving this quietly as our client has requested. I will send out word to my Irregulars. One of them might have heard something."

"So we should just wait here for news? In that case, I might pour myself a small drink. Would you like one?"

"There's no time for that. You are holding our most important clue, and we should investigate it at once."

I took out the necklace and studied it carefully. However, I couldn't see what he had spotted.

"No, not the necklace," said Holmes. "See here – in the box."

Inside, there was a piece of jeweller's cloth, to which the necklace had been pinned. He pointed to the edge of it, and I saw a tiny corner of card poking out. I pulled back the cloth to reveal a business card for a jewellery store, Chambers and Company in Bond Street.

The streets of London were quieter than usual. Many people had chosen to spend the day at home, out of the snow. I would have preferred to have done likewise, but instead I found myself in Bond Street, standing outside a shuttered jewellery shop.

For the third time, Holmes banged on the door, but still there was no response.

"We should come back tomorrow," I said.

However, Holmes ignored me and instead moved along the street to the next door.

"I don't see how disturbing the neighbours will help us," I said. "Even if there is anyone there, they aren't going to know anything."

Holmes pointed at a card that was neatly displayed next to the door.

"On the contrary, I believe that the resident of the rooms upstairs might be able to assist us. It would be a coincidence if the Mr. Chambers who lives here wasn't connected to the store that bears his name."

Holmes banged on that door, and was rewarded with the sound of grumbling and footsteps descending the stairs. The door opened slightly, and I was just about able to make out a short balding man peering through the gap.

"What do you want?"

"Are you the proprietor of this shop?" asked Holmes.

"I'm Chambers. What's the problem? Forgot to get the wife a Christmas present? Well, I'll be open tomorrow. You can come back then to get her something nice to make up for it."

Chambers started to push the door closed, but Holmes pushed back.

"It would be better if we could speak to you today."

"Better for you maybe, but I'm enjoying a day off. You will have to wait."

300

"Mr. Chambers," I said, "we have reason to believe that there might have been a robbery at your store last night. Please can you let us in so we can find out what has been taken?"

Without waiting to ask further questions, he lurched into motion. "A robbery? And on Christmas Day too. Wait here."

He closed the door, leaving us standing outside in the cold. A few minutes later he returned with a large bunch of keys and wearing a worn black overcoat. He closed the door to his residence and then made his way over to the shop's entrance. He was about to place a key in one of the locks when he paused.

"If you are right and there's been a robbery," he said, "I should be sending for the police, not talking to a pair of strangers about it. For all I know, this is some kind of trick so that you can rob the place yourselves."

"Do we look like a pair of common hoodlums?" asked Holmes. "Very well, send for the police, if you must, but I fear you will end up wasting your time and theirs."

"My good man," I said, "surely you have heard of Sherlock Holmes. This is him, and I can assure you that he is far more likely to retrieve any items that have been stolen from you than the Metropolitan Police Force."

Mr. Chambers looked us both up and down.

"I don't know about any detectives, but you two do look like proper gentlemen. Very well, I will let you in, but I'll be watching you both carefully."

He turned back to the door and started to tackle the first of three sturdy locks.

"I wonder how young Gooding managed to get in?" I whispered to Holmes. "I cannot see any sign of damage to the windows, and it seems unlikely he could have made it through this door."

"I doubt the boy has ever set foot in this establishment," replied Holmes. "It would have taken a master thief to break in undetected. However, your story about a break-in was a clever ruse. It should gain us access to the shop and its records much faster."

I had no doubt that Holmes's assessment would prove to be correct, but I felt bad that I had unwittingly misled Mr. Chambers. However, I would be glad if it meant our trip in the snow hadn't been wasted.

"There we go," said Mr. Chambers. While we had been talking, he had tackled the rest of the locks. "You'd better come in, gentlemen."

I kicked the snow off my boots and followed him inside. He walked through the shop quickly, establishing with a glance that the display cabinets were undisturbed, and made his way into the back office. It was only a couple of minutes before he emerged again.

"I don't know what you two are playing at, but I'm inclined to call the police like I should have done in the first place. There hasn't been any sort of robbery here. Everything is exactly where it should be. Even the safe is untouched."

"I am sorry for the mistake," said Holmes, "but we didn't come here without cause."

He took out the box and opened it to show the angry jeweller.

"This item was possibly stolen last night, and if so, we believe that it might have come from this shop."

Mr. Chambers took the box and examined the necklace with a jeweller's glass.

"Well, you're right this is one of mine, but it wasn't stolen from here. I had a few pieces in this design, but I sold the last of them at least nine months back."

"Do you have a record of who purchased them?" Holmes asked.

"I doubt it. I don't tend to keep track of my merchandise after it has left my shop."

"You don't have anything?" I asked.

"Well, if I delivered any of them I guess there would be a note in the ledger."

He went into the office and came out with a large black book.

"Let me see now. Yes, I was right, the last one went at the end of February. No notes on that one."

He started flicking back through the pages of the book.

"Here's another in December last, and two more in the November before that. I think four is all of them, but no notes about who bought any of them."

"That is unfortunate," said Holmes, and took out a calling card. "If you were to remember anything, I would be grateful if you could notify us."

"I have been approaching this the wrong way," Holmes said.

We had left Mr. Chambers, having apologised profusely for disturbing his holiday, and I was about to hail us a hansom back to Baker Street.

"What do you mean?"

"The jewellery store is the type of establishment a professional thief would target. They would have taken everything and swiftly passed it on to a reliable middleman to sell. Peter Gooding is the very antithesis of that breed of hardened criminal. He may have taken just one item of moderate value, only to hide it behind the Christmas tree in his own home. I believe the fastest way to reunite this necklace with its rightful owner is to speak to the boy ourselves."

"Do you have any idea where he might be? Mr. Gooding said his nephew had left the house, and it didn't sound like he was planning to return soon."

"I doubt he went far. If he isn't with his family, he is probably with those same friends whom Mr. Gooding feared were leading him astray. I imagine our client will have some idea where they might be found."

I sighed, resigning myself to the thought that I would not, as I had hoped, be returning to the comforts of home any time soon.

The snow had stopped falling by the time we reached Ealing. The local children were out playing on the Green, building snowmen and throwing snowballs at one another.

The Gooding family lived to the north of the green, in a moderately large house on Mount Park Crescent. Mrs. Gooding was surprised by our visit, but welcomed us warmly into their home.

"Is there news already?" she asked. "It would be a relief to have this horrid matter resolved, so that we could go back to enjoying our Christmas celebrations like yesterday."

"I'm sorry," said Holmes. "We don't have an answer for you yet. I was hoping to speak to your husband again. There is some further information I require."

"I'm afraid he's out at the moment, but you're welcome to wait for him."

She showed us into the drawing room. It was at the front of the house and had a large bay window looking out onto the street. However, at that time, the view was obscured by a large Christmas tree, decorated with baubles and paper chains. An elderly lady was sitting in an armchair in the corner of the room. She looked up at us as we entered, and smiled but didn't say anything.

"Mother," said Mrs. Gooding. "This is Mr. Holmes and Dr. Watson. They have come to help us deal with that necklace you found this morning."

"Such a lovely necklace. Your father has such good taste." Then the old woman turned to us. "I am afraid my husband isn't here right now, but he should return soon."

"No, mother," said Mrs. Gooding. "Daddy is gone. It is my husband, James, they have come to see."

"Of course, my dear." The old woman smiled us sweetly, but it was clear that she didn't really understand.

"I am sorry," said Mrs. Gooding. "Her memory has been bad for years, but since my father died just over a year ago it has become much worse."

"I have seen it all too often," I said, "and it is always hard on the family when it happens."

Mrs. Gooding was clearly struggling to contain her emotions, and made an excuse to leave.

"I'll get a pot of tea," she said, and hurried out of the room.

Holmes headed across the room towards the Christmas tree and proceeded to kneel down in front of it. After a moment, he called me over. He pointed to the floor, just to the left of the tree, in front of a tall dresser.

"You observe the glass on the floor?" he said to me.

It wasn't obvious at first, there were only the tiniest pieces there, but eventually I spotted the fragments he had discovered.

"What does it mean? Did somebody break in through the window? That would suggest that maybe Peter is not responsible. They could have dropped the box with the necklace inside, perhaps to hide it, or even to implicate him?"

"An intriguing, but fanciful notion," said Holmes. "Look at the window. None of the panes are broken, and the family could hardly have missed it if one had been. No, it is quite obvious that a glass was broken here."

"Oh dear! Did we miss some?"

Mrs. Gooding had returned while we were talking. She had brought with her, not just a pot of tea, but a trolley laden with treats both sweet and savoury.

"We broke a wine glass there yesterday. I thought we had cleared up all the pieces, but clearly we missed a bit. That will have to be seen to – otherwise the children might get hurt. Anyway, sit down please, gentlemen. Please help yourselves. I thought you might like a small snack with your drink. It's nothing much, just a few things we had left over from our celebrations yesterday."

"Is this all for us?" I asked, since there was enough food to feed a large party, not just two visitors.

She was about to answer, when we heard the front door slam.

"We're in the drawing room," Mrs. Gooding shouted, and a moment later Mr. Gooding joined us.

"Damn that boy! He won't listen to me. He won't even admit that he did it."

Then he turned and noticed us for the first time.

"Mr. Holmes, Dr. Watson. I hadn't expected to see you so soon. Have you found the owner of the necklace?"

"Not yet," said Holmes. "I was hoping to speak to your nephew. I take it that you know where we might find him?"

"He was at his club, with those friends of his. I say his 'club', as that is what they like to call it, but really it is just the upstairs room at a public house. The Plume of Feathers, on the Broadway. I imagine they will still be there. They didn't look like they planned to leave."

"Thank you," said Holmes. "If you will all excuse us, we must go and try to find him. Hopefully we'll have better luck persuading him of the seriousness of his position."

Holmes swept out of the room and I followed behind, after a last wistful glance at the tea trolley.

The Plume of Feathers was easy to find. It was a large building on a corner, near to the centre of town. It was quiet in the bar and the landlord greeted us enthusiastically.

"Come in out of the cold, gentlemen. What can I get for you this afternoon? A pint? Or maybe a warming bowl of soup? My wife made it fresh today."

"No, thank you," said Holmes. "We are looking for a young man, Peter Gooding, and have reason to believe he might be here."

"Master Gooding, you say? He is popular today. His uncle was also here looking for him not half-an-hour past. He isn't in some kind of trouble, is he?"

"I am afraid he might well be," replied Holmes.

"Well, you will find him and his friends upstairs."

He paused, then leant across the bar. His voice lowered, as though he was sharing some great secret, even though there was no one else there to hear.

"I don't know what you might have heard about them, but they are decent lads really. A little rebellious, and keen to leave their mark on the world, but which of us wasn't at their age? I wouldn't let them meet on my premises if I thought otherwise."

Then he stood up straight again and his voice returned to normal.

"Anyway, you can judge for yourselves. They'll be in the first room on the right."

We thanked him and headed upstairs. When we reached the top, Holmes didn't stop. Instead he pushed the door open and walked straight into the room. I heard someone inside shout out in protest.

"Hey! You can't do that. This is a private gathering."

I followed Holmes through the door just in time to see the young man who had spoken try to push him back. Holmes grabbed his would-be assailant by the wrist and, employing one of his Baritsu techniques, he hurled the man to the ground.

"Please let us have no more of this foolishness," Holmes said. "We simply wish to speak briefly with Peter Gooding, and then we'll be on our way."

I looked around the room. In addition to the individual on the floor, there were three other young gentlemen sitting round a table towards the back of the room. They were all holding playing cards and there was a small pot of money in the middle of the table.

"Another interruption, Peter," the young man on the left of the table said.

The person opposite him looked at us, then back to his friend.

"You can't blame me for this, Robert. I've never seen this pair before in my life."

"We've been employed by your uncle to try to save you from the trouble you have gotten yourself into," I said.

"See," said Robert, "it's your uncle again. I told you he wouldn't leave us alone. What are you two? Priests, or some other busy-bodies he has sent here to save our souls?"

"What if they're police?" asked the third man at the table, nervously. "Mr. Gooding did threaten to call them."

"The old man wouldn't do that," replied Robert. "He might not care about us, but he wouldn't want them to arrest young Peter here. Besides what would they charge us with? We haven't done anything wrong."

"Robbery is a serious crime," I said, "and if you aren't honest with Mr. Holmes, I will call the police here myself."

The man on the floor pulled himself up and stared at Holmes with an expression of fear mixed with awe.

"Mr. Holmes? I've heard of him," he said to his friends. "He's meant to be smarter than any of the detectives at Scotland Yard."

Then he turned to us.

"I'm sorry, Mr. Holmes. I wouldn't have tried to lay hands on you if I had known who you were."

"Where were you last night?" asked Holmes.

"We were all here," said Robert. "Well, all except for Henry."

The third man at the card table looked embarrassed.

"I told you, my mum would have killed me if I'd have gone out on Christmas Day."

"Anyway, the rest of us stayed until Edwin, the landlord, threw us out and we had to go back to our own homes."

306

"Then where did you acquire the necklace?" I asked Peter. "If you will just tell us now, we still might be able to clear up the whole affair before the police become involved."

Peter stood up from the card table.

"I will tell you what I keep telling my uncle: I hadn't ever seen that d--ned thing before he thrust it in my face this morning. I don't know why everyone assumes that I know where it came from. Why aren't you questioning my great-aunt? She's the one who was found wearing it. Or better still, ask my uncle. Perhaps he is making all this fuss to cover up his own wrong-doings. He probably bought it for his mistress, and decided to blame me when it was found."

"Your uncle has a mistress?" I asked.

"He could have. Why do you think that less likely than that I would have broken into a stranger's house on Christmas Night and run off with a piece of jewellery?"

"It is a fair question," said Holmes. "The entire case against you has been constructed on a foundation of assumptions, not facts."

"You think he is innocent then?" I asked.

"I think that this has been a small distraction on an otherwise dull day. However, the solution lies back at the house on Mount Park Crescent. Mr. Gooding, if you wish to establish your innocence, I would ask you to return with us now to your uncle's house."

"You might as well," said Roger. "You're too distracted for cards. A few more hands and I'll have cleaned you out."

Peter looked uncertain, but then he nodded.

"Very well, Mr. Holmes. Let us see if my uncle will give me the benefit of the doubt now that I have you on my side."

Mrs. Gooding was delighted to see that Peter had returned with us. He stood there awkwardly, with his arms by his side, as she gave him a big hug and a kiss on the cheek.

"I'm so pleased you came back," she said. "Whatever you have done, I am sure we can make it right with the help of these fine gentlemen."

Peter opened his mouth to object at the assumption of his guilt, but I stopped him.

"Now isn't the time," I said. "Let Mr. Holmes handle it."

Peter nodded and allowed himself to be led into the drawing room.

Things were much as we had left them, except for the addition of three young children and their nanny. A little girl holding a doll came over and stared at me for a moment before retreating to hide behind her father's chair. I recognised the ribbon in the doll's hair as being a match for the one spotted in Mr. Gooding's pocket when he visited us.

The youngest child sat quietly on the nanny's lap, but it was the middle child who drew everyone's attention. He was running around the room holding a metal toy train, shouting, "Choo choo!" as loudly as he could. The arrival of new people in the drawing room distracted him. He forgot where he was going for a moment, and crashed into the dresser. The tall piece of furniture wobbled and Mrs. Gooding cried out in alarm.

"Please be careful, Mark. We don't want another accident, do we?" Nanny, maybe you could take them upstairs to the nursery, while we speak with Mr. Holmes and Dr. Watson?"

The nanny stood, still holding the baby in one arm, while using the other arm to herd the children out of the room and upstairs.

"At least there were no glasses out today," said Mrs. Gooding, as she invited us all to sit down.

Mr. Gooding nodded in agreement. "Still, it shook everything in the cabinets," he said. "Mark is getting too big to run around in here like that."

"I'm sure nanny will calm him down," said Mrs. Gooding.

Then Mr. Gooding turned his attention to his nephew.

"Now then, Peter. Has Mr. Holmes finally managed to persuade you to tell us from where you got that necklace?"

"We're sure it was really just a foolish prank," said Mrs. Gooding, "but if we don't return it to its rightful owner soon, it's going to cause trouble."

Peter turned to us.

"I told you this was a waste of time," he said. "They're never going to believe me."

He started to stand, to leave again, but Holmes stopped him.

"I believe we can resolve this right now," he said, taking out the jewellery box and opening it. He took out the necklace, and walked over to Mrs. Gooding's mother, who was still sitting in the same seat where we had left her, smiling gently.

"I believe this belongs to you, Mrs. Overy," Holmes said, and fastened the necklace around her neck. She looked up at Holmes and beamed.

"Isn't it lovely," she said. "My John has the most exquisite taste."

"He does indeed," said Holmes, "and it goes with your earrings beautifully."

I looked closer and saw that the old woman was indeed wearing a pair of sapphire earrings, very similar in design to the necklace.

"What is going on here?" asked Mrs. Gooding. "I don't understand. That isn't mother's necklace. I'm certain she has never owned anything resembling it."

"You should have listened to her from the beginning," said Holmes, "and all this could have been avoided. It was her Christmas present, just as she said, only it wasn't just a day late arriving, but a year and a day."

Holmes sat down again, and continued to explain.

"Your father bought this necklace from a jewellers in Bond Street in November last year. He obviously intended it to be a present for his wife, matching the earrings, which I guess he also gave her?"

"That's right," said Mrs. Gooding. "They were his present to her on their last Christmas together. It is why she chose to wear them today and yesterday."

"Having purchased the gift, he carefully hid it. His hiding place was somewhere he knew nobody would think to look. He'd probably been using it for years. But then, tragically, he died before he could give her the present, and so it remained hidden – until yesterday."

He stood up, and dragged a chair over to the dresser.

"If I may," he said, and then without waiting for an answer he climbed up on to the chair he had moved and stretched until he could see what was on top of the dresser.

"As I suspected: There is a square patch near the corner here without any dust. You should thank your son, Mr. and Mrs. Gooding. His rowdy play yesterday knocked down more than a wine glass."

"That's impossible," said Mr. Gooding. "We would have noticed it when we were cleaning the floor. The glass went everywhere. There was certainly nothing under the tree when we finished."

"The box didn't land on the floor," replied Holmes. "At least, not straight away. First it fell *into* your Christmas tree, where it hung until late into the night. If you look closely, you can see where the weight of it tore the paper chains when it fell, making the noise that you heard in the night and mistook for your nephew."

"I told you I didn't steal anything," said Peter, angrily. "Why didn't you believe me?"

Mr. and Mrs. Gooding looked ashen.

"We're so sorry," she said.

"They may have doubted you for a moment," I said, "but you must never doubt that they love you. Rather than turn the matter over to the police, as they could have done, your uncle employed the services of Mr. Holmes in order to keep you safe. You are very lucky."

"I suppose I am," said Peter, his expression softening.

Holmes was still standing on the chair next to the dresser.

"Would somebody assist me, please?" he requested.

Peter went over to him, but instead of accepting a hand to help him get down, Holmes started passing him a selection of small boxes and bags.

309

"As I suspected," said Holmes, "Mr. Overy used this as a hiding place for more than one present over the years.

The Goodings started opening the packages, revealing a selection of small toys and sweet treats.

"You should be wary of the food," I said. "It has been up there for over a year."

However, even my overabundance of medical caution couldn't dampen the spirits of the family at this point.

"It's like Christmas Day all over again!" said Mrs. Gooding, tears of delight in her eyes.

Holmes climbed down and replaced the chair.

"We shall leave you to enjoy this time together then, as a family," he said. "I wish you a merry Boxing Day."

"And a happy feast of St. Stephen," I added, as we left the family to enjoy the final presents from their departed loved one.

A Fine Kettle of Fish
by Mike Hogan

"Something quite interesting occurred this morning," I said as I unwound my scarf and placed it on my desk with my hat and gloves.

He turned down a corner of his newspaper.

"At the fish counter of Harrod's."

Holmes raised an enquiring eyebrow.

"A magnificent turbot was on display, quite thirty inches in diameter, and as many pounds in weight. For a moment I was rashly tempted to purchase a fish instead of a goose for our New Year dinner – just for a change." I smiled. "I'm glad I resisted. Our landlady has just informed me in no uncertain terms that the house possesses no pot large enough to seethe such a beast, and she has laid in the sage, onions, and apples for the goose stuffing."

"Juvenal," said Holmes.

He returned to his newspaper, and no further explanation was forthcoming, but I was glad I had provoked a response, even an enigmatic one. For the last several days my friend had been in a dull humour, silent, almost morose. The recent collapse of the great Netherlands-Sumatra fraud trials on the Continent had been a bitter blow after the Herculean effort he had expended during the summer gathering evidence for the prosecution. And the Christmas period was always an ordeal for Holmes, who found what he considered the false bonhomie and relentless cheer galling, the decorations and seasonal fripperies irksome, and the dearth of serious crime deeply frustrating as everyone – even the criminal classes – celebrated with family and friends.

"The monster fish was also very expensive: A wild extravagance given the state of the year-end finances."

Holmes looked up. "The interesting occurrence?"

I settled myself in my usual chair by the fire. "It was quite extraordinary. On the counter beside the turbot was an arrangement of crabs, oysters, and other shellfish on ice, and a dish of caviar with a mother-of-pearl spoon. As I examined the turbot, a portly gentleman beside me reached across the display, scooped up a heap of caviar with the spoon, and ate it!"

I chuckled and looked in vain to Holmes for a reaction. "I, the Harrods staff, and the other shoppers gave the fellow deprecatory looks."

He raised an enquiring eyebrow. "And?"

"Then you'll never guess, ha ha. The fellow's face reddened. He gasped, choked, puffed up like a turkey, and let out a resounding cough, spluttering caviar that pinged across the glass display and sent bystanders ducking for cover!"

"Birdshot," Holmes said, flicking open his newspaper. "Harrods can't have several guineas worth of caviar sitting on display under the gas lamps every day, so they substitute lead shotgun pellets to simulate fish roe. Number eight shot would do very well for Beluga."

"Yes," I said, somewhat deflated. "So after helping the poor fellow to the Harrod's infirmary and administering a mustard-and-asafoetida enema, I bowed to tradition (and Mrs. Hudson) and ordered a goose for our New Year's Eve feast."

I reached for our account book. "I thought of investing in a *turbotiere*. You never know when it might come in handy. Was that the doorbell?"

A heavy tread came on the stairs, the door of the sitting room opened, and our page peeked in. "Visitor," he told us. "Maximilian Eldridge Allar – " Billy frowned at the calling card in his hand. "'*Allar* – '"

"Allardyce," said our visitor, easing Billy to one side so he could manoeuvre his considerable bulk though the doorway.

I started in astonishment as I recognised the stout gentleman who had eaten the birdshot caviar in Harrods.

"Doctor Watson," the gentleman said, holding out his hand. "How glad I am to have the opportunity to thank you again for your ministrations this morning. I was, as you will recall, quite incapacitated for some time and therefore unable to adequately express my heartily felt gratitude. You must have thought me abominably rude."

I stood and we shook hands. "Not at all, Mr. Allardyce. I hope you have quite recovered from your ordeal. May I present my friend, Mr. Sherlock Holmes?" I indicated Holmes, who was leaning back in his chair regarding our visitor, his fingers steepled before his face and a faint smile on his lips.

"Mr. Holmes requires no introduction," Mr. Allardyce said, bowing. He passed his silk hat, gloves, and scarf to our page and, with his help, shrugged off his overcoat, revealing a striped waistcoat under a fashionable grey frock-coat.

I ushered our guest to the sofa, the only seat in the room that would accommodate his ample proportions, and offered refreshments.

"I hope you will forgive my intrusion upon your domestic contentment, gentlemen." Mr. Allardyce said as he settled on the sofa and warmed his hands at our fire. "Particularly during the festive season." He encompassed in a wide gesture our homely sitting room with its yule branches across the mantelpiece and holly wreathes around the pictures on the walls – the few examples of Christmas cheer that Holmes would tolerate.

I made an appropriate remark, sent Billy to fetch coffee, and slipped into my chair.

"In the aftermath of the incident this morning," Mr. Allardyce continued, "I was fully preoccupied with the business of recuperation. It was not until I was myself again that I read your calling card and realised that my Good Samaritan was Doctor Watson, the author of the fascinating story in *Beeton's Christmas Review*." He frowned. "Ah, 'The Scarlet Letter', was it?"

I overrode the growl from Holmes with my correction. "*A Study in Scarlet*, in fact, in *Beeton's Christmas Annual*."

"Yes, that's the one. I read the story on the train one morning last week as I came up from my country place in Suffolk, and I was so engrossed that I settled into the station restaurant to finish it." Mr. Allardyce grimaced. "I dare not eat anything, of course, but I ventured on a glass of porter as a sop to the house. Really, the food at the terminus restaurant is a blot on the escutcheon of the Great Eastern Railway Company. My valet unwisely ate a bloater there last summer and was instantly laid low. He was unable to discharge his duties for several days, but the company refused compensation for the inconvenience."

Mr. Allardyce leaned back in the sofa with a creak of strained rattan. "I wrote a stinging rebuke to the letters page in *The Times*."

He considered for a moment, then addressed me in a sombre tone. "I believe I owe you not only my thanks, but also an apology and an explanation."

"Not at all. No apology – "

Mr. Allardyce held up a restraining hand. "Pray allow me to continue, Doctor. I am as mortified by what you may have perceived as my greed as by its unfortunate consequence."

I bowed, and Mr. Allardyce took a moment to collect himself before he continued. "I was for many years engaged in trade. I retired some twenty years ago. As other yearnings fell away with the passage of time, I acquired a passion for the culinary arts, or rather their culmination: Fine food, particularly the fruits of our bountiful rivers and oceans and their littoral precincts. I am a member of a small society of persons with similar interests, a discreet dining coterie composed of gentlemen of diverse backgrounds who come together to worship at the altar of the piscatorial Epicurus. I speak metaphorically."

Mr. Allardyce seemed to pause for a response.

"You refer to fish," I offered.

"I do. We take biannual turns arranging dinners focussed on fish and shellfish. I host the winter meeting tomorrow evening. An awkward date, as you will agree, in the dull hiatus between Christmas festivities and the celebration of New Year."

He sighed. "And our little club is not quite what it was. I am obliged to admit that gourmets, like other mortals, are subject to a spirit of competition that in the early years of our association was a healthy stimulus to our endeavours. Recently, however, the focus of attention among members has shifted from the *quality* of the food presented by the host to its *rarity* – the more exotic the fare, the more plaudits accrued. The host who offers his guests the most outlandish, the scarcest species of fish or shellfish is considered, if only in his own estimation, to be worthy of the plaudits of his fellows."

Mr. Allardyce patted his frock coat pockets. I offered our cigarette case, but he refused politely, proffering his cigar case. I held up my pipe, lit a taper from the fire, and we shared a light.

"I aim to eschew the bizarre while offering the connoisseur a memorable experience," he continued between puffs. "In that regard, I had hoped to procure a stingray for tomorrow's repast. Harrods were unable to fulfil my order for a mature ray – they cite a series of violent typhoons across the spawning grounds – but I had secured on deposit a Tasmanian specimen from Sherman's Emporium in Pinchin Lane. However, when Sherman learned – I know not how – that the beast was intended for consumption rather than companionship, he refused to countenance the sale."

Mr. Allardyce pursed his lips. "And thus, with just forty-eight hours before the club dinner, my desperate excursion to Harrods. In my haste to discover what the seafood department could offer, I left my house at an early hour, missing breakfast – aside from an egg or two and a crumb of toast. By mid-morning I was famished, and when I saw the caviar, I succumbed." He lowered his head in contrition.

"Perfectly understandable, old chap," I said. "A sustaining breakfast is the cornerstone on which a busy day must be erected."

Mr. Allardyce looked up and favoured me with a brave smile that I returned.

Holmes had been moving restlessly in his chair during our visitor's exposition, and I feared a dyspeptic eruption, but a distraction saved the day as Billy sidled into the room with coffee. He placed the tray on our breakfast table and leaned towards me. "Mrs. H. wants to know what to do with the fish," he whispered.

I blinked at him. "What fish?"

Mr. Allardyce evidently overheard me. "I noticed your interest in the turbot at Harrods," he said. "I had thought to purchase him for my little *soirée*, but in justice not only to your prior claim, but even more to your medical skills, I could not deprive you of that noblest of the piscatorial race."

"No, no, I cannot possibly accept such a princely gift."

Mr. Allardyce held up an admonitory hand. "I must insist, my dear doctor. Let it be a small token of my appreciation not only for your medical aid, but for the pleasure, and may I say enlightenment, you afforded me with your admirable American story." He frowned. "I left the fish with a lady downstairs, whom I presume is your housekeeper. She seemed disinclined to accept it into the house, making some reference to sage, onion, and apples in a context I could not quite follow."

"But what of your supper tomorrow?" I asked.

"Do not trouble yourself on that account. When I returned home from my uncomfortable shopping trip, I was apprised that a message awaited me from my agent at the port. A shipment I had thought delayed had in fact arrived, and with it came a certain delicacy that I will offer on my menu tomorrow. The turbot is therefore superfluous to my requirements."

"Nevertheless – "

"It would be churlish to refuse," Holmes said from his seat by the fire. He chuckled. "You might consider the fish an accolade to your literary acumen."

I withered Holmes with a steely glare.

"How would you recommend we prepare the turbot?" Holmes asked, unfazed.

"*À la anglais,*" Mr. Allardyce replied firmly. "Rubbed with lemon, steamed in fresh spring water, and served with a lobster *velouté* sauce. Not steamed for too long, gentlemen. In things epicurean, *tout est une question de synchronisme.*"

He stood. "I mentioned my supper tomorrow. The membership of my club is restricted to six, but two of our members are unable to attend, and it is within my power as host to replace them with guests of my choosing. I would therefore be honoured if you gentlemen would agree to join us. It's an informal affair – entirely masculine of course – with no political or philosophical bias. Judge Cresswell is one of our number, as is the Maharajah of Malapuram, ruler of a substantial portion of the Malabar Coast."

Mr. Allardyce caught my involuntary glance towards Holmes.

"But I hesitate," he said, addressing my friend. "I must presume, Mr. Holmes, that you, like the Iron Duke, are indifferent to concerns of the flesh, and your energies are focussed entirely within the intellectual sphere."

"Not at all," Holmes answered in a thankfully amicable tone. "There is a direct relationship between healthy eating and intellectual prowess."

Mr. Allardyce clapped his hands with delight. "Then you will come?"

"We will."

I helped our guest into his overcoat and, as he pulled on his gloves, he gave me details of the dinner venue. He paused at the sitting room door. "One small favour, Doctor. My lapse of judgement at Harrods today – the caviar did look so very alluring – might be viewed by my fellow Neptunians (as our little company style ourselves) with jaundiced eyes. Might I prevail on you not to mention the matter in their company?"

"It is forgotten, Mr. Allardyce," I assured him. Holmes waved a languid hand, and I saw our guest downstairs.

Holmes and I stood before the kitchen table on which the immense turbot lay on a bed of ice in a basket lined with butcher's paper. Mrs. Hudson and Billy regarded the scene from the doorway of the scullery, both with folded arms and stiff expressions.

"I had thought of purchasing a *turbotiere*," I said, "but it would have to be one of considerable dimensions to contain a fish of this immensity, even if we remove the fins – "

" – wings," said Holmes. "Turbots have wings, not fins."

" – and tail, it still won't fit in any pot we possess." I frowned. "You mentioned Juvenal?"

"The Roman satirist wrote of a fisherman who offered Emperor Nero an enormous turbot:

> *But when was joy unmixed? No pot is found,*
> *Capacious of the turbot's ample round.*

"Nero simply ordered a huge pot to be hastily manufactured." Holmes smiled. "God-emperors command resources unavailable to mere mortals. But we have the more modern example of Monsieur Brillat-Savarin, the French gourmet, who devised a simple solution to a similar problem. He had the fish laid in a capacious basket, enveloped in herbs, and covered with a washtub. The assembly was then hoisted in a hammock over a water boiler. *Eh voila*."

I brightened. "We have the Harrod's basket and a washtub. Billy can fetch a lobster from the fishmonger and the necessary herbs from the market. The laundry boiler will make a splendid steamer."

Mrs. Hudson stiffened as Holmes opened the larder door and peered inside. "We have peas and potatoes, and Mrs. Hudson can whip up a *velouté* sauce in a trice." He considered. "'Tis the season of bonhomie and gluttony. I will contribute a half-dozen of Condrieu. An aromatic white Rhône will go splendidly with this elegant fish."

"I am not very hungry," I commented as our cab turned into a side street near Leicester Square the following evening. Then, after a few moments, I added, "We shall be in exalted company today. Mr. Allardyce mentioned the Maharajah of Malapuram and Judge Cresswell. Isn't the judge presiding over the Sumatra fraud at the Old Bailey that we discussed over dinner?"

"Cresswell is directing the proceedings with an iron hand," Holmes answered. "I have no doubt the trial will end with stiff sentences for the minnows in custody: The sharks still swim free. I gave my evidence in Brussels earlier in the year and convictions were confidently predicted, but the tentacles of Baron Maupertuis, the mastermind behind the evil enterprise, penetrated every European agency and jurisdiction, spreading venality and corruption and obstructing the wheels of justice." Holmes peered out of the cab window. "The case collapsed. Ah, we're there – or rather, *here*."

I retrieved my silk hat from the seat opposite, and Holmes and I got down from the cab outside a building with a blue-and-white awning decorated with Oriental hieroglyphs and a huge red lantern hanging from the eaves. My heart sank. "I do hope we're not offered anything too peculiar."

"Tut tut, old man," Holmes answered with a smile. "You must eschew oversensitivity in the matter of food. The English cling to the dishes that graced the stodgy tables at our schools. The ubiquitous mutton chop and glutinous treacle tart. Our Continental cousins consume a much wider range of fare than we do, and they are demonstrably healthier. Our lower classes are more conservative in their eating habits, and thus hollow-chested weaklings form our thin red line compared with the strapping fellows in the French and Prussian armies. The wiry Chinese eat without injury anything that walks, runs, or slithers."

A lady in a kimono greeted us at the entrance of the restaurant and led us with mincing steps through a sliding paper door and along a narrow corridor. She opened another door, bowed, and ushered us into a small room styled in the Japanese manner.

"The cuisine we are to be offered is apparent," Holmes murmured.

A modern dining table laid for six stood in the centre of the room, with four seats occupied by elderly gentlemen. A kimono-clad lady in dead-white makeup knelt in a corner, plucking on a Japanese banjo.

Mr. Allardyce rose from his place at the head of the table and introduced us to each of the other three diners. We were indeed in high company. Seated between the judge and Maharajah was Colonel Redpath of the Foot Guards, the intrepid Andean explorer.

"Aside from his South American peregrinations, you will know the colonel from his widely acclaimed book, *Partial Xanthism in the Common Bream*," Mr. Allardyce assured us. "A memorandum that fluttered a number of dovecots in the piscatorial community."

Colonel Redpath held out his hand to Holmes. "Are you gentlemen fish fanciers?"

"Not exactly."

"I doubt Mr. Holmes has time for hobbies," Judge Cresswell said in a cold tone. "He is too busy nuzzling for tidbits of gossip. He is a professional snoop."

"A professional *consulting* snoop," Holmes said in an equable tone. "And the only nuzzling I have done recently has been at the behest of Her Majesty's prosecution in a matter currently before Your Honour at the Old Bailey, and therefore *sub judice*." He smiled and held a finger to his lips. "I am constrained from elaboration."

Judge Cresswell sniffed and turned away. Mr. Allardyce and the Maharajah shook hands with Holmes, and then with me.

I settled in my seat, took a sip of the fiery rice wine we were offered by a kimono-clad waitress, and consulted one of the ornate, hand-written menus that lay on each place-setting. "*Fugu sashimi* followed by *fugu nabe*."

"*Tetraodontidae*," Holmes said, "known colloquially as blowfish."

I blinked at my friend. "Isn't blowfish – "

"I say, this *fugu* fish is dashed poisonous," Colonel Redpath exclaimed, looking up from his menu. "Half a Japanese restaurant full of diners were killed in Hawaii just last year, or the year before."

Judge Cresswell chuckled. "My dear Allardyce, in your wish to surpass the *crabe de cocotier mornay* I offered at our summer gathering, you look to slaughter us."

Mr. Allardyce rang a tiny bell, summoning an Oriental-looking man in chef's garb who stood at his side and bowed.

"You are correct, Colonel," Mr. Allardyce said. "Certain organs of the *fugu* fish are infused with a poison a hundred times more toxic than cyanide. Those parts Chef Kimura-san has skilfully excised, leaving the delicate flesh that will be served today. Kimura-san has prepared *fugu* here

318

and in his native land for over thirty years, and he has yet to lose a customer."

"I, for one, have no intention of being the first," the colonel said, squinting at the Japanese chef through his monocle.

"You are perfectly safe, gentlemen" the chef assured us in heavily accented English. "I have personally tasted all of today's ingredients without ill effect."

Waitresses placed tiny bowls at each setting and filled them with a dark liquid. "Soy sauce," the chef explained.

Two large platters were laid on the table. On each, wafer-thin, almost translucent slices of fish were layered in a flower pattern.

"This first dish is *fugu sashimi*," the chef informed us, "that is, raw *fugu*. The second contains slices of raw grouper."

"For the faint-hearted among us," Judge Cresswell quipped.

"You dip each slice into the soy sauce, so." Mr. Allardyce used his chopsticks to grasp a delicate slice of *fugu* and dunk it in the sauce bowl. "The soy may be flavoured to taste by the addition of *wasabi* – Japanese mustard."

Four of our host's fellow diners regarded the *fugu* plate without enthusiasm, but Holmes took a slice, manipulating his chop sticks with dexterity. "I tasted *fugu* earlier in the year as the guest of the projector of the Japanese Exhibition in Knightsbridge. If prepared by an expert, there is little danger."

He popped the morsel into his mouth.

Mr. Allardyce beamed at Holmes. "The texture is extraordinary. The Japanese language has far more words describing textures than we do, and they consider that of *fugu* flesh to be the most exquisite of its kind."

I took a slice of *fugu* with considerable trepidation. It tasted of soy sauce with a hint of chicken.

The other diners also tried the *fugu*, and, as the rice wine was passed, the atmosphere thawed and became pleasantly convivial, particularly at my end of the table. A remark by Colonel Redpath on the silken kimonos worn by our waitresses led to a spirited discussion among the colonel, the Maharajah, and me on the relative softness of Japanese silk, the wool of the alpaca, and that of the Kashmiri goat.

I noticed that the judge and Mr. Allardyce were chatting on a topic that I couldn't quite catch, and that the judge was ignoring Mr. Allardyce's polite attempts to include Holmes in their conversation. I endeavoured to draw Holmes into our wool debate, but he smiled and concentrated on his plate.

Mr. Allardyce tapped his glass for attention as the table was cleared. "The second course today is *fugu nabe*." A great tureen was carried in and placed on a side table atop a charcoal burner. "The *nabe* is prepared in front of the diners. The stock is brought to a soft boil, then the *fugu* is added and let simmer before vegetables and *tofu* complete the stew."

Chef Kimura supervised as lacquerware bowls filled with aromatic sauce replaced our tiny soy bowls.

"The secret to a great *nabe* is the *ponzu* sauce in which the morsels are dipped," Mr. Allardyce continued, indicating the bowls. "This sauce was made to Komura-san's special recipe. We were unable to source fresh *sudachi*, but limes are a perfectly adequate substitute."

The judge sniffed.

"The *nabe* is eaten communally," Mr. Allardyce said as the steaming pot was placed on a wooden block in the centre of the table. "We pick pieces with our chopsticks, so, then dip the piping hot morsels into individual bowls filled with *ponzu* sauce. Grated radish and chopped scallions are on the side."

He nodded to the chef, who bowed to the company and left us.

I followed Holmes's lead and managed to manoeuvre a few pieces of fish and some vegetables to my bowl. The process was fiddly, and I soon resorted to using a small ceramic spoon I found beside my plate.

We ate, resuming our conversation, until Mr. Allardyce called us to order and announced that the broth remaining in the *nabe* would be served as a soup. Mr. Allardyce requested the judge's bowl, into which he poured a ladleful of fragrant liquid. He raised his eyebrows as the judge took a sip.

"Well enough," Judge Cresswell said. "A trifle over-salted."

Mr. Allardyce filled the judge's bowl, and I and the other guests passed ours in turn. The aroma of the soup was delightful, and the flavour was intense, dominated by a savoury tang and not fishy at all.

When we had emptied our bowls, Mr. Allardyce scooped the remaining vegetables and fish from the *nabe* and shared them among the company. "Finally, we return the broth to the boil, adding four cups of cooked rice. The rice thickens the soup, making a savoury porridge something like a risotto, called *zosui*." He took the pot from the heat, whisked three raw eggs, and added the mixture to the *nabe*, stirring the pot once before serving. "The flavours of the *nabe* are intensified. For my part, the *zosui* is the culmination of the meal."

I spooned some of the gruel and paused, frowning. I blinked at Holmes. "I am experiencing an odd sensation – a numbness of the lips and a feeling of light-headedness, almost intoxication. My tongue is partially numbed."

Holmes's eyes narrowed, and he seemed about to speak when Judge Cresswell's bowl and spoon dropped onto the table with a clatter. The judge swayed in his chair. "I feel a trifle – "

I half-rose, but the judge waved me down. "No, no, do not disturb yourself, sir. It's nothing, just – " He leaned forward and vomited.

I hurried around the table and helped him sit up. His face was pale, his brow beaded with sweat. I undid his cravat and loosened his collar. I felt his pulse racing.

"Doctor?"

I turned to Colonel Redpath, who was wiping his neck with his napkin. "I am feeling nauseous – " The colonel stood, clutched his stomach and stared at me wide-eyed. "Are we poisoned?" he gasped.

"How are you, Holmes?" I asked.

"I feel a faint prickling over my body, and a mild exhilaration, nothing more. You?"

"The same." I frowned. "The judge's heart is racing, and his muscles are stiffening. Assuming this is poisoning, we must encourage the patient to expel as much of the ingested material as possible and attempt to neutralise the toxin. Find some unused charcoal in the kitchen, Holmes. Hammer it to a powder and mix it with milk to make a suspension."

"I am having trouble – " the judge gasped, his face turning dark red. "I can't – "

"Is there no antidote?" I asked the chef who appeared in the doorway, his face as white as his uniform.

"None."

"Fetch asafetida. I will prepare an enema."

Mr. Allardyce stood and steadied himself with a hand on his chair back. He was as pale as the chef. "I too am unwell – dizzy, and – " He slid to the floor gasping for breath.

I ministered to the judge and Mr. Allardyce as well I could, inducing vomiting, then encouraging them to drink as much of the charcoal suspension as they could stand.

Colonel Redpath watched wide-eyed, gulping down the milk. "Are we dead men, Doctor?"

The Maharajah sipped his sake and called for more, humming to himself and seeming unperturbed. I realised that the girl in the corner continued to play her banjo, and I barked at her to leave.

Mr. Allardyce began to breathe more easily, and my own dizziness abated. I drained the milk jug into the judge's glass and called to Chef Kimura for more.

Holmes laid a hand on my arm and indicted the judge. "I don't think that will be necessary."

321

I turned to Judge Cresswell, checked his vital signs, and stood back, the energy draining from my limbs. "He has passed."

Holmes instructed a waitress to fetch the constable on fixed-point duty by Leicester Square Station. He requisitioned small bowls from the kitchen and took specimens from the pot, then from the soup bowls. "Let me have your pencil." He wrote labels for each bowl on slips torn from the menu.

"Police?" the Maharajah asked. "What business is this of the police?"

"How terrible," Colonel Redpath said in a quavering voice. "Terrible." He narrowed his eyes and pointed an accusing finger at Chef Kimura. "Murderer!"

Holmes addressed the chef. "Where was the fish prepared?"

Chef Kimura led us to the kitchen at the back of the building. A long wooden table stood in the centre of the room, an iron range occupied one wall and gleaming sinks and counters another. The waitresses were huddled in the far corner. They bowed, and then observed us in expressionless silence.

"I separated the gonads, liver, and other dangerous parts of the fish on this counter," Chef Kimura said in a quavering tone. "The safe portions I kept in this dish. At no point after removal did the poisonous entrails touch the edible flesh. I examined the entrails most carefully – they were whole and undamaged. No toxin can have seeped out. The counter, plate and the knife I used were then washed thoroughly and rinsed in boiling water, which I poured into the drain."

"And the toxic portions of the fish?" I asked.

"I threw on the fire." He rubbed his hands together. "Mr. Allardyce was with me the whole time. He saw that nothing was amiss."

Mr. Allardyce appeared in the doorway, mopping his brow with a napkin. "That is correct."

Holmes took the knife and dishes and wrapped them in clean towels, handling them with great care. He took specimens of the remaining raw fish, the soy sauce, and the *ponzu*. We trooped back into the dining room.

"What a ghastly accident," Mr. Allardyce said. "I cannot fathom how such a thing could have occurred. My – our – symptoms were relatively mild. Judge Cresswell must have been abnormally sensitive to the toxin. It is a catastrophe."

The Maharajah shrugged. "Such things occur. It is God's will – *kismet*. No need to make a fuss." He picked up his menu and addressed the chef. "What of the Lungfish and Black Truffle savoury? Surely that is not tainted."

A young, extravagantly moustached police sergeant arrived with the constable we had summoned and introduced himself as Sergeant Harris of

C Division of the Metropolitan Police. He frowned at the corpse. "Is that who I think it is?"

I nodded.

"Oh, deary, deary me."

Holmes and I gave our account of the affair to the sergeant, and then we helped carry Judge Cresswell's body outside to a four-wheeler. Holmes called a hansom and instructed the driver to follow the growler to the morgue.

"A horrible accident, don't you think?" I said as we settled in our seats.

"I do not."

I gaped at my friend. "You suspect foul play? By a club member with a grudge against a fellow Neptunian perhaps? But no one would kill another over something so trivial as rivalry in a dining club."

"The English take their hobbies seriously,"

I couldn't but agree. "How did the murderer stage the killing? If the raw fish or stew were poisoned, why were we and the other diners hardly affected? How could the murderer administer a lethal dose to his victim, leaving the other diners relatively unscathed? A targeted poisoning would surely assume the complicity of the chef, and possibly the waitresses, which seems most unlikely."

I went over the events of the evening in my mind as I gazed out of the cab window at empty streets and shuttered shops. The denizens of the metropolis were at home, girding their loins for a repeat of their yuletide excesses on the morrow, New Year's Eve. "The Maharajah was the only guest unaffected by the poison," I said at last. "Could he have taken an antidote? I know the chef said there is none, but it's common knowledge the shamans in India have access to arcane learning relating to toxins. One instinctively thinks of the Orient in that regard – "

"Not Lucrezia Borgia?"

I knitted my brows. "Wait – wait. We dined from communal dishes, but we received individual bowls of the *ponzu* sauce. That's the answer. The judge's sauce was spiked – but by whom? If not the Maharajah, was some outside agency involved? A person or persons not at our meal?"

Holmes tapped his cane against the cab roof. "Cabby! Stop at the district messengers' office at Trafalgar Square."

"The Japanese chef may have been involved," I continued. "He claimed to have tasted everything beforehand. Was that an exaggeration or a lie?"

After a brief stop for Holmes to send several messages, we continued to the morgue, arriving as Sergeant Harris and two mortuary assistants manhandled the corpse out of the cab and onto an ambulance trolly.

Coroner Ivor Purchase, who Holmes and I had met on an earlier case in the summer, supervised the transfer, smoking a long cigar. "Welcome, welcome, gentlemen, to my little abode."

We shook hands, and he offered cigars from his case.

"You're working late," I said after a brief narration of the events of the evening. "We expected to deal with your night staff."

The coroner smiled. "Like Bloggs the corner grocer, I live above the shop. My clerk has orders to fetch me for anything out of the ordinary." He patted the shoulder of the portly corpse. "This will make a change from the dreary stabbings and cracked skulls of the past few weeks." He turned to Holmes. "Really, I despair of our run-of-the-mill, home-grown assassins with their blunt traumas, slit throats, and speared kidneys. East End cosh-artists and stab merchants are regrettably devoid of homicidal imagination."

We followed the trolley into a dim, green-tiled tunnel that led to the morgue proper, a spacious, windowless room as brightly lit as a butcher's shop. The judge's corpse was heaved onto a slab, not without great difficulty, and a pair of assistants stripped the body.

"The festive season brings its share of domestic mayhem," Mr. Purchase said, indicating a dozen or so corpses arrayed on tables across the room. "Quarrels among relatives, fights over the thrupenny bit in the plum pudding, and the like. But nothing really engaging." He prepared his instruments, and I helped his assistant set up a camera and tripod and photograph the judge's corpse from several angles. Holmes leaned against an empty table, smoking one of the coroner's cigars.

"For drama one has to look to the Continent," Mr. Purchase continued. "Did you read of the Montrouge affair, gentlemen? In November of last year, a young lady of a certain type was found dismembered and displayed in chunks on the steps of a church. The Parisian police are still flummoxed, but they do not have recourse to a detective of the calibre of Mr. Holmes."

He bowed.

The coroner made his incision in the breast of the corpse. "This is only my second blowfish poisoning. The first victim was pickled, so my investigations were severely hampered."

I frowned.

"A sailor. His ship was at anchor in a port on the Malay coast and the crew passed their time fishing from the aft deck. One crew member barbecued his catch, and he and three others then ate the fish. Our fellow started feeling unwell, his condition rapidly deteriorated and he died, apparently in agony. His captain, anxious to allay suspicion – it seems there was bad blood between him and the dead fellow – had his body preserved in a barrel of vinegar."

"The other sailors weren't affected?" I asked.

"No." Mr. Purchase excised the judge's viscera and passed them to an assistant for weighing.

"That seems to be the case in this incident," I said. "This gentleman is the only casualty of six at table. We all ate the same meal, aside from individual portions of sauce. Was the judge predisposed by some characteristic or trait to be abnormally sensitive to *fugu* toxin? He was significantly obese."

"The pickled fisherman was a slender Malay." Mr. Purchase poked the judge's liver with his scalpel. "I see no evidence of a morphological cause of death, aside from a predictable sclerosis." He turned to me. "You suspect the sauce?"

I described the process of preparation, cooking in the pot, and serving the meal. "At no point was anything added to Judge Cresswell's bowl that wasn't shared with the others. All the guests were more or less affected (aside from the Maharajah), yet only the judge succumbed to the poison – if poison is the active agent. The dipping sauce for the fish stew was the sole item served in individual bowls." I glanced towards Holmes, who remained impassive, smoking his cigar. "That is the only possible way in which a fatal dose of the toxin could have been delivered to its victim."

"This much and only this I know from my reading," Mr. Purchase said. "Depending on the amount of toxin ingested, the onset of symptoms is within ten to forty minutes. The symptoms in order of appearance are numbness around the mouth, followed by localised paralysis, lack of co-ordination, and slurring of speech. Does that accord with your observations, Doctor?"

"It does. Widespread paralysis then manifested. The judge had more and more difficulty breathing, and finally died twenty minutes after ingestion."

"The victim was fully conscious during that time?"

"He was."

Mr. Purchase considered. "I shall swab the stomach contents, and we may compare them with Mr. Holmes's samples of the meal."

He led Holmes, Sergeant Harris, and me to his office, where he took a half-loaf of bread from a cupboard and several pipettes from another. We followed him to a hut in the backyard of the mortuary. As he opened the door a crescendo of squeaking assailed us.

"I keep a small menagerie for my experiments on cholera and typhus transmission," Mr. Purchase explained. "You may have seen my paper in last month's *Lancet* correcting some of Dr. Koch's wilder assertions on bacteria."

He soaked pieces of bread in Holmes's specimen of the *nabe* soup and offered it to the rats in one cage. He repeated the experiment at another cage with the residue of the judge's *ponzu* sauce, then fragments of raw *fugu*. The rats ate avidly and gibbered and squeaked for more. Then the creatures in the first cage, who had eaten the *nabe*, began to stagger, bumping into each other as if blinded, but within a few moments they had recovered and resumed their usual activity.

"And lastly, this dunked in the contents of the victim's stomach."

The rats fell on the bread fragments. In a matter of seconds they had flopped on their sides, quivered and lay still.

"There we are," the coroner said. "A conclusive result."

"How extraordinary," I said. "The stew is only mildly toxic, yet the judge's stomach contents are lethal." I turned to Holmes. "If not the *ponzu* sauce, then what?" I asked. "The result defies logic."

Holmes smiled one of his irritatingly enigmatic smiles.

Mr. Purchase echoed his smile. "Do I detect from your expression, Mr. Holmes, that you already have an answer?"

"There were one or two probabilities I was considering. Now that it is proven the contents of the judge's stomach are more toxic than the residue in the pot, only one solution remains."

Holmes, the sergeant, and I followed the coroner back to his office. "I will test for all the regular toxins," Mr. Purchase said, "in case someone used the blowfish dinner as cover for a more commonplace poisoning. I have no test for *tetraodontidae* poison. I do believe one exists."

Mr. Purchase knelt before his office fire, heaped coals, and administered fierce jabs with a poker. "Damned chimney." He produced a bottle of port from one cupboard, and a pan and block of cheese from another. "Toasted cheese, gentlemen? I understand your dinner was cut short. I usually have a light supper and a sustaining glass at about this time of the evening that I would be happy to share."

The sergeant accepted the offer, but Holmes stood, and I made our excuses.

Mr. Purchase held out his hand. "An interesting puzzle, Mr. Holmes – indeed, one that seems to me to be impenetrable. You yourselves are hearty testament to the relative innocence of the exotic fare you consumed. If it was mortally tainted, why are you, and as you inform me, the other diners, still with us?"

"How do you feel?" I asked as we travelled homewards in a hansom.

"My symptoms were slight." Holmes answered. "No worse than the aftermath of a hot curry."

"Very well. But we were both in imminent danger this evening, so the polite thing to do would be to share your conclusions on an affair that might have killed us."

Holmes steepled his fingers as he considered for a moment. "People often talk of the perfect murder. I have a feeling that you and I were privileged to witness a crime that may claim that appellation."

"So you don't know who did it."

"On the contrary, I do, and I know how it was accomplished." He smiled. "My work is therefore done."

"Not quite," I said, perhaps more stiffly than I had intended. "You must inform Sergeant Harris of your conclusions. A senior member of the judiciary was murdered before our eyes – "

Holmes raised his hand in a placating gesture. "I cannot offer a scintilla of direct evidence to support my conclusion – certainly nothing that would convince a jury. Nor do I have any hope that proof will be forthcoming."

"Still – "

"Still, I will furnish Sergeant Harris with both suspect and opportunity and leave him to extract a confession."

Our cab turned into Baker Street, and I directed the driver to stop outside our lodgings.

"What of motive?" I asked as we stepped down.

"I have my suspicions. Several enquiries are in train that may be of relevance."

I came down to breakfast on New Year's Eve morning to find Holmes at the table leafing through his *Times*.

"Judge Cresswell's demise made the front pages," he said. "Most reports are less than sympathetic. His Lordship wasn't loved, or even liked, and the manner of his passing excites little sympathy from more prudent diners. The Netherlands-Sumatra trial is suspended."

I glanced at the front page of my *Telegraph*. "I see the chef has been arrested." I helped myself to coffee. "One thing is clear. If this was foul play, then only the chef could have done the deed. The guests, with the possible but unlikely exception of the Maharajah, are perfectly innocent."

"Do you say so?"

I said nothing more, busying myself with breakfast. I had learned over the years as our acquaintance had matured into friendship that attempts to cajole Holmes into an explanation were wasted effort.

We settled in front of the fireplace with our morning pipes.

327

"While you were busy discussing alpaca wool with the colonel and Maharajah," Holmes said at last, puffing a stream of aromatic smoke across the room, "Judge Cresswell afforded Mr. Allardyce an interesting insight into the background of the Netherlands-Sumatra affair, and I listened in. Much couldn't be said, as the matter is *sub judice*, but the judge shared his frustration with the progress of the case and with the collapse of the trials on the Continent. The deception was on a colossal scale – scores of bank clerks and several senior officials were bribed or coerced into accepting forged certificates for sums amounting to a hundred-thousand pounds or more. There are rumours suggesting national banks, including the Bank of England, were compromised. Fiscal authorities here and abroad are reluctant to admit the true extent of the frauds for fear the public will lose confidence in the financial system.

"The gang responsible has scattered. The bigger fish darted into their hidey-holes where they believe they're beyond the reach of the law, leaving the small fry to be scooped up and brought to trial. Baron Maupertuis himself is said to have shed his identity and established himself in luxurious circumstances in the Balearic Islands. Judge Cresswell hoped his fierce admonitions from the bench would shame the government into a more active pursuit."

"You believe the judge was murdered to derail the fraud case?"

"I do."

"Was the chef an accomplice? Or the waitresses?"

"The *nabe* was the culprit. Yet it was completely innocent when it was brought to the table."

I allowed myself a mildly sceptical sniff. By what feat of legerdemain had the murderer introduced the poison into the judge's bowl with the other diners just an arm's length away?

The sitting room door opened, and Billy showed in Sergeant Harris. Holmes invited him to take a vacant seat at our breakfast table.

"I have done as you suggested, Mr. Holmes sir," the sergeant said in a doubtful tone, "although my superiors are clamouring for an explanation." He turned to me. "The foreign cook has been released, and I've requested Mr. Allardyce to come to the station for an interview at one o'clock."

Holmes stood. "I called you to witness a little demonstration, Sergeant. You, Watson, and Billy will be my guinea pigs." He instructed our page to clear our breakfast dishes and fetch a bowl, a ladle, three soup bowls and a jug of hot water.

Billy raced downstairs and back again, laying the items on our breakfast table.

"This bowl of water represents the soup course of the *nabe*, which I am convinced was properly prepared by Chef Kimura, and therefore untainted." Holmes held up the salt cellar. "This will simulate the poison."

Sergeant Harris, Billy and I watched as Holmes wet the inside of the ladle and dusted it with salt. "You see the salt coats the ladle. *Fugu* toxin is colourless and of such virulent toxicity that it was only necessary to rub the entrails inside the ladle bowl." Holmes dipped the ladle in the pot, half-filling it with hot water. "I swirl to dissolve the salt, and then pour into the boy's soup bowl. I add another scoop using the same swirling method. I then thoroughly stir the pot before I serve you and the sergeant, *comme ca.*"

He passed bowls to Billy, the sergeant and to me. "Billy's soup is now loaded with poison, and yours and the sergeant's are tainted by the residue on the ladle. Try it."

"Faintly saline," I said.

"Bit salty," said the inspector.

Billy grinned, gulped water from his cup, and instantly choked.

Holmes bowed. "*Eh voila!*"

I patted the boy on the back as he heaved and spluttered, and I sent him downstairs when he had recovered his wits. I retrieved my pipe from the mantel and relit it. "No doubt the Japanese chef's attention was directed elsewhere for a few minutes while Allardyce used the toxic offal to contaminate the ladle."

"No doubt," Holmes agreed. "Judge Cresswell was the intended victim, so he was served first. The smear of poison on the ladle was dissolved in the hot soup and his portion was heavily contaminated. Having delivered a lethal dose to his victim, Allardyce then served the colonel. He stirred the soup vigorously before he filled the colonel's bowl – to better appreciate the aroma, as he remarked. Any poison remaining was much diluted by swirling in the hot, un-poisoned soup in the tureen.

"Allardyce and the other diners received a much lower dose than the judge – sufficient to cause the mild symptoms we experienced, but not to kill. You will recall the rats: The *nabe* was slightly toxic, but nowhere near mortally so. The judge's stomach contents were deadly."

"But why did Allardyce wish to harm the judge?"

"I had no suspicion of murderous intent until too late, but my misgivings regarding our host were aroused by his persistence in questioning Judge Cresswell during dinner. Naturally, I did a little digging into our host's past – after the event unfortunately. Allardyce mentioned a background in trade, but my contacts in the Home Office suggest that his business was in fact in securities, and that he was deeply involved in the Sumatra-Netherlands affair. There is no evidence of deception against him. Nevertheless, I believe he was a prime mover in the English element of the fraud."

"One of the sharks," I suggested.

"You may borrow these visual aides, Sergeant," Holmes said. "Invite Allardyce to your office and lay before him the evidence of motive I have given you. Let him protest his innocence, doubtless echoing the objections Watson made to the possibility of murder by *nabe*. When he is done – "

"I stun him with the ladle trick." Sergeant Harris clapped his hands together and grinned.

"Exactly."

Sergeant Harris left, carrying the kitchenware, and Holmes and I settled once more by the fire.

I puffed on my pipe. "Allardyce took a terrible risk. If he had miscalculated, he might have killed us all! Surely it was very unwise of him to invite us – I mean *you* – to his feast."

"He needed a quorum of witnesses: Two of the club members dropped out," Holmes tapped out the tobacco dottle in his pipe and refilled it with shag. "And the murder left no trace. Persons who think they have devised the perfect murder often suffer from hubris, thinking themselves impregnable. We shall see."

He lit his pipe. "The murder was well-planned. You remarked that the tiny soy sauce thimbles were filled at the table one-by one by the charming waitresses, yet the larger *ponzu* bowls were filled in the kitchen before they were delivered to each diner – *Why?* I think we will find that Mr. Allardyce suggested that arrangement."

"Smoke and mirrors," I suggested, "to muddy the waters."

"The waitress will testify that she delivered the *ponzu* bowls randomly, but the suspicion will be there, and in a murder trial that element of doubt will favour the accused. You must give Allardyce credit. His was an ingenious scheme." Holmes smiled. "This is one of the rare times that I have been actually present at a murder. It was a stimulating experience."

"I say, Holmes – a chap died."

"In murder cases, someone invariably does."

I went over in my mind the sequence of events during the dinner. I could think of no other explanation that fit the facts. Holmes's demonstration had convinced me that the ladle was the only possible means of delivery for the poison. "The prosecution could sway a jury with your party trick. They might obtain a guilty verdict."

"I very much hope not."

I blinked at him.

"There isn't an atom of actual proof as to who contaminated the ladle. I should not like to see a man hanged by what you rightly refer to as my 'party trick'. No, I'm afraid Allardyce will get away with murder."

"Perhaps he will confess," I suggested.

"I can think of no earthly reason why he should."

I picked up my *Telegraph* and glanced at the headlines. "If Allardyce and I hadn't met at Harrods, we would have known nothing of this except what we read in the papers."

"Indeed so," Holmes answered. "Which makes me wonder whether your meeting was entirely fortuitous. His master, the vile Baron Maupertuis, may have ordered him to invite us. He likes to play games."

I flicked down my newspaper. "What did Allardyce mean by his comment on the Duke of Wellington? Was His Grace indifferent to food?"

"The story goes that during one of his campaigns, the Duke was so absorbed in his strategic thoughts that he breakfasted on a rotten egg without complaint. Neither he nor his noble adversary Napoleon were great trenchermen." Holmes stood. "We have one bottle of the Condrieu remaining. What do you say to opening it as an aperitif to our New Year's feast?"

"With all my heart."

Holmes drew the cork, and I fetched two glasses.

Billy put his head around the door. "Mrs. Hudson asks how can she serve her special pea-and-ham soup with no ladle and half the soup bowls missing, and she politely requests a dash of brandy for the bread-and-butter pudding." He grinned. "The goose is going on the fire any minute!"

I unlocked the tantalus and poured a glass of brandy from the decanter. "Walk, don't run."

Billy stalked downstairs, and I settled back in my chair, accepted a glass of wine from Holmes, and raised it. "To a prosperous and peaceful new year."

"As for prosperous, very well, but to achieve prosperity, I must hope for criminal mayhem next year on an epic scale." Homes lifted his glass. "I therefore amend your toast. To a prosperous and *tumultuous* New Year."

The Case of the Left Foot
by Stephen Herczeg

Christmas was fast approaching when I was finally able to begin tidying up my notes for a case from the previous February that would become known as "The Beryl Coronet". Sadly for my good friend Sherlock Holmes, it had been several weeks since he'd had an interesting case, and he'd descended through that December into a worrying state of *ennui*, in spite of the approaching holidays. With winter and Christmas now upon us, my concern for him began to manifest itself.

It was then that fortune shone upon us, like the coming of the Biblical Star, when I heard the doorbell ring downstairs that morning. Within moments I could hear Mrs. Hudson, our wonderful landlady, climbing the stairs to our apartments.

Not wishing to seem too eager, I waited until she finished rapping on the door before crossing to receive her.

"Hello, Doctor," she said softly, handing me a small envelope. "Telegram came for him." We both glanced at Holmes's name printed on the outside. "I do hope it brings him out of his room. I know that people get glum at this time of year . . ." she added before retreating downstairs.

Closing the door, I turned and carefully opened the envelope, sliding out the folded sheet. Opening it, the message I read brought a smile to my face. Lestrade needed Holmes's services – something that generally led to some level of intrigue, or at least interest, in my friend's mind.

Reinserting the note into the envelope, I turned to find Holmes entering the sitting room. He spied the message in my hand and said, "What have you there?"

Handing the telegram over, I said, "Hopefully something of a worthwhile distraction for you."

Quickly reading it, he replied, "As you have seen, there isn't much detail, but Lestrade wishes us to join him at Dufour's Place in Soho."

"Strange location to meet," I said.

"Not if there's someone for us to see in the mortuary."

"Of course," I said, remembering the establishment of such in that very place some years back.

"Well, shall we away?" Holmes asked, disappearing from the sitting room to get ready without another word.

When I rejoined him mere moments later, Holmes stood unconsciously tapping his foot in repressed impatience. The sniff of a mystery had brought all his senses and expectations to the fore.

We were soon trotting through the streets of Marylebone and eventually into the more decrepit area of Soho. The contrast was striking. In the area near our Baker Street lodgings, the shops were decorated for the season. There was an energy in the air, and a marked cheerfulness as well. This seemed to dissipate as we travelled to the southeast, where there was less opportunity or reason for those around us to celebrate. And yet, if one looked closely, there were still small efforts made to acknowledge the holiday.

The driver turned into the somewhat grim area near Dufour's Place and stopped outside a three-storey Georgian building with a tired, run-down appearance to it.

The structure brought a sense of nervousness to my disposition. Even though I had never attended there, I remembered its history. It had been procured by the St. James Parish well over thirty years before, and a mortuary established to deal with the overflow of victims of the cholera outbreak of the mid-1850's.

I was merely an infant at the time, but part of my medical studies required research and re-examination of such outbreaks and the lessons learned from their responses. Medical knowledge had advanced from those days, and I sincerely hoped that it was sufficient, but history shows that new variants of diseases are often encountered that force our knowledge and techniques to improve, generally at the cost of many lives in the early days of the process.

Standing before the mortuary, Holmes noticed my expression. "You look confused."

"I'm simply unsure why this building still functions as a mortuary. Surely there are better-resourced facilities."

"Ah, I have heard tell that the high rate of mortality for the area's inhabitants requires such a facility, even to this day. The Parish of St. James maintains the building as a way of helping those families that have suffered a death but have no means to pay the fees required at more salubrious establishments."

"That explains why it's so run down."

"Yes. I think the church's charity can only stretch so far. Renovations are probably well down the list of needs."

A short figure appeared in the doorway, rugged up with a thick coat and hat pulled down to his ears.

"Lestrade," Holmes called, receiving a nod and a wave of a gloved hand for us to join him inside.

Stepping inside the dim corridor, Lestrade's demeanour was dour at best. His responses were shorter than normal, giving me the impression that he was under great pressure over something.

"What do you have for us?" asked Holmes as we were led down the passageway towards a larger and slightly better-lit room at the end. A strong smell of decay and chemicals floated towards us, making my throat constrict for a moment, as it had been a while since my senses had been assaulted in such a way.

It wasn't until we entered the larger room that Lestrade finally answered Holmes's question. "This is a strange one, Mr. Holmes, and worrying." The room was large and rectangular, kept cold by the absence of heating. Several tables lined one wall. Each held objects covered in stained white sheets. I knew by their shape that they were recently deceased bodies, awaiting collection and burial.

My eyes then fell on the subject of Lestrade's despair.

In the middle of the room lay the examination table in question. Instead of the body of some poor unfortunate victim, a solitary shod foot sat in the middle of a clean white sheet. Even from where I stood, I could tell it was a woman's by the size and style of the shoe.

"My Lord," I gasped, stepping closer to peer at the dismembered appendage. It was a left foot, cut off just above the ankle, and wearing a shoe as if its owner had simply misplaced a body part as she strolled towards her place of employment, before being brought here to reside until she came to collect it like an item of lost baggage.

"We haven't examined it, Mr. Holmes," said the policeman. "I knew you'd want to look at it first."

Holmes stood nearby, a speculative expression on his face as he glanced down at the foot, gleaning as much initial information as he could. "Well, Lestrade," he said, "you have my attention. Do you wish to fill me in before I examine this item further?"

"I'll start at the beginning then." Coughing several times to clear his throat, and possibly loosen the built-up taste from the odours in the room, Lestrade reached into his pocket, starting to remove a notepad before shaking his head and simply telling us what he knew. "A little over a week ago, a young lass, Miss Elaine Waterson, employed as the personal assistant to Sir Lyndon Marsden, of Marsden's Fine Apparel for Women – "

"I know that place," I blurted out, receiving a withering look from Holmes. "It's in Mayfair, isn't it?" A harrumphing cough from Holmes stopped me speaking further.

"Inspector," he told Lestrade, "please continue."

334

"As Doctor Watson said, Sir Lyndon's business is in Mayfair. Very salubrious establishment it is, too, if I may add. I certainly won't be taking Mrs. Lestrade there any time soon. Anyway, Miss Waterson didn't come into work on the Monday of last week, and hasn't shown up since."

"Nothing untoward in that," said Holmes. "Possibly sick, or . . . ." His eyes joined mine in staring at the foot upon the examination table.

"I'll get to that in a moment," said Lestrade. Pulling a piece of paper from his pocket and carefully unfolding it, he placed the page on the white sheet. "This was received on Wednesday of last week."

Holmes and I stepped closer and read the note. It was written in a thin scrawl, and I saw that it was in a woman's hand:

Sir Lyndon Marsden,

    We have taken your assistant, Miss Elaine Waterson. She will come to no harm if you comply with our demands.

    A personal advertisement will be placed in tomorrow's Times. *The addressee will be Mr. Myron Betterman. You are to follow the directions indicated and deliver the sum of one-thousand pounds to the location mentioned.*

    If you fail to meet these demands, then the results will not be conducive to Miss Waterson's health.

    Do not involve the police.

    Ignore us at your peril.

I looked back at the dismembered foot and gasped.

"I presume that this Sir Lyndon fellow ignored them?" asked Holmes.

"Actually no. If it weren't for one of Miss Waterson's co-workers, we wouldn't have known about any of this."

Pointing at the foot, Holmes asked, "What led to this then?"

"Ah," said Lestrade, pulling a small piece of newsprint from his pocket and laying it next to the letter. "This is the personal advertisement as mentioned." I had to peer closer, but could make out the slightly smudged print.

Mr. Myron Betterman,

    Happy to have made your acquaintance. Leave the item of concern in a satchel before the north face of the statue

*of the woman in Berkeley Square at mid-day Monday.
Come alone. Don't be late.*

"Sir Lyndon didn't make it to Berkeley Square then?" I asked.

"He did, but . . . ." Lestrade trailed off for a moment before continuing, "We were informed not long after the first note was received – the lady's co-workers found out, and were concerned. We – a small contingent of plain-clothed constables and myself – spread out across the Square in anticipation of apprehending the kidnapper."

A wry grin crossed Holmes's face as he turned towards Lestrade. "He didn't show, did he?"

"No," Lestrade answered with downcast eyes. "No, he didn't."

"So it is now Wednesday – two days after this aborted transaction, which seems to have been upset because of the police presence – and more than a week after the lady was taken. You should know, Inspector, that even London's finest look like policemen no matter what their dress – even to the uninformed."

"It would seem that way," Lestrade replied.

"What was Sir Lyndon's response?"

"His rage knew no bounds. My superiors were immediately notified, and that's why I'm now asking for your help. Then there is this," said Lestrade, pulling another piece of paper from his pocket. Unfolding it and placing it next to the other sheets, he added, "This arrived with the foot, early this morning."

"Before I read that, how was the foot presented? Surely not just left on the doorstep."

Lestrade shook his head. "No, no it wasn't. It was neatly wrapped, like a Christmas present, complete with a red ribbon. A gift card on the outside said it was for Sir Lyndon. Naturally, the first staff member to arrive had no clew, took it inside, and placed it on Sir Lyndon's desk."

A grimace crossed Holmes's face. "So the wrapping would be a useless place to search for information. Too many hands would have had the opportunity to touch it."

Nodding to a small table nearby, Lestrade said, "You can still have a look. It has been placed there for your inspection." Pointing to the third sheet he'd laid out, he said, "Read that."

Holmes and I bent lower to read the note. I could see that the scrawl was certainly different from the original delicate scratching of a woman. This consisted of a much heavier set of letters, revealing that the author had found it quite a bit more difficult to manipulate the pen than had the person who prepared the first note:

336

Sir,

You have involved the police. For that, you will pay, as has Miss Waterson.

The sum is now five-thousand pounds.

Deliver this amount to the same location in Berkeley Square by three o'clock this afternoon.

Comply with our demands to the letter, or you will receive several more Christmas presents, each containing another piece.

Come alone.

If any policemen are detected, then you will receive all of your presents at once.

"That is quite the definitive demand," murmured Holmes.

"Yes," said Lestrade.

"I assume Sir Lyndon wasn't happy with this either."

"Not in the slightest. I was called in directly and suffered several minutes of his cursing and red-faced fury before he finally stormed from the room. I had these items brought here as quickly as possible, Dufour's being the closest mortuary to Mayfair, and a sight more discreet for such an affair."

"Can we assume your superiors are not amused either?"

"That's an understatement."

"It's a good thing you brought me into it then."

"Can you find the kidnapper, before it's too late?"

"We don't have much time, and I have some questions that need answering, but I truly believe I can find the kidnapper and the poor unfortunate Miss Waterson."

I saw a slight frown cross Holmes's face as he was casting an eye over the packaging before he turned back towards the disembodied foot. Pulling his glass from an inside pocket, he proceeded to bend closer, examining the wound area closely.

Moving up next to him, I found my gaze drawn to the raw, meaty protrusion sticking from the top of the shoe. After a few moments, Holmes mumbled, "What say you, Watson?"

"The foot size is around six or seven, which for an average woman puts her height at around five-foot-four inches."

"Do we know Miss Waterson's height, Inspector?"

"As the Doctor said: She is five-foot-four inches in height, and of very slight build."

337

Indicating the amputation site, I continued with my observations. "The cut is clean, but shows a slight roughness, with some tearing. I would suggest it was made with something like a wood saw." Holding my hand out towards Holmes, I said, "Can I borrow your glass for a moment?" Taking the proffered instrument, I focused on the bones themselves. Each had been sawn through roughly, confirming my suspicions. Handing the glass back and pointing at the protruding tibia and fibula, I said, "See here? The cut across the bones is slightly jagged, I would suggest that my observation is correct, and the saw had been dulled before this horrid business. The roughness indicates a bluntness to the blade."

"Excellent. I thought as much myself." Taking back the glass and holding it in front of the Achilles Tendon, Holmes continued. "What do you think of this?"

It took me a moment to understand what he meant, but then I moved to one side. A dark shade ran along the back of the protruding segment of leg, disappearing into the heel of the shoe. "I need to see the foot."

"I agree," said Holmes, "and I would also like to examine the shoe by itself."

Delicately, I unlaced the shoe and prized the foot from within it.

"That was a little more difficult than it should have been, wasn't it?" Holmes asked.

"Yes, it was. I would have expected the foot to have become slightly smaller due to loss of blood."

"Quite, so, "said Holmes, picking up the shoe and studying it. "This is piquing my interest more and more."

Turning my attention to the foot, I rotated it and examined the heel and the Achilles Tendon, following the dark subcutaneous shadow.

"It was removed *post mortem*, wasn't it?"

Surprised by Holmes's quick summation, I nodded in agreement. "Yes. The body lay for quite some time, several hours, I presume, before the removal of the limb." Pointing to the dark shadow on the heel, and the discolouration by the tendon, I added, "Blood pooled here, as indicated by the lividity." Picking up Holmes's discarded glass, I focused on the wound itself. "Yes, I can see a thicker area of coagulation at the site of the cut, which would have been the exit point of the saw if working from front to back of the leg – not something that would occur in a fresh amputation."

"Any idea how long she was dead?" asked Lestrade, his curiosity showing at our discovery.

"I would have to say two or three days, but perhaps more. It depends on whether she was kept cold or not."

"In this weather? I can hardly get warm myself, even by my fire at night."

"Yes. So it could be anywhere up to a week."

"Still, that means it could be our poor unfortunate Miss Waterson."

Nodding, I said, "Yes, sadly."

"Then we've already failed."

"Not so fast, Inspector," interrupted Holmes. "We've only established the fact that the foot was removed from a corpse. Further investigations will be needed to confirm from whom – we have no proof that the foot belonged to the woman in question. It could belong to anyone."

Holmes returned the shoe to the table before pointing to the foot itself. "The owner didn't have regular access to the sort of bathing or grooming facilities one might attribute to an assistant working for a high-end fashion house." Following the direction of his finger, I saw that the foot's toenails were split, and could be called filthy, as well as exhibiting a marked fungal infection. I had been so intent on the wound and blood settlement that I had failed to observe that point.

"And I presume you noticed the slight swelling in the foot?" Holmes continued.

"Yes, I did. I put it down to the lass being a shop steward. Those poor girls are renowned for problems with swelling of the feet."

"Ah, yes, but our Miss Waterson is a personal assistant. We will have to confirm it, but I would expect her to be seated for the majority of the day, with short walking journeys to fetch items for Sir Lyndon."

"Right you are, Mr. Holmes. So if this foot doesn't belong to Miss Waterson, whose is it?"

"If I were to hazard a guess," said Holmes, gazing at the appendage intently for a few moments, "I would say it belonged to one of the streetwalkers who go missing or are found dead at far too regular intervals in our fair city." Turning his attention back to the shoe, he added, "This is where it gets interesting, though."

"Why?"

Carefully picking up the shoe, Holmes examined every side for a moment before continuing. "This shoe doesn't quite fit the foot – it's a bit too small, which is why we had trouble removing it. And it comes from Cobram and Sons of Oxford Street. Their mark is on the underside of the sole."

"That's a very expensive place to purchase shoes," I remarked. "Even for – no offence to Miss Waterson – a personal assistant."

A smile grew on Holmes's face. "Yes, it is quite an expensive item for Miss Waterson to possess. So that leaves us to our next port of call."

"Which is?" asked Lestrade.

"Miss Waterson's house. But first, one last item. Can you find me a sheet of paper?" When Holmes took the foot from me and stepped across to the nearby sink. He dripped some water onto the tips of his gloved fingers, then dabbed them gently onto the underside of the toes and ball of the foot before placing it onto a clean sheet of paper. Once satisfied, he returned the foot to the examination table and held the paper, showing the partial print formed from the dampened ingrained dirt on the base of the amputated appendage.

"And that's for what exactly?" I asked.

"Comparison," he replied.

Twenty minutes later, we stepped from Lestrade's carriage in front of a quaint three-storey terraced house in the middle of Chelsea.

"She has the lease of the entire building," Lestrade explained.

"Curious," I exclaimed, gazing at the beautifully presented streetscape before me. "This is an expensive house for a simple secretary."

"Personal assistant," Holmes corrected. "It seems to be the title afforded our Miss Waterson."

"Still."

"Yes, you are quite right," said Holmes, stepping towards the ground-floor entryway. "I find it quite bemusing that the subject of our investigations could afford such a lovely home." He turned toward Lestrade. "And a large home as well. How many servants?"

Lestrade shook his head. "None. All that space, and she occupied it by herself." He extracted a key from his pocket and all three of us filed into the entranceway. Without a word, Holmes headed upstairs, intending to search the lady's bedroom. I decided to linger downstairs and moved from room to room, hoping to gain a sense of the woman that lived there.

The house was sparsely furnished but showed an exquisite taste. I was extremely impressed by Miss Waterson's studious adherence to order. In the kitchen, there was no sign of any used dishes, all having been returned to their places once washed and dried. The parlour was neat and tidy, with no ash spillage from the small fireplace, and no half-burnt coal in the hearth.

Several photographs lined the mantelpiece, each sitting in exquisite silver frames. They showed a rather lovely young woman that I took to be our Miss Waterson, plus a pair of older folk with sour expressions. I speculated that they were possibly her parents. Another lone photograph showed the same pretty woman, but now dressed all in black, with the saddest look on her face. She stood before the doorway of a terraced house, different from the one we had entered. It took me a moment to realise the woman was likely depicted during a mourning phase in her life, possibly for her parents or someone close to her.

After gaining an appreciation for the presentation of the house and its almost museum-display quality, I was disappointed to find a lone ashtray sitting at the far end of the mantel. The stub of a cigar sat within, having burned down after the smoker placed it on the edge until only a small end remained. Sniffing the remains, I recoiled at the bitter stench. It had the hallmarks of an item smoked in the seedy dens frequented by lower-class workers and drunks, rather than something that would be found in such a beautifully appointed home.

Leaving the parlour, I made my way upstairs, joining Holmes and Lestrade in the lady's bedroom. Again, I was met with a well-appointed and neat arrangement. Holmes stood before a free-standing wardrobe, examining the clothing and rack of shoes.

Not wishing to break his train of thought, I stood silently in the doorway and made my own study of the room. Next to the wardrobe was a small dressing table with a mirror. An array of bottles sat before the mirror, with a small jewellery stand to one side, holding a single but striking necklace consisting of a thin chain of gold with a gold heart pendant. The pendant itself held a clear stone in its centre that must have been diamond. The necklace drew my attention almost immediately, as it appeared simple, elegant, and expensive, all at the same time – something that could never have been afforded on a simple assistant's wage. "Had she inherited money, perhaps – enough to explain the necklace and the large house?"

"Not at all," said Lestrade, in answer to my question. "She came from common folk, somewhere here in London. Where she obtained her funds has not yet been established."

Gazing at the contents of the table, I could see that indications that items were missing. Some of the fine facial powder that Miss Waterson used had fallen to the surface, leaving imprints of objects that had been removed. At least two larger items were missing. From my elementary understanding, I speculated that these might be a powder jar and bottle of facial crème. The table was also devoid of a hairbrush, comb, and hand mirror – items I attributed to women of all ages.

I was about to mention this to Holmes when he stepped away from the wardrobe and approached the table. "Items are missing," I said, jumping in to voice my observations.

"Yes. I observed that earlier," he said, leaving me slightly deflated. With his hand pressed to his chin and a finger pointing upwards, he continued. "There are two pairs of shoes missing, and likely some items of clothing, though I can't tell how many."

Joining him near the wardrobe, I spotted the vacant spaces at the bottom of the cupboard.

"She left of her own accord then?" asked Lestrade.

"It would look that way," said Holmes. "But whether that is because she planned a trip, or if she went willingly with her supposed abductor is another matter altogether."

Glancing back at the array of shoes, it was apparent that these sported the same mix of elegance and practicality as that accompanying the amputated foot. Pointing towards a specific pair, I said, "Those look very much the same as the shoe we saw earlier."

Holmes reached for one of the shoes, examining its underside. Nodding, he said, "Yes. Cobram and Sons, inscribed on the base of the sole."

"That's impressive. Two pairs from that establishment."

"Actually," said Holmes, studying the shoe, "we can only be certain that these were hers, but we do now have confirmation that Miss Waterson possessed at least one pair." Turning the shoe around, he held his glass up to the dark writing on the inside of the heel. "Yes, the same size as well."

Carrying the shoe to the table, he pulled out the paper with the foot's imprint on it. Then he removed a small folding knife from his pocket and proceeded to slit the top of the shoe, so that he could then pull it apart and see the inside where the foot normally rested. Then he compared it to the dirty imprint of the detached foot before passing the shoe and the sheet to me.

"Do you see it?"

Lestrade bustled over and leaned in as well. "I do," said the inspector.

All three of us had come to the same conclusion: The feet were completely different, but it wasn't really a surprise, considering the condition of the amputated foot at the morgue. The big toe on the paper imprint was larger than that impressed into the bottom of this shoe, and it appeared to bend towards the right, an indication of the beginning of a deformity from standing too long on rough, slightly uneven ground. The other toes failed to line up evenly as well.

"The shoe at the morgue," explained Holmes, "definitely belonged to Miss Waterson. The patterns within it conform to this matching shoe here – and neither of the Cobram shoes have the same wear as what we see from the amputated foot. It isn't much, but this, combined with the probable evidence that the foot was amputated after death, plus the condition and slight swelling of the detached appendage, allow us to be essentially certain that the foot does not belong to Miss Waterson."

"Then who?" asked Lestrade.

"And why?" I added.

"I think extortion is still our main *modus operandi*. And as to who the foot belongs to, I think I shall make some further enquiries."

"Where?" asked Lestrade.

"I'm unsure as yet, but I believe I already generally know the source of the limb in question. However, there is no haste to determine that at this stage. Our immediate need is to find the whereabouts of Miss Waterson, as there is every chance that she is alive and in good health."

"Marvellous," said Lestrade, his face turning quickly to concern. "But where?"

"Ah, that I do not know," said Holmes as he turned and almost darted from the room in his haste to leave.

Lestrade and I followed him downstairs more slowly, where Holmes was standing at the mantel, examining the cigar stub and photographs. Sniffing the cigar remains, he noted that it was Jamaican in in origin – something rather rare in England, possibly indicating that the owner had brought it himself from the Caribbean. From there, he moved from room to room for some time before ducking into a small nook near the kitchen. The tiny room contained a roll-top desk which clattered when Holmes opened it by the handles. A small array of notes and bills lay upon the green leather of the desk's interior.

Holmes picked up several and quickly read and returned them before holding one before him. "Was there ever any mention of the lady having additional premises in Rotherhithe, Inspector?"

Lestrade shook his head. "No, why?"

"Well, Miss Waterson has several letters and bills, all bearing the same Rotherhithe address. This one," he indicated the page in his hand, "is the latest coal bill." Reading it, he added, "Not very high, which would indicate that the heating isn't used very often."

"Strange," Lestrade noted. "Why would she have bills from another address?"

"Perhaps it's her parents' old house?" I suggested. "There's evidence in the parlour that her parents are deceased. If she has found the money to pay for a residence of this station, she may have been able to afford to keep the other as well."

"Good point, Watson," Holmes said. "It also makes me wonder if Miss Waterson spends some of her time there – perhaps on the weekends when she doesn't need to attend to her employer."

"That might account for the missing items," I said. "And there is the photograph of her in mourning, depicted before another house. That could be this Rotherhithe place."

"Interesting," said Holmes. "I think we should visit it, just to ascertain if our Miss Waterson is there. But first, I feel that we should visit the

343

gentleman that has been maintaining this property for Miss Waterson's use."

"And who would that be?" asked Lestrade.

"Why, isn't that obvious?" asked Holmes, lifting one eyebrow as he turned to glance at Lestrade. "Sir Lyndon, of course."

Stepping from Lestrade's carriage for the second time that morning, we found ourselves before an impressive four-story, white-stoned Georgian mansion, taking up residence in the wealthy neighborhood of Belgravia. All around us, the houses were covered with Christmas decorations, but none could compare with Sir Lyndon's home – an enormous wreath upon the door, and smaller ones that matched on every ground floor window. Stretches of garland were draped along the front between the various upstairs windows. It was almost too much, but it certainly outshone the efforts of the neighbors.

"I'm in the wrong business," said Lestrade, glaring at the expansive premises before us. "There seems to be money in selling ladies dresses."

"I think you'll find that the work you do, Inspector," said Holmes, "far exceeds the amount of good created through Sir Lyndon's endeavours."

Lestrade nodded. "But it would be nice to treat the missus from time to time."

"Quite so, and I'm sure you will be able to work your way up to Chief Inspector or even Superintendent in the coming years, which should furnish you with more in the way of honest income to help supplement your lifestyle," said Holmes.

"Well, there's always hope, isn't there."

"It is a wonderful property, gentlemen," I pressed, feeling the nip in the air deep in my bones, "but it's also a bitterly cold day and time is of the essence. Shouldn't we move on?"

"Sorry," said Lestrade, moving up to the front door. The knocking on the door was soon met with a look of slight disdain from an elderly butler.

"Yes, may I help you?" he asked, his eyes peering down his nose towards the three of us.

"Inspector Lestrade of Scotland Yard. My colleagues, Mr. Holmes and Dr. Watson, and I would like to see Sir Lyndon. It is on a matter of urgency, and at his request."

"The master isn't in," began the butler, before a female voice broke out behind him.

"Who is it, Johnson?" the voice asked.

Before the man could turn, a woman that I presumed to be in her late fifties bustled to the front door, almost pushing the aging butler away. "Hello, gentlemen. Come in. It's frightfully horrid out there."

After we'd moved into the entranceway, decorated just as thickly for Christmas, Johnson took our coats and hats while the woman introduced herself. "I'm Lady Beryl Marsden." Indicating a nearby doorway, she added, "Please, let us adjourn to the parlour." Turning to the butler, she directed, "Johnson: Coffee, tea, and biscuits for our guests please." We left a slightly mystified Johnson and assembled in the adjacent room, a welcoming place where a warm fire glowed in the hearth. As we found our seats, I breathed deeply – somewhere in the house, treats were being baked for the holidays, and the odours from the distinctive spices filled the air. "Now," asked the lady, "what can I do for you gentlemen?"

Lestrade spoke up. "I am Inspector Lestrade of Scotland Yard, your Ladyship. Umm, I have been assigned to the delicate matter at your husband's workplace."

"Oh, yes? What matter?"

"Why, the case of a kidnapped employee."

"Oh, dear." Her face showed shock – I wasn't sure if it was from the newly acquired news or the fact her husband had possibly declined to share it with her. "Who? Not that lovely Mr. Benedict?"

"No, ma'am. It's Sir Lyndon's assistant, Miss Waterson."

At the mention of that name, Lady Beryl's face grew dark. "Oh," she said, with such disapproval that I was surprised she didn't rise and usher us from her house as fast as she could.

"You know Miss Waterson?" Holmes asked.

Turning towards him, Lady Beryl's face brightened, either through the application of a careful but well-rehearsed façade, or by way of a genuine interest in our presence. I was unsure.

"You would be Mr. Sherlock Holmes."

"That's correct."

"I'm happy to meet you, Mr. Holmes. I am a long-time friend of Honoria Westphail. I believe you would know her niece, Miss Helen Stoner. Honoria was most delighted by the way you helped her niece – I think it was four or five years ago now – and saved the young lass from a dreadful calamity. She was most effusive and described you in great detail," Then, turning towards me, she added, "And also you Dr. Watson."

Lestrade began to ask another question when Johnson arrived at the doorway. Lady Beryl turned towards him and said, "Ah, good – coffee and tea." Eyeing a small plate of pastries on the side, she thanked Johnson for his thoughtfulness and took the tray from him. Placing it on a nearby side table, she turned and asked us what we would prefer. Lestrade was becoming impatient at the delay, but I knew Holmes would be more than happy to engage Lady Beryl for some hidden details that we were unlikely to gain from Sir Lyndon himself.

Finally, after the coffee and cakes were served, Lestrade was able to ask his question. "Lady Beryl," he started, "we have come to apprise Sir Lyndon of our findings and ask him some more pertinent questions. He had asked that I make a report to him. Can you tell us where he has gone or when he will return? Time is of the essence."

"The last I saw of Lyndon was when he stormed back into the house earlier this morning, not long after the shop should have opened. Within moments, he left once again. He was in a frightful state, such that I didn't wish to even contemplate, let alone become involved. He has been in such a distasteful temper of late. We've hardly spoken a word."

"He hasn't confessed anything to you then?" asked Holmes.

"Confessed?" She gave him a speculative look. "About what? As I said, we've hardly spoken," Lady Beryl answered. "If there's something I should know about, then by all means, please tell me."

It was Lestrade who took the lead. "As we mentioned, there has been a kidnapping: Sir Lyndon's assistant, Miss Waterson."

"Most horrid, but that girl – " Lady Beryl started, but thought better of saying anything further and became quiet.

"Is there something about Miss Waterson that might be helpful?" I asked, assuming an air of innocence.

"Well," she replied, "kidnapping was the least of my worries where that girl is concerned."

"Why is that?" I prodded.

Lady Beryl stared into my face for a moment. Her eyes bore through me as if examining my reasons for the question before she relaxed and let the truth spill forth. By the end of her admission, my heart went out to this poor woman.

Dropping her head, she began to speak, slowly at first, and fighting her inner shame.

"It was around Christmas time last year – Can it have been a whole year? – that I first became aware . . . ." Then she gave a start and raised her eyes to stare at the far wall. "Lyndon and I have been married for many years. Our children are grown and gone off to make their way in the world. I had hoped that the time we now had alone together would re-engender a spark in our marriage, but . . . ." Stopping for a moment, she took a deep breath. I could tell that tears were welling behind her eyes, held in check through sheer force of will. "Last Christmas it was. One day I came home after Lyndon had already arrived, and as Johnson was busy, I put my coat on the rack. I bumped Lyndon's coat and noticed something in one of his

346

pockets. Finding a small box, I almost placed it back without further investigation, but curiosity gained the best of me, and I open it to find the most beautiful gold necklace – a delicate gold chain and a small gold heart pendant with a diamond in the centre. I couldn't believe it. Placing it back where I found it, I assumed that Lyndon had bought it for me, and when Christmas came around, I received a similar-sized box from him."

She took another deep breath and pulled a small kerchief from her sleeve, wiping at corners of her eyes before continuing. "My heart swelled as I unwrapped the little present, but then it sank into my shoes when all I found enclosed was a silk scarf. No sign of the necklace. He had bought it for another. It was then I truly knew that our marriage was nought but a sham."

"Oh, dear," I said.

"But that wasn't the worst of it," she added. "A week or so after Christmas, we had an engagement at the store – to welcome the New Year and congratulate the employees on a job well done for the previous year." Taking another deep breath, she finished off with, "It was then I realised who my 'replacement' was."

"Miss Waterson?" I asked.

Nodding, she continued. "Yes. There she was, as bright as day, dressed in a gown that she had no right to possess. And there around her neck – "

"The necklace," finished Holmes, already knowing the answer.

Turning towards my friend, the tears finally forming and sliding down her face, she nodded and dabbed at her eyes.

"We're so sorry," I stated, my concern for this woman trumping any care for the case at hand. "Have you confronted him?"

A small smile came to her face as she shook her head. "What else is there to do but accept it? I'm a matron, almost in my sixties. I have grown so used to this life. Over the last year, I have simply resolved myself to play the part of a loving, doting wife. I wouldn't wish to throw the spectre of scandal over the lives of my children, and I couldn't live with the shame in polite company."

This was something I had contemplated before. Even though the upper class live lives of affluence and influence, there is – even for them – a simmering underbelly of discontent within their ranks. In this house, it had been made all the more real by the events unfolding over the last week.

I was about to make such a comment when the bell rang. Lady Beryl moved to the connecting doorway to watch as Johnson attended to the newcomer. She must have recognised the visitor, as she sighed before stepping into the entranceway. Instead of waiting for the door to be opened, she turned toward the rear of the house and quickly walked away.

Within moments, a red-faced man appeared. He was portly, balding, and I made him to be in his mid-fifties. He was sweating profusely and breathing heavily from some unknown vigorous activity. As his eyes fell on the inspector, his thin voice bellowed out. "Lestrade, what in blazes are you doing here? Have you found her?" Taking a quick look at Holmes and me, he added, "And who are these two layabouts?"

"Sir Lyndon," Lestrade said, rising slowly to bring a sense of calm to the situation. "This is Sherlock Holmes and his colleague, Doctor John Watson. I've asked them to assist. I didn't think you would mind the added support."

"Holmes? The detective? You must be at your wit's end, Lestrade!" Anger began to bristle behind his thick eyebrows, countered when Holmes spoke up.

"Sir Lyndon, forgive our involvement, but we have already discovered an important fact."

"What?" he almost bellowed.

"We are extremely confident that the foot you received does not belong to Miss Waterson. She may be still alive – something that I believe may not have been the case if you had successfully paid the ransom."

Sir Lyndon's eyes opened wide in anger as he stared indignantly at Holmes. "What are you suggesting, sir?"

"In many of these cases, the kidnappers have no intention of returning their hostage. They merely wait for the funds to be given over, and then they execute the captive to remove any possibility of identification. Scotland Yard's involvement has prevented this occurrence, and probably ensured the continued health of young Miss Waterson."

"Nonsense. This is simply a business deal. This – " Sir Lyndon waved his hand through the air, searching for words. " – this *villain* has absconded with something I want. He has set his terms, and I am happy to meet them. Once I've paid up, he'll hand over Elaine. Simple as that."

"I beg you not to do that, Sir Lyndon," said Lestrade. "This 'villain', as you say, may not hold up his end of the bargain."

Sir Lyndon's face grew dire. "Of course that wasn't Elaine's foot – I never thought for a moment it was. And if you hadn't interfered, Elaine would be back in her rooms by now, and all this would be behind us."

Feeling the need to dissipate the ill feelings in the room and to satisfy my curiosity on one matter, I spoke up. "Sir Lyndon, you seemed very out of breath when you entered. I am a doctor – Is there any way in which I can help?"

His eyes fell on me, almost as if he hadn't taken account of my presence earlier. "I sped home from the bank. I'm afraid I'm a little out of shape. Too much work. Too much food. Why?"

348

"I had wondered if it was due to smoking. Cigars, perhaps."

I saw Holmes smile at my deftness at recalling the cigar found on the Miss Waterson's mantel. Yet the mystery deepened with Sir Lyndon's answer.

"Smoking? Filthy habit. I have never and would never smoke, and I'm incensed by your suggestion."

Holding my hands up in supplication, I said, "I do apologise. I am a medical man and simply seek to identify the most obvious causes of any malady. I congratulate you on such a stance."

Sir Lyndon's anger diminished slightly. He turned towards Lestrade and asked, "If the foot doesn't belong to Elaine, then who does it belong to?"

Holmes answered for the inspector. "That we don't know yet. But we have investigated Miss Waterson's Chelsea flat, and came here to report, but also to seek out further information."

"Yes?" The man seemed suddenly wary after the mention of the lady's residence.

"The Chelsea flat," continued Holmes. "You arranged that, of course, and you pay her rent and other bills."

Sir Lyndon looked shocked. He blustered his answer. "What? What do you mean? I . . . I don't know what you mean!"

"Come now, sir. It is certainly you who gives Miss Waterson an allowance for clothes, food, and other trivialities. You are a benevolent employer, but surely no one would expect that a mere personal assistant could afford the upkeep on such a residence. There is also the matter of how quickly you took it upon yourself to organise the monies to pay for Miss Waterson's ransom. That is something that any other employer would be very reticent to undertake."

Staring into Holmes's stoic expression for a moment, Sir Lyndon's face relaxed as he became resolved to his unmasking. He took a look towards the open doorway before striding across and shutting the door. Turning back, he answered, "Yes, yes you are right. I'm a damned fool, but have to admit I've fallen for the young lass. Things haven't been well between me and Lady Beryl for many years. I'm old, but still young enough . . . ."

He moved to a large, overstuffed chair and dropped wearily into it. "Elaine and I have formed a . . . a *relationship* over the last year or so. I moved her into the flat to . . . have a place where we can meet. When I found she was missing, and then that damned note arrived, I dropped everything to make sure I could get her back."

His downward gaze had hidden his expression, but as he lifted his face to us, I could see tears forming at the corners of his eyes. "When that

God-awful thing arrived, I realised that it could mean the worst, but I still hoped she was alive." Reaching into his jacket he pulled out a thick wad of notes. "I spent all morning arranging for the new ransom. Regardless of what you advise, Inspector, I will happily give it just to have her back safe and sound."

"I hope we won't need to pay it," responded Lestrade.

Staring at the policeman, Sir Lyndon said, "I don't care. I will get her back, no matter what it takes." Abruptly standing, he indicated the doorway. "Now gentlemen, I won't lie, but I have matters to attend to. By this evening I will have Elaine back, one way or another – with or without your help."

We shuffled out to find Johnson awaiting us with our coats and hats in his arms. As we prepared ourselves for the chill outside, Lestrade made one last appeal. "Sir Lyndon, I implore you to remain at home. Don't give in to these demands. It will not end well."

"Pish-posh!" was Sir Lyndon's only reply. He bustled us from his house, and that angry, red face that was the last sight I beheld there as the door closed quickly.

Holmes wore an expression of irritation before turning from the Marsden house and scanning the street. Then a grin grew on his face as he spied a young street urchin and hurried over toward him. Even from that distance, I realised that the boy must be one of his Irregulars – a fact that became clearer as the day grew long.

"He's just going to waste his money and get the girl killed," spat Lestrade, his impatience with Sir Lyndon spilling out from his normally calm but gruff exterior.

"Sir Lyndon will have observers of his own this time," said Holmes with a look in Lestrade's direction. "And they won't look like policemen." Pulling out his watch, he continued, "It's now just past one o'clock. We still have a good two hours before Sir Lyndon pays the ransom. Our next destination should provide some further intelligence as to the overall situation."

Some time later, as our carriage pulled into the more tightly packed and altogether unpleasant area of Rotherhithe, I started to worry that Holmes's optimism might be misplaced. Suspicious eyes followed us as we wound our way through the constricted streets, and I felt their stare stay upon me as we alighted before our destination.

The tiny, terraced house was worlds away from the two elegantly fronted addresses we had previously encountered. This whole section consisted of cramped three-storey buildings filled with various rooms let for lodging. Each of the buildings on this block sported yellowed and peeling paint with faded black trims to the windows. Unlike Sir Lyndon's extensively decorated digs, there was no sign of Christmas here whatsoever.

According to the information gathered at Miss Waterson's Chelsea abode, the apartment we sought was before us, at this address. Its darkened windows and worn and rotting woodwork gave it the appearance of abandonment, but I knew that it was actually a hive of local residents, as were the surrounding structures.

Thinking of the lady's fine Chelsea home, I asked, "Are we sure this is the place?" But I knew it was – this was the house in the photograph.

"This is the address upon the coal pedlar's bill," Holmes replied. Without waiting further, he led us up the stairs and tried to turn the door knob, but it was strangely locked. He tried again, and then knocked loudly. Silence greeted us until he repeated the announcement. Then the quiet was broken by a harsh voice from the basement alcove of the neighbouring house.

"She's gone out!" it cried.

The three of us turned and glanced towards the owner of the voice. There, below street level, sat the solitary figure of a woman, who I made out to be well into her seventies. She sat on a rotting armchair, surrounded by a cloud of smoke from the cigarette hanging from her lips.

"What do you mean, 'She'?" asked Lestrade. "How do you know who we're looking for?"

"Ain't but one lady lives in that building. She bought it somehow and kicked everyone else out – even the ones that had nowhere else to go. Keeps it locked up, except for when she comes by sometimes."

This was news. How could the lady have the resources to acquire this property – even as run-down and filthy as it was?

"Do you know when she will be back?" asked Lestrade.

"Why? What has she done now?"

"What does this lady look like?" asked Holmes. The woman was silent for a moment, weighing her suspicions, before relenting and giving a good description of the missing personal assistant."

"Do you know when she'll be back?" asked Lestrade again. "We simply wish to speak with her – to ensure that she's in good health."

"Looked pretty healthy to me. I'm more worried about why you men want to talk to her." Before anyone could answer, however, the old woman continued, blowing out a huge cloud of smoke. "It's none of my business. Her mother, God rest her soul, would turn in her grave, I tell you."

"And why would that be?" asked Holmes.

"Well, ever since Elaine started coming back, she's been – How d'you say? – not her mother's little girl."

"Elaine," asked Holmes. "Elaine Waterson?"

"That's her. Grew up here. That was her parent's house. They let the rooms until they died. Then she took it on. I kept an eye on it for her, but then a few weeks ago, she turned everybody out. I'm not surprised – she isn't much like her mother."

"A bit flighty?" I asked. "Irresponsible?"

"Umm, more a bit of a charva," she said. "And bringin' back the men? What would her mother think? It's like Kings Cross Station here, some weeks."

"Oh," I answered, suddenly taken aback.

"That new one's a big 'un though."

"New one?" asked Holmes.

"Gorgeous he is," the old woman said, a smile coming to her mouth, showing a severe lack of teeth. "Taller than all of you. Broad across the shoulders. Huge bushy beard, and the strangest thing – a length of hair at the back."

"Long like a queue?" asked Holmes. "Or is it tied up?"

"He leaves it long."

"Have you observed any tattoos?"

"I'm not the sort to stick my nose in, but now you mention it, I did. I bumped into them in the street a while back. The big fellow was holding a sack, but I saw letters tattooed on his knuckles. I could only make out an 'aitch on his left hand, but his right had the word *Sultan* on it."

"Hmm," murmured Holmes.

"What does it mean?" I asked.

"Well, the queue might be a tar, worn by Her Majesty's sailors, and the tattoo might be the name of a ship. Often sailor memorialize their first ship that way. Possibly his was the *HMS Sultan*. She was an ironclad in the channel fleet for many years. I think she's now in the Mediterranean."

Stroking his chin for a moment, Holmes finally said, "These new facts, added to the cigar stub we found, may mean that the man was in the Navy, but no longer. Possibly he's moved into the merchant trade." Staring upward into the clouded sky, Holmes thought for many moments, until Lestrade and I became agitated at his silence. I was aware that three o'clock, and the payment of the next ransom demand, was rapidly approaching.

I noticed the old lady gawking at us with a wry smile on her face as she puffed on another cigarette. Holmes finally broke the silence. "Inspector, you may need to send someone to the nearby docks to see which ships are leaving for the Caribbean today – possibly Jamaica."

"Why the rush?" Lestrade asked.

"Our quarry may be planning to leave England this evening, if the ransom demand is met this time. And the cigar is just the smallest indication that the man we seek has Caribbean ties."

Surprise on his face, Lestrade bustled back towards our carriage and spoke with the driver. Then he climbed aboard and they drove away. Holmes turned back towards the woman below us and said, "Thank you, Madam. As we said, we are here to see Miss Waterson. We shall bid you a good day and wait for her inside."

Indifferent, the woman simply continued to puff on her cigarette, adding, "I would take care around that fellow of hers. Big bloke. Seems to have a touch of anger about him too."

"Thank you," finished Holmes before moving again to the front door. Extracting his picks, he made short work of the old lock, and within moments we found ourselves inside.

The house smelled from a touch of hidden damp, and also the heavy tang of the same type of cigar that we'd found in the Chelsea flat. Holmes left me to bustle off toward the bowels of the house, seemingly with a singular idea front and centre in his mind.

I remained in the parlour, awaiting Lestrade's return. Soon he appeared in the doorway, a slight grin crossing his face as he spied me standing before him. "I assume that the front door was unlocked?" Understanding the intent of his question, I simply shrugged, causing an expulsion of breath and a slight shake of his head. "Mr. Holmes – what the devil is he playing at?"

When my eyes shifted to the passageway that Holmes had taken, the inspector started to move in that direction. I began to follow as he passed by, but a sharp retort from a female voice in the entranceway stopped us both.

"'Ere! What's the meaning of this?"

Lestrade and I spun at the sound of the voice and I spied one of the loveliest faces I had seen in my life. "Miss Waterson?" said Lestrade, to which the young woman nodded, tentatively. She was carrying a sack which, from the bit I could see, contained something wrapped in butcher's paper, and one or two green vegetables.

"Yes, and who would you be?" she said, her reaction to our impertinence strong in her voice.

"Inspector Lestrade of Scotland Yard, and this is Doctor John Watson. He is helping me with my investigations."

"Pleased to meet you, Miss," I said, my eyes dropping to her untouched left foot. "I'm glad that you are in full health."

Miss Waterson's eyes followed my gaze, before darting back towards Lestrade. She looked as if she might turn and bolt. "Why are you here? My Trevor will be very mad when he returns."

Presuming that "Trevor" was the fellow described by the neighbor, my retort was cut off by Holmes's arrival in the parlour. "That's if your Trevor returns at all," he said.

All eyes turned towards him. "What do you mean?" said Miss Waterson. "Why wouldn't he return? And who are you now?"

Stepping further into the room, Holmes took a slight bow and said, "I am Sherlock Holmes, consulting detective. I'm helping Inspector Lestrade in the matter of your supposed kidnapping." Holmes's eyes dropped to the woman's left foot, a wry grin came to his face as he said, "And you are Miss Elaine Waterson. It's good to see you fully intact."

"Why do you gentlemen keep saying that? And why are you so interested in my feet?" She glanced down and then asked, "And why won't Trevor return?"

"First things first, I suppose," said Holmes. "The condition of the bedroom seems to indicate that this Trevor, if that is his name, has removed both his items and himself from this abode."

"What?" Miss Waterson cried, before bursting past the three of us and heading into the rear of the house. Moments later she returned, a look of intense shock on his face. "All of his clothes. Everything. Gone. His bag – gone." Tears welled in the corners of her eyes as she glanced up at us. "Is he gone?"

I moved across, taking the sack from her, setting it upon the floor, and guiding the stricken woman to a nearby seat. As we passed, Holmes pulled out his watch and, checking the time, said, "Not quite, but it probably won't be long." Glancing at Lestrade, he continued. "Inspector, it's now two o'clock. We still have time, but it will be close thing."

"What's going on?" I heard the poor woman whimper.

"Ah," said Holmes, "now that's an interesting tale."

We related all that had happened so far. Miss Waterson's face remained placid during the story of the first ransom note, leaving me with a sense that none of that part was new. It was when Lestrade mentioned the delivery of the amputated foot that the lady's eyes grew wide in shock bordering on terror. "A foot? A real foot?" she exclaimed. "Who's was it?"

"Well, supposedly it was meant to be yours, but obviously," Holmes explained, indicating Miss Waterson's intact appendage, "it isn't."

"That's horrible. Why would Trevor . . . ?" Suddenly she went quiet. Her simple retort told Holmes and Lestrade almost everything they needed to know.

354

"It may be pertinent, at this juncture, for you to relate everything you know on the matter," suggested Holmes.

Miss Waterson seemed to deflate as the pent-up anxiety bled from her body. "It was Trevor's idea. He's lovely. I met him about three months ago. We had a bit of a fling before he was back on ship. When he came home to port, two weeks ago, he told me all about his idea."

"I can only assume that it was you who wrote the first ransom note," Holmes asked. When she nodded, he continued. "Does Sir Lyndon know about this Trevor?"

A shocked look crossed Miss Waterson's face. "No, of course not. Why would I tell him? He'd cut me off straight away." Her eyes grew wide, and tears began to form at the edges. "It's just that Sir Lyndon is kind, but . . . ." her face twisted into a little grimace. "I'm so much younger than him. I . . . I need to be with someone my age."

"Please tell us the rest," I said.

"Trevor wants to leave the sea life. That's all he's ever really known, but he doesn't want to stay in the city. He has hopes to buy a farm in the Cotswolds. We're going to live in the fresh air. Raise some sheep." She hesitated for a moment. "And some children." Looking from face to face, tears fell down her cheek. "I didn't think Sir Lyndon would miss the money. He's been so good to me, and he's so well off.

"He was so very angry on Monday, but I thought it was because his captain said he needed to do one more trip to see out his contract. So he didn't get the ransom?"

"He did not," Holmes replied. "That was when your Trevor devised his second plan – one that was all his idea." He looked at Lestrade. "The heavier script of the second note, with the intent of the Christmas present and the haste to receive the ransom."

"Must have been," answered Miss Waterson. "He's been so quiet since. Kept disappearing for hours on end. Once we sent the note . . . asking for the money . . . we agreed that I couldn't go back to Sir Lyndon. We've been here ever since, in my parents' old house. I woke up this morning and Trevor was nowhere to be seen. I had to duck out to get something for his tea. I wanted it to be nice when he got back. I bought a bit of beef. I thought he'd be here, but – " Sobs broke out of her, followed by a stream of tears. "He's gone!"

It took some time to calm the poor woman down. Holmes pulled out his pocket watch once again and I knew that time was passing. Somewhere Trevor was waiting to pick up the ransom, which would certainly be paid this time by Sir Lyndon.

It wasn't until a knock on the door that Miss Waterson came back to herself. Looking up, she exclaimed, "Trevor?"

355

It was Lestrade that opened the door to reveal his driver. After a few moments of whispered conversation, he motioned for Holmes and me to join him, away from the young lady. In hushed tones related his news. "There are two Caribbean cargo ships in port. Both are moored nearby – only five minutes away." He looked at his watch. "Nearly three. This Trevor will be retrieving the money now, and heading that way. We can be there well before he turns up." Nodding towards the young woman, he asked, "What about her?

Although we agreed that from a legal perspective, Lestrade had every right to arrest Miss Waterson for her involvement in the original kidnapping plot, we also agreed to defer doing so until we had dealt with the actual mastermind behind the crime.

As we left the house and drove to the docks, Miss Waterson gave us more information about her errant beau, as she now seemed to have turned against him completely upon realizing that he had no intention of returning to her once he had Sir Lyndon's money. The man's full name was Trevor Farnsley, and her description matched that provided by the old woman next door, and included a confirmation that the tattoos on Farnsley's knuckles indeed read *H.M.S. Sultan*. He had described his previous Navy service aboard that ship to her, and after he was discharged several years earlier, he'd found work plying his trade between England and the Caribbean.

The most useful piece of information that Miss Waterson provided was the name of Farnsley's current ship, the *Batavia*, whose home port was Kingston in Jamaica.

The trip in Lestrade's carriage was swift. We arrived at around a quarter-past-three. Leaving Miss Waterson in the custody of his driver, Lestrade went in search of additional reinforcements. After he returned, we went straight to the *Batavia*'s berth and consulted the Chief Steward. The man had the aged look of one who had spent most of his life at sea. A quick conversation confirmed that Farnsley wasn't yet on board, but was due before the ship weighed anchor at four o'clock.

As we deliberated on our next course of action, two more carriages appeared on the dock, filled with officers. Lestrade quickly instructed the constables aboard to make themselves scarce and wait for his signal. The carriages were driven away and hidden behind some nearby buildings.

A few minutes later, a small, filthy-looking lad appeared around the corner of one of the large warehouses. He glanced once behind himself, then over at Holmes before running for all his worth towards my good friend. A short, but agitated conversation ensued before Holmes motioned towards the opposite corner and followed behind the boy. As Holmes passed me, he whispered, pointing down the roadway leading onto the

356

docks. "The lad was there when the ransom was retrieved. Farnsley is on his way – he's coming in a hansom."

"How did he know where to find you?" Lestrade asked.

"I told the Irregulars to deliver a message to any ships leaving this afternoon for the Caribbean. We were bound to be at one of them."

Following behind Holmes, we ducked down the tight alleyway and waited. Lestrade took up station at the closest point and kept watch around the corner. "Here he comes."

Just as the hansom stopped near the gangway, Lestrade hurried away, with Holmes and me hot on his heels. As we closed in, the hansom moved off, revealing a large cloud of cigar smoke circling the tall well-built figure of a man speaking with the Chief Steward.

Lestrade wasted no time, stopping only a few yards from the pair and speaking loud and clear. "Trevor Farnsley, I am Inspector Lestrade of Scotland Yard. We have reason to believe you are involved in the kidnap of Miss Elaine Waterson, and extortion of Sir Lyndon Marsden."

Turning to face the policeman, Farnsley's expression was a mix of horror and rage. He turned in an attempt to gain the gangway, but the Chief Steward swiftly blocked his way. Pointing at Lestrade, he said, "I think you should talk to the policeman first. We don't want no trouble on board."

Rather than talk, Farnsley threw his rucksack to the ground and balling his fists, strode towards the shorter Lestrade. "I've done nothing. Elaine is in her house in Rotherhithe. No harm has been done to her."

"There is the matter of five-thousand pounds that you have extorted from her employer," Lestrade said, keeping his eyes on the larger man.

Shrugging, Farnsley said, "What money? I haven't taken any money." Throwing his hands to the side, he continued, "Search me if you like. I got nothing but a few pounds."

"Ah, but that isn't quite true, is it?" said Holmes stepping forward, his hand grasping his revolver. "I had you followed from Berkeley Square all the way here." He nodded towards the little fellow peeking around the building corner that we occupied moments before. "My spies tell me that you picked up a small leather satchel at the base of the statue in Berkeley Square before hiring a hansom and heading here, with a brief stop at an address in Limehouse. I'm sure we could find the key if needs be, and at that address, a quick search should reveal the satchel, with its rich contents awaiting your return."

Farnsley's expression turned completely to rage, his eyes darting around for a quick exit. As he made to run, Lestrade pulled a police whistle from his pocket and gave two long blasts. Within seconds, the squad of blue-coated bobbies appeared from around several corners and headed

357

towards us. The cigar fell from Farnsley's mouth as he gaped at the constables.

"You're knicked, Farnsley," said Lestrade. "We'll get all the details from you back at the station, but you aren't going nowhere for a long time."

The tall man bellowed with rage and started again towards Lestrade, but the sight of Holmes's revolver stopped him in his tracks. He swore and cursed under his breath until the paddy wagon arrived to take him to the Yard.

"So Farnsley confirmed that he never intended to take Miss Waterson with him?"

"No," said Lestrade, leaning back and taking a sip of tea. We were sitting in Baker Street, and around us were a substantial amount of Christmas decorations – holly and ivy and seasonal candles, all brought in by Mrs. Hudson once she'd been able to make the effort while Holmes was away. I knew that he found them distasteful at best, but it pleased our landlady to celebrate the season, and therefore he would put up with it for a while.

"After we began to question him, it all came out. He met Miss Waterson several months ago, in a tiny pub down in Limehouse. His ship was in port. He was out with some of the other boys. They struck up a conversation and then a relationship. On the next voyage away, Farnsley came up with his plan and convinced the girl to go along with it."

"But not all of it?" asked Holmes.

"No. She agreed to ask for the thousand pounds, but knew nothing more about the rest of it. She had dreams of moving to the country – dreams that Farnsley used to his advantage. She thought that he'd already collected the ransom, and that they would leave London soon. But in the end, he only had eyes for the money."

"The cad," I exclaimed.

"Precisely. Well, he'll be at Her Majesty's pleasure for some time to come."

"I have one last question."

"Yes, Doctor?"

"The foot? Whose was it?"

"Ah," said Holmes. "I can answer that, and the inspector can correct me if I'm wrong." Lestrade nodded his approval. "I've made some enquiries, including at a similar building to the Dufour's Mortuary which is set up in Poplar near the parish church. As with many of the city's mortuaries, they overflow with the dead, from disease and the cold weather. I've had word that disreputable attendants have been selling off

358

bodies to medical schools, and even individual students. Procuring a foot would not be difficult if one has the right connections.

"Given the proximity of Poplar to Farnsley's separate Limehouse residence, I'm sure that he had those. The original owner of the foot was probably a poor streetwalker or local resident, which will be easy enough to confirm. Hence, that's why the body had probably been dead for almost as long as Miss Waterson was missing. In order to add veracity to his trick, Farnsley put it into one of the Miss Waterson's shoes – which Sir Lyndon would recognize, since he saw them every day, and in fact paid for."

"Ghastly," I said. "And what of the lady?"

"I would think that she has been through enough," said Lestrade, surprisingly. "In this matter, she did intend to extort money from her employer – or lover, whichever term you'd like to use. But in my opinion, was that any more tragic than the situation she was already in? Indebted, and enamoured by a man twice her age, with no convenient way out of the arrangement? If she's honest with him, he will simply sack her and throw her out of the Chelsea apartment. I've left her to her own reconnaissance in this matter. Hopefully, it will be a lesson hard learnt."

He took another sip of tea. "And after all – it is Christmas. A little seasonal charity isn't amiss."

"Difficult," I said. "But fair."

"Agreed," said Holmes. "And this will stay with her as a Christmas to remember for many years to come."

"Amen to that," I said, staring into the flames burning in our little grate while the sound of carolers echoed up from the street below.

The Case of the
Golden Grail
by Roger Riccard

NOTE: From the notes gleaned on this investigation, it appears that Sherlock Holmes attempted to have Watson include textbook-like instructions on how a detective should proceed to follow a case – something he often felt lacking in the Doctor's "romanticized" stories. I have attempted to include the detective's observations as they were attached. – R.R.

Chapter I

My notes indicate that it was the latter part of December in 1888, the week before Christmas in fact, when an exalted person requested an audience with my companion, the consulting detective, Sherlock Holmes. This request came by way of a letter delivered by the early afternoon post and brought upstairs by our landlady, Mrs. Hudson.

Having just finished lunch, Holmes was preoccupied with a chemical experiment. Therefore, I accepted the envelope from her at the doorway to our sitting room. Glancing at the addressee and seeing it was for my friend, I carried it over and set it on the arm of his favorite chair by the fireplace, there being no safe space on his laboratory table.

I stirred the fire and added more coal on this chilly afternoon. Then I sat in my usual seat across the way. I had just opened the newspaper when Holmes spoke without looking up. "Who is it from?"

I looked over the top of my paper toward him and replied, "Someone named Arthur Campbell. Baron of Ayrshire."

That seemed to catch his attention. Holmes was never impressed by titles, but the fact that a Scottish Baron was reaching out to him suggested the possibility of a case, and Holmes was anxious for a new problem to solve. Inaction was the bane of his existence. More than once I had heard him cry in exasperation, "Give me data, give me problems, give me the most abstract of puzzles to solve! My brain craves exercise!"

He removed his goggles and gloves and came over to sit in his chair. He picked up the envelope and began an examination which was quite familiar to me. This time, however, he requested me to make notes of his actions.

360

"Watson," said he, as he picked up the envelope, "I'm tempted to have you record my processes for future use as an instruction manual for Scotland Yard. Please take this down."

I retrieved pencil and paper from the writing desk and assumed a writing position.

Holmes proceeded to speak as follows:

1. *When receiving a written request, determine how it was delivered. Did it come by post? Was it hand-delivered and by whom – the potential client or a confederate or servant of such client, or a messenger service? Was it in the form of a telegram?*
   If hand delivered by messenger, make a thorough examination of the outside of the envelope for any possible contaminants which might indicate a poisonous substance within.

2. *If delivered by an agency, determine from whence it came by examining the postmark or telegraph office address. This will also tell you when it was sent and may give you a hint as to its urgency. This particular letter is postmarked two days ago in Ayrshire, Scotland.*

3. *Also note the return address and the sender's name. Is the full name used or a shortened version? Is there a title? Is it pre-printed stationery or hand-written? This can give you insights into the sender's character and status. It may determine a level of wealth, which may vary in spite of titles. As I recall, you once received a letter from a moderately wealthy friend who handwrote "Alex" in the return address, instead of the more formal "Alexander". This indicated someone who did not stand upon his station, but was more informal in his manner. Here we have a pre-printed, high-quality envelope noting the name and title: Baron Arthur Campbell, Bellrose Castle, Ayrshire, Scotland.*

4. *Next, examine the outside of the envelope itself for quality of paper and any telltale marks such as a thumb impression, makeup, tear stains, and the like. This can give you an idea of the person's wealth, the presence of a woman, or the emotional state of the sender.*

5. *At this point you should feel the envelope thoroughly. Use your middle finger, as it is more sensitive to touch and more likely to discover any small enclosure. I have*

> received coins, locks of hair, and all sorts of items people perceived as clues.
>
> 6. *Now open the envelope carefully. In this case, the envelope has been sealed with wax and the clan seal has been used to impress it. Therefore, we shall preserve the seal by carefully slitting the envelope along the top.*

Holmes did so with his penknife and carefully removed the sheet of paper within.

> 7. *The paper matches the envelope in age and quality, and also includes the clan crest. Had it not been a good match, then one must be on the lookout for a possible forgery by someone who was able to steal an envelope.*
> 8. *Again, check for any identifying features, tear stains and the like. Do not forget to check for any tell-tale scent such as perfume or other odor which may help identify the sender or where it was sent from. Now examine the handwriting.*

He looked over the top of the page at me and said, "I've mentioned my monograph to you on handwriting interpretations. It should be noted as a separate reference tool. This particular message was written by an elderly, right-handed gentleman suffering from arthritis. There are several hesitation points throughout which could be due to his condition or a pause to gather his thoughts. However, the signature is quite bold and exudes pride."

I should note to the reader of this tale that the actions described above are so natural to Holmes that this entire process takes him less than one minute. I bade him to please read the note, for by now I was overcome by curiosity. His eyes shifted back and forth across the page for several seconds until I said in exasperation, "Out loud, if you please!"

Holmes smirked, his impish sense of humour apparently brought forth by what he had read. He stood, handed me the paper, and walked over to his indexes. He came back to his chair with a volume which included the letter "*C*".

Meanwhile, I read as follows:

Dear Mr. Sherlock Holmes,

> *Greetings and felicitations of the Season. Allow me to introduce myself. I am Arthur Campbell, Baron of Ayrshire,*

and titular head of my branch of the Campbell Clan at Bellrose Castle.

To get straight to the matter, I have been the victim of a crime of theft, such that, it is not merely against myself, but against my family, now and for generations to come.

The local police are befuddled. In desperation, I wrote to the police at the capital in Edinburgh, hoping they might have more formidable resources. In reply, you were recommended to me by an official named Ewan Gibson.

The item stolen is a Golden Grail. Family tradition says it is The Holy Grail, entrusted to King Arthur's descendants by Sir Bors, the companion of Sir Galahad. As you may know, certain Campbell branches claim direct lineage with King Arthur.

I realize that this sounds fanciful. However, this Grail has been in our family as far back as records are known. While it certainly has not bestowed eternal life upon any member of the clan, no male member in my line, from time immemorial, has failed to live to at least the age of seventy. There are some clan records indicating miraculous actions that saved our men in battle. But that was long ago and I cannot confirm them.

Whatever the case, it is a treasured possession and its value in gold alone is worth several hundred pounds.

If you should be inclined to assist, please telegraph particulars as to your fee and expenses. I shall be happy to extend an advance to allow your purchase of train fare. We have several guest rooms available to you here at Bellrose.

I hope you will be amenable to my plea. If you are unable, I would appreciate your thoughts as to other investigators who may be capable.

In all sincere hopes,
Arthur Campbell

I peered across to my friend and queried, "An interesting situation. Who is this Ewan Gibson who recommended you?"

Holmes declined to look up from his examination of his index and merely answered, "Hmm? Gibson? Oh, just an old classmate from university. I assisted him with a little problem at school and on a case a few years ago, after he joined the police force in Edinburgh. *

"Please enter this instruction into your notes, Doctor:

9.   *Investigate the sender's identity through independent means. Rolls of peerage, business directories, newspaper articles, library sources, government records, trusted individuals, etc.*

I made the note, then asked, "And what do your files tell you about Arthur Campbell?"

Holmes finally looked up and answered, "I have more than one individual by that name in my file. However, the Baron of Ayrshire does happen to be one of them."

He then read thusly:

Campbell, Arthur Byron: Born 28 February, 1821. Succeeded as 11th Baron of Ayrshire, 1 September 1858 upon death of his father, Byron Bruce Campbell, at age 72. Widower, one daughter, Elise, married to Roy Lennox. Twin nephews, Harold and Henry Fraser, sons of his sister, Brenda and husband, Donald Fraser.

Member, 92nd Regiment of Foot (Gordon Highlanders), served in the Crimean War and the Indian Rebellion, rising to the rank of Major.

Peerage of Scotland. Retired from Parliament 1885.

Residence: Bellrose Castle, Holmston, Ayrshire, Scotland.

Barony of Ayrshire was created 20 September, 1623 by King James I (aka: James VI, King of Scots). First holder: Alexander Campbell. Crest: Yellow boar's head on golden buckler. Motto: Ne Obliviscaris (Forget Not). Clan Tartan: Plaid of light green, light blue and black.

Holmes closed the book and laid it upon his crossed legs as he leaned to one side, elbow impressing upon the arm of his chair. Resting his chin upon his right thumb while his index finger formed a cross with his lips, he descended into a contemplative mood. Although I had questions, I knew better than to interrupt his train of thought and held my tongue.

At last he sat up. Then he stood, returned the index to his shelves, and remarked, "It poses an interesting diversion, I should think. I need to consult with some of the sources I've listed for you. Should I be inclined to travel to Ayrshire, would you be amenable to accompany me, or do you have holiday plans?"

364

"Nothing firm. I should be happy to join you if I may be of assistance. It would be agreeable to spend Christmas in the land of my ancestors."

"Capital! If my enquiries merit my involvement, I shall telegraph Baron Campbell this afternoon and we can leave on the morrow."

With that he threw on his ulster, scarf, and hat. With umbrella in hand, he went out to brave the threatening weather. I looked over the list of sources he had requested me to write down. My deductions concluded that he would likely be headed to the British Library, the Records Office, and possibly the British Museum. I also recalled that, earlier that year, he had introduced me to Thomas Kent, a reporter for *The Daily Telegraph*, while we were investigating the fate of Andrew Etherege. However, as I thought it out, it seemed unlikely that Kent, whose primary role was as a theatre critic with occasional reporting on crime stories which Holmes brought to him, would have much information regarding a Scottish Baron.

I stood and walked over to the window. The dark grey skies were threatening to let loose their moisture at any moment. Previous days' storms had resulted in deposits of snow which now lay, blackened by soot, in piles along the kerbs of Baker Street where it had been shoveled off payment and plowed off streets. Despite Christmas decorations in shop windows attempting to create a festive mood, it made for a dreary and depressing atmosphere. Yes, it would be good to be relieved of the dark days of winter in London. I found myself suddenly hopeful for the opportunity to spend Christmas in the Scottish countryside where snow would be clean and white. Even a blizzard upon an open landscape would be preferable to the crowded and polluted capital.

Chapter II

I decided to put my time to good use whilst I awaited my friend's return. As he went about looking into the character of our potential client, I chose to research the object of his investigation. I supposed this would be his next instruction:

> 10. *If the crime in question be a theft, learn all possible about the missing object. Is it something which retains its value only if left intact, such as a painting or other work of art or a document? Does it have historical significance? Could its disappearance have a deleterious effect upon the owner or the heirs, such as a missing deed or will? Is it something which can be converted into something of more transportable value, such as a gold or silver object which could be melted*

down? Is its primary value as an object which can be held for ransom?

Thus I went through our meagre library of books to find what I could about King Arthur and the legend of the Holy Grail. I retrieved my copy of Sir Thomas Malory's *Le Morte d'Arthur* and began perusing its pages for those which were relevant to the search for the golden artifact.

I was intrigued by the fact that Baron Campbell perpetuated the Grail legend as a part of his family history. While I was well aware that the legend of King Arthur himself was historically challenging, there is, I think, an inherent need in the human psyche to believe in something greater than ourselves. While for most people, their religion and God fill that void, for many, even beyond that, there still exists a need to believe in legends and heroes. We apparently want an example of someone who can prevail against the travails of life, real or imaginary – even if they have flaws as we all do.

I found my eyes caught by certain passages as I searched through the pages of Mallory's work. This had the unfortunate effect of distracting me from my goal as I re-read segments I'd read years ago. I lost count of the number of times I had to shake myself from reverie to continue my quest for the disposition of the Holy Grail.

Darkness was fast approaching, sped along by the heavy skies now pouring snow upon the streets. I was required to turn up more lights to read, and took no little time in wondering how Sherlock Holmes was faring in his enquiries.

At last I completed my investigation. I closed the heavy tome just as Mrs. Hudson knocked on the door to enquire about dinner.

"I am assuming Holmes will be here," I stated. "He didn't mention any expectation of being late."

"Hmmpf! Just the same, I'll turn down the heat in case he's delayed. I can always turn it up again, thanks to that new gas stove."

She returned down to her kitchen. I reflected on the fact that the gas lines we took for granted for our lighting were now allowing her to have better control over her cooking. It struck me as odd that we had these modern conveniences of science at our disposal while we were about to investigate the theft of something purported to be nearly two-thousand years old.

I put the book away and went to the sideboard to prepare an *aperitif* to enjoy before dinner. Just as I resumed my seat by the fire, Sherlock Holmes came through the door. He had left his wet outer garments and umbrella down in the foyer and quickly strode to the fireplace to regain some warmth to his limbs.

I peered up at my friend as he reached for his pipe and the Persian slipper which held his tobacco. Raising my own glass I asked, "Care for some inner warmth?"

The detective nodded. "A brandy will do nicely, thank you." He then knelt by the fire and used the tongs to pluck a coal with which to light his briar. Settling into his chair, he took a long pull. A stream of blue haze soon ascended toward the ceiling, discolored after so much tobacco smoke over the years.

I returned from the sideboard and handed him his snifter. He gratefully took a healthy sip. "Ah, that is better! Well, Watson, I trust the passing hours have not given you second thoughts regarding a journey to the Scottish coast. I have telegraphed Campbell, advising him of my need for your assistance. I've told him that we shall leave on tomorrow's train and he can reimburse our travel expense afterward. Here is another instruction for your notes, which I passed on to the Baron:

> 11. It is imperative that police or client be advised of the necessity to preserve the location of a crime as pristine as possible, and that detailed observation be conducted at the soonest moment.

When I finished making note of his statement, I advised him of my own comment regarding the provenance of the stolen item in the case of a theft. He nodded in approval and replied, "You do have a gift for the turn of a phrase, Doctor. You proposed a clear and precise instruction without embellishment or romance. I am gratified that you have this capability. I only wish that you had confined yourself to it when you published *A Study in Scarlet* last year. I trust you'll remember this writing method, should you pursue the publication of future cases."

This compliment seemed somewhat backhanded. However, having known Holmes for some years now, I chose to concentrate upon the positive aspect of his statement and merely said, "Thank you."

"I perceive by the disturbance of the dust upon our bookshelves that you followed through upon this instruction. What did your research reveal?"

I took a final swallow of my drink to clear my throat and replied, "Having only Mallory's work to consult, the results were unsatisfactory. He does not continue the story of the Grail beyond the ascension of Galahad to heaven. His companion knights, Percival and Bors, witness this event, but the fate of the Grail is not communicated."

Holmes nodded, "I admit, I fared little better in that department. An acquaintance of mine at the British Museum indicated that Sir Bors de

Ganis is the only knight to return to England from the Grail quest, but the fate of the object itself is unknown. There are several religious establishments throughout Europe who claim to possess this holy artifact. I remind you, Watson, I care nothing for legends, especially supernatural ones, as you well know. However, their existence as a matter of motive cannot be ignored. In this particular case, if the thief believes the Grail provides healing powers and eternal life, it increases our chances of finding it intact. Otherwise, with so many days gone by, it could easily be melted down and redeemed for its metallic value by now."

I replied, sardonically, "Then let us hope the thief isn't quite as cynical about legends as yourself. What other information did your afternoon sojourn provide?"

"In addition to the museum, I spent some time at the Records Office, looking into this branch of the Campbell clan. I fleshed out a few more details which may, or may not, prove significant."

Recalling my earlier thoughts, I asked, "Did you happen to call upon that newspaper fellow, Thomas Kent?"

Holmes tilted his head to the side momentarily, then replied, "I understand your thinking, as I did mention newspapers as a source of information. However, I have journalistic sources other than Kent who are more likely to have information regarding former members of Parliament, retired soldiers, and Scottish barons. I've spoken with one of them. I also telegraphed Gibson to get his take on the situation and expect an answer tonight."

A knock upon our door was followed by the presence of our landlady, "I saw your things in the hallway, Mr. Holmes. Dinner is warm and can be ready whenever you are."

"Your timing is impeccable, Mrs. Hudson," answered my companion. "We are ready to eat at your convenience. Also, we should prefer an early breakfast tomorrow, if not inconvenient. We shall be leaving on the seven o'clock train and shall be out of town for a few days."

"As you wish, gentlemen. I shall take the opportunity to give these rooms a proper scrubbing in your absence. You should also be aware that I shall be spending four days with my sister over the holidays, starting on Christmas Eve morning. Therefore, I shall wish you felicitations of the season now. Do try to enjoy your holidays while you're off chasing criminals."

Chapter III

Tuesday morning broke with fresh snowfall being plowed off the streets as we attempted to circumvent the drifts to flag down a cab to take us to Euston Station. Fortunately, the skies themselves now showed some few blue patches peeking through light grey clouds. The temperature wasn't quite so cold, yet chilly enough and I was glad when we were finally ensconced in our private compartment for the long trip ahead.

Holmes had advised me that we could well be riding the rails for nearly twelve hours, having to change trains once we arrived at Glasgow Central Station for the trip south along the west coast of Scotland to Ayr. Therefore, I had brought along *Le Morte d'Arthur* and another novel I had been reading, as well as the latest medical journal. For his part, Holmes bought the morning papers to help pass the time. The trip north was at least interesting in its variety of geography and weather. Once out of London, the land became a patchwork of greens, browns, and snow-covered landscapes. We passed through farmlands, rolling hills, and the mountains of southern Scotland.

During the early part of the journey, Holmes suggested a few more instructions to be added to my narrative.

> 12. *Proceed to the location of the crime with due haste and bring with you the following instruments, if possible:*
>
> A. *A powerful magnifying lens.*
> B. *Several small envelopes with which to gather evidence.*
> C. *A pencil and notebook with which to make observations and sketches for future reference.*
> D. *Matches, a small dusting brush, measuring tape, multiplex pocket knife.*
> E. *A weapon appropriate to the situation: Leaded bludgeon, heavy-topped cane, fighting knife, etc. In extreme or unknown situations, a small revolver is recommended. Handcuffs as well.*

Arriving in Glasgow mid-afternoon, we changed trains for the southbound ride to Ayr and we picked up the city's afternoon papers. Headed west out of Glasgow, we made a wide arc as the locomotive slowly changed its course southward along the western coast. After passing through Irvine, the Firth of Clyde came into view, but the Isle of Arran was hidden from site by low clouds that pelted our railcar intermittently with rain.

Being so close to the shortest day of the year, darkness was quickly descending when we pulled into Ayr Station. A light snow was falling, but, unlike London, that which was already on the rooftops and roads retained its natural whiteness and gave an eerie glow in the twilight. Disembarking the train, Holmes led us straight to the station telegraph office and enquired as to whether a message had arrived in his name.

There was such a message from Mrs. Hudson. Knowing that our departure might be in advance of a reply from Baron Campbell, Holmes had asked our landlady to forward any answers sent to Baker Street to the Ayr Station telegraph office. Quickly reading it he handed me the paper.

It read as follows, *"You and Watson welcome. Enquire Holmston Livery upon arrival. Driver arranged."* As I was reading, Holmes asked the telegrapher directions to Holmston Livery and found it was just a short walk down the street. The owner turned us over to a young fellow named Malcolm, with a bright face and eager smile, who doffed his cap and led us to an enclosed carriage hitched to a fine pair of white-stockinged, bay Clydesdales bedecked with ribbons and bells befitting to the holiday.

He drove us along a road which paralleled the River Ayr for about two miles where the river turned north. Just as we were coming to the change in the river's course that took it due east again, Bellrose Castle came into view. It was the stereotype of thirteenth-century Scottish castles, with the exception of it being triangular shaped, much like Caerlaverock Castle near Dumfries. Located on the bend of the river, it took advantage of its proximity, and a moat was dredged from the river to protect the eastern and southern sides of the grounds while the river acted as a natural barrier to the north and west. Thus, in effect, Bellrose was its own island. Our carriage rattled across an old-fashioned drawbridge into a courtyard where modern touches first made their appearance with several gas lamps providing illumination.

We stepped out of the carriage, Holmes in his grey ulster and ear-flapped traveling cap, and I in my black overcoat and derby. Malcom took up our bags before we could retrieve them and led the way to the massive door under the main house portico. There was a large wreath upon the door and boughs of holly with bright red berries hung over the frame.

A double tap of the ringed knocker brought a butler to the door in mere seconds and we were ushered inside. Malcolm made the introductions, "Sherlock Holmes and Dr. Watson to see the Baron. Gentlemen, this is Aames, Chief of Staff for Sir Arthur."

Aames was a stout, broad-shouldered fellow about five-foot-eight. In appearance I judged him to be roughly fifty years of age with greying hair and moustache. His sharp blue eyes took us in quickly and a courteous smile crossed his lips as he bowed to us. He told Malcolm to leave the luggage there in the foyer and he would have it attended to. Then he offered the young man to attend to the kitchen for some hot coffee before he drove back into town. To us he bid welcome. Having a maid take our hats and coats and a servant our luggage, he asked that we follow him to meet the Baron.

Modern conveniences did not end with the gas lamps outside. The house itself appeared to be well-heated in spite of its cold stone exterior. I noted heating vents strategically placed, in addition to a good sized fireplace in many rooms. More holly boughs and other Christmas trimmings gave the interior a cheery countenance. Baron Campbell was in his library, where another fireplace roared with dancing flames. He was sitting behind a large oak-inlayed desk with exquisitely carved legs and a scallop-edged top which shone from years of polishing.

I had a picture of him in my mind, based upon the age Holmes had discovered in his index and his service in the military. However, I was pleasantly presented with a fine figure of a man who stood ramrod straight as we entered the room. For a man who would be sixty-eight in two months, he didn't look his age at all. He was taller than I, at about six feet, and maintained a healthy weight. He bore a full head of iron grey hair with just a slight remnant of red, parted on the right and neatly trimmed. He was clean-shaven, wearing a smoking jacket patterned after his clan tartan, and black trousers.

When he spoke there was a fine Scottish burr to his tone. "Mr. Holmes, Dr. Watson, I wasn't expecting ye until much later, more likely tomorrow. Ye couldn't have gotten my telegram this morning and arrived this quickly."

Holmes replied, "Your case intrigues me, Lord Campbell. I confess, we left at the earliest opportunity, I instructed our landlady to forward any telegrams to the Ayr Station. Thus we learned of your instructions."

"I like a man who takes the initiative," smiled the Baron, sticking out his hand in greeting.

Such was his commanding presence that I nearly snapped to attention. Even so, I subconsciously stood a little taller and measured my steps, as if in march formation. Holmes, no great respecter of titles, merely strode forward and clasped the welcome of our host. When it was my turn, I found my hand in a strong grip. Green eyes gazed into mine as he asked, "You've a military air about ye, Doctor. Or should I call ye 'Captain?' Where did ye serve?"

Automatically I replied, "'Doctor' is fine, sir. I was in Afghanistan as an army surgeon with the 5th Northumberland Fusiliers and the Berkshires until the Battle of Maiwand."

"A bloody mess, that. Wounded I take it?"

"Yes, sir. Shoulder during the battle while I was tending to wounded, and my leg during the retreat."

"I thought I detected a slight limp. Cold weather aggravates it, I imagine."

"On occasion, sir. However, I can generally get by with my cane."

"Very well. Shall we sit by the fire?" Looking back to Holmes, he waved us over to a sitting area where a dark green leather sofa and four royal blue stuffed chairs were arranged in a rectangle open to the welcome blaze. Holmes and I took chairs to the left while Lord Campbell sat opposite us.

"I appreciate your quick response to my communique, gentlemen. Inspector Gibson seems to have great confidence in your powers, Mr. Holmes. He says ye be more worthy than any policeman he knows and can solve cases that others refuse as impossible."

Holmes crossed his leg across his knee and folded his hands in his lap, assuming a casual air. I have seen him take this position often to show his client, or suspect, that he isn't intimidated by rank or position.

"Gibson is a fine policeman in his own right, but he makes too much of my powers. They are not supernatural. However, some may consider them more than natural due to the fact that so few people use the totality of the senses given to them. As I have often declared to the police and others, 'You see, but you do not observe'. Observation is what makes deduction possible, and deductions lead to conclusions."

"How interesting," Lord Campbell replied. "Can ye give me an example?"

Holmes tilted his head to one side, "I would prefer to examine the setting of the crime as quickly as possible, Sir Arthur. Should the thief be a member of the household, our arrival may cause him to take further steps to attempt to cover it up. If you will lead us to the location, I shall be happy to explain my methods as we walk."

The former army major slapped his knees with both hands and stood, "Charge right into the action! I appreciate that, Mr. Holmes. Follow me, gentlemen."

As we walked along with the Baron, Holmes explained his observation process. "You may wish to make note of this for your references, Watson:

13. *When meeting someone who may be involved in the case, no matter how peripherally, it is important to observe mannerisms, traits, and physical characteristics. One must use these to ascertain the personality and character of the person.*

14. *As you observe this person, it is important to notice trouser knees, shoes, shirt cuffs, elbows, and collars.*

Take into account wear patterns and size or fit. The style and age of the clothing and how comfortable they are while wearing it.

15. *Notice the hands. Note the position, size, and age of any callouses or blisters. Look out for ink stains or any other discoloration. Overall, you should also note the skin complexion and the degree of exposure to sun. Be aware of scars, no matter how small. Eyes are also important. The presence or absence of glasses or pince-nez can indicate a degree of vanity, or the accuracy of the observations they report to you. Ears should be well-observed, as they can indicate possible relationships between parties.*

Lord Campbell interrupted, "This is all fascinating, Mr. Holmes. By your account, ye must have already made several deductions since your arrival."

We were turning into the entrance to what must have once been the armory when Holmes answered, "Allow me to give a brief demonstration. Your Chief of Staff, Aames, is a proud man and former military himself. Likely he was an officer's batman at some point, though not yours. He is Scottish by birth but attended school in England.

"He is a strict but fair leader over the household and will work side by side with them when necessary. He runs an efficient house, showing excellent foresight and planning skills. He is respected and even liked by the town tradesmen. He uses reading glasses, but will not wear them during the normal course of the day. He was once a smoker, but now uses snuff."

The Baron had unlocked and was pushing open two wide double doors and started to make a remark about Holmes's comments, but the detective first asked, "Are these doors kept shut and locked at night?"

Lord Campbell replied, "We usually keep the doors shut, as there is no need to heat this room, but we do air it out once a week. I've had no occasion to lock these doors in many a year. However, since the burglary, the police have recommended that I lock them, and your friend, Gibson, suggested I keep everyone out of the room until ye had a chance to examine it."

My companion gazed briefly at the floor, then charged ahead, "I perceive this is where the Grail was kept."

We had reached a pedestal about four feet tall, with a glass case roughly one foot cubed. There was no lock on the case. It merely lifted off the pedestal where it was fitted into grooves which kept it from sliding if bumped. A felt Campbell tartan covered the top of the pedestal. There was a slight indented circle where the Grail had rested upon it. On either side, low, glass-topped cases exhibited various items of Campbell historical items.

Lord Campbell was still digesting Holmes's findings regarding Aames and took a second to answer. "Aye, that pedestal was its display case. I must say, your assessment of Aames is amazing."

"That is my profession, Sir Arthur. Years of study and experience has made such observations and deductions second nature. It is as familiar to me as saddling and riding your horse is to you."

The floor was flagstone with a few rugs here and there, so footmarks were highly unlikely to be found, especially after so many days. I could discern no fingermarks or smudges upon the glass cube itself, but Holmes began a closer examination with his magnifying lens. The cube was an oak-framed glass case. He checked the case and the pedestal for any markings, all the way down to the floor itself. As he did so, he asked a question.

"Did the thief put the case back upon the pedestal, or did one of your servants do so before I requested that nothing be touched?"

The Baron, who was now standing to one side with his hands clasped behind his back, replied, "'Tis exactly as it was when it was found."

Holmes nodded, then began examining the tops of the counters to either side. On the left side he found marks of some type and noted, "It appears the thief set the glass case down here, removed the Grail, and set it next to it, then replaced the cube. That is telling in itself. Someone thought that returning the glass could buy some time. He or she likely believed that someone walking through the room might take no notice of the missing Grail as long as everything else was in place and no one looked directly toward it."

"May I offer a further suggestion?" remarked the Baron.

"By all means," replied Holmes. "The more data I have, the better."

In his pleasant baritone voice, the Baron continued, "At this time of year, we often loan the Grail out to the local church for their Christmas pageant. It is possible that someone knowing this might restore the case, so that anyone other than myself or Aames would assume that its absence was due to that situation. I do not come in here every day, and the castle is large enough that Aames likely doesn't either, as he inspects the other servants' work."

As he was making this remark, I was surveying the room itself. Higher up on the wall where the display cases were, there hung various tapestries of historical events where the Campbell clan had been involved. There was a long faded scene of King Arthur and the Knights at the Round

Table. Another was of a lad pulling a sword from a stone, although whether it was Arthur or Galahad wasn't clear. There were battle scenes of Stirling Bridge and Bannockburn, as well as the more local battle of Largs against the invading Norwegians in 1263. There was even a fanciful rendition of James VI, bestowing the baronetcy and knighthood upon Alexander Campbell.

The opposite wall was lined with suits of armor, military uniforms, shields, coats-of-arms and various weaponry. On one end of the room there were paintings of various Campbells down through the ages, including the most recent, Arthur Campbell himself in his finest kilted uniform. The other end featured narrow windows looking out upon the Rive Ayr

There was one other entrance to the room, from the corner farthest from that which we had come. That door appeared to be bolted from the inside. Two ancient candle chandeliers hung from the ceiling. However, they were not lit. Gas lamps encircled the room every few feet and provided excellent illumination.

"Watson," said Holmes, breaking my concentration, "I see you are examining the room itself. Please note for instruction:

16. *Examine the room where the crime took place thoroughly. Include all walls, ceilings, and floors. Look for secret passages, check windows, and other closets or anterooms. Be especially observant of any locks and their condition.*

17. *When examining the location of the crime itself, whether theft or murder, the perpetrator may have left some indication behind. Check for footprints, fingermarks, snagged pieces of cloth, smudges of mud, dirt, ink, chemicals, or some such left behind. If footprints are noted, measure for size and note the tread pattern and any unusual wear.*

Finishing this dictation, Holmes went on with his examination of the room, following the steps he had just outlined. Coming to the other door he enquired, "Is this door always kept locked from this side?"

Lord Campbell replied, "Generally not. The police recommended it after their examination, in case the thief came back."

"Highly unlikely I should think," I commented.

The retired Major nodded, "I believe they just wanted to make it appear as if they were doing something. Their lack of progress was embarrassing, to say the least."

"I'm sure they did their best, Sir Arthur," said Holmes as he checked the floor by the other door. "It is an unfortunate fact that today's British police force isn't as thoroughly trained as they should be. This is why I'm asking Watson to take note of my instructions. I'm hopeful that we can create a teaching tool for them."

Looking in disgust at the floor rugs, he lamented, "They also tend to blunder about like a herd of lost elephants. I count no less than four sets of footprints left by what are certainly policemen's boots. Finding the culprit's prints in this morass will be highly unlikely.

Chapter IV

At that moment, Aames entered the room and stated, "Pardon me, your Lordship. Mrs. Galway is asking what time you wish to have dinner. She doesn't want to interrupt your meeting."

Campbell looked to Holmes, who replied, "I should be finished here in another fifteen minutes, Sir Arthur."

"Then we shall give ye and Dr. Watson some time to refresh yourselves and dress for dinner," he replied. Turning to Aames he directed, "Tell cook we shall be ready in forty-five minutes."

True to his word, Holmes had completed his task in the allotted time and we were shown to our rooms on an upper floor. Mine had a view which looked out upon the River Ayr, currently frozen over and bordered by snow banks. There was a half-moon showing through the broken clouds and the snowfall itself had stopped. I cleaned up and changed. Then, as I had a few minutes to spare, I looked over the notes I had taken thus far. Holmes's instructions along the way weren't going to be easy to weave into a narrative style and I wasn't sure if my agent, Doyle, or any London publisher would accept this unique way of telling a story.

I was in this contemplation when a knock came to my door and I answered. "Come in."

It was my companion, formally dressed for dinner. His fashionable appearance, however, didn't match his mood. "We've work to do, Watson! This delay of several days since the time of the theft gives us not a minute to lose. I would as soon forgo this dinner in favor of continuing our investigation."

"Our host may construe that as an insult to good manners," I noted.

"Yes, but I do hope you'll assist me in whatever steps I may take to move things along."

"I should be happy to conspire with you."

He shot me a look, "Conspire. An interesting word, that. It is one of many things we must consider. For now, to keep from interrupting our dinner and extending it, please note the following for your record:

18. *When brought into a case, take special note of all the possible players in your game of wits. Include all members of the family, all the household staff, even those who only come in for specific tasks or times. Also any close family friends or suitors who may have had access to the scene, however improbable. Check with local authorities to discern if any similar crimes have occurred in the area.*
19. *Look into any feuds or grudges, no matter how ancient, as well as any business or property disputes.*
20. *Check into any local work being done in the area by government workers or private contractors.*

After ensuring I had written these down, Holmes led the way to the dining room where we arrived after the Baron. We all remained standing for the arrival of his daughter, Elise, her husband, Roy Lennox, and their son, Fergus. Once all were in place we sat – Sir Arthur at the head of the table, Roy and Elise to his left, Fergus at his right hand, then Holmes and myself beyond the boy.

Fergus was a short, skinny lad who appeared to be about ten years old but, we later learned, was actually thirteen. He exhibited the red hair of his father and the pale complexion of his mother. Elise was an attractive woman in her mid-thirties with soft, curly brown hair that surrounded her thin pale face, from which hazel eyes flitted about carelessly. Her husband, Roy Lennox, was also quite thin with a shock of red hair just beginning to show some grey as he appeared to be entering his forties. All were well-dressed in splendid finery which bespoke of the family fortune.

After the Baron made introductions and while the first course was being served, Mr. Lennox asked the obvious question of my friend. "Mr. Holmes, how can you hope to solve this theft after so many days, and succeed where the police have failed?"

"I have often succeeded where police have failed," replied the detective. "However, the passage of time is working against us. Even after the thief is discovered, he may well have disposed of the item in a way that will make it impossible to retrieve."

"How do you mean, sir?" asked Elise Lennox, who was sitting directly across from my friend.

377

"It depends upon the thief's motive, Madam. If the theft is merely out for personal gain, then he or she could have had it melted down strictly for its gold value. Or there could be a plan put in motion to get it into the hands of a private collector who will stash it away for what may be decades."

"What would be the point of that?" she asked innocently.

Holmes indulged her further and replied, "There are people of a certain bent of mind who merely wish to possess what others don't have. They derive some perverse pleasure in ownership, even though no one else knows they own it."

"Really?" asked young Fergus, his eyes wide with alarm.

"I'm afraid I've known more than a few such criminals," answered Holmes. "However, we are speculating in a vacuum. I need much more detail as to the circumstances of the theft."

He turned to our host and asked, "Sir Arthur, could you please tell me exactly which date and approximately what time frame the theft took place, and who was in the house at the time?"

"A moment if you please, Mr. Holmes. Let us first ask the Lord's blessing upon our food."

The servants had finished serving the first course by this point, yet no one had deigned to touch their plate. Minding the manners of good guests, we, likewise, had refrained from eating until our host had begun. Baron Campbell's prayer was heartfelt and recalled to me my own Presbyterian youth.

Once his petitions to God were complete, each person began to eat. Sir Arthur turned to Holmes and made his reply.

"'Twas a week ago, sometime between late Saturday afternoon and Sunday afternoon, when we returned from church. Pastor Reynolds had enquired of me if they might continue to have use of the Grail in the Annual Christmas Pageant."

I interrupted, much to Holmes's chagrin I imagined, and asked, "Excuse me, Lord Campbell. It was my understanding that, traditionally, the Grail was used at the last supper and the crucifixion. What purpose would it serve at Christmas?"

The Baron smiled at this chance to tell the story, "One of the ancient traditions is that it represents the gift of gold, given by one of the wise men to Mary at Jesus' birth. This story has her bringing it to Jerusalem during the final journey. Christ uses it at the last supper and she retains possession. She catches drops of her son's blood in it as he is hanging on the cross. Then she turns it over to Joseph of Arimathea, who has volunteered his own tomb for Christ's body."

"I see. Thank you, Baron."

"Fascinating as this is," said Holmes, barely hiding his scowl at my interruption, "I presume that when you returned home and looked in upon the Grail, you found it missing."

"Exactly that, Mr. Holmes. One of our maids had dusted the Grail and its case on Saturday sometime after lunch. No one had occasion to go into the room after that until I found it missing the next day."

"Did you have any visitors that weekend, or were just you and the household staff in attendance?"

"Elise and her family live with me here," stated the Baron. "Roy is my estate manager. That particular weekend my sister Brenda and her husband, Donald Fraser, were here, as well as my nephew, Henry, with his wife Allison. Other than that, no one."

Lennox spoke up, somewhat indignantly, when his father-in-law had finished. "Surely you don't suspect a family member would do this, Mr. Holmes?"

Holmes steepled his long fingers under his chin, "In my profession, Mr. Lennox, I must suspect everyone until I have excluded them by process of elimination. Far too often family members, or servants with many years of loyal service, have taken actions which no one would have thought possible. Tell me, was the drawbridge taken up that night?"

"No," answered the estate manager, "We keep it oiled and will raise and lower it on occasion, to ensure it's in proper working order. But since there is no particular need to keep invading Englishmen out in this day and age – " (He looked pointedly at Holmes.) " – we generally leave it down."

My friend smiled and replied, "Thank you. Fortunately I have my good Scottish companion, Watson, here to help me mind my manners."

He took a sip of wine and began a cursory attempt at eating. The meal went on with much lighter conversation after that. Holmes merely made some few enquiries as to the servants and their length of time with the Baron. When the main dishes were cleared, Holmes discreetly tapped my leg, signaling that he was going to attempt to excuse us from dessert in order to continue his examination of the castle in the areas around the area of the crime.

However, before he could speak, Baron Campbell called his name, "Mr. Holmes, ye made some remarkable deductions regarding Mr. Aames here." The Chief of staff stood stiffly at attention by the Baron's side as he was overseeing the serving of dessert. He looked upon his employer and then at Holmes with a puzzled expression.

Campbell smiled, "Nothing shocking, Aames, I assure you. However, I should like Mr. Holmes to explain his observations that led to his deductions about ye."

My companion sighed as he placed his napkin upon the table before him. "What you are asking, Sir Arthur, is the equivalent of a magician revealing the secrets of his trade. Once explained, the mystique is gone. I cannot begin to tell you how often I have done so, only to find the person who asked the question reply, 'How absurdly simple!'"

The old major leaned forward, forearms upon the edge of the table, "I promise to make no such statement, Mr. Holmes. The deductions ye made were far too unique to be reduced to such a remark."

Holmes glanced at me and gave a slight shake of his head in resignation, "Very well. As I recall, I stated he was Scottish by birth, but attended school in England. This is revealed by his speech. Though he retains his Scottish burr, certain pronunciations are distinctly English and some are unique to the higher educational institutes such as Oxford, Cambridge, and the like. As to his affording such an education, I have insufficient data, but would speculate that a benefactor provided the necessary funds. Perhaps the parents of the officer to whom he was attached as batman.

"His former military service is evident by his mannerisms and the watch chain upon his waistcoat. There aren't many men of his station who own their own watch. However, as a batman to a military officer, it would be essential for him to possess such an instrument, and it was likely given him upon his entering that officer's service. The deduction the officer wasn't you was indicated by the Chinese coin and service medallion of the Second China War hung upon the chain. It indicates his service was likely in the British protectorate of Hong Kong. You, Major Campbell, according to peerage records, served in the Crimea and India.

"The fact that he treats the household staff fairly and assists as necessary was indicated by the servants' attitudes who picked up our luggage. Their smiles and countenance was one of respect, not fear. His own white gloves, though primarily pristine, had a small smudge of silver polish where likely he was engaged in this task which would normally be below his station. The fact our rooms were ready indicates foresight on his part in that he couldn't have known what time we would arrive. The house itself is well maintained as to cleanliness. The easy camaraderie between him and our driver indicated an attitude of friendly respect and appreciation.

"There are slight indentations on either side of his nose indicating the occasional use of glasses. For a man of his age, that is likely for reading, as his eyesight seems perfectly well suited to other normal pursuits.

"While it is common for soldiers to smoke, a man in Aames position needs to avoid the staining of his gloves, an unpleasant odor on his breath, and the smell of tobacco permeating his clothes. Thus, I perceive that the outline of the small box in his right waistcoat pocket is a snuff box and the few small grains of powder near it are, in fact, snuff. This would assist his desire for the chemicals found in tobacco without having to indulge in the act of smoking."

Upon completion of his explanations, we had the pleasant experience of the Baron's appreciation as he raised his wineglass. "Well done, sir! Every link of the chain proves true. Anyone who calls such a feat as 'simple' is sadly mistaken. I only hope this power is sufficient to find our thief."

Holmes returned the compliment with a sip of his own wine and replied, "As to that end, Sir Arthur, I should like to continue my observations around the house and question the servants at your convenience. Watson and I are in no need of desserts to expand our waistlines. So if we may be excused?"

Campbell nodded. "I cannot argue with your logic, sir. Ye have the run of the manor. I merely ask that ye have a family member present should ye wish to examine any bedrooms. Aames will make the servants available as ye see fit."

Holmes stood and I reluctantly joined him, enviously eyeing the dessert cart containing a sweet smelling Dundee cake. Mrs. Lennox, noting my expression said, "Not to worry, Doctor. I'll see that a slice is saved for you in the kitchen."

I returned her smile with a nod and we excused ourselves, making our way back toward the armory.

Chapter V

The gas lamps were burning low when we re-entered the armory. I started to restore full illumination when Holmes stopped me. "Leave it be for a moment. I wish to observe the room as our culprit may have, if he removed the item after the household had retired."

Holmes led the way toward the pedestal as I followed. At one point, I nearly fell when I stubbed my toe upon the edge of one of the flagstones. Holmes, acting as if he expected me to do so, caught my arm and kept me upright. "A telling point, Watson. A stranger to this room may well have fallen as you nearly did with the lights this low. You should make another note for your instructions:

> 21. *If at all possible, attempt to reconstruct or investigate the setting of the crime in a manner which most closely resembles the conditions at the time of the incident. This may assist in revealing the culprit's familiarity with the*

site or the victim. It also may be telling as to the physical prowess of the criminal.

We finished making our way to the pedestal, where Holmes examined it again under the low light. As it was directly beneath one of the wall lamps, even the low light provided sufficient illumination to perform the necessary tasks. After a brief inspection, he requested me to turn up the lights again. I retreated to the double doors of the room's main entrance and did so.

As there were display cases intermittently running down the center of the room, one couldn't approach the opposite door without circumnavigating the room's perimeter. This was where Holmes had gone while I was turning up the lights. As I did so, I walked past the windows on the far end, which happened to face the river. These were several in number but narrow in breadth – wide enough for an archer to shoot through from inside, but not for an invader to enter, should he make it across the river. The hinged glass opened inward like a door and I could see that the light coat of dust on the sill hadn't been disturbed recently.

When at last I caught up to my friend, he was examining the floor outside the single door in this corner of the armory. "See here. The police have made a capital mistake."

I looked upon the floor where he had waved his hand. This area was carpeted. Being a much later addition to the castle's décor, there was a wide arc corresponding to where the door brushed the carpet as it swung out into the corridor.

"The door has obliterated any footprints there might have been," I observed, knowing that my friend saw more than I, but playing the role he expected.

"Just as the police thought," he confirmed. "Thus they failed to take any further steps. Literally. Look here, beyond the arc."

I stepped out onto the tamped down carpet and knelt to get a better look. If I found just the right angle, I could see a trace of footprints. The fact that the carpet fibers were bent in the same direction as the path left by carpet sweepers made their discernment nearly impossible.

"I can just make out what appear to be footprints," I remarked, "but they seem rather small. Could they not have been left by the maid who ran the carpet sweep over this area?"

"Possible, but unlikely," replied Holmes. "The most efficient way to run a carpet sweep is to begin against one wall and pull toward you. As you go back and forward in this manner, you walk backwards, thus sweeping over your own footprints and any dirt your shoes leave behind. These prints had to be left after the last time this carpet was swept."

Keeping to one side, we followed the path until we arrived at the common area at the base of the back stairwell. Here numerous prints obliterated each other and it was impossible to tell which direction was taken by our possible thief. Off to the right would have taken them toward the dining room, kitchen, and the servants quarters beyond. To the left would lead back toward the main living area, containing drawing room, library, parlour, foyer, and great room. Of course, if the thief were a family member, he or she could merely return to their room upstairs.

Retracing our steps, Holmes peered deeply at the floor until he found what seemed to be the clearest impression. He knelt and took his tape measure from his pocket, carefully noting all dimensions at various widths along the foot as well as the overall length. He pulled some tracing paper from his inner breast pocket and made a careful outline of the shoe print itself. I noticed the length was a mere eight-and-one-half inches. From my medical knowledge, I realized this was approximately a woman's size three shoe, which corresponds roughly to someone around five-feet tall, give-or-take a couple of inches. If this was our culprit, it was certainly not among the men of the house.

Being skeptical at the thought of one of the women being the thief, I stated, "We don't know if these are, in fact, our thief's footprints. We only know someone made them after the carpet was swept. It could have been someone who came this way to go into the armory, found the door locked, and returned to go around the other way."

"No," replied my friend. "Had that been the case, the prints would have been found on the carpet outside the door, not brushed away when the door was open the last time by the police. We shall have to question the servants about when this sweeping occurred."

There being little more to examine in this area of the house, Holmes chose to seek out Aames and arrange for interviews of the staff. We found him eating his own dinner in the kitchen. Seeing the man *sans* coat and gloves as he ate a well-proportioned meal, I could better appreciate the personality Holmes had prescribed to him. He started to stand upon our entrance, but Holmes waved him back to his seat. "Pray do not let us interrupt your meal, Mr. Aames. I merely wish to arrange some interviews with the staff. If possible, I should like to begin with the maid-servants.

"Easily done, Mr. Holmes," answered silver–haired gentleman. Turning toward the cook he said, "Mrs. Galway, would you have Mrs. Kenworth gather the housemaids for Mr. Holmes? Thank you."

The cook wiped her hands of the soapy dishwater and left the room. Turning back to us, Aames remarked, "Your deductions about me were intriguing, Mr. Holmes. You were correct in your surmise that my education was paid for by a benefactor. I was the son of servants to Sir

Robert Douglas. He perceived I was a bright boy and I had grown up with his son, Clyde. When Clyde went off to Oxford, I was sent with him. He rose to the rank of captain, but died while we were still in China, and I mustered out. After I returned home, Sir Robert recommended me to Lord Campbell, and I've worked my way up to my current position."

While I found this story interesting, Holmes was more concerned with the case in hand. "Thank you for your verification, Mr. Aames. However, my current concern is with your master's missing artifact."

The Chief of Staff sat back in his chair in a most informal posture as he gazed upon us, almost disapprovingly. I took this as a feeling that he felt his age required as much respect from us as his station required his respect for us. Holmes took up this aspect of leveling the field, so to speak, and spoke to the man in a more confidential tone than a servant would normally command.

"As a former soldier and person of authority, do you have any thoughts on the subject? Is there anyone among the staff, for instance, who is in dire need of funds?"

Aames' Scottish burr came out in his answer. "Nay, Mr. Holmes. All of our lads and lassies came with high recommendations. The only one I don't know all that well is our newest addition, Fiona Blair. She's the downstairs maid and does sweeping and dusting. She started with us just before last Christmas. She's a quiet sort. Keeps to herself mostly, but does good work."

Holmes nodded, "I take it she's about five-feet tall, rather thin, and wears Oxford shoes?"

Aames, looked upon my companion with amazement. "How do ye do that, Mr. Holmes? Have ye already seen her?"

"No, but I should very much like to interview her first."

Chapter VI

Aames guided us to the parlour where we took seats near a pleasant fire in soft leather wingback chairs. After an early morning, a strenuous ride on the rails, the stiff carriage from town, and the wooden dining chairs, this was the most comfortable I had felt all day – even more so than the chairs in the Baron's office. As I sank deeply into the soft leather, the effects of a full meal and long day wore on me, and I could feel my eyes closing. My stiff muscles were relaxing as I was being swallowed up by the luxury of the chair. This reverie was brief, of course, for Holmes had more instructions for me to write.

"For your notes," said he, apparently oblivious to the comfort the chairs offered.

22. When interviewing a suspect, there are a variety of techniques that can be used, depending upon the station, personality, and intelligence level of your quarry. Please refer to my monograph regarding this subject. Briefly there are three main methods, with several sub-contexts for each: One – You put your subject at ease. Maintain a friendly manner as if this were just routine, in order to show you covered all possibilities. Two – Treat the subjects as equals. Pretend to take them into your confidence. Ask their advice or opinion on various aspects to see if they know more than they should. Three – Usually the least effective and unfortunately, the one police use most often, though sometimes the situation calls for it. Bully the suspects with an overload of facts, sometimes even ones you make up. By revealing a good deal of your hand, you may convince them you know all, and their only hope of leniency is to make a clean breast of everything. It may also raise their temper and they slip up during their denial, revealing some salient fact that actually leads to their guilt.

At this point, Aames arrived with a young girl in tow, whom he introduced as Fiona Blair. We had stood upon their entrance and Holmes offered his chair to the maidservant. To myself I thought, he was obviously going with method Number One in this instance.

Miss Blair was quite young, certainly not yet twenty. She was petite, roughly five-feet tall, and thin as a rail. Soft brown curls extended beyond the frilled edges of her white mop cap. She had brown, doe-like eyes, a small nose, and thin lips. Her overall countenance bespoke innocence.

As Holmes has so often said, however, "Looks can be deceiving, dear fellow." Thus, I vowed to keep an open mind and took up my pad and pencil to make notes. She had sat in the chair my friend offered, but didn't relax into it, tempting as it was. She sat on the edge, back straight as a rod, and dainty hands folded neatly in her lap. In this position, I couldn't make note of her shoes, as her long grey dress brushed the floor around them.

Holmes, in his most charming tone, spoke up, "Thank you, Miss Blair. We shan't keep you long. I have just a few minor questions for you."

Her sweet face turned up toward the detective as she replied, "As you wish, sir."

Holmes went on to ask her about her duties on the Saturday prior to the theft: What she did and when she did it. From this he gleaned the last time the Grail had been touched prior to the theft, and also what time she ran the carpet sweep along the back corridor.

"Just one more thing, Miss. May I see your right shoe?"

Confused but cooperative, the girl put out her right foot beyond her dress with the toe facing up and the back of the heel dug into the rug. It was a shiny black shoe of the Oxford style. The bottom was well worn, indicating some age to it, but the leather was in good condition.

Holmes retrieved his tape measure from his pocket and knelt before her. Instinctively, she pulled her foot back and fearfully asked, "What are you doing, sir?"

She looked up to Aames, as in a plea against any untoward act this guest was attempting. The former soldier patted her shoulder and said, "'Tis all right, lass. He'll not hurt ye. I promise."

Holmes, likewise, spoke in soothing tones, "I just need to measure the bottom of your shoe, Miss Blair. I shall not touch you in any way. I merely need to compare your shoes with some footprints I found on the hall carpet."

Hesitantly, she extended her foot again, using her hands to keep her dress tightly wrapped around her ankle. Holmes took his measurements and stood. She withdrew her foot quickly back under her dress.

Holmes wrote the numbers down on the paper where he had recorded his earlier measurements and said, "There now, all done. I have one further question of you at this time, Miss Blair. Did you return to the back hallway after you swept the carpet?

"No, sir, I did not."

"Thank you. You may return to your duties."

She arose quickly and stepped over to Aames' side, keeping a watchful eye on the detective the whole time. Aames, exhibiting a more fatherly tone, merely said, "Everything is fine, lass. Back to your chores now."

She bowed her head to him, shot a bewildered look at Holmes, and hurried from the room. Aames folded his hands behind his back and questioned my companion, "Must ye be doing this with all the female staff, Mr. Holmes? I would have appreciated a warning. Our ladies are all quite modest. It is a trait we insist upon when hiring them."

"I only need to check the shoes of anyone approximately her size, Mr. Aames," replied the detective. "Is there any other such person, man or woman?"

"No, she is by far the shortest person on our staff, and has the daintiest feet."

Holmes nodded, "Very well, then. Perhaps we can reduce the time for these interviews if you can tell me the whereabouts of each staff member throughout that Saturday afternoon, after Miss Blair cleaned the Grail."

Aames replied, "The police already asked that question. Each staff member had specific duties which would have kept them quite busy, and nowhere near the armory on that day. And, aye, all those duties were performed to perfection. No one had time to detour into the armory and make off with the grail. The police also searched all of our quarters and found nothing. Anything else?"

Aames had obviously taken some affront at Holmes's methods or questions and was now exhibiting a more belligerent attitude. Whether this was in response to Holmes not communicating his intentions, or at being used as a guinea pig in his demonstration of his powers, I couldn't discern. There was also the possibility that he was somehow involved in the theft.

"Just one more question," continued Holmes, ignoring the man's tone. "Is the Baron's sister, or his niece, of a similar stature to Miss Blair?"

Aames reddened as he brought his hands to his side, fists balled up as he attempted to control his temper. "Miss Allison is petite as well. But I will thank ye not to accuse any member of the family in this mishap. No one would betray Lord Campbell in that fashion, and if ye persist in such a ridiculous persecution, I shall recommend the Baron throw ye out of this house!"

Before Holmes could reply, Aames spun on his heel and strode quickly from the room. I looked up from my chair at my friend. He stared at the retreating back of the Chief of Staff until the door was brutally shut behind him. Then he pulled his pipe and tobacco pouch from his pocket and charged his briarwood as he finally settled into the chair opposite me, allowing its texture to form around his lean frame.

I looked at my friend and asked, "To paraphrase the Bard, 'Dost he protest too much?'"

In an oddly playful mood, Holmes smiled as he replied, "Methinks not. I believe he is merely protecting the household against my 'slings and arrows'. His statements alone do not eliminate any suspects, as he may be in league with someone and providing an alibi for that person. However, we shall, for the present, work along the hypothesis that he is telling the truth until we can prove otherwise."

"So where does that leave us?" I asked. "Do you question the Baron about possible motives by his niece, or do you look harder at the chance of an outside intruder?"

"I shall have to smoke a pipe or two upon it. Tomorrow's daylight will provide me with an opportunity to examine the outer grounds for possible intrusion. But I must eliminate the household as well. I shall need some time to myself. I suggest you seek out that slice of cake saved for you in the kitchen. I shall see you at breakfast."

My taste buds won out over the comfort of the chair and I arose and left Holmes to his pipe. I knew he was likely to smoke several, depending upon how the facts in his mind coalesced into some semblance of order which revealed the thief.

Chapter VII

The next morning, I arose, put on slippers and dressing gown against the cold, and went over to throw open the deep blue curtains to look out upon the day. The sun was too far south to be seen from my north-facing window, but the sky was a high, faded blue with scattered clouds. The snowscape from my window was pristine in its whiteness, and the river a glass-like grey with drifts scattered about. Off in the distance I could see the smoke of chimneys some two-hundred yards away. The houses themselves were unseen behind a copse of trees, but judging by the smoke, there must have been a closely built neighborhood of several dwellings, rather than just a single farm or estate.

Looking down, I could see Holmes standing on the snow-covered lawn, staring at the windows of the armory which were below our rooms. I performed my ablutions, dressed, and went downstairs. Knowing where the kitchen was, I popped in to see if I could obtain a cup of coffee to warm myself until breakfast. Mrs. Galway was most obliging, after my compliments to her Dundee cake the night before. She also told me Holmes had already passed through and was out on the grounds.

Preferring the warmth of the house, I drank my coffee in the kitchen where a hot breakfast was being prepared. When finished, I set my cup in the sink. The lady advised me breakfast would be ready in twenty minutes and I should go retrieve my friend. Already being outfitted in my overcoat, hat, scarf, and gloves, I went out through the servants' door and made my way around to the side of the house where I had last seen Holmes.

He was examining the ground beneath the windows. I hadn't noticed the evening before, but because the lawn sloped down to the river, the bottom of the windows were a good six feet above ground. Apparently hearing my approach, Holmes spoke without looking up. "It won't do. These windows are too high up to be entered without a ladder of sorts, even if someone were slim enough to fit through them, and there is no sign of any disturbance below them. They are the only other way into that room besides the doors. The walls aren't thick enough for any secret passage, and the floor is solid stone in that part of the house. Another note for your instructions, Doctor:

23. *Note the weather conditions on the day of the criminal act. They may provide the means of some clue, or they may have obliterated crucial evidence.*

We circled around the east end of the manor through a garden and came again to the courtyard and the front door. Here we found the lad, Fergus, building a snowman. He had a fairly large base already rolled into place and was working on the middle section as we approached. We surprised him, as he wasn't expecting anyone about this early. "Mr. Holmes, Doctor – What are you doing here?"

Holmes seemed lost in thought and so I answered, "A detective's work is never done, Fergus. Mr. Holmes has been examining the grounds around the house to see if anyone may have entered through a window, or by some other means."

"Oh," replied the lad.

Before he could expand upon that answer, the front door opened and Aames called out, "Master Fergus, time for breakfast! Gentlemen, if you care to join the family, the meal is about to be served."

He turned upon his heel and left the door open for the boy. Fergus brushed off his gloved hands and the knees of his trousers, then made for the door. I took a step to follow, but realized my friend was still mentally off somewhere. I reached out and grabbed his elbow to pull him along. He seemed to snap out of his reverie with a wisp of a smile that was here and then gone in the blink of an eye.

We cleaned up and joined the family at the breakfast table. At one point, when Aames was out of the room, Holmes asked the Baron, "Sir Arthur, you've mentioned the men in your family appear to have enjoyed long lives thanks to the Grail. Just how does that work?"

The Baron set down his coffee cup and replied, "It has become tradition that everyone of this branch of the Campbell bloodline, starting when they are sixteen, drinks wine from the Grail every year on their birthday."

"Does that include the women as well?" asked Holmes.

"Aye, if they be in the bloodline. My sister, for example, but not her husband. Elise," he nodded at his daughter, "but not Roy. Ye can't marry into the tradition. Fergus will be included when he is of age." At this he smiled at the lad.

The boy nodded and replied with a quiet, "Yes, sir."

Holmes folded his hands under his chin and announced, "If you could be so good as to provide a trap for us, I believe Watson and I could put good use of our time in town today. I have matters to discuss with the police and wish to follow up with some of the pawn shops in town."

"Certainly, Mr. Holmes," replied the Baron. "I'll have my groom drive ye in at your convenience."

Holmes held up a palm in supplication, "I would prefer that we go in alone, Sir Arthur. We may have to venture into some seedier parts of town, and I shouldn't wish to put any of your staff at risk, nor be distracted by worrying about their safety. Watson and I have done this sort of thing before and are quite capable working in tandem."

Lord Campbell tilted his head at the detective, frowned, but then acquiesced, "Very well. I shall have our phaeton harnessed and available for you within the hour."

He rang for Aames. The Chief of Staff came and received instructions to relate to the groom. While he was there, Holmes posed a question. "Aames, since the night of the theft, have you noticed anything amiss in the wine cellar?"

All eyes turned upon Holmes at this apparently incongruous statement. Finally Aames replied, "Nothing that I recall. Why?"

"Just a curiosity. Whoever stole the Grail may have thought its powers only worked with a Campbell's wine. It might provide a clue as to motive. If such were the case, then we may have hope that the theft was for the Grail's powers and not for its monetary value. Thus we may still find it intact.

"At any rate, please thank Mrs. Galway for an excellent breakfast. I believe our journey into town shall require that we luncheon there, but we certainly expect to be back well before dark and dinner."

As we each left the table to go our separate ways, I noted that Elise went toward the kitchen, Roy reminded his son he had schoolwork to do in his room, and he could play outside after lunch. Then he went down a hallway to where we knew he had his office. The Baron went to his study and Aames off to deliver the message to the groom to prepare our ride.

Holmes and I ascended the stairs to our rooms. Just before I entered my door, he turned and made an unusual request of me. "I would most appreciate it if, in addition to your revolver, you would also bring your medical bag. I'll meet you at the stable in fifteen minutes."

I cocked my head at him, questioningly, but he was already stepping into his room. As I prepared for our journey, I slipped my old army Webley into my overcoat pocket and pulled my leather medical bag from the closet.

I half-expected to run into my friend on the way to the stable, but found I had actually beaten him there. The groom had hitched a fine pair to the Baron's phaeton, which was just large enough for two to travel comfortably and provide some little protection from precipitation, though not much from wind. Fortunately the skies were blue with high scattered clouds. I only hoped they would remain so for the duration of our sojourn.

When my companion arrived, he carried an extra blanket wrapped around his left arm, "I thought we could use a little extra protection against the cold. Would you be so kind as to drive?"

Since we weren't involved in a high-speed chase through the streets of London, which Holmes knows backwards and forward, this wasn't all that unusual. Often he preferred to not be distracted by physical activity while he was confirming the facts of a case in his mind. I set my medical bag on the floor, took up the reins, asked the groom for directions to the Ayr Police Station, and set the horses upon a trot.

We drove out to the Holmston Road. There was a copse of trees about three-hundred yards south of the castle, just as the road turned west with the river. My friend bid me to pull to the side and looked carefully about.

"Your medical bag if you please," he said. Then he unwrapped the blanket and used it to shield the fact that he was now placing the stolen Grail into the leather case!

"Holmes!" I cried, then lowered my voice to a whisper at his silent admonition. "Where did you find it?"

"Drive on please. I will tell you the tale as we continue our little ruse."

Chapter VIII

I whipped up the horses again and we made for town at a moderate pace, since there seemed to be no actual hurry. Holmes explained what he had done while I was in my room, preparing for our journey. He began his tale by admonishing me that I couldn't publish this particular case until after the death of the current Baron.

"What about all the instructions you have had me include, Holmes? This was to be your magnum opus for future generations."

"I am sure we will find other occasions to include my teachings. I have made a promise that I must enjoin you not to break."

"As you wish," I replied. Secretly, however, I was relieved. I hadn't yet determined how I was to weave his teachings into a story that publishers would feel to be appealing to the masses.

Holmes began his explanation. "You noticed my distraction when we were outside after coming upon Fergus constructing his snowman. I had come upon an idea that was highly improbable, but then, the circumstances of this theft were already *outré* to begin with.

"While it wasn't a certainty, the most likely explanation of the tracks upon the carpet of the back hallway was that they were left by the thief.

391

The size indicated a person of small stature. Thus the search among the female staff. Miss Blair isn't our thief. Though her shoes are the proper size, as I observed her walk she is slightly duck-footed. The tracks in the hall didn't turn out as her feet would. If Aames is to be believed, only the Baron's niece, Allison, who isn't a blood-relative, would be the next likely suspect.

"However, as you are well-aware, Oxford-style shoes are favored by both genders under certain circumstances. Fergus stature is small for his age, and thus his feet are the proper size. I noted this fact when I saw his footprints in the snow."

"Fergus is the thief?" I asked, incredulously. "But, why? Isn't he the next heir to the baronetcy? The Grail would be his eventually."

"It isn't the grail itself that he craved," said my friend. "Let me repeat the story I learned while you were getting ready for our little day trip."

Sherlock Holmes had retrieved a blanket from his room after breakfast and walked down the hall to the bedroom of Fergus Lennox. Receiving permission to come in upon his knock, he found the lad seated at a desk by the window. A book was open and he was writing on a piece of paper by the natural sunlight that shone through when the curtains were opened.

At first, Fergus seemed confused his visitor wasn't one of the servants or his mother. Then he stood, a look of panic that a thirteen year old couldn't hide upon his face. "Mr. Holmes! What do you want . . . sir?"

"I wish to tell you a story, Fergus, may I sit?"

The lad swallowed hard and nodded as he sat back down. Holmes sat on the edge of the bed facing the boy and began a tale which he hadn't even shared with me.

"When I was your age, I was also about your size. This was rather unfortunate, for I had an older brother who was already six feet tall. We were always rather competitive, and he often drove me to temper that resulted in my fruitless attempts at physical assault upon him. Naturally, in spite of the fact that he wasn't athletic, he easily rendered me harmless. This, of course, made me all the more frustrated. I would have done anything to be able to best him physically.

"I believe we share that frustration. While I have noticed that you are well-coordinated, your size likely keeps you from competing as well as you would hope at school."

"It isn't fair!" cried Fergus. "I can beat anybody my size at anything. But they always put me up against larger boys because of my age and I can never win because they are all taller, heavier, and stronger."

The detective looked with sympathy at lad, then replied, "So you thought drinking from the Grail would give you some sort of extra power due to its purported supernatural properties."

He made this statement so matter-of-factly that Fergus took it as a known fact rather than a question and said, "Yes! If all the stories I've been told are true, then it should help me. I couldn't wait until I was sixteen. Who made that rule up anyway? I needed help now! So I snuck down the back stairs in the middle of the night and took up the Grail. Then I went to the kitchen and poured some of the wine Mrs. Galway uses to cook with into the cup. I didn't want to be caught in the kitchen, so I rushed back up here and drank it behind closed doors. I was going to take the Grail back down with no one the wiser, but the wine made me sleepy and the next thing I knew, it was morning. There was no way to put the cup back without being seen. Then the police came and the room was always locked after that."

"Where is the Grail now?" asked Holmes.

Fergus reached down and opened the bottom drawer of his desk. He pulled out the Grail which was wrapped in an old shirt and handed it over to Holmes. "What will you do Mr. Holmes? You won't tell Grandfather will you?"

Holmes looked upon the artifact with interest and replied, "I will keep your secret if I can, Master Fergus. I have a plan which I believe will satisfy everyone."

He stood and draped the blanket over the golden cup. "I'm going into town with Dr. Watson. I'll then bring the Grail back to your grandfather with a convincing tale and no one the wiser. But I leave you with this thought: As I said, I was about your height when I was thirteen. By the time I was fourteen, I had grown five inches. I kept growing until I was as tall as I am now by the time I was twenty. So, take heart young man. Patience is a virtue and is its own reward."

By the time Holmes finished his story, I was bringing our horses to a stop at the local police station. I turned to my friend and asked, "Since you already have the Grail, what are you going to tell the police?"

"Nothing," he replied.

At my surprised look he expanded upon his answer, "Well, I may give them a few hints on how to better conduct future investigations. Primarily though, I shall introduce us to the local Chief Inspector and ask about the location of local pawn shops or fences where the Grail may find its way. This will coincide with the tale I am weaving for Sir Arthur."

Thus, we spent the day traveling to various pawn shops and making discreet inquiries. We enjoyed an excellent lunch of fried steak, tomatoes, potatoes, and onions at Tudor's Grill. Afterward, Holmes took the reins and drove us down to the seashore.

The harbor at Ayr isn't exceptionally large. However, in our favor, there were two boats heading out that day which suited Holmes's purpose. One for Belfast, and one for Oslo, Norway.

By three o'clock we were on our way back to Bellrose Castle. Holmes rehearsing with me the tale we would tell the Baron upon our return. The weather had held, and had actually approached fifty-five degrees Fahrenheit around two o'clock, but was now steadily dropping and the wind was picking up.

It was nearly gale force by the time we gained the courtyard at Bellrose, and the groom rushed to open the stable door so we could pull in safely out of the weather. Fortunately, among the later renovations to the manor was an enclosed walkway had been constructed from the stables to the main house along the west wall. We were able to reach the house in relative comfort.

This path brought us into the kitchen and the cook graciously offered us hot coffee. We thanked her, but Holmes insisted we take it with us so we could report to Sir Arthur immediately. This being in keeping with the story Holmes was about to tell.

Sweeping into Lord Campbell's library where we had first met him, Holmes cried out. "Success, Sir Arthur! Watson, if you please?"

I opened my medical bag and produced the Grail, setting it gently upon the polished surface of the Baron's desk. He stood in amazement and snatched it up, holding it reverently to his breast for several seconds. Then he raised it up and examined it closely for any damage or missing jewels. Finally, he reached out and shook each of our hands. "Mr. Holmes, Dr. Watson, how can I thank ye? I confess I was grasping at straws when I called ye in on this case. Ye have exceeded expectations. Whatever your fee, sir, I will pay it gladly!"

Holmes cocked his head and I wondered what price he would put upon what turned out to be a fairly simple retrieval. The number he offered was far below his normal fee. In fact, it was barely enough to cover our train tickets and the meal we had enjoyed in town.

Lord Campbell shook his head. "No, no. Surely you're time alone is worth more than that."

Holmes waved his hand and replied, "The matter turned out to be quite simple, though interesting as an exercise. I have named my fee, Sir Arthur. You may do as you see fit. Now that we have completed our task, we shall be returning to London on tomorrow's train."

"But how did ye find it? Where was it? Did ye face any danger? I am used to receiving full reports of actions taken, sir,"

394

Holmes shook his head, "I am not one of your soldiers, Major. However, I shall be happy to report all, though I do not wish to repeat myself. Let us discuss it at dinner so the whole family can be satisfied."

Later that evening, all were seated around the dinner table and even Aames was in attendance as he stood to one side. Once the meal was served and Lord Campbell had offered the grace, he turned to Holmes and said, "Now, Mr. Holmes, please tell us how you were able to recover the Grail."

Holmes weaved a tale, as only he can, about how we obtained information from the police and spent the day tracking down various places where the Grail may have been sold. By his reckoning, at one pawn shop we entered just as the owner was saying "No" to a particularly rough-looking fellow. As this chap walked out in a huff, we approached the pawnbroker regarding the Grail and was told that the man who just left was trying to sell it to him. He knew stolen goods when he saw them and put the fellow off. We then supposedly rushed out the door and gave chase. Holmes stayed on this man's heels while he waved me to try and cut him off from across the street.

When the rough turned in my direction, I had used my old rugby skills and brought him down. He dropped the bag holding the Grail. My leg though, had given out and Holmes had to help me out of the street from harm's way of the passing traffic. We saw the fellow snag a cab but had trouble finding one ourselves. It must have been a good two or three minutes that gave the thief a head start. He seemed to be heading for the docks, so we instructed our driver to do so as well. As we arrived, a small steam vessel was just pulling away. Checking with the harbor master, we found that two boats were supposed to be heading out at that time. One for Belfast and one for Oslo. We didn't know for certain if our thief was on either boat. The description we were able to glean from our running observation and the pawnbroker was that of a dark, swarthy fellow of lean build and short stature.

"So you see, Sir Arthur," said Holmes. "While I was able to gain some interesting facts about the case, notably that he must have picked the lock on the kitchen entrance, for there were no tracks about any of the windows. It was merely old fashion police work that retrieved your artifact."

Baron Campbell nodded. "Well, even if it wasn't your extraordinary powers which secured the Grail, you did retrieve it for us, and we are most grateful. "Pastor Reynolds will be as well, come Christmas."

"Here! Here!" said Lennox, and the rest of the family, including young Fergus, raised their glasses to us.

"How is your leg after all that, Doctor Watson?" asked Elise, ever the concerned mother-figure.

I cleared my throat and replied, "The cold weather always has a detrimental effect upon it, Mrs. Lennox. It will be all right again in a day or two."

We stuffed ourselves that evening and again we were treated to a magnificent Dundee cake. The next morning, we packed early, but chose to breakfast with the family before catching a ten o'clock train. Before breakfast, I wandered out to the courtyard to see how Fergus was progressing with his snowman. He had nearly finished it the day before, but it still lacked arms, face, or clothing when we had returned the previous afternoon.

What I found, however, was Sherlock Holmes with the boy on a patch of snow on what would normally be grass, thus providing a softer surface. He was teaching the boy some unique wrestling moves and Fergus was picking them up quickly. He had just put Holmes on his backside when I walked up. "Shall I make note of this for your instruction manual, Holmes? How not to be bested by an opponent in wrestling, perhaps?"

My friend stood, frowned at me then, smiled at the lad. "I am just showing Master Fergus how to use an opponent's size and weight against him. The battle does not always go to the strong, remember."

We said our goodbyes after breakfast and were driven to Ayr Station. Once alone on the train I remarked to my friend, "You seem to have once again sacrificed truth for the greater good, Holmes."

My companion smiled, "After this experience, it is unlikely the lad will ever steal anything again. Justice is not always served by the letter of the law, Watson. Often mercy can be the greater solution."

"A most admirable attitude for the Christmas season, Holmes," I replied, pulling a flask of brandy from my coat and offering it to him saying in my best Scots burr, "*Nollik Chree-hel Blee-una va oor*".

He took a swig and returned it saying, "Thank you for playing along with my little game, Doctor, and I wish you a Merry Christmas, and Happy New Year as well!"

NOTE

*   That case was "Mrs. Forrester's Complication" in *The MX Book of New Sherlock Holmes Stories – Part XI: Some Untold Cases (1880-1891)* (MX Publishing, 2018) and *Sherlock Holmes Alphabet of Cases Volume Three* (Baker Street Studios, 2019). That case would later involve them with Mary Morstan, Watson's future wife, in *The Sign of the Four*.

398

400

About the Contributors

The following contributors appear in this volume:
The MX Book of New Sherlock Holmes Stories
Part XXVIII – More Christmas Adventures (1869-1888)

Deanna Baran lives in a remote part of Texas where cowboys may still be seen in their natural habitat. A librarian and former museum curator, she writes in between cups of tea, playing *Go*, and trading postcards with people around the world.

Brian Belanger is a publisher, editor, illustrator, author, and graphic designer. In 2015, he co-founded Belanger Books along with his brother, author Derrick Belanger. He designs the covers for every Belanger Books release, and his illustrations have appeared in the MacDougall Twins with Sherlock Holmes series, as well as *Dragonella, Scones and Bones on Baker Street*, and *Sherlock Holmes: A Three-Pipe Problem*. Brian has published a number of Sherlock Holmes anthologies, as well as new editions of August Derleth's classic Solar Pons mysteries. Since 2016, Brian has written and designed letters for the *Dear Holmes* series, and illustrated a comic book for indie band The Moonlight Initiative. In 2019, Brian received his investiture in the PSI as "Sir Ronald Duveen". Find him online at *www.belangerbooks.com, www.zhahadun.wixsite.com/221b*, and *www.redbubble.com/people/zhahadun*

Thomas A. Burns Jr. writes *The Natalie McMasters Mysteries* from the small town of Wendell, North Carolina, where he lives with his wife and son, four cats, and a Cardigan Welsh Corgi. He was born and grew up in New Jersey, attended Xavier High School in Manhattan, earned B.S degrees in Zoology and Microbiology at Michigan State University, and a M.S. in Microbiology at North Carolina State University. As a kid, Tom started reading mysteries with The Hardy Boys, Ken Holt, and Rick Brant, then graduated to the classic stories by authors such as A. Conan Doyle, Dorothy Sayers, John Dickson Carr, Erle Stanley Gardner, and Rex Stout, to name a few. Tom has written fiction as a hobby all of his life, starting with *The Man from U.N.C.L.E.* stories in marble-backed copybooks in grade school. He built a career as technical, science, and medical writer and editor for nearly thirty years in industry and government. Now that he's a full-time novelist, he's excited to publish his own mystery series, as well as to write stories about his second most favorite detective, Sherlock Holmes. His Holmes story, "The Camberwell Poisoner", recently appeared in the March-June issue of *The Strand Magazine*. Tom has also written a Lovecraftian horror novel, *The Legacy of the Unborn*, under the pen name of Silas K. Henderson – a sequel to H.P. Lovecraft's masterpiece *At the Mountains of Madness*.

Martin Daley was born in Carlisle, Cumbria in 1964. He cites Doyle's Holmes and Watson as his favourite literary characters, who continue to inspire his own detective writing. His fiction and non-fiction books include a Holmes pastiche set predominantly in his home city in 1903. In the adventure, he introduced his own detective, Inspector Cornelius Armstrong, who has subsequently had some of his own cases published by MX Publishing. For more information visit *www.martindaley.co.uk*

Sir Arthur Conan Doyle (1859-1930) *Holmes Chronicler Emeritus*. If not for him, this anthology would not exist. Author, physician, patriot, sportsman, spiritualist, husband and

401

father, and advocate for the oppressed. He is remembered and honored for the purposes of this collection by being the man who introduced Sherlock Holmes to the world. Through fifty-six Holmes short stories, four novels, and additional Apocryphal entries, Doyle revolutionized mystery stories and also greatly influenced and improved police forensic methods and techniques for the betterment of all. *Steel True Blade Straight.*

Steve Emecz's main field is technology, in which he has been working for about twenty-five years. Steve is a regular speaker at trade shows and his tech career has taken him to more than fifty countries – so he's no stranger to planes and airports. In 2008, MX published its first Sherlock Holmes book, and MX has gone on to become the largest specialist Holmes publisher in the world with over 500 books. MX is a social enterprise and supports three main causes. The first is Happy Life, a children's rescue project in Nairobi, Kenya, where he and his wife, Sharon, spend every Christmas at the rescue centre in Kasarani. They have written two editions of a short book about the project, *The Happy Life Story.* The second is Undershaw, Sir Arthur Conan Doyle's former home, which is a school for children with learning disabilities for which Steve is a patron. Steve has been a mentor for the World Food Programme for several years, and was part of the Nobel Peace Prize winning team in 2020.

Mark A. Gagen BSI is co-founder of Wessex Press, sponsor of the popular *From Gillette to Brett* conferences, and publisher of *The Sherlock Holmes Reference Library* and many other fine Sherlockian titles. A life-long Holmes enthusiast, he is a member of *The Baker Street Irregulars* and *The Illustrious Clients of Indianapolis*. A graphic artist by profession, his work is often seen on the covers of *The Baker Street Journal* and various BSI books.

Tim Gambrell lives in Exeter, Devon, with his wife, two young sons, three cats and nine chickens. He has previously contributed to Parts XIII, XVI, XIX, XXIII, & XXVII of *The MX Book of New Sherlock Holmes Stories* from MX Publishing, as well as *Sherlock Holmes and Dr Watson: The Early Adventures, Sherlock Holmes and the Occult Detectives,* and *Sherlock Holmes: After the East Wind Blows,* all from Belanger Books. Outside of the world of Holmes, Tim has written extensively for *Doctor Who* spin-off ranges. He is the range editor of Candy Jar Books' *UNIT* series, and has written several novels and short stories for their *Lethbridge-Stewart* and *Lucy Wilson Mysteries* ranges. He has also written a novel, *The Way of The Bry'hunee,* for the *Erimem* range from Thebes Publishing. Tim has written audiobooks for Big Finish Productions, including *Blake's 7: The Palluma Project* (2021), *Signifiers of the Verphidiae* in *Bernice Summerfield: The Christmas Collection* (2020) and *Stockholm from Home* in *Bernice Summerfield: True Stories* (2017).

Dick Gillman is an English writer and acrylic artist living in Brittany, France with his wife Alex, Truffle, their Black Labrador, and Jean-Claude, their Breton cat. During his retirement from teaching, he has written over twenty Sherlock Holmes short stories which are published as both e-books and paperbacks. His initial contribution to the superb MX Sherlock Holmes collection, published in October 2015, was entitled "The Man on Westminster Bridge" and had the privilege of being chosen as the anchor story in *The MX Book of New Sherlock Holmes Stories – Part II (1890-1895).*

John Atkinson Grimshaw (1836-1893) was born in Leeds, England. His amazing paintings, usually featuring twilight or night scenes illuminated by gas-lamps or moonlight, are easily recognizable, and are often used on the covers of books about The Great

402

Detective to set the mood, as shadowy figures move in the distance through misty mysterious settings and over rain-slicked streets.

Liz Hedgecock grew up in London, England (a train and a tube ride away from Baker Street), did an English degree, and then took forever to start writing. Now Liz travels between the nineteenth and twenty-first centuries, murdering people. To be fair, she does usually clean up after herself. Liz's reimaginings of Sherlock Holmes, the Caster & Fleet, and Maisie Frobisher Victorian mystery series, and the Magical Bookshop and Pippa Parker contemporary mystery series are available in eBook and paperback. Liz lives in Cheshire with her husband and two sons, and when she's not writing you can usually find her reading, going for walks, or cooing over stuff in museums and art galleries. That's her story, anyway, and she's sticking to it.

Stephen Herczeg is an IT Geek, writer, actor, and film-maker based in Canberra Australia. He has been writing for over twenty years and has completed a couple of dodgy novels, sixteen feature-length screenplays, and numerous short stories and scripts. Stephen was very successful in 2017's International Horror Hotel screenplay competition, with his scripts *TITAN* winning the Sci-Fi category and *Dark are the Woods* placing second in the horror category. His three-volume short story collection, *The Curious Cases of Sherlock Holmes*, will be published in 2021. His work has featured in *Sproutlings – A Compendium of Little Fictions* from Hunter Anthologies, the *Hells Bells* Christmas horror anthology published by the Australasian Horror Writers Association, and the *Below the Stairs*, *Trickster's Treats*, *Shades of Santa*, *Behind the Mask*, and *Beyond the Infinite* anthologies from *OzHorror.Con*, *The Body Horror Book*, *Anemone Enemy*, and *Petrified Punks* from Oscillate Wildly Press, and *Sherlock Holmes In the Realms of H.G. Wells* and *Sherlock Holmes: Adventures Beyond the Canon* from Belanger Books.

Paul Hiscock is an author of crime, fantasy, horror, and science fiction tales. His short stories have appeared in a variety of anthologies, and include a seventeenth century whodunnit, a science fiction western, a clockpunk fairytale, and numerous Sherlock Holmes pastiches. He lives with his family in Kent (England) and spends his days taking care of his two children. He mainly does his writing in coffee shops with members of the local NaNoWriMo group or in the middle of the night when his family has gone to sleep. Consequently, his stories tend to be fuelled by large amounts of black coffee. You can find out more about Paul's writing at *www.detectivesanddragons.uk*.

Mike Hogan writes mostly historical novels and short stories, many set in Victorian London and featuring Sherlock Holmes and Doctor Watson. He read the Conan Doyle stories at school with great enjoyment, but hadn't thought much about Sherlock Holmes until, having missed the Granada/Jeremy Brett TV series when it was originally shown in the eighties, he came across a box set of videos in a street market and was hooked on Holmes again. He started writing Sherlock Holmes pastiches several years ago, having great fun re-imagining situations for the Conan Doyle characters to act in. The relationship between Holmes and Watson fascinates him as one of the great literary friendships. (He's also a huge admirer of Patrick O'Brian's Aubrey-Maturin novels). Like Captain Aubrey and Doctor Maturin, Holmes and Watson are an odd couple, differing in almost every facet of their characters, but sharing a common sense of decency and a common humanity. Living with Sherlock Holmes can't have been easy, and Mike enjoys adding a stronger vein of "pawky humour" into the Conan Doyle mix, even letting Watson have the second-to-last word on occasions. His books include *Sherlock Holmes and the Scottish Question, The Gory Season – Sherlock Holmes, Jack the Ripper and the Thames Torso Murders*, and the *Sherlock Holmes & Young Winston 1887 Trilogy* (*The Deadwood Stage, The Jubilee Plot,* and *The Giant Moles*), He has also written the following short story collections: *Sherlock Holmes: Murder at the Savoy and Other Stories, Sherlock Holmes: The Skull of Kohada Koheiji and Other Stories,* and *Sherlock Holmes: Murder on the Brighton Line and Other Stories,* among others. *www.mikehoganbooks.com*

Nancy Holder, BSI, is a *New York Times* bestselling author who lives in Washington state. She has received 6 Bram Stoker Awards from the Horror Writers Association and the 2019 Grand Master "Faust" Award from the International Association of Media Tie-in Writers. She has written numerous Sherlockian pastiches and articles and is a member of several Sherlockian societies including *The Sound of the Baskervilles* and *The Sherlock Holmes Society of London.* She also writes and edits comic books and pulp fiction. Forthcoming works include two new comic book and graphic novel series with her writing partner, Alan Philipson.

Roger Johnson BSI, ASH is a retired librarian, now working as a volunteer assistant at the Essex Police Museum. In his spare time, he is commissioning editor of *The Sherlock Holmes Journal,* an occasional lecturer, and a frequent contributor to *The Writings about the Writings.* His sole work of Holmesian pastiche was published in 1997 in Mike Ashley's anthology *The Mammoth Book of New Sherlock Holmes Adventures,* and he has the greatest respect for the many authors who have contributed new tales to the present mighty trilogy. Like his wife, Jean Upton, he is a member of both *The Baker Street Irregulars* and *The Adventuresses of Sherlock Holmes.*

John Lawrence served for thirty-eight years as a staff member in the U.S. House of Representatives, the last eight as Chief of Staff to Speaker Nancy Pelosi (2005-2013). He has been a Visiting Professor at the University of California's Washington Center since 2013. He is the author of *The Class of '74: Congress After Watergate and the Roots of Partisanship* (2018), and has a Ph.D. in history from the University of California (Berkeley).

Jeffrey Lockwood spent youthful afternoons darkly enchanted by feeding grasshoppers to black widows in his New Mexican backyard, which accounts for his scientific and literary affinities. He earned a doctorate in entomology and worked as an ecologist at the University of Wyoming before metamorphosing into a Professor of Natural Sciences & Humanities in the departments of philosophy and creative writing. He considers Sherlock Holmes a model of scientific prowess, integrating exquisite observational skills with incisive abductive (not deductive) reasoning.

David Marcum plays *The Game* with deadly seriousness. He first discovered Sherlock Holmes in 1975 at the age of ten, and since that time, he has collected, read, and chronologicized literally thousands of traditional Holmes pastiches in the form of novels, short stories, radio and television episodes, movies and scripts, comics, fan-fiction, and unpublished manuscripts. He is the author of nearly ninety Sherlockian pastiches, some published in anthologies and magazines such as *The Strand,* and others collected in his own books, *The Papers of Sherlock Holmes, Sherlock Holmes and A Quantity of Debt, Sherlock Holmes – Tangled Skeins, Sherlock Holmes and The Eye of Heka,* and *The Complete Papers of Sherlock Holmes.* He has edited over sixty books, including several dozen traditional Sherlockian anthologies, such as the ongoing series *The MX Book of New Sherlock Holmes Stories,* which he created in 2015. This collection is now up to 30 volumes, with more in preparation. He was responsible for bringing back August Derleth's

404

Solar Pons for a new generation, first with his collection of authorized Pons stories, *The Papers of Solar Pons*, and then by editing the reissued authorized versions of the original Pons books, and then volumes of new Pons adventures. He has done the same for the adventures of Dr. Thorndyke, and has plans for similar projects in the future. He has contributed numerous essays to various publications, and is a member of a number of Sherlockian groups and Scions. His irregular Sherlockian blog, *A Seventeen Step Program*, addresses various topics related to his favorite book friends (as his son used to call them when he was small), and can be found at *http://17stepprogram.blogspot.com/* He is a licensed Civil Engineer, living in Tennessee with his wife and son. Since the age of nineteen, he has worn a deerstalker as his regular-and-only hat. In 2013, he and his deerstalker were finally able make his first trip-of-a-lifetime Holmes Pilgrimage to England, with return Pilgrimages in 2015 and 2016, where you may have spotted him. If you ever run into him and his deerstalker out and about, feel free to say hello!

Mark Mower is a crime writer and historian whose passion for tales about Sherlock Holmes and Dr. Watson began at the age of twelve, when he watched an early black-and-white film featuring the unrivalled screen pairing of Basil Rathbone and Nigel Bruce. Hastily seeking out the original stories of Sir Arthur Conan Doyle, and continually searching for further film and television adaptations, his has been a lifelong obsession. Now a member of the Crime Writers' Association, The Sherlock Holmes Society of London, and The Solar Pons Society of London, he has written numerous crime books. Mark has contributed to over 20 Holmes anthologies, including 13 parts of *The MX Book of New Sherlock Holmes Stories*, *The Book of Extraordinary New Sherlock Holmes Stories* (Mango Publishing) and *Sherlock Holmes – Before Baker Street* (Belanger Books). His own books include *A Farewell to Baker Street, Sherlock Holmes: The Baker Street Case-Files*, and *Sherlock Holmes: The Baker Street Legacy*, and *Sherlock Holmes: The Baker Street Epilogue* (all with MX Publishing).

Will Murray has been writing about popular culture since 1973, principally on the subjects of comic books, pulp magazine heroes, and film. As a fiction writer, he's the author of over 70 novels featuring characters as diverse as Nick Fury and Remo Williams. With the late Steve Ditko, he created the Unbeatable Squirrel Girl for Marvel Comics. Murray has written numerous short stories, many on Lovecraftian themes. Currently, he writes The Wild Adventures of Doc Savage for Altus Press. His acclaimed Doc Savage novel, *Skull Island*, pits the pioneer superhero against the legendary King Kong. This was followed by *King Kong vs. Tarzan* and two Doc Savage novels guest-starring The Shadow, and *Tarzan, Conqueror of Mars*, a crossover with John Carter of Mars. He is the author of the short story collecdtion *The Wild Adventures of Sherlock Holmes. www.adventuresinbronze.com* is his website.

Sidney Paget (1860-1908), a few of whose illustrations are used within this anthology, was born in London, and like his two older brothers, became a famed illustrator and painter. He completed over three-hundred-and-fifty drawings for the Sherlock Holmes stories that were first published in *The Strand* magazine, defining Holmes's image forever after in the public mind.

Roger Riccard's family history has Scottish roots, which trace his lineage back to Highland, Scotland. This British Isles ancestry encouraged his interest in the writings of Sir Arthur Conan Doyle at an early age. He has authored the novels *Sherlock Holmes & The Case of the Poisoned Lilly*, and *Sherlock Holmes & The Case of the Twain Papers.* In addition, he has produced several short stories in *Sherlock Holmes Adventures for the*

Twelve Days of Christmas, and in November 2021 his fifth and final volume of *A Sherlock Holmes Alphabet of Cases* will be released. All of his books have been published by Baker Street Studios. Having earned Bachelor of Arts Degrees in both Journalism and History from California State University, Northridge, his career has progressed from teaching into business, where he has used his writing skills in various aspects of employee communications. He has also contributed to newspapers and magazines and has earned some awards for his efforts. He currently lives in a suburb of Los Angeles, California with his wife/editor/inspiration, Rosilyn.

Brenda Seabrooke's stories have been published in a number of reviews, journals, and anthologies. She has received grants from the National Endowment for the Arts and Emerson College's Robbie Macauley Award. She is the author of twenty-three books for young readers including *Scones and Bones on Baker Street: Sherlock's (maybe!) Dog and the Dirt Dilemma*, and *The Rascal in the Castle: Sherlock's (possible!) Dog and the Queen's Revenge*. Brenda states: "*It was fun to write from Dr. Watson's point of view and not have to worry about fleas, smelly pits, ralphing, or scratching at inopportune times.*"

Joseph W. Svec III is retired from Oceanography, Satellite Test Engineering, and college teaching. He has lived on a forty-foot cruising sailboat, on a ranch in the Sierra Nevada Foothills, in a country rose-garden cottage, and currently lives in the shadow of a castle with his childhood sweetheart and several long coated German shepherds. He enjoys writing, gardening, creating dioramas, world travel, and enjoying time with his sweetheart.

Amy Thomas is a member of the *Baker Street Babes* Podcast, and the author of *The Detective and The Woman* mystery novels featuring Sherlock Holmes and Irene Adler. She blogs at *girlmeetssherlock.wordpress.com*, and she writes and edits professionally from her home in Fort Myers, Florida.

Thomas A. (Tom) Turley has been "hooked on Holmes" since finishing *The Hound of the Baskervilles* at about the age of twelve. However, his interest in Sherlockian pastiches didn't take off until he wrote one. *Sherlock Holmes and the Adventure of the Tainted Canister* (2014) is available as an e-book and an audiobook from MX Publishing. It also appeared in *The Art of Sherlock Holmes – USA Edition 1*. In 2017, two of Tom's stories, "A Scandal in Serbia" and "A Ghost from Christmas Past" were published in Parts VI and VII of this anthology. "Ghost" was also included in *The Art of Sherlock Holmes – West Palm Beach Edition*. Meanwhile, Tom is finishing a collection of historical pastiches entitled *Sherlock Holmes and the Crowned Heads of Europe*, to be published in 2021 The first story, "Sherlock Holmes and the Case of the Dying Emperor" (2018) is available from MX Publishing as a separate e-book. Set in the brief reign of Emperor Frederick III (1888), it inaugurates Sherlock Holmes's espionage campaign against the German Empire, which ended only in August 1914 with "His Last Bow". When completed, *Sherlock Holmes and the Crowned Heads of Europe* will also include "A Scandal in Serbia" and two additional historical tales. Although he has a Ph.D. in British history, Tom spent most of his professional career as an archivist with the State of Alabama. He and his wife Paula (an aspiring science fiction novelist) live in Montgomery, Alabama. Interested readers may contact Tom through MX Publishing or his Goodreads author's page.

Emma West is the Acting Headteacher at Undershaw (formerly Stepping Stones), a school for special needs students located at Undershaw, one of Sir Arthur Conan Doyle's former homes in Hindhead, England.

*The following contributors appear
in the companion volumes:*
Part XXIX – More Christmas Adventures (1889-1896)
Part XXX – More Christmas Adventures (1897-1928)

Ian Ableson is an ecologist by training and a writer by choice. When not reading or writing, he can reliably be found scowling at a clipboard while ankle-deep in a marsh somewhere in Michigan. His love for the stories of Arthur Conan Doyle started when his grandfather gave him a copy of *The Original Illustrated Sherlock Holmes* when he was in high school, and he's proud to have been able to contribute to the continuation of the tales of Sherlock Holmes and Dr. Watson.

Wayne Anderson was born and raised in the beautiful Pacific Northwest, growing up in Alaska and Washington State. He discovered Sherlock Holmes around age ten and promptly devoured the Canon. When it was all gone, he tried to sate the addiction by writing his own Sherlock Holmes stories, which are mercifully lost forever. Sadly, he moved to California in his twenties and has lived there since. He has two grown sons who are both writers as well. He spends his time writing or working on the TV pilots and patents which will someday make him fabulously wealthy. When he's not doing these things, he is either reading to his young daughter from The Canon or trying to find space in his house for more bookshelves.

Derrick Belanger, PSI is an author and educator most noted for his books and lectures on Sherlock Holmes and Sir Arthur Conan Doyle, as well as his writing for the blogs *I Hear of Sherlock Everywhere* and *Belanger Books Sherlock Holmes and Other Readings Blog*. Both volumes of his two-volume anthology, *A Study in Terror: Sir Arthur Conan Doyle's Revolutionary Stories of Fear and the Supernatural* were #1 best sellers on the Amazon.com U.K. Sherlock Holmes book list, and his *MacDougall Twins with Sherlock Holmes* chapter book, *Attack of the Violet Vampire!* was also a #1 bestselling new release in the U.K. Through his press, Belanger Books, he has released a number of Sherlock Holmes anthologies as well as new editions of August Derleth's original Solar Pons series. In 2019, Mr. Belanger received his investiture in the PSI as "Albert, the Dove". In January 2020, Mr. Belanger was awarded the Susan Z. Diamond Award in recognition of outstanding efforts to introduce young people to Sherlock Holmes. Mr. Belanger dedicates "The Man of Miracles" to teacher extraordinaire Kimberly Kubsch, for introducing him to the wonderful world of Magical Realism.

Andrew Bryant was born in Bridgend, Wales, and now lives in Burlington, Ontario. His previous publications include *Poetry Toronto, Prism International, Existere, On Spec, The Dalhousie Review*, and *The Toronto Star*. His first Holmes story was published in *The MX Book of New Sherlock Holmes Stories - Part XIII*, with the second in *Part XVI*. The two stories in this collection are the third and fourth. Andrew's interest in Holmes stems from watching the Basil Rathbone and Nigel Bruce films as a child, followed by collecting The Canon, and a fascinating visit to 221B Baker Street.

Chris Chan is a writer, educator, and historian. He works as a researcher and "International Goodwill Ambassador" for Agatha Christie Ltd. His true crime articles, reviews, and short fiction have appeared (or will soon appear) in *The Strand, The Wisconsin Magazine of History, Mystery Weekly, Gilbert!, Nerd HQ*, Akashic Books' *Mondays are Murder* web series, *The Baker Street Journal*, and *Sherlock Holmes Mystery Magazine*. His latest book is *Sherlock and Irene: The Secret Truth Behind "A Scandal in Bohemia"*. He is also the

407

author of *Murder Most Grotesque: The Comedic Crime Fiction of Joyce Porter*, published by Level Best Books. His first novel, *Sherlock's Secretary*, is published by MX Publishing.

Barry Clay is a graduate of Shippensburg University with a BA in English. He's dug ditches, stocked grocery shelves, tutored for room and board, cleaned restrooms, mopped floors, taught cartooning, worked in a bank, asked if you'd like fries with that (and cooked the fries to boot), ordered carpet for cars, and worked commission sales at Sears. Currently, he is a thirty-two year veteran of the Federal employee workforce. He has been writing all his life in different genres, and he has written thirteen books ranging from Christian theology, anthologies, speculative fiction, horror, science fiction, and humor. His Sherlockian volumes include *The Darkened Village* and *The Leveson-Gower Theft*. He volunteers as conductor of a local student orchestra and has been commissioned to write music. His first two musicals were locally produced. He is the husband of one wife, father of four children, and "Opa" to one granddaughter. He is honored to have been asked to contribute to this collection.

Craig Stephen Copland confesses that he discovered Sherlock Holmes when, sometime in the muddled early 1960's, he pinched his older brother's copy of the immortal stories and was forever afterward thoroughly hooked. He is very grateful to his high school English teachers in Toronto who inculcated in him a love of literature and writing, and even inspired him to be an English major at the University of Toronto. There he was blessed to sit at the feet of both Northrup Frye and Marshall McLuhan, and other great literary professors, who led him to believe that he was called to be a high school English teacher. It was his good fortune to come to his pecuniary senses, abandon that goal, and pursue a varied professional career that took him to over one-hundred countries and endless adventures. He considers himself to have been and to continue to be one of the luckiest men on God's good earth. A few years back he took a step in the direction of Sherlockian studies and joined the *Sherlock Holmes Society of Canada* – also known as *The Toronto Bootmakers*. In May of 2014, this esteemed group of scholars announced a contest for the writing of a new Sherlock Holmes mystery. Although he had never tried his hand at fiction before, Craig entered and was pleasantly surprised to be selected as one of the winners. Having enjoyed the experience, he decided to write more of the same, and is now on a mission to write a new Sherlock Holmes mystery that is related to and inspired by each of the sixty stories in the original Canon. He currently lives and writes in Toronto and Dubai, and looks forward to finally settling down when he turns ninety.

Harry DeMaio is a *nom de plume* of Harry B. DeMaio, successful author of several books on Information Security and Business Networks, as well as the seventeen-volume *Casebooks of Octavius Bear*. He is also a published author of Solar Pons stories and stories included in the MX Sherlock Holmes series edited by David Marcum. His latest offering for Belanger Books is a seven-story collection: *The Adventures of Sherlock Holmes and the Glamorous Ghost*. A retired business executive, former consultant, information security specialist, elected official, private pilot, disk jockey and graduate school adjunct professor, he whiles away his time traveling and writing preposterous books, articles, and stories. He has appeared on many radio and TV shows and is an accomplished, frequent public speaker. Former New York City natives, he and his extremely patient and helpful wife, Virginia, live in Cincinnati (and several other parallel universes.) They have two sons, living in Scottsdale, Arizona and Cortlandt Manor, New York, both of whom are quite successful and quite normal, thus putting the lie to the theory that insanity is hereditary. His books are available on Amazon, Barnes and Noble, directly from Belanger Books and MX Publishing, and at other fine bookstores. His e-mail is *hdemaio@zoomtown.com*

You can also find him on Facebook. His website is *www.octaviusbearslair.com*

Tim Gambrell *also has a story in Part XXX*

Jayantika Ganguly BSI is the General Secretary and Editor of the *Sherlock Holmes Society of India*, a member of the *Sherlock Holmes Society of London*, and the *Czech Sherlock Holmes Society*. She is the author of *The Holmes Sutra* (MX 2014). She is a corporate lawyer working with one of the Big Six law firms.

Paul D. Gilbert was born in 1954 and has lived in and around London all of his life. His wife Jackie is a Holmes expert who keeps him on the straight and narrow! He has two sons, one of whom now lives in Spain. His interests include literature, ancient history, all religions, most sports, and movies. He is currently employed full-time as a funeral director. His books so far include *The Lost Files of Sherlock Holmes* (2007), *The Chronicles of Sherlock Holmes* (2008), *Sherlock Holmes and the Giant Rat of Sumatra* (2010), *The Annals of Sherlock Holmes* (2012), *Sherlock Holmes and the Unholy Trinity* (2015), *Sherlock Holmes: The Four Handed Game* (2017), *The Illumination of Sherlock Holmes* (2019), and *The Treasure of the Poison King* (2021).

Arthur Hall was born in Aston, Birmingham, UK, in 1944. He discovered his interest in writing during his schooldays, along with a love of fictional adventure and suspense. His first novel, *Sole Contact*, was an espionage story about an ultra-secret government department known as "Sector Three", and was followed, to date, by three sequels. Other works include six Sherlock Holmes novels, *The Demon of the Dusk, The One Hundred Percent Society, The Secret Assassin, The Phantom Killer, In Pursuit of the Dead*, and *The Justice Master*, as well as two collections of Holmes *Further Little-Known Cases of Sherlock* Holmes, and *Tales from the Annals of Sherlock Holmes*. He has also written other short stories and a modern detective novel. He lives in the West Midlands, United Kingdom.

Paula Hammond has written over sixty fiction and non-fiction books, as well as short stories, comics, poetry, and scripts for educational DVD's. When not glued to the keyboard, she can usually be found prowling round second-hand books shops or hunkered down in a hide, soaking up the joys of the natural world.

Christopher James was born in 1975 in Paisley, Scotland. Educated at Newcastle and UEA, he was a winner of the UK's National Poetry Competition in 2008. He has written three full length Sherlock Holmes novels, *The Adventure of the Ruby* Elephant, *The Jeweller of Florence*, and *The Adventure of the Beer Barons*, all published by MX.

Paul Hiscock *also has a story in Part XXX*

Naching T. Kassa is a wife, mother, and writer. She's created short stories, novellas, poems, and co-created three children. She lives in Eastern Washington State with her husband, Dan Kassa. Naching is a member of the *Horror Writers Association*, Head of Publishing and Interviewer for *HorrorAddicts.net*, and an assistant and staff writer for Still Water Bay at Crystal Lake Publishing. She has been a Sherlockian since the age of ten and is a member of *The Sound of the Baskervilles*. You can find her work on Amazon. *https://www.amazon.com/Naching-T-Kassa/e/B005ZGHTI0*

Susan Knight's newest novel from MX publishing, *Mrs. Hudson Goes to Ireland*, is a follow-up to her well-received collection of stories, *Mrs. Hudson Investigates* of 2019. She is the author of two other non-Sherlockian story collections, as well as three novels, a book of non-fiction, and several plays, and has won several prizes for her writing. She lives in Dublin where she teaches Creative Writing. Her next Mrs. Hudson novel is already a gleam in her eye.

Gordon Linzner is founder and former editor of *Space and Time Magazine*, and author of three published novels and dozens of short stories in *F&SF*, *Twilight Zone*, *Sherlock Holmes Mystery Magazine*, and numerous other magazines and anthologies, including *Baker Street Irregulars II*, *Across the Universe*, and *Strange Lands*. He is a member of *HWA* and a lifetime member of *SFWA*.

Michael Mallory is the Derringer-winning author of the "Amelia Watson" (The Second Mrs. Watson) series and "Dave Beauchamp" mystery series, and more than one-hundred-twenty-five short stories. An entertainment journalist by day, he has written eight nonfiction books on pop culture and more than six-hundred newspaper and magazine articles. Based in Los Angeles, Mike is also an occasional actor on television.

David Marcum *also has stories in Parts XXIX and XXX*

J. Lawrence Matthews has contributed fiction to the *New York Times* and *NPR's All Things Considered*, and is the author of three non-fiction books as Jeff Matthews. *One Must Tell the Bees: Abraham Lincoln and the Final Education of Sherlock Holmes*, his first novel, combines his passion for the original Sherlock Holmes stories of Sir Arthur Conan Doyle with his interest in American history as told on the battlefields of the Civil War. Matthews is now researching the sequel, which follows Sherlock Holmes a bit further afield – to Florence, Mecca and Tibet – but readers may contact him at *jlawrencematthews@gmail.com*. Those interested in the history behind *One Must Tell the Bees* will find it at *jlawrencematthews.com*.

Julie McKuras ASH, BSI discovered Sherlock Holmes at the age of eleven through the late night magic of the Basil Rathbone and Nigel Bruce films. It was a bonus to learn there were actually books written by Sir Arthur Conan Doyle. She served as the President of *The Norwegian Explorers of Minnesota* for nine years, and has been on the board of *The Friends of the Sherlock Holmes Collections* since 1997, editing their quarterly newsletter since 1999. Julie was the first editor of *The BSI Trust* newsletter as well. She is a frequent contributor to the *Friends* newsletter, and has had articles published in the *Baker Street Journal*, London's *Sherlock Holmes Journal*, *Through the Magic Door*, and *The Serpentine Muse*. Her essays have been included in *The Norwegian Explorers Christmas Annuals*, *Sir Arthur Conan Doyle and Sherlock Holmes: Essays and Art on The Doctor and The Detective*, "A Note on the Sherlock Holmes Collections" published in *The Horror of the Heights*, *Violets and Vitriol*, and *Sherlock Holmes in the Heartland: The Illustrious Clients Fifth Casebook*. She is a co-editor of *The Missing Misadventures of Sherlock Holmes*, and with Susan Vizoskie, she co-edited *Sherlockian Heresies*. Julie has been a speaker at a number of conferences and events, such as *The Sherlock Holmes Society of London*'s Statue Festival, Holmes Under the Arch, the Newberry Library, From Gillette to Brett, and the 2014 Reichenbach Irregulars Conference in Davos. She lives in Apple Valley, Minnesota with her husband, Mike, and with her children, their spouses, and her three grandchildren nearby.

Tracy J. Revels, a Sherlockian from the age of eleven, is a professor of history at Wofford College in Spartanburg, South Carolina. She is a member of *The Survivors of the Gloria Scott* and *The Studious Scarlets Society*, and is a past recipient of the Beacon Society Award. Almost every semester, she teaches a class that covers The Canon, either to college students or to senior citizens. She is also the author of three supernatural Sherlockian pastiches with MX (*Shadowfall*, *Shadowblood*, and *Shadowwraith*), and a regular contributor to her scion's newsletter. She also has some notoriety as an author of very silly skits: For proof, see "The Adventure of the Adversarial Adventuress" and "Occupy Baker Street" on YouTube. When not studying Sherlock, she can be found researching the history of her native state, and has written books on Florida in the Civil War and on the development of Florida's tourism industry.

Dan Rowley is a retired lawyer who practiced for over forty years in private practice and in house for a large international corporation. He lives in Erie, Pennsylvania, with his wife Judy. His father introduced him to the love of mysteries a long time ago. He inherited his creativity and writing ability from his children, Jim and Katy, now enhanced by Sherry and Prince.

J.S. Rowlinson grew up on the Staffordshire/Derbyshire border, in the heart of England, near the market town of Uttoxeter where his story is set. He is now an art teacher in Plymouth, with the Mayflower steps to the south and Dartmoor to the north. Conan Doyle, for a short time, had a medical practice in the city, on Durnford Street. When not teaching or writing, he is a freelance illustrator, a singer of traditional English folk songs and ballads, and can often be found walking the desolate beauty of the moor with his dog, Jessie.

Jane Rubino is the author of *A Jersey Shore* mystery series, featuring a Jane Austen-loving amateur sleuth and a Sherlock Holmes-quoting detective, *Knight Errant*, *Lady Vernon and Her Daughter*, (a novel-length adaptation of Jane Austen's novella *Lady Susan*, co-authored with her daughter Caitlen Rubino-Bradway, *What Would Austen Do?*, also co-authored with her daughter, a short story in the anthology *Jane Austen Made Me Do It*, *The Rucastles' Pawn*, *The Copper Beeches from Violet Turner's POV*, and, of course, there's the Sherlockian novel in the drawer – who doesn't have one? Jane lives on a barrier island at the New Jersey shore.

Geri Schear is a novelist and short story writer. Her work has been published in literary journals in the U.S. and Ireland. Her first novel, *A Biased Judgement: The Diaries of Sherlock Holmes 1897* was released to critical acclaim in 2014. The sequel, *Sherlock Holmes and the Other Woman* was published in 2015, and *Return to Reichenbach* in 2016. She lives in Kells, Ireland.

Frank Schildiner is a martial arts instructor at Amorosi's Mixed Martial Arts in New Jersey. He is the writer of the novels, *The Quest of Frankenstein, The Triumph of Frankenstein, Napoleon's Vampire Hunters, The Devil Plague of Naples, The Klaus Protocol*, and *Irma Vep and The Great Brain of Mars*. Frank is a regular contributor to the fictional series *Tales of the Shadowmen* and has been published in *From Bayou to Abyss: Examining John Constantine, Hellblazer, The Joy of Joe, The New Adventures of Thunder Jim Wade, Secret Agent X* Volumes 3, 4, 5, and 6, *The Lone Ranger and Tonto: Frontier Justice*, and *The Avenger: The Justice Files*. He resides in New Jersey with his wife Gail, who is his top supporter, and two cats who are indifferent on the subject.

411

Shane Simmons is the author of the occult detective novels *Necropolis* and *Epitaph*, and the crime collection *Raw and Other Stories*. An award-winning screenwriter and graphic novelist, his work has appeared in international film festivals, museums, and lectures about design and structure. He was born in Lachine, a suburb of Montreal best known for being massacred in 1689 and having a joke name. Visit Shane's homepage at *eyestrainproductions.com* for more.

Kevin Thornton is the author of more than a dozen Holmes short stories, as well as other crimonous fare. He has been short-listed quite a few times for awards. He has never won. He has written for *The New York Times* and has been in a top-selling anthology, but he is not an *NYT* best -selling writer. His singular achievement so far has been the locked room mystery he wrote where the door was not, in fact, locked. But that is not in this collection. He lives in Northern Canada. When asked, he will agree that it is quite cold.

DJ Tyrer is the person behind Atlantean Publishing, and has had fiction featuring Sherlock Holmes published in volumes from MX Publishing and Belanger Books, and an issue of *Awesome Tales*, and has a forthcoming story in *Sherlock Holmes Mystery Magazine*, as well as non-Sherlockian mysteries in anthologies such as *Mardi Gras Mysteries* (Mystery and Horror LLC) and *The Trench Coat Chronicles* (Celestial Echo Press).
DJ Tyrer's website is at *https://djtyrer.blogspot.co.uk/*
His Facebook page is at *https://www.facebook.com/DJTyrerwriter/*
The Atlantean Publishing website is at *https://atlanteanpublishing.wordpress.com/*

Margaret Walsh was born Auckland, New Zealand and now lives in Melbourne, Australia. She is the author of *Sherlock Holmes and the Molly-Boy Murders*, *Sherlock Holmes and the Case of the Perplexed Politician*, and *Sherlock Holmes and the Case of the London Dock Deaths*, all published by MX Publishing. Margaret has been a devotee of Sherlock Holmes since childhood and has had several Holmesian related essays printed in anthologies, and is a member of the online society *Doyle's Rotary Coffin*. She has an ongoing love affair with the city of London. When she's not working or planning trips to London. Margaret can be found frequenting the many and varied bookshops of Melbourne.

I.A. Watson was shattered when he failed in his life's ambition to become a Christmas Elf, and turned for solace to writing stories of Sherlock Holmes (which are known to be Santa's favourites). In hopes of being allowed at least a turn as a reindeer, he has produced the books *Holmes and Houdini* and *The Incunabulum of Sherlock Holmes*, and over thirty short stories about the Great Detective, along with eight other novels and many novellas and short stories on less-Sherlockian subjects (most recently *The Death of Persephone*). Having to generate so many "About the Author" paragraphs requires additional eccentric author blurb – but heck, it's Christmas! An up-to-date list of I.A. Watson's work is online at: *http://www.chillwater.org.uk/writing/iawatsonhome.htm*

Matthew White is an up-and-coming author from Richmond, Virginia in the USA. A lifelong devotee of Sherlock Holmes, he maintains a Sherlockian blog, Baker Street Forever, at *https://bakerstreetforever.wordpress.com*. He can be reached at *matthewwhite.writer@gmail.com*.

Marcia Wilson is a freelance researcher and illustrator who likes to work in a style compatible for the color blind and visually impaired. She is Canon-centric, and her first MX offering, *You Buy Bones*, uses the point-of-view of Scotland Yard to show the unique talents of Dr. Watson. This continued with the publication of *Test of the Professionals: The*

412

Adventure of the Flying Blue Pidgeon and *The Peaceful Night Poisonings.* She can be contacted at: *gravelgirty.deviantart.com*

414

416

The MX Book of New Sherlock Holmes Stories
Edited by David Marcum
(MX Publishing, 2015-   )

"This is the finest volume of Sherlockian fiction I have ever read, and I have read, literally, thousands." – Philip K. Jones

"Beyond Impressive . . . This is a splendid venture for a great cause!
– Roger Johnson, Editor, *The Sherlock Holmes Journal,*
The Sherlock Holmes Society of London

Part I: 1881-1889
Part II: 1890-1895
Part III: 1896-1929
Part IV: 2016 Annual
Part V: Christmas Adventures
Part VI: 2017 Annual
Part VII: Eliminate the Impossible (1880-1891)
Part VIII – Eliminate the Impossible (1892-1905)
Part IX – 2018 Annual (1879-1895)
Part X – 2018 Annual (1896-1916)
Part XI – Some Untold Cases (1880-1891)
Part XII – Some Untold Cases (1894-1902)
Part XIII – 2019 Annual (1881-1890)
Part XIV – 2019 Annual (1891-1897)
Part XV – 2019 Annual (1898-1917)
Part XVI – Whatever Remains . . . Must be the Truth (1881-1890)
Part XVII – Whatever Remains . . . Must be the Truth (1891-1898)
Part XVIII – Whatever Remains . . . Must be the Truth (1898-1925)
Part XIX – 2020 Annual (1882-1890)
Part XX – 2020 Annual (1891-1897)
Part XXI – 2020 Annual (1898-1923)
Part XXII – Some More Untold Cases (1877-1887)
Part XXIII – Some More Untold Cases (1888-1894)
Part XXIV – Some More Untold Cases (1895-1903)
Part XXV – 2021 Annual (1881-1888)
Part XXVI – 2021 Annual (1889-1897)
Part XXVII – 2021 Annual (1898-1928)
Part XXVIII – More Christmas Adventures (1869-1888)
Part XXIX – More Christmas Adventures (1889-1896)
Part XXX – More Christmas Adventures (1897-1928)
<u>In Preparation</u>
Part XXXI (and XXXII and XXXIII???) – 2022 Annual

. . . and more to come!

The MX Book of New Sherlock Holmes Stories
Edited by David Marcum
(MX Publishing, 2015-   )

Publishers Weekly says:

Part VI: *The traditional pastiche is alive and well . . . .*

Part VII: *Sherlockians eager for faithful-to-the-canon plots and characters will be delighted.*

Part VIII: *The imagination of the contributors in coming up with variations on the volume's theme is matched by their ingenious resolutions.*

Part IX: *The 18 stories . . . will satisfy fans of Conan Doyle's originals. Sherlockians will rejoice that more volumes are on the way.*

Part X: *. . . new Sherlock Holmes adventures of consistently high quality.*

Part XI: *. . . an essential volume for Sherlock Holmes fans.*

Part XII: *. . . continues to amaze with the number of high-quality pastiches.*

Part XIII: *. . . Amazingly, Marcum has found 22 superb pastiches . . . This is more catnip for fans of stories faithful to Conan Doyle's original*

Part XIV: *. . . this standout anthology of 21 short stories written in the spirit of Conan Doyle's originals.*

Part XV: *Stories pitting Sherlock Holmes against seemingly supernatural phenomena highlight Marcum's 15th anthology of superior short pastiches.*

Part XVI: *Marcum has once again done fans of Conan Doyle's originals a service.*

Part XVII: *This is yet another impressive array of new but traditional Holmes stories.*

Part XVIII: *Sherlockians will again be grateful to Marcum and MX for high-quality new Holmes tales.*

Part XIX: *Inventive plots and intriguing explorations of aspects of Dr. Watson's life and beliefs lift the 24 pastiches in Marcum's impressive 19th Sherlock Holmes anthology*

Part XX: *Marcum's reserve of high-quality new Holmes exploits seems endless.*

Part XXI: *This is another must-have for Sherlockians.*

Part XXII: *Marcum's superlative 22nd Sherlock Holmes pastiche anthology features 21 short stories that successfully emulate the spirit of Conan Doyle's originals while expanding on the canon's tantalizing references to mysteries Dr. Watson never got around to chronicling.*

Part XXIII: *Marcum's well of talented authors able to mimic the feel of The Canon seems bottomless.*

Part XXIV: *Marcum's expertise at selecting high-quality pastiches remains impressive.*

The MX Book of New Sherlock Holmes Stories
Edited by David Marcum
(MX Publishing, 2015-   )

420

MX Publishing

MX Publishing is the world's largest specialist Sherlock Holmes publisher, with over five-hundred titles and over two-hundred authors creating the latest in Sherlock Holmes fiction and non-fiction

The catalogue includes several award winning books, and over two-hundred-and-fifty have been converted into audio.

MX Publishing also has one of the largest communities of Holmes fans on Facebook, with regular contributions from dozens of authors.

www.mxpublishing.com

@mxpublishing on Facebook, Twitter and Instagram

422

423